Isaac Asimov's Magical Worlds of Fantasy

WITCHES & WIZARDS

Isaac Asimov's
Magical Worlds of Fantasy

WITCHES
&
WIZARDS

Two Volumes in One
Introductions by Isaac Asimov

Edited by Isaac Asimov, Martin H. Greenberg
and Charles G. Waugh

BONANZA BOOKS

NEW YORK

ACKNOWLEDGMENTS

My Mother Was a Witch by William Tenn. Copyright © 1966 by William Tenn. Reprinted by permission of the author and his agent, Virginia Kidd.

A Message From Charity by William Lee. Copyright © 1967 by Mercury Press, Inc. from *The Magazine of Fantasy and Science Fiction*. Reprinted by permission of the agents for the author's estate, the Scott Meredith Literary Agency, Inc., 845 Third Avenue, New York, N.Y. 10022.

The Witch by A.E. van Vogt. Copyright © 1942 by Street & Smith Publications, Inc., renewed 1970 by A. E. van Vogt. Reprinted by permission of Forrest J. Ackerman, 2495 Glendower Avenue, Hollywood, CA 90027.

The Witches of Karres by James H. Schmitz. Copyright © 1949 by Street & Smith Publications, Inc. Reprinted by permission of the agents for the author's estate, the Scott Meredith Literary Agency, Inc., 845 Third Avenue, New York, N.Y. 10022.

Spree by Barry N. Malzberg. Copyright © 1984 by Barry N. Malzberg. By permission of author.

Devil's Henchman by Murray Leinster (writing as Will F. Jenkins). Copyright © 1952 by Will F. Jenkins. Reprinted by permission of the agents for the author's estate, the Scott Meredith Literary Agency, Inc., 845 Third Avenue, New York, N.Y. 10022.

Malice in Wonderland by Rufus King. Copyright © 1957 by Davis Publications, Inc. Reprinted from the book *Malice in Wonderland* by Rufus King by permission of Doubleday & Compnay, Inc.

Operation Salamander by Poul Anderson. Copyright © 1957 by Mercury Press, Inc. From *The Magazine of Fantasy and Science Fiction*. Reprinted by permission of the Scott Meredith Literary Agency, Inc., 845 Third Avenue, New York, N.Y. 10022.

Wizard's World by Andre Norton. Copyright © 1967 by Galaxy Publishing Corporation. Reprinted by permission of Larry Sternig Literary Agency.

Sweets to the Sweet by Robert Bloch. Copyright © 1947 by Short Stories, Inc.; copyright renewed by the author. Reprinted by permission of Kirby McCauley, Ltd.

Poor Little Saturday by Madeleine L'Engle. Copyright © 1956 by King-Size Publications. Reprinted by permission of The Lescher Agency.

Squeakie's First Case by Margaret Manners. Copyright © 1943 by Margaret Manners. Reprinted by arrangment with the Scott Meredith Literary Agency, Inc., 845 Third Avenue, New York, N.Y. 10022. Every effort has been made to locate the copyright holder. Heir to the Manners estate please contact the above Agency for payment.

The Ipswich Phial by Randall Garrett. Copyright © 1976 by Condé Nast Publications. Reprinted by arrangement with the Scott Meredith Literary Agency, Inc., 845 Third Avenue, New York, N.Y. 10022.

Mazirian the Magician by Jack Vance. Copyright © 1950 by Jack Vance; copyright renewed. Reprinted by permission of Kirby McCauley, Ltd.

Acknowledgments continue on page 651 which
serves as an extension of this copyright page.

Library of Congress of Cataloging in Publication Data
Main entry under title:

Isaac Asimov's magical worlds of fantasy.

Previously published in 2 separate volumes as: Isaac Asimov's magical worlds of fantasy #1, wizards, and Isaac Asimov's magical worlds of fantasy #2, witches.
1. Fantastic fiction, American. 2. Witchcraft — Fiction. 3. Magic — Fiction. I. Asimov, Isaac, 1920– . II. Greenberg, Martin Harry. III. Waugh, Charles. IV. Isaac Asimov's magical worlds of fantasy #1, Wizards. V. Isaac Asimov's magical worlds of fantasy #2, witches.

PS648.F318 1985   813'.0876'08   85-9917
ISBN: 0-517-47669-X

h g f e d c b a

Contents

Volume One

Witches

INTRODUCTION *by Isaac Asimov*   9

MY MOTHER WAS A WITCH *by William Tenn*   12

A MESSAGE FROM CHARITY *by William M. Lee*   18

THE WITCH *by A.E. van Vogt*   37

THE WITCHES OF KARRES *by James H. Schmitz*   58

SPREE *by Barry N. Malzberg*   99

DEVIL'S HENCHMAN *by Murray Leinster*   107

MALICE IN WONDERLAND *by Rufus King*   121

OPERATION SALAMANDER *by Poul Anderson*   140

WIZARD'S WORLD *by Andre Norton*   166

SWEETS TO THE SWEET *by Robert Bloch*   212

POOR LITTLE SATURDAY *by Madeleine L'Engle*   221

SQUEAKIE'S FIRST CASE *by Margaret Manners*   236

THE IPSWICH PHIAL *by Randall Garrett*   258

BLACK HEART AND WHITE HEART
    by H. Rider Haggard   303

Volume Two

Wizards

INTRODUCTION *by Isaac Asimov*   353

MAZIRIAN THE MAGICIAN *by Jack Vance*   357

PLEASE STAND BY *by Ron Goulart*   373

WHAT GOOD IS A GLASS DAGGER? *by Larry Niven*   395

THE EYE OF TANDYLA *by L. Sprague de Camp*   430

THE WHITE HORSE CHILD *by Greg Bear*   453

SEMLEY'S NECKLACE *by Ursula K. Le Guin*   472

AND THE MONSTERS WALK *by John Jakes*   491

THE SEEKER IN THE FORTRESS
    by Manly Wade Wellman   528

THE WALL AROUND THE WORLD
    by Theodore Cogswell   550

THE PEOPLE OF THE BLACK CIRCLE
    by Robert E. Howard   576

Volume One

WITCHES

Introduction

WITCHES
by Isaac Asimov

In Anglo-Saxon times, a magician was called a "wicca." At least, a male magician was. A female magician was a "wicce," the feminine form of the word. In modern English, the word became "witch." You might think that we would use the modern English system for deriving a female from a male noun and speak of a male magician as a "witch" and a female magician as a "witchess." After all, we talk of "enchanters" and "enchantresses"; of "sorcerers" and "sorceresses."

But it doesn't work for "witch." That term is always used for a female magician. We simply don't think of males as "witches."

On the other hand, a "wizard" is always a male magician, and no one uses the term "wizardess."

For that reason, in modern English we think of "wizard" and "witch" as the male and female version, respectively, of the same word. After all, we don't have to have every female word formed by adding the "-ess" suffix. We may have "prince/princess," and "count/countess," but we don't have "king/kingess." Instead we have "king/queen" and, for that matter, "gentleman/lady," "boy/girl," "bull/cow." Why not, then, "wizard/witch"?

You can use each word in the original meaning of magician, or in a modern diluted meaning. A wizard can be merely some man who is extraordinarily clever or good at his task. A witch can be merely some woman who is so roguishly lovely that men cannot resist her. Both are so good at what they do that they seem to use magic.

Yet there is an important difference, too, an asymmetry. If we consider the words in the original meaning of someone who makes use of magic to accomplish some aim, that aim might be either a good or an evil one in intention and in fact. In the case of a wizard, it is liable to be good (to our casual thinking) as often as bad. The greatest wizard in literature is the one in the Arthurian legends—Merlin. And he is certainly considered to be

9

on the side of good. The most popular wizard in modern children's literature is the Wizard of Oz, and he is also on the side of good.

Witches, too, might be either good or evil, and in the Oz books, Glinda is a good witch. However, that is quite exceptional. We almost always think of witches as evil. In the movie *The Wizard of Oz*, we tend to forget the pale, washed-out Billie Burke as the wholly improbable good witch, and remember only the magnificent performance of Margaret Hamilton as the Wicked Witch of the West. In literature generally, the most memorable witches are the three weird sisters in *Macbeth*, and they, too, are clearly evil phenomena.

Why, then, are witches so much more likely to be viewed as evil than wizards are? There, the fault might lie with the Bible. Witches, wizards, and all varieties of enchanters and magicians were thought to use the powers of demons and devils, and therefore to be working in opposition to God, so that they were considered to be evil virtually as a matter of course. Their tampering with the supernatural was held to be a capital offense in the Bible. The Hebrew word for such tamperers was translated into the English of the King James Bible as "witch," so that we have the verse: "Thou shalt not suffer a witch to live" (Exodus 22:18). A word equivalent to "witch" was used in the translation of that verse into other European languages.

As a result, during the first century or so after the Protestant Reformation, when Europe was torn by religious wars, and everyone was tense over religious differences, a virtual witch-hunting mania swept over Europe, and thousands of essentially innocent people were tortured and killed. A few men were, but the vast majority who suffered were women.

Though educated people no longer believe in witches (in the sense of thinking that there are people who can truly manipulate supernatural entities), the aura of evil remains in connection with witches rather than with wizards.

A woman may be a witch at any age. After all, what's to stop a young woman from dealing with demons? (Thus, in this anthology of stories about witches, there are young as well as old witches.)

Nevertheless, when we think of witches, we generally think of old women. What's more, in the sad days when witches were being hunted down by the hundreds, old women suffered in numbers far out of proportion to their occurrence in the general population.

The witches in *Macbeth* are always pictured as old women; the traditional witches with which we are presented in Halloween illustrations are always old women. Why old?

Here's what I think—

Up to about a century and a half ago, the average life expectancy was only thirty-five at the most, and old people generally made up a considerably smaller percentage of the population than they do now. What's more, in addition to the causes of death that dealt with either sex indiscriminately, women frequently died in childbirth, too. For that reason, there were fewer old women than old men.

The face changes with age. For one thing, it becomes wrinkled and withered. For another, teeth disappear. In the days when teeth weren't cleaned and were certainly never cared for properly, it was probably a rare human being who had any teeth left after the age of forty.

In the case of old men, the wrinkled face and the toothless gums were hidden by the beard which almost all men wore. Old women, however, had no beards, and the few that existed must have looked very odd, and even frightening, with their faces so different from those of younger people. And since difference is often equated with evil, old women were easy to think of as evil.

Look at the old witches of Halloween. Invariably, they have pointed noses and chins that approach each other. That is virtually the trademark of the witch. However, when there are no teeth in the mouth, the nose and chin naturally approach each other more closely than when teeth serve as a barrier. The Halloween witch is merely a toothless old woman.

I wonder if modern dentistry may not have done more to wipe out fear of witches than any amount of education. That and the fact that with the general extension of the life span, old people— and old women, in particular—have grown too common to chill one.

—But in stories, they still exist, and they can still frighten, so welcome to this anthology.

My Mother Was a Witch
by William Tenn

"William Tenn" is a pseudonym for Philip Klass, a professor of English at Penn State University. He was one of the most important writers associated with the social/satirical science fiction of the 1950s, a man both funny and bitter, with the ability to step back from the society in which he lived and see its dark side. His total output has been disappointingly small, but his major stories (he has produced very little since 1970) can be found in a half-dozen of the best collections in the field, including The Human Angle *(1956),* The Square Root of Man *(1971), and* The Wooden Star (1968). A Lamp for Medusa *is a delightful short novel first published in 1968. In addition, Mr. Klass is one of the best before/during/after-dinner speakers in science fiction.*

I spent most of my boyhood utterly convinced that my mother was a witch. No psychological trauma was involved; instead, this belief made me feel like a thoroughly loved and protected child.

My memory begins in the ragged worst of Brooklyn's Brownsville—also known as East New York—where I was surrounded by witches. Every adult woman I knew was one. Shawled conventions of them buzzed and glowered constantly at our games from nearby "stoops." Whenever my playmates swirled too boisterously close, the air turned black with angry magic: immense and complicated curses were thrown.

"May you never live to grow up" was one of the simpler, cheerier incantations. "But if you do grow up, may it be like a radish, with your head in the ground and your feet in the air." Another went: "May you itch from head to foot with scabs that drive you crazy—but only after your fingernails have broken off so you can't scratch."

These remarks were not directed at me; my mother's counter-magic was too widely feared, and I myself had been schooled in every block and parry applicable to little boys. At bedtime, my mother spat thrice, forcing the Powers with whom she was in constant familiar correspondence to reverse curses aimed at me that day back on their authors' heads threefold, as many times as she had spit.

A witch in the family was indeed a rod and a staff of comfort.

My mother was a Yiddish witch, conducting her operations in that compote of German, Hebrew, and Slavic. This was a serious handicap: she had been born a Jewish cockney and spoke little Yiddish until she met my father, an ex-rabbinical student and fervent Socialist from Lithuania. Having bagged him in London's East End on his way to America, she set herself with immediate, wifely devotion to unlearn her useless English in place of what seemed to be the prevailing tongue of the New World.

While my father trained her to speak Yiddish fluently, he cannot have been of much help to her and their firstborn in that superstitious Brooklyn slum. He held science and sweet reason to be the hope of the world; her casual, workaday necromancy horrified him. Nary a spell would he teach her: idioms, literary phrases and fine Yiddish poetry, by all means, but no spells, absolutely no spells.

She needed them. A small boy, she noted, was a prime target for malice and envy, and her new neighbors had at their disposal whole libraries of protective cantrips. Cantrips, at first, had she none. Her rank on the block was determined by the potency of her invocations and her ability—when invoked upon—to knock aside or deftly neutralize. But she sorely lacked a cursing tradition passed for generations from mother to daughter; she alone had brought no such village lore to the United States wrapped in the thick bedspreads and sewed into goosedown-stuffed pillows. My mother's only weapons were imagination and ingenuity.

Fortunately her imagination and ingenuity never failed her—once she had gotten the hang of the thing. She was a quick study too, learning instruments of the occult as fast as she saw them used.

"Mach a feig!" she would whisper in the grocer's as a beaming housewife commented on my health and good looks. Up came my fist, thumb protruding between forefinger and middle-finger in the ancient male gesture against the female evil eye. *Feigs* were my reserve equipment when alone: I could make them at any cursers and continue playing in the serene confidence that all unpleasant wishes had been safely pasteurized. If

an errand took me past threatening witch faces in tenement doorways, I shot *feigs* left and right, all the way down the street.

Still, my mother's best would hardly have been worth its weight in used pentagrams if she had not stood up worthily to Old Mrs. *Mokkeh*. *Mokkeh* was the lady's nickname (it is Yiddish for plague or pestilence) and suggested the blood-chilling imprecations she could toss off with spectacular fluency.

This woman made such an impression on me that I have never been able to read any of the fiercer fairy tales without thinking of her. A tiny, square female with four daughters, each as ugly and short as she, Mrs. *Mokkeh* walked as if every firmly planted step left desolated territory forever and contemptuously behind. The hairy wart on the right side of her nose was so large that behind her back—only behind her back; who knew what she'd wish on you if she heard you?—people giggled and said, "Her nose has a nose."

But that was humor's limit; everything else was sheer fright. She would squint at you, squeezing first one eye shut, then the other, her nose wart vibrating as she rooted about in her soul for an appropriately crippling curse. If you were sensible, you scuttled away before the plague that might darken your future could be fully fashioned and slung. Not only children ran, but brave and learned witches.

Old Mrs. *Mokkeh* was a kind of witch-in-chief. She knew curses and spells that went back to antiquity, to the crumbled ghettoes of Babylon and Thebes, and she reconstructed them in the most novel and terrible forms.

When we moved into the apartment directly above her, my mother tried hard to avoid a clash. Balls must not be bounced in the kitchen; indoor running and jumping were strictly prohibited. My mother was still learning her trade at this time and had to be cautious. She would frequently scowl at the floor and bite her lips worriedly. "The *mokkehs* that woman can think up!" she would say.

There came a day when the two of us prepared to visit cousins in the farthest arctic regions of the Bronx. Washed and scrubbed until my skin smarted all over, I was dressed in the good blue serge suit bought for the High Holy Days recently celebrated. My feet were shod in glossy black leather, my neck encircled by a white collar that had been ultimately alloyed with starch. Under this collar ran a tie of brightest red, the intense shade our neighborhood favored for burning the sensitive retina of the Evil Eye.

As we emerged from the building entrance upon the stone

stoop, Mrs. *Mokkeh* and her eldest, ugliest daughter, Pearl, began climbing it from the bottom. We passed them and stopped in a knot of women chatting on the sidewalk. While my mother sought advice from her friends on express stops and train changes, I sniffed like a fretful puppy at the bulging market bags of heavy oilcloth hanging from their wrists. There was onion reek, and garlic, and the fresh miscellany of "soup greens."

The casual, barely noticing glances I drew did not surprise me; a prolonged stare at someone's well-turned-out child invited rapid and murderous retaliation. Staring was like complimenting—it only attracted the attention of the Angel of Death to a choice specimen.

I grew bored; I yawned and wriggled in my mother's grasp. Twisting around, I beheld the witch-in-chief examining me squintily from the top of the stoop. She smiled a rare and awesomely gentle smile.

"That little boy, Pearlie," she muttered to her daughter. "A darling, a sweet one, a golden one. How nice he looks!"

My mother heard her and stiffened, but she failed to whirl, as everyone expected, and deliver a brutal riposte. She had no desire to tangle with Mrs. *Mokkeh*. Our whole group listened anxiously for the Yiddish phrase customarily added to such a compliment if good will had been at all behind it—*a leben uff em*, a long life upon him.

Once it was apparent that no such qualifying phrase was forthcoming, I showed I had been well-educated. I pointed my free right hand in a spell-nullifying *feig* at my admirer.

Old Mrs. *Mokkeh* studied the *feig* with her narrow little eyes. "May that hand drop off," she intoned in the same warm, low voice. "May the fingers rot one by one and wither to the wrist. May the hand drop off, but the rot remain. May you wither to the elbow and then to the shoulder. May the whole arm rot with which you made a *feig* at me, and may it fall off and lie festering at your feet, so you will remember for the rest of your life not to make a *feig* at me."

Every woman within range of her lilting Yiddish malediction gasped and gave a mighty head-shake. Then stepping back, they cleared a space in the center of which my mother stood alone.

She turned slowly to face Old Mrs. *Mokkeh*. "Aren't you ashamed of yourself?" she pleaded. "He's only a little boy—not even five years old. Take it back."

Mrs. *Mokkeh* spat calmly on the stoop. "May it happen ten times over. Ten and twenty and a hundred times over. May he wither, may he rot. His arms, his legs, his lungs, his belly. May he vomit green gall and no doctor should be able to save him.''

This was battle irrevocably joined. My mother dropped her eyes, estimating the resources of her arsenal. She must have found them painfully slender against such an opponent.

When she raised her eyes again, the women waiting for action leaned forward. My mother was known to be clever and had many well-wishers, but her youth made her a welterweight or at most a lightweight. Mrs. *Mokkeh* was an experienced heavy, a pro who had trained in the old country under famous champions. If these women had been in the habit of making book, the consensus would have been: even money she lasts one or two rounds; five to three she doesn't go the distance.

"Your daughter, Pearlie—" my mother began at last.

"Oh, momma, no!" shrieked the girl, suddenly dragged from noncombatant status into the very eye of the fight.

"Shush! Be calm," her mother commanded. After all, only green campaigners expected a frontal attack. My mother had been hit on her vulnerable flank—me—and was replying in kind. Pearl whimpered and stamped her feet, but her elders ignored this: matters of high professional moment were claiming their attention.

"Your daughter, Pearlie," the chant developed. "Now she is fourteen—may she live to a hundred and fourteen! May she marry in five years a wonderful man, a brilliant man, a doctor, a lawyer, a dentist, who will wait on her hand and foot and give her everything her heart desires."

There was a stir of tremendous interest as the kind of curse my mother was kneading became recognizable. It is one of the most difficult forms in the entire Yiddish thaumaturgical repertoire, building the subject up and up and up and ending with an annihilating crash. A well-known buildup curse goes, "May you have a bank account in every bank, and a fortune in each bank account, and may you spend every penny of it going from doctor to doctor, and no doctor should know what's the matter with you." Or: "May you own a hundred mansions, and in each mansion a hundred richly furnished bedrooms, and may you spend your life tossing from bed to bed, unable to get a single night's sleep on one of them."

To reach a peak and then explode it into an avalanche—that is the buildup curse. It requires perfect detail and even more perfect timing.

"May you give your daughter Pearlie a wedding to this wonderful husband of hers, such a wedding that the whole world will talk about it for years.'' Pearlie's head began a slow submergence into the collar of her dress. Her mother grunted like a boxer who has been jabbed lightly and is now dancing away.

"This wedding, may it be in all the papers, may they write about it even in books, and may you enjoy yourself at it like never before in your whole life. And one year later, may Pearlie, Pearlie and her wonderful, her rich, her considerate husband— may they present you with your first grandchild. And, *masel tov*, may it be a boy.''

Old Mrs. *Mokkeh* shook unbelievingly and came down a step, her nose wart twitching and sensitive as an insect's antenna.

"And this baby boy,'' my mother sang, pausing to kiss her fingers before extending them to Mrs. *Mokkeh*, "what a glorious child may he be! Glorious? No. Magnificent! Such a wonderful baby boy no one will ever have seen before. The greatest rabbis coming from all over the world only to look upon him at the *bris,* so they'll be able to say in later years they were among those present at his circumcision ceremony eight days after birth. So beautiful and clever he'll be that people will expect him to say the prayers at his own *bris*. And this magnificent first grandson of yours, just one day afterward, when you are gathering happiness on every side, may he suddenly, in the middle of the night—''

"Hold!'' Mrs. *Mokkeh* screamed, raising both her hands. "Stop!''

My mother took a deep breath. "And why should I stop?''

"Because I take it back! What I wished on the boy, let it be on my own head, everything I wished on him. Does that satisfy you?''

"That satisfies me,'' my mother said. Then she pulled my left arm up and began dragging me down the street. She walked proudly, no longer a junior among seniors, but a full and accredited sorceress.

A Message from Charity
by *William M. Lee*

*The late William Lee published only a few stories in the
science fiction magazines, most for* The Magazine of
Fantasy and Science Fiction. *In addition to the present
selection, "Sea Home" (F&SF, June 1968), and
"Trouble on Kort" (F&SF, April 1969) are both well
worth reading.*

That summer of the year 1700 was the hottest in the memory of
the very oldest inhabitants. Because the year ushered in a new
century, some held that the events were related and that for a
whole hundred years Bay Colony would be as torrid and steamy
as the Indies themselves.

There was a good deal of illness in Annes Towne, and a score
had died before the weather broke at last in late September. For
the great part they were oldsters who succumbed, but some of
the young were sick too, and Charity Payne as sick as any.

Charity had turned eleven in the spring and had still the figure
and many of the ways of thinking of a child, but she was tall and
strong and tanned by the New England sun, for she spent many
hours helping her father in the fields and tryng to keep some sort
of order in the dooryard and garden.

During the weeks when she lay bedridden and, for a time,
burning up with the fever, Thomas Carter and his good wife
Beulah came as neighbors should to lend a hand, for Charity's
mother had died abirthing and Obie Payne could not cope all
alone.

Charity lay on a pallet covered by a straw-filled mattress
which her father, frantic to be doing something for her and
finding little enough to do beyond the saying of short fervent
prayers, refilled with fresh straw as often as Beulah would allow.
A few miles down Harmon Brook was a famous beaver pond
where in winter the Annes Towne people cut ice to be stored
under layers of bark and chips. It had been used heavily early in

18

the summer, and there was not very much ice left, but those families with sickness in the home might draw upon it for the patient's comfort. So Charity had bits of ice folded into a woolen cloth to lay on her forehead when the fever was bad.

William Trowbridge, who had apprenticed in medicine down in Philadelphia, attended the girl, and pronounced her illness a sort of summer cholera which was claiming victims all up and down the brook. Trowbridge was only moderately esteemed in Annes Towne, being better, it was said, at delivering lambs and foals than at treating human maladies. He was a gruff and notional man, and he was prone to state his views on a subject and then walk away instead of waiting to argue and perhaps be refuted. Not easy to get along with.

For Charity he prescribed a diet of beef tea with barley and another tea, very unpleasant to the taste, made from pounded willow bark. What was more, all her drinking water was to be boiled. Since there was no other advice to be had, they followed it and in due course Charity got well.

She ran a great fever for five days, and it was midway in this period when the strange dreams began. Not dreams really, for she was awake though often out of her senses, knowing her father now and then, other times seeing him as a gaunt and frightening stranger. When she was better, still weak but wholly rational, she tried to tell her visitors about these dreams.

"Some person was talking and talking," she recalled. "A man or perchance a lad. He talked not to me, but I could hear or understand all that he said. 'Twas strange talk indeed, a porridge of the King's English and other words of no sense at all. And with the talk I did see some fearful sights."

"La, now, don't even think of it," said Dame Beulah.

"But I would fen both think and talk of it, for I am no longer afeared. Such things I saw in bits and flashes, as 'twere seen by a strike of lightning."

"Talk and ye be so minded, then. There's naught impious in y'r conceits. Tell me again about the carriages which traveled along with nary horse."

Annes Towne survived the Revolution and the War of 1812, and for a time seemed likely to become a larger, if not an important community. But when its farms became less productive and the last virgin timber disappeared from the area, Annes Towne began to disappear too, dwindling from twoscore of homes to a handful, then to none; and the last foundation had crumbled to rubble and been scattered a hundred years before it could have been nominated a historic site.

In time dirt tracks became stone roads, which gave way to black meanderings of macadam, and these in their turn were displaced by never-ending bands of concrete. The crossroads site of Annes Towne was presently cleared of brambles, sumac and red cedar, and overnight it was a shopping center. Now, for mile on spreading mile the New England hills were dotted with ranch houses, salt boxes and split-level colonial homes.

During four decades Harmond Brook had been fouled and poisoned by a textile bleach and dye works. Rising labor costs had at last driven the small company to extinction. With that event and increasingly rigorous legislation, the stream had come back to the extent that it could now be bordered by some of these prosperous homes and by the golf course of the Anniston Country Club.

With aquatic plants and bullfrogs and a few fish inhabiting its waters, it was not obvious to implicate the Harmon for the small outbreak of typhoid which occurred in the hot dry summer of 1965. No one was dependent on it for drinking water. To the discomfort of a local milk distributor, who was entirely blameless, indictment of the stream was delayed and obscured by the fact that the organisms involved were not a typical strain of *Salmonella typhosa*. Indeed they ultimately found a place in the American Type Culture Collection, under a new number.

Young Peter Wood, whose home was one of those pleasantly situated along the stream, was the most seriously ill of all the cases, partly because he was the first, mostly because his symptoms went unremarked for a time. Peter was sixteen and not highly communicative to either parents or friends. The Wood Seniors both taught, at Harvard and Wellesley respectively. They were intelligent and well-intentioned parents, but sometimes a little offhand, and like many of their friends, they raised their son to be a miniature adult in as many ways as possible. His sports, tennis and golf, were adult sports. His reading tastes were catholic, ranging from Camus to Al Capp to science fiction. He had been carefully held back in his progress through the lower grades so that he would not enter college more than a year or so ahead of his age. He had an adequate number of friends and sufficient areas of congeniality with them. He had gotten a driver's license shortly after his sixteenth birthday and drove seriously and well enough to be allowed nearly unrestricted use of the second car.

So Peter Wood was not the sort of boy to complain to his family about headache, mild nausea and other symptoms. Instead, after they had persisted for forty-eight hours, he telephoned for an appointment on his own initiative and visited the family doctor. Suddenly, in the waiting room, he became much worse, and was given a cot in an examining room until Dr. Maxwell was free to drive him home. The doctor did not seriously suspect typhoid, though it was among several possibilities which he counted as less likely.

Peter's temperature rose from 104° to over 105° that night. No nurse was to be had until morning, and his parents alternated in attendance in his bedroom. There was no cause for alarm, since the patient was full of wide-spectrum antibiotic. But he slept only fitfully with intervals of waking delirium. He slapped at the sheet, tossed around on the bed and muttered or spoke now and then. Some of the talk was understandable.

"There's a forest," he said.

"What?" asked his father.

"There's a forest the other side of the stream."

"Oh."

"Can you see it?"

"No, I'm sitting inside here with you. Take it easy, son."

"Some deer are coming down to drink, along the edge of Weller's pasture."

"Is that so?"

"Last year a mountain lion killed two of them, right where they drank. Is it raining?"

"No, it isn't. It would be fine if we could have some."

"It's raining. I can hear it on the roof." A pause. "It drips down the chimney."

Peter turned his head to look at his father, momentarily clear-eyed.

"How long since there's been a forest across the stream?"

Dr. Wood reflected on the usual difficulty of answering explicit questions and on his own ignorance of history.

"A long time. I expect this valley has been farm land since colonial days."

"Funny," Peter said. "I shut my eyes and I can see a forest. Really big trees. On our side of the stream there's a kind of a garden and an apple tree and a path goes down to the water."

"It sounds pleasant."

"Yeah."

"Why don't you try going to sleep?"

"OK."

The antibiotic accomplished much less than it should have done in Peter's case, and he stayed very sick for several days. Even after diagnosis, there appeared no good reason to move him from home. A trained nurse was on duty after that first night, and tranquilizers and sedatives reduced her job to no more than keeping a watch. There were only a few sleepy communications from her young patient. It was on the fourth night, the last one when he had any significant fever, that he asked.

"Were you ever a girl?"

"Well, thanks a lot. I'm not as old as all that."

"I mean, were you ever inside a girl?"

"I think you'd better go back to sleep, young man."

He uttered no oddities thereafter, at least when there was anyone within hearing. During the days of his recovery and convalescence, abed and later stretched out on a chaise longue on the terrace looking down toward Harmon Brook, he took to whispering. He moved his lips hardly at all, but vocalized each word, or if he fell short of this, at least put each thought into carefully chosen words and sentences.

The idea that he might be in mental communication with another person was not, to him, very startling. Steeped in the lore of science fiction whose heroes were, as like as not, adepts at telepathy, the event seemed almost as an expected outcome of his wishes. Many nights he had lain awake sending out (he hoped) a mental probe, trying and trying to find the trick, for surely there must be one, of making a contact.

Now that such a contact was established he sought, just as vainly, for some means to prove it. How do you know you're not dreaming, he asked himself. How do you know you're not still delirious?

The difficulty was that his communication with Charity Payne could be by mental route only. Had there been any possibility for Peter to reach the girl by mail, by telephone, by travel and a personal visit, their rapport on a mental level might have been confirmed, and their messages cross-checked.

During their respective periods of illness, Peter and Charity achieved a communion of a sort which consisted at first of brief glimpses, each of the other's environment. They were not—then— seeing through one another's eyes, so much as tapping one another's visual recollections. While Peter stared at a smoothly plastered ceiling, Charity looked at rough-hewn beams. He, when his aching head permitted, could turn on one side and watch a television program. She, by the same movement, could see a small smoky fire in the monstrous stone fireplace, where water was heated and her beef and barley broth kept steaming.

Instead of these current images, current for each of them in their different times, they saw stored-up pictures, not perfect, for neither of them was remembering perfectly; rather like pictures viewed through a badly ground lens, with only the objects of principal interest in clear detail.

Charity saw her fearful sights with no basis for comprehension —a section of dual highway animated by hurtling cars and trucks and not a person, recognizable as a person, in sight; a tennis court, and what on earth could it be; a jet plane crossing the sky; a vast and many-storied building which glinted with glass and the silvery tracings of untarnished steel.

At the start she was terrified nearly out of her wits. It's all very well to dream, and a nightmare is only a bad dream after you waken, but a nightmare is assembled from familiar props. You could reasonably be chased by a dragon (like the one in the picture that St. George had to fight) or be lost in a cave (like the one on Parish Hill, only bigger and darker). To dream of things which have no meaning at all is worse.

She was spared prolongation of her terror by Peter's comprehension of their situation and his intuitive realization of what the experience, assuming a two-way channel, might be doing to her. The vignettes of her life which he was seeing were in no way disturbing. Everything he saw through her mind was within his framework of reference. Horses and cattle, fields and forest, rutted lanes and narrow wooden bridges were things he knew, even if he did not live among them. He recognized Harmon Brook because, directly below their home, there was an immense granite boulder parting the flow, shaped like a great bearlike animal with its head down, drinking. It was strange that the stream, in all those years, had neither silted up nor eroded away to hide or change the seaming of the rock, but so it was. He saw it through Charity's eyes and knew the place in spite of the forest on the far hill.

When he first saw this partly familiar, partly strange scene, he heard from somewhere within his mind the frightened cry of a little girl. His thinking at that time was fever-distorted and incoherent. It was two days later after a period of several hours of normal temperature when he conceived the idea—with sudden virtual certainty—these pastoral scenes he had been dreaming were truly something seen with other eyes. There were subtle perceptual differences between those pictures and his own seeing.

To his mother, writing at a table near the windows, he said, "I think I'm feeling better. How about a glass of orange juice?"

She considered. "The doctor should be here in an hour or so. In the meantime you can make do with a little more icewater. I'll get it. Drink it slowly, remember."

Two hundred and sixty-five years away, Charity Payne thought suddenly, "How about a glass of orange juice?" She had been drowsing, but her eyes popped wide open. "Mercy," she said aloud. Dame Beulah bent over the pallet.

"What is it, child?"

"How about a glass of orange juice?" Charity repeated.

"La, 'tis gibberish." A cool hand was laid on her forehead. "Would ye like a bit of ice to bite on?"

Orange juice, whatever that might be, was forgotten.

Over the next several days Peter Wood tried time and again to address the stranger directly, and repeatedly failed. Some of what he said to others reached her in fragments and further confused her state of mind. What she had to say, on the other hand, was coming through to him with increasing frequency. Often it was only a word or a phrase with a quaint twist like a historical novel, and he would lie puzzling over it, trying to place the person on the other end of their erratic line of communication. His recognition of Bear Rock, which he had seen once again through her eyes, was disturbing. His science fiction conditioning led him naturally to speculate about the parallel worlds concept, but that seemed not to fit the facts as he saw them.

Peter reached the stage of convalescence when he could spend all day on the terrace and look down, when he wished, at the actual rock. There for the hundredth time he formed the syllables. "Hello, who are you?" and for the first time received a response. It was a silence, but a silence reverberating with shock, totally different in quality from the blankness which had met him before.

"My name is Peter Wood."

There was a long pause before the answer came, softly and timidly.

"My name is Charity Payne. Where are you? What is happening to me?"

The following days of enforced physical idleness were filled with exploration and discovery. Peter found out almost at once that, while they were probably no more than a few feet apart in their respective worlds, a gulf of more than a quarter of a thousand years stretched between them. Such a contact through time was a greater departure from known physical laws, certainly, than the mere fact of telepathic communication. Peter reveled in his growing ability.

In another way the situation was heartbreaking. No matter how well they came to know one another, he realized, they could never meet, and after no more than a few hours of acquaintance he found that he was regarding this naïve child of another time with esteem and a sort of affection.

They arrived shortly at a set of rules which seemed to govern and limit their communications. Each came to be able to hear the other speak, whether aloud or subvocally. Each learned to perceive through the other's senses, up to a point. Visual perception became better and better especially for direct seeing while, as they grew more skillful, the remembered scene became less clear. Tastes and odors could be transmitted, if not accurately, at least with the expected response. Tactile sensations could not be perceived in the slightest degree.

There was little that Peter Wood could learn from Charity. He came to recognize her immediate associates and liked them, particularly her gaunt, weather-beaten father. He formed a picture of Puritanism which, as an ethic, he had to respect, while the supporting dogma evoked nothing put impatience. At first he exposed her to the somewhat scholarly agnosticism which prevailed in his own home, but soon found that it distressed her deeply and he left off. There was so much he could report from the vantage of 1965, so many things he would show her which did not conflict with her tenets and faith.

He discovered that Charity's ability to read was remarkable, though what she had read was naturally limited—the Bible from cover to cover, *Pilgrim's Progress*, several essays and two of Shakespeare's plays. Encouraged by a schoolmaster who must have been an able and dedicated man, she had read and reread everything permitted to her. Her quite respectable vocabulary was gleaned from these sources and may have equaled Peter's own in size. In addition she possessed an uncanny word sense which helped her greatly in underatanding Peter's jargon.

She learned the taste of bananas and frankfurters, chocolate ice cream and Coke, and displayed such an addiction to these delicacies that Peter rapidly put on some of the pounds he had lost. One day she asked him what he looked like.

"Well, I told you I am sixteen, and I'm sort of thin."

"Does thee possess a mirror?" she asked.

"Yes, of course."

At her urging and with some embarrassment he went and stood before a mirrored door in his mother's bedroom.

"Marry," she said after a dubious pause, "I doubt not thee is comely. But folk have changed."

"Now let me look at you," he demanded.

"Nay, we have no mirror."

"Then go and look in the brook. There's a quiet spot below the rock where the water is dark."

He was delighted with her appearance, having remembered Hogarth's unkind representations of a not much later period and being prepared for disappointment. She was in fact very much prettier by Peter's standards than by those of her own time, which favored plumpness and smaller mouths. He told her she was a beauty, and her tentative fondness for him turned instantly to adulation.

Previously Peter had had fleeting glimpses of her slim, smoothly muscled body, as she had bathed or dressed. Now, having seen each other face to face, they were overcome by embarrassment and both of them, when not fully clothed, stared resolutely into the corners of the room.

For a time Charity believed that Peter was a dreadful liar. The sight and sound of planes in the sky were not enough to convince her of the fact of flying, so he persuaded his father to take him along on a business flight to Washington. After she had recovered from the marvels of airplane travel, he took her on a walking tour of the Capitol. Now she would believe anything, even that the American Revolution had been a success. They joined his father for lunch at an elegant French restaurant and she experienced, vicariously, the pleasures of half of a half bottle of white wine and a chocolate eclair. Charity was by way of getting spoiled.

Fully recovered and with school only a week away, Peter decided to brush up his tennis. When reading or doing nothing in particular, he was always dimly aware of Charity and her immediate surroundings, and by sharpening his attention he could bring her clearly to the forefront of his mind. Tennis displaced her completely and for an hour or two each day he was unaware of her doings.

Had he been a few years older and a little more knowledgeable and realistic about the world, he might have guessed the peril into which he was leading her. Fictional villainy abounded, of course, and many items in the news didn't bear thinking about, but by his own firsthand experience, people were well intentioned and kindly, and for the most part they reacted to events with reasonable intelligence. It was what he expected instinctively.

A first hint of possible consequences reached him as he walked home from one of his tennis sessions.

"Ursula Miller said an ill thing to me today."

"Oh?" His answer was abstracted since, in all truth, he was

beginning to run out of interest in the village gossip which was all the news she had to offer.

"Yesterday she said it was an untruth about the thirteen states. Today she avowed that I was devil-ridden. And Ursula has been my best friend."

"I warned you that people wouldn't believe you and you might get yourself laughed at," he said. Then suddenly he caught up in his thinking. "Good Lord—Salem."

"Please, Peter, thee must stop taking thy Maker's name."

"I'll try to remember. Listen, Charity, how many people have you been talking to about our—about what's been happening?"

"As I have said. At first to Father and Aunt Beulah. They did believe I was still addled from the fever."

"And to Ursula."

"Aye, but she vowed to keep it secret."

"Do you believe she will, now that she's started name-calling?"

A lengthy pause.

"I fear she may have told the lad who keeps her company."

"I should have warned you. Damn it, I should have laid it on the line."

"Peter!"

"Sorry. Charity, not another word to anybody. Tell Ursula you've been fooling—telling stories to amuse her."

" 'Twould not be right."

"So what. Charity, don't be scared, but listen. People might get to thinking you're a witch."

"Oh, they couldn't."

"Why not?"

"Because I am not one. Witches are—oh, no, Peter."

He could sense her growing alarm.

"Go tell Ursula it was a pack of lies. Do it now."

"I must milk the cow."

"Do it now."

"Nay, the cow must be milked."

"Then milk her faster than she's ever been milked before."

On the Sabbath, three little boys threw stones at Charity as she and her father left the church. Obadiah Payne caught one of them and caned him, and then would have had to fight the lad's father save that the pastor intervened.

It was on the Wednesday that calamity befell. Two tight-lipped men approached Obadiah in the fields.

"Squire wants to see thy daughter Charity."

"Squire?"

"Aye. Squire Hacker. He would talk with her at once."

"Squire can talk to me if so be he would have her reprimanded. What has she been up to?"

"Witchcraft, that's what," said the second man, sounding as if he were savoring the dread news. "Croft's old ewe delivered a monstrous lamb. Pointly pinched-up face and an extra eye." He crossed himself.

"Great God!"

" 'Twill do ye no good to blaspheme, Obadiah. She's to come with us now."

"I'll not have it. Charity's no witch, as ye well know, and I'll not have her converse with Squire. Ye mind the Squire's lecherous ways."

"That's not here nor there. Witchcraft is afoot again and all are saying 'tis your Charity at bottom of it."

"She shall not go."

First one, then the other displayed the stout truncheons they had held concealed behind their backs.

" 'Twas of our own good will we told thee first. Come now and instruct thy daughter to go with us featly. Else take a clout on the head and sleep tonight in the gaol house."

They left Obie Payne gripping a broken wrist and staring in numbed bewilderment from his door stoop, and escorted Charity, not touching her, walking at a cautious distance to either side, to Squire Hacker's big house on the hill. In the village proper, little groups of people watched from doorways and, though some had always been her good friends, none had the courage now to speak a word of comfort.

Peter went with her each reluctant step of the way, counting himself responsible for her plight and helpless to do the least thing about it. He sat alone in the living room of his home, eyes closed to sharpen his reading of her surroundings. She offered no response to his whispered reassurances and perhaps did not hear them.

At the door her guards halted and stood aside, leaving her face to face with the grim-visaged squire. He moved backward step by step, and she followed him, as if hypnotized, into the shadowed room.

The squire lowered himself into a high-backed chair. "Look at me."

Unwillingly she raised her head and stared into his face.

Squire Hacker was a man of medium height, very broad in the shoulder and heavily muscled. His face was disfigured by deep pock marks and the scar of a knife cut across the jaw, souvenirs of his earlier years in the Carib Islands. From the Islands he had also brought some wealth which he had since increased manyfold by the buying of land, share cropping and money lending.

"Charity Payne," he said sternly, "take off thy frock."

"No. No, please."

"I command it. Take off thy garments, for I must search thee for witch marks."

He leaned forward, seized her arm and pulled her to him. "If thee would avoid public trial and condemnation, thee will do as I say." His hands began to explore her body.

Even by the standards of the time, Charity regularly spent extraordinary hours at hard physical labor and she possessed a strength which would have done credit to many young men. Squire Hacker should have been more cautious.

"Nay," she shouted and drawing back her arm, hit him in the nose with all the force she could muster. He released her with a roar of rage, then, while he was mopping away blood and tears with the sleeve of his ruffled shirt and shouting imprecations, she turned and shot out the door. The guards, converging, nearly grabbed her as she passed but, once away, they stood no chance of catching her and for a wonder none of the villagers took up the chase.

She was well on the way home and covering the empty road at a fast trot before Peter was able to gain her attention.

"Charity," he said, "Charity, you mustn't go home. If that s. o. b. of a squire has any influence with the court, you just fixed yourself."

She was beginning to think again and could even translate Peter's strange language.

"Influence!" she said. "Marry, he is the court. He is the judge."

"Ouch!"

"I wot well I must not be found at home. I am trying to think where to hide. I might have had trial by water. Now they will burn me for surety. I do remember what folk said about the last witch trials."

"Could you make your way to Boston and then maybe to New York—New Amsterdam?"

"Leave my home forever! Nay. And I would not dare the trip."

"Then take to the woods. Where can you go?"

"Take to—? Oh. To the cave, mayhap."

"Don't too many people know about it?"

"Aye. But there is another across the brook and beyond Tom Carter's freehold. I do believe none know of it but me. 'Tis very small. We must ford the brook just yonder, then walk that fallen tree. There is a trail which at sundown will be tromped by a herd of deer.''

''You're thinking about dogs?''

''Aye, on the morrow. There is no good pack in Annes Towne.''

''You live in a savage age, Charity.''

''Aye,'' she said wryly. '' 'Tis fortunate we have not invented the bomb.''

''Damn it,'' Peter said, ''I wish we'd never met. I wish I hadn't taken you on the plane trip. I wish I'd warned you to keep quiet about it.''

''Ye could not guess I would be so foolish.''

''What can you do out here without food?''

''I'd liefer starve than be in the stocks, but there is food to be had in the forest, some sorts of roots and toadstools and autumn berries. I shall hide myself for three days, I think, then seek out my father by night and do as he tells me.''

When she was safely hidden in the cave, which was small indeed but well concealed by a thicket of young sassafras, she said:

''Now we can think. First, I would have an answer from thy superior wisdom. Can one be truly a witch and have no knowledge of it?''

''Don't be foolish. There's no such thing as a witch.''

''Ah well, 'tis a matter for debate by scholars. I do feel in my heart that I am not a witch, if there be such creatures. That book, Peter, of which ye told me, which recounts the history of these colonies.''

''Yes?''

''Will ye look in it and learn if I came to trial and what befell me?''

''There'd be nothing about it. It's just a small book. But—''

To his parents' puzzlement, Peter spent the following morning at the Boston Public Library. In the afternoon he shifted his operations to the Historical Society. He found at last a listing of the names of women known to have been tried for witchcraft between the years 1692 and 1697. Thereafter he could locate only an occasional individual name. There was no record of any Charity Payne in 1700 or later.

He started again when the reading room opened next day, interrupting the task only momentarily for brief exchanges with Charity. His lack of success was cheering to her, for she overestimated the completeness of the records.

At close to noon he was scanning the pages of a photostated doctoral thesis when his eye caught a familiar name.

"Jonas Hacker," it read. "Born Liverpool, England, date uncertain, perhaps 1659, was the principal figure in a curious action of law which has not become a recognized legal precedent in English courts.

"Squire Hacker, a resident of Annes Towne (cf. Anniston), was tried and convicted of willful murder and larceny. The trial was posthumous, several months after his decease from natural causes in 1704. The sentence pronounced was death by hanging which, since it could not be imposed, was commuted to forfeiture of his considerable estate. His land and other possessions reverted to the Crown and were henceforward administered by the Governor of Bay Colony.

"While the motivation and procedure of the court may have been open to question, evidence of Hacker's guilt was clear cut. The details are these. . . ."

"Hey, Charity." Peter rumbled in his throat.

"Aye?"

"Look at this page. Let me flatten it out."

"Read it please, Peter. Is it bad news?"

"No. Good, I think." He read the paragraphs on Jonas Hacker.

"Oh, Peter, can it be true?"

"It has to be. Can you remember any details?"

"Marry, I remember well when they disappeared, the ship's captain and a common sailor. They were said to have a great sack of gold for some matter of business with Squire. But it could not be, for they never reached his house."

"That's what Hacker said, but the evidence showed that they got there—got there and never got away. Now here's what you must do. Late tonight, go home."

"I would fen do so, for I am terrible athirst."

"No, wait. What's your parson's name?"

"John Hix."

"Can you reach his house tonight without being seen?"

"Aye. It backs on a glen."

"Go there. He can protect you better than your father can until your trial."

"Must I be tried?"

"Of course. We want to clear your name. Now let's do some planning."

The town hall could seat no more than a score of people, and the day was fair; so it was decided that the trial should be held on the common, in discomforting proximity to the stocks.

Visitors came from as far as twenty miles away, afoot or in carts, and nearly filled the common itself. Squire Hacker's own armchair was the only seat provided. Others stood or sat on the patchy grass.

The squire came out of the inn presently, fortified with rum, and took his place. He wore a brocaded coat and a wide-brimmed hat and would have been more impressive if it had not been for his still swollen nose, now permanently askew.

A way was made through the crowd then, and Charity, flanked on one side by John Hix, on the other by his tall son, walked to the place where she was to stand. Voices were suddenly stilled. Squire Hacker did not condescend to look directly at the prisoner, but fixed a cold stare on the minister: a warning that his protection of the girl would not be forgiven. He cleared his throat.

"Charity Payne, is thee willing to swear upon the Book?"

"Aye."

"No mind. We may forgo the swearing. All can see that ye are fearful."

"Nay," John Hix interrupted. "She shall have the opportunity to swear to her word. 'Twould not be legal otherwise." He extended a Bible to Charity, who placed her fingers on it and said, "I do swear to speak naught but the truth."

Squire Hacker glowered and lost no time coming to the attack. "Charity Payne, do ye deny being a witch?"

"I do."

"Ye do be one?"

"Nay, I do deny it."

"Speak what ye mean. What have ye to say of the monstrous lamb born of Master Croft's ewe?"

"I know naught of it."

"Was't the work of Satan?"

"I know not."

"Was't then the work of God?"

"I know not."

"Thee holds then that He might create such a monster?"

"I know naught about it."

"In thy own behalf will thee deny saying that this colony and its neighbors will in due course make wars against our King?"

"Nay, I do not deny that."

There was a stir in the crowd and some angry muttering.

"Did ye tell Mistress Ursula Miller that ye had flown a great journey through the air?"

"Nay."

"Mistress Ursula will confound thee in that lie."

"I did tell Ursula that someday folk would travel in that wise. I did tell her that I had seen such travel through eyes other than my own."

Squire Hacker leaned forward. He could not have hoped for a more damning statement. John Hix's head bowed in prayer.

"Continue."

"Aye. I am blessed with a sort of second sight."

"Blessed or cursed?"

"God permits it. It cannot be accursed."

"Continue. What evil things do ye see by this second sight?"

"Most oftentimes I see the world as it will one day be. Thee said evil. Such sights are no more and no less evil than we see around us."

Hacker pondered. There was an uncomfortable wrongness about this child's testimony. She should have been gibbering with fear, when in fact she seemed self-possessed. He wondered if by some strange chance she really had assistance from the devil's minions.

"Charity Payne, thee has confessed to owning second sight. Does thee use this devilish power to spy on thy neighbors?"

It was a telling point. Some among the spectators exchanged discomfited glances.

"Nay, 'tis not devilish, and I cannot see into the doings of my neighbors—except—"

"Speak up, girl. Except what?"

"Once I did perceive by my seeing a most foul murder."

"Murder!" The squire's voice was harsh. A few in the crowd made the sign of the cross.

"Aye. To tell true, two murders. Men whose corpses do now lie buried unshriven in a dark cellar close onto this spot. 'Tween them lies a satchel of golden guineas."

It took a minute for the squire to find his voice.

"A cellar?" he croaked.

"Aye, a root cellar, belike the place one would keep winter apples." She lifted her head and stared straight into the squire's eyes, challenging him to inquire further.

The silence was ponderous as he strove to straighten out his thoughts. To this moment he was safe, for her words described every cellar in and about the village. But she knew. Beyond any question, she knew. Her gaze, seeming to penetrate the darkest corners of his mind, told him that, even more clearly than her words.

Squire Hacker believed in witches and considered them evil and deserving of being destroyed. He had seen and shuddered at the horrible travesty of a lamb in farmer Croft's stable yard, but he had seen like deformities in the Caribbee and did not hold the event an evidence of witchcraft. Not for a minute had he thought Charity a witch, for she showed none of the signs. Her wild talk and the growing rumors had simply seemed to provide the opportunity for some dalliance with a pretty young girl and possibly, in exchange for an acquittal, a lien upon her father's land.

Now he was unsure. She must indeed have second sight to have penetrated his secret, for it had been stormy that night five years ago, and none had seen the missing sailors near to his house. Of that he was confident. Further, shockingly, she knew how and where they lay buried. Another question and answer could not be risked.

He moved his head slowly and looked right and left at the silent throng.

"Charity Payne," he said, picking his words with greatest care, "has put her hand on the Book and sworn to tell true, an act, I opine, she could scarce perform, were she a witch. Does any person differ with me?"

John Hix looked up in startled hopefulness.

"Very well. The lambing at Master Croft's did have the taint of witchcraft, but Master Trowbridge has stated his belief that some noxious plant is growing in Croft's pasture, and 'tis at the least possible. Besides, the ewe is old and she has thrown runty lambs before.

"To quote Master Trowbridge again, he holds that the cholera which has afflicted us so sorely comes from naught but the drinking of bad water. He advises boiling it. I prefer adding a little rum."

He got the laughter he sought. There was a lessening of tension.

"As to second sight." Again he swept the crowd with his gaze. "Charity had laid claim to it, and I called it a devilish gift to test her, but second sight is not witchcraft, as ye well know. My own grandmother had it, and a better woman ne'er lived. I hold it to be a gift of God. Would any challenge me?

"Very well. I would warn Charity to be cautious in what she sees and tells, for second sight can lead to grievous disputations. I do not hold with her story of two murdered men although I think that in her own sight she is telling true. If any have aught of knowledge of so dire a crime, I adjure him to step forth and speak."

He waited. "Nobody? Then, by the authority conferred on me

by his Excellency the Governor, I declare that Charity Payne is innocent of the charges brought. She may be released.''

This was not at all the eventuality which a few of Squire Hacker's cronies had foretold. The crowd had clearly expected a day-long inquisition climaxed by a prisoner to bedevil in the stocks. The Squire's about-face and his abrupt ending of the trial surprised them and angered a few. They stood uncertain.

Then someone shouted hurrah and somone else called for three cheers for Squire Hacker, and all in a minute the gathering had lost its hate and was taking on the look of a picnic. Men headed for the tavern. Parson Hix said a long prayer to which few listened, and everybody gathered around to wring Obie Payne's good hand and to give his daughter a squeeze.

At intervals through the afternoon and evening Peter touched lightly on Charity's mind, finding her carefree and happily occupied with visitors. He chose not to obtrude himself until she called.

Late that night she lay on her mattress and stared into the dark.

"Peter," she whispered.

"Yes, Charity."

"Oh, thank you again."

"Forget it. I got you into the mess. Now you're out of it. Anyway, I didn't really help. It all had to work out the way it did, because that's the way it had happened. You see?"

"No, not truly. How do we know that Squire won't dig up those old bones and burn them?"

"Because he didn't. Four years from now somebody will find them."

"No, Peter, I do not understand, and I am afeared again."

"Why, Charity?"

"It must be wrong, thee and me talking together like this and knowing what is to be and what is not."

"But what could be wrong about it?"

"That I do not know, but I think 'twere better you should stay in your time and me in mine. Goodbye, Peter."

"Charity!"

"And God bless you."

Abruptly she was gone and in Peter's mind there was an emptiness and a knowledge of being alone. He had not known that she could close him out like this.

With the passing of days he became skeptical and in time he might have disbelieved entirely. But Charity visited him again. It was October. He was alone and studying, without much interest.

"Peter."

"Charity, it's you."

"Yes. For a minute, please, Peter, for only a minute, but I had to tell you. I—" She seemed somehow embarrassed. "There is a message."

"A what?"

"Look at Bear Rock, Peter, under the bear's jaw on the left side."

With that, she was gone.

The cold water swirled around his legs as he traced with one finger the painstakingly chiseled message she had left: a little-girl message in a symbol far older than either of them.

The Witch

by A. E. van Vogt

A. E. van Vogt, along with Isaac Asimov, Robert A. Heinlein, and Theodore Sturgeon, was one of the major figures of science fiction's Golden Age—roughly 1939–1943. His inventive and complex novels like Slan *(1946),* The Weapon Makers *(1947),* The Book of Ptah *(1947), and* The World of A *(1948), all of which appeared earlier as serials, were highlights of this period and were tremendously influential in the development of the field. However, a long diversion into L. Ron Hubbard's Dianetics cost him many potentially productive years, and he never fully regained his earlier stature. His many short stories are equally inventive and outstanding, and can be found in some sixteen collections, including* The Best of A. E. Van Vogt *(1976).*

From where he sat, half hidden by the scraggly line of bushes, Marson watched the old woman. It was minutes now since he had stopped reading. The afternoon air hung breathless around him. Even here, a cliff's depth away from the sparkling tongue of sea that curled among the rocks below, the heat was a material thing, crushing at his strength. But it was the letter in his pocket, not the blazing sunlight, that weighed on Marson's mind. Two days now since that startling letter had arrived, and he still hadn't the beginning of the courage necessary to ask for an explanation. Frowning uncertainly—unsuspected—unsuspecting —he watched.

The old woman basked in the sun. Her long, thin, pale head drooped in sleep. On and on she sat, moveless, an almost shapeless form in her black sack of a dress. The strain of looking hurt his eyes; his gaze wandered; embraced the long, low, tree-protected cottage with its neat, white garage and its aloneness there on that high, green hill overlooking the great spread of city. Marson had a brief, cozy sense of privacy—then he turned back to the old woman.

For a long moment, he stared at the spot where she had been. He was conscious of a dim, intellectual surprise, but there was not a real thought in his head. After a brief period he grew aware of the blank, and he thought: Thirty feet to the front door from where she had been sitting; and she would have had to cross his line of vision to get there. An old woman, capable of moving— well, thirty feet a minute.

Marson stood up. There was a searing pain where an edge of the sun had cut into his shoulders. But that passed. From his upright position, he saw that not a solitary figure was visible on the steeply mounting sidewalk. And only the sound of the sea on the rocks below broke the silence of that hot Saturday afternoon. Where had the old wretch disappeared to?

The front door opened, and Joanna came out. She called to him: "Oh, there you are, Craig. Mother Quigley was just asking where you were."

Marson came silently down from the cliff's edge. Almost meticulously, he took his wife's words, figuratively rolled them over in his mind, and found them utterly inadequate. The old woman couldn't have been *just* asking for him, because the old woman had *not* gone through that door and therefore hadn't asked anyone anything for the last twenty minutes.

At last he said, "Where's Mother Quigley now?"

"Inside." He saw that Joanna was intent on the flower box on the window beside the door. "She's been knitting in the living room for the last half hour."

Amazement in him yielded to sharp annoyance. There was too damn much old woman in his mind since that letter had come less than forty-eight hours before. He drew it out, and stared bleakly at the scrawl of his name on the envelope.

It was simple enough, really, that this incredible letter had come to him. After the old woman's arrival nearly a year before, an unexpected nightmare, he'd mentally explored all the possible reverberations that might accrue from her presence in his home. And the thought had come that if she'd left any debts in the small village where she'd lived, he'd better pay them. A young man, whose appointment to the technical school principalship had been severely criticized on the grounds of his youth, couldn't afford to have *anything* come back on him. And so a month before he'd leisurely written the letter to which this was the answer.

Slowly, he drew the note from its envelope and once more read the mind-staggering words:

Dear Mr. Marson:

As I am the only debtor, the postmaster handed me your letter; and I wish to state that when your great grandmother died last year I buried her myself and in my capacity as gravestone marker I carved a stone for her grave. I did this at my own expense, being a God-fearing man, but if there is a relative, I feel you should bear the cost of same, which is eighteen (18) dollars. I hope to hear from you, as I need the money just now.

Pete Cole.

Marson stood for a long moment, then he turned to speak to Joanna—just in time to see her disappearing into the house. Once more undecided, he climbed to the cliff's edge, thinking: The old scoundrel! The nerve of a perfect stranger of an old woman walking into a private home and pulling a deception like that.

His public situation being what it was, his only solution was to pay her way into an institution; and even that would require careful thought. Frowning blackly, he hunched himself deeper into his chair there on the cliff's edge and deliberately buried himself in his book. It was not until much later that memory came of the way the old woman had disappeared from the lawn. Funny, he thought then, it really was damned funny.

Blankly sat the old woman.

Supper was over; and, because for years there had been no reserves of strength in that ancient body, digestion was an almost incredible process, an all-out affair. She sat as one dead, without visible body movement, without thought in her brain, even the grim creature purpose that had brought her here to this house lay like a stone at the bottom of the black pool that was her mind. It was as if she had always sat there in that chair by the window overlooking the sea, like an inanimate object, like some horrible mummy, like a wheel that, having settled into position, seemed now immovable.

After an hour, awareness began to creep into her. The creature mind of her, the strange, inhuman creature mind behind that parchment-like, sharp-nosed mask of human flesh, stirred into

life. It studied Marson at the living room table, his head bent
thoughtfully over the next term curriculum he was preparing.
Toothless lips curled finally into a contemptuous sneer.

The sneer faded as Joanna slipped softly into the room. Half-
closed, letching eyes peered then, with an abruptly ravenous,
beastlike lust, at the slim, lithe, strong body. Pretty, pretty body,
soon now to be taken over. In the three-day period of the first
new moon after the summer solstice . . . in nine days exactly—

Nine days! The ancient carcass shuddered and wriggled ecstati-
cally with the glee of the creature. Nine short days, and once
again the age-long cycle of dynamic existence would begin.
Such a pretty body, too, capable of vibrant, world-ranging life.
Thought faded as Joanna went back into the kitchen. Slowly, for
the first time, awareness came of the sea.

Contentedly sat the old woman. Soon now, the sea would hold
no terrors, and the blinds wouldn't have to be down, nor the
windows shut. She would even be able to walk along the shore at
midnight, as of old; and *they*, whom she had deserted so long
ago, would once more shrink from the irresistible energy aura of
her new, young body.

The sound of the sea came to her, where she sat so quietly;
calm sound at first, almost gentle in the soft sibilation of each
wave thrust. Farther out, the voices of the water were louder,
more raucous, blatantly confident, but the meaning of what they
said was blurred by the distance, a dim, clamorous confusion
that rustled discordantly out of the gathering night. Night! She
shouldn't be aware of night falling, when the blinds were drawn.
With a little gasp, she twisted toward the window beside which
she sat. Instantly, a blare of hideous fear exploded from her lips.

The ugly sound bellowed into Marson's ears, and brought him
lurching to his feet. It raged through the door into the kitchen,
and Joanna came running as if it were a rope pulling at her. The
old woman screeched on; and it was Marson who finally penetrated to the desire behind that mad terror.

"Good Lord!" he shrugged. "It's the windows and the blinds.
I forgot to put them down when dusk fell." He stopped, irritated,
then: "Damned nonsense! I've a good mind to—"

"For Heaven's sake!" his wife urged. "We've got to stop that
noise. I'll take this side of the room; you take the windows next
to her."

Marson shrugged again, acquiescently. He was thinking: They
wouldn't have this to put up with much longer. As soon as the
summer holidays arrived, he'd make arrangements to put her in

the Old Folks Home. And that would be that. Less than two weeks now.

His wife's voice broke almost sharply across the silence that came as Mother Quigley settled back into her chair. "I'm surprised at you forgetting a thing like that. You're usually so thoughtful."

"It was so damned hot!" Marson complained.

Joanna said no more; and he went back to his chair. But he was thinking suddenly: Old woman who fears the sea and the night, why did you come to this house by the sea, where the street lamps are far apart and the nights almost primevally dark? The gray thought passed. His mind returned with conscientious intentness to the preparation of the curriculum.

Startled sat the old woman! All the swift rage of the creature burned within her. That wretched man, daring to forget. And yet— "You're usually so thoughtful!" his wife had said. It was true. Not once in eleven months had he forgotten to look after the blinds—until tonight. Was it possible that he suspected? That somehow, now that the time for the change was so near, an inkling of her purpose had dripped from her straining brain? It had happened before. In the past, she had had to fight for her bodies against terrible, hostile men who had nothing but dreadful suspicion.

Jet-black eyes narrowed to pinpoints. With this man, there would have to be more than suspicion. Being what he was, practical, skeptical, cold-brained, not all the telepathic vibrations, nor the queer mind storms with their abnormal implications—if he had yet had any—would touch him or remain with him of themselves. Nothing but facts would rouse this man.

What facts? Was it possible that, in her intense concentration of thought, she had unwittingly permitted images to show? Or had he made inquiries? Her body shook, and then, slowly, purpose formed: She must take no chances. Tomorrow was Sunday, and the man would be home. So nothing was possible. But Monday—

That was it. Monday morning while Joanna slept—and Joanna always went back to bed for an hour's nap after her husband had gone to work—on Monday morning she would slip in and prepare the sleeping body so that, seven days later, entry would be easy. No more wasting time trying to persuade Joanna to take the stuff voluntarily. The silly fool with her refusal of home remedies, her prating of taking only doctor's prescriptions. Forcible feeding would be risky, but not half so risky as expecting this wretched, doting wreck of a body to survive another year.

Implacable sat the old woman.

In spite of herself, she felt the toll of the hours of anticipation. At Monday's breakfast, she drooled with the inner excitement of her purpose. The cereal fell from her misshaped mouth, milk and saliva spattered over the tablecloth—and she couldn't help it. Old hands shook, mouth quivered; in everything her being yielded to that dreadful anility of body.

With a start, she saw that the man was pushing clear of the table, and there was such a white look on his face that she scarcely needed his words, as he said:

"There's something I've been intending to say to Mother Quigley"—his voice took on a rasping note—"and right now, when I'm feeling thoroughly disgusted, is a darned good time to say it."

"For Heaven's sake, Craig"—Joanna cut in sharply, and the old woman snatched at the interruption, and began queasily to get to her feet—"what's made you so irritable these last few days? Now, be a good lover and go to school. Personally, I'm not going to clean up this mess till I've had my nap, and I'm certainly not going to let it get me down. 'By.'"

A kiss; and she was gone into the hallway. Almost instantly, she vanished into the master bedroom; and then, even as the old woman struggled desperately to get farther out of her chair, Marson was turning to her, eyes bleak and determined. Cornered, she stared up at him like a trapped animal, dismayed by the way this devilish body had betrayed her in an emergency, distorting her will. Marson said:

"Mother Quigley—I shall continue to call you that for the moment—I have received a letter from a man who claims to have carved a stone for the body he himself buried in your grave. What I would like to know is this: Who is occupying that grave?"

It was his own phrasing that brought Marson to startled silence. He stood strangely taut, struck rigid by a curious, alien horror, unlike anything he had ever known. For a long, terrible moment, his mind seemed to lie naked and exposed to the blast of an icy inner wind that whirled at him out of some nether darkness. Thoughts came, a blare of obscene mental vaporings, unwholesome, black with ancient, incredibly ancient evil, a very seething mass of unsuspected horrors. With a start he came out of that grisly world of his own imagination and grew aware that the old crone was pouring forth harsh, almost eager words:

"It wasn't me that was buried. There were two of us old ones in the village, and when she died, I made her face to look like

mine, and mine to look like hers, and I took her money and . . .
I used to be an actress, you know, and I could use makeup.
That's how it was, yes, yes, makeup; and that's the whole
explanation and I'm not what you think at all, but just an old
woman who was poor. That's all, just an old woman to be
pitied—''

She would have gone on endlessly if the creature-logic in her
had not, with dreadful effort, forced her quiet. She stood then,
breathing heavily, conscious that her voice had been too swift,
too excited, her tongue loose with the looseness of old age, and
her words had damned her with every syllable. It was the man
who brought surcease to her desperate fear; the man saying
explosively:

"Good heavens, woman, do you mean to stand there and tell
me you did a thing like that—''

Marson stopped, overwhelmed. Every word the old woman
had spoken had drawn him further back from the strange, unsettling morass of thoughts that had briefly flooded his mind, back
into the practical world of his own reason, and his own ethics.
He felt almost physically shocked, and it was only after a long
moment that he was able to go on. He said finally, slowly:

"You actually confess to the ghoulish deed of disfiguring a
dead body for the purpose of stealing money."

His voice collapsed before that abyss of unsuspected moral
degradation. Here was a crime of the baser sort, an unclean,
revolting thing that, if it were ever found out, would draw the
censure of an entire nation, and ruin any school principal alive.
He shuddered. He said hastily:

"I haven't time to go into this now." With a start, he saw that
she was heading toward the hallway that led to her bedroom.
More firmly, he called: "And there's another thing. Saturday
afternoon, you were sitting out on the lawn—''

A door closed softly. Behind it, the old woman stood, gasping
from her exertions, but with a growing conviction of triumph.
The silly, stupid man still didn't suspect. What did she care what
he thought of her? Only seven days remained, and if she could
last them, nothing else mattered. The danger was that her position would become more difficult every day. That meant, when
the time came, a quick entry would be absolutely necessary.
That meant—the woman's body must be prepared now! Joanna,
healthy Joanna, would be already asleep. So it was only a matter
of waiting for that miserable husband to get out. She waited.

The sweet sound came at last from the near distance—the
front door opening and then shutting. Like a stag at bay, the old

woman quivered. Her body shook with the sick thrill of imminent action. She had made some preparation to offset disaster, but if she failed, if she were discovered—

The spasm of fear passed. With a final, reassuring fumble into the flat, black bosom of her dress, where the little bag of powder hung open, she glided forth. For the tiniest instant, she paused in the open doorway of Joanna's bedroom. Her gimlet eyes dwelt with a glitter of satisfaction on the sleeping figure. And then, she was in the room.

The morning wind from the sea struck Marson like a blow as he opened the door. He shut it with a swift burst of strength, and stood in the dully lighted hallway, indecisive. It wasn't that he wasn't going out. There were too many things to do before the end of the school year. It was just that the abrupt resistance of the wind had crystallized a thought: Ought he to leave without telling Joanna about the letter from the gravestone maker? After all, the old woman now knew that he knew. In her cunning eagerness to defend herself and the security she must consider threatened, she might mention the subject to Joanna, and Joanna would know nothing.

Still undecided, Marson took several slow steps, then paused again just inside the living room. Damn it, the thing could probably wait till noon, especially as Joanna would be asleep by now. Even as it was, he'd have to go by car or streetcar if he hoped to reach the school at his usual early hour.

His thought twisted crazily as the black form of the old woman glided ghostlike across the bedroom hallway straight into Joanna's room. Senselessly, a yell quivered on Marson's lips— senselessly, because there was in him no reasoned realization of alienness. The sound froze unuttered because abruptly that icy, unnatural wind out of blackness was blowing again in his mind. Abnormal, primordial things echoed and raged. He had no consciousness of running, but suddenly, there was the open bedroom door, and there was the old woman. And at that last instant, though he had come with noiseless speed, the creature sensed him.

She jumped with a sheer physical dismay that was horrible to see. Her fingers that had been hovering over Joanna's mouth jerked spasmodically, and a greenish powder in them sprayed partly on the bed, mostly on the little rug beside the bed.

And then, Marson was on top of her. That loathsome mind-wind was blowing stronger, colder; and in him was an utter, deadly conviction that demonic muscles would resist his strength to the limit. For a moment, that certainty prevailed even over reality. For there was nothing.

Thin, bony arms yielded instantly to his devastatingly hard thrust; a body that was like old, rotten paper crumbled to the floor from his murderous rush. For a moment, the incredibly easy victory gave Marson pause. But no astonishment could genuinely cancel that unnatural sense of unhuman things; no totality of doubt at this instant could begin to counterbalance his fury at what he had seen.

The old woman lay at his feet in a shapeless, curled-up blob. With a pitiless ferocity, a savage intent beyond any emotion he had ever known, Marson snatched her from the floor. Light as long-decayed wood, she came up in his fingers, a dangling, inhuman, black-clothed thing. He shook it, as he would have shaken a monster; and it was then, when his destroying purpose was a very blaze of unreasoning intensity, that the incredible thing happened.

Images of the old woman flooded the room. Seven old women, all in a row, complete in every detail from black, sacklike dress to semi-bald head, raced for the door. Three exact duplicates of the old woman were clawing frantically at the nearest window. The eleventh replica was on her knees desperately trying to squeeze under the bed. With an astounded gasp, Marson dropped the thing in his hands. It fell squalling, and abruptly the eleven images of the old woman vanished like figments of a nightmare.

"Craig!"

In a dim way, he recognized Joanna's voice. But still he stood, like a log of wood, unheeding. He was thinking piercingly: That was what happened Saturday on the lawn—an image of the old woman unwittingly projected by her furiously working mind as she sat in the living room knitting. Unwitting images had they been now, of a certainty. The old woman's desperately fearful mind seeking ways of escape. God, what was he thinking? There was—there *could* be nothing here but his own disordered imagination. The thing was impossible.

"Craig, what is all this anyway? What's happened?"

He scarcely heard; for suddenly, quite clearly, almost calmly, his mind was coordinating around a single thought, simple, basic, and terrible:

What did a man do with a witch in A. D. 1948?

The hard thought collapsed as he saw, for the first time, that Joanna was half-sitting, half-kneeling in the taut position she had jerked herself into when she wakened. She was swaying the slightest bit, as if her muscle control was incomplete. Her face was creased with the shock of her rude awakening. Her eyes, he saw, were wide and almost blank; and they were staring at the old woman. With one swift glance he followed that rigid gaze, and alarm struck through him. Joanna had not wakened till the old woman screamed. She *hadn't* seen the images at all. She would have only the picture of a powerful, brutal young man standing menacingly over the moaning form of an old woman— and by Heaven, he'd have to act fast.

"Look!" Marson began curtly, "I caught her slipping a green powder on your lips."

It was putting the thing into words that struck him dumb. His mind reeled before the tremendous fact that a witch had tried to feed dope to Joanna—*his* Joanna! In some incomprehensible way, Joanna was to be a victim, and he must convince her now of the action they must take. Before that purpose, rage fled. Hastily, he sank down on the bed beside Joanna. Swiftly, he launched into his story. He made no mention of the images or of his own monstrous suspicions. Joanna was even more practical than he. It would only confuse the issue to let her get the impression that he was crazy. He finished finally:

"I don't want any arguments. The facts speak for themselves. The powder alone damns her; the letter serves to throw enough doubt on her identity to relieve us of any further sense of obligation. Here's what we're going to do. First, I shall phone my secretary that I may not be in till late. Then I'll call up the Old Folks Home. I have no doubt under normal conditions there are preliminaries to entry, but money ought to eliminate all red tape. We're getting rid of her today and—"

Amazingly, Joanna's laughter interrupted him, a wave of laughter that ended in a sharp, unnormal, hysterical note. Marson shook her.

"Darling," he began anxiously.

She pushed him away, scrambled off the bed, and knelt with a curious excitement beside the old woman.

"Mother Quigley," she said, and her voice was so high-pitched that Marson half-climbed to his feet. He sank down again as she went on: "Mother Quigley, answer one question: That powder you were placing in my mouth—was it that ground seaweed remedy of yours that you've been trying to feed me for my headaches?"

The flare of hope that came to the old woman nearly wrecked her brain. How could she have forgotten her long efforts to make Joanna take the powder voluntarily? She whispered:

"Help me to my bed, dearie. I don't think anything is broken, but I'll have to lie down . . . yes, yes, my dear, that was the powder. I was so sure it would help you. We women, you know, with our headaches, have to stick together. I shouldn't have done it, of course, but—'' A thought, a blaze of anxiety, struck her. She whimpered, ''You won't let him send me away, will you? I know I've been a lot of trouble and—''

She stopped, because there was a queer look on Joanna's face; and enough was enough. Victory could be overplayed. She listened with ill-suppressed content as Joanna said swiftly:

''Craig, hadn't you better go? You'll be late.''

Marson said sharply, ''I want the rest of that weed powder. I'm going to have it analyzed.''

But he avoided his wife's gaze; and he was thinking, stunned: ''I'm crazy. I was so dizzy with rage that I had a nightmare of hallucinations.''

Wasn't it Dr. Lycoming who had said that the human mind must have racial memory that extended back to the nameless seas that spawned man's ancestors? And that under proper and violent stress, these memories of terror would return? His shame grew as the old woman's shaking fingers produced a little canvas bag.

Without a word, he took the container and left the room.

Minutes later, with the soft purr of his car throbbing in his ears, eyes intent on the traffic, the whole affair seemed as remote and unreal as any dream. He thought: ''Well, what next? I still don't want her around but—'' It struck him with a curious, sharp dismay that there was not a plan in his head.

Tuesday morning the old woman awakened with a start and lay very still. Hunger came, but her mind was made up. She would not dress or eat until after the man was gone to work, and she would not come out at noon, or after school hours, but would remain in this room, with the door shut, whenever he was around.

Six days before she could act, six days of dragging minutes, of doubts and fears.

Wednesday at 4:30 p.m., Marson's fingers relaxed on the shining knob of the front door as the laughter of women tinkled from inside. He recalled that he had been warned of an impending tea. Like an unwelcome intruder, he slipped off down the street, and it was seven o'clock before he emerged from the ''movie'' and headed homewards. He was thinking for the hundredth time: ''I saw those old woman images. I know I saw them. It's my civilized instinct that makes me want to doubt, and so keeps me inactive.''

The evening paper was lying on the doorstep. He picked it up;

and later, after a supper of left-over sandwiches and hot coffee, he glanced through it. A paragraph from an anti-communist editorial caught, first his eyes, and then his mind.

> The enemy has not really fooled us. We know that all his acts, directly or indirectly, have been anti-*us*. The incredible and fantastic thing is this knowing all we know and doing nothing.
>
> If an individual had as much suspicion, as much evidence, that someone was going to murder him at the first opportunity, he would try to prevent the act from being committed; he would not wait for the full, bloody consummation.
>
> The greater fact is that there will come a time when everything possible is too little, even all-out effort too late.

With a start, Marson allowed the paper to fall. The ideology of the editorial was already out of his mind. But the theme, the inmost meaning of that editorial was for him and for his problem. *Knowing what he knew and doing nothing.*

Uneasily, but with sudden determination, he climbed to his feet. "Joanna," he began, and realized that he was talking to an empty room. He peered into the bedroom. Joanna lay on the bed, fully dressed, sound asleep. Marson's grimness faded into an understanding smile. Preparing that afternoon tea had taken its toll. After an hour, she was still asleep, and so very quietly, very gently, he undressed her and put her to bed. She did not waken even when he kissed her good night.

Thursday: By noon, his mind was involved with a petty-larceny case, a sordid, miserable affair of a pretty girl caught stealing. He saw Kemp, the chemistry assistant, come in; and then withdraw quietly. In abrupt fever of excitement, he postponed the unwelcome case, and hastened after Kemp. He found the man putting on his hat to go to lunch. The young chemistry instructor's eyes lighted as they saw Marson, then he frowned.

"That green powder you gave me to analyze, Mr. Marson, it's been a tough assignment. I like to be thorough, you know."

Mr. Marson nodded. He knew the mettle of this man, which was why he had chosen him rather than his equally obliging chief. Kemp was young, eager; and he knew his subject.

"Go on," said Marson.

"As you suggested," Kemp continued, "it was ground weed. I took it up to Biology Bill . . . I mean, I took it up to Mr. Grainger."

In spite of himself, Marson smiled. There had been a time when he had said "Biology Bill" as a matter of course. "Go on," was all he said now.

"Grainger identified it as a species of seaweed known as *Hydrodendon Barelia*."

"Any special effects if taken into the human system?" Marson was all casualness.

"No-o! It's not dangerous, if that's what you mean. Naturally, I tried it on the dog, meaning myself, and it's rather unpleasant, not exactly bitter but sharp."

Marson was silent. He wondered whether he ought to feel disappointed or relieved. Or what? Kemp was speaking again:

"I looked up its history, and surprisingly, it has quite a story. You know how in Europe they make you study a lot of stuff about the old alchemists and all that kind of thing, to give you an historical grounding."

"Yes."

Kemp laughed. "You haven't got a witch around your place by any chance?"

"Eh!" The exclamation almost burned Marson's lips. He fought to hide the tremendousness of that shock.

Kemp laughed again. "According to *Die Geschichte der Zauberinnen*, by the Austrian Karl Gloeck, *Hydrodendon Barelia* is the modern name for the sinister witch's weed of antiquity. I'm not talking about the special witches of our Christian lore, with their childish attributes, but the old tribe of devil's creatures that came out of prehistory, regular full-blooded sea witches. It seems when each successive body gets old, they choose a young woman's body, attune themselves to it by living with the victim, and take possession any time after midnight of the first full-moon period following the 21st of June. Witch's weed is supposed to make the entry easier. Gloeck says . . . why, what's the matter, sir?"

His impulse, his wild and terrible impulse, was to babble the whole story to Kemp. With an effort, he stopped himself; for Kemp, though he might talk easily of witches, was a scientist to the depths of his soul. And what he—Marson—might have to do must not be endangered by the knowledge that some practical, doubting person suspected the truth. The mere existence of suspicion would corrode his will, and, in the final issue, undermine his decision to act.

He heard himself muttering words of thanks. Minutes later, on his way, he was thinking miserably: What could he say, how could he convince Joanna that the old woman must be gotten rid of? And there was one more thing that he had to clear up before he would dare risk everything in the only, unilateral action that remained. One more thing—

All Saturday morning, the sun shone brilliantly, but by afternoon black clouds rode above his racing car. At six in the evening it rained torrentially for ten minutes; and then, slowly, the sky cleared.

His first view of the village was from a hill, and that, he thought, relieved, should make it easier. From a group of trees he surveyed the little sprawl of houses and buildings. It was the church that confused him at first. He kept searching in its vicinity with his field glasses. And it was nearly half an hour before he was convinced that what he sought was not there. Twilight was thick over the world now, and that brought surging panic. He couldn't possibly go down to the village and inquire where the graveyard was. Yet—hurry, hurry! He walked deeper into the woods along the edge of the hill. There was a jutting point of ground farther along, from where he would be able to sweep the countryside. These villages sometimes had their graveyards a considerable distance away.

The little roadway burst upon him abruptly, as he emerged from the brush; and there, a few scant feet away, was a trellised gate. Beyond it, in the gathering shadows, simple crosses gleamed, an angel stood whitely, stiffly, poised for flight; and several great, shining granite stones reared rigidly from a dark, quiet earth.

Night lay black and still on the graveyard when his cautiously used flashlight at last picked out the headstone he sought. The inscription was simple:

Mrs. Quigley
Died July 7, 1945
Over 90 years old

He went back to the car, and got the shovel; and then he began to dig. The earth was strong; and he was not accustomed to digging. After an hour, he had penetrated about a foot and a half. Breathless, he sank down on the ground, and for a while he lay there under the night sky with its shifting panoply of clouds. A queer, intellectual remembrance came that the average weight of university presidents and high school principals was around one hundred eighty pounds, according to Young. But the devil of it was, he thought grimly, it was all weight and no endurance. Nevertheless, he had to go on if it took all night.

At least, he was sure of one thing. Joanna wasn't home. It had been a tough job persuading her to accept that week-end invitation alone, tougher still to lie about the duties that would take him out of the city until Sunday morning; and he had had to promise faithfully that he would drive out Sunday to get her. The simplest thing of all had been getting the young girl to look after the old woman over the week-end.

The sound of a car passing brought him to his feet in one jerky movement. He frowned. It wasn't that he was worried, or even basically alarmed. His mind felt rock-steady; his determination was an unshaken thing. Here in this dark, peaceful setting, disturbance was as unlikely as his own ghoul-like incursion. People simply didn't come to graveyards at night.

The night sped as he dug on and on, nearer to that secret he must have before he could take the deadly action that logic dictated even now. And he didn't feel like a ghoul. There was no feeling at all, only his purpose; and there was the dark night, the quietness, broken only by the swish of dirt thrown upward and outward. His life, his strength flowed on here in this little, tree-grown field of death; and his watch showed twenty-five minutes to two when at last the spade struck wood.

It was after two when his flashlight glowed eerily into the empty wooden box. For long seconds, he stared; and now that the reality was here, he didn't know what he had expected. Obviously, only too obviously, an image had been buried here—and vanished gleefully as the dirt began to thud in the filling of the grave. But why a burial at all? Who was she trying to fool? His mind grew taut. Reasons didn't matter now. *He knew;* that was what counted. And his actions must be cold and deadly as was the purpose of the creature that had fastened itself on his household.

His car glided onto the deserted early-morning highway. The gray dawn came out of the east to meet him as he drove; and only his dark purpose, firmer, icier each minute, an intellectualized thing as unquenchable as sun fire, kept him companion.

It was deep into the afternoon when his machine, in its iron-throated second gear, whirred up the steep hill and twisted into the runway that led to the garage. He went into the house and for a while he sat down. The girl whom Joanna had left in charge was a pretty, red-haired thing named Helen. She was quite fragilely built, he noted with grim approval; he had suggested her for the week-end with that very smallness in mind. And yes, she wouldn't mind staying another night if they didn't come home. And when was he leaving to get his wife?

"Oh, I'm going to have a nap first," Marson replied. "Had rather a hard drive. And you . . . what are you going to do while I sleep?"

"I've found some magazines," the girl said. "I'm going to sit here and read. I'll keep very quiet, I assure you."

"Thank you," Marson said. "It's just for a couple of hours, you know."

He smiled bleakly to himself as he went into the bedroom and closed the door. Men with desperate plans had to be bold, had to rely on the simplest, most straightforward realities of life—such as the fact that people normally stayed away from cemeteries at night. And that young women didn't make a nuisance of themselves by prowling around when they had promised not to. He took off his shoes, put on his slippers, and then he waited for five long minutes to give her time to settle down.

Finally, softly, he went through the bathroom door that led to the hallway that connected kitchen and bedrooms. The kitchen door creaked as he went out, but he allowed himself no qualms; not a trace of fear entered into the ice-cold region that was his brain.

The car was parked at the side of the house, where there was only one window. He took the five-gallon tin of gasoline out of the back seat, carried it through the kitchen down into the basement. He covered it with some old cloth, then he was up again through the kitchen. He reached the bedroom, thinking tensely: It was these details that must paralyze most people planning murder. Tonight when he came back, he wouldn't be able to drive the car up the hill, because it was to be a very special, unseen, ghostly trip. The car would be parked at least a mile away, and obviously, it would be fantastically risky, and tiring, to lug a five-gallon tin of gas a whole mile through back alleys. And what a nightmare it would be to blunder with such a tin through the kitchen and into the basement at midnight. Impossible, too, he had found, to get anything past Joanna without her seeing.

Murder had its difficulties; and quite simply, of course, murder it must be. And by fire. All that he ever heard about witches showed the overwhelming importance of fire. And just let lightly built Helen try to break down the old woman's door after the fire had started and he had locked that door from the outside.

He lay for a while quietly on the bed, and the thought came that no man would seem a greater scoundrel than he if all that he had done and all that he intended to do was ever found out. For a moment, then, a fear came black as pitch; and as if the picture was there before his eyes, he saw the great school slipping from him, the greater college beyond fading like the dream it was, fading into the mists that surrounded a prison cell.

He thought: It would be so easy to take half measures that would rid him and Joanna of the terrible problem. All he needed to do next day was to take her to the Old Folks Home while Joanna was still away, and ruthlessly face down all subsequent objections. The old woman would escape, perhaps, but she would never come back to them.

He could retreat, then, into his world of school and Joanna; existence would flow on in its immense American way—and somewhere soon there would be a young woman witch, glowing with the strength of ancient, evil life renewed; and somewhere too there would be a human soul shattered out of its lawful body, a home where an old woman had blatantly, skillfully, intruded.

Knowing what he did, and doing nothing short of everything!

He must have slept on that thought, the demanding sleep of utterly weary nerves, unaccustomed to being denied their rest. He wakened with a shock. It was pitch dark, he saw, and—

The bedroom door opened softly. Joanna came tiptoeing in. She saw him by the light that streamed from the hall. She stopped and smiled. Then she came over and kissed him.

"Darling," she said, "I'm so glad that you hadn't started out to get me. A delightful couple offered to drive me home, and I thought, if we met you on the way, at least it would have saved you that much, after your long, tiring week-end. I've sent Helen home. It's after eleven, so just undress and go straight to bed. I'm going to have a cup of tea myself; perhaps you'd like one too."

Her voice barely penetrated through the great sounds that clanged in his brain, the pure agony of realization. *After eleven*— less than an hour to the midnight that, once a year, began the fatal period of the witch's moon. The whole world of his plans was crashing about his ears.

He hovered about her while she put the kettle on. It was half-past eleven when they finished tea, and still he couldn't speak, couldn't begin to find the beginning that would cover all the things that had to be said. Wretchedly, he grew aware of her eyes watching him as she puffed at her cigarette.

He got up and started to pace the floor; and now there was dark puzzlement in her fine brown eyes. Twice, she started to speak, but each time cut herself off. And waited. He could almost feel her waiting in that quiet, earnest way of hers, waiting for him to speak first.

The impossibility, he thought, the utter impossibility of convincing this calm, practical, tender-hearted wife of his. And yet, it *had* to be done; now before it was too late, before even all-out effort would be too little. The recurrence of that phrase from the editorial started a streak of cold perspiration down his face. He stopped short, stopped in front of her; and his eyes must have been glaring pools, his rigid posture terrifying; for she shrank back.

"Craig—"

"Joanna, I want you to take your hat and coat and go to a hotel."

It needed no imagination to realize that his words must sound insane. He plunged on with the volubility of a child telling an exciting story. And that was the way he felt—like a child talking to a tolerant grown-up. But he couldn't stop. He omitted only his grim murder purpose. She would have to absorb the shock of that later when it was all over. When he had finished, he saw that her gaze was tender.

"You poor darling," she said. "So that's been bothering you. You were worried about me. I can just see how everything would work on your mind. I'd have felt the same, if it were you apparently in danger."

Marson groaned. So that was the angle she was taking—sweet understanding; humoring his natural alarm; believing not a word. He caught his mind into a measure of calm. He said in a queer, shaky voice:

"Joanna, think of Kemp's definite analysis of it as witch's weed, and the fact that the body is not in the grave."

Still there was no fire in her eyes, no flame of basic fear. She was frowning; she said:

"But why would she have to go to all that trouble of burying one of her images, when all she had to do was get on the train and come here? Physically, that is what she did; why that enormous farce of a burial?"

Marson flared, "Why the lie she told me about having put makeup on someone else who was buried there? Oh, darling, don't you see—"

Slowly, reasonably, Joanna said, "There may have been some connivance, Craig, perhaps between the man, Pete Cole, who wrote you the letter, and Mother Quigley. Have you thought of that?"

If she had been with him, he thought, when he opened that dark grave. If she had seen the incredible images— If, if, if—

He stole a glance at the clock on the wall. It was seventeen minutes to twelve, and that nearly twisted his brain. He shuddered, and fought for control of his voice. There were arguments he could think of, but the time for talk was past, far past. Only one thing mattered.

"Joanna," he said, and his voice was so intense that it shocked him, "you'll go to the hotel for three days, for my sake?"

"Why, of course, darling." She looked serene, as she stood up. "My night bag is still packed. I'll just take the car and—" A thought seemed to strike her. Her fine, clear brow creased. "What about you?"

"I'll stay here of course," he said, "to see that she stays here. You can phone me up at school tomorrow. Hurry, for Heaven's sake."

He felt chilled by the way that her gaze was appraising him. "Just a minute," she said, and her voice was slow, taut. "Originally, you planned to have me out of the way only until tomorrow. What—are you—planning to do—tonight?"

His mind was abruptly sullen, rebellious, his mouth awkward, as if only the truth could come easily from it. Lies had always been hard for him. But he tried now.

"All I wanted was to get you out of the way while I visited the grave. I didn't really figure beyond that."

Her eyes didn't believe him; her voice said so, but just what words she used somehow didn't penetrate. For an odd steadiness was coming to him, realization that the time must be only minutes away and that all this talk was worthless. Only his relentless purpose mattered. He said simply, almost as if he were talking to himself:

"I intended to lock her door from the outside, and burn the house, but I can see now that isn't necessary. You'd better get going, darling, because this is going to be messy, and you mustn't see it. You see, I'm going to take her out to the cliff's edge, and throw her to the night sea she fears so violently."

He stopped because the clock, incredibly, said eight minutes to twelve. Without a sound, without waiting for the words that seemed to quiver on her lips, he whirled and raced into the bedroom corridor. He tried the old woman's door. It was locked. A very fury of frustration caught at his throat.

"Open up!" he roared.

There was silence within the room. He felt Joanna's fingers tugging at his sleeve. And then he was flinging the full weight of his hundred and eighty pounds at that door. Two bone-wrenching thrusts, and it went down with an ear-splitting crash. His fingers fumbled for the light switch. There was a click, and then—

He stopped, chilled, half-paralyzed by what the light revealed: Twelve old women, twelve creatures snarling at him from every part of the room. The witch was out in the open. And ready.

The queerest thing of all in that tremendous moment was the sheer glow of triumph that swept him—the triumph of a man who has indisputably won an argument with his wife. He felt a crazy, incredible joy; he wanted to shout: "See! see! wasn't I right? Wasn't it exactly as I told you?"

With an effort, he caught hold of himself; and the shaky realization came that actually he was on the verge of madness. He said unsteadily:

"This is going to take a little time. I'll have to carry them one by one to the cliff; and the law of averages says that I'll strike the right one sooner or later. We won't have to worry about her slipping away in between, because we know her horrible fear of the night. It's only a matter of perseverance.''

His voice faltered the faintest bit, for suddenly the ghastly reality of what was here struck his inner consciousness. Some of the creatures sat on the bed, some on the floor; two stood, their arms around each other; and half of them were gibbering in a fantastic caricature of terror. With a start, he grew aware of Joanna behind him. She was pale, incredibly pale for Joanna, and her voice, when she spoke, quavered. She said:

"The trouble with you, Craig, is that you're not practical. You want to do physical things like throwing her onto the rocks at the bottom of the cliff, or burning her. It proves that even yet your basic intellect doesn't believe in her. Or you'd know what to do.''

She was pressing against him, staring wide-eyed over his shoulder at that whimpering, terrified group. Now, before he could realize her intention, she slipped under his arm, and was into the room. Her shoulder bumped him slightly in passing, and threw him off balance. It was only for a moment, but when he could look again, eight squalling crones had Joanna surrounded.

He had a brief glimpse of her distorted face. Six gnarled hands were clawing to open her mouth; a tangle of desperate old women's hands were clutching at her arms and her legs, trying to hold her flailing, furious body. *And they were succeeding!* That was the terrifying reality that drove him into the midst of that brew of old women with battering fists—and pulled Joanna clear.

Immense anger grew out of his fear. "You silly fool!" he

raged. "Don't you realize it must be after midnight?" Then, with an abrupt, fuller realization that she had actually been attacked, piercingly:

"Are you all right?"

"Yes." Shakily. "Yes."

But *she* would have said that too. He glared at her with mad eyes, as if by the sheer intensity of his gaze he would see through her face into her brain. She must have seen his terrible thought in his straining countenance, for she cried:

"Don't you see, darling? The blinds, the windows—pull them up. That's what I intended to do. Let in the night. Let in the things she fears. If she exists, then so must they. Don't you see?"

He took Joanna with him, kicking at the creatures with his fists and feet, with a grim merciless ferocity. He tore the blind from its hooks; one thrust of his foot smashed the whole lower pane of the window. And then, back at the door, they waited.

Waited!

There was a whisper of water splattering on the window sill. A shape without shape silhouetted abnormally against the blue-black sky beyond the window. And then, the water was on the floor, trickling from a misty shape that seemed to walk. A voice sighed, or was it a thought?

"You nearly fooled us, Niyasha, with that false burial. We lost sight of you for months. But we knew that only by the sea and from the sea could your old body draw the strength for the change. We watched, as we watched so long for so many of the traitors; and so at last you answer the justice of the ancient waters."

There was no sound but the sibilation of water trickling. The old women were silent as stones; and they sat like birds fascinated by a snake. And suddenly, the images were gone, snuffed out. One fragile, lonely-looking old woman sat on the floor directly in the path of the mist-thing. Almost primly, she gathered her skirts about her.

The mist enveloped her form. She was lifted into it, then instantly dropped. Swiftly, the mist retreated to the window. It was gone. The old woman lay flat on her back, eyes open and staring; her mouth open, too, unprettily.

That was the overall effect—the utter lack of anything beautiful.

The Witches of Karres
by James H. Schmitz

The late (1911–1981) James H. Schmitz became a full-time writer only in 1961, at the age of fifty, but he quickly established himself as an excellent craftsman, especially adept at depicting convincing aliens and their environments. He also developed a very popular telepathic female series character, Telzey Amberdon, who came along at just about the same time as the James Bond films, not a bad coincidence for a secret-agent-type protagonist. Her exploits are recorded in such books as The Universe Against Her *(1964),* The Lion Game *(1973), and* The Telzey Toy *(1973). "The Witches of Karres" is perhaps his most famous story.*

I

It was around the hub of the evening on the planet of Porlumma that Captain Pausert, commercial traveler from the Republic of Nikkeldepain, met the first of the witches of Karres.

It was just plain fate, so far as he could see.

He was feeling pretty good as he left a high-priced bar on a cobbly street near the spaceport, with the intention of returning straight to his ship. There hadn't been an argument, exactly. But someone grinned broadly, as usual, when the captain pronounced the name of his native system; and the captain had pointed out then, with considerable wit, how much more ridiculous it was to call a planet Porlumma, for instance, than to call it Nikkeldepain.

He proceeded to collect a gradually increasing number of pained stares by a detailed comparison of the varied, interesting and occasionally brilliant role Nikkeldepain had played in history with Porlumma's obviously dull and dumpy status as a sixth-rate Empire outpost.

In conclusion, he admitted frankly that he wouldn't care to be found dead on Porlumma.

Somebody muttered loudly in Imperial Universum that in that case it might be better if he didn't hang around Porlumma too long. But the captain only smiled politely, paid for his two drinks and left.

There was no point in getting into a rhubarb on one of these border planets. Their citizens still had an innocent notion that they ought to act like frontiersmen—but then the Law always showed up at once.

He felt pretty good. Up to the last four months of his young life, he had never looked on himself as being particularly patriotic. But compared to most of the Empire's worlds, Nikkeldepain was downright attractive in its stuffy way. Besides, he was returning there solvent—would they ever be surprised!

And awaiting him, fondly and eagerly, was Illyla, the Miss Onswud, fair daughter of the mighty Councilor Onswud, and the captain's secretly affianced for almost a year. She alone had believed in him!

The captain smiled and checked at a dark cross-street to get his bearings on the spaceport beacon. Less than half a mile away. He set off again. In about six hours, he'd be beyond the Empire's space borders and headed straight for Illyla.

Yes, she alone had believed! After the prompt collapse of the captain's first commercial venture—a miffel-fur farm, largely on capital borrowed from Councilor Onwud—the future had looked very black. It had even included a probable ten-year stretch of penal servitude for "willful and negligent abuse of intrusted monies." The laws of Nikkeldepain were rough on debtors.

"But you've always been looking for someone to take out the old *Venture* and get her back into trade!" Illyla reminded her father tearfully.

"Hm-m-m, yes! But it's in the blood, my dear! His great-uncle Threbus went the same way! It would be far better to let the law take its course," Councilor Onswud said, glaring at Pausert, who remained sulkily silent. He had *tried* to explain that the mysterious epidemic which suddenly wiped out most of the stock of miffels wasn't his fault. In fact, he more than suspected the tricky hand of young Councilor Rapport, who had been wagging futilely around Illyla for the last couple of years!

"The *Venture*, now—!" Councilor Onswud mused, stroking his long, craggy chin. "Pausert can handle a ship, at least," he admitted.

That was how it happened. Were they ever going to be surprised! For even the captain realized that Councilor Onswud was unloading all the dead fish that had gathered the dust of his warehouses for the past fifty years on him and the *Venture*, in a last, faint hope of getting *some* return on those half-forgotten investments. A value of eighty-two thousand maels was placed on the cargo; but if he'd brought even three-quarters of it back in cash, all would have been well.

Instead—well, it started with that lucky bet on a legal point with an Imperial Official at the Imperial capitol itself. Then came a six-hour race fairly won against a small, fast private yacht—the old *Venture* 7333 had been a pirate-chaser in the last century and could still produce twice as much speed as her looks suggested. From there on, the captain was socially accepted as a sporting man and was in on a long string of jovial parties and meets.

Jovial and profitable—the wealthier Imperials just couldn't resist a gamble; and the penalty he always insisted on was that they had to buy!

He got rid of the stuff right and left! Inside of twelve weeks, nothing remained of the original cargo except two score bundles of expensively built but useless tinklewood fishing poles and one dozen gross bales of useful but unattractive allweather cloaks. Even on a bet, nobody would take them! But the captain had a strong hunch those items had been hopefully added to the cargo from his own stocks by Councilor Rapport; so his failure to sell them didn't break his heart.

He was a neat twenty percent net ahead, at that point—

And finally came this last-minute rush-delivery of medical supplies to Porlumma on the return route. That haul alone would have repaid the miffel-farm losses three times over!

The captain grinned broadly into the darkness. Yes, they'd be surprised—but just where was he now?

He checked again in the narrow street, searching for the port-beacon in the sky. There it was—off to his left and a little behind him. He'd got turned around somehow!

He set off carefully down an excessively dark little alley. It was one of those towns where everybody locked their front doors at night and retired to lit-up, enclosed courtyards at the backs of the houses. There were voices and the rattling of dishes nearby, and occasional whoops of laughter and singing all around him; but it was all beyond high walls which let little or no light into the alley.

It ended abruptly in a cross-alley and another wall. After a moment's debate, the captain turned to his left again. Light spilled out on his new route a few hundred yards ahead, where a courtyard was opened on the alley. From it, as he approached, came the sound of doors being violently slammed, and then a sudden, loud mingling of voices.

"Yeeee-eep!" shrilled a high, childish voice. It could have been mortal agony, terror, or even hysterical laughter. The captain broke into an apprehensive trot.

"Yes, I see you up there!" a man shouted excitedly in Universum. "I caught you now—you get down from those boxes! I'll skin you alive! Fifty-two customers sick of the stomachache—YOW!"

The last exclamation was accompanied by a sound as of a small, loosely built wooden house collapsing, and was followed by a succession of squeals and an angry bellowing, in which the only distinguishable words were: ". . . threw the boxes on me!" Then more sounds of splintering wood.

"Hey!" yelled the captain indignantly from the corner of the alley.

All action ceased. The narrow courtyard, brightly illuminated under its single overhead bulb, was half covered with a tumbled litter of what appeared to be empty wooden boxes. Standing with his foot temporarily caught in one of them was a very large, fat man dressed all in white and waving a stick. Momentarily cornered between the wall and two of the boxes, over one of which she was trying to climb, was a smallish, fair-haired girl dressed in a smock of some kind, which was also white. She might be about fourteen, the captain thought—a helpless kid, anyway.

"What *you* want?" grunted the fat man, pointing the stick with some dignity at the captain.

"Lay off the kid!" rumbled the captain, edging into the courtyard.

"Mind your own business!" shouted the fat man, waving his stick like a club. "I'll take care of her! She—"

"I never did!" squealed the girl. She burst into tears.

"Try it, Fat and Ugly!" the captain warned. "I'll ram the stick down your throat!"

He was very close now. With a sound of grunting exasperation, the fat man pulled his foot free of the box, wheeled suddenly and brought the end of the stick down on the top of the captain's cap. The captain hit him furiously in the middle of the stomach.

There was a short flurry of activity, somewhat hampered by shattering boxes everywhere. Then the captain stood up, scowling and breathing hard. The fat man remained sitting on the ground, gasping about ". . . the law!"

Somewhat to his surprise, the captain discovered the girl standing just behind him. She caught his eye and smiled.

"My name's Maleen," she offered. She pointed at the fat man. "Is he hurt bad?"

"Huh—no!" panted the captain. "But maybe we'd better—"

It was too late! A loud, self-assured voice became audible now at the opening to the alley:

"Here, here, here, here, here!" it said in the reproachful situation-under-control tone that always seemed the same to the captain, on whatever world and in whichever language he heard it.

"What's all this about?" it inquired rhetorically.

"You'll all have to come along!" it replied.

Police Court on Porlumma appeared to be a business conducted on a very efficient, around-the-clock basis. They were the next case up.

Nikkeldepain was an odd name, wasn't it, the judge smiled. He then listened attentively to the various charges, countercharges, and denials.

Bruth the Baker was charged with having struck a citizen of a foreign government on the head with a potentially lethal instrument—produced in evidence. Said citizen had admittedly attempted to interfere as Bruth was attempting to punish his slave Maleen—also produced in evidence—whom he suspected of having added something to a batch of cakes she was working on that afternoon, resulting in illness and complaints from fifty-two of Bruth's customers.

Said foreign citizen had also used insulting language—the captain admitted under pressure to "Fat and Ugly."

Some provocation could be conceded for the action taken by Bruth, but not enough. Bruth paled.

Captain Pausert, of the Republic of Nikkeldepain—everybody but the prisoners smiled this time—was charged (a) with said attempted interference, (b) with said insult, (c) with having frequently and severely struck Bruth the Baker in the course of the subsequent dispute.

The blow on the head was conceded to have provided a provocation for charge (c)—but not enough.

Nobody seemed to be charging the slave Maleen with anything. The judge only looked at her curiously, and shook his head.

"As the Court considers this regrettable incident," he remarked, "it looks like two years for you, Bruth; and about three for you, captain. Too bad!"

The captain had an awful sinking feeling. He had seen something and heard a lot of Imperial court methods in the fringe systems. He could probably get out of this three-year rap; but it would be expensive.

He realized that the judge was studying him reflectively.

"The Court wishes to acknowledge," the judge continued, "that the captain's chargeable actions were due largely to a natural feeling of human sympathy for the predicament of the slave Maleen. The Court, therefore, would suggest a settlement as follows—subsequent to which all charges could be dropped:

"That Bruth the Baker resell Maleen of Karres—with whose services he appears to be dissatisfied—for a reasonable sum to Captain Pausert of the Republic of Nikkeldepain."

Bruth the Baker heaved a gusty sigh of relief. But the captain hesitated. The buying of human slaves by private citizens was a very serious offense in Nikkeldepain! Still, he didn't have to make a record of it. If they weren't going to soak him too much—

At just the right moment, Maleen of Karres introduced a barely audible, forlorn, sniffling sound.

"How much are you asking for the kid?" the captain inquired, looking without friendliness at his recent antagonist. A day was coming when he would think less severely of Bruth; but it hadn't come yet.

Bruth scowled back but replied with a certain eagerness: "A hundred and fifty m—" A policeman standing behind him poked him sharply in the side. Bruth shut up.

"Seven hundred maels," the judge said smoothly. "There'll be Court charges, and a fee for recording the transaction—" He appeared to make a swift calculation. "Fifteen hundred and forty-two maels—" He turned to a clerk: "You've looked him up?"

The clerk nodded. "He's right!"

"And we'll take your check," the judge concluded. He gave the captain a friendly smile. "Next case."

The captain felt a little bewildered.

There was something peculiar about this! He was getting out of it much too cheaply. Since the Empire had quit its wars of expansion, young slaves in good health were a high-priced article. Furthermore, he was practically positive that Bruth the Baker had been willing to sell for a tenth of what the captain actually had to pay!

Well, he wouldn't complain. Rapidly, he signed, sealed and

thumbprinted various papers shoved at him by a helpful clerk; and made out a check.

"I guess," he told Maleen of Karres, "we'd better get along to the ship."

And now what was he going to do with the kid, he pondered, padding along the unlighted streets with his slave trotting quietly behind him. If he showed up with a pretty girl-slave in Nikkeldepain, even a small one, various good friends there would toss him into ten years or so of penal servitude-immediately after Illyla had personally collected his scalp. They were a moral lot.

Karres—?

"How far off is Karres, Maleen?" he asked into the dark.

"It takes about two weeks," Maleen said tearfully.

Two weeks! The captain's heart sank again.

"What are you blubbering about?" he inquired uncomfortably.

Maleen choked, sniffed, and began sobbing openly.

"I have two little sisters!" she cried.

"Well, well," the captain said encouragingly. "That's nice— you'll be seeing them again soon. I'm taking you home, you know!"

Great Patham—now he'd said it! But after all—

But this piece of good news seemed to be having the wrong effect on his slave! Her sobbing grew much more violent.

"No, I won't," she wailed. "They're here!"

"Huh?" said the captain. He stopped short. "Where?"

"And the people they're with are mean to them, too!" wept Maleen.

The captain's heart dropped clean through his boots. Standing there in the dark, he helplessly watched it coming:

"You could buy them awfully cheap!" she said.

II

In times of stress, the young life of Karres appeared to take to the heights. It might be a mountainous place.

The Leewit sat on the top shelf of the back wall of the crockery and antiques store, strategically flanked by two expensive-looking vases. She was a doll-sized edition of Maleen; but her eyes were cold and gray instead of blue and tearful. About five or six, the captain vaguely estimated. He wasn't very good at estimating them around that age.

"Good evening," he said, as he came in through the door. The Crockery and Antiques Shop had been easy to find. Like

Bruth the Baker's, it was the one spot in the neighborhood that was all lit up.

"Good evening, sir!" said what was presumably the store owner, without looking around. He sat with his back to the door, in a chair approximately at the center of the store and facing the Leewit at a distance of about twenty feet.

". . . and there you can stay without food or drink till the Holy Man comes in the morning!" he continued immediately, in the taut voice of a man who has gone through hysteria and is sane again. The captain realized he was addressing the Leewit.

"Your other Holy Man didn't stay very long!" the diminutive creature piped, also ignoring the captain. Apparently, she had not yet discovered Maleen behind him.

"This is a stronger denomination—much stronger!" the store owner replied, in a shaking voice but with a sort of relish. *"He'll* exorcise you, all right, little demon—you'll whistle no buttons off him! Your time is up! Go on and whistle all you want! Bust every vase in the place—"

The Leewit blinked her gray eyes thoughtfully at him.

"Might!" she said.

"But if you try to climb down from there," the store owner went on, on a rising note, "I'll chop you into bits—into little, little bits!"

He raised his arm as he spoke and weakly brandished what the captain recognized with a start of horror as a highly ornamented but probably still useful antique battle-ax.

"Ha!" said the Leewit.

"Beg your pardon, sir!" the captain said, clearing his throat.

"Good evening, sir!" the store owner repeated, without looking around. "What can I do for you?"

"I came to inquire," the captain said hesitantly, "about that child."

The store owner shifted about in his chair and squinted at the captain with red-rimmed eyes.

"You're not a Holy Man!" he said.

"Hello, Maleen!" the Leewit said suddenly. "That him?"

"We've come to buy you," Maleen said. "Shut up!"

"Good!" said the Leewit.

"Buy it? Are you mocking me, sir?" the store owner inquired.

"Shut up, Moonell!" A thin, dark, determined-looking woman had appeared in the doorway that led through the back wall of the store. She moved out a step under the shelves; and the Leewit leaned down from the top shelf and hissed. The woman moved hurriedly back into the doorway.

"Maybe he means it," she said in a more subdued voice.

"I can't sell to a citizen of the Empire," the store owner said defeatedly.

"I'm not a citizen," the captain said shortly. This time, he wasn't going to name it.

"No, he's from Nikkel—" Maleen began.

"Shut up, Maleen!" the captain said helplessly in turn.

"I never heard of Nikkel," the store owner muttered doubtfully.

"Maleen!" the woman called shrilly. "That's the name of one of the others—Bruth the Baker got her. He means it, all right! He's buying them—"

"A hundred and fifty maels!" the captain said craftily, remembering Bruth the Baker. "In cash!"

The store owner looked dazed.

"Not enough, Moonell!" the woman called. "Look at all it's broken! Five hundred maels!"

There was a sound then, so thin the captain could hardly hear it. It pierced at his eardrums like two jabs of a delicate needle. To right and left of him, two highly glazed little jugs went *"Clink-clink,"* showed a sudden veining of cracks, and collapsed.

A brief silence settled on the store. And now that he looked around more closely, the captain could spot here and there other little piles of shattered crockery—and places where similar ruins apparently had been swept up, leaving only traces of colored dust.

The store owner laid the ax down carefully beside his chair, stood up, swaying a little, and came towards the captain.

"You offered me a hundred and fifty maels!" he said rapidly as he approached. "I accept it here, now, see—before witnesses!" He grabbed the captain's right hand in both of his and pumped it up and down vigorously. "Sold!" he yelled.

Then he wheeled around in a leap and pointed a shaking hand at the Leewit.

"And NOW," he howled, "break something! Break anything! You're his! I'll sue him for every mael he ever made and ever will!"

"Oh, do come help me down, Maleen!" the Leewit pleaded prettily.

For a change, the store of Wansing, the jeweler, was dimly lit and very quiet. It was a sleek, fashionable place in a fashionable shopping block near the spaceport. The front door was unlocked, and Wansing was in.

The three of them entered quietly, and the door sighed quietly shut behind them. Beyond a great crystal display-counter, Wansing was moving about among a number of opened shelves, talking softly to himself. Under the crystal of the counter, and in close-packed rows on the satin-covered shelves, reposed a many-colored gleaming and glittering and shining. Wansing was no piker.

"Good evening, sir!" the captain said across the counter.

"It's morning!" the Leewit remarked from the other side of Maleen.

"Maleen!" said the captain.

"We're keeping out of this," Maleen said to the Leewit.

"All right," said the Leewit.

Wansing had come around jerkily at the captain's greeting, but had made no other move. Like all the slave owners the captain had met on Porlumma so far, Wansing seemed unhappy. Otherwise, he was a large, dark, sleek-looking man with jewels in his ears and a smell of expensive oils and perfumes about him.

"This place is under constant visual guard, of course!" he told the captain gently. "Nothing could possibly happen to me here. Why am I so frightened?"

"Not of me, I'm sure!" the captain said with an uncomfortable attempt at geniality. "I'm glad your store's still open," he went on briskly. "I'm here on business—"

"Oh, yes, it's still open, of course," Wansing said. He gave the captain a slow smile and turned back to his shelves. "I'm making inventory, that's why! I've been making inventory since early yesterday morning. I've counted them all seven times—"

"You're very thorough," the captain said.

"Very, very thorough!" Wansing nodded to the shelves. "The last time I found I had made a million maels. But twice before that, I had lost approximately the same amount. I shall have to count them again, I suppose!" He closed a shelf softly. "I'm sure I counted those before. But they move about constantly. Constantly! It's horrible."

"You've got a slave here called Goth," the captain said, driving to the point.

"Yes, I have!" Wansing said, nodding. "And I'm sure she understands by now I meant no harm! I do, at any rate. It was perhaps a little—but I'm sure she understands now, or will soon!"

"Where is she?" the captain inquired, a trifle uneasily.

"In her room perhaps," Wansing suggested. "It's not so bad when she's there in her room with the door closed. But often she sits in the dark and looks at you as you go past—" He opened another drawer, and closed it quietly again. "Yes, they do move!'' he whispered, as if confirming an earlier suspicion. ''Constantly—''

''Look, Wansing,'' the captain said in a loud, firm voice. ''I'm not a citizen of the Empire. I want to buy this Goth! I'll pay you a hundred and fifty maels, cash.''

Wansing turned around completely again and looked at the captain. ''Oh, you do?'' he said. ''You're not a citizen?'' He walked a few steps to the side of the counter, sat down at a small desk and turned a light on over it. Then he put his face in his hands for a moment.

''I'm a wealthy man,'' he muttered. ''An influential man! The name of Wansing counts for a great deal on Porlumma. When the Empire suggests you buy, you buy, of course—but it need not have been I who bought her! I thought she would be useful in the business—and then, even I could not sell her again within the Empire. She has been here for a week!''

He looked up at the captain and smiled. ''One hundred and fifty maels!'' he said. ''Sold! There are records to be made out—'' He reached into a drawer and took out some printed forms. He began to write rapidly. The captain produced identifications.

Maleen said suddenly: ''Goth?''

''Right here,'' a voice murmured. Wansing's hand jerked sharply, but he did not look up. He kept on writing.

Something small and lean and bonelessly supple, dressed in a dark jacket and leggings, came across the thick carpet of Wansing's store and stood behind the captain. This one might be about nine or ten.

''I'll take your check, captain!'' Wansing said politely. ''You must be an honest man. Besides, I want to frame it.''

''And now,'' the captain heard himself say in the remote voice of one who moves through a strange dream, ''I suppose we could go to the ship.''

The sky was gray and cloudy; and the streets were lightening. Goth, he noticed, didn't resemble her sisters. She had brown hair cut short a few inches below her ears, and brown eyes with long, black lashes. Her nose was short and her chin was pointed. She made him think of some thin, carnivorous creature, like a weasel.

She looked up at him briefly, grinned, and said: ''Thanks!''

''What was wrong with *him*?'' chirped the Leewit, walking backwards for a last view of Wansing's store.

''Tough crook,'' muttered Goth. The Leewit giggled.

''You premoted this just dandy, Maleen!'' she stated next.

"Shut up," said Maleen.

"All right," said the Leewit. She glanced up at the captain's face. "You been fighting!" she said virtuously. "Did you win?"

"Of course, the captain won!" said Maleen.

"Good for you!" said the Leewit.

"What about the takeoff?" Goth asked the captain. She seemed a little worried.

"Nothing to it!" the captain said stoutly, hardly bothering to wonder how she'd guessed the takeoff was the one operation on which he and the old *Venture* consistently failed to cooperate.

"No," said Goth, "I meant when?"

"Right now," said the captain. "They've already cleared us. We'll get the sign any second."

"Good," said Goth. She walked off slowly down the hall towards the back of the ship.

The takeoff was pretty bad, but the *Venture* made it again. Half an hour later, with Porlumma dwindling safely behind them, the captain switched to automatic and climbed out of his chair. After considerable experimentation, he got the electric butler adjusted to four breakfasts, hot, with coffee. It was accomplished with a great deal of advice and attempted assistance from the Leewit, rather less from Maleen, and no comments from Goth.

"Everything will be coming along in a few minutes now!" he announced. Afterwards, it struck him there had been a quality of grisly prophecy about the statement.

"If you'd listened to me," said the Leewit, "we'd have been done eating a quarter of an hour ago!" She was perspiring but triumphant—she had been right all along.

"Say, Maleen," she said suddenly, "you premoting again?"

Premoting? The captain looked at Maleen. She seemed pale and troubled.

"Spacesick?" he suggested. "I've got some pills—"

"No, she's premoting," the Leewit said scowling. "What's up, Maleen?"

"Shut up," said Goth.

"All right," said the Leewit. She was silent a moment, and then began to wriggle. "Maybe we'd better—"

"Shut up," said Maleen.

"It's all ready," said Goth.

"What's all ready?" asked the captain.

"All right," said the Leewit. She looked at the captain. "Nothing," she said.

He looked at them then, and they looked at him—one set each of gray eyes, and brown, and blue. They were all sitting around the control room floor in a circle, the fifth side of which was occupied by the electric butler.

What peculiar little waifs, the captain thought. He hadn't perhaps really realized until now just how *very* peculiar. They were still staring at him.

"Well, well!" he said heartily. "So Maleen 'premotes' and gives people stomachaches."

Maleen smiled dimly and smoothed back her yellow hair.

"They just thought they were getting them," she murmured.

"Mass history," explained the Leewit, offhandedly.

"Hysteria," said Goth. "The Imperials get their hair up about us every so often."

"I noticed that," the captain nodded. "And little Leewit here—she whistles and busts things."

"It's *the* Leewit," the Leewit said, frowning.

"Oh, I see," said the captain. "Like *the* captain, eh?"

"That's right," said the Leewit. She smiled.

"And what does little Goth do?" the captain addressed the third witch.

Little Goth appeared pained. Maleen answered for her.

"Goth teleports mostly," she said.

"Oh, she does?" said the captain. "I've heard about that trick, too," he added lamely.

"Just small stuff really!" Goth said abruptly. She reached into the top of her jacket and pulled out a cloth-wrapped bundle the size of the captain's two fists. The four ends of the cloth were knotted together. Goth undid the knot. "Like this," she said and poured out the contents on the rug between them. There was a sound like a big bagful of marbles being spilled.

"Great Patham!" the captain swore, staring down at what was a cool quarter-million in jewel stones, or he was still a miffel-farmer.

"Good gosh," said the Leewit, bouncing to her feet. "Maleen, we better get at it right away!"

The two blondes darted from the room. The captain hardly noticed their going. He was staring at Goth.

"Child," he said, "don't you realize they hang you without trial on places like Porlumma, if you're caught with stolen goods?"

"We're not on Porlumma," said Goth. She looked slightly annoyed. "They're for you. You spent money on us, didn't you?"

"Not that kind of money," said the captain. "If Wansing noticed— They're Wansing's, I suppose?"

"Sure!" said Goth. "Pulled them in just before takeoff!"

"If he reported, there'll be police ships on our tail any—"

"Goth!" Maleen shrilled.

Goth's head came around and she rolled up on her feet in one motion. "Coming," she shouted. "Excuse me," she murmured to the captain. Then she, too, was out of the room.

But again, the captain scarcely noticed her departure. He had rushed to the control desk with a sudden awful certainty and switched on all screens.

There they were! Two sleek, black ships coming up fast from behind, and already almost in gun range! They weren't regular police boats, the captain recognized, but auxiliary craft of the Empire's frontier fleets. He rammed the *Venture*'s drives full on. Immediately, red-and-black fire blossoms began to sprout in space behind him—then a finger of flame stabbed briefly past, not a hundred yards to the right of the ship.

But the communicator stayed dead. Porlumma preferred risking the sacrifice of Wansing's jewels to giving them a chance to surrender! To do the captain justice, his horror was due much more to the fate awaiting his three misguided charges than to the fact that he was going to share it.

He was putting the *Venture* through a wildly erratic and, he hoped, aim-destroying series of sideways hops and forward lunges with one hand, and trying to unlimber the turrets of the nova guns with the other, when suddenly—!

No, he decided at once, there was no use trying to understand it—there were just no more Empire ships around. The screens all blurred and darkened simultaneously; and, for a short while, a darkness went flowing and coiling lazily past the *Venture*. Light jumped out of it at him once, in a cold, ugly glare, and receded again in a twisting, unnatural fashion. The *Venture*'s drives seemed dead.

Then, just as suddenly, the old ship jerked, shivered, roared aggrievedly, and was hurling herself along on her own power again!

But Porlumma's sun was no longer in evidence. Stars gleamed and shifted distantly against the blackness of deep space all about. The patterns seemed familiar, but he wasn't a good enough navigator to be sure.

The captain stood up stiffly, feeling a heavy cloud. And at that moment, with a wild, hilarious clacking like a metallic hen, the electric butler delivered four breakfasts, hot, one after the other, right onto the center of the control room floor.

The first voice said distinctly: "Shall we just leave it on?"

A second voice, considerably more muffled, replied: "Yes, let's! You never know when you need it—"

The third voice, tucked somewhere in between them, said simply: *"Whew!"*

Peering about the dark room in bewilderment, the captain realized suddenly that the voices had come from the speaker of an intership communicator, leading to what had once been the *Venture*'s captain's cabin.

He listened; but only a dim murmuring came from it now, and then nothing at all. He started towards the hall, then returned and softly switched off the communicator. He went quietly down the hall until he came to the captain's cabin. Its door was closed.

He listened a moment, and opened it suddenly.

There was a trio of squeals:

"Oh, don't! You spoiled it!"

The captain stood motionless. Just one glimpse had been given him of what seemed to be a bundle of twisted black wires arranged loosely like the frame of a truncated cone on—or was it just above?—a table in the center of the cabin. Where the tip of the cone should have been burned a round, swirling, orange fire. About it, their faces reflecting its glow, stood the three witches.

Then the fire vanished; the wires collapsed. There was only ordinary light in the room. They were looking up at him variously—Maleen with smiling regret, the Leewit in frank annoyance, Goth with no expression at all.

"What out of Great Patham's Seventh Hell was that?" inquired the captain, his hair bristling slowly.

The Leewit looked at Goth; Goth looked at Maleen. Maleen said doubtfully: "We can just tell you its name—"

"That was the Sheewash Drive," said Goth.

"The what-drive?" asked the captain.

"Sheewash," repeated Maleen.

"The one you have to do it with yourself," the Leewit said helpfully.

"Shut up," said Maleen.

There was a long pause. The captain looked down at the handful of thin, black, twelve-inch wires scattered about the table top. He touched one of them. It was dead-cold.

"I see," he said. "I guess we're all going to have a long talk." Another pause. "Where are we now?"

"About three light-years down the way you were going," said Goth. "We only worked it thirty seconds."

"Twenty-eight!" corrected Maleen, with the authority of her years. "The Leewit was getting tired."

"I see," said Captain Pausert carefully. "Well, let's go have some breakfast."

III

They ate with a silent voraciousness, dainty Maleen, the exquisite Leewit, supple Goth, all alike. The captain, long finished, watched them with amazement and—now at last—with something like awe.

"It's the Sheewash Drive," explained Maleen finally, catching his expression.

"Takes it out of you!" said Goth.

The Leewit grunted affirmatively and stuffed on.

"Can't do too much of it," said Maleen. "Or too often. It kills you sure!"

"What," said the captain, "*is* the Sheewash Drive?"

They became reticent. People did it on Karres, said Maleen, when they had to go somewhere else fast. Everybody knew how there.

"But of course," she added, "we're pretty young to do it right!"

"We did it pretty good!" the Leewit contradicted positively. She seemed to be finished at last.

"But how?" said the captain.

Reticence thickened almost visibly. If you couldn't do it, said Maleen, you couldn't understand it either.

He gave it up, for the time being.

"I guess I'll have to take you home next," he said; and they agreed.

Karres, it developed, was in the Iverdahl System. He couldn't find any planet of that designation listed in his maps of the area, but that meant nothing. The maps were old and often inaccurate, and local names changed a lot.

Barring the use of weird and deadly miracle drives, that detour was going to cost him almost a month in time—and a good chunk of his profits in power used up. The jewels Goth had illegally teleported must, of course, be returned to their owner, he explained. He'd intended to look severely at the culprit at that point; but she'd meant well, after all! They were extremely peculiar children, but still children—they couldn't really understand.

He would stop off en route to Karres at an Empire planet with banking facilities to take care of that matter, the captain added. A planet far enough off so the police wouldn't be likely to take any particular interest in the *Venture*.

A dead silence greeted this schedule. It appeared that the representatives of Karres did not think much of his logic.

"Well," Maleen sighed at last, "we'll see you get your money back some other way then!"

The junior witches nodded coldly.

"How did you three happen to get into this fix?" the captain inquired, with the intention of changing the subject.

They'd left Karres together on a jaunt of their own, they explained. No, they hadn't run away—he got the impression that such trips were standard procedure for juveniles in that place. They were on another planet, a civilized one but beyond the borders and law of Empire, when the town they were in was raided by a small fleet of slavers. They were taken along with most of the local youngsters.

"It's a wonder," he said reflectively, "you didn't take over the ship."

"Oh, brother!" exclaimed the Leewit.

"Not that ship!" said Goth.

"That was an Imperial Slaver!" Maleen informed him. "You behave yourself every second on those crates."

Just the same, the captain thought as he settled himself to rest in the control room on a couch he had set up there, it was no longer surprising that the Empire wanted no young slaves from Karres to be transported into the interior! Oddest sort of children—but he ought to be able to get his expenses paid by their relatives. Something very profitable might even be made of this deal—

Have to watch the record entries though! Nikkeldepain's laws were explicit about the penalties invoked by anything resembling the purchase and sale of slaves.

He'd thoughtfully left the intership communicator adjusted so he could listen in on their conversation in the captain's cabin. However, there had been nothing for some time beyond frequent bursts of childish giggling. Then came a succession of piercing shrieks from the Leewit. It appeared she was being forcibly washed behind the ears by Maleen and obliged to brush her teeth, in preparation for bedtime.

It had been agreed that he was not to enter the cabin, because—for reasons not given—they couldn't keep the Sheewash Drive on in his presence; and they wanted to have it ready, in case of an emergency. Piracy was rife beyond the Imperial borders, and the *Venture* would keep beyond the border for a good part of the trip, to avoid the more pressing danger of police pursuit instigated by Porlumma. The captain had explained the potentialities of the nova guns the *Venture* boasted, or tried to. Possibly, they hadn't understood. At any rate, they seemed unimpressed.

The Sheewash Drive! Boy, he thought in sudden excitement, if he could just get the principles of that. Maybe he would!

He raised his head suddenly. The Leewit's voice had lifted clearly over the communicator:

". . . not such a bad old dope!" the childish treble remarked.

The captain blinked indignantly.

"He's not so old," Maleen's soft voice returned. "And he's certainly no dope!"

He smiled. Good kid, Maleen.

"Yeah, yeah!" squeaked the Leewit offensively. "Maleen's sweet onthu-ulp!"

A vague commotion continued for a while, indicating, he hoped, that someone he could mention was being smothered under a pillow.

He drifted off to sleep before it was settled.

If you didn't happen to be thinking of what they'd done, they seemed more or less like normal children. Right from the start, they displayed a flattering interest in the captain and his background; and he told them all about everything and everybody in Nikkeldepain. Finally, he even showed them his treasured pocket-sized picture of Illyla—the one with which he'd held many cozy conversations during the earlier part of his trip.

Almost at once, though, he realized that was a mistake. They studied it intently in silence, their heads crowded close together.

"Oh, brother!" the Leewit whispered then, with entirely the wrong kind of inflection.

"Just what did you mean by that?" the captain inquired coldly.

"Sweet!" murmured Goth. But it was the way she closed her eyes briefly, as though gripped by a light spasm of nausea.

"Shut up, Goth!" Maleen said sharply. "I think she's very swee . . . I mean, she looks very nice!" she told the captain.

The captain was disgruntled. Silently, he retrieved the maligned Illyla and returned her to his breast pocket. Silently, he went off and left them standing there.

But afterwards, in private, he took it out again and studied it worriedly. His Illyla! He shifted the picture back and forth under the light. It wasn't really a very good picture of her, he decided. It had been bungled! From certain angles, one might even say that Illyla did look the least bit insipid.

What was he thinking, he thought, shocked.

He unlimbered the nova gun turrets next and got in a little firing practice. They had been sealed when he took over the *Venture* and weren't supposed to be used, except in absolute emergencies. They were somewhat uncertain weapons, though very effective, and Nikkeldepain had turned to safer forms of armament many decades ago. But on the third day out from Nikkeldepain, the captain made a brief notation in his log:

"Attacked by two pirate craft. Unsealed nova guns. Destroyed one attacker; survivor fled—"

He was rather pleased by that crisp, hard-bitten description of desperate space adventure, and enjoyed rereading it occasionally. It wasn't true, though. He had put in an interesting four hours at the time pursuing and annihilating large, craggy chunks of sub-stance of a meteorite cloud he found the *Venture* plowing through. Those nova guns were fascinating stuff! You'd sight the turrets on something; and so long as it didn't move after that, it was all right. If it did move, it got it—unless you relented and deflected the turrets first. They were just the thing for arresting a pirate in midspace.

The *Venture* dipped back into the Empire's borders four days later and headed for the capital of the local province. Police ships challenged them twice on the way in; and the captain found considerable comfort in the awareness that his passengers foregathered silently in their cabin on these occasions. They didn't tell him they were set to use the Sheewash Drive—somehow it had never been mentioned since that first day; but he knew the queer orange fire was circling over its skimpy framework of twisted wires there and ready to act.

However, the space police waved him on, satisfied with routine identification. Apparently, the *Venture* had not become generally known as a criminal ship, to date.

Maleen accompanied him to the banking institution that was to return Wansing's property to Porlumma. Her sisters, at the captain's definite request, remained on the ship.

The transaction itself went off without a visible hitch. The jewels would reach their destination in Porlumma within a month. But he had to take out a staggering sum in insurance—"Piracy, thieves!'' smiled the clerk. "Even summary capital punishment won't keep the rats down.'' And, of course, he had to register name, ship, home planet, and so on. But since they already had all that information in Porlumma, he gave it without hesitation.

On the way back to the spaceport, he sent off a sealed message by radio-relay to the bereaved jeweler, informing him of the action taken, and regretting the misunderstanding.

He felt a little better after that, though the insurance payment had been a severe blow! If he didn't manage to work out a decent profit on Karres somehow, the losses on the miffel farm would hardly be covered now.

Then he noticed that Maleen was getting uneasy.

"We'd better hurry!'' was all she would say, however. Her face grew pale.

The captain understood. She was having another premonition! The hitch to this premoting business was, apparently, that when something was brewing you were informed of the bare fact but had to guess at most of the details. They grabbed an aircab and raced back to the spaceport.

They had just been cleared there when he spotted a small group of uniformed men coming along the dock on the double. They stopped short and then scattered, as the *Venture* lurched drunkenly sideways into the air. Everyone else in sight was scattering, too.

That was a very bad takeoff—one of the captain's worst! Once afloat, however, he ran the ship promptly into the nightside of the planet and turned her nose towards the border. The old pirate-chaser had plenty of speed when you gave her the reins; and throughout the entire next sleep period, he let her use it all.

The Sheewash Drive was not required that time.

Next day, he had a lengthy private talk with Goth on the Golden Rule and the Law, with particular reference to individual property rights. If Councilor Onswud had been monitoring the sentiments expressed by the captain, he could not have failed to rumble surprised approval. The delinquent herself listened impassively; but the captain fancied she showed distinct signs of being rather impressed by his earnestness.

It was two days after that—well beyond the borders again—when they were obliged to make an unscheduled stop at a mining moon. For the captain discovered he had already miscalculated the extent to which the prolonged run on overdrive after leaving the capital was going to deplete the *Venture*'s reserves. They would have to juice up—

A large, extremely handsome Sirian freighter lay beside them at the Moon station. It was half a battlecraft really, since it dealt regularly beyond the borders. They had to wait while it was being serviced; and it took a long time. The Sirians turned out to be as unpleasant as their ship was good-looking—a snooty, conceited, hairy lot who talked only their own dialect and pretended to be unfamiliar with Imperial Universum.

The captain found himself getting irked by their bad manners—particularly when he discovered they were laughing over his argument with the service superintendent about the cost of repowering the *Venture*.

"You're out in deep space, captain!" said the superintendent. "And you haven't juice enough left even to travel back to the Border. You can't expect Imperial prices here!"

"It's not what you charged *them*!" The captain angrily jerked his thumb at the Sirian.

"Regular customers!" the superintendent shrugged. "You start coming by here every three months like they do, and we can make an arrangement with you, too."

It was outrageous—it actually put the *Venture* back in the red! But there was no help for it.

Nor did it improve the captain's temper when he muffled the takeoff once more—and then had to watch the Sirian floating into space, as sedately as a swan, a little behind him!

An hour later, as he sat glumly before the controls, debating the chance of recouping his losses before returning to Nikkeldepain, Maleen and the Leewit hurriedly entered the room. They did something to a port screen.

"They sure are!" the Leewit exclaimed. She seemed childishly pleased.

"Are what?" the captain inquired absently.

"Following us," said Maleen. She did not sound pleased. "It's that Sirian ship, Captain Pausert—"

The captain stared bewilderedly at the screen. There *was* a ship in focus there. It was quite obviously the Sirian and, just as obviously, it was following them.

"What do they want?" he wondered. "They're stinkers but they're not pirates. Even if they were, they wouldn't spend an hour running after a crate like the *Venture*!"

Maleen said nothing. The Leewit observed: "Oh, brother! Got their bow-turrets out now—better get those nova guns ready!"

"But it's all nonsense!" the captain said, flushing angrily. He turned suddenly towards the communicators. "What's that Empire general beam length?"

".0044," said Maleen.

A roaring, abusive voice flooded the control room immediately. The one word understandable to the captain was "*Venture*." It was repeated frequently, sometimes as if it were a question.

"Sirian!" said the captain. "Can you understand them?" he asked Maleen.

She shook her head. "The Leewit can—"

The Leewit nodded, her gray eyes glistening.

"What are they saying?"

"They says you're for stopping," the Leewit translated rapidly, but apparently retaining much of the original sentence-structure. "They says you're for skinning alive . . . ha! They says you're for stopping right now and for only hanging. They says—"

Maleen scuttled from the control room. The Leewit banged the communicator with one small fist.

"Beak-Wock!" she shrieked. It sounded like that, anyway. The loud voice paused a moment.

"Beak-Wock?" it returned in an aggrieved, demanding roar.

"Beak-Wock!" the Leewit affirmed with apparent delight. She rattled off a string of similar-sounding syllables. She paused.

A howl of inarticulate wrath responded.

The captain, in a whirl of outraged emotions, was yelling at the Leewit to shut up, at the Sirian to go to Great Patham's Second Hell—the worst—and wrestling with the nova gun adjustors at the same time. He'd had about enough! He'd—

SSS-whoosh!

It was the Sheewash Drive.

"And where are we now?" the captain inquired, in a voice of unnatural calm.

"Same place, just about," said the Leewit. "Ship's still on the screen. Way back though—take them an hour again to catch up." She seemed disappointed; then brightened. "You got lots of time to get the guns ready!"

The captain didn't answer. He was marching down the hall towards the rear of the *Venture*. He passed the captain's cabin and noted the door was shut. He went on without pausing. He was mad clean through—he knew what had happened!

After all he'd told her, Goth had teleported again.

It was all there, in the storage. Items of half a pound in weight seemed to be as much as she could handle. But amazing quantities of stuff had met that one requirement—bottles filled with what might be perfume or liquor or dope, expensive-looking garments and cloths in a shining variety of colors, small boxes, odds, ends and, of course, jewelry!

He spent half an hour getting it loaded into a steel space crate. He wheeled the crate into the rear lock, sealed the inside lock and pulled the switch that activated the automatic launching device.

The outside lock clicked shut. He stalked back to the control room. The Leewit was still in charge, fiddling with the communicators.

"I could try a whistle over them," she suggested, glancing up. She added: "But they'd bust somewheres, sure."

"Get them on again!" the captain said.

"Yes, sir," said the Leewit surprised.

The roaring voice came back faintly.

"SHUT UP!" the captain shouted in Imperial Universum.

The voice shut up.

"Tell them they can pick up their stuff—it's been dumped out in a crate!" the captain told the Leewit. "Tell them I'm proceeding on my course. Tell them if they follow me one light-minute beyond that crate, I'll come back for them, shoot their front end off, shoot their rear end off, and ram 'em in the middle."

"Yes, SIR!" the Leewit sparkled. They proceeded on their course.

Nobody followed.

"Now I want to speak to Goth," the captain announced. He was still at a high boil. "Privately," he added. "Back in the storage—"

Goth followed him expressionlessly into the storage. He closed the door to the hall. He'd broken off a two-foot length from the tip of one of Councilor Rapport's overpriced tinklewood fishing poles. It made a fair switch.

But Goth looked terribly small just now! He cleared his throat. He wished for a moment he were back on Nikkeldepain.

"I warned you," he said.

Goth didn't move. Between one second and the next, however, she seemed to grow remarkably. Her brown eyes focused on the captain's Adam's apple; her lip lifted at one side. A slightly hungry look came into her face.

"Wouldn't try that!" she murmured.

Mad again, the captain reached out quickly and got a handful of leathery cloth. There was a blur of motion, and what felt like a small explosion against his left kneecap. He grunted with anguished surprise and fell back on a bale of Councilor Rapport's all-weather cloaks. But he had retained his grip—Goth fell half on top of him, and that was still a favorable position. Then her head snaked around, her neck seemed to extend itself; and her teeth snapped his wrist.

Weasels don't let go—

"Didn't think he'd have the nerve!" Goth's voice came over the communicator. There was a note of grudging admiration in it. It seemed that she was inspecting her bruises.

All tangled up in the job of bandaging his freely bleeding wrist, the captain hoped she'd find a good plenty to count. His knee felt the size of a sofa pillow and throbbed like a piston engine.

"The captain is a brave man," Maleen was saying reproachfully. "You should have known better—"

"He's not very *smart*, though!" the Leewit remarked suggestively.

There was a short silence.

"Is he? Goth? Eh?" the Leewit urged.

"Perhaps not very," said Goth.

"You two lay off him!" Maleen ordered. "Unless," she added meaningly, "you want to *swim* back to Karres—on the Egger Route!"

"Not me," the Leewit said briefly.

"You could still do it, I guess," said Goth. She seemed to be reflecting. "All right—we'll lay off him. It was a fair fight, anyway."

IV

They raised Karres the sixteenth day after leaving Porlumma. There had been no more incidents; but then, neither had there been any more stops or other contacts with the defenseless Empire. Maleen had cooked up a poultice which did wonders for his knee. With the end of the trip in sight, all tensions had relaxed; and Maleen, at least, seemed to grow hourly more regretful at the prospect of parting.

After a brief study, Karres could be distinguished easily enough by the fact that it moved counterclockwise to all the other planets of the Iverdahl System.

Well, it would, the captain thought.

They came soaring into its atmosphere on the dayside without arousing any visible interest. No communicator signals reached them; and no other ships showed up to look them over. Karres, in fact, had all the appearance of a completely uninhabited world. There were a larger number of seas, too big to be called lakes and too small to be oceans, scattered over its surface. There was one enormously towering ridge of mountains that ran from pole to pole, and any number of lesser chains. There were two good-sized icecaps; and the southern section of the planet was speckled with intermittent stretches of snow. Almost all of it seemed to be dense forest.

It was a handsome place, in a wild, somber way.

They went gliding over it, from noon through morning and into the dawn fringe—the captain at the controls, Goth and the Leewit flanking him at the screens, and Maleen behind him to do the directing. After a few initial squeals, the Leewit became oddly silent. Suddenly the captain realized she was blubbering.

Somehow, it startled him to discover that her homecoming had affected the Leewit to that extent. He felt Goth reach out behind him and put her hand on the Leewit's shoulder. The smallest witch sniffled happily.

" 'S beautiful!" she growled.

He felt a resurge of the wondering, protective friendliness they had aroused in him at first. They must have been having a rough time of it, at that. He sighed; it seemed a pity they hadn't got along a little better!

"Where's everyone hiding?" he inquired, to break up the mood. So far, there hadn't been a sign of human habitation.

"There aren't many people on Karres," Maleen said from behind his shoulder. "But we're going to The Town—you'll meet about half of them there!"

"What's that place down there?" the captain asked with sudden interest. Something like an enormous lime-white bowl seemed to have been set flush into the floor of the wide valley up which they were moving.

"That's the Theater where . . . *ouch!*" the Leewit said. She fell silent then but turned to give Maleen a resentful look.

"Something strangers shouldn't be told about, eh?" the captain said tolerantly. Goth glanced at him from the side.

"We've got rules," she said.

He let the ship down a little as they passed over "the Theater where—" It was a sort of large, circular arena, with numerous steep tiers of seats running up around it. But all was bare and deserted now.

On Maleen's direction, they took the next valley fork to the right and dropped lower still. He had his first look at Karres animal life then. A flock of large, creamy-white birds, remarkably Terrestrial in appearance, flapped by just below them, apparently unconcerned about the ship. The forest underneath had opened out into a long stretch of lush meadowland, with small creeks winding down into its center. Here a herd of several hundred head of beasts was grazing—beasts of mastodonic size and build, with hairless, shiny black hides. The mouths of their long, heavy heads were twisted up into sardonic, crocodilian grins as they blinked up at the passing *Venture*.

"Black Bollems," said Goth, apparently enjoying the captain's expression. "Lots of them around; they're tame. But the gray mountain ones are good hunting."

"Good eating, too!" the Leewit said. She licked her lips daintily. "Breakfast—!" she sighed, her thoughts diverted to a familiar track. "And we ought to be just in time!"

"There's the field!" Maleen cried, pointing. "Set her down there, captain!"

The "field" was simply a flat meadow of close-trimmed grass running smack against the mountainside to their left. One small vehicle, bright blue in color, was parked on it; and it was bordered on two sides by very tall, blue-black trees.

That was all.

The captain shook his head. Then he set her down.

The town of Karres was a surprise to him in a good many ways. For one thing, there was much more of it than you would have thought possible after flying over the area. It stretched for miles through the forest, up the flanks of the mountain and across the valley—little clusters of houses or individual ones, each group screened from all the rest and from the sky overhead by the trees.

They liked color on Karres; but then they hid it away! The houses were bright as flowers, red and white, apple-green, golden-brown—all spick and span, scrubbed and polished and aired with that brisk, green forest smell. At various times of the day, there was also the smell of remarkably good things to eat. There were brooks and pools and a great number of shaded vegetable gardens to the town. There were risky-looking treetop playgrounds, and treetop platforms and galleries which seemed to have no particular purpose. On the ground was mainly an enormously confusing maze of paths—narrow trails of sandy soil snaking about among great brown tree roots and chunks of gray mountain rock, and half covered with fallen needle leaves. The first six times the captain set out unaccompanied, he'd lost his way hopelessly within minutes, and had to be guided back out of the forest.

But the most hidden of all were the people! About four thousand of them were supposed to live in the town, with as many more scattered about the planet. But you never got to see more than three or four at any one time—except when now and then a pack of children, who seemed to the captain to be uniformly of the Leewit's size, would burst suddenly out of the undergrowth across a path before you, and vanish again.

As for the others, you did hear someone singing occasionally; or there might be a whole muted concert going on all about, on a large variety of wooden musical instruments which they seemed to enjoy tootling with, gently.

But it wasn't a real town at all, the captain thought. They didn't live like people, these Witches of Karres—it was more like a flock of strange forest birds that happened to be nesting in the same general area. Another thing: they appeared to be busy enough—but what was their business?

He discovered he was reluctant to ask Toll too many questions about it. Toll was the mother of his three witches; but only Goth really resembled her. It was difficult to picture Goth becoming smoothly matured and pleasantly rounded; but that was Toll. She had the same murmuring voice, the same air of sideways observation and secret reflection. And she answered all the captain's questions with apparent frankness; but he never seemed to get much real information out of what she said.

It was odd, too! Because he was spending several hours a day in her company, or in one of the next rooms at any rate, while she went about her housework. Toll's daughters had taken him home when they landed; and he was installed in the room that belonged to their father—busy just now, the captain gathered, with some sort of research of a geological nature elsewhere on Karres. The arrangement worried him a little at first, particularly since Toll and he were mostly alone in the house. Maleen was going to some kind of school; she left early in the morning and came back late in the afternoon; and Goth and the Leewit were just plain running wild! They usually got in long after the captain had gone to bed and were off again before he turned out for breakfast.

It hardly seemed like the right way to raise them! One afternoon, he found the Leewit curled up and asleep in the chair he usually occupied on the porch before the house. She slept there for four solid hours, while the captain sat nearby and leafed gradually through a thick book with illuminated pictures called "Histories of Ancient Yarthe." Now and then, he sipped at a cool, green, faintly intoxicating drink Toll had placed quietly beside him some while before, or sucked an aromatic smoke from the enormous pipe with a floor rest, which he understood was a favorite of Toll's husband.

Then the Leewit woke up suddenly, uncoiled, gave him a look between a scowl and a friendly grin, slipped off the porch and vanished among the trees.

He couldn't quite figure that look! It might have meant nothing at all in particular, but—

The captain laid down his book then and worried a little more. It was true, of course, that nobody seemed in the least concerned about his presence. All of Karres appeared to know about him, and he'd met quite a number of people by now in a casual way. But nobody came around to interview him or so much as dropped in for a visit. However, Toll's husband presumably would be returning presently, and—

How long had he been here, anyway?

Great Patham, the captain thought, shocked. He'd lost count of the days!

Or was it weeks?

He went in to find Toll.

"It's been a wonderful visit," he said, "but I'll have to be leaving, I guess. Tomorrow morning, early—"

Toll put some fancy sewing she was working on back in a glass basket, laid her thin, strong witch's hands in her lap, and smiled up at him.

"We thought you'd be thinking that," she said, "and so we— You know, captain, it was quite difficult to find a way to reward you for bringing back the children?"

"It was?" said the captain, suddenly realizing he'd also clean forgotten he was broke! And now the wrath of Onswud lay close ahead.

"Gold and jewel stones would have been just right, of course!" she said, "but unfortunately, while there's no doubt a lot of it on Karres somewhere, we never got around to looking for it. And we haven't money—none that you could use, that is!"

"No, I don't suppose you do," the captain agreed sadly.

"However," said Toll, "we've all been talking about it in the town, and so we've loaded a lot of things aboard your ship that we think you can sell at a fine profit!"

"Well now," the captain said gratefully, "that's fine of—"

"There are furs," said Toll, "the very finest furs we could fix up—two thousand of them!"

"Oh!" said the captain, bravely keeping his smile. "Well, that's wonderful!"

"And essences of perfume!" said Toll. "Everyone brought one bottle of their own, so that's eight thousand three hundred and twenty-three bottles of perfume essences—all different!"

"Perfume!" said the captain. "Fine, fine—but you really shouldn't—"

"And the rest of it," Toll concluded happily, "is the green Lepti liquor you like so much, and the Wintenberry jellies!" She frowned. "I forgot just how many jugs and jars," she admitted, "but there were a lot. It's all loaded now. And do you think you'll be able to sell all that?" she smiled.

"I certainly can!" the captain said stoutly. "It's wonderful stuff, and there's nothing like it in the Empire."

Which was very true. They wouldn't have considered miffel-furs for lining on Karres. But if he'd been alone he would have felt like he wanted to burst into tears.

The witches couldn't have picked more completely unsalable items if they'd tried! Furs, cosmetics, food and liquor—he'd be shot on sight if he got caught trying to run that kind of merchandise into the Empire. For the same reason that they couldn't use it on Nikkeldepain—they were that scared of contamination by goods that came from uncleared worlds!

He breakfasted alone next morning. Toll had left a note beside his plate, which explained in a large, not too legible script that she had to run off and fetch the Leewit; and that if he was gone before she got back she was wishing him good-bye and good luck.

He smeared two more buns with Wintenberry jelly, drank a large mug of cone-seed coffee, finished every scrap of the omelet of swan hawk eggs and then, in a state of pleasant repletion, toyed around with his slice of roasted Bollem liver. Boy, what food! He must have put on fifteen pounds since he landed on Karres.

He wondered how Toll kept that sleek figure.

Regretfully, he pushed himself away from the table, pocketed her note for a souvenir, and went out on the porch. There a tear-stained Maleen hurled herself into his arms.

"Oh, captain!" she sobbed. "You're leaving—"

"Now, now!" the captain murmured, touched and surprised by the lovely child's grief. He patted her shoulders soothingly. "I'll be back," he said rashly.

"Oh, yes, do come back!" cried Maleen. She hesitated and

added: "I become marriageable two years from now. Karres time—"

"Well, well," said the captain, dazed. "Well, now—"

He set off down the path a few minutes later, with a strange melody tinkling in his head. Around the first curve, it changed abruptly to a shrill keening which seemed to originate from a spot some two hundred feet before him. Around the next curve, he entered a small, rocky clearing full of pale, misty, early-morning sunlight and what looked like a slow-motion fountain of gleaming rainbow globes. These turned out to be clusters of large, vari-hued soap bubbles which floated up steadily from a wooden tub full of hot water, soap and the Leewit. Toll was bent over the tub; and the Leewit was objecting to a morning bath, with only that minimum of interruptions required to keep her lungs pumped full of a fresh supply of air.

As the captain paused beside the little family group, her red, wrathful face came up over the rim of the tub and looked at him.

"Well, Ugly," she squealed, in a renewed outburst of rage, "who you staring at?" Then a sudden determination came into her eyes. She pursed her lips.

Toll up-ended her promptly and smacked the Leewit's bottom.

"She was going to make some sort of a whistle at you," she explained hurriedly. "Perhaps you'd better get out of range while I can keep her head under. And good luck, captain!"

Karres seemed even more deserted than usual this morning. Of course, it was quite early. Great banks of fog lay here and there among the huge dark trees and the small bright houses. A breeze sighed sadly far overhead. Faint, mournful bird-cries came from still higher up—it could have been swan hawks reproaching him for the omelet.

Somewhere in the distance, somebody tootled on a wood-instrument, very gently.

He had gone halfway up the path to the landing field, when something buzzed past him like an enormous wasp and went *CLUNK!* into the hole of a tree just before him.

It was a long, thin, wicked-looking arrow. On its shaft was a white card; and on the card was printed in red letters:

STOP, MAN OF NIKKELDEPAIN!

The captain stopped and looked around slowly and cautiously. There was no one in sight. What did it mean?

He had a sudden feeling as if all of Karres were rising up

silently in one stupendous, cool, foggy trap about him. His skin began to crawl. What was going to happen?

"Ha-ha!" said Goth, suddenly visible on a rock twelve feet to his left and eight feet above him. "You did stop!"

The captain let his breath out slowly.

"What else did you think I'd do?" he inquired. He felt a little faint.

She slid down from the rock like a lizard and stood before him. "Wanted to say good-bye!" she told him.

Thin and brown, in jacket, breeches, boots, and cap of gray-green rock-lichen color, Goth looked very much in her element. The brown eyes looked up at him steadily; the mouth smiled faintly; but there was no real expression on her face at all. There was a quiverful of those enormous arrows slung over her shoulder, and some arrow-shooting gadget—not a bow—in her left hand.

She followed his glance.

"Bollem hunting up the mountain," she explained. "The wild ones. They're better meat—"

The captain reflected a moment. That's right, he recalled; they kept the tame Bollem herds mostly for milk, butter, and cheese. He'd learned a lot of important things about Karres, all right!

"Well," he said, "good-by, Goth!"

They shook hands gravely. Goth was the real Witch of Karres, he decided—more so than her sisters, more so even than Toll. But he hadn't actually learned a single thing about any of them.

Peculiar people!

He walked on, rather glumly.

"Captain!" Goth called after him. He turned.

"Better watch those takeoffs," Goth called, "or you'll kill yourself yet!"

The captain cussed softly all the way up to the *Venture*.

And the takeoff was terrible! A few swan hawks were watching but, he hoped, no one else.

V

There wasn't the remotest possibility, of course, of resuming direct trade in the Empire with the cargo they'd loaded for him. But the more he thought about it now, the less likely it seemed that Councilor Onswud was going to let a genuine fortune slip through his hands on a mere technicality of embargoes. Nikkel-depain knew all the tricks of interstellar merchandising; and the councilor himself was undoubtedly the slickest unskinned miffel in the Republic.

More hopefully, the captain began to wonder whether some sort of trade might not be made to develop eventually between Karres and Nikkeldepain. Now and then, he also thought of Maleen growing marriageable two years hence, Karres time. A handful of witch-notes went tinkling through his head whenever that idle reflection occurred.

The calendric chronometer informed him he'd spent three weeks there. He couldn't remember how their year compared with the standard one.

He found he was getting remarkably restless on this homeward run; and it struck him for the first time that space travel could also be nothing much more than a large hollow period of boredom. He made a few attempts to resume his sessions of small-talk with Illyla, via her picture; but the picture remained aloof.

The ship seemed unnaturally quiet now—that was the trouble! The captain's cabin, particularly, and the hall leading past it had become as dismal as a tomb.

But at long last, Nikkeldepain II swam up on the screen ahead. The captain put the *Venture* 7333 on orbit, and broadcast the ship's identification number. Half an hour later, Landing Control called him. He repeated the identification number, and added the ship's name, his name, owner's name, place of origin and nature of cargo.

The cargo had to be described in detail.

"Assume Landing Orbit 21,203 on your instruments," Landing Control instructed him. "A customs ship will come out to inspect."

He went on the assigned orbit and gazed moodily from the vision ports as the flat continents and oceans of Nikkeldepain II as they drifted by below. A sense of equally flat depression overcame him unexpectedly. He shook it off and remembered Illyla.

Three hours later, a ship ran up next to him; and he shut off the orbital drive. The communicator began buzzing. He switched it on.

"Vision, please!" said an official-sounding voice. The captain frowned, located the vision-stud of the communicator screen and pushed it down. Four faces appeared in vague outline on the screen, looking at him.

"Illyla!" the captain said.

"At least," young Councilor Rapport said unpleasantly, "he's brought back the ship, Father Onswud!"

"Illyla!" said the captain.

Councilor Onswud said nothing. Neither did Illyla. They both seemed to be staring at him, but the screen wasn't good enough to permit the study of expression in detail.

The fourth face, an unfamiliar one above a uniform collar, was the one with the official-sounding voice.

"You are instructed to open the forward lock, Captain Pausert," it said, "for an official investigation."

It wasn't till he was releasing the outer lock to the control room that the captain realized it wasn't Customs who had sent a boat out to him, but the police of the Republic.

However, he hesitated for only a moment. Then the outer lock gaped wide.

He tried to explain. They wouldn't listen. They had come on board in contamination-proof repulsor suits, all four of them; and they discussed the captain as if he weren't there. Illyla looked pale and angry and beautiful, and avoided looking at him.

However, he didn't want to speak to her before the others anyway.

They strolled back to the storage and gave the Karres cargo a casual glance.

"Damaged his lifeboat, too!" Councilor Rapport remarked.

They brushed past him down the narrow hallway and went back to the control room. The policeman asked to see the log and commercial records. The captain produced them.

The three men studied them briefly. Illyla gazed stonily out at Nikkeldepain II.

"Not too carefully kept!" the policeman pointed out.

"Surprising he bothered to keep them at all!" said Councilor Rapprt.

"But it's all clear enough!" said Councilor Onswud.

They straightened up and then and faced him in a line. Councilor Onswud folded his arms and projected his craggy chin. Councilor Rapport stood at ease, smiling faintly. The policeman became officially rigid.

Illyla remained off to one side, looking at the three.

"Captain Pausert," the policeman said, "the following charges—substantiated in part by this preliminary investigation—are made against you—"

"Charges?" said the captain.

"Silence, please!" rumbled Councilor Onswud.

"First: material theft of a quarter-million value of maels of jewels and jeweled items from a citizen of the Imperial Planet of Porlumma—"

"They were returned!" the captain protested.

"Restitution, particularly when inspired by fear of retribution, does not affect the validity of the original charge," Councilor Rapport quoted, gazing at the ceiling.

"Second," continued the policeman. "Purchase of human slaves, permitted under Imperial law but prohibited by penalty of ten years to lifetime penal servitude by the laws of the Republic of Nikkeldepain—"

"I was just taking them back where they belonged!" said the captain.

"We shall get to that point presently," the policeman replied. "Third, material theft of sundry items in the value of one hundred and eighty thousand maels from a ship of the Imperial Planet of Lepper, accompanied by threats of violence to the ship's personnel—"

"I might add in explanation of the significance of this particular charge," added Councilor Rapport, looking at the floor, "that the Regency of Sirius, containing Lepper, is allied to the Republic of Nikkeldepain by commercial and military treaties of considerable value. The Regency has taken the trouble to point out that such hostile conduct by a citizen of the Republic against citizens of the Regency is likely to have an adverse effect on the duration of the treaties. The charge thereby becomes compounded by the additional charge of a treasonable act against the Republic—"

He glanced at the captain. "I believe we can forestall the accused's plea that these pilfered goods also were restored. They were, in the face of superior force!"

"Fourth," the policeman went on patiently, "depraved and licentious conduct while acting as commercial agent, to the detriment of your employer's business and reputation—"

"WHAT?" choked the captain.

"—involving three of the notorious Witches of the Prohibited Planet of Karres—"

"Just like his great-uncle Threbus!" nodded Councilor Onswud gloomily. "It's in the blood, I always say!"

"—and a justifiable suspicion of a prolonged stay on said Prohibited Planet of Karres—"

"I never heard of that place before this trip!" shouted the captain.

"Why don't you read your Instructions and Regulations then?" shouted Councilor Rapport. "It's all there!"

"Silence, please!" shouted Councilor Onswud.

"Fifth," said the policeman quietly, "general willful and

negligent actions resulting in material damage and loss to your employer to the value of eighty-two thousand maels.''

"I've still got fifty-five thousand. And the stuff in the storage," the captain said, also quietly, "is worth half a million, at least!"

"Contraband and hence legally valueless!" the policeman said. Councilor Onswud cleared his throat.

"It will be impounded, of course," he said. "Should a method of resale present itself, the profits, if any, will be applied to the cancellation of your just debts. To some extent, that might reduce your sentence." He paused. "There is another matter—"

"The sixth charge," the policeman said, "is the development *and* public demonstration of a new type of space drive, which should have been brought promptly and secretly to the attention of the Republic of Nikkeldepain!"

They all stared at him—alertly and quite greedily.

So *that* was it—the Sheewash Drive!

"Your sentence may be greatly reduced, Pausert," Councilor Onswud said wheedlingly, "if you decide to be reasonable now. What have you discovered?"

"Look out, father!" Illyla said sharply.

"Pausert," Councilor Onswud inquired in a fading voice, "what is that in your hand?"

"A Blythe gun," the captain said, boiling.

There was a frozen stillness for an instant. Then the policeman's right hand made a convulsive movement.

"Uh-uh!" said the captain warningly.

Councilor Rapport started a slow step backwards.

"Stay where you are!" said the captain.

"Pausert!" Councilor Onswud and Illyla cried out together.

"Shut up!" said the captain.

There was another stillness.

"If you'd looked," the captain said, in an almost normal voice, "you'd have seen I've got the nova gun turrets out. They're fixed on that boat of yours. The boat's lying still and keeping its little yap shut. You do the same—"

He pointed a finger at the policeman. "You got a repulsor suit on," he said. "Open the inner port lock and go squirt yourself back to your boat!"

The inner port lock groaned open. Warm air left the ship in a long, lazy wave, scattering the sheets of the *Venture*'s log and commercial records over the floor. The thin, cold upper atmosphere of Nikkeldepain II came eddying in.

"You next, Onswud!" the captain said.

And a moment later: "Rapport, you just turn around—"

Young Councilor Rapport went through the port at a higher velocity than could be attributed reasonably to his repulsor units. The captain winced and rubbed his foot. But it had been worth it.

"Pausert," said Illyla in justifiable apprehension, "you are stark, staring mad!"

"Not at all, my dear," the captain said cheerfully. "You and I are now going to take off and embark on a life of crime together."

"But, Pausert—"

"You'll get used to it," the captain assured her, "just like I did. It's got Nikkeldepain beat every which way."

"Pausert," Illyla said, whitefaced, "we told them to bring up revolt ships!"

"We'll blow them out through the stratosphere," the captain said belligerently, reaching for the port-control switch. He added, "But they won't shoot anyway while I've got you on board!"

Illyla shook her head. "You just don't understand," she said desperately. "You can't make me stay!"

"Why not?" asked the captain.

"Pausert," said Illyla, "I am Madame Councilor Rapport."

"Oh!" said the captain. There was a silence. He added, crestfallen: "Since when?"

"Five months ago, yesterday," said Illyla.

"Great Patham!" cried the captain, with some indignation. "I'd hardly got off Nikkeldepain then! We were engaged!"

"Secretly . . . and I guess," said Illyla, with a return of spirit, "that I had a right to change my mind!"

There was another silence.

"Guess you had, at that," the captain agreed. "All right—the port's still open, and your husband's waiting in the boat. Beat it!"

He was alone. He let the ports slam shut and banged down the oxygen release switch. The air had become a little thin.

He cussed.

The communicator began rattling for attention. He turned it on.

"Pausert!" Councilor Onswud was calling in a friendly but shaking voice. "May we not depart, Pausert? Your nova guns are still fixed on this boat!"

"Oh, that—" said the captain. He deflected the turrets a trifle. "They won't go off now. Scram!"

The police boat vanished.

There was other company coming, though. Far below him but climbing steadily, a trio of revolt ships darted past on the screen, swung around and came back for the next turn of their spiral. They'd have to get a good deal closer before they started shooting; but they'd try to stay under him so as not to knock any stray chunks out of Nikkeldepain.

He sat a moment, reflecting. The revolt ships went by once more. The captain punched in the *Venture*'s secondary drives, turned her nose towards the planet and let her go. There were some scattered white puffs around as he cut through the revolt ships' plane of flight. Then he was below them, and the *Venture* groaned as he took her out of the dive.

The revolt ships were already scattering and nosing over for a counter-maneuver. He picked the nearest one and swung the nova guns towards it.

"—and ram them in the middle!" he muttered between his teeth.

SSS-whoosh!

It was the Sheewash Drive—but, like a nightmare now, it kept on and on!

VI

"Maleen!" the captain bawled, pounding the locked door of the captain's cabin. "Maleen—shut it off! Cut it off! You'll kill yourself. Maleen!"

The *Venture* quivered suddenly throughout her length, then shuddered more violently, jumped and coughed; and commenced sailing along on her secondary drives again. He wondered how many light-years from everything they were by now. It didn't matter!

"Maleen!" he yelled. "Are you all right?"

There was a faint *thump-thump* inside the cabin, and silence. He lost almost a minute finding the right cutting tool in the storage. A few seconds later, a section of door panel sagged inwards; he caught it by one edge and came tumbling into the cabin with it.

He had the briefest glimpse of a ball of orange-colored fire swirling uncertainly over a cone of oddly bent wires. Then the fire vanished, and the wires collapsed with a loose rattling to the table top.

The crumpled small shape lay behind the table, which was

why he didn't discover it at once. He sagged to the floor beside it, all the strength running out of his knees.

Brown eyes opened and blinked at him blearily.

"Sure takes it out of you!" Goth grunted. "Am I hungry!"

"I'll whale the holy, howling tar out of you again," the captain roared, "if you ever—"

"Quit your bawling!" snarled Goth. "I got to eat."

She ate for fifteen minutes straight, before she sank back in her chair, and sighed.

"Have some more Wintenberry jelly," the captain offered anxiously. She looked pretty pale.

Goth shook her head. "Couldn't—and that's about the first thing you've said since you fell through the door, howling for Maleen. Ha-ha! Maleen's *got* a boy friend!"

"Button your lip, child," the captain said. "I was thinking." He added, after a moment: "Has she really?"

"Picked him out last year," Goth nodded. "Nice boy from town—they get married as soon as she's marriageable. She just told you to come back because she was upset about you. Maleen had a premonition you were headed for awful trouble!"

"She was quite right, little chum," the captain said nastily.

"What were you thinking about?" Goth inquired.

"I was thinking," said the captain, "that as soon as we're sure you're going to be all right, I'm taking you straight back to Karres!"

"I'll be all right now," Goth said. "Except, likely, for a stomachache. But you can't take me back to Karres."

"Who will stop me, may I ask?" the captain asked.

"Karres is gone," Goth said.

"Gone?" the captain repeated blankly, with a sensation of not quite definable horror bubbling up in him.

"Not blown up or anything," Goth reassured him. "They just moved it! The Imperialists got their hair up about us again. But this time, they were sending a fleet with the big bombs and stuff, so everybody was called home. But they had to wait then till they found out where we were—me and Maleen and the Leewit. Then you brought us in; and they had to wait again, and decide about you. But right after you'd left . . . *we'd* left, I mean . . . they moved it."

"Where?"

"Great Patham!" Goth shrugged. "How'd I know? There's lots of places!"

* * *

There probably were, the captain admitted silently. A scene came suddenly before his eyes—that lime-white, arenalike bowl in the valley, with the steep tiers of seats around it, just before they'd reached the town of Karres—"the Theater where—"

But now there was unnatural night-darkness all over and about that world; and the eight thousand-some Witches of Karres sat in circles around the Theater, their heads bent towards one point in the center, where orange fire washed hugely about the peak of a cone of curiously twisted girders.

And a world went racing off at the speeds of the Sheewash Drive! There'd be lots of places, all right. What peculiar people!

"Anyway," he sighed, "if I've got to start raising you—don't say 'Great Patham' any more. That's a cuss word!"

"I learned it from you!" Goth pointed out.

"So you did, I guess," the captain acknowledged. "I won't say it either. Aren't they going to be worried about you?"

"Not very much," said Goth. "We don't get hurt often—especially when we're young. That's when we can do all that stuff like teleporting, and whistling, like the Leewit. We lose it mostly when we get older—they're working on that now so we won't. About all Maleen can do right now is premote!"

"She premotes just dandy, though," the captain said. "The Sheewash Drive—they can all do that, can't they?"

"Uh-huh!" Goth nodded. "But that's learned stuff. That's one of the things they already studied out." She added, a trace uncomfortably: "I can't tell you about that till you're one yourself."

"Till I'm what myself?" the captain asked, becoming puzzled again.

"A witch, like us," said Goth. "We got our rules. And that won't be for four years, Karres time."

"It won't, eh?" said the captain. "What happens then?"

"That's when I'm marriageable age," said Goth, frowning at the jar of Wintenberry jelly. She pulled it towards her and inspected it carefully. "I got it all fixed," she told the jelly firmly, "as soon as they started saying they ought to pick out a wife for you on Karres, so you could stay. I said it was me, right away; and everyone else said finally that was all right then—even Maleen, because she had this boy friend."

"You mean," said the captain, stunned, "this was all planned out on Karres?"

"Sure," said Goth. She pushed the jelly back where it had been standing, and glanced up at him again. "For three weeks, that's about all everyone talked about in the town! It set a perceedent—"

She paused doubtfully.

"That would explain it," the captain admitted.

"Uh-huh," Goth nodded relieved, settling back in her chair. "But it was my father who told us how to do it so you'd break up with the people on Nikkeldepain. He said it was in the blood."

"What was in the blood?" the captain said patiently.

"That you'd break up with them. That's Threbus, my father," Goth informed him. "You met him a couple of times in the town. Big man with a blond beard—Maleen and the Leewit take after him."

"You wouldn't mean my great-uncle Threbus?" the captain inquired. He was in a state of strange calm by now.

"That's right," said Goth. "He liked you a lot."

"It's a small Galaxy," said the captain philosophically. "So that's where Threbus wound up! I'd like to meet him again someday."

"We'll start after Karres four years from now, when you learn about those things," Goth said. "We'll catch up with them all right. That's still thirteen hundred and seventy-two Old Sidereal days," she added, "but there's a lot to do in between. You want to pay the money you owe back to those people, don't you? I got some ideas—"

"None of those teleporting tricks now!" the captain warned.

"Kid stuff!" Goth said scornfully. "I'm growing up. This'll be fair swapping. But we'll get rich."

"I wouldn't be surprised," the captain admitted. He thought a moment. "Seeing we've turned out to be distant relatives, I suppose it is all right, too, if I adopt you meanwhile—"

"Sure," said Goth. She stood up.

"Where you going?" the captain asked.

"Bed," said Goth. "I'm tired." She stopped at the hall door. "About all I can tell you about us till then," she said, "you can read in those Regulations, like the one man said—the one you kicked off the ship. There's a lot about us in there. Lots of lies, too, though!"

"And when did you find out about the communicator between here and the captain's cabin?" the captain inquired.

Goth grinned. "A while back," she admitted. "The others never noticed!"

"All right," the captain said. "Good night, witch—if you get a stomachache, yell and I'll bring the medicine."

"Good night," Goth yawned. "I will, I think."

"And wash behind your ears!" the captain added, trying to remember the bedtime instructions he'd overheard Maleen giving the junior witches.

"All right," said Goth sleepily. The hall door closed behind her—but half a minute later, it was briskly opened again. The captain looked up startled from the voluminous stack of "General Instructions and Space Regulations of the Republic of Nikkeldepain" he'd just discovered in one of the drawers of the control desk. Goth stood in the doorway, scowling and wide-awake.

"And you wash behind yours!" she said.

"Huh?" said the captain. He reflected a moment. "All right," he said. "We both will, then."

"Right," said Goth, satisfied.

The door closed once more.

The captain began to run his finger down the lengthy index of K's—or could it be under W?

Spree

by Barry N. Malzberg

*In an incredible burst of creativity, that extended through-
out the 1970s, Barry Malzberg produced several dozen
memorable science fiction novels and more than one
hundred short stories. No one had ever maintained this
kind of pace with consistently high quality before, at
least over so long a period. Particularly outstanding
were* Beyond Apollo *(1972 winner of the John W.
Campbell, Jr., Memorial Award),* Herovit's World
(1973), Guernica Night *(1974), and* The Destruction of
the Temple *(1974). These and other books extended the
genre, a field he has written about with great perception in* The Engines of the Night *(1982), a landmark
work of criticism. Many readers feel that he is even
better at the shorter lengths.*

At the International Artists & College Graduates Singles Mixer I
meet a registered nurse named Gloria Weinstein and decide to
tell her the truth. I am so sick of the secret, sick of it, it leaches
through the corridors of being, burbles with the blood, intersects
with the powers of speech; I have fought the revelation for all
this time and I can no longer do it. Will no longer do it. "I'm a
warlock," I say, holding a scotch on the rocks and facing her
squarely, her shoulders to the wall, her own drink bright in her
hand; her eyes drifting through the room to see if there might be
anyone more promising at the International Artists (there is not; I
can say this for a fact). "I can produce magical incantations. I
can change the scope and substance, the meaning and direction
of lives; I can even raise the dead, although this is one power I
have not yet explored."

She stares at me. If nothing else I have focused her intention.
"I've heard lines," she said, "I've been on this circuit for two
years now and I've aged before my time, but—"

"It's not a line," I say earnestly, "it's the truth. I just can't

99

hold back the truth anymore. I mean, I'm a graduate student on a fellowship and all that, I live a very ordinary life, to look at me you'd detect nothing strange at all, but truth is truth—''

"Graduate student where?"

"NYU," I say. I swallow the scotch convulsively; it mingles with the blood, spreads splinters of warmth and implication. "I'm afraid," I say, "afraid of the power, of the possibility—"

"So what are you saying to me?" Gloria Weinstein asks. She is moderately pretty, I suppose, five feet six or seven, dark hair, round full eyes, nurse's breasts ponderous through the thin sweater she wears, nurse's hands thin and charged with power as they surround the glass, although it is not these qualities which have attracted me to her so much as a certain vulnerability and accessibility, an openness to her posture, some small hints and breaks in her composure which have indicated to me, even before I began to talk, that she might listen, she might understand. "You're a warlock and you know magical incantations and I'm supposed to go to bed with you? To hear the spells and all that?" She shakes her head. "Yes indeed," she says, "that's a new one all right," but encouragingly she makes no move to leave, her posture against the wall remains easeful, her eyes, dense and accepting, rest now on mine. "I don't care," she says, "I've met them all. I've met interns and rapists and a truckdriver who was on the way to being an audited clear and a bartender who had been a trapeze artist with the circus. I've met a second violinist in the New York Philharmonic who was tone-deaf and a dancer with the New York City Ballet who had three knee operations, so I don't see why a warlock should be anything really special. That's a male witch, right? A warlock?"

"Something like that. It isn't quite that simple; it's a separate strain, a different archetype—"

"Hey," Gloria Weinstein says to me and puts her drink down on a ledge, then extends a hand to me, "I don't really need to hear about it, you don't have to tell me no more. Do you want to get out of here?"

"Yes," I say, "of course I'd like to get out of here. The only purpose of these things is to get out of them. Like life itself."

"Then let's go," she says. "I have three roommates and there's always one of them off-shift sleeping, so you can forget that. You got a place?"

"I've got a furnished one-and-a-half on West 123rd Street," I say and think of the cluttered room, the incense, the piles of debris, the stones and magical books scattered on the shelves and the floor, "but I don't know if you'd want to go there, I haven't really cleaned it up."

"A warlock can't clean his room? You can't just point a finger and make a spell?"

"It isn't that simple," I say. "None of it is that simple. You're making fun of me, but I told you simply because I can't keep it secret anymore, I can't deal with it, I can't carry it all alone, there comes a time finally when you have to share—"

"It's all right," she says. She takes my hand. "I'm a *nurse*, remember. I'm big on sympathy. Let's get out of here." She leads me through the thin clumps of International Artists & Singles through the heavy odors of the room and through the doors; possessed, enchanted, I follow.

"A warlock," she says as we wait for our coats at the checkroom. "A warlock with magical spells and incantations. In a furnished room near Columbia University. Hey, why don't you live near NYU if you're going there?"

"They threw me out of Columbia in the fall," I said. "I just barely worked it out at NYU, but I've got all my things in the room; I couldn't just move."

"Why did they throw you out?"

"Why don't we just get our coats and go uptown?" I say.

Power fills me, the terrible rising power, scrolls and screed lurk in the darkness of consciousness as slowly I move upon her whispering the incantations, my dread choked off in the back of the throat emerges as small, hawklike cries in the darkness, then growing, mounting, spreading like blood, the blood rising, pulsing in the darkness, and the brisk collision is incidental to the rising of that blood, I bounce off stone, stone incident to circumstance, and move through, beating, beating, the smell of ozone suddenly high and hard in the air, dense, overtaking me—

"My God," she says as if from a far distance, "my God, you weren't kidding, were you?"

Falling, falling upon her I batter at the voice, there are more words, words fluttering like insects in the air, but I penetrate their center, move to the pool of darkness, now there are different sounds, flutelike, disparate, but I part them too, the collisions heavier, coming at me, walls tumbling, the splitting of the earth, and in the center of all of that a small chink of light. I concentrate upon one aspect of that light, working myself toward it, forcing it to expand, and slowly the darkness implodes, light leaching at the corridors, sounds all around, shrieks and the power comes from me then in an enormous incantation of speed and scurrying, I wedge myself all the way through and in the dazzle of circumstance am finally alone, free, in that high empty place which I have sought and which is at last mine, I seek purchase within it—

Inside the described pentagram the demon totters, falls to his haunches, crouches with difficulty, his taloned hands spread against the earth. "This has got to stop, you know," he says. "This can't go on. You're going to have to get hold of yourself, control the situation, find some kind of resolution, stop calling for help."

"I'm not calling for help," I say. Fires ring the demon; carefully I feed one of the magic parchments to the near flame, grant it sustenance. Within the ring of fire the demon cowers, but if the fire were ever to go out, if it were to go out, if it were—

"There is no help," the demon says, "there is only the flame over and again." His skin is damp against the heat; his sweat has the odor of sacred text. "Let me go," he says. "I'm in terrible pain."

"Pain from hell?" I try to laugh, but the hollow explosion of sound racks me. "What do you know of pain? Can pain feel pain? Give me the incantation," I say. "Give it to me now and you are free."

"You don't understand," the demon says. "There is no incantation, there is no magic, there is only yourself known over and again. Why do you think that I would have the answer?"

"From walking to and fro upon the earth and up and down within it; from the exile and the circumstance—"

"Oh come on," the demon says, "come on, come on, come on," his little voice beating and beating against the wall of flame, "come on, stop being a fool, demonology is not the answer, this is your *life*." His little shrieks and taunts inflame me. I put my hand through the fire to squeeze him and take what vengeance I can, but the pentagram resists my hand with sudden and awful power and I feel it open, feel the strength draining. The heat comes into the unprotected joints and I scream with the sudden pain, pull my hand out, retreat, stumble from that center and cower against a wall while the demon regards me with enormous, solemn eyes not untinged now with sympathy as I begin to understand what he has said: that even in hell, that in hell of all places and for its creatures, there must be the quality of pain.

*   *   *

In Washington Square Park, on a bench, watching the derelicts assemble beyond one gate to compute the endless circumstance of their lives while in other sections of the park more
vigorous if useless attempts are made to come to terms with
urban shock; in Washington Square Park on a bench I contem-
plate my life and what has taken me to this condition and what if
anything I can do about it. Unaware of my power until the age of
fourteen, brought suddenly to terrible terms with it, attempting
for a decade thereafter to deny it, finally accepting in my twenty-
fourth year the dreadful circumstance: pursuit of the old texts,
retreat into medievalism, the conversion of a degree in account-
ing to an application for fellowship in philosophy, the months at
Columbia, the disgraceful confrontation in the corridor with
senior faculty and subsequent breakdown which brought me
here, the circles of my life, the pit of my belief, the solemnity
and terror of my obligation . . . I think and think of all of these
things on the bench until I begin to tremble with implication; a
warlock should not be in this position, I think, no warlock
worthy of the name would be in a condition of this sort; he
would invoke his powers and through spiritual decree free himself . . . and yet the concept of the warlock entrapped overcomes
me; in or out of time there is no end to the entrapment: *power
achieved is only the power to further entrap*, and this insight
bolts me upright from the bench. It is as if for the first time I see
things clearly (I have had this illusion before), have some purchase on circumstance, have some true and final understanding
of what I have achieved, and I move toward the gates rapidly, in
haste to somehow commit this insight to action. It is only action
that will save me now, only action that can at last bring me
through this to some deeper understanding. One of the derelicts
looks up, spits at me, I feel his saliva hitting my face like a
blow, and I raise my hand, wheel on him, whisper the Word; his
face caves in, he crumples upon himself, falls to the ground, the
others stare at him, then at me, I raise my hand again. "Don't do
it," one of them cries, "don't do it, sonny," and for just an
instant I feel the pure and sentencing fire that will take me free
but I hold back. This is not the way to do it, there will be
another time and I will not waste my power upon derelicts. I turn
and stalk from the park, they murmur behind me. High above I
hear the birdlike cries of sustenance; from the cloudless and
terrible sky the Elders have observed and once again have passed
their judgment. In or out of time, in or out of power there is no
end to judgment; to know this is to know it again and again and
again.

*   *   *

In hunched and crowded sleep I dream of Gloria, the thin pressure of her body against me, the high and haunting sound of her voice as she took my measure, and I think in the dream that I perceive her with the mask torn and her pure witch's face glinting out at me. Gloria a witch then living under cover as I no longer can, Gloria living her terrible secret in the hospital corridors, in the International Artists Mixer, in the open and closed spaces of the city. "You've got to survive," she says to me, "don't you understand that, you can't tell them what you are. This is the end of the second millennium, the beginning of the third, technology, rationality, the machines, the terrible and barbarous circumstances of power, the knives and steel of the machines will kill if you tell them who you are.

"You must be like me," she says in the dream, rising then to confront me, her eyes dark and shrouded. "You must never tell, you must tell them nothing," and I enfold her with my arms, drag her down again to the sheets. "Don't tell," she says, "don't *tell tell tell*," and I want to scream to her that this is possible for her but not possible for me, that something has ripped, broken, the armament has been destroyed, and that absent of guile, stripped of concealment, I must not only invoke but describe my power. "Power denied turns against the bearer," I say to her, "power becomes then only the power to die," and hard and heavy against her I begin to scrapple in the motions of generation, still earnest even at this terrible time. Power does indeed seize me, in power I turn and I rise and I rise, it is as if in this elevation I will purchase at last an answer but instead am ripped free only of the fabric of the dream itself and come to consciousness in my cold room on a high floor in the tenement of life, staring out at the river, the cold frozen gray burning into sensibility, and Gloria dwindles, wraps the dream about herself and is destroyed. Alone and alone in the spaces of the room I look upon the texts and the bottles and the potions and the cryptograms which I have sped against the wall and think yes, the gleaming machinery, the steel and the knives will be the end of all of us if I emerge and yet if I were not to emerge they will kill us unbidden. One more try. One more try for the Pentagram. One more try at last for the Word which will strike not only at derelicts but at the hearts and souls of my countrymen, the living and the dead, the shallow and the spoken and bring them all to rise in that judgment which invoked awaits all of us, and I began once again with the paints to construct the circle . . .

* * *

Within which the demon poises chattering, his skin cold now, no more protective sweat as the fires shrivel him to stone. "You don't understand," he says, "you don't really understand any of this, do you?"

"Give me the word," I say. "Give it now."

"There is no word, there is no judgment—"

"I want it now," I say. Remorselessness fills me; I know that I have been denied for the last time. "Give it to me now or I will douse the fires and let the saints do with you what they will; I won't wait any longer, there's no time, there's never been any time from the beginning. Give it to me," I say.

The demon says, "You misunderstand, you misunderstand totally, don't you see—"

"Now," I say, "now or I'll call the father of hell himself to pronounce a judgment and if I do that then there will be nothing for any of us, all of it will be gone but you will pay and you will pay—"

The demon says, "You're a fool," and slowly stands within the circle. His eyes are enormous; the rest of him has contracted to that terrible stare. "I'll give you the word then but it won't make things any easier, it's only going to make them more terrible, don't you see that, don't you understand what you've done? You could have had it the easy way all your life, you could have used it to advantage but instead you allowed it to overtake—"

"The word," I say. "The Word."

The demon looks at me. He licks his lips; little wings sprout from his back, his eyes fill with luster and intensity.

"You fool," he says again.

He gives me the Word.

In hard embrace against Gloria I move into the splitting rock of circumstance waiting now for the proper time; the Word is within my possession and I can use it to advantage but only at the optimum point; it would be wrong to employ it when I cannot get the maximum effect. Poised, chattering, I hear her beginning to whisper once again, witch's secrets, ancient and debilitating oaths which will cut to the center of my power and—"Shut up, you bitch," I say, "shut up now." But she cannot stop, once unleashed a witch's confidences cannot so easily be denied, and rage fills me, rage at all of those forces which drove me toward revelation and then at last to demand the Word itself, and in the sudden, cool center of that rage I find the strength to do as I must. "I warned you," I say to her. "I warned you that it would be this way, *you made me do it.*" And then, stricken, I utter the Word itself, mumbling it at first under the tongue and then as her body begins to come to fire under its sound I say it again, louder, louder yet, begin to scream it, the syllables ripped out of my throat, great hawking cries. The room splits, it opens wings like a bird, and I am catapulted into a sudden open space where free at enormous height I seem to look down upon all of them, the knives and the steel, the poised machinery waiting below to consume. But I will not yield, I will not land. Instead I cry out the Word once more in all of its ancient and terrible powers and the seas and the cities collapse and run against one another, all mingles, all dwells . . .

And they come in the morning with solemn hands and solemn hearts and tell me what I did and wait politely while I assemble my clothing and join them at the door to be taken off. Because there is absolutely nothing left to do.

And because, with the word at last delivered, there is absolutely nothing left to say.

Devil's Henchman
by Murray Leinster

*Murray Leinster (1896–1975) was at one time the proud
possessor of the title "Dean of Science Fiction." His
was truly a remarkable and lengthy career, which began with his first sale in 1913 and continued almost
without interruption until his retirement in 1967. Although he worked in all genres, most of his production
was science fiction, where he is fondly remembered as
a pioneer of the "parallel world" story and the author
of the popular and award-winning "Med Service" series of stories.* The Best of Murray Leinster *(1978)
indeed shows him at his best. "Devil's Henchman"
was originally published under the author's real name,
Will F. Jenkins.*

When Joe Burchard wore the witch ring from the outland country
and fought with the devil in Ben Harper's body, the morning
didn't start out any different from any other. The sun rose over
the mountains, and the shadows were long and sprawling, and all
the spider webs shone like diamonds. The wind blew overhead,
going from yonder to some other place. Smoke from the cabins
all up and down the valley streaked out long and low. It was a
mighty nice day to be twenty-one years old in, like Joe was.
He'd licked every man but one in a day's walking, and he'd
courted and kissed every girl but two.

He didn't know a thing about the witch ring that morning,
though. He sat in his granny's cabin and ate the breakfast she'd
cooked him. He felt purely fine, like a body does when he's
twenty-one and tall and broad and hasn't got a care in the world.
He breathed in, and it felt good. He breathed out, and it felt even
better.

His granny looked at him sharp whilst he was eating his
breakfast. She'd been a witching woman once and she could see
more in a peek than most in a gape, and Joe was her only kin
and she loved him like nobody but a granny is able to. He had on

his store-going red wool shirt and his Saturday pants. That meant he'd be going down to Crowder's Store, where three roads crossed and the young men loafed around to show off to each other and the girls that came to the store with their mas.

"Huh!" says Joe's granny.

"Dressed up! You aim to be kissing some young girl and fighting some young man this morning. I know the signs."

He grinned at her. "Now," he says, "the fella ain't so young. He's Ben Harper. And the girl—I ain't sure, but Letty Smith asked me to stop by her folks' cabin for a letter she'd like to get mailed."

His granny thumped the floor with her stick, fretful.

"Foolish! Foolish! Foolish!" she says. "To you, it's fun, but Ben Harper's been craving Letty since she was old enough to look cornerways. He wouldn't fight no fist fight with somebody he thought she favored! He's got black eyes and no lobes to his ears, and that's a sign he ain't no fist-fighting man. He'll take to a knife or worse, he will!"

"Shucks!" says Joe. "There's the law, granny. Them days are long gone. He'd as soon take to witching."

"He might do that," says Joe's granny, peevish. "You're young yet, honey. You don't know what can happen inside a man when a girl he craves laughs at him. And if a man's heart is wrong and his cravings hot, there's ways of turning to witchery. But you, now—supposing you do kiss Letty at her folks' cabin and lick Ben Harper down to the store?"

Joe laughed, and he wiped his mouth.

"That's something I ain't figured out yet," he says.

His granny snapped, "There's Sally." Sally Walker was the only girl besides Letty in a day's walking that Joe hadn't courted and kissed, and Joe's granny thought a lot of Sally. But Joe didn't look up.

"No—o," says Joe. "I've known her all my born days. It wouldn't be no fun to court Sally or to kiss her. She's pretty enough. She's sweet. She's a right nice girl. But I just ain't got a mind to her."

His granny says, angry, "I was a witchin' woman once, before I got religion and married your grandpa. I know what's the matter. You're scared Sally wouldn't like you kissing her. You're—scared! I'd ought to do a little witchin'—"

Joe laughed and he got up and he went over and gave his granny a hug.

"You wouldn't witch me," he says.

"I wouldn't witch nobody," says his granny, peevish. "I promised your grandpa and I promised the Lord. Else I'd show you. Go along with you."

She gave him a shove and he laughed again and went over to the mirror that his granny kept tacked up on the wall. It was a sign and a reminder of what she'd given up, because a witching woman can't abide a mirror. Joe bent down to look in it, and he took a comb and he parted his straight black hair because he'd be stopping by Letty's folks' cabin, and she'd be there by her lone.

Then he went out of the cabin and striding on his way, and the sun was shining bright and a bobwhite called somewheres off in the woods, and the sky was so blue even a young man had to notice it. It felt purely good to be alive and young and a-walking to kiss a girl another man pined for, and fight that man and lick him after. Joe didn't take his granny's fussing serious. She'd got religion and married Joe's grandpa and he was waiting for her over Jordan and she wouldn't disappoint him. So Joe went on his way with nothing on his mind but the pleasure it was to be alive. He didn't think about the witching ring, that's sure. He didn't know there was such a thing.

But presently he thought about Sally. Her folks' cabin was the nearest to his granny's and when his own ma and pa died off while he was small he came to live with his granny. He could remember Sally from when neither of them was knee-high to a duck. And now he was grown-up, thinking of Sally gave him a queer kind of sad feeling, and a yearning feeling, and a scared feeling, too. So he backed down from thinking about her as much as he could.

The speckled shadows passed over as he walked. Birds chirped and katydids whirred all about. He went uphill and down, and all of a sudden he looked and there was Letty Smith's folks' cabin up above him and the gray rocks sticking out of the hillside all around. And sudden-like he knew that he didn't want to kiss Letty, but he was bounden to. He was going to fight Ben Harper, and Ben Harper craved Letty so bad that his eyes shone wild when they looked at her, and he'd never got religion. But she'd told Joe that her ma and her pa were going over the mountains to hear the new preacher and she'd have to stay home to look after the stock, and would he stop by to get a letter to mail for her down at Crowder's.

Joe stopped short and grunted to himself. He kind of fumed, because all of a sudden he didn't care a thing about kissing

Letty. And that wasn't natural, with him being twenty-one. He caught himself thinking. "If it was Sally, now—" and then he thought suspicious of his granny. She could make him feel this way if she liked. A spell muttered over a crumb of cornbread he'd eat the rest of out in the yard because of the mirror on the wall.

But he knew his granny wouldn't witch him even for his own good. She'd got religion years ago.

So Joe took a deep breath and climbed up the hillside, frowning to himself because it was funny he didn't want to kiss a pretty girl. But still he wasn't thinking about witchery, and least of all about the witch ring.

He stepped over the stile and went across the pasture to the cabin. There wasn't any noise but the chickens pecking and clucking and the wind above the Hollow. He opened his mouth to call, but the door opened and there was Letty looking at him. Her hair was straggly and she wasn't primped up. She looked white and scared and half crazy with crying and grief. She didn't say a word. Her hands were shaking.

"What's the matter?" says Joe, uncomfortable. "You sick?"

She didn't say a word, just looked at him imploring. And Joe felt queer.

He says, suspicious, "You sure act funny, Letty. You act like you was witched."

And that was what had to be said before Letty could speak. She put her face in her hands and she moaned.

"I *am* witched!" she cried. "That's it, Joe—I am!"

Now, Joe wasn't scared of witchery like some people, because his granny had told him—and she'd ought to know—that witchery hasn't got any power over a man unless his heart is wrong.

So Joe says, curious, "How does it take you, Letty? How does it feel?"

"I'm pins and needles all over," says Letty, pitiful, "and I itch and I ache to go to the one that's witched me, and nobody else can come near me without a pain in my heart and my breath stopping. So don't come near me, Joe. I'm witched and if you do I'll fall down dead." But she cried, heartbroken.

Joe shifted his weight from one foot to the other. Letty looked mighty pitiful, and she looked at him so pleading that it was right much of a dare for a young man that was twenty-one years old.

"My granny says," says Joe, "that witching ain't got any power if your heart's right."

Then Letty cried harder.

"I know," she says bitter. "I know all that. But I've had hate in my heart a long time. I hated Ben Harper because he craved me to love him and he wasn't the right one. I hated the girls you courted, because they wasn't me. There's no harm telling you because I'm witched, but I've laid awake nights thinking of you and I—I—" She says, heartbroke, "I've tried to witch you to dream love dreams of me and that's give witchery the power over me. And if you was to come near me now I'd have a pain in my heart and my breath would stop and I'd drop down dead."

Then she wrung her hands and cried desperate but her eyes went to him pleading. And Joe shifted his weight back to the foot he'd been standing on before. It's a mighty fine thing to be twenty-one, but Joe knew better than to fool with witchery. He thought hard, fidgeting. Letty'd been trying to witch him into loving her, and that was what gave witchery the power over her, so she was witched because of him.

She was a pretty girl, too, when she wasn't crying. Joe knew better than to look too close, but he did know that she was thin where a girl had ought to be thin, and where a girl oughtn't to be, she wasn't. She'd be nice to go buggy riding with or a-courting, but Joe hadn't ever thought of wanting to marry her.

"Who witched you?" says Joe, unhappy. "If I'm what made the trouble you're in, I'd ought to try to get you out."

"It's Ben Harper," says Letty. "He boiled a black cat in a kettle and threw the bones in a running stream, and he gave up crossing over Jordan and a man came and told him what to do. He told me. So I got to go to him, Joe. Please help me. So long as he's living, unless he takes the witching off, I'm suffering, and flesh and blood can't stand but so much!"

Then she twitched and she shivered and she gasped and she panted like she was going to have a fit.

Joe backed away, considerate, and he says, "I was figuring on seeing him down to the store today and he's the last man in a day's walking that I ain't licked. But if he's been fooling with a black cat's bones and started witching, it ain't no ordinary flesh and blood can lick him. My granny—"

"She won't help none," says Letty, a-wringing her hands. "She's got religion. And there ain't anything else can help me but Ben Harper dying or taking the witching off of me. But you could make him, Joe. There ain't anything I won't do for you, Joe, if only you'll do that for me!"

"You hold on," says Joe, "and I'll do it. You go stand on a

rock in a running stream. That'll weaken the witchery and I'll tend to Ben Harper.''

And he turned and he left her. And first off he started straight for Ben's cabin, figuring that Ben wouldn't be going to no store that Saturday morning if he'd put a spell on Letty so's she'd have to come to him. Ben would be waiting up in his cabin for his spell to work.

Then Joe began to realize that if Ben was a witch it wouldn't do no good to go after him alone, because, leaving out stronger witchery, there's just three things witching can't stand against. One's a purely good heart, and one's a bullet fired across still water, and one's the law and the Grand Jury. So Joe turned and headed back to talk to his granny. If it'd been Sally that had been itching and aching and crying and wringing her hands because Ben Harper'd witched her, Joe wouldn't have turned aside. He'd have gone straight to Ben Harper, and he'd have been raging, and somehow he'd've managed to kill Ben with his own bare hands before any spell could stop him. But this was Letty, so it was different.

The sky didn't look so blue to him, because he didn't see it. He thought about Letty, crying pitiful, and it was because of him that she'd been witched, and he thought about Sally Walker that may be Ben might turn his mind to witch some day.

He went tramping across the pasture and he went past the well. He stomped up on the porch and his eyes were hot and angry, and he went inside—and there was Sally Walker a-setting and talking with his granny. She'd seen him start off to Crowder's Store from her own folks' cabin up the mountainside, and she'd come over to visit.

The two of them, Sally and his granny, turned around and stared when Joe came stomping in.

He says, furious, "Granny, Letty Smith's been witched!"

Then the words poured out as he told them, raging, all about it. His granny sniffed.

"Huh!" she says. "When I was a witching woman, before I got religion, *I* woulda handled this!"

Joe says, "It's on account of me, Granny! He couldn't have witched her, but her heart ain't been right on account of me! She's been hating the girls I courted and she tried witching me to make me dream love dreams of her. She told me. And that gave witchery the power over her. I can't let Letty go be a witch's woman on account of me.''

His granny thumped her stick and looked at Sally, a-setting

there white and pale and twisting her fingers in her lap as she looked at Joe. Joe's granny says, "I told you he didn't have the sense he was born with!"

But she didn't move to do a thing. And Joe says, fierce, "I know you won't do no witching, Granny. So it looks like I got to get Ben Harper in my sights over still water. And I got to do it right away. I got to, Granny, because it's on account of me!"

His granny says, "What'll the law do? The sheriff don't pay no mind to witchin'. They'll hang you, and it'd serve you right for fooling around like you been doing."

"I'll go on a journey, after," says Joe. "They won't never catch me. But I'd never sleep nights thinking of Letty as a witch's woman and a-crying in the dark because she couldn't never pass over Jordan. I got to do it, Granny. I got to!"

"I promised," his granny says, peevish, "but Lord knows it's a temptation! Away back before there was any people living in this Hollow and before the ships come across the ocean to this land, the great-grandpappy of my grandpa was foolin' with witchery, and it's in the blood. But I promised—and I aim to cross over Jordan. I won't do a thing."

"Then," says Joe, "I'll get my rifle. Nothing else to do."

His granny thumped the floor with her stick. "You, Joe!" she says, angry, "I didn't say I wouldn't tell you what to do. This is a witchin' family, and there's things come down from long ago. Up in the attic there's one of them. When I burnt my witchin' things I wouldn't touch it because it couldn't be burnt, and after I got religion I wouldn't touch a witch thing excep' to burn it. And it's full of peril. But if your heart is right, you can take it an' fight Ben Harper and he won't never be able to witch nobody any more."

Joe, he says, miserable, "I don't know how right my heart is, but I don't want a thing from Letty, not even a thank you. All I want is to be able to sleep nights and not think of somebody cryin' in the dark because they won't never cross over Jordan, and it my fault."

Joe's granny sniffs and says, "Go up in the attic," she says. "High up where the bricks get narrow, and make a shelf. All the way in back there's a iron box. It's rusty and it's old. You fetch it here."

Joe went and climbed up to the attic. It was crowded with things from past times and long ago. There were boxes with quilts and comforters in them, and a spinning wheel Joe's granny had used when she was a girl, and what might've been a loom.

There was an old bed, all apart, and a flintlock musket, and all the things that pile up in a attic when folks live in the same house for generations. Joe had to step careful, but he got to the chimney, and he reached far back and up high, and he felt a little box all furry with cobwebs. Something ran over his fingers when he stirred it, but he brushed the cobwebs off and went back downstairs.

"There's a ring in that box," says Joe's granny, grim. "It's rusty because it's iron. There's paper in the box hand-writ, and there's no use tryin' to read it. You go outside and put on the ring. Then you can go fight Ben Harper and he can't do a thing to you by his witchin'. If you lick him, he won't never be able to witch no more. But I'm warnin' you, don't never let anybody you love see you while you wear that ring!"

Then Sally spoke, for the only time. Her voice was shaky. "If he—puts it on—can he cross over Jordan after?"

Joe's granny sniffed. "It's outland witchery," she says. "My grandma warned me—she that was never happy again after grandpa saw her wearin' the ring. There's witchery that meant turnin' your back to the Lord, and your heart has to be black to take pleasure in it. But there's witchery that has to be done with a good heart. It's full of peril, because to feel sure your heart is right is presumin' before the Lord. I trust I'm goin' over Jordan, but I know I'm a schemin' old woman and I wouldn't never dare to put on that ring. But Joe," she says, "he's bound and determined, and I wouldn't want to see him hung even for shootin' a witch."

She looked at Joe, stern, and he went out of the house. The box was iron, with designs on it, and he had to hit it a couple of licks with the axhead before the top opened up reluctant. And there was a ring in it, like his granny had said, and there was paper in it—only it wasn't paper but like rabbit skin with the fur off, and old and dry and yellow. He could read the writing, but it was spelled funny and it didn't make sense at all.

"By ye arte of alchymie," was what he made out, "I Thomas Dee, Doctor, have made ye ringe of veritie under ye signe of Saturne, but yt ys a sadde discouerie . . ."

Joe didn't try to read any more. He shut up the box and he put the ring on his finger. It fitted pretty good.

He didn't feel a mite different until he happened to look down at the ground. Then he was scared.

He shivered a minute and took the ring off fast. But then he thought about Letty all alone and itching and aching and crying because she knew she couldn't hold out forever. So he started off toward Ben Harper's cabin, holding the ring tight.

It wasn't far beyond where Letty lived, and the way was near. Tramping through the fallen leaves and pushing aside the bushes, it came to Joe Burchard that Letty'd be strengthened to fight the witchery if she knew his errand. So he turned aside a little and presently there were her folks' cabin on the hillside, with the gray rocks sticking up out of the earth all around. He stepped over the stile and up the sloping pasture, and when he was ten yards from the cabin he hollered.

There wasn't any answer. Not a sound but the clucking of the chickens and a bobwhite somewhere. Joe hollered again.

Still no answer. And then the sweat came out on Joe Burchard all over. It was plain enough. Letty was toilin' over the hills to Ben Harper, crying and wringing her hands as she went because she couldn't help herself.

Joe took out after her. He went fast. He carried the witch ring in his hand, not on his finger, and he vaulted the rail fence of the pasture, and he went running over the slanting ground, and once he stumbled and went crashing into a dead tree that crumbled to dust when he hit it, and then he knew that witchery was working on him to keep him from catching up to Letty to help her. The ring had fallen out of his hand.

It took him minutes to find it again, and Lord knows if he'd been thinking anything but good he wouldn't never have found it at all. He hunted and hunted desperate, and then he says, agonized, "Lord, help Your servant, because I don't want to do this for myself, being the only girl I purely care about is Sally. But I'm the cause of Letty bein' witched—" And there was the witch ring before him, laying on the ground in plain sight. He picked it up and put it on his finger and he run.

He flung through brushwood and he flung through briars. He climbed up steep ways and he slid down slopes. He waded waist-deep in hollows where the leaves had gathered, and he hauled himself up rockfalls by the vines that grew down over them. He came to a place where the path led to Ben Harper's cabin. He turned into that path and he run.

He hadn't gone a quarter of a mile when he saw Letty. She was moving along the path with her hands over her face, and she was crying bitter. There was sobbings that choked her, and sometimes she took down her hands from her face to wring them. And she was gasping, "I don't want to go. . . . I ain't goin'. . . . I'm goin' to stop when I get to that bush. . : . I'm a-goin' to set right down here an' not move a step. . . ."

But she went right on walking, slow and heavy and leaning back and crying, like somebody trying to walk in a freshet. Ben Harper's witching was strong!

Then Joe came up to her, panting, and he says, "Letty!"

And she turned her despairing eyes to him, and she fell down on the path and hid her face. She didn't know him. And Joe remembered that if he was to go near her she'd have a pain in her heart and her breath would stop. There couldn't nobody touch Letty but the one that had witched her. And she didn't know Joe. She lay on the ground, crying and shivering because she'd seen Joe Burchard with the witch ring on his finger, and she took on pitiful. So Joe began to realize how perilous it was to wear this ring, but he went on.

He run on down the path before her, and he brushed through briars and he pushed through brush, and there was Ben Harper's cabin. And Ben Harper sat on the steps before his door.

His eyes glittered and the sunshine seemed to dodge falling on him, and he was a strong, stout man and Joe had put him off to the last to lick, because licking Ben Harper without no witchery would be a hard job. But this was worse. Joe knew right away that he wouldn't have no chance at all without the witch ring.

Ben's eyes were glittering and his mouth was slobbering and he was an awful sight to look at. He'd turned his back on the Lord to have Letty for his own in this life, and he knew she was coming to him. He was waiting for his reward for turning witch, and it was terrible to see. But Joe knew, all of a sudden, that Ben wasn't alone, because right there in his body with him, a-gloating over what Ben thought, a-sharing everything he saw and knew and felt, there was the devil. He was right there in Ben's body, possessing it, and Ben didn't know. But Joe knew, for certain, and he felt almost sorry for Ben. So it was Ben he spoke to.

"Ben," he says, "look at my shadow."

Ben Harper looked—and the devil in his body looked, too. Then he screeched. And then he bounced up and come for Joe like a panther cornered in a henhouse will come for a man that opens the door. The devil in Ben Harper's body knew that he'd got power over any creature that casts a shadow except a man or woman whose heart is right. But he knew, and Ben knew, too, that when somebody that don't cast a shadow stands before him, it's time for the ending of evil and witchery, too. And with the witch ring on his finger, Joe didn't cast no shadow.

Ben Harper was a big man. He wasn't as tall as Joe, but he

was broader. His legs were like tree trunks and his arms were thick with muscle. His eyes glared hate, and his teeth showed like a snarling dog's, and he came panting to fight for his witchery and his meannesses and the pleasures he'd turned witch to have. And the devil stayed in his body to help him. Ben was fighting for Letty, wringing her hands and crying because she couldn't help herself from coming to him. He was fighting for the devil like a preacher fights for the Lord, only he fought with fists and boots and fingers and teeth, biting and gouging and frothing at the mouth because he was fighting for what he'd give up crossing over Jordan for.

And that was a fight! If it wasn't that the witch ring was a good fit on Joe Burchard's finger, Ben woulda got it off and trompled on it, and there would've been nothing left of Joe at all. They fought on the tromped clear space before Ben's cabin door, and they fought in the brush beyond the clearing. They fought into the rail fence around the pigsty, and they knocked it down and they fought in the mud and the mire and the hogs run squealing off into the pine thicket around.

Once Ben got both hands around Joe's throat, and the misty dark shapes all around grew thicker and crowded close. But Joe—with his eyes going black from lack of breath—managed to get hold of just one of Ben's fingers, and he bent it back and broke it, and Ben let go.

And presently they were up, beating at each other with their fists, gasping in each other's faces, and the blows they struck making smacking noises in the stillness that seemed to hold everywhere near by. And Joe felt his knees weakening, and he lurched ahead and gripped Ben around the waist and flung him to the ground, and then he pounded Ben's head on a mite of rock that stuck up out of the ground right there, and he hammered Ben's head on it, and he hammered and he hammered. And Joe must've been mighty dazed by the fighting he'd been through, because he sudden-like heard himself panting. "The Lord is my shepherd—" *Thump!* That was Ben's head on the rock. "I shall not want." *Thump!* "He leadeth me beside the still waters—" *Thump!*

And then Ben give a monstrous shudder and lay still.

He wasn't dead, because he was still breathing, but his eyes were closed and his arms were limp and his fingers hung loose and empty. There wasn't a quiver in him when Joe got up, panting.

He looked all around. The sunshine played over everything

plain and clear. It shone on Ben Harper, and there wasn't any more mistiness anywhere. Joe heard the birds singing. He heard Ben's hogs grunting a little way off, so he panted a while and then heaved Ben up off the ground and carried him into the cabin, so as not to leave him laying like dead for the hogs to find. And in the cabin he saw Something that the devil must've told Ben Harper to make, and Joe Burchard felt mighty sick at his stomach. But he kicked it to pieces and flung it in the fireplace and stirred up the embers to make it burn. And then he knew, from what his granny had told him, that Ben Harper couldn't never be a witch again, no matter what he did. So he'd better try mighty hard to get religion.

Then Joe went out of the cabin and down the path. He saw Letty Smith running away, swarming over fallen logs and running through the brush, with the witching off her so she didn't itch or ache or need to be fearful any more. And she was crying still, but it was with joy, and she'd get to somebody's cabin, crying with gladness, and get them to take her quick to a preacher so she could get religion and nevermore be like she'd been.

But Joe, he headed back to his granny's. It'd been a mighty hard fight. Where he wasn't scratched, he was black and blue. Where he wasn't sore, he stung, and where he didn't sting he ached pretty bad. And he was all wore out. But he started back for his granny's and there was something that his mind clung to. Letty'd seen him, she cried out and fell down an' hid her face. When Ben Harper saw him, he'd screeched and come despairing to fight. And his granny had said for Joe never to let anybody he cared about see him with the ring on his finger. That was a thing Joe had to find out about, being he was twenty-one.

When he came to his granny's cabin, he went past the well. He went up on the porch and he went in the door. And he turned to the mirror that his granny had tacked up on the wall for a proof and a reminder that she'd give up all her witching ways. He looked in that mirror to see what he looked like that he had scared Letty so bad, and made Ben Harper screech and fight. He figured he was going to see something mighty fearful.

But he didn't see a thing. He looked right through his own image and at the wall behind him. He was invisible in the mirror like he didn't cast a shadow in the sun. He stood there, staring at the mirror that didn't show him back at all.

Then his granny says, stern, "You Joe! Take off that there ring! Didn't I tell you not to let nobody see you with it on?"

Joe wrenched it off his finger, and he swallowed. He turned. And there was Sally Walker still setting in the chair where she'd been visiting with his granny. Joe groaned. He stumbled to a chair, and he put his face in his hands and felt like crying while his granny got up and went to get some rags and arnica for the beating he'd got whilst he was licking Ben. And Joe could've cried. He was twenty-one years old and he'd licked every man in a day's walking and he'd fought the devil besides, that day, and he'd won. But Sally Walker'd seen him with the witch ring on his finger and Joe didn't see any good in anything.

Then she said soft and anxious in his ear, "Joe, do you hurt bad anywheres?"

He jumped. He looked at her and she didn't look scared of him. She looked worried, but that was all. And Joe felt so good at seeing that, he went plain out of his head.

His granny's stick, thumping on the floor, brought him back to where he was and made him stop what he was doing.

"Huh!" says his granny, sniffing. "Now you licked every man in a day's walking and kissed every girl but one! Now what're you goin' to do?"

And Joe Burchard grinned like his throat would split, and he didn't mind the hurt at all. He held Sally Walker close and he says, "Granny, I reckon I'm going to settle down an' get married."

And he did. And it was a long time before he learned any more about the witch ring. His granny wouldn't talk about it, and Sally didn't know, but it stayed in Joe's mind. And one day his granny took sick and she looked triumphant because she'd kept her promise to Joe's grandpa and to the Lord, and she knew she'd be going over Jordan. So she lay in her bed, and Joe says:

"Granny," he says, "if you don't tell me I'll never know, and till I know I'll fret. When I was wearing that witch ring I scared Letty Smith and I scared Ben Harper, but when I looked in that mirror I looked right through my image and I couldn't see myself at all. How come?"

His granny grinned at him, laying there in the bed, waiting to pass over Jordan.

"Huh!" she says. "That ring is perilous, honey, because it makes folks see you like you really are. That's what Letty and Ben Harper saw. But no man can't never see himself like he really is, so you couldn't see a dawgoned thing!"

And Joe, he thought it over, and he says, "But you and Sally, you saw me with the witch ring on! You saw me like I really was, and it didn't scare neither of you."

But his granny just sniffed at him, while she looked at him soft—just as soft as Sally ever did. And she says, "You won't understand, honey. But we was two women that purely loved you. So it didn't matter a bit."

And Joe's granny was right. He didn't understand. Never till the day he died.

Malice in Wonderland
by Rufus King

The late (1893–1966) Rufus King was a major contributor to the pulp magazines in the 1920s and beyond. Although he worked primarily in the mystery field he also contributed stories to many other genre publications. He is best remembered for his novels about Lieutenant Valcour, a New York City detective of French Canadian origin. King wrote more than twenty mystery novels as well as four very good story collections, the last of which, The Faces of Danger, *appeared in 1964. He also worked as a playwright, scripting* Murder at the Vanities, *a musical comedy with music by John Green that was produced in New York in 1933.*

When Alice Wickershield was a little girl of nine and still believed in all the childhood wonderlands with their fantasy inhabitants, she was given a birthday party by an old woman whom she firmly considered to be a witch.

Alice frequently remarked to her best friend, Elsie Grunwald, "The tip of Mrs. Fleury's nose almost touches her chin, and that is a sign."

Elsie, who was of a similar age but completely disillusioned as to the fey, would answer practically, "That is because she hates wearing false teeth."

There the matter would drop until some later event would again bring Mrs. Fleury under scrutiny. Naturally, with Mrs. Fleury being the hostess, the birthday party brought the subject of her cabalistic specialty into focus once more.

Alive lived with her father (her mother was dead) in a house of Early-Boom design in the town of Halcyon, on the Florida coast to the north of Miami. Their neighbors on the west were the Grunwalds, whose only child, Elsie, was Alice's best friend; and on the other side was the sorceress with her old-fashioned,

121

galleried home appropriately shrouded in dank grounds of somber tropical plantings.

The birthday party was in late June, and as school was over for the season, the festivities were able to get under way shortly after the noon hour with a series of mildly competitive games under the palm and ficus trees that smothered the grounds with their shade. It was at the conclusion of the games and the distribution of prizes, with each of the children miraculously having won one, that luncheon was served on the patio and Mrs. Fleury's witchery meshed into gear and determined, eleven years later, the question of Alice's fate.

Dessert for the luncheon was a delicious treat put up especially for Mrs. Fleury by a local company. It consisted of ice-cream tropical fish of various flavors and colors with each mold resting artistically on a foamy wave of spun sugar. At the side of each plate with its chill confection was a cracker bonbon, or snapper, that went bang when its ends were sharply pulled and which contained a favor and a strip of paper on which was printed a motto, that was presumed to shed a prophetic light on the puller's future.

"Children," Mrs. Fleury said, while these final temptations were being placed on the table, "I am going to command a test for your powers of self-control—Jefferson Hollingsworth, put down that cracker bonbon until you hear what I have to say."

"This is *it*," whispered Alice to Elsie. "Look at her chin."

Mrs. Fleury waited until Jefferson Hollingsworth, a handsome youngster with liquid chestnut eyes, reluctantly replaced his snapper beside a frozen version of a pistachio-and-raspberry carp.

"I am going to ask that each little guest take his or her cracker bonbon home, and that you do not tear it open until some moment of the most *desperate nature* may come to you during your lifetimes. As you know, the crackers conceal a printed motto and it is my wish for you—and for Alice in particular because it is her birthday anniversary—that the message conveyed in the motto shall guide you during this future crisis of either joy or sorrow to do the right, the happy thing."

"She is asking one hell of a lot from kids," Harold Grunwald said to his wife Sidonia after Elsie had returned from the party and reported the odd incident. "I'd say the old bat has lost her marbles."

"Well," Sidonia laughed, "it was too much for Elsie, and where that child gets her I.Q. from I wouldn't know. She produced a logical enough crisis out of a hat."

"She gets her I.Q. from me. At her age I had mastered the Morse code in preparation for becoming an international spy, and last month I merely mentioned the fact and Elsie picked out Mata Hari as her dream career in womanhood and can already take six words a minute in Morse. She uses her pal Alice as a receiving set."

"So that's why they've been tapping on things and looking remote."

"It is, and what's this about a logical crisis?"

"Just that Elsie opened her cracker bonbon before she even set foot in the house. She claimed the rich food at the party made her feel critically bilious, so she ripped out the motto."

"And what was the prophetic suggestion? Citrate of magnesia?"

"No, it was a rather horrid quotation from Shakespeare. *Open, locks, whoever knocks!*"

"What's so horrible in that?"

Sidonia, who was tons more intellectual than her husband (she had majored in English at Barry College), said, "It doesn't give the entire quotation. It's simply taken out of context."

"Put it back in again."

"It goes, *By the prickling of my thumbs, something wicked this way comes. Open, locks, whoever knocks!*"

Mr. Grunwald, becoming bored with the matter and wanting to get on with the Do-It-Yourself parakeet cage he was making, said, "All that superstitious rubbish is silly."

"I don't know. I honestly don't know, Hal. Sometimes I wonder."

Two weeks later Elsie, while presumably stitching up a ball costume for her favorite doll in the seclusion of the Grunwald's alamanda-draped gazebo, totally disappeared.

With the exception of Alice, all the children had followed Elsie's impulse and torn open their favors. They had read the time-weary little mottoes, been momentarily captivated by the tissue-paper hats, the modest souvenirs, and then had thrown the whole works into a wastebasket and out of their minds.

Not Alice.

Because she still believed in the wondrous, Alice had put her cracker bonbon in her treasure chest—a cardboard show box fancifully pasted over with Christmas wrappings—along with her diary, a dried toadstool highly favored as a parasol by elves, and sundry other articles of enduring sentiment.

It was only natural that being her most intimate companion, Alice should have been questioned more patiently and closely than any of the other children after Elsie had "gone away"—that phrasing being considered as best suitable by their elders to cover the desperately serious reality. Alice bore the questioning stoically and only broke down once, when she asked Mrs. Grunwald whether she might keep the doll's ball gown that Elsie had been sewing on in the gazebo to remember Elsie by.

"But Elsie is coming back, dear," Sidonia said, restraining by the greatest willpower her own tears of torture and doubt.

"No, she isn't, Mrs. Grunwald. She was put under a spell by Mrs. Fleury and that's the end of her."

"A spell, Alice?" Sidonia repeated as her eyes narrowed speculatively that herein might lie some clue, however preposterous, to the fate of her lost child. "What do you mean by a spell, dear?"

"Mrs. Fleury is a witch and Elsie disobeyed her *express command* by opening her cracker bonbon on such a silly excuse. A stomachache is not a crisis."

Alice left the interview, taking with her the doll's unfinished ball gown with its needle and length of unused thread still stuck in lemonade-colored satin. She wrapped the dress around her own cracker bonbon, as both seemed to be linked in their special magical field, and returned them to the treasure chest where they were to lie fallow in their diablerie for many years to come.

When Hal Grunwald came home that night after a harrowing day spent with the police, the sheriff's deputies, and the road patrols, all of whom were searching for Elsie during this second day of her disappearance, Sidonia told him what Alice had said about Mrs. Fleury being a witch and he hit the ceiling.

He then collapsed dog-tired into a chair and held his hot head in his hands and said, "Oh, my God, Sid, you could listen to childish drivel while we're moving heaven and earth to find her."

"I'd listen to any sort of drivel if I thought it would do any good. After all, Hal, what *do* we know about Mrs. Fleury?"

"We know what she has told us."

"That's exactly what I mean about our life here. The friends we make come from all over the country and we don't know a thing about them except what they tell us themselves."

Sidonia, who had been holding her control by superhuman effort during the past tragical days and nights, grew hysterical, and her voice broke in odd high notes.

"We exercise more judgment about our servants than we do about our friends," she went on with those shrillish overtones. "We check servants, look up references—why, they even have

police cards of identity! But our friends? We let our children
associate with them and we don't know *what they are*. Mrs. Fleury?
From Cleveland, she says—widowed—her husband left her well
off—and we smile and swallow it. She might be a mass poisoner
for all we know! Alice claims she's a witch and you laugh. Well, a
child's judgment might be better than our judgment. A child's eyes
see things clearly, not through a fog of polite social conventions."

"Sid, knock it off, will you? We're both carrying all the
traffic will bear without getting sidetracked into black magic."

The ransom note came that night.

With the vivid ears of childhood, Alice arranged all the fragments of overheard talks between her father and his friends into a
factual whole. A ransom had been demanded, $50,000 had been
paid, and Elsie still had not returned home.

"She can't," Alice said to Sidonia when they met by chance
at the hibiscus border that divided the Wickershield and Grunwald
properties. "She can't come back because she's dead."

"Darling, don't say it. Oh, don't even think it!" Sidonia
plunged through the hedge and getting down on her knees gripped
Alice's hands so hard that the bones felt all together. "You must
tell me—I am begging this of you, Alice—isn't there something
you know? Something real?"

"Witches are real."

Sidonia looked at the child searchingly, half convinced in the
torture-ridden uncertainties of her cracking mind that the fateful
motto just might have had something to do with their loss.

"You really believe that, Alice, don't you?"

"It's dangerous not to."

"Then destroy it. Burn your cracker bonbon. Get it now and
burn it up."

"I can't."

"Why not?"

"Because it isn't time."

So intense is the power of public opinion that Mrs. Fleury
began feeling it on all sides—to the extent that she concluded the
only answer lay in selling her place and leaving Halcyon.

The children beleaguered her with cries from a safe distance of
witch-witch-witch, and the elders forming her circle of friends
were electrically artificial in their greetings and perfunctory smiles.

Even the police thoroughly checked her whereabouts during
the hour when Elsie had been sewing by herself in the gazebo.
They handled the inquiry discreetly, of course, and no mention
of it was made public officially; but the fact was shortly general
knowledge that Mrs. Fleury had an ironclad alibi. She had been

undergoing the rack of a hair and facial treatment at the shop of Halcyon's best and most talkative beautician.

In Alice's opinion this absolute alibi was futile for a witch, they being a breed notoriously famous for their astral ability to be in two different places at the same time, and she announced as much to the other children, who promptly stepped up their campaign of torment instead of dropping it.

Mrs. Fleury was unable to fight back, any more than she could have fought the invisible vapors from a swamp with her bare fists. Fortunately she found a ready buyer for her home in Dr. Jessup Hollingsworth, whose adopted son Jefferson had had to be cautioned at the birthday party against a premature snapping of his cracker bonbon.

Since coming to Halcyon over a year ago, Dr. Hollingsworth had been living with Jeff in the sterile splendor of a beach hotel. The doctor had reached the age of retirement and wanted to settle down.

"I want roots," he said to Haidee Glosser in her real estate office in town. "Not so much for myself as for Jefferson. My wife's tragic death made it impossible to continue living in our former home in New York."

"I understand," Miss Glosser murmured with sympathy while mentally pocketing a fat commission for the Fleury estate.

Within less than a week the deal was closed. Mrs. Fleury moved to the west coast and settled in St. Petersburg, which was, so far as east coast Floridians were concerned, as far away as the moon.

And Alice acquired a new best friend.

She and young Jeff Hollingsworth were classmates in elementary school, it was true, but there had been none of the special affinity that goes with a friendship on a next-door basis, once the initial ice of propinquity is melted—and at the age of nine the thaw comes fast.

"How do you like being adopted?" Elsie asked during the preliminaries.

"There's not much feeling about it," Jeff said.

"What happened to your adopted mother?"

"Foster mother."

"Foster. Thank you."

"Don't mention it. She was killed by a hit-and-run driver right after my adoption papers went through. I only remember her looks."

"What did she look like?"

"Like anybody."

"What are you going to be, Jeff, when you grow up?"

"A botanist."

"Why?"

"Because plants. and trees and flowers are important. They can be like people, only nicer. I've got leaves and specimens of about almost everything around here. Each one is dried and labeled from where I found it."

"Have you ever met any elves while you were gathering them?"

"No."

"Do you believe in them, Jeff?"

"Maybe."

Inevitably, as the years of childhood and the ensuing 'teens dreamed by, Alice and Jeff drew more seriously toward each other in their affections, and only Sidonia Grunwald of the people who knew them tried to put a damper on the intimacy.

Sidonia had never given up, nor would she, no matter how earnestly Hal begged her to resign herself to the inevitable. Elsie was gone but they, he said, were left and had their lives together to be lived.

"She isn't gone," Sidonia would say with a kind of fierceness. "She's someplace."

Yes, Hal would think in his own emptiness, Elsie was some place all right, and a stomach-wrenching vision would come to him of their darling's small bones lying unshrived in some secret desolation of the everglades or under the water of rockpits or hyacinth-smothered canals, year after lonely year in their whitening.

"I cannot get it out of my head," Sidonia would say wildly, "that that place, that that woman had something to do with it."

"I wish you'd stop poking around over there. I know you do at night, and apart from the fact that I'm sure it annoys Doctor Hollingsworth, it just isn't healthy, Sid."

"You can't be healthy with an empty heart."

This fixed idea formed the basis for Sidonia's corroding reaction to the romance between Alice, whom she feverishly loved because there seemed to cling to the girl a lingering of her lost Elsie, and young Jeff. Actually, Sidonia was a little deranged on the subject, feeling herself constantly drawn to the old Fleury grounds (she never thought of it as the Hollingsworth place), and it was true, as Hal said, that she would steal over there and search around beneath its dank canopies especially when the moon was full.

She had convinced herself of the half-dented syllogism that the grounds were under a curse, therefore Jeff and his foster father, since they lived within the influence of their baleful star, were also accursed. Sidonia wanted no part of this disastrous magic to rub off on Alice, not even through the medium of young love.

The college years brought no hiatus in the serious intentions between Alice and Jeff. She went to Barry in Miami Shores and he attended the University of Miami in nearby Coral Gables. There Jeff delved deeply into the structure, physiology, and distribution of the members of the vegetable kingdom, with an ultimate aim of specializing in plant morphology. With this broadened knowledge Jeff, among later interests, had carefully emended his collections of boyhood specimens which were still methodically kept on file in the small laboratory he had equipped at home.

Rather because she wanted to be near him than from any curiosity about botany, Alice would often stay with Jeff in the laboratory while he worked, and one day when he was reclassifying some specimens of his childhood collection, her interest was caught by a closely set cluster of fine slender branches.

"It looks like a little broom, Jeff."

"It should. It's *hexenbesen,* more commonly known as witches'-broom."

The name aroused stirrings of many years ago.

"Did you find it here? When Mrs. Fleury owned the place?"

"Not actually."

He had picked it up, Jeff told her, from his foster father's bedroom floor in the beach hotel they had then been staying at. He imagined it must have fallen from a cuff of Dr. Hollingsworth's trousers when he had taken them off the night before.

"I remember asking him about it. It's an unusual find and I wanted to trace its source. It's an outgrowth caused by a plant parasite or fungus."

"Did you?"

"Did I what?"

"Trace its source?"

"Not until after we'd moved here."

Dr. Hollingsworth had told him, when questioned, that he might have picked it up while looking over the grounds with the real estate agent just before purchasing them.

"I finally located it," Jeff said, "after we'd moved in and I'd remembered that witches'-brooms sometimes appear on ferns—low enough to be caught in a cuff."

"So it did come from here. Funny."

"Why funny?"

"Don't you remember our thinking old Mrs. Fleury was a witch? At least I certainly did."

"All kids think crazy stuff."

"I know it and I realize now what a little fool I was about it. I'd like to see Mrs. Fleury again and tell her I'm sorry for having caused her to be pestered, for making her give up her home, really. Jeff—I wonder if she's still alive?"

"What makes you say that?"

"Just a feeling. A funny feeling, Jeff."

They were to be married shortly after graduation, and Mr. Wickershield, Alice's father, finally persuaded Sidonia in her self-assumed role of proxy mother to Alice to handle all the intricate arrangements for the wedding.

"I still feel," Sidonia said to Hal after she had reluctantly consented to Mr. Wickershield's urging, "that it is a mistake. It's—it's sinister, malign."

"Oh, please, Sid!"

Hal had grown stout and comfortable, and instead of continuing to be sympathetic he was getting irritated with what he thought of as Sidonia's perpetual mania and her occasional Ophelia-like nocturnal driftings around the old Fleury grounds. He had loved their lost Elsie with all his heart and he still loved her memory, but grief cannot live forever. If it did, he thought philosophically, all life on earth would die.

Dr. Hollingsworth, in his role of foster father, arranged the bachelor dinner for Jeff at a beach club of correct splendor, the groom's gift for the best man and the ushers being platinum cufflinks from Tiffany, the food and the wines compatible; and Jeff, whose familiarity with champagne was only on a nodding basis, got socked straight into left field. Unfortunately he remained on his feet, his talk was intelligible, and his good night to the doorman who brought his car sounded (as the doorman later testified) all right.

A milkman making his delivery shortly after sunup to the rear of Dr. Hollingsworth's house found Sidonia lying crumpled under the hibiscus that edged the driveway to the garage. He was not a man to panic, thanks to Korea, and having determined that she was still alive, he roused the house. All that is, but Jeff, who was still sprawled fully dressed across his bed in stuporous sleep.

. . . In the news of local interest [a Fort Lauderdale newscaster announced] the Halcyon police report an alleged drunk-driving accident on the grounds of Dr. Jessup Hollingsworth, formerly the old Fleury estate. The victim is a Mrs. Grunwald, a nearby neighbor whose daughter Elsie was kidnapped a decade ago and presumably killed by her abductor after a ransom of $50,000 had been paid. The old kidnapping case remains unsolved. According to her husband and her close friends, this tragedy continued to prey on Mrs. Grunwald and caused her to take walks at night around the Hollingsworth grounds which, they say, she associated in some fashion with her child's disappearance. The police believe that she was on such an excursion last night when Dr. Hollingsworth's adopted son Jefferson drove home from a bachelor dinner in a drunken condition and struck her. James Cray, 2714 Northeast Hempstead Court, who delivers the morning milk, found her lying under an hibiscus hedge where she had been flung by the impact. She is now at Memorial and her condition is critical . . .

The world came to an end but Alice did not break down. With Jeff released under a $5,000 bail bond, Sidonia's life spun on with a thread above the valley of death. Alice would make Jeff sit out the foreboding hours with her in the privacy of the Grunwalds' alamanda-draped gazebo where they were reasonably sheltered from the press and even from their friends. When evening fell each would go home to face the night with such courage as could be summoned.

"I don't suppose," Alice's father said to her, cupping the mouthpiece of a telephone on the second night following the accident, "that you would care to talk with her? She's peculiarly insistent."

"Who, Papa?"

"That woman who used to live next to us. You remember, a Mrs. Fleury. She's calling from St. Petersburg."

Alice rushed to the phone.

"Alice, dear child," Mrs. Fleury's (again) familiar voice came from the receiver, "I have been reading all about it and you will think me a silly old woman but I felt compelled to telephone. I want to ask you just one question."

"Yes, Mrs. Fleury?"

"Call me a superstitious old fool if you wish—I remember how you were childishly positive I was a witch," Mrs. Fleury paused to give a forgiving, paperish little laugh, "and perhaps I *am* one, because while I was reading about your fiancé's critical predicament, the most singular, almost clairvoyant vision popped

into my mind. It made me feel exactly like one of the weird
sisters and I simply leaped on my witch's broom and flew to call
you up. Now tell me, Alice, do you remember the birthday
party?''

"Of course, Mrs. Fleury."

"Do you recall the cracker bonbons and my nonsensically
mysterious instructions about them?''

"Yes."

"Well, do you by the wildest chance still have yours?''

"Yes."

"Is it still unopened?''

"Yes."

"Then open it now."

And the wire went dead.

Alice felt her father still standing near the telephone, with Mr.
Wickershield silently wondering just what the call had been all
about in order to have affected his daughter in such an odd
manner.

"I swear to you, Hal," he told Harold Grunwald afterward,
"she positively drifted from the room as if she'd been put under
a spell. . . ."

The cardboard treasure chest with its Christmas wrappings of
holly gold and stars had for years been lying undisturbed in the
bottom drawer of a dresser in Alice's room.

Alice got it out and put it on a desk where the shaft from a
metal cone-shaded lamp made startling the colors' holiday
brilliance. With a reluctance that combined the fear ever present
when brushing the unnatural, and a hope that she did not dare
feel too strongly because of the impossible qualities that draped
it, she took out the cracker bonbon in its covering of the doll's
ball gown, and pushed the treasure chest aside.

Then in her sudden eagerness Alice felt a finger pricked by the
needle which was still caught in what had been Elsie's last stitch,
and a drop of blood stained a pea-sized circle of red on the
lemonade-colored satin of the little dress. Alice removed the
dress and with no further ado took both ends of the cracker
bonbon and pulled them sharply apart. The report, to her now
more adult ears, produced but a trivial effect.

With a scissors she slit the white paper cover, and discarding a
gay red paper hat and a miniature metal fire engine, she came at
last to the strip of paper on which the motto was printed. An
ugly wave of disappointment engulfed Alice as she read it. She
had been expecting something truly prophetic—like Elsie's *Open,*

locks, whoever knocks! which she later had learned had been out of dire context.

The motto dropped from her fingers and came to rest on the ball gown beside the needle. Beside the drop of blood. She had hoped so much, Alice now admitted to herself—she had been hoping all along with her desperate heart for some sign—and now all her hopes had come to this childlike ending of—of—

Her eyes darted from the motto to the blood drop, to the needle, to the line of stitches, in the last one of which the needle had been left. Clear under the cone-shafted light, they were visible in their good straight line. There was only one thing the matter with it, Alice decided critically. The line ran diagonally across the front panel of the gown and therefore, from a dressmaker's point of view, not only served no purpose but was the act of a seamstress gone suddenly mad.

Never would Elsie, as Alice remembered her lost best friend, with her fine capabilities in so many of the childhood arts, have been guilty of such botchery. Unless it were purposely done. And rarely had anything ever been done by Elsie that lacked purpose.

Alice's pulse quickened as a ripple of strange excitement caught her brain, and she examined more closely the misplaced line of stitching. Not only was the line misplaced but the stitches themselves were uneven in their spacing—another unthinkable thing for Elsie to have done.

Unless, again, it were *purposely* done.

So steeped was Alice in the flood made by the years rolled back that Elsie became real—with their best-friend loveship and all their secrets of shattering importance and their fearless preparations for facing the entrancing vistas of adult life to come. Yes, Alice remembered, their last projected career had been to become Mata Hari, with all her fascinating background of international intrigue.

And for which they had both learned the Morse code.

Her eyes flew to the line of unevenly spaced stitches. Dots and dashes, sewn in chartreuse thread on lemonade-colored satin. The pencil in her fingers automatically put the letters down on the spread-open white paper wrapper of the cracker bonbon. DRHOLCRZYHLPM—then nothing more.

So intense, so feverish, was Alice's excitement that little meant anything to her but that here was Elsie's last message on earth, and that within it undoubtedly lay a clue to her disappearance and, according to Mrs. Fleury, a help in Jeff's and Alice's present deadly crisis.

Taking the ball gown with her and leaving the rest of the

magical properties on the desk, with her heart going suffocatingly in hopeful thumps, Alice ran from her room and out of the house with no thought in her head other than to find and tell Jeff.

A lamp was lighted on the lower front gallery of the old Fleury house, and Dr. Hollingsworth was seated beside it in a wicker chair. He was smoking a cigar and reading.

"Alice, dear girl!" he said as she rushed up the steps and paused breathless before him. His professional training took a clinical look at her eyes, at the tremor in her fingers that held, as if with an ague, the edge of a piece of satin. "You have had a shock."

"Yes, Doctor—this."

He took it from her outstretched hand.

"It looks like—it's a doll's dress, isn't it?"

"It's the one Elsie was sewing on in the gazebo just before she disappeared."

"Elsie? Oh, of course—the little Grunwald girl."

"I must show it to Jeff!"

"But why?"

"There is a message stitched on it in Morse code. We had both learned the code together. It's Elsie's last message, Doctor—"

"Amazing!"

Alice took the gown from his fingers and said, "I'll go right in, if you don't mind, and tell Jeff."

"He isn't home."

Delay was a blow.

"Do you know where he is?"

"No. Jeff has been taking long walks these nights. Alone. Trying to knock himself out physically so that he can get some sleep. Alice, sit down. Since you can't tell Jeff, tell me."

This Alice did, from the birthday party down to the call from Mrs. Fleury and the motto and the stitches in Morse.

"What was your father's reaction? Is he getting in touch with the sheriff?"

"He knows nothing about it. It hit me so hard, Doctor, that I simply raced over here to tell Jeff. If I'd met Father on the way out I'd naturally have told him, but I didn't."

"What did the message say, Alice?"

"I haven't decoded it yet," Alice said, "because I'm waiting to do it with Jeff. I'm certain it will give us a clue to Elsie's kidnapping, and I know this sounds fantastic but I honestly believe that Mrs. Fleury is right and that it will help Jeff, too. Do you think that sentimental, Doctor?"

"Not that you feel that way, no. As I recall it, you were

firmly convinced that Mrs. Fleury was a witch. I'd simply say
that your subconscious was getting in a few old licks.''

"I'm almost ready to believe in her sorcery again, Doctor.
Take her telephoning, the cracker bonbon and the motto—she
even *spoke* of a witch's broom—oh, it's not only Mrs. Fleury
herself, it's the whole atmosphere of this place where she lived.''

"Witch's broom?''

"Yes. Witches'-broom is a growth that looks like a little
broom. Of course you don't remember, but you caught some in
the cuff of your trousers when you were looking over the grounds
here with the real estate agent, and Jeff found it on the floor of
your bedroom in the hotel.''

"Yes, now I do remember him asking me about it, and I
remember that when he moved in here he located the spot it
came from. A clump of ferns. Serpent ferns, I think he called
them.''

"Do you remember where they are?''

"I believe so, in a general way. They're back quite a distance
in this tropical jungle. Why?''

"I want to go there. Could we go there, Doctor? Now? While
we're waiting for Jeff?''

"I suppose we could. But why?''

"I don't know why. This is crazy, but it's almost as if Mrs.
Fleury were urging me to.''

Dr. Hollingsworth looked at Alice judicially, as if he were
trying to determine a proper course of therapy for her very
evident emotional state.

"You are overstrung, Alice. The walk might be good for you
at that.''

"Then you'll show me?''

"I'll get a flashlight,'' Dr. Hollingsworth said.

Mr. Wickershield had been in the library selecting a book for
a quiet hour's reading when he was conscious, as he thought, of
a screen door slamming. Alice? Scarcely. Alice did not allow
screen doors to slam. Still, that phone call from Mrs. Fleury
had—just what had it done? Sort of knocked her for a loop, he
decided.

Mr. Wickershield left the library and rapped on Alice's door,
then went inside. She wasn't there. The only light on was the
desk lamp with its cone of brilliance from the metal shade.
Inescapably, his attention was drawn to the doll and to the flattened wrapper of the cracker bonbon. He went to the desk and he
sat down. Clearly, vividly, as though it were today, recognition

came and he recalled the whole grim episode, of the birthday party, the kidnapping of Elsie, and of that child of nine who had believed in the wondrous and was now his grown-up daughter Alice.

Something was missing. Of course, the doll dress that Elsie had been sewing and in which Alice had wrapped the cracker bonbon. Had she taken it with her when, judging from the screen door slam, she had pelted from the house? To show Jeff? Most likely.

The end of the motto strip was exposed beneath the cracker bonbon wrapper and he pulled it out. He reread it. Thoughtfully, he read it again.

Mr. Wickershield had served in Army Intelligence during the war, and his brain was experienced in appraisal and deduction well beyond that of an untrained man. Alice had found some clue in the doll's dress to Elsie's disappearance and had rushed over to discuss it with Jeff—that line of deduction was almost obvious.

He then recalled the children's plunge into Morse code—so the connection between the motto and some probable stitching on the doll dress and the penciled letters on the paper wrapper suggested itself at once.

His experience with decoding in Intelligence had been superficial, but he saw immediately that this message—that must, he thought, have been stitched with such haste and yet such care, and under God knew what a pall of terror—was scarcely a code at all.

Ice sluggished his blood as he read it, and as he started out at a brisk pace for the Grunwald house to pick up Hal.

The flashlight was powerful—one of those two-foot, heavy, cylindrical cases that could throw a beam an eighth of a mile, much farther than was needed for the job on hand.

"Well, there it is," Dr. Hollingsworth said. "The serpent ferns and the witches'-broom. Tell me, Alice, what really made you want to come here? I don't mind admitting that I am interested in extrasensory perception, but in all actuality I'm an out-and-out realist. Putting Mrs. Fleury's alleged witchery aside, why did you want to come?"

"Because there is something here."

"What?"

"Doctor, I don't know. That it is connected with Elsie I *do* know, even though I don't know the reason."

Alice parted the serpent ferns and took several hesitant steps within the large, lush clump.

"No need to be definite," Dr. Hollingsworth said. "Just tell me what you feel?"

"I feel a grave. I feel it is Elsie's, but I can't explain."

Dr. Hollingsworth moved the light shaft from the serpent ferns full upon Alice's face.

"That answer is simple, Alice," he said. "You are standing on it now."

Both Mr. Wickershield and Hal had wasted no time. To reach the steps of the old Fleury house front gallery was but a matter of minutes. Hal knocked on the screen door, through which they could see a dimly lighted stretch of empty hall. They waited a moment, then went inside.

"Anybody home?" Hal shouted, his voice unnaturally loud under the pressure of their dangerous urgency.

A door at the end of the hallway opened and Jeff came out.

"Who's shouting?" he said. "Oh—oh, hello. I've been working in my lab and I thought the house was coming down."

"Where is the Doctor?" Mr. Wickershield asked tensely.

"I left him reading on the gallery about an hour ago. I've been shut up in the lab since then. Why?"

"Where's Alice?"

"I've no idea. Why?"

"She ran over here to see you. Ten or fifteen minutes ago."

"Then where is she? I never heard a thing in the lab until your shout. What's the matter? What's happened?"

Mr. Wickershield explained tersely, while blood receded from Jeff's face in an ebbing tide.

"Where would he have taken her?" Mr. Wickershield asked.

"We'll search the grounds," Jeff said.

Pinned like a specimen bug in the harsh shaft of the flashlight, still having no knowledge of what Elsie's last message had meant, but no longer needing that knowledge now that the implication in Dr. Hollingsworth's statement about the grave was so plain, every muscle in Alice strained toward flight. But her control was gone. She stood like a statue among the serpent ferns, marbleized by shock and fright.

"You killed Elsie," she said, in someone else's voice.

"Yes."

"But you had everything. Money—position— Why?"

"I had no money. I had spent the small fortune I killed my wife for. I needed more."

"Your wife—then it wasn't a hit-and-run?"

"No. It was arranged."

"But Elsie—a little child—"

"I suggest you think of her rather in terms of fifty thousand dollars. A sum I have pyramided through legitimate business channels into a comfortable fortune. There was no need to continue with crime. Only Sidonia Grunwald's erratic prying around here offered a threat. Well, an appropriate opportunity presented itself and I took advantage of it."

"You involved Jeff. You are making him pay. Don't you love him? If you don't, if you never have, why did you adopt him?"

"For a front."

"Front?"

"Like the flower shops the Chicago gangsters used to run. Gave them a legitimate surface of respectability. Jeff did that for me."

"How?"

"As a son he gave me the desirable standing of being a family man, a good, kind father to a well-brought-up boy. A lone bachelor, or a widower, is always an object of speculative curiosity, whereas a father with a child is hardly ever suspected. Having reached my goal, however, Jeff became expendable."

"You arranged it so that they would believe he had hit Mrs. Grunwald."

"Of course. He stopped the car and passed out at the start of the driveway. Sidonia was going on with her act that night. I trailed her as I usually had, heard the car, saw Jeff's condition as he slumped over the wheel, and appreciated the perfect setup." Dr. Hollingsworth added matter-of-factly, "Before arranging her in the condition in which she was found I hit her with this flashlight."

Although the moon was at the full its blue-white brightness rinsed but sparsely through the tropical overhead as Jeff led the way.

"Move quietly so as not to startle him," Mr. Wickershield warned, the words thick from dread. "There may still be time."

Shortly, Jeff stopped.

"They're over there," he said. "Step here and you can see the beam from his flashlight—there, through that break in the shrubs."

Mr. Wickershield moved beside Jeff and saw it—saw it focused on Alice's rigid face.

Then saw it go out.

"Run for it!" he said.

It was Jeff who caught Dr. Hollingsworth's upraised arm before the torch could crash down again. . . .

The following evening, feeling somewhat like Madame Récamier with her famous levees à la chaise longue, Alice lay on a bamboo counterpart in the company of her father, Jeff, and Bill Duggan, chief investigator for the sheriff's department. Hal was at Memorial with Sidonia, who had passed the crisis and was given by the doctors a more than excellent chance for complete recovery.

Alice herself was fairly over the effects from the blow of the flashlight that had landed glancingly on her head before Jeff had put an end to the murderous attack.

"Evidence?" Duggan was saying. "We're glutted with it. The District Attorney looks like a canary-stuffed cat. That ransom note, the one the Grunwalds got eleven years ago, was still on file. The B.C.I. boys knew back then that it was written on a blank leaf torn from a book. From some particular book among the hundreds of thousands within the area, so that got them noplace. Now it does. Once the message stitched on the doll dress put the finger on him, Dr. Hollingsworth's library was inspected and the leaf was found to have been torn from a book on forensic medicine—a reference work he would have hesitated to throw away, even if he hadn't felt so sure of himself. Even the printing on the note, although he tried to disguise it, had been identified by an expert graphologist as being his."

"Did the witches'-broom help?" Alice asked. "The specimen Jeff kept?"

"Definitely. It puts him at the grave."

"Why do you suppose he picked that special spot?" Jeff asked.

"He told me. It's all down in his statement. He picked the Fleury grounds because, for one thing, they were handy. After a very bad attempt at trying to wheedle Elsie into going to a movie with him, and obviously frightening her enough by his manner and insistence into stitching her message for help, he killed her. Then he carried her from the gazebo, and the large clump of serpent ferns hid her nicely until he buried her in the center of them that night. Naturally, he could move about freely. There was no earthly reason why any suspicion would point to him."

"Wouldn't the everglades have been safer?" Mr. Wickershield asked. "Some far-off place?"

"He said he thought of that, then he thought that if the body ever were discovered under the ferns, Mrs. Fleury herself would provide an excellent suspect, what with her somewhat odd habits. Of course, he didn't know then that she had a perfect alibi. Nobody knew, until a couple of days later after we had turned up the fact that she was in the beauty shop."

"I can see why he bought the place as soon as it was put up for sale," Mr. Wickershield said. "He wouldn't want other tenants to have it. Their possible ideas on altering the landscaping could conceivably have uncovered the grave. I can even see how he might have got a perverted kick out of it, although Sidonia's prowlings must have kept him somewhat on edge."

"No, they kind of amused him for a while, but the night he fixed up the drunk-driving deal on Jeff was different. He felt it was time to call quits. You see, he'd been tailing her as usual and she did something that night she had never done before. Signed her own death warrant, you might say."

"What was it?"

"She went into the utility room by the garage and came out with a shovel."

Much later at night Duggan got home and told his wife all about it.

"Like a fairy tale," he said. "Only a damn grim one. Take that coded message, and the uncanny way the motto pointed toward the sewing on the doll dress. Here—here's a copy. Mr. Wickershield spotted it right off as simple contraction."

Mrs. Duggan looked at the slip of paper.

DRHOLCRZYHLPM
DR/HOL/CRZY/HLP/M
DOCTOR HOLLINGSWORTH
CRAZY HELP ME

"And the motto?" she asked.
"A stitch in time saves nine."

Operation Salamander

by Poul Anderson

Poul Anderson has been entertaining readers of high-quality science fiction and fantasy for more than thirty-five years. He has consistently combined excellent writing with interesting ideas, and is still going strong. His many honors include six Hugoes, two Nebulas, and the Tolkien Memorial Award. He also served as President of the Science Fiction Writers of America and was Guest of Honor at the World Science Fiction Convention in 1959. He has worked effectively at all story lengths, but he excels at the novella. Among his fantasy works he is best known for two wonderful novels—Three Hearts and Three Lions (1961) and A Midsummer's Tempest (1974).

The sky was full of broomsticks and the police were going nuts trying to handle the traffic. The Homecoming game always attracts an overflow crowd, also an overflow of high spirits. These I did not share. I edged my battered pre-war Chevvy past a huge 200-dragonpower Lincoln with sky-blue handle, polyethylene straw, and blatting radio. It sneered at me, but I got to the vacant rack first. Dismounting, I pocketed the runekey and mooched glumly through the mob.

The Weather Bureau kachinas are obliging about game nights. There was a cool crisp tang to the air, and dry leaves scrittled across the sidewalks. A harvest moon was rising like a big yellow pumpkin over the darkened buildings of Trismegistus University. I thought of Midwestern fields and woods, damp earthy smells and streaming mists, out beyond the city, and the wolf part of me wanted to be off and away after jackrabbits. But with proper training a were can control his reflexes, and polarized light doesn't have to cause more than a primitive tingle along his nerves.

For me, the impulse was soon lost in bleaker thoughts. Ginny,

my darling! She should have been walking beside me, face lifted
to the wind and long hair crackling in the thin frost; but the only
consolation I had was an illegal hip-flask. Why the hell was I
attending the game anyhow?

Passing Teth Caph Sameth frat house, I found myself on the
campus proper. Trismegistus was founded after the advent of
modern science, and its layout reflects that fact. The largest
edifice houses the Language Department, because exotic tongues
are necessary for the more powerful spells (which is why so
many African and Asian students come here to learn American
slang); but there are two English halls, one for the arts college
and one for Engineering Poetics. Nearby is the Therianthropology
Building, which always has interesting displays of foreign
technique: this month it was Eskimo, in honor of the visiting
agekok Dr. Ayingalak. A ways off is Zoology, carefully isolated
inside its pentagonal fence, for some of those long-legged beast-
ies are not pleasant neighbors. The medical school has a shiny
new research center, courtesy of the Rockefeller Foundation,
from which have already come such stunning advances as the
polaroid filter-lenses that make it possible for those afflicted with
the Evil Eye to lead normal lives.

Only the law school is unaffected. Their work has always been
of the other world.

Crossing the Mall, I went by the grimy little Physical Sciences
Building just in time for Dr. Griswold to hail me. He came
puttering down the steps, a small wizened fellow with goatee and
merry blue eyes. Somewhere behind their twinkle lay a look of
hurt bafflement, as of a child who could never quite understand
why no one else was really interested in his toys.

"Ah, Mr. Matuchek," he said. "Are you attending the game?"

I nodded, not especially wanting company, but he tagged
along and I had to be sociable. Not that I was apple-polishing—I
was in his chemistry and physics classes, but they were snaps. I
simply didn't have the heart to rebuff a nice, lonely old geezer.

"Me too," he went on. "I understand the cheerleaders have
planned something spectacular between halves."

"Yeh?"

He cocked his head and gave me a birdlike glance. "If there is
any difficulty, Mr. Matuchek . . . if I can help you . . . it's what
I'm here for, you know."

"It's OK," I lied. "Thanks anyway, sir."

"It can't be easy for a mature man, a combat veteran and a
famous actor, to start in with a lot of giggling freshmen," he
said. "I remember how you helped me in that . . . ah . . .

unfortunate incident last month. Believe me, Mr. Matuchek, I am grateful.''

"Oh, hell, it's nothing. I came here to get an education." *And to be with Virginia Graylock—but that's impossible now.*

I saw no reason to load the details on him. It was simple enough. After we beat the kaftans off the Caliphate, I returned to Metro-Goldwyn-Merlin and resumed werewolfing for them. But the same exploit which introduced me to Ginny had left me bobtailed, and a brushpiece is a nuisance. I had medals, sure, but war heroes were a dime a coven—not that I claim an undue share of courage, events had merely flogged me into doing what I did. I couldn't get real conviction into my role in *Abbott and Costello Meet Paracelsus;* I don't look down on pure entertainment, but I discovered a newborn wish to do something more significant.

Ginny could get me into the Arcane Agency of which she was head witch, and I could work on that control of paranatural forces on which the whole world now depends. To be precise, I shared the common dream of taming Fire and Air enough to hitch them to a ship and reach the planets. But first I needed professional training. So Stephen Matuchek and MGM parted company with noises of mutual esteem, and I went to college on my savings and my G.I.

Ginny herself wanted a Ph.D.—she already had an M.A. from Congo—and Trismegistus offered her an instructorship while she took an extended leave of absence from the agency. Same school . . . we'd be together all our free hours, and I could probably talk her into an early marriage. Wonderful setup.

Like hell.

Griswold sighed, perhaps understanding my withdrawal. "There are times when I feel altogether useless," he said.

"Not at all, sir," I answered with careful heartiness. "How on Middle Earth would—oh, say alchemy—be practical without a grounding in chemistry and nuclear physics? You'd produce poisonous compounds, or blow up half a country."

"Of course, of course. You understand. You know something of the world—more than I, in all truth. But the students . . . well, I suppose it's only natural. They want to speak a few words, make a few passes, and get what they desire, just like that, without bothering to learn the Sanskrit grammar or the periodic table. They haven't realized that you never get something for nothing."

"They will. They'll grow up."

"Even the administration . . . this university just doesn't appreciate the need for physical science. Now at California,

they're getting a billion-volt Philosopher's Stone, but here—"
Griswold shrugged. "Excuse me. I despise self-pity."

We came to the stadium, and I handed over my ticket but
declined the night-seeing spectacles. They'd given me witch-
sight in basic training. My seat was on the 30-yard line, between
a fresh-faced coed and an Old Grad already hollering himself
raw. An animated tray went by, and I bought a hot dog and
rented a crystal ball. But that wasn't to follow the details of play.
I muttered over the globe and peered into it and saw Ginny.

She was seated on the 50, opposite side, the black cat Svartalf
on her lap, her hair a shout of red against the human drabness
around. That witchcraft peculiarly hers was something more old
and strong than the Art in which she was so adept. Even across the
field and through the cheap glass gazer, she made my heart
stumble.

The problem was simply this: Trismegistus' President Malzius
was a pompous mediocrity whose chief accomplishment had
been to make the trustees his yes-men. What he said, went. And
it was his arrogant idea to insist that all personnel take a geas to
obey every University regulation while their contracts were in
force. He had still corralled a pretty good faculty, for the salaries
were good and the rules the ordinary ones. Ginny had signed her
contract a month before I enrolled and not felt the kicker till too
late.

Students and faculty members, right down to the instructor
level, were not permitted to date each other.

Naturally I had stormed my way into Malzius' office and
demanded an exception. No use. He wasn't going to revise the
book for me—"bad precedent, Mr. Matuchek, bad precedent"—
and I agreed sulkily that it was, indeed, a bad president. The
rule would have had to be stricken completely, as the geas didn't
allow special dispensations. Nor did it allow for the case of a
student from another school, so it was pointless for me to
transfer. The only solution, till Ginny's contract expired in June,
would have been for me to drop out entirely, and with that
cold-iron determination of hers she wouldn't hear of that. Lose a
whole year? What was I, a wolf or a mouse? We had quite a
quarrel about it, right out in public. And when you can only
meet at official functions, it isn't just easy to kiss and make up.

Oh, sure, we were still engaged and still saw each other at
smokers, teas . . . really living it up. Meanwhile, as she pointed
out with that icy logic I knew was defensive but never could
break past, we were human. From time to time she would be

going out with some bachelor colleague, wishing he were me, and I'd squire an occasional girl around. . . .

Tonight she was with Dr. Alan Abercrombie, Assistant Professor of Comparative Nigromancy, sleek, blond, handsome, the lion of the tiffins. He'd been paying her a lot of attention while I smoldered alone.

Quite alone. I think Svartalf the cat considers my morals no better than his. I had every intention of fidelity, but when you've parked your broomstick in a moonlit lane and a cute bit of fluff is snuggled up against you . . . those round yellow eyes glowing from a nearby tree are remarkably style-cramping. I soon gave up and spent my evenings studying or drinking beer.

Heigh-ho. I drew my coat tighter about me and shivered in the wind. There was a smell of wrongness to the air . . . probably only my bad mood, I thought, but I'd sniffed trouble up in the future before now.

The Old Grad blasted my ears off as the teams trotted out into the moonlight, Trismegistus' Gryphons and the Albertus Magnus Wyverns. The very old grads say they can't get used to so many four-eyed runts wearing letters—apparently a football team was composed of dinosaurs back before the so-called Thaumaturgic Age. But of course the Art is essentially intellectual and has given its own tone to sports.

This game had its interesting points. The Wyverns levitated off and their skinny little quarterback turned out to be a werepelican. Dushanovitch, in condor shape, nailed him on our 20. Andrevski is the best line werebuck in the Big Ten, and held them for two downs. On the third, Pilsudski got the ball and became a kangaroo. His footwork was beautiful as he dodged a tackle (the guy had a Tarnkappe, but you could see the footprints advance) and passed to Mstislav. The Wyverns swooped low, expecting Mstislav to turn the ball into a raven for a field goal, but with lightning a-crackle as he fended off their counterspells, he made it into a pig . . . greased. (These were minor transformations, of course, a quick gesture at an object already sensitized, not the great and terrible Words I was to hear before dawn.)

A bit later, unnecessary roughness cost us 15 yards: Domingo accidentally stepped on a scorecard which had blown to the field and drove his cleats right through several of the Wyverns' names. But no great harm was done, and they got the same penalty when Thorsson was carried away by the excitement and tossed a thunderbolt. At the end of the first half, the score was Trismegistus 13, Albertus Magnus 6, and the crowd was nearly ripping up the benches.

I pulled my hat back off my ears, gave the Old Grad a dirty look, and stared into the crystal. Ginny was more of a fan than I; she was still jumping and hollering, hardly seeming to notice that Abercrombie had his arms around her. Or perhaps she didn't mind . . . ? I took a long resentful drag at my flask.

The cheering squad paraded out onto the field. Their instruments wove through an elaborate aerial maneuver, drumming and tootling, as they made the traditional march up to the Campus Queen. I'm told it's also traditional that she ride forth on a unicorn to meet them, but for some reason that was omitted this year.

The hair rose stiff on my neck and I felt the blind instinctive tug of Skinturning. Just in time I pulled myself back toward human and sat in a cold shudder. The air was rotten with danger. Couldn't *anyone* else smell it?

I focused my crystal on the cheering squad, looking for the source, only dimly aware of the yell—

> *Aleph, beth, gimel, daleth, he, vau,*
> *Nomine Domini, blow, wow, wow!*
> *Melt 'em in the fire and stick 'em with pins,*
> *Trismegistus always wins. . . .*
> MACILWRAITH!

"Hey . . . what's wrong, mister?" The coed shrank from me, and I realized I was snarling.

"Oh. Nothing . . . I hope." With an effort I composed my face and kept it human.

The fattish blond kid down among the rooters didn't look harmful, but there was a sense of lightning-shot blackness about his future. I'd dealt with him before, and—

I didn't snitch on him at the time, but it was he who had almost broken up Griswold's chemistry class. Pre-med freshman, rich boy, not a bad guy at heart but with an unfortunate combination of natural aptitude for the Art and total irresponsibility. Medical students are notorious for merry little pranks such as waltzing an animated skeleton through the girls' dorm, and he wanted to start early.

Griswold had been demonstrating the action of a catalyst, and MacIlwraith had muttered a pun-spell to make a cat boil out of the test tube. Only he slipped up quantitatively and got a saber-toothed tiger. Because of the pun, it listed to starboard, but it was still a vicious, panic-raising thing. I ducked into a closet, used my pocket moonflash, and transformed; as a werewolf I chased Pussy out the window and up a tree till somebody could call the Exorcism Department.

Having seen MacIlwraith do it, I looked him up and warned him that if he disrupted the class again I'd chew him out in the most literal sense. Fun is fun, but not at the expense of students who really want to learn and a pleasant elderly anachronism who's trying to teach them.

"TEAM!"

The cheerleader waved his hands and a spurt of many-colored fire jumped out of nothingness. Taller than a man it lifted, a leaping glory of red, blue, yellow, haloed with a wheel of sparks. Slitting my eyes, I could just discern the lizardlike form, white-hot and supple, within the aura.

The coed squealed. "Thrice blessed Hermes," choked the Old Grad. "What is it? A demon?"

"No, a fire elemental," I muttered. "Salamander. Hell of a dangerous thing to fool around with."

My gaze ran about the field as the burning shape began to do its tricks, bouncing, tumbling, spelling out words in long flamebands. Yes, they had a fireman down there in full canonicals, making the passes that kept the thing harmless. It ought to be all right. . . . I lit a cigaret, shakily. It is not well to call up Loki's pets, and the stink of menace to come was acrid in my nostrils.

A good show, but— The crystal revealed Abercrombie clapping, but Ginny with a worried frown between the long green eyes. She didn't like it any better than I. Switch the ball back to MacIlwraith, fun-loving MacIlwraith.

I was probably the only one in the stadium who saw it. The boy gestured at his baton. It sprouted wings. The fat fireman, swaying back and forth with his gestures, was a natural target for a good healthy goose.

"*Yeowp!*"

He rocketed heavenward. The salamander wavered. All at once it sprang up, thinning out till it towered over the walls. There was a spinning, dazzling blur, and the thing was gone.

My cigaret burst luridly into flame and I tossed it from me. Hardly thinking, I jettisoned my hipflask. It exploded from a touch of incandescence and the alcohol burned blue. The crowd howled, hurtling away their smokes, slapping at pockets where matches had kindled, getting rid of bottles. The Campus Queen shrieked as her thin dress caught fire. She got it off in time to prevent serious injury and went wailing across the field. Under different circumstances, I would have been very interested.

The salamander stopped its lunatic shuttling and materialized between goal posts that began to smoke—an intolerable blazing that scorched the grass and roared. The fireman dashed toward it, shouting the spell of extinguishment. From the salamander's mouth licked a tongue of fire. I heard a distinct Bronx cheer, then it was gone again.

The announcer, who should have been calming the spectators, screeched as it flickered before his booth. That touched off the panic! In one heartbeat, fifty thousand people were clawing and trampling, choking each other in the gates, blind with horror and trying only to fight their way out.

I vaulted across benches and an occasional head, down to the field. There was death on those jammed tiers. "Ginny! Ginny, come here where it's safe!"

She couldn't have heard me above the din, but came of herself, dragging a terrorized Abercrombie by one wrist. We faced each other in a ring of ruin.

The Gryphons came boiling out of their locker room. Boiling is the right word: the salamander had materialized down there and playfully wrapped itself around the shower pipes.

Sirens hooted under the moon and police broomsticks shot above us, trying to curb the stampede. The elemental flashed for a moment across one of the besoms. Its rider dove it low enough to jump off, and the burning stick crashed on the grass.

"God!" exclaimed Abercrombie. "It's loose!"

"Tell me more," I snorted. "Ginny, you're a witch. Can you do anything about this?"

"I can extinguish the brute if it'll hold still long enough for me to recite the spell," she said. Disordered ruddy hair had tumbled past her pale, high-boned face to the fur-clad shoulders. "That's our only chance—the binding charm is broken, and it knows that!"

I whirled, remembering friend MacIlwraith, and collared him. "Were you possessed?" I shouted.

"I didn't do anything—" he gasped. His teeth rattled as I shook him.

"Don't hand me that guff. I saw it!"

He collapsed on the ground. "It was just for fun," he whimpered. "I didn't know—"

Well, I thought grimly, that was doubtless true. It's the trouble with the Art—with any blind powerful force man uses, fire or dynamite or atomic energy or thaumaturgy. Any meathead can learn enough to begin something; these days, they start them in the third grade with spelling bees. But it's not always so easy to halt the something.

Student pranks were a standing problem at Trismegistus, as at all colleges. They were usually harmless enough—sneaking into the dorms with Tarnkappen, or 'chanting female lingerie out through the windows. Sometimes they could be rather amusing, like the time the statue of a revered and dignified former president was animated and went downtown singing bawdy songs. Often they fell quite flat, as when the boys turned Dean Hornsby into stone and it wasn't noticed for three days.

This one had gotten out of hand. The salamander was quite capable of igniting the whole city.

I turned to the fireman, who was jittering about trying to flag down a police broom. In the dim shifty light, none of the riders saw him. "What d'you figure to do?" I asked.

"I gotta report back for duty," he said harshly. "And then we'll need a water elemental, I guess."

"I have experience with the Hydros," offered Ginny. "I'll come along."

"Me too," I said at once.

Abercrombie glowered. "What can *you* do?"

"I'm were," I snapped. "In wolf shape I can't easily be harmed by fire. That might turn out useful."

"All right, Steve!" Ginny smiled at me, the old smile which had so often gone between us. Impulsively, I grabbed her to me and kissed her.

She didn't waste energy on a slap. I collected an uppercut that tumbled me on my tocus. "Not allowed," she clipped. That double-damned geas! I could see misery caged within her eyes, but her mind was compelled to obey Malzius' rules.

"It's . . . ah . . . no place for a woman—a lady as charming as you," murmured Abercrombie. "Let me take you home, my dear."

"I've got work to do," she said impatiently. "What the devil is wrong with those cops? We've got to get a lift out of here."

"Then I shall come too," said Abercrombie. "I am not unacquainted with blessings and curses, though—ha!—I fear that ever-filled purses are a trifle beyond my scope. In any event, the Treasury Department frowns on them."

Even in that moment, with riot thundering and hell let loose on earth, I was pleased to note that Ginny paid no attention to his famous wit. She scowled abstractedly and looked around. The Campus Queen was huddled near the benches, wearing somebody's overcoat. Ginny grinned and waved her wand. The Campus Queen shucked the coat and ran toward us. Thirty seconds later, three police broomsticks had landed. The fireman commandeered them and we were all whirled over the stadium and into the street.

During that short hop, I saw three houses ablaze. The salamander was getting around!

We gathered at the district police station, a haggard and sooty crew with desperate eyes. The fire and police chiefs were there, and a junior officer going crazy at the switchboard. Ginny, who had picked up her own broom and come via her apartment, arrived with Svartalf on one shoulder and the *Handbook of Alchemy and Metaphysics* under her arm. Abercrombie was browbeating the terrified MacIlwraith till I told him to lay off.

"My duty—" he began. "I'm a proctor, you know."

I suppose it's necessary to have witchsmellers on campus, to make sure the boys don't 'chant up liquor in the frat houses or smuggle in succubi. And every year somebody tries to get by an exam with a familiar under his coat whispering the answers from a crib-sheet. Nevertheless, I don't like professional nosy parkers.

"You can deal with him later," I said, and gave the boy a push out the door. "The salamander can fight back."

President Malzius huffed into the room. "What is the meaning of this?" he demanded. His pince-nez bobbed above full jowls. "I'll have you know, sir, I was preparing a most important address. The Lions Totem is holding a luncheon tomorrow, and—"

"Might not be any lunch," grunted the cop who had fetched him. "There's a salamander loose around here."

"Sala— No! It's against the rules! It is positively forbidden to—"

The man at the switchboard looked up. "It's just kindled the Methodist church at 14th and Elm," he said. "And my God, all our equipment is already working—"

"Impossible!" cried Malzius. "A demon can't go near a church."

"How stupid does a man have to be to get your job?" Ginny fairly spat·it. "This *isn't* a demon. It's an elemental." Her temper was again sheathed in ice, and she continued slowly: "We haven't much hope of using a Hydro to put out the salamander, but we can raise one to help fight the fires. It'll always be three jumps behind, but at least the whole city won't be ruined."

"Unless the salamander gets too strong," cut in Abercrombie. His face was colorless and he spoke through stiff lips. "Then it can evaporate the Hydro."

"Call up two water beings," stammered Malzius. "Call up a hundred. I'll waive the requirement of formal application for permission to—"

"There's a limit, sir," Abercrombie told him. "The restraining force required is an exponential function of the total embodied mass. There probably aren't enough adepts in this town to control more than three at a time. If we raised four . . . we'd flood the city, and the salamander need only skip elsewhere."

"Alan—" Ginny laid her handbook on the desk and riffled its pages. Abercrombie leaned over her shoulder, remembering to rest one hand carelessly on her hip. I choked back my prize cuss-words. "Alan, just for a starter, can you summon one Hydro and put it to work?"

"Of course, gorgeous one," he smiled. "It is a—ha!—elemental problem."

She gave him a worried glance. "They can be as tricky as Fire or Air," she warned. "It's not enough just to know the theory."

"I have some small experience," he preened. "During the war— After this is over, come up to my place for a drink and I'll tell you about it." His lips brushed her cheek.

"Mr. Matuchek!" wailed Malzius. "Will you please stop growing fangs?"

I shook myself and suppressed the rage which had been almost as potent as moonlight.

"Look here," said the police chief. "I gotta know what's going on. You longhairs started this trouble and I don't want you making it worse."

Seeing that Ginny and Pretty Boy were, after all, legitimately busy, I sighed and whistled up a cigaret. "Let me explain," I offered. "I learned a few things about the subject, during the war. An elemental is not the same as a demon. Any kind of demon is a separate being, as individual as you and I. An elemental is part of the basic force involved: in this case, fire, or more accurately energy. It's raised out of the basic energy matrix, given temporary individuality, and restored to the matrix when the adept is through with it."

"Huh?"

"Like a flame. A flame exists only potentially till someone lights a fire, and goes back to merely potential existence when you put the fire out. And of course the second fire you light, even on the same log, is not identical with the first, so you can understand why an elemental isn't exactly anxious to be dismissed. If it ever breaks loose, as this one did, it'll do its damnedest to stay in this world and to increase its own power."

"But how come it can burn a church?"

"Because it's soulless, a mere physical force. Any true individual, human or otherwise, is under certain constraints of a . . . a moral nature. A demon is allergic to holy symbols. A man who does wrong has to live with his conscience in this world and face judgment in the next. But what does a fire care? And that's all the salamander is—a glorified fire. It's bound only by the physical laws of nature and paranature."

"So how do you, uh, put it out?"

"A Hydro of corresponding mass could do it—mutual annihilation. Earth could bury it or Air withdraw from its neighborhood. Trouble is, Fire is the swiftest of them all; it can flick out of an area before any other sort of elemental can injure it. So we're left without the dismissal spell. But that has to be said in the salamander's presence, and it takes about two minutes."

"Yeah . . . and when it hears you start the words, it'll burn you down or scram. *Very* nice. What're we gonna do?"

"I don't know, chief," I said, "except it's like kissing a sheep dog." I blew hard and smacked my lips. "You got to be quick. Every fire the critter starts feeds it more energy and makes it that much stronger. There's a critical point somewhere at which it becomes too powerful for anything to affect it."

"And then what happens?"

"Ragnarok."

I saw Ginny turn from the desk. Abercrombie was chalking a pentagram on the floor while a sputtering Malzius had been deputized to sterilize a pocket knife with a match—blood is a substitute for the usual powders, since it has the same proteins. The girl laid a hand on mine. "Steve, it'll take too long to get hold of all the local adepts and organize them," she said. "God knows what the salamander will be doing meanwhile. Are you game to track it down?"

"Sure," I agreed. "It can't hurt me—if I'm careful—till it gets big enough to burn up all the world's oxygen. But you're staying here!"

"Ever hear about the oath of my order? Come on."

As we went out the door, I gave Abercrombie a smug look. He had nicked his wrist and sprinkled the Signs; now he was well into the invocation. I felt cold dampness swirl through the room.

Outside, the night was still autumnally sharp, the moon high. Roofs were a sawtoothed silhouette against the leaping red glare at a dozen points around us, and sirens howled in the streets. Up overhead, across the small indifferent stars, I saw what looked like the whirl of dry leaves, refugees fleeing on their sticks.

Svartalf jumped to the front end of Ginny's Cadillac, and I took the saddle behind. We rode skyward.

Below us, blue fire sat and the station lights went out. Water poured into the street, a solid roar of it with President Malzius bobbing like a cork in the torrent.

"Unholy Sathanas!" I choked. "What's happened now?"

Svartalf ducked the stick low. "That idiot," groaned Ginny. "He let the Hydro slop all over the floor . . . short circuits . . ." She made a few rapid passes with her wand. The stream quieted, drew into herself, became a ten-foot-high blob glimmering in the moonlight. Abercrombie scuttled out and started it squelching toward the nearest fire.

I laughed. "Go on up to his place and listen to him tell about his vast experience," I said.

"Don't kick a man when he's down," Ginny snapped. "You've pulled your share of boners, Steve Matuchek."

Svartalf whisked the broom up again and we went low above the chimneypots. *Oof!* I thought. Could she really be falling for that troll? A regular profile, a smooth tongue, and proximity . . . I bit back an inward sickness and squinted ahead, trying to find the salamander.

"There!" Ginny yelled it over the whistle of cloven air. Svartalf bottled his tail and hissed.

The University district is shabby-genteel: old pseudo-Gothic caves of wood which have slipped from mansions to rooming houses, flyspecked with minor business establishments. It was burning merrily, a score of angry red stars flickering in the darkness between street lamps. As I watched, one of the stars exploded in a puff of steam—the Hydro must have clapped a sucker onto a fireplug and blanketed the place. I had a brief heretical thought that the salamander was doing a public service by eliminating those architectural teratologies . . . but of course lives and property were involved—

Tall and terrible, the elemental wavered beside the house on which it was feeding. It had doubled in size, and its core was too bright to look at. Flames whirled about the reptile head.

Svartalf braked and we hovered a few yards off, twenty feet in the air and level with the hungry mouth. Ginny was etched wild against night by that intolerable radiance. She braced herself in the stirrups and began the spell, her voice almost lost in the roar as the roof caved in. *"O Indra, Abaddon, Lucifer, Moloch, Hephaestos, Loki . . ."*

It heard. The seething eyes swung toward us and it leaped.

Svartalf squalled as his whiskers shriveled—perhaps it was only hurt vanity—and put the stick through an Immelmann turn and whipped away. The salamander bawled with the voice of a hundred blazing forests. Suddenly the heat scorching my back was gone, and the thing had materialized in front of us.

"That way!" I hollered, pointing. "In there!"

I covered Ginny's eyes and buried my own face against her back as we went through the plate-glass front of Stub's Beer Garden. The flame-tongue licked after us, recoiled, and the salamander ramped beyond the door.

We tumbled off the broom and looked around. The place was empty, full of a fire-spattered darkness. Everyone had fled. I saw a nearly full glass of beer on the counter and tossed it off.

"You might have offered me a drink," said Ginny. "Alan would have." Before I could recover enough to decide whether she was taunting or teasing me, she went on in a rapid whisper: "It isn't trying to escape. It's gained power—confidence—it means to kill us!"

Even then, I wanted to tell her that tousled red hair and a soot smudge across an aristocratic nose were particularly enchanting. But the occasion didn't seem appropriate. "Can't get in here," I panted. "Can't do much much more than ignite tthe building by thermal radiation, and that'll take a while. We're safe for the moment."

"Why . . . oh, yes, of course. Stub's is cold-ironed. All these college beer parlors are, I'm told."

"Yeh." I peered out the broken window. The salamander peered back, and spots danced before my eyes. "So the clientele won't go jazzing up the brew above 3.2—Quick, say your spell."

Ginny shook her head. "It'll just flicker away out of earshot. Maybe we can talk to it, find out—"

She trod forth to the window, and the thing crouched in the street extended its neck and hissed at her. I stood behind my girl, feeling boxed and useless. Svartalf, lapping spilled beer off the counter, looked up and sneered.

"Ohé, Child of Light!" she cried.

A ripple went down the salamander's back. Its tail switched restlessly, and a tree across the way kindled. I can't describe the voice that answered . . . crackling, bellowing, sibilant, it was

Fire given a brain and a throat. "Daughter of Eve, what have you to say to the likes of Me?"

"I command you by the Most High, return to your proper bonds and cease from troubling the world."

"Ho—oh, ho, ho, ho!" The thing sat back on its haunches (asphalt bubbled) and shuddered its laughter into the sky. *"You* command Me, combustible one?"

"I have at my beck powers so mighty they could wither your little spark into the nothingness whence it came. Cease and obey, lest worse befall you than dismissal."

I think the salamander was, for a moment, honestly surprised. "Greater than *Me?"* Then it howled so the tavern shook. "You dare say there are mightier forces than Fire? Than Me, Who am going to consume all the earth?"

"Mightier and more beautiful, O Ashmaker. Think—you cannot even enter this house. Water will extinguish you, Earth will smother you, Air alone can keep you alive. Best you surrender now—"

I remembered the night we had faced an afreet together. Ginny must be pulling the same trick—feeling out the psychology of the thing that raged and flared beyond the door—but what could she hope to gain?

"More beautiful!" The salamander's tail beat furrows in the street. It threw out bursting fireballs and a rain of sparks, red, blue, yellow, a one-being Fourth of July. I thought crazily of a child kicking the floor in a tantrum.

"More beautiful! Stronger! You dare say— Haaaaa—" Teeth of incandescence gleamed in a mouth that was jumping fire. "We shall see how beautiful you are when you lie a choked corpse!" Its head darted to the broken glass front. It could not pass the barrier of cold iron, but it began to suck air, in and out. A furnace wave of heat sent me gasping back.

"My God . . . it's going to use up all our oxygen. . . . Stay here!" Hardly thinking, I sprang for the door. Ginny shrieked, but I scarcely heard her "No!" as I went through.

Moonlight flooded me, cool and tingling between the unrestful guttering fires. I crouched to the hot sidewalk and felt a shudder as my body changed.

Wolf I was, and a wolf which only silver could kill . . . I hoped. My abbreviated tail thrust against the seat of my pants, and I remembered that some injuries are beyond the healing powers of even the were shape.

Pants! Hell and damnation! Have you ever tried being a wolf

while wrapped in shirt, trousers, underwear, and topcoat designed for a man?

I went flat on my moist black nose. My suspenders slid down and wrapped themselves about my hind legs. My tie tripped me up in front and my coat gleefully wrapped itself around the whole bundle.

Frantic, I snapped at the cloth, rolling over and tearing with my fangs. The salamander grew aware of me, and its tail slapped contemptuously across my back. For a moment of searing agony, hair and skin went up with the fabric . . . then I was free, and the fluid molecules rebuilt themselves. Hardly knowing what I did, I picked up a shoe which had dropped from my now smaller foot, laid it on the salamander's white-hot toe, and bore down.

It roared and swung about to attack me. Those jaws gaped wide enough to bite me in half. I skittered away. It paused, gauged the distance, flicked into nothingness, and materialized right on top of me.

I *think* I got a tooth-grip in the obvious place to bite a salamander when it is sitting on you, but the pain was too great for me to know. Then it was gone, the street lay bare and quiet between burning houses, and I gasped my way back toward wholeness.

Sanity returned. My shaggy head was in Ginny's lap, and she was stroking it and crying. Feebly, I licked her hand. Strength flowed back. As a man, I'd naturally have stayed where I was, but being a wolf with lupine instincts, I sat up and yipped.

"Steve . . . Almighty Father, Steve you saved our lives," whispered Ginny. "Another minute and we'd have been suffocating. My lungs still feel like mummy dust."

Svartalf trotted from the bar, looking as smug as a cat with singed whiskers can. He meowed. Ginny gave a trembling laugh and explained:

"But you owe Svartalf a pint of cream or something. He saved you too. A few more seconds and you'd have been dead—but he showed me how to drive the beast off."

I cocked my ears inquiringly.

"He manned the beer taps," she said. "I filled stein after stein and went out and threw them at the salamander. Not enough to do more than discommode it . . . but added to the trouble you were making, enough to make it skip."

Horrible waste of beer, I thought. But there was still work to do.

Penalties attach to everything. The trouble with being were is that in the other shape you have, essentially, an animal brain, with only a superficial layer of human personality. Or in plain language, as a wolf I'm a rather stupid man. I was only able to think I'd better reassume human form . . . and I did.

Ever see a cat grin? "Omi-gawd!" I groaned, and started to change back.

"Never mind that," said Ginny crisply, peeling off her fur coat. I broke all records donning it. Pretty tight fit around the shoulders, but it went low enough . . . if I was careful. The night wind nipped my shanks, but my face was of salamander temperature.

"Now where?" I asked quickly. "The damned critter could be anyplace."

"I think it will hang around the campus," she said. "Plenty of grazing, and it's not very smart. Let's get back on our stick."

She fetched it from the smoldering barroom and we lifted. "All we've done so far," I said, "is lose time."

"No, not entirely. I did get a line on its mind." Ginny turned her head back to face me as we cleared the rooftops. "I wasn't sure into just what form it had been conjured—you can mold the elemental forces into almost anything. But apparently the cheerleader was satisfied to give it a knowledge of English and a rudimentary intelligence. Add to that the volatile nature of Fire, and what have you got? A child."

"Some child," I muttered, hugging her coat to me.

"No, no, Steve, this is important. It has all the child's traits. Improvidence, complete lack of foresight . . . a wise salamander would lie low, gathering strength slowly, and would never think of burning the entire planet. Because what would it use for oxygen when that was finished? You'll note, too, its fantastic vanity; it went into an insane rage when I said there were powers stronger and more beautiful than it, and the crack about beauty hurt as much as the one about strength. Short span of attention . . . it could have smothered us easily before attending to as minor a nuisance as you provided. At the same time, within that span of attention, it focuses on one issue only, to the exclusion of everything else." She nodded thoughtfully, and the long blowing hair tickled my face. "I don't know just how, but some way its psychology must provide us with a lever."

My own vanity is not small. "I wasn't such a minor nuisance," I grumbled.

Ginny smiled and reached around to pat my cheek. "All right, Steve, all right. I love you just the same, and now I *know* you'll make a good husband."

That left me in a comfortable glow until I wondered precisely what she was thinking of.

We spotted the salamander below us, igniting a theater, but it flicked away even as I watched, and a mile off it appeared next to the medical research center. Glass brick doesn't burn very well. As we neared, I saw it petulantly kick the wall and vanish again. Ignorant and impulsive . . . a child . . . a brat from Hell!

Sweeping over the campus, we saw lights in the Administration Building. "Probably that's HQ for our side now," said Ginny. "We'd better report." Svartalf landed us on the Mall in front of the place and strutted ahead toward the steps.

A squad of cops armed with fire extinguishers guarded the door. "Hey, there!" One of them barred our path. "Where you going?"

"To the meeting," said Ginny, smoothing her tangled hair.

"Yeh?" The policeman's eye fell on me. "All dressed up for it, too, aren't you? Haw, haw, haw!"

I'd had about enough for one night. I wered and peeled off his own trousers. As he lifted his billy, Ginny turned it into a small boa constrictor. I switched back to human, we left the squad to its own problems and went down the hall.

The faculty meeting room was packed. Malzius had summoned all his professors. As we entered, I heard his orotund tones: ". . . disgraceful. The authorities won't even listen to me. Gentlemen, it is for us to vindicate the honor of Gown against Town." He blinked when Ginny and Svartalf came in, and turned a beautiful Tyrian purple as I followed in the full glory of mink coat and stubby chin. *"Mister* Matuchek!"

"He's with me," said Ginny curtly. "We were out fighting the salamander while you sat here."

"Possibly something more than brawn, even lupine brawn, is required," smiled Dr. Alan Abercrombie. "I see that Mr. Matuchek lost his pants in a more than vernacular sense."

Like Malzius, he had changed his wet clothes for the inevitable tweeds. Ginny gave him a cold look. "I thought you were directing the Hydro," she said.

"Oh, we got enough adepts together to use three water elementals," he said. "Mechanic's work. I felt my job was here. We can control the fires easily enough—"

"—if the salamander weren't always lighting fresh ones," clipped Ginny. "And every blaze it starts, it gets bigger and stronger, while you sit here looking beautiful."

"Why, thank you, my dear," he laughed.

I jammed my teeth together so it hurt. She had actually smiled back at him.

"Order, order!" boomed President Malzius. "Please be seated, Miss Graylock. Have you anything to contribute to the discussion?"

"Yes. I understand the salamander now." She took a place at the end of the table. It was the last vacant chair, so I hovered miserably in the background wishing her coat had more buttons.

"Understand it well enough to extinguish it?" asked Professor van Linden of Alchemy.

"No. But I know how it thinks—"

"We're more interested in how it operates," said van Linden. "How can we make it hold still long enough to hear a dismissal?" He cleared his throat. "Obviously, we must first know by what process it shuttles around so fast—"

"Oh, that's simple enough," piped up little Griswold timidly. He was drowned by van Linden's fruity bass:

"—which is, of course, by the well-known affinity of Fire for Quicksilver. Since virtually every home these days has at least one thermometer—"

"With all due respect, my good sir," interrupted Vittorio of Astrology, "you are talking utter hogwash. It is a simple matter of the conjunction of Mercury and Neptune in Scorpio—"

"You're wrong, sir!" declared van Linden. "Dead wrong! Let me show you the *Ars Thaumaturgica*." He glared around after his copy, but of course it had been mislaid and he had to use an adaptation of the Dobu yam-calling chant to find it. Meanwhile Vittorio was screaming:

"No, no, no! The conjunction, with Uranus opposing in the ascendant, as I can easily prove—" He went to the blackboard and started drawing a diagram.

"Oh, come now!" snorted Jasper of Metaphysics. "I don't understand how you can both be so wrong. As I showed in my paper read at the last A.A.A.S. meeting, the intrinsic nature—"

"That was disproved ten years ago!" roared van Linden. "The affinity—"

"—*Ding an sich*—"

"—up Uranus—"

I sidled over and tugged at Griswold's sleeve. He pattered into a corner with me. "Just how *does* the bloody thing work?" I asked.

"Oh . . . merely a question of wave mechanics." he whispered. "According to the Heisenberg Uncertainty Principle, a photon has a finite probability of being at any point of space. The salamander uses a simple diffraction process to change the spatial coordinates of psi squared, in effect going from point to point without crossing the intervening space, much like an electron making a quantum jump, though of course the analogy is not precise due to the modifying influence of—"

"Never mind," I sighed. "This confab is becoming a riot. Wouldn't we do better to—"

"—stick by the original purpose," agreed Abercrombie, joining us. Ginny followed. Van Linden blacked Vittorio's eye while Jasper threw chalk at both of them. Our little group went over near the door.

"I've already found the answer to our problem," said Abercrombie, "but I'll need help. A transformation spell—turn the salamander into something we can handle more easily."

"That's dangerous," said Ginny. "You'll need a really strong T-spell, and that sort can backfire. Just what happens then is unpredictable."

Abercrombie straightened himself with a look of pained nobility. "For you, my dear, no hazard is too great."

She regarded him with admiration. It does take guts to use the ultimate runes. "Let's go," she said. "I'll help."

Griswold plucked at my arm, "I don't like this, Mr. Matuchek," he confided. "The Art is too unreliable. There ought to be some method grounded in nature and nature's quantitative laws."

"Yeh," I said disconsolately. "But what?" I paddled out after Ginny and Abercrombie, who had their heads together over the handbook. Griswold marched beside me and Svartalf made a gesture with his tail at the Trismegistus faculty. They were too embroiled to notice.

We went out past an enraged but well-cowed squad of cops. The Physical Sciences hall was nearby, and its chemistry division held stuff that would be needed. We entered an echoing gloom.

The freshman lab, a long room full of workbenches, shelves, and silence, was our goal. Griswold switched on the lights and Abercrombie looked around. "But we'll have to bring the salamander here," he said. "We can't do anything except in its actual presence."

"Go ahead and make ready," the girl told him. "I know how to fetch the beast. A minor transformation—" She laid out some test tubes, filled them with various powders, and sketched her symbols on the floor. Those ball-point wands are useful.

"What's the idea?" I asked.

"Oh, get out of the way," she snapped. I told myself she was only striking at her own weariness and despair, but it hurt. "We'll use its vanity, of course. I'll prepare some Roman candles and rockets and stuff—shoot them off, and naturally it'll come to show it can do more spectacular things."

Griswold and I withdrew into a corner. This was big-league play. I was frankly scared, and the little scientist's bony knees were beating a tattoo in march time. Even Ginny—yes, there was sweat beading that smooth forehead. If this didn't work, we were probably all done for: either the salamander or the backlash of the spell could finish us. And we had no way of knowing whether the beast had grown too strong for a transformation.

The witch got her fireworks prepared, and went to an open window and leaned out. Hissing balls of blue and red, streamers of golden sparks, flew up and exploded.

Abercrombie had completed his diagrams. He turned to smile at us. "It's all right," he said. "Everything under control. I'm going to turn the salamander's energy into matter. E equals mc squared, you know. Just light me a Bunsen burner, Matuchek, and set a beaker of water over it. Griswold, you turn off these lights and use the polaroid bulbs. We need polarized radiation."

We obeyed—and I hated to see an old and distinguished man acting as lab assistant to this patronizing slickpaper adman's dream. "You *sure* it'll work?" I asked.

"Of course," he smiled. "I've had experience. I was in the Quartermaster Corps during the war, till they tapped me for the propaganda division . . . broadcasting nightmares, you know."

"Yeh," I said, "but turning dirt into K-rations isn't the same thing as transforming that hell-born monster. You and your experience!"

Suddenly and sickly, remembering how he had bungled with the Hydro, I realized the truth. Abercrombie was confident, unafraid—because he didn't *know* enough!

For a minute I couldn't unfreeze my muscles. Griswold stood fiddling unhappily with some metallic samples. He'd been using them only the other day for freshman experiments, trying to teach us the chemical properties—Lord, it seemed a million years ago . . .

"Ginny!" I stumbled toward her where she stood at the window throwing rainbows into the air. "My God, darling, stop—"

Crack! The salamander was in the room with us.

I lurched back from it, half blinded. Grown hideously bigger, it filled the other end of the lab, and the bench tops smoked.

"Oh, so!" The voice of Fire blasted our eardrums. Svartalf shot up to a shelf top and began upsetting bottles of acid onto the varmint. It didn't notice. "So, small moist pests, you would try to outdo Me!"

Abercrombie and Ginny lifted their wands and shouted the few brief words of transformation.

Crouched back into my corner, peering through a sulfurous reek of fumes, I saw Ginny cringe and them jump for safety. She must have sensed the backlash. There was a shattering explosion and the air was full of flying glass.

My body shielded Griswold, and the spell didn't do more to me than turn me lupine. I saw Ginny nearby on her hands and knees, behind a bench, half unconscious . . . but unhurt, unhurt, praise all Powers forever. Svartalf—a Pekingese dog yapped on the shelf. Abercrombie was gone, but a chimpanzee in baggy tweeds scuttered wailing toward the door.

A fire-blast rushed before the ape. He whirled, screamed, and shinnied up a steam pipe. The salamander arched its back and howled with laughter.

"You would use your tricks on Me? Almighty Me, terrible Me, beautiful me? Ha, they bounce off like water from a hot skillet! And I, I, I am the skillet which is going to fry you!"

Somehow, the low-grade melodrama of its speech was not at all ridiculous. For this was the childish, vainglorious, senselessly consuming thing which was loose on earth to turn our broad fair home into one white blaze among the planets.

Under the polaroids, I switched back to human and stood up behind the bench. Griswold turned on a water faucet and squirted a jet with his finger. The salamander hissed in annoyance—yes, water still hurt, but there wasn't enough liquid here to quench it, you'd need a whole lake by this time. . . . It swung its head, gape-mouthed, and aimed at Griswold and drew a long breath.

All is vanity. . . .

I reeled over to the Bunsen burner that was heating a futile beaker of water. Ginny sat up and looked at me through scorched locks. The room shimmered in heat, my lungs were one great anguish. I didn't have any flash of genius, I acted on raw instinct and tumbled memories.

"Kill us," I croaked. "Kill us if you dare. Our servant is more powerful than you. He'll hound you to the ends of creation."

"Your servant?" Flame wreathed the words.

"Yeh . . . I mean yes . . . our servant, that Fire which fears not water!"

The salamander stepped back a pace, snarling. It was still not so strong that the very name of water didn't make it flinch. "Show Me!"it chattered. "Show Me! I dare you!"

"Our servant . . . small, but powerful," I rasped. "Brighter and more beautiful than you, and above taking harm from the Wet Element." I staggered to the jars of metal samples and got a pair of tongs. "Have you the courage to look on him?"

The salamander bristled. "Have I the *courage?* Ask rather, does it dare confront Me?"

I flicked a glance from the corner of my eye. Ginny had risen and was gripping her wand. She scarcely breathed, but her eyes were narrowed.

There was a silence. It hung like a world's weight in that long room, smothering what noises remained: the crackle of fire, Abercrombie's simian gibber, Svartalf's indignant yapping. I took a strip of magnesium in the tongs and held it to the burner flame.

It burst into a blue-white actinic radiance from which I turned dazzled eyes. The salamander was not so viciously brilliant. I saw the brute accomplish the feat of simultaneously puffing itself up and shrinking back.

"Behold!" I lifted the burning strip. Behind me, Ginny's rapid mutter came: *"O Indra, Abaddon, Lucifer . . ."*

The child mind, incapable of considering more than one thing at a time . . . but for how long a time? I had to hold its full attention for the hundred and twenty seconds required.

"Fire," said the salamander feverishly. "Only another fire, only a little piece of that Force from which I came."

"Can you do this, buster?"

I plunged the strip into the beaker. Steam puffed from the water, it boiled and bubbled—and the metal went on burning!

". . . abire ex orbis terrestris . . ."

"Mg plus H_2O yields Mg_1O plus H_2," whispered Griswold reverently.

"Keek-eek!" said Abercrombie.

"Yip-yip-yip!" said Svartalf.

"It's a trick!" screamed the salamander. "It's impossible! If even I cannot— *No!*"

"Stay where you are!" I barked in my best Army manner. "Do you doubt that my servant can follow you where you may flee?"

"I'll kill that little monster!"

"Go right ahead, chum," I agreed. "Want to have the duel fought under the sea?"

Whistles skirled above the racketing fire. The police had seen through our windows.

"I'll show you, I will!" There was almost a sob in the rear. I ducked behind the bench, pulling Griswold with me, as a geyser of flame rushed where I had been.

"Nyaah, nyaah, nyaah," I called. "You can't catch me! Scaredy cat!"

Svartalf gave me a hard look.

The floor trembled as the elemental came toward me, not going around the benches but burning its way through them. Heat clawed at my throat. I spun down toward darkness.

And it was gone. Ginny cried her triumphant *"Amen!"* and displaced air cracked like thunder.

I lurched to my feet. Ginny fell into my arms. The police entered the lab and Griswold hollered something about calling the fire department before his whole building went up in smoke. Abercrombie scampered out a window and Svartalf jumped down from the shelf. He forgot that a Pekingese isn't as agile as a cat, and his pop eyes bubbled with righteous wrath.

Outside, the Mall was cool and still. We sat on dewed grass and looked at the moon and thought what a great and simple wonder it is to be alive.

The geas held us apart, but tenderness lay on Ginny's lips. We scarcely noticed when somebody ran past us shouting that the salamander was gone, nor when church bells began pealing the news to all men.

Svartalf finally roused us with his barking. Ginny chuckled. "Poor fellow. I'll change you back as soon as I can, but there's more urgent business now. Come on, Steve."

Griswold, assured that his priceless hall was safe, followed us at a tactful distance. Svartalf merely sat where he was . . . too shocked to move, I guess, at the idea that there could be more important affairs than turning him back into a cat.

Dr. Malzius met us halfway, under one of the campus elms. Moonlight spattered his face and gleamed on the pince-nez. "My dear Miss Graylock," he began, "is it indeed true that you have overcome that menace to society? Most noteworthy. Accept my congratulations. The glorious annals of this great institution of which I have the honor to be president—"

Ginny faced him, arms akimbo, and nailed him with the chilliest gaze I have ever seen. "The credit belongs to Mr. Matuchek and Dr. Griswold," she said. "I shall so inform the press. Doubtless you'll then see fit to recommend a larger appropriation for Dr. Griswold's outstanding work."

"Oh, now, really," stammered the scientist. "I didn't—"

"Be quiet, you ninnyhammer," hissed Ginny. Aloud: "Only through his courageous and farsighted adherence to the basic teachings of natural law— Well, you can fill in the rest for yourself, Malzius. I don't think you'd be very popular if you went on starving his department."

"Oh . . . indeed . . . after all . . ." The president blew himself up. "I have given careful consideration to the matter. Was going to recommend it at the next meeting of the board, in fact."

"I'll hold you to that," said Ginny. "Now there is this stupid rule against student-faculty relationships. Mr. Matuchek is shortly going to be my husband—"

Whoosh! I tried to regain my breath.

"My dear Miss Graylock," sputtered Malzius, "decorum . . . propriety . . . why, he isn't even decent!"

I realized with horror that somehow, in all the excitement, I'd lost Ginny's expensive mink coat.

A pair of cops approached, dragging a small hairy form that struggled in their arms. One of them carried the garments the chimp had shed. "Begging your pardon, Miss Graylock." The tone was pure worship. "We found this monkey loose and—"

"Oh, yes." She laughed. "We'll have to restore him. But not right away. Steve needs those pants worse."

I got into them in a hurry. Ginny turned back to smile with angelic sweetness at Malzius.

"Poor Dr. Abercrombie," she sighed. "These things will happen when you deal with paranatural forces. Now I believe, sir, that there is no rule against faculty members conducting research."

"Oh, no," said the president shakily. "Of course not. On the contrary! We expect our people to publish—"

"To be sure. Now I have in mind a most interesting research project involving transformations. I'll admit it's just the least bit dangerous. It could backfire as Dr. Abercrombie's spell did." Ginny leaned on her wand and regarded the turf thoughtfully. "It could even . . . yes, there's even a small possibility that it could turn *you* into an ape, dear Dr. Malzius. Or, perhaps, a worm. A long slimy one. But we mustn't let that stand in the way of Science, must we?"

"What? But—"

"Naturally," purred the witch, "if I were allowed to conduct myself as I wish with my fiancé, I shouldn't have time for research."

It took Malzius a bare fifty words to admit surrender. He stumped off in tottery grandeur while the last fire-glow died above the campus roofs.

Ginny gave me a long slow glance. "The rule can't officially be stricken till tomorrow," she murmured. "Think you can cut a few classes then?"

"Keek-eek-eek," said Dr. Alan Abercrombie. Then Svartalf showed up full of resentment and chased him up the tree.

Wizard's World

by Andre Norton

Andre Norton is one of the most popular of contemporary science fiction and fantasy writers, with a very high percentage of her more than one hundred books currently in print. She is also a highly honored writer, the recipient of two of the highest awards her field can offer: the Grand Master of Fantasy Award, bestowed by the World Fantasy Convention in 1977, and the Gandalf Award, given her by the World Science Fiction Convention in 1978. Although many of her novels are technically "juveniles," they can be enjoyed by readers of all ages. Appropriately, her most famous books are those of the "Witch World" series, including such outstanding works as Sorceress of the Witch World *(1968). She was also one of the first important sf writers to consistently feature female protagonists in her books.*

I

Craike's swollen feet were agony, every breath he drew fought a hot band imprisoning his laboring lungs. He clung weakly to a rough spur of rock in the canyon wall, swayed against it, raking his flesh raw on the stone. That weathered red and yellow rock was no more unyielding than the murderous wills behind him. And the stab of pain in his calves no less than the pain of their purpose in his dazed mind.

He had been on the run so long, ever since he had left the E-Camp. But until last night—no, two nights ago—when he had given himself away at the gas station, he had not known what it was to be actually hunted. The will-to-kill which fanned from those on his trail was so intense it shocked his Esper senses, panicking him completely.

Now he was trapped in wild country, and he was city-born.

166

Water—Craike flinched at the thought of water. Espers should control their bodies, that was what he had been taught. But there come times when cravings of the flesh triumph over will.

He winced, and the spur grated against his half-naked breast. They had a "hound" on him right enough. And that brain-twisted Esper slave who fawned and served the mob masters would have no difficulty in trailing him straight to any pocket into which he might crawl. A last remnant of rebellion sent Craike reeling on over the gravel of the long-dried stream bed.

Espers had once been respected for their "wild talents," then tolerated warily. Now they were used under guard for slave labor. And the day was coming soon when the fears of the normals would demand their extermination. They had been trying to prepare against that.

First they had worked openly, petitioning to be included in spaceship crews, to be chosen for colonists on the Moon and Mars; then secretly when they realized the norms had no intention of allowing that. Their last hope was flight to the waste spots of the world, those refuse places resulting from the same atomic wars which had brought about the birth of their kind.

Craike had been smuggled out of an eastern E-Camp, provided with a cover, sent to explore the ravaged area about the onetime city of Reno. Only he had broken his cover for the protection of a girl, only to learn, too late, she was bait for an Esper trap. He had driven a stolen speeder until the last drop of fuel was gone, and after that he had kept blindly on, running, until now.

The contact with the Esper "hound" was clear; they must almost be in sight behind. Craike paused. They were not going to take him alive, wring from him knowledge of his people, recondition him into another "hound." There was only one way, he should have known that from the first.

His decision had shaken the "hound." Craike bared teeth in a death's-head grin. Now the mob would speed up. But their quarry had already chosen a part of the canyon wall where he might pull his tired and aching body up from one hold to another. He moved deliberately now, knowing that when he had lost hope, he could throw aside the need for haste. He would be able to accomplish his purpose before they brought a gas rifle to bear on him.

At last he stood on a ledge, the sand and gravel some fifty feet below. For a long moment he rested, steadying himself with both hands braced on the stone. The weird beauty of the desert country was a pattern of violent color under the afternoon sun.

Craike breathed slowly; he had regained a measure of control. There came shouts as they sighted him.

He leaned forward and, as if he were diving into the river which had once run there, he hurled himself outward to the clean death he sought.

Water, water in his mouth! Dazed, he flailed water until his head broke surface. Instinct took over, and he swam, fought for air. The current of the stream pulled him against a boulder collared with froth, and he arched an arm over it, lifting himself, to stare about in stupefied bewilderment.

He was close to one bank of a river. Where the colorful cliff of the canyon had been there now rolled downs thickly covered with green growth. The baking heat of the desert had vanished; there was even a slight chill in the air.

Dumbly Craike left his rock anchorage and paddled ashore, to lie shivering on sand while the sun warmed his battered body. What *had* happened? When he tried to make sense of it, the effort hurt his mind almost as much as had the "hound's" probe.

The Esper "hound!" Craike jerked up, old panic stirring. First delicately and then urgently, he cast a thought-seek about him. There was life in plenty. He touched, classified and disregarded the flickers of awareness which mingled in confusion—animals, birds, river dwellers. But nowhere did he meet intelligence approaching his own. A wilderness world without man as far as Esper ability could reach.

Craike relaxed. Something had happened. He was too tired, too drained to speculate as to what. It was enough that he was saved from the death he had sought, that he was *here* instead of *there*.

He got stiffly to his feet. Time was the same, he thought—late afternoon. Shelter, food—he set off along the stream. He found and ate berries spilling from bushes where birds raided before him. Then, squatting above a side eddy of the stream, he scooped out a fish, eating the flesh raw.

The land along the river was rising, he could see the beginning of a gorge ahead. Later, when he had climbed those heights, he caught sight through the twilight of the fires. Four of them burning some miles to the southwest, set out in the form of a square!

Craike sent out a thought probe. Yes—men! But an alien touch. This was no hunting mob. And he was drawn to the security of the fires, the camp of men in the dangers of the night. Only, as Esper, he was not one with them but an outlaw. And he dare not risk joining them.

He retraced his path to the river and holed up in a hollow not large enough to be termed a cave. Automatically he probed again for danger. Found nothing, but animal life. He slept at last, drugged by exhaustion of mind and body.

The sky was gray when he roused, swung cramped arms, stretched. Craike had awakened with the need to know more of that camp. He climbed once again to the vantage point, shut his eyes to the early morning and sent out a seeking.

A camp of men far from home. But they were not hunters. Merchants—traders! Craike located one mind among the rest, read in it the details of a bargain to come. Merchants from another country, a caravan. But a sense of separation grew stronger as the fugitive Esper sorted out thought streams, absorbed scraps of knowledge thirstily. A herd of burden-bearing animals, nowhere any indication of machines. He sucked in a deep breath—he was—he was in another world!

Merchants traversing a wilderness—a wilderness? Though he had been driven into desert the day before, the land through which he had earlier fled could not be termed a wilderness. It was overpopulated because there were too many war-poisoned areas where mankind could not live.

But from these strangers he gained a concept of vast, barren territory broken only by small, sparse strips of cultivation. Craike hurried. They were breaking camp. And the impression of an unpeopled land they had given him made him want to trail the caravan.

There was trouble! An attack—the caravan animals stampeded. Craike received a startlingly vivid mind picture of a hissing, lizard thing he could not identify. But it was danger on four scaled feet. He winced at the fear in those minds ahead. There was a vigor of mental broadcast in these men which amazed him. Now, the lizard thing had been killed. But the pack animals were scattered. It would take hours to find them. The exasperation of the master trader was as strong to Craike as if he stood before the man and heard his outburst of complaint.

The Esper smiled slowly. Here—handed to him by Fate—was his chance to gain the good will of the travelers. Breaking contact with the men, Craike cast around probe webs, as a fisher might cast a net. One panic-crazed animal and then another—he touched minds, soothed, brought to. bear his training. Within moments he heard the dull thud of hooves on the mossy ground, no longer pounding in a wild gallop. A shaggy mount, neither pony nor horse of his knowledge, but like in ways of each, its dull hide marked with a black stripe running from the root of shaggy mane to the base of its tail, came toward him, nickered questioningly. And then fell behind Craike, to be joined by another and another, as the Esper walked on—until he led the full train of runaways.

He met the first of the caravan men within a quarter of a mile and savored the fellow's astonishment at the sight. Yet, after the first surprise the man did not appear too amazed. He was short, dark of skin, a black beard of wiry, tightly curled hair clipped to a point thrusting out from his chin. Leggings covered his limbs, and he wore a sleeveless jerkin laced with thongs. This was belted by a broad strap gaudy with painted designs, from which hung a cross-hilted sword and a knife almost as long. A peaked cap of silky white fur was drawn far down so that a front flap shaded his eyes, and another, longer strip brushed his shoulders.

"Many thanks, Man of Power—" the words he spoke were in a clicking tongue, but Craike read their meaning mind to mind.

Then, as if puzzled on his closer examination of the Esper, the stranger frowned, his indecision slowly turning hostile.

"Outlaw! Begone, horned one!" The trader made a queer gesture with two fingers. "We pass free from your spells—"

"Be not so quick to pass judgment, Alfric—

The newcomer was the Master Trader. As his man, he wore leather, but there was a gemmed clasp on his belt. His sword and knife hilt were of precious metal, as was a badge fastened to the fore of his yellow and black fur head gear.

"This one is no local outlaw." The Master stood, feet apart, studying the fugitive Esper as if he were a burden pony offered as a bargain. "Would such use his power for our aid? If he is a horned one—he is unlike any I have seen."

"I am not what you think—" Craike said slowly, fitting his tongue to the others' alien speech.

The Master Trader nodded. "That is true. And you intend us no harm; does not the sun-stone so testify?" His hand went to the badge on his cap. "In this one is no evil, Alfric, rather does he come to us in aid. Have I not spoken the truth to you, stranger from the wastes?"

Craike broadcast good will as strongly as he could. And they must have been somewhat influenced by that.

"I feel—he *does* have the power!" Alfric burst forth.

"He has power," the Master corrected him. "But has he striven to possess our minds as he could do? We are still our own men. No—this is no renegade Black Hood. Come!"

He beckoned to Craike, and the Esper, the animals still behind him, followed on into the camp, where the rest of the men seized upon the ponies to adjust their packs.

The Master filled a bowl from the contents of a three-legged pot set in the coals of a dying fire. Craike gulped an excellent and filling stew. When he had done, the Master indicated himself.

"I am Kaluf of the Children of Noe, a far trader and trail master. Is it your will, Man of Power, to travel this road with us?"

Craike nodded. This might all be a wild dream. But he was willing to see it to its end. A day with the caravan, the chance to gather more information from the men here, should give him some inkling as to what had happened to him and where he now was.

II

Craike's day with the traders became two and then three. Esper talents were accepted by this company matter-of-factly, even asked in aid. And from the travelers he gained a picture of this world which he could not reconcile with his own.

His first impression of a large continent broken by widely separated holdings of a frontier type remained. In addition there was knowledge of a feudal government, petty lordlings holding title to lands over men of lesser birth.

Kaluf and his men had a mild contempt for their customers. Their own homeland lay to the southeast, where, in some coastal cities, they had built up an overseas trade, retaining its cream for their own consumption, peddling the rest in the barbarous hinterland. Craike, his facility in their click speech growing, asked questions which the Master answered freely enough.

"These inland men know no difference between Saludian silk and the weaving of the looms in our own Kormonian quarter." He shrugged in scorn at such ignorance. "Why should we offer Salud when we can get Salud prices for Kormon lengths and the buyer is satisfied? Maybe—if these lords ever finish their private quarrels and live at peace so that there is more travel and they themselves come to visit in Larud or the other cities of the Children of Noe, then shall we not make a profit on lesser goods"

"Do these Lords never try to raid your caravans?"

Kaluf laughed. "They tried that once or twice. Certainly they saw there was the profit in seizing a train and paying nothing. But we purchased trail rights from the Black Hoods, and there was no more trouble. How is it with you, Ka-rak? Have you lords in your land who dare to stand against the power of the Hooded Ones?''

Craike, taking a chance, nodded. And knew he had been right when some reserve in Kaluf vanished.

"That explains much, perhaps even why such a man of power as you should be adrift in the wilderness. But you need not fear in this country, your brothers hold complete rule—"

A colony of Espers! Craike tensed. Had he, through some weird chance, found here the long-hoped-for refuge of his kind? But where *was* here? His old bewilderment was lost in a shout from the fore of the train.

"The outpost has sighted us and raised the trade banner." Kaluf quickened pace. "Within the hour we'll be at the walls of Sampur. Illif!''

Craike made for the head of the line. Sampur, by the reckoning of the train, was a city of respectable size, the domain of a Lord Ludicar with whom Kaluf had had mutually satisfactory dealings for some time. And the Master anticipated a profitable stay. But the man who had ridden out to greet them was full of news.

Racially he was unlike the traders, taller, longer of arm. His bare chest was a thatch of blond-red hair as thick as a bear's pelt, long braids swung across his shoulders. A leather cap, reinforced with sewn rings of metal, was crammed down over his wealth of hair, and he carried a shield slung from his saddle pad. In addition to sword and knife, he nursed a spear in the crook of his arm, from the point of which trailed a banner strip of blue stuff.

"You come in good time, Master. The Hooded Ones have proclaimed a horning, and all the outbounders have gathered as witnesses. This is a good day for your trading, the Cloudy Ones have indeed favored you. But hurry, the Lord Ludicar is now riding in and soon there will be no good place from which to watch—"

Craike fell back. Punishment? An execution? No, not quite that. He wished he dared ask questions. Certainly the picture which had leaped into Kaluf's mind at the mention of "horning" could not be true!

Caution kept the Esper aloof. Sooner or later his alien origin must be noted, though Kaluf had supplied him with a fur cap, leather jerkin, and boots from the caravan surplus.

The ceremony was to take place just outside the main gate of the stockade, which formed the outer rampart of the town. A group of braided, ring-helmed warriors hemmed in a more imposing figure with a feather plume and a blue cloak, doubtless Lord Ludicar. Thronging at a respectful distance were the townfolk. But they were merely audience; the actors stood apart.

Craike's hands went to his head. The emotion which beat at him from that party brought the metallic taste of fear to his mouth, aroused his own memories. Then he steadied, probed. There was terror there, broadcast from two figures under guard. Just as an impact of Esper power came from the three black-hooded men who walked behind the captives.

He used his own talent carefully, dreading to attract the attention of the men in black. The townsfolk opened an aisle in their ranks, giving free passage to the open moorland and the green stretch of forest not too far away.

Fear—in one of those bound, stumbling prisoners it was abject, the same panic which had hounded Craike into the desert. But, though the other captive had no hope, there was a thick core of defiance, a desperate desire to strike back. And something in Craike arose to answer that.

Other men, wearing black jerkins and no hoods, crowded about the prisoners. When they stepped back Craike saw that the drab clothing of the two had been torn away. Shame, blotting out fear, came from the smaller captive. And there was no mistaking the sex of the curves that white body displayed. A girl, and very young. A violent shake of her head loosened her hair to flow, black and long, clothing her nakedness. Craike drew a deep breath as he had before that plunge into the canyon. Moving quickly he crouched behind a bush.

The Black Hoods went about their business with dispatch, each drawing in turn certain designs and lines in the dust of the road until they had created an intricate pattern about the feet of the prisoners.

A chant began in which the townspeople joined. The fear of the male captive was an almost visible cloud. But the outrage and anger of his feminine companion grew in relation to the chant, and Craike could sense her will battling against that of the assembly.

The watching Esper gasped. He could not be seeing what his eyes reported to his brain! The man was down on all fours, his legs and arms stretched, a mist clung to them, changed to red-brown hide. His head lengthened oddly, horns sprouted. No man, but an antlered stag stood there.

And the girl—?

Her transformation came more slowly. It began and then

faded. The power of the Black Hoods held her, fastening on her the form they visualized. She fought. But in the end a white doe sprang down the path to the forest, the stag leaping before her. They whipped past the bush where Craike had gone to earth, and he was able to see through the illusion. Not a red stag and a white doe, but a man and woman running for their lives, yet already knowing in their hearts there was no hope in their flight.

Craike, hardly knowing why he did it or who he could aid, followed, sure that mind touch would provide him with a guide.

He had reached the murky shadow of the trees when a sound rang from the town. At its summoning he missed a step before he realized it was directed against those he trailed and not himself. A hunting horn! So this world also had its hunted and its hunters. More than ever he determined to aid those who fled.

But it was not enough to just run blindly on the track of stag and doe. He lacked weapons. And his wits had not sufficed to save him in his own world. But there he had been conditioned against turning on his hunters, hampered, cruelly designed from birth to accept the quarry role. That was not true here.

Esper power—Craike licked dry lips. Illusions so well done they had almost enthralled him. Could illusion undo what illusion had done? Again the call of the horn, ominous in its clear tone, rang in his ears, set his pulses to pounding. The fear of those who fled was a cord, drawing him on.

But as he trotted among the trees Craike concentrated on his own illusion. It was not a white doe he pursued but the slim, young figure he had seen when they stripped away the clumsy stuff which had cloaked her, before she had shaken loose her hair veil. No doe, but a woman. She was not racing on four hooved feet, but running free on two, her hair blowing behind her. No doe, but a maid!

And in that moment, as he constructed that picture clearly, he contacted her in thought. It was like being dashed by sea-spray, cool, remote, very clean. And, as spray, the contact vanished in an instant, only to return.

"Who are you?"

"One who follows," he answered, holding to his picture of the running girl.

"Follow no more, you have done what was needful!" There was a burst of joy, so overwhelming a release from terror that it halted him. Then the cord between them broke.

Frantically Craike cast about seeking contact. There was only a dead wall. Lost, he put out a hand to the rough bark of the nearest tree. Wood things lurked here, them only did his mind touch. What did he do now?

His decision was made for him. He picked up a wave of panic again—spreading terror. But this was the fear of feathered and furred things. It came to him as ripples might run on a pool.

Fire! He caught the thought distorted by bird and beast mind. Fire which leaped from tree crown to tree crown, cutting a gash across the forest. Craike started on, taking the way west, away from the menace.

Once he called out as a deer flashed by him, only to know in the same moment that this was no illusion but an animal. Small creatures tunneled through the grass. A dog fox trotted, spared him a measuring gaze from slit eyes. Birds whirred, and behind them was the scent of smoke.

A mountain of flesh, muscle and fur snarled, reared to face him. But Craike had nothing to fear from any animal. He confronted the great red bear until it whined, shuffled its feet and plodded on. More and more creatures crossed his path or ran beside him for a space.

It was their instinct which brought them, and Craike, to a river. Wolves, red deer, bears, great cats, foxes and all the rest came down to the saving water. A cat spat at the flood, but leaped in to swim. Craike lingered on the bank. The smoke was thicker, more animals broke from the wood to take to the water. But the doe—where was she?

He probed, only to meet that blank. Then a spurt of flame ran up a dead sapling, advance scout of the furnace. He yelped as a floating cinder stung his skin and took to the water. But he did not cross, rather did he swim upstream, hoping to pass the flank of the fire and pick up the missing trail again.

III

Smoke cleared as Craike trod water. He was beyond the path of the fire, but not out of danger. For the current against which he had fought his way beat here through an archway of masonry. Flanking that arch were two squat towers. As an erection it was far more ambitious than anything he had seen during his brief glimpse of Sampur. Yet, as he eyed it more closely, he could see it was a ruin. There were gaps in the narrow span across the river, a green bush sprouted from the summit of the far tower.

Craike came ashore, winning his way up the steep bank by handholds of vine and bush no alert castellan would have allowed to grow. As he reached a terrace of cobbles stippled with bunches of coarse grass, a sweetish scent of decay drew him around the base of the tower to look down at a broad ledge extending into the river. Piled on it were small baskets and bowls, some so rotted that only outlines were visible. Others new and all filled with moldering food stuffs. But those who left such offerings must have known that the tower was deserted.

Puzzled, Craike went back to the building. The stone was undressed, yet the huge blocks which formed its base were fitted together with such precision that he suspected he could not force the thin blade of a pocket knife into any crack. There had been no effort at ornamentation, at any lightening of the impression of sullen, brute force.

Wood, split and insect-bored, formed a door. As he put his hand to it Craike discovered the guardian the long-ago owners of the fortress had left in possession. His hands went to his head, the blow he felt might have been physical. Out of the stronghold before him came such a wave of utter terror and dark promise as to force him back. But no farther than the edge of the paved square about the building's foundation.

Grimly he faced that challenge, knowing it for stored emotion and not the weapon of an active will. He had his own defense against such a formless enemy. Breaking a dead branch from a bush, he twisted about it wisps of the sun-bleached grass until he had a torch of sorts. A piece of smoldering tinder blown from the fire gave him a light.

Craike put his shoulder to the powdery remnants of the door, bursting it wide. Light against dark. What lurked there was nourished by dark, fed upon the night fears of his species.

A round room, bare except for some crumbling sticks of wood, a series of steps jutting out from the wall to curl about and vanish above. Craike made no move toward further exploration, holding up the torch, seeking to see the real, not the threat of this place.

Those who had built it possessed Esper talents. And they had used that power for twisted purposes. He read terror and despair trapped here by the castellans' art, horror, an abiding fog of what his race considered evil.

Tentatively Craike began to fight. With the torch he brought light and heat into the dark and cold. Now he struggled to offer peace. Just as he had pictured a girl in flight in place of the doe, so did he now force upon those invisible clouds of stored suffering calm and hope. The gray window slits in the stone were uncurtained to the streaming sunlight.

Those who had set that guardian had not intended it to hold

against an Esper. Once he began the task, Craike found the opposition melting. The terror seeped as if it sank into the floor wave by wave. He stood in a room which smelt of damp and, more faintly, of the rotting food piled below its window slits; but now it was only an empty shell.

Craike was tired, drained by his effort. And he was puzzled. Why had he fought for this? Of what importance to him was the cleansing of a ruined tower?

Though to stay here had certain advantages. It had been erected to control river traffic. Though that did not matter for the present, just now he needed food more—

He went back to the rock of offerings, treading a wary path through the disintegrating stuff. Close to the edge he came upon a clay bowl containing coarsely ground grain and, beside it, a basket of wilted leaves filled with overripe berries. He ate in gulps.

Grass made him a matted bed in the tower, and he kindled a fire. As he squatted before its flames, he sent out a questing thought. A big cat drank from the river. Craike shuddered away from that contact with blood lust. A night-hunting bird provided a trace of awareness. There were small rovers and hunters. But nothing human.

Tired as he was Craike could not sleep. There was the restless sensation of some demand about to be made, some task waiting. From time to time he fed the fire. Towards morning he dozed, to snap awake. A night creature drinking, a screech overhead. He heard the flutter of wings echo hollowly through the tower.

Beyond—darkness—blank, that curious blank which had fallen between him and the girl. Craike got to his feet eagerly. That blank could be traced.

Outside it was raining, and fog hung in murky bands among the river hollows. The blank spot veered. Craike started after it. The tower pavement became a trace of old road he followed, weaving through the fog.

There was the sour smell of old smoke. Charred wood, black muck clung to his feet. But his guide point was now stationary as the ground rose, studded with outcrops of rock. So Craike came to a mesa jutting up into a steel gray sky.

He hitched his way up by way of a long-ago slide. The rain had stopped, but there was no hint of sun. And he was unprepared for the greeting he met as he topped the lip of a small plateau.

A violent blow on the shoulder whirled him halfway around, and only by a finger's width did he escape a fall. A cry echoed his, and the blank broke. She was there.

Moving slowly, using the same technique he knew to sooth frightened animals, Craike raised himself again. The pain in his shoulder was sharp when he tried to put much weight upon his left arm. But now he saw her clearly.

She sat cross-legged, a boulder at her back, her hair a rippling cloud of black through which her hands and arms shown starkly white. She had the thin, three-cornered face of a child who has known much harshness; there was no beauty there—the flesh had been too much worn by spirit. Only her eyes, watchful-wary as those of a feline, considered him bleakly. In spite of his beam of good will, she gave him no welcome. And she tossed another stone from hand to hand with the ease of one who had already scored with such a weapon.

"Who are you?" She spoke aloud.

"He who followed you." Craike fingered the bruise wound on his shoulder, not taking his eyes from hers.

"You are no Black Hood." It was a statement not a question. "But you, also, have been horned." Another statement.

Craike nodded. In his own time and place he had indeed been "horned."

Just as her thrown stone had struck without warning, so came her second attack. There was a hiss. Within striking distance a snake flickered a forked tongue.

Craike did not give ground. The snake head expanded, fur ran over it; there were legs, a plume of tail fluffed. A dog fox yapped once at the girl and vanished. Craike read her recoil, the first faint uncertainty.

"You have the power!"

"I have power," he corrected her.

But her attention was no longer his. She was listening to something he could hear with neither ear nor mind. Then she ran to the edge of the mesa. He followed.

On this side the country was more rolling, and across it now came mounted men moving in and out of mist pools. They rode in silence, and over them was the same blanketing of thought as the girl had used.

Craike glanced about. There were loose stones, and the girl had already proven her marksmanship with such. But they would be no answer to the weapons the others had. Only flight was no solution either.

The girl sobbed once, a broken cry so unlike the iron will she had shown that Craike started. She leaned perilously over the drop, staring down at the horsemen.

Then her hands moved with desperate speed. She tore hairs from her head, twisted and snarled them between her fingers, breathed on them, looped them with a stone for weight, casting the tangled mass out to land before the riders.

The mist curled, took on substance. Where there had been only rock there was now a thicket of thorn, so knotted that no fleshed creature could push through it. The hunters paused, then they rode on again, but now they drove a reeling, naked man, a man kept going by a lashing whip whenever he faltered.

Again the girl sobbed, burying her face in her hands. The wretched captive reached the thorn barrier. Under his touch it melted. He stood there, weaving drunkenly.

A whip sang. He went to his knees under its cut, a trapped animal's wail on the wind. Slowly, with a blind seeking, his hands went out to small stones about him. He gathered them, spread them anew in patterns. The girl had raised her head, watched dry-eyed, but seething with hate and the need to strike back. But she did not move.

Craike dared lay a hand on her narrow shoulder, feeling through her hair the chill of her skin, while the hair itself clung to his fingers as if it had the will to smother and imprison. He tried to pull her away, but he could not move her.

The naked man crouched in the midst of his pattern, and now he chanted, a compelling call the girl could not understand. She wrenched free of Craike's hold. But as she went she spared a thought for the man who had tried to save her. She struck out, her fist landing on the stone bruise. Pain sent him reeling back as she went over the rim of the mesa, her face a mask which no friend nor enemy might read. But there was no resignation in her eyes as she was forced to the meeting below.

IV

By the time Craike reached a vantage point the girl stood in the center of the stone ring. Outside crouched the man, his head on his knees. She looked down at him, no emotion showing on her wan face. Then she dropped her hand on his thatch of wild hair. He jerked under that touch as he had under the whip which had printed the scarlet weals across his back and loins. But he raised his head, and from his throat came a beast's mournful howl. At her gesture he was quiet, edging closer to her as if seeking some easement of his suffering.

The Black Hoods drew in. Craike's probe could make nothing of them. But they could not hide their emotions as well as they concealed their thoughts. And the Esper recoiled from the avid blood lust which lapped at the two by the cliff.

A semicircle of the black-jerkined retainers moved too. And the man who had led them lay on the earth now, moaning softly. But the girl faced them, head unbowed. Craike wanted to aid her. Had he time to climb down the cliff? Clenching his teeth against the pain movement brought to his shoulder, the Esper went back, holding a mind shield as a frail protection.

Directly before him now was one of the guards. His mount caught Craike's scent, stirred uneasily, until the quieting thought of the Esper held it steady. Craike had never been forced into such action as he had these past few days; he had no real plan now, it must depend upon chance and fortune.

As if the force of her enemies' wills had slammed her back against the rock, the girl was braced by the cliff wall, a black-and-white figure.

Mist swirled, took on half substance of a monstrous form, was swept away in an instant. A clump of dried grass broke into flame, sending the ponies stamping and snorting. It was gone, leaving a black smudge on the earth. Illusions, realities—Craike watched. This was so far beyond his own experience that he could hardly comprehend the lightning moves of mind against mind. But he sensed these others could beat down the girl's resistance at any moment they desired, that her last futile struggles were being relished by those who decreed this as part of her punishment.

And Craike, who had believed that he could never hate more than he had when he had been touched by the fawning "hound" of the mob, was filled with a rage tempered into a chill of steel determination.

The girl went to her knees, still clutching her hair about her, facing her tormenters with her still-held defiance. Now the man who had wrought the magic which had drawn her there crawled, all humanity gone out of him, wriggling on his belly back to his captors.

Two of the guards jerked him up. He hung limp in their hands, his mouth open in an idiot's grin. Callously, as he might tread upon a worm, the nearest Black Hood waved a hand. A metal axe flashed, and there came the dull sound of cracking

bone. The guards pitched the body from them so that the blood-
ied head almost touched the girl.

She writhed, a last frenzied attempt to break the force which
pinned her. Without haste the guards advanced. One caught at
her hair, pulling it tautly from her head.

Craike shivered. The thrill of her agony reached him. This
was what she feared most, fought so long to prevent. If ever he
must move now. And that part of his brain which had been
feverishly seeking a plan went into action.

Ponies pawed, reared, went wild with panic. One of the Black
Hoods swung around to face the terrorized animals. But his own
mount struck out with teeth and hooves. Guardsmen shouted,
and above their cries arose the shrill squeals of the animals.

Craike stood his ground, keeping the ponies in terror-stricken
revolt. The guard who held the handful of hair slashed at the
tress with his knife, severing it at a palm's distance away from
her head. But in that same movement she moved. The knife
leaped free from the man's grasp, while the severed hair twined
itself about his hands, binding them until the blade buried itself
in his throat; and he went down.

One of the Black Hoods was also finished, tramped into a
feebly squirming thing by the ponies. Then from the ground
burst a sheet of flame which split into balls, drifting through the
air or rolling along the earth.

The Esper wet his lips—that was not his doing! He did not
have to feed the panic of the animals now; they were truly mad.
The girl was on her feet. Before his thought could reach her she
was gone, swallowed up in a mist which arose to blanket the
fireballs. Once more she cut their contact; there was a blank void
where she had been.

Now the fog thickened. Through it came one of the ponies,
foam dripping from its blunt muzzle. It bore down on Craike,
eyes gleaming red through a tangled forelock. With a scream it
reared.

Craike's hand grabbed a handful of mane as he leaped, avoiding teeth and hooves. Then, somehow, he gained the pad saddle,
locking his fingers in the coarse hair, striving to hold his seat
against the bucking enraged beast. It broke into a run, and the
Esper plastered himself to the heaving body. For the moment he
made no attempt at mind control.

Behind, the Black Hoods came out of their stunned bewilderment. They were questing feverishly, and he had to concentrate
on holding his shield against them. A pony fleeing in terror

would not excite them; a pony under control would provide them with a target.

Later he could circle about and try to pick up the trail of the witch girl. Flushed with success, Craike was sure he could provide her with a rear guard no Black Hood could pass.

The fog was thick, and the pace of the pony began to slacken. Once or twice it bucked halfheartedly, giving up when it could not dislodge its rider. Craike drew his fingers in slow, soothing sweeps down the sweating curve of its neck.

There were no more trees about, and the unshod hooves pounded on sand. They were in a dried watercourse, and Craike did not try to turn from that path. Then his luck ran out.

What he had ignorantly supposed to be a rock ahead heaved up seven feet or more. A red mouth opened in a great roar. He had believed the bear he had seen fleeing the fire to be a giant, but this one was a nightmare monster.

The pony screamed with an almost human note of despair and whirled. Craike gripped the mane again and tried to mind-control the bear. But his surprise had lasted seconds too long. A vast clawed paw struck, ripping across pony hide and human thigh. Then Craike could only cling to the running mount.

How long he was able to keep his seat he never knew. Then he slipped; there was a throb of pain as he struck the ground, to be followed by blackness.

It was dusk when he opened his eyes, fighting agony in his head, his leg. But later there was moonlight. And that silver-white spotlighted a waiting shape. Green slits of eyes regarded him remotely. Dizzily he made contact.

A wolf—hungry—yet with a wariness which recognized in the prone man an enemy. Craike fought for control. The wolf whined, then it arose, its prick ears sharp-cut in the moonlight, its nose questing for the scent of other, less disturbing prey, and it was gone.

Craike edged up against a boulder and sorted out sounds. The rush of water. He moved a paper-dry tongue over cracked lips. Water to drink—to wash his wounds—water!

With a groan Craike worked his way to his feet, holding fast to the top of the rock when his torn leg threatened to buckle under him. The same inner drive which had kept him going through the desert brought him down to the river.

By sunrise he was seeking a shelter, wanting to lie up, as might the wolf, in some secret cave until his wounds healed. All chance of finding the witch girl was lost. But as he crawled along the shingle, leaning on a staff he had found in drift wood, he kept alert for any trace of the Black Hoods.

It was midmorning on the second day that his snail's progress brought him to the river towers. And it took another hour for him to reach the terrace. Gaunt and worn, his empty stomach complaining, he wanted nothing more than to sink down in the nest of grass he had gathered and cease to struggle.

Perhaps he might have done so had not a click-clack of sound from the river put him on the defensive, his staff now a club. But these were not Black Hoods. Farmers, local men bound for the market of Sampur with products of their fields. They had paused, were making a choice among the least appetizing of their wares for a tribute to be offered to the tower demon.

Craike hitched stiffly to a point where he could witness that sacrifice. But when he assessed the contents of their dugout, the heaping basket piled between the paddlers, his hunger took command.

Fob off a demon with a handful of meal and a too-ripe melon, would they? With three haunches of cured meat and all that other stuff on board!

Craike voiced a roar which could have done credit to the red bear, a roar which altered into a demand for meat. The paddlers nearly lost control of their crude craft. But one reached for a haunch and threw it blindly on the refuse-covered rock, while his companion added a basket of small cakes into the bargain.

"Enough, little men—" Craike's voice boomed hollowly. "You may pass free."

They needed no urging, they did not look at those threatening towers as their paddles bit into the water, adding impetus to the pull of the current.

Craike watched them well out of sight before he made a slow descent to the rock. The effort he was forced to expend warned him that a second such trip might be impossible, and he inched back to the terrace dragging both meat and cakes.

The cured haunch he worried into strips, using his pocket knife. It was tough, not too pleasant to the taste and unsalted. But he found it more appetizing than the cakes of baked meal. With this supply he could afford to lie up and favor his leg.

About the claw rents the flesh was red and puffed. Craike had no dressing but river water and the leaves he had tied over the tears. Sampur was beyond his power to reach, and to contact men traveling on the river would only bring the Black Hoods.

He lay in his grass nest and tried to sort out the events of the past few days. This was a land in which Esper powers were allowed free range. He had no idea of how he had come here, but it seemed to his feverish mind that he had been granted another chance—one in which the scales of justice were more balanced in his favor. If he could only find the girl, learn from her—

Tentatively, without real hope, he sent out a questing thought. Nothing. He moved impatiently, wrenching his leg, so that his head swam with pain. Throat and mouth were dry. The lap of water sounded in his ears. Water—he was thirsty again. But he could not crawl downslope and up once more. Craike closed his eyes wearily.

V

Craike's memory of the hours which followed thereafter was dim. *Had* he seen a demon in the doorway? A slavering wolf? A red bear?

Then the girl sat there, cross-legged as he had seen her on the mesa, her cloak of hair about her. A hand emerged from the cloak to lay wood on the fire. Illusions?

But would an illusion turn to him, put firm, cool fingers upon his wound, somehow driving out by touch the pain and fire which burned there? Would an illusion raise his head, cradling it against her so that the soft silk of her hair lay against his cheek and throat, urging on him liquid out of a crude bowl? Would an illusion sing softly to herself while she drew a fish-bone comb back and forth through her hair, until the song and the sweep of the comb lulled him into a sleep so deep that no dream walked there?

He awoke, clear-headed. Yet that last illusion lingered. For she came from the sun-drenched world without, a bowl of fruit in her hand. For a long moment she stood gazing at him searchingly. But when he tried mind contact, he met that wall. Not unheeding—but a refusal to answer.

Her hair was now braided. But about her face the lock which the guardsman had shorn made an untidy fringe. While around her thin body was a strip of hide, purposefully arranged to mask all femininity.

"So," Craike spoke rustily, "you are real—"

She did not smile. "I am real. You no longer dream with fever."

"Who are you?" He asked the first of his long hoarded questions.

"I am Takya." She added nothing to that.

"You are Takya, and you are a witch—"

"I am Takya, and I have the power." It was an assertion of fact rather than agreement.

She settled in her favorite cross-legged position, selected a fruit from her bowl and examined it with the interest of a housewife who has shopped for supplies on a limited budget. Then she placed it in his hand before she chose another for herself. He bit into the plumlike globe. If she would only drop her barrier, let him communicate in the way which was fuller and deeper than speech.

"You also have the power—"

Craike decided to be no more communicative than she. He replied to that with a curt nod.

"Yet you have not been horned—"

"Not as you have been. But in my own world, yes."

"Your world?" Her eyes held some of the feral glow of a hunting cat's. "What world, and why were you horned there, man of sand and ash power?"

Without knowing why Craike related the events of the days past. Takya listened, he was certain, with more than ears alone. She picked up a stick from the pile of firewood and drew patterns in the sand and ash, patterns which had something to do with her listening.

"Your power was great enough to break a world wall." She snapped the stick between two fingers, threw it into the flames.

"A world wall?"

"We of the power have long known that different worlds lie together in such a fashion." She held up her hand with the fingers tight lying one to another. "Sometimes there comes a moment when two touch so closely that the power can carry one through if at that moment there is a desperate need for escape. But those places of meeting cannot be readily found, and the moment of their touch can lie only for an instant. Have you in your world no reports of men and women who have vanished almost in sight of their fellows?"

Remembering old tales, he nodded.

"I have seen a summoning from another world," she continued with a shiver, running both hands down the length of her braids as if so she evoked a shield for both mind and body. "To summon so is a great evil, for no man can hold in check the power of something alien. You broke the will of the Black Hoods when I was a beast running from their hunt. When I made the serpent to warn you off, you changed it into a fox. And when the Black Hoods would have shorn my power''—she looped the braids about her wrists, caressing, treasuring them against her small breasts—''again you broke their hold and set me free for a second time. But this you could not have done had you been born into this world, for our power must follow set laws. Yours lies outside our patterns and can cut across those laws—even as the knife cut this—'' She touched the rough patch of hair at her temple.

''Follow patterns? Then it was those patterns in stone which drew you down from the mesa?''

''Yes. Takyi, my womb-brother, whom they slew there, was blood of my blood, bone of my bone. When they crushed him, then they could use him to draw me, and I could not resist. But in the slaying of his husk they freed me—to their great torment, as Tousuth shall discover in time.''

''Tell me of this country. Who are the Black Hoods and why did they horn you? Are you not of their breed since you have the power?''

But Tayka did not answer at once in words. Nor did she, as he had hoped, lower her mind barrier.

Her fingers now held one long hair she had pulled from her head, and this she began to weave in and out, swiftly, intricately, in a complicated series of loops and crossed strands. After a moment Craike did not see the white fingers, nor the black hair they passed in loops from one to another. Rather did he see the pictures she wrought in her weaving.

A wide land, largely wilderness. The impressions he had gathered from Kaluf and the traders crystalized into vivid life. Small holdings here and there, ruled by petty lords, new settlements carved out by a scattered people moving up from the south in great wheeled wains, bringing flocks and herds, their carefully treasured seed. Stopping here and there for a season to sow and reap, until they decided upon a site for their final rooting. Tiny city-states, protected by the Black Hoods—the Esper born who purposefully interbred their own gifted stock, keeping their children apart.

Takya and her brother coming, as was sometimes—if rarely— true, from the common people. Carefully watched by the Black Hoods. Then discovered to be a new mutation, condemned as such to be used for experimentation. But for a while protected by the local lord who wanted Takya.

But he might not take her unwilling. For the power that was

hers as a virgin was wholly rift from her should she be forced. And he had wanted that power, obedient to him, as a check upon the monopoly of the Black Hoods. So with some patience he had set himself to a peaceful wooing. But the Black Hoods had moved first.

Had they accomplished her taking, the end they had intended for her was not as easy as death. And she wove a picture of it, with all its degradation and shame stark and open, for Craike's seeing.

"Then the Hooded Ones are evil?"

"Not wholly." She untwisted the hair and put it with care into the fire. "They do much good, and without them people would suffer. But I, Takya, am different. And after me, when I mate, there will be others also different. How different we are not yet sure. The Hooded Ones want no change, by their thinking that means disaster. So they would use me to their own purposes. Only I, Tayka, shall not be so used!"

"No, you shall not." The vehemence of his own outburst startled him. Craike wanted nothing so much at that moment as to come to grips with the Black Hoods, who had planned this systematic hunt.

"What will you do now?" he asked more calmly, wishing she would share her thoughts with him.

"This is a strong place. Did you cleanse it?"

He nodded impatiently.

"So I thought. That was also a task one born to this world might not have performed. But those who pass are not yet aware of the cleansing. They will not trouble us, but pay tribute."

Craike found her complacency irritating. To lie up here and live on the offerings of river travelers did not appeal to him.

"This stone piling is older work than Sampur and much better," she continued. "It must have been a fortress for some of those forgotten ones who held lands and then vanished long before we came from the south. If it is repaired no lord of this district would have so good a roof."

"Two of us to rebuild it?" he laughed.

"Two of us—working thus."

A block of stone, the size of a brick, which had fallen from the sill of one of the needle-narrow windows, arose slowly in the air, settled into the space from which it had tumbled. Illusion or reality? Craike got to his feet and lurched to the window. His hand fell upon the stone, which moved easily in his grasp. He took it out, weighed it, and then gently returned it to its place. Not illusion.

"But illusion too—if need be." There was, for the first time, a warmth not of amusement in her tone. "Look on your tower, river lord!"

He limped to the door. Outside it was warm, sunny, but it was a site of ruins. Then the picture changed. Brown drifts of grass vanished from the terrace, the fallen stone was all in place. A hard-faced sentry stood wary-eyed on a repaired river arch. Another guardsman led out ponies saddle-padded and ready, other men were about garrison tasks.

Craike grinned. The sentry on the arch lost his helm, his jerkin. He now wore the tight tunic of the Security Police, his spear was a gas rifle. The ponies misted, and in their place a speedster sat on the stone. He heard her laugh.

"*Your* guard, *your* traveling machine. But how grim, ugly. This is better!"

Guards, machine, all were swept away. Craike caught his breath at the sight of delicate winged creatures dancing in the air, displaying a joy of life he had never known. Fawns, little people of the wild, came to mingle with such shapes of beauty and desire that at last he turned his head away.

"Illusion." Her voice was hard, mocking.

But Craike could not believe that what he had seen had been born from hardness and mockery.

"All illusions. We shall be better now with warriors. As for plans, can you suggest any better than to remain here and take what fortune sends—for a space?"

"Those winged dancers—where?"

"Illusions!" she returned harshly. "But such games tire one. I do not think we shall conjure up any garrison before they are needed. Come, do not tear open those wounds of yours anew, for healing is no illusion and drains one even more of the power."

The clawed furrows were healing cleanly, though he would bear their scars for life. He hobbled back to the grass bed and dropped upon it, but regretted the erasure of the sprites she had shown him.

Once he was safely in place, Takya left with the curt explanation she had things to do. But Craike was restless, too much so to remain long inside the tower. He waited until she had gone and then, with the aid of his staff, climbed to the end of the span above the river. From here the twin tower on the other bank looked the same as the one from which he had come. Whether it was also haunted Craike did not know. But, as he looked about, he could see the sense of Tayka's suggestion. A few illusion sentries would discourage any ordinary intrusion.

Takya's housekeeping had changed the rock of offerings. All the rotting debris was gone and none of the odor of decay now offended the nostrils at a change of wind. But at best it was a most uncertain source of supply. There could not be too many farms up river, nor too many travelers taking the water away.

As if to refute that, his Esper sense brought him sudden warning of strangers beyond the upper bend. But, Craike sensed, these were no peasants bound for the market at Sampur. Fear, pain, anger, such emotions heralded their coming. There were three, and one was hurt. But they were not Esper, nor did they serve the Black Hoods. Though they were, or had been, fighting men.

A brutal journey over the mountains where they had lost comrades, the finding of this river, the theft of the dugout they now used so expertly—it was all there for him to read. And beneath that something else, which, when he found it, gave Craike a quick decision in their favor—a deep hatred of the Black Hoods! Outlaws, very close to despair, keeping on a hopeless trail because it was not in them to surrender.

Craike contacted them subtly. They must not think they were heading into an Esper trap! Plant a little hope, a faint suggestion that there was a safe camping place ahead, that was all he could do at present. But so he drew them on.

"No!" A ruthless order cut across his line of contact, striking at the delicate thread with which he was playing the strangers in. But Craike stood firm. "Yes, yes, and yes!"

He was on guard instantly. Takya, mistress of illusion as she had proved herself to be, might act. But surprisingly she did not. The dugout came into view, carried more by the current than the efforts of its crew. One lay full-length in the bottom, while the bow paddler had slumped forward. But the man in the stern was bringing them in. And Craike strengthened his invisible, unheard invitation to urge him on.

VI

But Takya had not yet begun to fight. As the dugout swung in toward the offering ledge one of the Black Hoods' guardsmen appeared there, his drawn sword taking fire from the sun. The fugitive steersman faltered until the current drew his craft on.

Craike caught the full force of the stranger's despair, all the keener for the hope of moments before. The Esper irritation against Takya flared into anger.

He made the illusion reel back, hands clutching at his breast from which protruded the shaft of an arrow. Craike had seen no bows here, but it was a weapon to suit this world. And this should prove to Takya he meant what he had said.

The steersman was hidden as the dugout passed under the arch. There was a scrap of beach, the same to which Craike had swum on his first coming. He urged the man to that, beaming good will.

But the paddler was almost done, and neither of his companions could aid him. He drove the crude craft to the bank, and its bow grated on the rough gravel. Then he crawled over the bodies of the other two and fell rather than jumped ashore, turning to pull up the canoe as best he could.

Craike started down. But he might have known that Takya was not so easily defeated. Though they maintained an alliance of sorts she accepted no order from him.

A brand was teleported from the tower fire, striking spearwise in the dry brush along the slope. Craike's mouth set. He tried no more arguments. They had already tested power against power, and he was willing to so battle again. But this was not the time. However, the fire was no illusion, and he could not fight it, crippled as he was. Or could he?

It was not spreading too fast—though Takya might spur it by the forces at her command. Now—there was just the spot! Craike steadied himself against a mound of fallen masonry and swept out his staff, dislodging a boulder and a shower of gravel. He had guessed right. The stone rolled to crush out the brand, and the gravel he continued to push after it smothered the creeping flames.

Red tongues dashed spitefully high in a sheet of flame, and Craike laughed. *That* was illusion. She was angry. He produced a giant pail in the air, tilted it forward, splashed its contents into the heart of that conflagration. He felt the lash of her rage, standing under it unmoved. So might she bring her own breed to heel, but she would learn he was not of that ilk.

"Holla!" That call was no illusion, it begged help.

Craike picked a careful path downslope until he saw the dugout and the man who had landed it. The Esper waved an invitation, and at his summons the fugitive covered the distance between them.

He was a big man of the same brawny race as those of Sampur, his braids of reddish hair hanging well below his wide shoulders. There was the raw line of a half-healed wound down the angle of his jaw, and his sunken eyes were very tired. For a moment he stood downslope from Craike, his hands on his hips, his head back, measuring the Esper with the shrewdness of a canny officer who had long known how to judge and handle raw levies.

"I am Jorik of the Eagles' Tower." The statement was made with the same confidence as the announcement of rank might have come from one of the petty lords. "Though," he shrugged, "the Eagles' Tower stands no more with one stone upon the other. You have a stout lair here—" He hesitated before he concluded, "—friend."

"I am Craike," the Esper answered as simply, "and I am also one who has run from enemies. This lair is an old one, though still useful."

"Might the enemies from whom you run wear black hoods?" countered Jorik. "It seems to me that things I have just seen here have the stink of that about them."

"You are right. I am no friend to the Black Hoods."

"But you have the power—"

"I have power." Craike tried to make the distinction clear. "You are welcome, Jorik. So all are welcome here who are no friends to Black Hoods."

The big warrior shrugged. "We can no longer run. If the time has come to make a last stand, this is as good a place as any. My men are done." He glanced back at the two in the dugout. "They are good men, but we were pressed when they caught us in the upper pass. Once there were twenty hands of us." He held up his fist and spread the fingers wide for counting. "They drew us out of the tower with their sorcerers' tricks, and then put us to the hunt."

"Why did they wish to make an end to you?"

Jorik laughed shortly. "They dislike those who will not fit into their neat patterns. We are free mountain men, and no Black Hood helped us win the Eagles' Tower; none aided us to hunt. When we took our furs down to the valley they wanted to levy tribute. But what spell of theirs trapped the beasts in our deadfalls, or brought them to our spears? We pay not for what we have not bought. Neither would we have made war on them. Only, when we spoke out and said it so, there were others who were encouraged to do likewise, and the Black Hoods must put an end to us before their rule was broken. So they did."

"But they did not get all of you," Craike pointed out. "Can you bring your men up to the tower? I have been hurt and cannot walk without support or I would lend you a hand."

"We will come." Jorik returned to the dugout. Water was splashed vigorously into the face of the man in the bow, arousing him to crawl ashore. Then the leader of the fugitives swung the third man out of the craft and over his shoulder in a practiced carry.

When Craike had seen the unconscious man established on his own grass bed, he stirred up the fire and set out food while Jorik returned to the dugout to bring in their gear.

Neither of the other men was of the same size as their leader. The one who lay limp, his breath fluttering between his slack lips, was young, hardly out of boyhood, his thin frame showing bones rather than muscled flesh under the rags of clothing. The other was short, dark-skinned, akin by race to Kaluf's men, his jaw sprouting a curly beard. He measured Craike with suspicious glances from beneath lowered red lids, turning that study to the walls about him and the unknown reaches at the head of the stair.

Craike did not try mind touch. These men were rightly suspicious of Esper arts. But he did attempt to reach Takya, only to meet that nothingness with which she cloaked her actions. Craike was disturbed. Surely now that she was convinced he was determined to give the harborage to the fugitives, she would not oppose him. They had nothing to fear from Jorik and his men, but rather would gain by joining forces.

Until his wounds were entirely healed he could not go far. And without weapons they would have to rely solely upon Esper powers for defense. Having witnessed the efficiency of the Hooded Ones' attack, Craike doubted a victory in any engagement to which those masters came fully prepared. He had managed to upset their spells merely because they had not known of his existence. But the next time he would have no such advantage.

On the other hand the tower could be defended by force of arms. With bows—Craike savored the idea of archers giving a Hooded force a devastating surprise. The traders had had no such arm, as sophisticated as they were. And he had seen none among the warriors of Sampur. He'd have to ask Jorik if such were known.

In the meantime he sat among his guests, watching Jorik feed the semiconscious boy with soft fruit pulp and the other man wolf down dried meat. When the latter had done, he hitched himself closer to the fire and jerked a thumb at his chest.

"Zackuth," he identified himself.

"From Larud?" Craike named the only city of Kaluf's people he could remember.

The dark man's momentary surprise had no element of suspicion. "What do you know of the Children of Noe, stranger?"

"I journeyed the plains with one called Kaluf, a Master Trader of Larud."

"A fat man who laughs much and wears a falcon plume in his cap?"

"Not so." Craike allowed a measure of chill to ice his reply. "The Kaluf who led this caravan was a lean man who knew the edge of a good blade from its hilt. As for cap ornaments—he had a red stone to the fore of his. Also he swore by the Eyes of the Lady Lor."

Zackuth gave a great bray of laughter. "You are no stream fish to be easily hooked, are you, tower dweller? I am not of Larud, but I know Kaluf, and those who travel in his company do not wear one badge one day and another the next. But, by the looks of you, you have fared little better than we lately. Has Kaluf also fallen upon evil luck?"

"I traveled safely with his caravan to the gates of Sampur. How it fared with him thereafter I cannot tell you."

Jorik grinned and settled his patient back on the bed. "I believe you must have parted company in haste, Lord Ka-rak?"

Craike answered that with the truth. "There were two who were horned. I followed them to give what aid I could."

Jorik scowled, and Zackuth spat into the fire.

"We were not horned; we have no power," the latter remarked. "But they have other tricks to play. So you came here?"

"I was clawed by a bear," Craike supplied a meager portion of his adventures, "and came here to lie up until I can heal me of that hurt."

"This is a snug hole." Jorik was appreciative. "But how got you such eating?" He popped half a fruit into his mouth and licked his juicy fingers. "This is no wilderness feeding."

"The tower is thought to be demon-haunted. Those taking passage downstream leave tribute."

Zackuth slapped his knee. "The Gods of the Waves are good to you, Lord Ka-rak, that you should stumble into such fortune. There is more than one kind of demon for the haunting towers. How say you, Lord Jorik?"

"That we have also come into luck at last, since Lord Ka-rak has made us free of this hold. But perhaps you have some other thought in your head?" He spoke to the Esper.

Craike shrugged. "What the clouds decree shall fall as rain or snow," he quoted a saying of the caravan men.

It was close to sunset, and he was worried about Takya. He could not believe that she had gone permanently. And yet, if she returned, what would happen? He had been careful not to use Esper powers. Takya would have no such compunctions.

He could not analyze his feelings about her. She disturbed him, awoke emotions he refused to face. There was a certain way she had of looking sidewise— But her calm assumption of superiority pricked beneath his surface armor. And the antagonism fretted against the feeling which had drawn him after her from the gates of Sampur. Once again he sent out a quest-thought and, to his surprise, was answered.

"They must go!"

"They are outlaws, even as we. One is ill, the others worn with long running. But they stood against the Black Hoods. As such they have a claim on roof, fire and food from us."

"They are not as we!" Again arrogance. "Send them or I shall drive them. I have the power—"

"Perhaps you have the power, but so do I!" He put all the assurance he could muster into that. "I tell you, no better thing could happen than for us to give these men aid. They are proven fighters—"

"Swords cannot stand against the power!"

Craike smiled. His plans were beginning to move even as he carried on this voiceless argument. "Not swords, no, Takya. But all fighting is not done with swords nor spears. Nor with the power either. Can a Black Hood think death to his enemy when he himself is dead, killed from a distance, and not by mind power his fellows could trace and be armored against?"

He had caught her attention. She was acute enough to know that he was not playing with words, that he knew of what he spoke. Quickly he built upon that spark of interest. "Remember how your illusion guard died upon the offering rock when you would warn off these men?"

"By a small spear." She was contemptuous again.

"Not so." He shaped a picture of an arrow and then of an archer releasing it from the bow cord, of its speeding true across the river to strike deep into the throat of an unsuspecting Black Hood.

"You have the secret of this weapon?"

"I do. And five such arms are better than two, is that not the truth?"

She yielded a fraction. "I will return. But they will not like that."

"If you return, they will welcome you. These are no hunters of witch maidens—" he began, only to be disconcerted by her obvious amusement. Somehow he had lost his short advantage over her. Yet she did not break contact.

"Ka-rak, you are very foolish. No, these will not try to mate with me, not even if I willed it so. As you will see. Does the eagle mate with the hunting cat? But they will be slow to trust me, I think. However, your plan has possibilities, and we shall see."

VII

Takya had been right about her reception by the fugitives. They knew her for what she was, and only Craike's acceptance of her kept them in the tower. That and the fact, which Jorik did not try to disguise, that they could not hope to go much farther on their own. But their fears were partly allayed when she took over the nursing of the sick youngster, using on him the same healing power she had produced for Craike's wound. By the new day she was feeding him broth and demanding service from the others as if they had been her liegemen from birth.

The sun was well up when Jorik came in whistling from a dip in the river.

"This is a stout stronghold, Lord Ka-rak. And with the power aiding us to hold it, we are not likely to be shaken out in a hurry. Doubly is that true if the Lady aids us."

Takya laughed. She sat in the shaft of light from one of the narrow windows, combing her hair. Now she looked over her shoulder at them with something approaching a pert archness. In that moment she was more akin to the women Craike had known in his own world.

"Let us first see how the Lord Ka-rak proposes to defend us." There was mockery in that, enough to sting, as well as a demand that he make good his promise of the night before.

But Craike was prepared. He discarded his staff for a hold on Jorik's shoulder, while Zackuth slogged behind. They climbed into the forest. Craike had never fashioned a bow, and he did not doubt that his first attempts might be failures. But, as the three made their slow progress, he explained what they must look for and the kind of weapon he wanted to produce. They returned within the hour with an assortment of wood lengths with which to experiment.

After noon Zackuth grew restless and went off, to come back with a deer, visibly proud of his hunting skill. Craike saw bowstrings where the others saw meat and hide for the refashioning of foot wear. For the rest of the day they worked with a will. It was Takya who had the skill necessary for the feathering of the arrows after Zackuth netted two black river birds.

Four days later the tower community had taken on the aspect of a real stronghold. Many of the fallen stones were back in the walls. The two upper rooms of the tower had been explored, and a vast collection of ancient nests had been swept out. Takya chose the topmost one for her own abode and, aided by her convalescing charge, the boy Nickus, had carried armloads of sweat scented grass up for both carpeting and bedding. She did not appear to be inconvenienced by the bats that still entered at dawn to chitter out again at dusk. And she crooned a welcome to the snowy owl that refused to be dislodged from a favorite roost in the very darkest corner of the roof.

River travel had ceased. There were no new offerings on the rock. But Jorik and Zackuth hunted. And Craike tended the smoking fires which cured the extra meat against coming need, while he worked on the bows. Shortly they had three finished and practiced along the terrace, using blunt arrows.

Jorik had a true marksman's eye and took to the new weapon quickly, as did Nickus. But Zackuth was more clumsy, and Craike's stiff leg bothered him. Takya was easily the best shot when she would consent to try. But while agreeing it was an excellent weapon, she preferred her own type of warfare and would sit on the wall, braiding and rebraiding her hair with flying fingers, to watch their shooting at marks and applaud or jeer lightly at the results.

However, their respite was short. Craike had the first warning of trouble. He awoke from a dream in which he had been back in the desert panting ahead of the mob. Awoke, only to discover that some malign influence filled the tower. There was a compulsion on him to get out, to flee into the forest.

He tested the silences about him tentatively. The oppression which had been in the ancient fort at his first coming had not returned, that was not it. But what?

Someone moved restlessly in the dark.

"Lord Ka-rak?" Nickus' voice was low and hoarse, as if he struggled to keep it under control.

"What is it?"

"There is trouble—"

A bulk which could only belong to Jorik heaved up black against the faint light of the doorway.

"The hunt is up," he observed. "They move to shake us out of here like rats out of a nest."

"They did this before with you?" asked the Esper.

Jorik snorted. "Yes. It is their favorite move to battle. They would give us such a horror of our tower that we will burst forth and scatter. Then they can cut us down as they wish."

But Craike could not isolate any thought beam carrying that night terror. It seeped from the walls about them. He sent probes unsuccessfully. There was the pad of feet on the stairs, and then he heard Takya call:

"Build up the fire, foolish ones. They may discover that they do not deal with those who know nothing of them."

Flame blossomed from the coals to light a circle of sober faces. Zackuth caressed the spear lying across his knees, but Nickus and Jorik had eyes only for the witch maid as she knelt by the fire, laying out some bundles of dried leaf and fern. Her thoughts reached Craike.

"We must move or these undefended ones will be drawn out from here as nut meats are picked free from the shell. Give me of your power—in this matter I must be the leader."

Though he resented anew her calm assumption of authority, Craike also recognized in it truth. But he shrank from the task she demanded of him. To have no control over his own Esper arts, to allow her to use them to feed hers—it was a violation of a kind, the very thing he had so feared in his own world that he had been willing to kill himself to escape it. Yet now she asked it of him as one who had the right!

"Forced surrender is truly evil—but given freely in our defense this is different." Her thoughts swiftly answered his wave of repulsion.

The command to flee the tower was growing stronger. Nickus got to his feet as if dragged up. Suddenly Zackuth made for the door, only to have Jorik reach forth a long arm to trip him.

"You see," Takya urged, "they are already half under the spell. Soon we shall not be able to hold them, either by mind or body. And then they shall be wholly lost—for ranked against us now is the high power of the Black Hoods."

Craike watched the scuffle on the floor and then, still reluctant and inwardly shrinking, he limped around the fire to her side, lying down at her gesture. She threw on the fire two of her bundles of fern, and a thick, sweet smoke curled out to engulf them. Nickus coughed, put his hands uncertainly to his head and slumped, curling up as a tired child in deep slumber. And the struggle between Jorik and his man subsided as the fumes reached them.

Takya's hand was cool as it slipped beneath Craike's jerkin, resting over his heart. She was crooning some queer chant, and, though he fought to hold mind contact, there was a veil between them as tangible to his inner senses as the fern smoke was to his outer ones. For one wild second or two he seemed to see the tower room through her eyes instead of his own, and then the room was gone. He sped bodiless across the night world, casting forth as a hound on the trail.

All that had been solid in his normal sight was now without meaning. But he was able to see the dark cloud of pressure closing in on the tower and trace that back to its source, racing along the slender thread of its spinners.

There was another fire, and about it four of the Black Hoods. Here, too, was scented smoke to free minds from bodies. The essence which was Craike prowled about that fire, counting guardsmen who lay in slumber.

With an effort of will which drew heavily upon his strength, he concentrated on the staff which lay before the leader of the company, setting upon it his own commands.

It flipped up into the air, even as its master roused and clutched at it, falling into the fire. There was a flash of blue light, a sound which Craike felt rather than heard. The Hooded Ones were on their feet as their master stared straight across the flames to Craike's disembodied self. His was not an evil face, rather did it hold elements of nobility. But the eyes were pitiless, and Craike knew that now it was not only war to the death between them, but war beyond death itself. The Esper sensed that this was the first time that other had known of his existence, had been able to consider him as a factor in the tangled game.

There was a flash of lightning knowledge of each other, and then Craike was again in the dark. He heard once more Takya's crooning, was conscious of her touch resting above the slow, pulsating beat of his heart.

"That was well done," her thought welcomed him. "Now they must meet us face to face in battle."

"They will come." He accepted the dire promise that Black Hood had made.

"They will come, but now we are more equal. And there is not the Rod of Power to fear."

Craike tried to sit up and discovered that the weakness born of his wounds was nothing to that which now held him.

Takya laughed with some of her old mockery. "Do you think you can make the Long Journey and then romp about as a fawn, Ka-rak? Not three days on the field of battle can equal this. Sleep now and gather again the inner power. The end of this venture is still far from us."

He could no longer see her face, the glimmer of her hair veiled it, and then that shimmer reached his mind and shook him away from consciousness; and he slept.

It might have been early morning when he had made that strange visit to the camp of the Black Hoods. By the measure of the sun across the floor it was late afternoon when he lifted heavy eyelids again. Takya gazed down upon him. Her summons had brought him back, just as her urging had sent him to sleep. He sat up with a smile, but she did not return it.

"All is right?"

"We have time to make ready before we are put to the test. Your mountain captain is not new to this game. Matters of open warfare he understands well, and he and his men have prepared a rude welcome for those who come. And," her faint smile deepened, "I, too, have done my poor best. come and see."

He limped out on the terrace and for a moment was startled. Illusion, yes, but some of it was real.

Jorik laughed at the expression on Craike's face, inviting the Esper with a wave of the hand to inspect the force he captained. For there were bowmen in plenty, standing sentinel on the upper walls, arch, and tower, walking beats on the twin buildings across the river. And it took Craike a few seconds to sort out the ones he knew from those who served Takya's purposes. But the real had been as well posted as their illusionary companions. Nickus, for his superior accuracy with the new weapon, held a vantage point on the wall, and Zackuth was on the river arch where his arrows needed only a short range to be effective.

"Look below," Jorik ugred, "and see what shall trip them up until we can pin them."

Again Craike blinked. The illusion was one he had seen before, but that had been a hurried erection on the part of a desperate girl; this was better contrived. For all the ways leading to the river towers were cloaked with a tangled mass of thorn trees, the spiked branches interlocking into a wall no sword, no spear could hope to pierce. It might be an illusion, but it would require a weighty counterspell on the part of the Hooded Ones to clear it.

"She takes some twigs Nickus finds, and a hair, and winds them together, then buried all under a stone. After she sings over it—and we have this!" Jorik babbled. "She is worth twenty hands—no, twice twenty hands, or fighting men, is the Lady Takya! Lord Ka-rak, I say that there is a new day coming for this land when such as you two stand up against the Hooded Ones."

"Aaaay—" the warning was soft but clear, half whistle, half call, issuing from Nickus' lofty post. "They come!"

"So do they!" That was a sharp echo from Zackuth, "and down river as well."

"For which we have an answer," Jorik was undisturbed.

Those in the tower held their fire. To the confident attackers it was as such warfare had always been for them. If half their company was temporarily halted by the spiny maze, the river party had only to land on the offering rock and fight their way in, their efforts reinforced by the arts of their Masters.

But, as their dugout nosed in, bow cords sang. There was a voiceless scream which tore through Craike's head as the hooded man in its bow clutched at the shaft protruding from his throat and fell forward into the river. Two more of the crew followed him, and the rest stopped paddling, dismayed. The current pulled them on under the arch, and Zackuth dropped a rock to good purpose. It carried one of the guardsmen down with it as it hit the craft squarely. The dugout turned over, spilling all the rest into the water.

Zackuth laughed; Jorik roared.

"Now they learn what manner of bloodletting lies before them!" he cried so that his words must have reached the ears of the besiegers. "Let us see how eagerly they come to such feasting."

VIII

It was plain that the Black Hoods held their rulership by more practical virtues than just courage. Having witnessed the smashing disaster of the river attack, they made no further move. Night was coming, and Craike watched them withdraw downstream with no elation. Nor did Jorik retain his cheerfulness.

"Now they will try something else. And since we did not fall easily into their jaws, it will be harder to face. I do not like it that we must so face it during the hours of dark.''

"There will be no dark," Takya countered. One slim finger pointed at a corner of the terrace, and up into the gathering dusk leaped a pencil of clear light. Slowly she turned and brought to life other torches on the roof of the tower over river, on the arch spanning the water, on the parapet—and in that radiance nothing could move unseen.

"So!" Her fingers snapped, and the beacons vanished. "When they are needed, we shall have them."

Jorik blinked. "Well enough, Lady. But honest fire is also good, and it provides warmth for a man's heart as well as light for his eyes."

She smiled as a mother might smile at a child. "Build your fire, Captain of Swords. But we shall have ample warning when the enemy comes." She called. A silent winged thing floated down and alighted on the arm she held out to invite it. The white owl, its eyes seeming to observe them all with intelligence, snapped its wicked beak as Takya stared back at it. Then with a flap of wings, it went.

"From us they may hide their thoughts and movements. But they cannot close the sky to those things whose natural home it is. Be sure we shall know, and speedily, when they move against us."

They did not leave their posts, however. And Zackuth readied for action by laying up pieces of rubble which might serve as well as his first lucky shot.

It was a long night, wearing on the tempers of all but Takya. Time and time again Craike tried to probe the dark. But a blank wall was all he met. Whatever moves the Black Hoods considered, they were protected by an able barrier.

Jorik took to pacing back and forth on the terrace, five strides one way, six the other, and he brought down his bow with a little click on the time-worn stones each time he turned.

"They are as busy hatching trouble as a forest owl is in hatching an egg! But what kind of trouble?"

Craike had schooled himself into an outward patience. "For the learning of that we shall have to wait. But why do they delay—?"

Why did they? The more on edge he and his handful of defenders became, the easier meat they were. And he had no doubt that the Black Hoods were fertile in surprise. Though, judging by what Takya and Jorik reported, they were not accustomed to such determined and resourceful opposition to their wills. Such opposition would only firm their desire to wipe out the rebels.

"They move," Takya's witch fires leaped from every point she had earlier indicated. In that light she sped across the terrace to stand close to Jorik and Craike, close to the parapet wall. "This is the lowest hour of the night when the blood runs slow and resistance is at its depth. So they choose to move—"

Jorik snapped his bow cord, and the thin twang was a harp's note in the silence. But Takya shook her head.

"Only the Hooded Ones come, and they are well armored. See!" She jumped to the parapet and clapped her hands.

The witch light shone down on four standing within the thorn barrier, staring up from under the shadow of their hoods. An arrow sang, but it never reached its mark. Still feet away from the leader's breast it fell to earth.

But Jorik refused to accept defeat. With all the force of his arm he sent a second shaft after the first. And it, too, landed at the feet of the silent four. Craike grasped at Takya, but she eluded him, moving to call down to the Hooded Ones:

"What would you, men of power—a truce?"

"Daughter of evil, you are not alone. Let us speak with your lord."

She laughed, shaking out her unbound hair, rippling it through her fingers, gloatingly. "Does this show that I have taken a lord, men of power? Takya is herself, without division, still. Let that hope die from your hearts. I ask you again, what is it you wish—a truce?"

"Set forth your lord, and with him we will bargain."

She smoothed back her hair impatiently. "I have no lord, I and my power are intact. Try me and see, Tousuth. Yes, I know you, Tousuth, the Master, and Salsbal, Bulan, Yily—" she told them off with a pointed forefinger, a child counting out in some game.

Jorik stirred and drew in a sharp breath, and the men below shifted position. Craike caught thoughts—to use a man's name in the presence of hostile powers, that was magic indeed.

"Takya!" It was a reptile's hiss.

Again she laughed. "Ah, but the first naming was mine, Tousuth. Did you believe me so poor and power lost that I would obey you tamely? I did not at the horning, why should I now when I stand free of you? Before you had to use Takyi to capture me. But Takyi is gone into the far darkness, and over me now you can lay no such net! Also I have summoned one beside me—'' Her hand closed on Craike's arm, drawing him forward.

He faced the impact of those eyes meeting them squarely. Raising his hand he told them off as the girl had done:

"Tousuth, Master of women baiters, Salsbal, Bulan, Yily, the wolves who slink behind him. I am here, what would you have of me?"

But they were silent, and he could feel them searching him out, making thrusts against his mind shield, learning in their turn that he was of their kind; he was Esper born.

"What would you have?" he repeated more loudly. "If you do not wish to treat—then leave the night undisturbed for honest men's sleep."

"Changling!" It was Tousuth who spat that. It was his turn to point a finger and chant a sentence or two, his men watching him with confidence.

But Craike, remembering that other scene before Sampur, was trying a wild experiment of his own. He concentrated upon the man Takya had named Yily. Black cloak, black hood making a vulture's shadow against the rock. Vulture—vulture!

He did not know that he had pointed to his chosen victim, nor that he was repeating that word aloud in the same intonation as Tousuth's chant. "Vulture!"

Cool hand closed about his other wrist, and from that contact power flowed to join his. It was pointed, launched—

"Vulture!"

A black bird flapped and screamed, arose on beating wings to fly at him, raw red head outstretched, beak agap. There was the twang of a bow cord. A scream of agony and despair and a black-cloaked man writhed out his life on the slope by the thorn thicket.

"Good!" Takya cried. "That was well done, Ka-rak, very well done! But you cannot use that weapon a second time."

Craike was filled with a wild elation, and he did not listen to her. His finger already indicated Bulan and he was chanting: "Dog—"

But to no purpose. The Black Hood did not drop to all fours, he remained human; and Craike's voice faded. Takya spoke in swift whisper:

"They are warned, you can never march against them twice by the same path. Only because they were unprepared did you succeed. Ho, Tousuth," she called, "do you now believe that we are well armed? Speak with a true tongue and say what you want of us.''

"Yes,'' Jorik boomed, "you cannot take us, Master of power. Go your way, and we shall go ours—''

"There cannot be two powers in any land, as you should know, Jorik of the Eagles' towers, who tried once before to prove that and suffered thereby. There must be a victor here— and to the vanquished—naught!''

Craike could see the logic in that. But the Master was continuing: "As to what we want here—it is a decision. Match your power against ours, changling. And since you have not taken the witch, use her also if you wish. In the end it will come to the same thing, for both of you must be rendered helpless.''

"Here and now?'' asked Craike.

"Dawn comes, it will soon be another day. By sun or shadow, we care not in such a battle.''

The elation of his quick success in that first try was gone. Craike fingered the bow he had not yet used. He shrank inwardly from the contest the other proposed, he was too uncertain of his powers. One victory had come from too little knowledge. Takya's hand curled about his stiff fingers once again. The impish mockery was back in her voice, ruffling his temper, irritating him into defiance.

"Show them what you can do, Lord Ka-rak, you who can master illusions.''

He glanced down at her, and the sight of that cropped lock of hair at her temple gave him an odd confidence. Neither was Takya as all-powerful as she would have him believe.

"I accept your challenge,'' he called "Let it be here and now.''

"*We* accept your challenge!'' Takya's flash of annoyance, her quick correction, pleased him. Before the echo of her words died away she hurled her first attack.

Witchfire leaped downslope to ring in the three men, playing briefly along the body of the dead Yily. It flickered up and down about their feet and legs so they stood washed in pallid flame, while about their heads darted winged shapes which might have been owls or other night hunters.

There was a malignant hissing, and the slope sprouted reptiles, moving in a wave. Illusions? All—or some. But designed, Craike understood, to divert the enemy's minds. He added a few of his own—a wolfish shape crouching in the shadow—leaping—to vanish as its paws cut the witchfire.

Swift as had been Takya's attack, so did those below parry.

An oppressive weight, so tangible that Craike looked up to see if some mountain threatened them from overhead, began to close down upon the parapet. He heard a cry of alarm. There *was* a black cloud to be seen now, a giant press closing upon them.

Balls of witchfire flashed out of the light pillars, darted at those on the parapet. One flew straight at Craike's face, its burning breath singeing his skin.

"Fool!" Takya's thought was a whip lash, "Illusions are only real for the believer."

He steadied, and the witch ball vanished. But he was badly shaken. This was outside any Esper training he had had, it was the very thing he had been conditioned against. He felt slow, clumsy, and he was ashamed that upon Takya must the burden of their defense now rest.

Upon her—Craike's eyes narrowed. He loosened her hold on him, did not try to contact her. There was too much chance of self-betrayal in that. His plan was utterly wild, but it had been well demonstrated that the Black Hoods could only be caught by the unexpected.

Another witch ball hurtled at him, and he leaped to the terrace, landing with a force which sent a lance of pain up his healing leg. But on the parapet a Craike still stood, shoulder to shoulder with Takya. To maintain that illusion was a task which made him sweat as he crept silently away from the tower.

He had made a security guard to astonish Takya, the wolf, all the other illusions. But they had been only wisps, things alive for the moment with no need for elaboration. To hold this semblance of himself was in some ways easier, some ways harder. It was easier to make, for the image was produced of self-knowledge, and it was harder, for it was meant to deceive masters of illusion.

Craike reached the steps to the rock of the offerings. The glow of the witch lights here was pale, and the ledge below dark. He crept down, one arrow held firmly in his hand.

Here the sense of oppression was a hundredfold worse, and he moved as one wading through a flood which entrapped limbs and brain. Blind, he went to all fours, feeling his way to the river.

He set the arrow between his teeth in a bite which indented its shaft. A knife would have been far better, but he had no time to beg Jorik's. He slipped over, shivering as the chill water took him. Then he swam under the arch.

It was comparatively easy to reach the shingle where the dugout of the Black Hoods had turned over. As he made his way to the shore he brushed against water-soaked cloth and realized he shared this scrap of gravel with the dead. Then, arrow still between his teeth, Craike climbed up behind the Black Hoods' position.

IX

The thorn hedge cloaked the rise above him. But he concentrated on the breaking of that illusion, wading on through a mass of thorns, intact to his eyes, thin air at his passing. Then he was behind the Black Hoods. Takya stood, a black-and-white figure on the wall above, beside the illusion Craike.

Now!

The illusion Craike swelled a little more than life size, while his creator gathered his feet under him, preparatory to attack. The Craike on the wall altered—anything to hold the attention of Tousuth for a crucial second or two. Monster grew from man, wings, horns, curved tusks, all embellishments Craike's imagination could add. He heard shouts from the tower.

But with the arrow as a dagger in his hand, he sprang, allowing himself in that moment to see only, to think only of a point on Tousuth's back.

The head drove in and in, and Tousuth went down on his knees, clutching at his chest, coughing. While Craike, with a savagery he had not known he possessed, leaned on the shaft to drive it deeper.

Fingers hooked about Craike's throat, cutting off air, dragging him back. He was pulled from Tousuth, loosing his hold on the arrow shaft to tear at the hands denying him breath. There was a red fog which even the witch lights could not pierce and the roaring in his head was far louder than the shouts from the tower.

Then he was flat on the ground, still moving feebly. But the hands were gone from his throat, and he gasped in air. Around him circled balls of fire, dripping, twirling, he closed his eyes against their glare.

"Lord—Lord!"

The hail reached him only faintly. Hands pulled at him, and he tried to resist. But when he opened his eyes it was to see Jorik's brown face. Jorik was at the tower—how had Craike returned there? Surely he *had* attacked Tousuth? Or was it all illusion?

"He is not dead."

Whether or not that was said to him, Craike did not know. But his fingers were at his throat and he winced from his own touch. Then an arm came under his shoulders, lifting him, and he had a dizzy moment until earth and gray sky settled into their proper places.

Takya was there, with Nickus and Zackuth hovering in the background of black-jerkined guardsmen who stared back at her sullenly over the bodies of the dead. For they were all dead—the Hooded Ones. There was Tousuth, his head in the sand. And his fellows crumpled beside him.

The witch girl chanted, and in her hands was a cat's cradle of black strands. The men who followed Tousuth cringed, and their fear was a cloud Craike could see. He grabbed at Jorik, won to his feet, and tried to hail Takya. But not even a croak came from his tortured throat. So he flung himself at her, one hand out like a sword blade to slash. It fell across that wicked net of hair, breaking it, and went to close upon Takya's wrist in a crushing grip.

"Enough!" He could get out that command mind to mind.

She drew in upon herself as a cat crouches for a spring, and spat, her eyes green with feral lusting fire. But he had an answer to that, read it in her own spark of fear at his touch. His hands twined in her hair.

"They are men," he pulled those black strands to emphasize his words, "they only obeyed orders. We have a quarrel with their masters, but not with them!"

"They hunted, and now they shall be hunted!"

"I have been hunted, as have you, witch woman. And while I live there shall be no more such hunts—whether I am hound or quarry."

"While you live—" Her menace was ready.

Suddenly Craike forced out a hoarse croak meant for laughter. "You, yourself, Takya, have put the arrow to this bow cord!"

He kept one hand tangled in her hair. But with the other he snatched from her belt the knife she had borrowed from Nickus and not returned. She screamed, beat against him with her fists, tried to bite. He mastered her roughly, not loosing his grip on that black silk. And then in sweeps of that well-whetted blade he did what the Black Hoods had failed in doing, he sawed through those lengths.

"I am leaving you no weapons, Takya. You shall not rule here as you have thought to do—" The exultation he had known when he had won his first victory against the Black Hoods was returning a hundredfold. "For a while I shall pull those pretty claws of yours!" He wondered briefly how long it would take her hair to regrow. At least they would have a breathing spell before her powers returned.

Then, his arm still prisoning her shoulders, the mass of her hair streaming free from his left hand, he turned to face the guardsmen.

"Tell them to go," he thought, "taking their dead with them."

"You will go, taking these with you," she repeated aloud, stony calm.

One of the men dropped to his knees by Tousuth's body, then abased himself before Craike.

"We are your hounds, Master."

Craike found his voice at last. "You are no man's hound—for you are a man. Get you gone to Sampur and tell them that the power is no longer to make hind nor hound. If there are those who wish to share the fate of Tousuth, perhaps when they look upon him as dead they will think more of it."

"Lord, do you come also to Sampur to rule?" the other asked timidly.

Craike laughed. "Not until I have established my lordship elsewhere. Get you back to Sampur and trouble us no more."

He turned his back on the guardsmen and, drawing the silent Takya, still within the circle of his arm, with him, started back to the tower. The bowmen remained behind, and Craike and the girl were alone as they reached the upper level. He paused then and looked down into her set, expressionless face.

"What shall I do with you?"

"You have shamed me and taken my power from me. What does a warrior do with a female slave?" She formed a stark mind picture, hurling it at him as she had hurled the stone on the mesa.

With his left hand he whipped her hair across her face, smarting under that taunt.

"I have taken no slave, nor any woman in that fashion, nor shall I. Go your way, Takya, and fight me again if you wish when your hair has grown."

She studied him, and her astonishment was plain. Then she laughed and clutched at the hair, tearing it free from his grasp, bundling it into the front of her single garment.

"So be it, Ka-rak. It is war between us. But I am not departing hence yet a while." She broke away, and he could hear the scuff of her feet on the steps as she climbed to her own chamber in the tower.

"They are on their way, Lord, and they will keep to it." Jorik came up. He stretched. "It was a battle not altogether to my liking. For the honest giving of blows from one's hand is better than all this magic, potent as it is."

Craike sat down beside the fire. He could not have agreed more heartily with any suggestion. Now that it was over he felt drained of energy.

"I do not believe they will return," he wheezed hoarsely, very conscious of his bruised throat.

Nickus chuckled, and Zackuth barked his own laughter.

"Seeing how you handled the Lady, Lord, they want nothing more than to be out of your grasp and that as speedily as possible. Nor, when those of Sampur see what they bring with them, do I think we shall be sought out by others bearing drawn swords. Now," Jorik slapped his fat middle, "I could do with meat in my belly. And you, Lord, have taken such handling as needs good food to counter."

There was no mention of Takya, nor did any go to summon her when the meat was roasted. And Craike was content to have it so. He was too tired for any more heroics.

Nickus hummed a soft tune as he rubbed down his unstrung bow before wrapping it away from the river damp. And Craike was aware that the younger man glanced at him slyly when he thought the Esper's attention elsewhere. Jorik, too, appeared highly amused at some private thoughts, and he had fallen to beating time with one finger to Nickus' tune. Craike shifted uncomfortably. He was an actor who had forgotten his lines, a novice required to make a ritual move he did not understand. What they wanted of him he could not guess, for he was too tired to mind-touch. He only wanted sleep, and that he sought as soon as he painfully swallowed his last bite. But he heard through semistupor a surprised exclamation from Nickus.

"He goes not to seek her—to take her!"

Jorik's answer held something of approval in it. "To master such as the Lady Takya he will need full strength of power and limb. His is the wisest way, not to gulp the fruits of battle before the dust of the last charge is laid. She is his by shearing, but she is no meek ewe to come readily under any man's hand."

Takya did not appear the next day, nor the next. And Craike made no move to climb to her. His companions elaborately did not notice her absence as they worked together, setting in place fallen stones, bringing the tower into a better state of repair, or killing deer to smoke the meat. For as Jorik pointed out:

"Soon comes the season of cold. We must build us a snug place and have food under our hands before then." He broke off and gazed thoughtfully down stream. "This is also the fair time when countrymen bring their wares to market. There are traders in Sampur. We could offer our hides, even though they be newly fleshed, for salt and grain. And a bow—this Kaluf of whom you have spoken, would he not give a good price for a bow?"

Craike raised an eyebrow. "Sampur? But they have little cause to welcome us in Sampur."

"You and the Lady Takya, Lord, they might take arms against in fear. But if Zackuth and I went in the guise of wandering hunters—and Zackuth is of the Children of Noe, he could trade privately with his kin. We must have supplies, Lord, before the coming of the cold, and this is too fine a fortress to abandon."

So it was decided that Jorik and Zackuth were to try their luck with the traders. Nickus went to hunt, wrecking havoc among the flocks of migrating fowl, and Craike held the tower alone.

As he turned from seeing them away, he sighted the owl wheel out from the window slit of the upper chamber, its mournful cry sounding loud. On sudden impulse he went inside to climb the stair. There had been enough of her sulking. He sent that thought before him as an order. She did not reply. Craike's heart beat faster. Was—had she gone? The rough outer wall was it possible to climb down that?

He flung himself up the last few steps and burst into the room. She was standing there, her shorn head high as if she and not he had been the victor. When he saw her Craike stopped. Then he moved again, faster than he had climbed those stairs. For in that moment the customs of this world were clear, he knew what he must do, what he wanted to do. If this revelation was some spell of Takya's he did not care.

Later he was aroused by the caress of silk on his body, felt her cool fingers as he had felt them drawing the poison from his wounds. It was a black belt, and she was making fast about him, murmuring words softly as she interwove strand with strand about his waist until there was no beginning nor end to be detected.

"My chain on you, man of power." Her eyes slanted down at him.

He buried both his hands in the ragged crop of hair from which those threads had been severed and so held her quiet for his kiss.

"My seal upon you, witch."

"What Tousuth would have done, you have accomplished for him," she observed pensively when he had given her a measure of freedom once again. "Only through you may I now use my power."

"Which is perhaps well for this land and those who dwell in it," he laughed. "We are now tied to a common destiny, my lady of river towers."

She sat up running her hands through her hair with some of her old caress.

"It will grow again," he consoled.

"To no purpose, except to pleasure my vanity. Yes, we are tied together. But you do not regret it, Ka-rak—"

"Neither do you, witch." There was no longer any barrier between their minds, as there was none between their bodies. "What destiny will you now spin for the two of us?"

"A great one. Tousuth knew my power-to-come. I would now realize it." Her chin went up. "And you with me, Ka-rak. By this," her hand rested lightly on the belt.

"Doubtless you will set us up as rulers over Sampur?" he said lazily.

"Sampur!" she sniffed. "This world is wide—" Her arms went out as if to encircle all which lay beyond the tower walls.

Craike drew her back to him jealously. "For that there is more than time enough. This is an hour for something else, even in a warlock's world."

Sweets to the Sweet
by Robert Bloch

Robert Bloch has been scaring the daylights out of people for more than forty years. He got his start as a member of the famous "Lovecraft Circle" of correspondents and soon moved on to the pulp magazines, where he specialized in both supernatural and psychological horror. His book Psycho (1959) *was made into an immortal film by Alfred Hitchcock; more recently, he has given us* Psycho II (1983). *In many ways he still remains an underrated writer, although he has been honored by his readers and his peers with a Hugo Award and an Edgar Allan Poe Award.* The Best of Robert Bloch *contains some of his most outstanding work, but it would take several volumes to accommodate all his most worthy stories.*

Irma didn't look like a witch.

She had small, regular features, a peaches-and-cream complexion, blue eyes, and fair, almost ash-blond hair. Besides, she was only eight years old.

"Why does he tease her so?" sobbed Miss Pall. "That's where she got the idea in the first place—because he always insists on calling her a little witch."

Sam Steever bulked his paunch back into the squeaky swivel chair and folded his heavy hands in his lap.

His fat lawyer's mask was immobile, but he was really quite distressed.

Women like Miss Pall should never sob. Their glasses wiggle, their thin noses twitch, their creasy eyelids redden, and their stringy hair becomes disarrayed.

"Please, control yourself," coaxed Sam Steever. "Perhaps if we could just talk this whole thing over sensibly—"

"I don't care!" Miss Pall sniffled. "I'm not going back there again. I can't stand it. There's nothing I can do, anyway. The man is your brother, and she's your brother's child. It's not my responsibility. I've tried—''

"Of course you've tried." Sam Steever smiled benignly, as if Miss Pall were foreman of a jury. "I quite understand. But I still don't see why you are so upset, dear lady."

Miss Pall removed her spectacles and dabbed at her eyes with a floral-print handkerchief. Then she deposited the soggy ball in her purse, snapped the catch, replaced her spectacles, and sat up straight.

"Very well, Mr. Steever," she said. "I shall do my best to acquaint you with my reasons for quitting your brother's employ."

She suppressed a tardy sniff.

"I came to John Steever two years ago in response to an advertisement for a housekeeper, as you know. When I found that I was to be governess to a motherless six-year-old child, I was at first distressed. I knew nothing of the care of children."

"John had a nurse the first six years." Sam Steever nodded. "You know Irma's mother died in childbirth."

"I am aware of that," said Miss Pall primly. "Naturally, one's heart goes out to a lonely, neglected little girl. And she was so terribly lonely, Mr. Steever—if you could have seen her, moping around in the corners of that big, ugly old house—"

"I have seen her," said Sam Steever hastily, hoping to forestall another outburst. "And I know what you've done for Irma. My brother is inclined to be thoughtless, even a bit selfish, at times. He doesn't understand."

"He's cruel!" declared Miss Pall, suddenly vehement. "Cruel and wicked. Even if he is your brother, I say he's no fit father for any child. When I came there, her little arms were black-and-blue from beatings. He used to take a belt—"

"I know. Sometimes I think John never recovered from the shock of Mrs. Steever's death. That's why I was so pleased when you came, dear lady. I thought you might help improve the situation."

"I tried," Miss Pall whimpered. "You know I tried. I never raised a hand to that child in two years, though many's the time your brother told me to punish her. 'Give the little witch a beating,' he used to say. 'That's all she needs—a good thrashing.' And then she'd hide behind my back and whisper to me to protect her. But she wouldn't cry, Mr. Steever. Do you know, I've never seen her cry."

Sam Steever felt vaguely irritated and a bit bored. He wished the old hen would get on with it. So he smiled and oozed treacle.

"But just what exactly is your problem, dear lady?"

"Everything was all right when I came there. We got along just splendidly. I started to teach Irma to read—and was surprised to find that she had already mastered reading. Your brother disclaimed having taught her, but she spent hours curled up on the sofa with a book. 'Just like her,' he used to say. 'Unnatural little witch. Doesn't play with the other children. Little witch.'

"That's just the way he kept talking, Mr. Steever. As if she were some sort of . . . I don't know what. And she so sweet and quiet and pretty!

"Is it any wonder she read? I used to be that way myself when I was a girl, because— But never mind.

"Still, it was a shock that day I found her looking through the *Encyclopaedia Britannica*. 'What are you reading, Irma?' I asked her. And she showed me. It was the article on witchcraft.

"You see what morbid thoughts your brother has inculcated in her poor little head?

"I did my best. I went out and bought her some toys—she had absolutely nothing, you know, not even a doll. She didn't even know how to *play!* I tried to get her interested in some of the other little girls in the neighborhood, but it was no use. They didn't understand her, and she didn't understand them. There were scenes. Children can be cruel, thoughtless. And her father wouldn't let her go to public school. I was to teach her.

"Then I brought her the modeling clay. She liked that. She would spend hours just making faces with clay. For a child of six, Irma displayed real talent.

"We made little dolls together, and I sewed clothes for them. That first year was a happy one, Mr. Steever. Particularly during those months when your brother was away in South America. But this year, when he came back—oh, I can't bear to talk about it!"

"Please," said Sam Steever. "You must understand. John is not a happy man. The loss of his wife, the decline of his import trade, and his drinking—but you know all that."

"All I know is that he hates Irma," snapped Miss Pall suddenly. "He hates her. He wants her to be bad, so he can whip her. 'If you don't discipline the little witch, I shall,' he always says. And then he takes her upstairs and thrashes her with his belt. You must do something, Mr. Steever, you must—or I'll go to the authorities myself."

The crazy old biddy would, at that, Sam Steever thought. Remedy—more treacle. "But about Irma," he persisted.

"She's changed, too. Ever since her father returned this year. She won't play with me anymore. Hardly looks at me. It's as though I failed her, Mr. Steever, in not protecting her from that man. Besides—she thinks she's a witch.''

Crazy. Stark, staring crazy. Sam Steever creaked upright in his chair.

"Oh, you needn't look at me like that, Mr. Steever. She'd tell you so herself—if you ever visited the house!''

He caught the reproach in her voice and assuaged it with a deprecating nod.

"She told me, all right: If her father wants her to be a witch, she'll be a witch. And she won't play with me or anyone else, because witches don't play. Last Halloween she wanted me to give her a broomstick. Oh, it would be funny if it weren't so tragic.

"Just a few weeks ago, I thought she'd changed. That's when she asked me to take her to church one Sunday. 'I want to see the baptism,' she said. Imagine that—an eight-year-old interested in baptism! Reading too much, that's what does it.

"Well, we went to church, and she was as sweet as can be, wearing her new blue dress and holding my hand. I was proud of her, Mr. Steever, really proud.

"But after that, she went right back into her shell. Reading around the house, running through the yard at twilight, talking to herself.

"Perhaps it's because your brother wouldn't bring her a kitten. She was pestering him for a black cat, and he asked why, and she said, 'Because witches always have black cats.' Then he took her upstairs.

"I can't stop him, you know. He beat her again the night the power failed and we couldn't find the candles. He said she'd stolen them. Imagine that—accusing an eight-year-old child of stealing candles!

"That was the beginning of the end. Then today, when he found his hairbrush missing—''

"You say he beat her with his hairbrush?''

"Yes. She admitted having stolen it. Said she wanted it for her doll.''

"But didn't you say she has no dolls?''

"She made one. At least, I think she did. I've never seen it. She won't show us anything anymore; won't talk to us at table. It's just impossible to handle her.

"But this doll she made—it's a small one, I know, because at times she carries it tucked under her arm. She talks to it and pets it, but she won't show it to me or to him. He asked her about the hairbrush, and she said she took it for the doll.

"Your brother flew into a terrible rage—he'd been drinking in his room again all morning; don't think I don't know it!—and she just smiled and said he could have it now. She went over to her bureau and handed it to him. She hadn't harmed it in the least; his hair was still in it, I noticed.

"But he snatched it up, and then he started to strike her about the shoulders with it, and he twisted her arm, and then he—"

Miss Pall huddled in her chair and summoned great racking sobs from her thin chest.

Sam Steever patted her shoulder, fussing about her like an elephant over a wounded canary.

"That's all, Mr. Steever. I came right to you. I'm not even going back to that house to get my things. I can't stand any more—the way he beat her—and the way she didn't cry, but just giggled and giggled and giggled. Sometimes I think she *is* a witch—that he made her into a witch. . . ."

Sam Steever picked up the phone. The ringing had broken the relief of silence after Miss Pall's hasty and not unwelcome departure.

"Hello—that you, Sam?"

He recognized his brother's voice, somewhat the worse for drink.

"Yes, John."

"I suppose the old bat came running straight to you to shoot her mouth off."

"If you mean Miss Pall, I've seen her, yes."

"Pay no attention to her. I can explain everything."

"Do you want me to stop in? I haven't paid you a visit in months."

"Well—not right now. Got an appointment with the doctor this evening."

"Something wrong?"

"Pain in my arm. Rheumatism or something. Getting a little diathermy. But I'll call you tomorrow, and we'll straighten this whole mess out."

"Right."

But John Steever did not call his brother the next day. Along about suppertime, Sam called him.

Surprisingly enough, Irma answered the phone.

Her thin, squeaky little voice sounded faintly in Sam's ear.

"Daddy's upstairs sleeping," she said. "He's been sick."

"Well, don't disturb him. What is it—his arm?"

"His back, now. He has to go to the doctor again in a little while."

"Tell him I'll call tomorrow, then. Uh—everything all right, Irma? I mean, don't you miss Miss Pall?"

"No. I'm glad she went away. She's stupid."

"Oh. Yes. I see. But you phone me if you want anything. And I hope your daddy's better."

"Yes. So do I," said Irma. Then she began to giggle, and then she hung up.

There was no giggling the following afternoon when John Steever called Sam at the office. His voice was sober—with the sharp sobriety of pain.

"Sam—for the love of heaven, get over here. Something's happening to me!"

"What's the trouble?"

"The pain—it's killing me! I've got to see you. Quickly!"

"There's a client in the office, but I'll get rid of him. Say, wait a minute. Why don't you call the doctor?"

"That quack can't help me. He gave me diathermy for my arm, and yesterday he did the same thing for my back."

"Didn't it help?"

"The pain went away, yes. But it's back now. I feel . . . as if I'm being crushed. Squeezed, here in the chest. I can't breathe."

"Sounds like pleurisy. Why don't you call him?"

"It isn't pleurisy. He examined me. Said I was sound as a dollar. No, there's nothing organically wrong. And I couldn't tell him the real cause."

"Real cause?"

"Yes. The pins. The pins that little fiend is sticking into the doll she made. Into the arm, the back. And now heaven only knows how she's causing *this*."

"John, you mustn't—"

"Oh, what's the use of talking? I can't move off the bed here. She has me now. I can't go down and stop her, get hold of the doll. And nobody else would believe it. But it's the doll, all right, the one she made with the candle wax and the hair from my brush. Oh—it hurts to talk—that cursed little witch! Hurry, Sam. Promise me you'll do something—anything to get that doll from her—get that doll—"

*   *   *

Half an hour later, at four-thirty, Sam Steever entered his brother's house.

Irma opened the door.

It gave Sam a shock to see her standing there, smiling and unperturbed, pale blond hair brushed immaculately back from the rosy oval of her face. She looked just like a little doll. A little doll—

"Hello, Uncle Sam."

"Hello, Irma. Your daddy called me; did he tell you? He said he wasn't feeling well—"

"Yes, I know. But he's all right now. He's sleeping."

Something happened to Sam Steever; a drop of icewater trickled down his spine.

"Sleeping?" he croaked. "Upstairs?"

Before she opened her mouth to answer, he was bounding up the steps to the second floor and striding down the hall to his brother John's bedroom.

John lay on the bed. He was asleep—only alseep. Sam Steever noted the regular rise and fall of his chest as he breathed. His face was calm, relaxed.

Then the drop of icewater evaporated, and Sam could afford to smile—and even to murmur, "Nonsense!" under his breath as he turned away.

As he went downstairs, he hastily improvised plans. A six-month vacation for his brother; avoid calling it a "cure." An orphanage for Irma; give her a chance to get away from this morbid old house, all those books. . . .

He paused halfway down the stairs. Peering over the banister through the twilight, he saw Irma on the sofa, cuddled up like a little white ball. She was talking to something she cradled in her arms, rocking it to and fro.

Then there was a doll, after all.

Sam Steever tiptoed very quietly down the stairs and walked over to Irma.

"Hello," he said.

She jumped. Both arms rose to cover completely whatever it was she had been fondling. She squeezed it tightly.

Sam Steever thought of a doll being squeezed across the chest. . . .

Irma stared up at him, her face a mask of innocence. In the half-light her face did resemble a mask. The mask of a little girl, covering—what?

"Daddy's better now, isn't he?" lisped Irma.

"Yes, much better."

"I knew he would be."

"But I'm afraid he's going to have to go away for a rest—a long rest."

A smile filtered through the mask. "Good," said Irma.

"Of course," Sam went on, "you couldn't stay here all alone. I was wondering—maybe we could send you off to school or to some kind of home—"

Irma giggled. "Oh, you needn't worry about me," she said. She shifted about on the sofa as Sam sat down, then sprang up quickly as he came close to her.

Her arms shifted with the movement, and Sam Steever saw a pair of tiny legs dangling below her elbow. There were trousers on the legs, and little bits of leather for shoes.

"What's that you have, Irma?" he asked. "Is it a doll?"

Slowly he extended his pudgy hand.

She pulled back.

"You can't see it," she said.

"But I want to. Miss Pall said you made such lovely ones."

"Miss Pall is stupid. So are you," Irma said. "Go away."

"Please, Irma. Let me see it."

But even as he spoke, Sam Steever was staring at the top of the doll, momentarily revealed when she backed away. It was a head, all right, with wisps of hair over a white face. Dusk dimmed the features, but Sam recognized the eyes, the nose, the chin.

He could keep up the pretense no longer.

"Give me that doll, Irma!" he snapped. "I know what it is. I know *who* it is—"

For an instant, the mask slipped from Irma's face, and Sam Steever stared into naked fear.

She knew. She knew he knew.

Then, just as quickly, the mask was replaced.

Irma was only a sweet, spoiled, stubborn little girl as she shook her head merrily and smiled with impish mischief in her eyes.

"Oh, Uncle Sam," she giggled, "you're so silly! Why, this isn't a *real* doll."

"What is it, then?" he muttered.

Irma giggled once more, raising the figure as she spoke. "Why, it's only—candy!" she said.

"Candy?"

Irma nodded. Then, very swiftly, she slipped the tiny head of the image into her mouth.

And bit it off.

There was a single piercing scream from upstairs.

As Sam Steever turned and ran up the steps, little Irma, still gravely munching, skipped out of the front door and into the night beyond.

Poor Little Saturday
by Madeleine L'Engle

Madeleine L'Engle is one of the most popular contemporary children's writers. Her most famous books for young people are both fantasies: A Wrinkle in Time *(1963), which won the Newbery Medal as the outstanding children's book of that year; and* A Swiftly Tilting Planet, *winner of the National Book Award for Children's Literature in 1980. Both of these are part of her "Time" trilogy, the middle book being* A Wind in the Door *(1973). Another fantasy for younger readers is* A Ring of Endless Light *(1980). "Poor Little Saturday" appeared in the October 1956 issue of the late and lamented* Fantastic Universe, *and is her only known publication in the genre magazines.*

The witch woman lived in a deserted, boarded-up plantation house, and nobody knew about her but me. Nobody in the nosy little town in south Georgia where I lived when I was a boy knew that if you walked down the dusty main street to where the post office ended it, and then turned left and followed that road a piece until you got to the rusty iron gates of the drive to the plantation house, you could find goings-on would make your eyes pop out. It was just luck that I found out. Or maybe it wasn't luck at all. Maybe the witch woman wanted me to find out because of Alexandra. But now I wish I hadn't because the witch woman and Alexandra are gone forever and it's much worse than if I'd never known them.

Nobody'd lived in the plantation house since the Civil war when Colonel Londermaine was killed and Alexandra Londermaine, his beautiful young wife, hung herself on the chandelier in the ballroom. A while before I was born some northerners bought it but after a few years they stopped coming and people said it was because the house was haunted. Every few years a gang of boys or men would set out to explore the house but nobody ever found anything, and it was so well boarded up it was hard to force an entrance, so by and by the town lost interest in it. No one climbed the wall and wandered around the grounds except me.

I used to go there often during the summer because I had bad spells of malaria when sometimes I couldn't bear to lie on the iron bedstead in my room with the flies buzzing around my face, or out on the hammock on the porch with the screams and laughter of the other kids as they played torturing my ears. My aching head made it impossible for me to read, and I would drag myself down the road, scuffling my bare sunburned toes in the dust, wearing the tattered straw hat that was supposed to protect me from the heat of the sun, shivering and sweating by turns. Sometimes it would seem hours before I got to the iron gates near which the brick wall was lowest. Often I would have to lie panting on the tall prickly grass for minutes until I gathered strength to scale the wall and drop down on the other side.

But once inside the grounds it seemed cooler. One funny thing about my chills was that I didn't seem to shiver nearly as much when I could keep cool as I did at home where even the walls and the floors, if you touched them, were hot. The grounds were filled with live oaks that had grown up unchecked everywhere and afforded an almost continuous green shade. The ground was covered with ferns which were soft and cool to lie on, and when I flung myself down on my back and looked up, the roof of leaves was so thick that sometimes I couldn't see the sky at all. The sun that managed to filter through lost its bright pitiless glare and came in soft yellow shafts that didn't burn you when they touched you.

One afternoon, a scorcher early in September, which is usually our hottest month (and by then you're fagged out by the heat anyhow), I set out for the plantation. The heat lay coiled and shimmering on the road. When you looked at anything through it, it was like looking through a defective pane of glass. The dirt road was so hot that it burned even through my calloused feet and as I walked clouds of dust rose in front of me and mixed with the shimmying of the heat. I thought I'd never make the plantation. Sweat was running into my eyes, but it was cold sweat, and I was shivering so that my teeth chattered as I walked. When I managed finally to fling myself down on my soft green bed of ferns inside the grounds I was seized with one of the worst chills I'd ever had in spite of the fact that my mother had given me an extra dose of quinine that morning and some

666 malaria medicine to boot. I shut my eyes tight and clutched the ferns with my hands and teeth to wait until the chill had passed, when I heard a soft voice call:

"Boy."

I thought at first I was delirious, because sometimes I got light-headed when my bad attacks came on; only then I remembered that when I was delirious I didn't know it; all the strange things I saw and heard seemed perfectly natural. So when the voice said, "Boy," again, as soft and clear as the mockingbird at sunrise, I opened my eyes.

Kneeling near me on the ferns was a girl. She must have been about a year younger than I. I was almost sixteen so I guess she was fourteen or fifteen. She was dressed in a blue-and-white gingham dress; her face was very pale, but the kind of paleness that's supposed to be, not the sickly pale kind that was like mine showing even under the tan. Her eyes were big and very blue. Her hair was dark brown and she wore it parted in the middle in two heavy braids that were swinging in front of her shoulders as she peered into my face.

"You don't feel well, do you?" she asked. There was no trace of concern or worry in her voice. Just scientific interest.

I shook my head. "No," I whispered, almost afraid that if I talked she would vanish, because I had never seen anyone here before, and I thought that maybe I was dying because I felt so awful, and I thought maybe that gave me the power to see the ghost. But the girl in blue-and-white-checked gingham seemed as I watched her to be good flesh and blood.

"You'd better come with me," she said. "She'll make you all right."

"Who's she?"

"Oh—just Her," she said.

My chill had begun to recede by now, so when she got up off her knees, I scrambled up, too. When she stood up her dress showed a white ruffled petticoat underneath it, and bits of green moss had left patterns on her knees and I didn't think that would happen to the knees of a ghost, so I followed her as she led the way towards the house. She did not go up the sagging, half-rotted steps which led to the veranda about whose white pillars wisteria vines climbed in wild profusion, but went around to the side of the house where there were slanting doors to a cellar. The sun and rain had long since blistered and washed off the paint, but the doors looked clean and were free of the bits of bark from the eucalyptus tree which leaned nearby and which had dropped its bits of dusty peel on either side; so I knew that these cellar stairs must frequently be used.

The girl opened the cellar doors. "You go down first," she said. I went down the cellar steps, which were stone, and cool against my bare feet. As she followed me she closed the cellar doors after her and as I reached the bottom of the stairs we were in pitch darkness. I began to be very frightened until her soft voice came out of the black.

"Boy, where are you?"

"Right here."

"You'd better take my hand. You might stumble."

We reached out and found each other's hands in the darkness. Her fingers were long and cool and they closed firmly around mine. She moved with authority as though she knew her way with the familiarity born of custom.

"Poor Sat's all in the dark," she said, "but he likes it that way. He likes to sleep for weeks at a time. Sometimes he snores awfully. Sat, darling!" she called gently. A soft, bubbly, blowing sound came in answer, and she laughed happily. "Oh, Sat, you are sweet!" she said, and the bubbly sound came again. Then the girl pulled at my hand and we came out into a huge and dusty kitchen. Iron skillets, pots and pans were still hanging on either side of the huge stove, and there was a rolling pin and a bowl of flour on the marble-topped table in the middle of the room. The girl took a lighted candle off the shelf.

"I'm going to make cookies," she said as she saw me looking at the flour and the rolling pin. She slipped her hand out of mine. "Come along." She began to walk more rapidly. We left the kitchen, crossed the hall, went through the dining room, its old mahogany table thick with dust although sheets covered the pictures on the walls. Then we went into the ballroom. The mirrors lining the walls were spotted and discolored; against one wall was a single delicate gold chair, its seat cushioned with pale rose and silver-woven silk; it seemed extraordinarily well preserved. From the ceiling hung the huge chandelier from which Alexandra Londermaine had hung herself, its prisms catching and breaking up into a hundred colors the flickering of the candle and the few shafts of light that managed to slide in through the boarded-up windows. As we crossed the ballroom the girl began to dance by herself, gracefully, lightly, so that her full blue-and-white-checked gingham skirts flew out around her. She looked at herself with pleasure in the old mirrors as she danced, the candle flaring and guttering in her right hand.

"You've stopped shaking. Now what will I tell Her?" she

said as we started to climb the broad mahogany staircase. It was very dark, so she took my hand again, and before we had reached the top of the stairs I obliged her by being seized by another chill. She felt my trembling fingers with satisfaction. "Oh, you've started again. That's good." She slid open one of the huge double doors at the head of the stairs.

As I looked into what once must have been Colonel Londermaine's study I thought that surely what I saw was a scene in a dream or a vision in delirium. Seated at the huge table in the center of the room was the most extraordinary woman I had ever seen. I felt that she must be very beautiful, although she would never have fulfilled any of the standards of beauty set by our town. Even though she was seated I felt that she must be immensely tall. Piled up on the table in front of her were several huge volumes, and her finger was marking the place in the open one in front of her, but she was not reading. She was leaning back in the carved chair, her head resting against a piece of blue-and-gold-embroidered silk that was flung across the chair back, one hand gently stroking a faun that lay sleeping in her lap. Her eyes were closed and somehow I couldn't imagine what color they would be. It wouldn't have surprised me if they had been shining amber or the deep purple of her velvet robe. She had a great quantity of hair, the color of mahogany in firelight, which was cut quite short and seemed to be blown wildly about her head like flame. Under her closed eyes were deep shadows, and lines of pain about her mouth. Otherwise there were no marks of age on her face, but I would not have been surprised to learn that she was any age in the world—a hundred, or twenty-five. Her mouth was large and mobile and she was singing something in a deep, rich voice. Two cats, one black, one white, were coiled up, each on a book, and as we opened the doors a leopard stood up quietly beside her, but did not snarl or move. It simply stood there and waited, watching us.

The girl nudged me and held her finger to her lips to warn me to be quiet, but I would not have spoken—could not, anyhow, my teeth were chattering so from my chill which I had completely forgotten, so fascinated was I by this woman sitting back with her head against the embroidered silk, soft deep sounds coming out of her throat. At last these sounds resolved themselves into words, and we listened to her as she sang. The cats slept indifferently, but the leopard listened, too:

"I sit high in my ivory tower,
　The heavy curtains drawn.
I've many a strange and lustrous flower,
　A leopard and a fawn

Together sleeping by my chair
　And strange birds softly winging,
And ever pleasant to my ear
　Twelve maidens' voices singing.

Here is my magic maps' array,
　My mystic circle's flame.
With symbol's art He lets me play,
　The unknown my domain,

And as I sit here in my dream
　I see myself awake,
Hearing a torn and bloody scream,
　Feeling my castle shake . . ."

Her song wasn't finished but she opened her eyes and looked at us. Now that his mistress knew we were here the leopard seemed ready to spring and devour me at one gulp, but she put her hand on his sapphire-studded collar to restrain him.

"Well, Alexandra," she said, "Who have we here?"

The girl, who still held my hand in her long, cool fingers, answered, "It's a boy."

"So I see. Where did you find him?"

The voice sent shivers up and down my spine.

"In the fern bed. He was shaking. See? He's shaking now. Is he having a fit?" Alexandra's voice was filled with pleased interest.

"Come here, boy," the woman said.

As I didn't move, Alexandra gave me a push, and I advanced slowly. As I came near, the woman pulled one of the leopard's ears gently, saying, "Lie down, Thammuz." The beast obeyed, flinging itself at her feet. She held her hand out to me as I approached the table. If Alexandra's fingers felt firm and cool, hers had the strength of the ocean and the coolness of jade. She looked at me for a long time and I saw that her eyes were deep blue, much bluer than Alexandra's, so dark as to be almost black. When she spoke again her voice was warm and tender: "You're burning up with fever. One of the malaria bugs?" I nodded. "Well, we'll fix that for you."

When she stood and put the sleeping faun down by the leopard, she was not as tall as I had expected her to be; nevertheless she gave an impression of great height. Several of the bookshelves in one corner were emptied of books and filled with various-shaped bottles and retorts. Nearby was a large skeleton. There was an acid-stained washbasin, too; that whole section of the room looked like part of a chemist's or physicist's laboratory. She selected from among the bottles a small amber-colored one, and poured a drop of the liquid it contained into a glass of water. As the drop hit the water there was a loud hiss and clouds of dense smoke arose. When it had drifted away she handed the glass to me and said, "Drink. Drink, my boy!"

My hand was trembling so that I could scarcely hold the glass. Seeing this, she took it from me and held it to my lips.

"What is it?" I asked.

"Drink it," she said, pressing the rim of the glass against my teeth. On the first swallow I started to choke and would have pushed the stuff away, but she forced the rest of the burning liquid down my throat. My whole body felt on fire. I felt flame flickering in every vein, and the room and everything in it swirled around. When I had regained my equilibrium to a certain extent I managed to gasp out again, "What is it?"

She smiled and answered,

"Nine peacocks' hearts, four bats' tongues,
A pinch of moondust and a hummingbird's lungs."

Then I asked a question I would never have dared ask if it hadn't been that I was still half drunk from the potion I had swallowed, "Are you a witch?"

She smiled again, and answered, "I make it my profession."

Since she hadn't struck me down with a flash of lightning, I went on. "Do you ride a broomstick?"

This time she laughed. "I can when I like."

"Is it—is it very hard?"

"Rather like a bucking bronco at first, but I've always been a good horsewoman, and now I can manage very nicely. I've finally progressed to sidesaddle, though I still feel safer astride. I always rode my horse astride. Still, the best witches ride sidesaddle, so . . . Now run along home. Alexandra has lessons to study and I must work. Can you hold your tongue or must I make you forget?"

"I can hold my tongue."

She looked at me and her eyes burnt into me like the potion she had given me to drink. "Yes, I think you can," she said.

"Come back tomorrow if you like. Thammuz will show you out."

The leopard rose and led the way to the door. As I hesitated, unwilling to tear myself away, it came back and pulled gently but firmly on my trouser leg.

"Good-bye, boy," the witch woman said. "And you won't have any more chills and fever."

"Good-bye," I answered. I didn't say thank you. I didn't say good-bye to Alexandra. I followed the leopard out.

She let me come every day. I think she must have been lonely. After all, I was the only thing there with a life apart from hers. And in the long run the only reason I have had a life on my own is because of her. I am as much a creation of the witch woman's as Thammuz the leopard was, or the two cats, Ashtaroth and Orus (it wasn't until many years after the last day I saw the witch woman that I learned that those were the names of the fallen angels).

She did cure my malaria, too. My parents and the townspeople thought that I had outgrown it. I grew angry when they talked about it so lightly and wanted to tell them that it was the witch woman, but I knew that if ever I breathed a word about her I would be eternally damned. Mamma thought we should write a testimonial letter to the 666 Malaria Medicine people, and maybe they'd send us a couple of dollars.

Alexandra and I became very good friends. She was a strange, aloof creature. She liked me to watch her while she danced alone in the ballroom or played on an imaginary harp—though sometimes I fancied I could hear the music. One day she took me into the drawing room and uncovered a portrait that was hung between two of the long boarded up windows. Then she stepped back and held her candle high so as to throw the best light on the picture. It might have been a picture of Alexandra herself, or Alexandra as she might be in five years.

"That's my mother," she said. "Alexandra Londermaine."

As far as I knew from the tales that went about town, Alexandra Londermaine had given birth to only one child, and that stillborn, before she had hung herself on the chandelier in the ball room—and anyhow, any child of hers would have been Alexandra's mother or grandmother. But I didn't say anything because when Alexandra got angry she became ferocious like one of the cats, and was given to leaping on me, scratching and biting. I looked at the portrait long and silently.

"You see, she has on a ring like mine," Alexandra said, holding out her left hand, on the fourth finger of which was the most beautiful sapphire-and-diamond ring I had ever seen, or rather, that I could ever have imagined, for it was a ring apart from any owned by even the most wealthy of the townsfolk. Then I realized that Alexandra had brought me in here and unveiled the portrait simply that she might show me the ring to better advantage, for she had never worn a ring before.

"Where did you get it?"

"Oh, she got it for me last night."

"Alexandra," I asked suddenly, "how long have you been here?"

"Oh, a while."

"But how long?"

"Oh, I don't remember."

"But you must remember."

"I don't. I just came—like Poor Sat."

"Who's Poor Sat?" I asked, thinking for the first time of whoever it was that had made the gentle bubbly noises at Alexandra the day she found me in the fern bed.

"Why, we've never shown you Sat, have we!" she exclaimed. "I'm sure it's all right, but we'd better ask her first."

So we went to the witch woman's room and knocked. Thammuz pulled the door open with his strong teeth and the witch woman looked up from some sort of experiment she was making with test tubes and retorts. The fawn, as usual, lay sleeping near her feet. "Well?" she said.

"Is it all right if I take him to see Poor Little Saturday?" Alexandra asked her.

"Yes, I suppose so," she answered. "But no teasing," and turned her back to us and bent again over her test tubes as Thammuz nosed us out of the room.

We went down to the cellar. Alexandra lit a lamp and took me back to the corner furthest from the doors, where there was a stall. In the stall was a two-humped camel. I couldn't help laughing as I looked at him because he grinned at Alexandra so foolishly, displaying all his huge buck teeth and blowing bubbles through them.

"She said we weren't to tease him," Alexandra said severely, rubbing her cheek against the preposterous splotchy hair that seemed to be coming out, leaving bald pink spots of skin on his long nose.

"But what—" I started.

"She rides him sometimes." Alexandra held out her hand while he nuzzled against it, scratching his rubbery lips against the diamond and sapphire of her ring. "Mostly She talks to him.

She says he is very wise. He goes up to Her room sometimes and they talk and talk. I can't understand a word they say. She says it's Hindustani and Arabic. Sometimes I can remember little bits of it, like: *iderow, sorcabatcha,* and *anna bihed bech.* She says I can learn to speak with them when I finish learning French and Greek.''

Poor Little Saturday was rolling his eyes in delight as Alexandra scratched behind his ears. "Why is he called Poor Little Saturday?" I asked.

Alexandra spoke with a ring of pride in her voice. "I named him. She let me."

"But why did you name him that?"

"Because he came last winter on the Saturday that was the shortest day of the year, and it rained all day so it got light later and dark earlier than it would have if it had been nice, so it really didn't have as much of itself as it should, and I felt so sorry for it I thought maybe it would feel better if we named him after it . . . She thought it was a nice name!" she turned on me suddenly.

"Oh, it is! It's a fine name!" I said quickly, smiling to myself as I realized how much greater was this compassion of Alexandra's for a day than any she might have for a human being. "How did She get him?" I asked.

"Oh, he just came."

"What do you mean?"

"She wanted him so he came. From the desert."

"He *walked!*"

"Yes. And swam part of the way. She met him at the beach and flew him here on the broom stick. You should have seen him. She was still all wet and looked so funny. She gave him hot coffee with things in it."

"What things?"

"Oh, just things."

Then the witch woman's voice came from behind us. "Well, children?"

It was the first time I had seen her out of her room. Thammuz was at her right heel, the fawn at her left. The cats, Ashtaroth and Orus, had evidently stayed upstairs. "Would you like to ride Saturday?" she asked me.

Speechless, I nodded. She put her hand against the wall and a portion of it slid down into the earth so that Poor Little Saturday was free to go out. "She's sweet, isn't she?" the witch woman asked me, looking affectionately at the strange, bumpy-kneed, splay-footed creature. "Her grandmother was very good to me in Egypt once. Besides, I love camel's milk."

"But Alexandra said she was a he!" I exclaimed.

"Alexandra's the kind of woman to whom all animals are he except cats, and all cats are she. As a matter of fact, Ashtaroth and Orus are she, but it wouldn't make any difference to Alexandra if they weren't. Go on out, Saturday. Come on!"

Saturday backed out, bumping her bulging knees and ankles against her stall, and stood under a live oak tree. "Down," the witch woman said. Saturday leered at me and didn't move. "Down, sorcabatcha!" the witch woman commanded, and Saturday obediently got down on her knees. I clambered up onto her, and before I had managed to get at all settled she rose with such a jerky motion that I knocked my chin against her front hump and nearly bit my tongue off. Round and round Saturday danced while I clung wildly to her front hump and the witch woman and Alexandra rolled on the ground with laughter. I felt as though I were on a very unseaworthy vessel on the high seas, and it wasn't long before I felt violently seasick as Saturday pranced among the live oak trees, sneezing delicately.

At last the witch woman called out, "Enough!" and Saturday stopped in her traces, nearly throwing me, and kneeling laboriously. "It was mean to tease you," the witch woman said, pulling my nose gently. "You may come sit in my room with me for a while if you like."

There was nothing I liked better than to sit in the witch woman's room and to watch her while she studied from her books, worked out strange-looking mathematical problems, argued with the zodiac, or conducted complicated experiments with her test tubes and retorts, sometimes filling the room with sulphurous odors or flooding it with red or blue light. Only once was I afraid of her, and that was when she danced with the skeleton in the corner. She had the room flooded with a strange red glow and I almost thought I could see the flesh covering the bones of the skeleton as they danced together like lovers. I think she had forgotten that I was sitting there, half hidden in the wing chair, because when they had finished dancing and the skeleton stood in the corner again, his bones shining and polished, devoid of any living trappings, she stood with her forehead against one of the deep red velvet curtains that covered the boarded-up windows and tears streamed down her cheeks. Then she went back to her test tubes and worked feverishly. She never alluded to the incident and neither did I.

As winter drew on she let me spend more and more time in the room. Once I gathered up courage enough to ask her about herself, but I got precious little satisfaction.

"Well, then, are you maybe one of the northerners who bought the place?"

"Let's leave it at that, boy. We'll say that's who I am. Did you know that my skeleton was old Colonel Londermaine? Not so old, as a matter of fact; he was only thirty-seven when he was killed at the battle of Bunker Hill—or am I getting him confused with his great-grandfather, Rudolph Londermaine? Anyhow he was only thirty-seven, and a fine figure of a man, and Alexandra only thirty when she hung herself for love of him on the chandelier in the ballroom. Did you know that the fat man with the red mustaches has been trying to cheat your father? His cow will give sour milk for seven days. Run along now and talk to Alexandra. She's lonely."

When the winter had turned to spring and the camellias and azaleas and Cape jessamine had given way to the more lush blooms of early May, I kissed Alexandra for the first time, very clumsily. The next evening when I managed to get away from the chores at home and hurried out to the plantation, she gave me her sapphire-and-diamond ring, which she had swung for me on a narrow bit of turquoise satin. "It will keep us both safe," she said, "if you wear it always. And then when we're older we can get married and you can give it back to me. Only you mustn't let anyone see it, ever, ever, or She'd be very angry."

I was afraid to take the ring but when I demurred Alexandra grew furious and started kicking and biting and I had to give in.

Summer was almost over before my father discovered the ring hanging about my neck. I fought like a witch boy to keep him from pulling out the narrow ribbon and seeing the ring, and indeed the ring seemed to give me added strength and I had grown, in any case, much stronger during the winter than I had ever been in my life. But my father was still stronger than I, and he pulled it out. He looked at it in dead silence for a moment and then the storm broke. That was the famous Londermaine ring that had disappeared the night Alexandra Londermaine hung herself. That ring was worth a fortune. Where had I got it?

No one believed me when I said I had found it in the grounds near the house—I chose the grounds because I didn't want anybody to think I had been in the house or indeed that I was able to get in. I don't know why they didn't believe me; it still seems quite logical to me that I might have found it buried among the ferns.

It had been a long, dull year, and the men of the town were all

bored. They took me and forced me to swallow quantities of
corn liquor until I didn't know what I was saying or doing.
When they had finished with me I didn't even manage to reach
home before I was violently sick and then I was in my mother's
arms and she was weeping over me. It was morning before I was
able to slip away to the plantation house. I ran pounding up the
mahogany stairs to the witch woman's room and opened the
heavy sliding doors without knocking. She stood in the center of
the room in her purple robe, her arms around Alexandra, who
was weeping bitterly. Overnight the room had completely changed.
The skeleton of Colonel Londermaine was gone, and books filled
the shelves in the corner of the room that had been her laboratory.
Cobwebs were everywhere, and broken glass lay on the floor;
dust was inches thick on her work table. There was no sign of
Thammuz, Ashtaroth or Orus, or the fawn, but four birds were
flying about her, beating their wings against her hair.

She did not look at me or in any way acknowledge my
presence. Her arm about Alexandra, she led her out of the room
and to the drawing room where the portrait hung. The birds
followed, flying around and around them. Alexandra had stopped
weeping now. Her face was very proud and pale and if she saw
me miserably trailing behind them she gave no notice. When the
witch woman stood in front of the portrait the sheet fell from it.
She raised her arm; there was a great cloud of smoke; the smell
of sulphur filled my nostrils, and when the smoke was gone,
Alexandra was gone, too. Only the portrait was there, the fourth
finger of the left hand now bearing no ring. The witch woman
raised her hand again and the sheet lifted itself up and covered
the portrait. Then she went, with the birds, slowly back to what
had once been her room, and still I tailed after, frightened as I
had never been before in my life, or have been since.

She stood without moving in the center of the room for a long
time. At last she turned and spoke to me.

"Well, boy, where is the ring?"

"They have it."

"They made you drunk, didn't they?"

"Yes."

"I was afraid something like this would happen when I gave
Alexandra the ring. But it doesn't matter . . . I'm tired . . ."
She drew her hand wearily across her forehead.

"Did I—did I tell them everything?"

"You did."

"I—I didn't know."

"I know you didn't know, boy."

"Do you hate me now?"

"No, boy, I don't hate you."

"Do you have to go away?"

"Yes."

I bowed my head. "I'm so sorry . . ."

She smiled slightly. "The sands of time . . . Cities crumble and rise and will crumble again and breath dies down and blows once more . . ."

The birds flew madly about her head, pulling at her hair, calling into her ears. Downstairs we could hear a loud pounding, and then the crack of boards being pulled away from a window.

"Go, boy," she said to me. I stood rooted, motionless, unable to move. *"Go!"* she commanded, giving me a mighty push so that I stumbled out of the room. They were waiting for me by the cellar doors and caught me as I climbed out. I had to stand there and watch when they came out with her. But it wasn't the witch woman, my witch woman. It was *their* idea of a witch woman, someone thousands of years old, a disheveled old creature in rusty black, with long wisps of gray hair, a hooked nose, and four wiry black hairs springing out of the mole on her chin. Behind her flew the four birds and suddenly they went up, up, into the sky, directly in the path of the sun until they were lost in its burning glare.

Two of the men stood holding her tightly, although she wasn't struggling, but standing there, very quiet, while the others searched the house, searched it in vain. Then as a group of them went down into the cellar I remembered, and by a flicker of the old light in the witch woman's eyes I could see that she remembered, too. Poor Little Saturday had been forgotten. Out she came, prancing absurdly up the cellar steps, her rubbery lips stretched back over her gigantic teeth, her eyes bulging with terror. When she saw the witch woman, her lord and master, held captive by two dirty, insensitive men, she let out a shriek and began to kick and lunge wildly, biting, screaming with the blood-curdling, heart-rending screams that only a camel can make. One of the men fell to the ground, holding a leg in which the bone had snapped from one of Saturday's kicks. The others scattered in terror, leaving the witch woman standing on the veranda supporting herself by clinging to one of the huge wistaria vines that curled around the columns. Saturday clambered up onto the veranda, and knelt while she flung herself between the two humps. Then off they ran, Saturday still screaming, her knees knocking together, the ground shaking as she pounded along.

Down from the sun plummeted the four birds and flew after them.

Up and down I danced, waving my arms, shouting wildly until Saturday and the witch woman and the birds were lost in a cloud of dust, while the man with the broken leg lay moaning on the ground beside me.

Squeakie's First Case

by Margaret Manners

*The late Margaret Manners was a fine mystery and
suspense writer who wrote for such markets as* Street &
Smith's Detective Story Magazine, Alfred Hitchcock's
Mystery Magazine, *and* Ellery Queen's Mystery Maga-
zine. *She published more than forty stories, including
"Death Is My Legacy," "Trial by Fire," and "An
Instrument of Justice." A collection of her best work
would make an excellent book. "Squeakie's First Case,"
one of her rare ventures into fantasy, is from* EQMM,
May 1943.

I'll never forget that night, not if I live to be as old as Methuselah
and have as many wives as Solomon, God forbid!

Squeakie was brushing her hair and counting. She's been
doing a hundred strokes lately. I usually put pink-wax stopples in
my ears, but that night I was too busy trying to lay down the law to
her. A husband has some rights and one of them ought to be a
power of veto, especially if his wife goes in for learned courses
in anything from Shakespeare to hobgoblins. The last time it was
psychology and she was "handling" me.

Squeakie (her real name is Desdemona, her father was mad
. . . about Shakespeare, so is she) is difficult to approach in
these matters; the effect is about the same as if you walk on a
step that isn't there.

Squeakie's voice went on. "Twenty-two, twenty-three . . ."

"But look, Squeakie," I said, "I don't want you to ride a
broomstick."

"Twenty-eight, twenty-nine. Don't be silly, David."

"I don't know why you of all people should want me not to be
silly," I said.

She peeped at me between the strands of hovering hairs that
were trying to follow the brush that attracted them. She made a
good-looking witch.

236

"I don't intend to ride any broomstick. I've told you over and over. The idea is to get a complete historic view of the insides of people. Thirty-four, thirty-five."

I stared at her. Where had thirty to thirty-three gone? Had she been counting by remote control? "Insides of people" suggested lots of things.

She said, "I wish you wouldn't wear those purple pajamas. I always have nightmares when you do. Thirty-nine, forty."

I said sternly, "They're not purple, they're mauve. Anyway, you bought them." Then I came down as I thought to brass tacks.

"I won't have any more of this foolishness; you've got to give it up."

She turned away from the mirror and shook her curly brown mop at me. "Brushing is doing wonders. Can't you see the life in it?" she said seriously.

I was caught off guard. I said, "Yes," and began to look for the life in it. Then I ground my teeth and sprang off the bed. "Squeakie! I don't mean the hair. You know what I'm talking about. I mean that so-called esoteric study—"

She smiled and interrupted me. "Oh, that. I've been trying to tell you. It helps me to understand people. You can't understand people's minds in the tenth century or in any other century unless you can share their thoughts. You know—what they believed, their superstitions, their crimes. It's a kind of mythology. Every age has one. As a reporter that should be clear to you. For example, everyone today believes in microbes and germs. Causing disease, you know."

"But Squeakie," I gasped, "that's not a superstition. Bacteria do cause disease."

Her sweet little face became darkly prophetic under the halo of electrified hair. "Ha!" she said triumphantly. "Living today, that's what you think. But what will people think two hundred years from now?"

I bit the cuff of the mauve pajamas and gave up.

She looked at the clock and began counting again. "Sixty-one, sixty-two."

I couldn't stand it any longer. "Squeakie," I said gently.

"Mmmmm? Sixty-four, sixty-five . . ."

"How do you know it's sixty-one? You stopped counting strokes at forty. How do you know?"

She pointed to the leather-framed clock.

"The clock? Squeakie!"

"Oh, David, don't you see? I look at the second hand when I stop counting. I allow one second per stroke. It's easy."

There was something wrong somewhere. "But," I said, "you can't add, darling!"

"David, don't be silly. Of course I can add. I just don't do it your way. I subtract. Eighty-two . . ."

"Kiss me goodnight, darling," I said, "I want to go to sleep."

She's wonderful. But sometimes I get a little confused.

The last thing I remembered was Squeakie saying "ninety-two." I was listening to her chest with a huge stethoscope, begging her to say ninety-nine. But she wouldn't. Then I tried to pull the stethoscope out of my ears. There was a terrible noise in my head, like a siren shrieking, but the ear pieces wouldn't come out. I shook them and shook them and . . .

I opened my eyes and felt as if the top of my head were coming off.

Squeakie was shaking me. "David! David! Wake up!"

I spoke through the layers of fur in my mouth. "Huh? What is it?"

She was scared; her nails were digging into my arms. I pushed her away and sat up.

"David, a woman in the next house screamed. It was terrible!"

I was awake now, enough to be sore. "What do you want me to do, scream back?"

But she was trembling, so I put my arms around her. "What's the matter, darling?"

"David, she was being killed, I know it."

I took my arms away again, quick. That's just like Squeakie. Give her an inch . . . Before I could recover she took more territory and I hardly had room to stand up in. I was lying in bed, of course, but you see what I mean.

She said, "David, call Gregory!"

I'd better stop here for a minute. Gregory Sawyer is a good friend of ours and in addition he's a police lieutenant on New York's Homicide Squad. He likes Squeakie too.

I glanced at the clock. "Darling," I said. My voice was full of what I hoped was convincing authority and disapproval. "If you hear a scream in New York at twelve midnight, even in a nice early-to-bed neighborhood like this, you don't call a lieutenant of the Homicide Squad. At the most you call the local precinct and report it. Get into bed, you'll catch cold."

Not Squeakie. She couldn't do anything that simple. She

shook all over until her teeth chattered. "It's raining," she moaned. "Listen!"

I listened obligingly. After all, that was easy. It was pouring outside, nasty chill March rain. You could hear it splashing and plopping in the courtyard between the two houses. The soft swish of wheels in the wet street made bed seem a good place to be in.

We live in a very quiet street in that part of Manhattan which just stops being the Village and starts to be Chelsea. Contrary to all you've read and heard, we're quiet, nice, working people. The long-haired Bohemian is a vanishing race. They paint camouflage these days, I suppose, and get paid for it.

I sat up higher in bed and tried to see 313, the house across the court, but the angle was wrong, and anyway it was pitch-black outside.

We live in 315, its companion house, and the court runs in from the street, giving us light, air and street noises. However, the kids can't get in and play there, thank the lord. We have a high board fence, nicely painted battleship-gray, spanning the space between the two houses and shielding us from the public eye when we take our sunbaths in summer.

The door in the fence can't be entered from the outside, but you can always get out from the inside—a sort of latch arrangement. Small shrubs and fancy fire escapes, New Orleans wrought-iron style, leading down to our glorified playpen, take the curse off concrete and raise the rent. But iron balustrades are too stagy for us; we use the basement door to enter the court.

Do you follow me? For the sake of the story I had to make it clear about the houses.

Now back to Squeakie. She fidgeted while I listened to the rain. Then she went to the window.

"The second floor across the court has a light on," she said. "Oh, it's gone out. David, it was a horrible scream. Please call Gregory."

I stalled for time. "He's probably asleep. Squeakie, I don't want to wake a hardworking police officer."

"It's not late. Besides, he never goes to bed early. He's probably not at home anyway. You don't need to be scared."

I'd been caught that way before. "If you are worried," I pointed out, "why don't *you* call the police station? You're a citizen too."

To make a long story short I found myself dialing Gregory's number. His phone rang twice. "There," I said, "he's not in. I'll just . . . ."

Before I could slam down the receiver Squeakie stayed my hand. "Give him time," she said, a cold glitter in her eye.

I gave him time.

"Hullo, what is it?" he said.

Just my luck! This had to be the night he went to bed early. He sounded fuzzy, and I felt like a fool.

"Squeakie wanted me to call you," I said weakly.

I waited for the sound and fury at his end, but he just said, "Oh, it's you." Very unencouraging.

I tried again. "Squeakie heard a scream."

"Really?"

"Oh, hell!" I said. "You don't think I wanted to call you, do you?"

"I wouldn't know."

Squeakie glared at me and snatched the phone. She had intended to do the talking all along, and we both knew it.

I was glad to see she wasn't doing any too well. The horrendous tale failed to impress. She hung up sadly. "He told me to go back to bed."

"Good," I said. "That's fine. Let's get some sleep."

"No," she said, tight-lipped. "I'm going to get dressed and make some coffee. We'll probably need it tonight."

"Squeakie, darling!" I wailed. "There's no murder. There's no fire. No tired minions of the law will troop in here for refreshment. Why do you want to make coffee?"

"Don't scream at me, David. How do you know?"

"How do I know what?"

"That there hasn't been a murder?"

She had donned her air-raid-warden slacks and and a sweater. She's prepared, all right.

"How do you know there has?" I asked.

She looked at me somberly. "By the prickling of my thumb."

I thought she was swearing. "By the what?"

"By the prickling of my thumb. That's how I know. It's from *Macbeth*. The witch says it. Well, are you getting up?"

"I am not."

She marched out to the kitchen. I could hear the rattle of pots as she went about making coffee.

The phone rang.

I picked up the receiver with fear in my heart. It was Gregory.

"Apologize to your wife."

"My God, no!"

"Yes. Two of your neighbors heard the scream and phoned the police. A man went over and broke down a door. Found a woman murdered. I'm coming right down. Looks like an all-night job. Tell Squeakie to put the coffee on, will you?''

I said dully, "She has," and hung up.

Squeakie came in self-consciously trying not to look smug. "There, I was right, wasn't I? Oh, darling, isn't it dreadful?" She suddenly looked frightened and pitifully incapable of dealing with this harsh world. But you can't fool one of the people all of the time. I just looked at her little pink thumb. Then I said, "You ought to keep that out of other people's business."

Even that was too much. She gave me a lecture on my moral duties as a citizen.

I was very meek while we waited for Gregory. There was something I wanted to do, but I wanted to do it alone. Squeakie was sitting over the coffeepot, looking like a superefficient "Angel of Mercy."

"How was she killed, David?"

"I don't know. Gregory didn't say."

"Well, anyway, she wasn't shot."

I stared at her. "Did your thumb tell you that?"

"O David, you don't think!" (*I* don't think!) "If I heard the scream I'd have heard the shot, wouldn't I?"

I flattered her by looking wonder and admiration—hard. Then I put on my act.

"Good Lord!" I exclaim. "I'd almost forgotten that I'm a newspaperman. I think I'll just step over and find out who it is, etc., so that I can phone the paper. I'll be back in a few minutes."

Squeakie pours a cup of coffee and hands it to me. "Good idea, I think I'll come along."

"Swell," I say heartily, "put on your raincoat." But I don't let her get that far. "Darn it!" I add, pulling a long face. "We're forgetting, Squeakie. You can't leave the apartment." I imply that she shoulders a great responsibility. "Gregory will be here any minute."

Believe it or not, she really thinks Gregory will fly to her before he even peeps at the corpse. To consult the oracle of her thumb, I have no doubt. After that she folds up, forlorn as a wet umbrella, and I am free to do a little quiet snooping.

There were cars parked outside 313. Doc Evans and his little black bag were upstairs, and so was Haley with a couple of the boys. Gregory was probably still on his way.

I studied the names and the apartment numbers displayed in the mail boxes. This was the arrangement:

First floor:	1A VERA GRAY
	1B LEONARD S. COBALT
Second floor:	2A JONATHAN WEST
	2B MARY ELLEN MEREDITH
Third floor:	3A Vacant
	3B JUDYTHA PERRY
Fourth floor:	4A ARISTODEMUS KORDIS
	4B JOHN SLATER

Then I peeked into the hallway through the thinly curtained glass panel of the door.

Standing near the open door of apartment 1B was a middle-aged couple. They looked worried and at the isn't-it-dreadful-you-never-know stage. I tapped on the glass and showed my police card. Reluctantly Papa Cobalt opened the door.

"It's all right," I told him. "I live next door. David Meadow. I'm a reporter. *Herald.* My wife heard the scream. What happened?"

Mrs. Cobalt answered for him. Now that I come to think of it, I never did hear her husband's voice, but then there are women like that. "She's been murdered. Miss Perry's been murdered!" She whispered the word.

"Miss Perry?" I said. "Oh, you mean the one in apartment 3B. Did you know her? What did she do?"

Mrs. Cobalt shook her head. "I don't know, but she was a friend of Miss Gray across the hall and you know who *she* is."

I disclaimed all knowledge.

Mrs. Cobalt warmed to the task. "She's an actress. In that new hit play at the Village Little Theater. You know the one about ghosts; been in the papers such a lot lately. *Dark World.* Miss Gray plays the dead wife."

"But look here," I protested. "Vivian Gaylord plays that zombie."

Mrs. Cobalt smiled. "That's her stage name. She's really Vera Gray. Lucky girl!" She glanced with benevolent interest at the door marked 1A.

Lucky girl was right. The Little Theater had struggled on tiny subsidies for years and then out of a clear sky some striving Villager had written a hit for them. Vivian Gaylord! No one had ever heard of her till she was discovered in one of its eerie roles, not the lead but still . . .

I moved over to 1A.

"She's not there," Mrs. Cobalt offered. "She's telling the policeman what happened."

Someone was coming down the stairs. I looked up and saw a slender young woman with a white, set face looking down and through us. She was wearing one of those new hats that have a brim and then yards of stuff hanging around the face and swathing the chin.

"Miss Gaylord," I said. But Mama Cobalt was too quick for me.

"Poor child," she said, and advanced to take the actress to her bosom.

Gray, alias Gaylord, was not tall, but she looked really tiny sobbing on the Cobalt bust.

Again there was a step on the stairs, and this time a heavy one. Sergeant Haley lumbered down to us. He offered me his hand and spoke to Mrs. Cobalt.

"She's had a nasty shock," he said, glancing at the draped head under Mrs. Cobalt's chin. "Take her in and give her a cup of tea. Don't let her go to bed yet; the lieutenant will want to talk to her again."

The Cobalts, looking heavily co-operative, withdrew into 1B and closed the door.

Tim Haley, otherwise known as "The Comet," gave me the eye. "You reporters waste more good time," he said, gently reproving me. "Whyn't you come up and ask me?"

I agreed with him and tried to follow his suggestion.

He shook his head. "Wait'll the lieutenant gets here. I don't wanna tell it twice."

"Well, tell me how she was killed," I said as we were going upstairs.

"She was lying in bed. Her skull was beaten in with a base of a marble statue. Diana the Huntress."

"Diana the Huntress?"

"Sure. Don't you know your mythology? The lady with the bow. It's a copy of the one in the Metropolitan."

Haley is occasionally quite surprising. Now when and why would he have ever been in a museum? But we were at the door of 3B. He remarked that Doc Evans was inside.

"Well," said I, "it can't have been premeditated."

His hand on the doorknob, Haley looked at me.

"Because of the weapon," I added.

"That doesn't always follow," he said, and opened the door.

The layout of the apartment was like ours, but in reverse. We crossed the hall to the large bedroom, the one with windows on the court fire escape. But before we went in, the hall door opened behind us and there was Gregory. Squeakie says with emphasis that he's "very attractive." He's the rugged but well-washed-behind-the-ears type. The boys under him think he's swell. I do and I don't. I mean you can appreciate a guy and still not be blind to his faults.

Haley was just drawing himself up and getting ready to make his report when there was a loud thump at the door. I had dire forebodings, and alas, my instincts were right.

When Gregory opened the door there stood Squeakie. From somewhere about her person, which was well hung with flashlights, first-aid kits, spare parts and divers other things to help us beat the enemy, she produced a stenographer's notebook and pencil.

"I thought you might like nice transcribed reports of your investigation," she chirped at him.

Haley looked pleased: he hates to take down anything. But Gregory played hard to get.

"Now, Squeakie, you can't fool around with this. It's a murder case."

She opened her big blue eyes very wide and registered shocked surprise. "Why, Gregory! You know how serious I am about things like this. You'll have to question people. Can't I be your secretary? I won't say a word."

I flagged him behind her back and shook my head till it rattled. But in a few seconds she had him neatly tied up. No rescue was possible.

"I'm going to phone the paper," I said, and left.

When I returned Squeakie was sitting in the apartment hallway on a kitchen chair. The door to the bedroom was closed.

"Where are Gregory and The Comet?" I asked.

She shivered. "In there with the . . ."

"Corpse?" I said. "Squeakie, you are a sweet little ghoul." Which struck home. For the next five minutes she stared past me at a spot on the wall behind my left ear.

Gregory came out of the bedroom. "Go sit in the living room, Squeakie." He pointed to the front of the house. "We're going to bring out the body." She fled down the hall.

Doc Evans came out and said hello, and I went in. I saw the face before it was covered up. The head was badly battered. The face I had seen before, casually now and then, on the street. It was long and very white, but the mouth which on the street was usually a hard crimson gash was now revealed thin, tight and bloodless. The eyes were long and oval with pale lashes which hardly showed without the mascara. The hair was a greenish-bronze and spilled out in a kind of tangled bloodstained mass on the pillow. It was a strong handsome face, but it was not a kind face. I looked around the bedroom as they carried her out.

It was identical with ours in size and shape but was very pretentiously decorated. There was a lot of green around mingled with hot blues and reds. It was well done yet definitely theatrical, a setting.

The fire-escape window was open and the curtain blew hard. The rain was slanting into the room and the rug was wet.

I noted the ornate desk and dressing table and a heavy walnut Spanish-type chest. A straight two-edged sword, shining and unsheathed, hung from a crimson cord on the wall above the chest. I tried the lid. It was open. Inside were packets of letters. Each marked with a name which was followed by a series of figures. What the fair Perry had done was no longer a mystery. The packets were tumbled about a bit as if somebody had looked for something hurriedly. I let the lid fall.

Haley pointed to something lying beside the bed. "Exhibit A," he said.

It was a heavy-based marble statue of Diana. There was an irregular purplish stain on one corner of the pedestal.

It was pretty clear to the three of us that Judytha Perry was a clever girl. The apartment furnishings had cost her plenty. She had done well for herself, she and her little collection of letters.

Haley showed us that somebody had left the apartment via the fire escape. Though the "fresh scrapings" he pointed out did not impress me as conclusive evidence, they seemed to satisfy Gregory. Especially after he had discovered that those marks in the damp rug were footprints—large and masculine.

Squeakie burst in on us.

"Look, David, she had a copy of the book I'm studying." She waved a too, too familiar volume under my nose, *Medieval Witchcraft in Modern Practice*. "I found it in her bookcase; she has a wonderful collection . . . !"

"Squeakie!" I thundered. She subsided with a contrite little "Oh."

Haley made his report then. He'd been trying to ever since Gregory arrived. Squeakie wandered about the bedroom poking in drawers and looking in closets while he talked.

I sum up Haley's report: People in the two houses on the court had been startled or awakened, as the case may be, by a scream at a few minutes after midnight. Calls from the Cobalts, who had been playing gin rummy, and from Greerson, on the top floor of our house, had started the investigation. Miss Gray had been returning from the theater and was about to open her apartment door when she heard the scream. She thought she recognized her friend's voice and ran up the stairs. But there was no answer and she couldn't get into the apartment. She started upstairs for Mr. Slater, remembered he was working nights in defense and went downstairs to get help. She met the Cobalts coming up.

Miss Meredith on the second floor stuck her head out the door as they passed. She said she had been awakened by what she thought was a scream. She had not connected it with the apartment above her because as she raised her head from the pillow she had been attracted by a movement on the second-floor fire escape of the house across the court (our house, 315). Her fears had been dissipated (the phraseology is Haley's) when she saw that it was only the curtain of the open window blowing out in the rain. She would have gone back to sleep but the sound of running feet (the Cobalts and Miss Gray) aroused her curiosity. She was sitting below in her apartment and would be glad to answer any questions, but she didn't know what she could possibly add.

Suddenly we all looked up startled. Squeakie was speaking.

"I wonder where her cold cream is." She was tapping her lips and staring at an array of vermilion-capped bottles and jars on the dressing table. "Look, she had everything—astringent, mask, grits, lotion, foundation cream—but no cleansing cream and no cold cream. She must have had a jar."

Haley stared at me and I stared at Haley. But Gregory went over and with infinite patience . . .

"Of course she had some, Squeakie. She just used it more often than the other things, and she used it all up." He turned back to us. But he didn't know Squeakie like I know Squeakie.

"Well," said she, "if she used it up where's the jar? The government says we ought to keep them for refills. Conservation, you know."

I raised my eyebrows and shrugged my shoulders trying vainly to indicate that I was in no way responsible for the behavior of my wife. She went on rooting around in things. The sword seemed to fascinate her.

"It has a copper hilt!" she announced as if confiding to us something of great significance.

Haley went over to her. Deliberately ignoring the dramatic wall decoration he stared down at Squeakie. She fluttered a bit and was still.

As she turned away from him she stumbled awkwardly. Then she stooped and picked something from the floor. "Look!" She held it up. "A little doll!"

"Doll me eye," Haley growled. He snatched it out of her hand. "It's not a doll, Mrs. Meadow. It's a pin cushion."

He held the miniature female figure out and we all saw the pins sticking in the head. Squeakie gasped as he placed it with a careful eye for position on the dressing table.

"It's a real cute one, too. They think up all sorts of crazy things like that to sell for ladies' boudoirs," he instructed her.

"Cute! I think it's ugly," Squeakie said.

"Well, I'll be . . . !" Gregory jumped on Haley. "Are we playing house here, Sergeant?"

The Comet answered stolidly, "No, sir."

"All right, let's go down and interview Miss Gray. I suppose we'd better say Miss Gaylord. Squeakie, if you can't be seen and not heard, please don't come."

We called at the Cobalts' and found Miss Gaylord waiting for us. She led us across the hall to her apartment and Gregory questioned her. As she took off her hat with its draped blinkers I noticed she looked pale and washed-out. She sat, her head propped on her hand, her elbow resting on the table. She seemed to be answering automatically, not thinking about what she was saying at all.

Squeakie was very attentive and conspicuously quiet, which was very nice for all of us.

Gaylord's story only repeated in detail what she had told Haley. I select the important points. The play was an unusually long one, but Gaylord did not appear in the last act. However, she rarely left the theater immediately. One had to remove one's makeup. She smiled apologetically for mentioning it. I remembered then, and Squeakie, who had seen the play, was obviously on pins and needles to say so, that Gaylord as the dead wife wore a striking. phosphorescent makeup that glowed like ectoplasm on a dimmed stage. She explained that it took only a few seconds to remove it, but that she loafed around in her dressing room. It was her habit to leave the theater at about eleven-forty and walk home. She arrived as she had done tonight, around midnight. She doubted whether anyone at the theater had seen her leave; they were all on stage at the time.

Doorman? We evidently had no idea of the size of the Little Theater. They didn't have a doorman. Of course if this run kept up they'd move to a larger house; you never could tell.

Gregory nodded and Squeakie's fingers flew. That she's as fast as a court stenographer has always amazed me.

Then Gregory hit something.

He asked the routine questions about knowing anyone who knew the victim and if she could help them in any way.

She hesitated and seemed ill at ease. "Why, no," she said, "I guess not." Then, "Oh, I don't know." She twisted her fingers and peered at us in an agony of uncertainty.

Gregory said, "Miss Gaylord, there is no compulsion on you to speak at this moment. But I do advise you that nothing is too slight to tell us, especially if you are in doubt." He leaned forward and spoke earnestly. "I don't need to remind you that your friend has been murdered. Murder rules out all minor considerations. Nothing you can say will harm anyone who is innocent."

She answered him reluctantly and in a whisper. "I knew someone who knew her well a few years ago, still knows her, I suppose . . . but . . ."

Gregory waited.

Her voice grew firmer and she went on. "His name is Bob Morgan. He used to be quite fond of Judy. I think a few years ago they were—well—they went around together a lot." She hesitated again. "I wish you'd talk to him. I don't like to say anything further, especially as I'm not very sure."

"Do you know where he lives?"

She raised her head and looked straight at Gregory, yet I had the impression that she was looking beyond him. It was a concentrated vagueness that I couldn't explain.

"Yes, I know. He lives next door in 315."

We all stiffened like hounds on a live scent. It was too much for Squeakie. She forgot all about not being heard.

"You don't mean that nice-looking young man who has the apartment below us!" she exclaimed.

Haley coughed warningly. Miss Gaylord ignored her. Only Gregory spoke.

He said, "Under you, Squeakie?" He glanced at Haley, who nodded.

"That's right, Lieutenant. That's the apartment Miss Meredith saw, with the fire-escape window open."

"Is there anything else, Miss Gaylord? Anything you think would be of use to us?" He rose and Gaylord looked up at him.

"No," she said quickly. "I really have a dreadful headache. I'd like to lie down if I may."

"Do," he said. Then he spoke rather diffidently. I could see what Squeakie meant when she said he has charm. "I had intended to ask you more about Miss Perry, her past life, and the usual things that policemen have to ask, but I think I'll try Mr.

Morgan who seems to have been an old friend too. If I don't get what I want, I wonder—I know it's an imposition at this hour—but may I call back to see you again?''

She smiled wanly, but nodded her head as if she didn't much care.

"Oh, just one thing more, Miss Gaylord." He stopped halfway to the door. "How does it happen that Miss Perry and Mr. Morgan lived so close to one another? It wasn't chance, I take it."

Her face was haggard under the pale-gold hair. "No," she said very softly, "it wasn't chance. Judytha and I shared an apartment when we moved here. She insisted that we move. She said she wanted to keep an eye on Bob. I took a separate apartment later when the show did so well. Judytha was nervous and wanted to be alone."

She spoke in such a frightened tone that I was sure she was holding something back.

At the apartment door Squeakie turned and said gently, "You suffer with headaches, Miss Gaylord?"

Gaylord narrowed her eyes as if making an effort to see Squeakie. "Yes," she said. "Well, not really, just sometimes."

"It's your eyes," said Squeakie, paying no attention to Gregory, who was waiting impatiently at the door.

Gaylord gave a scared bleat. "No, it isn't. It can't be my eyes!" Her hands were shaking.

Squeakie went on. "I don't think it's serious. But you are frightfully nearsighted. You'll have to wear glasses someday. You'd relieve yourself if you'd do it now."

Gaylord went white. She turned on Gregory. "Take her out of here," she said huskily. "She gets on my nerves." Then to Squeakie, "For God's sake leave me alone. Is the police department short manpower?"

Outside, Gregory gave Squakie a piece of his mind. She took it without a murmur. "Squeakie, you tactless, scatter-brained little . . ."

When he had finished, Squeakie said, "Well, it's silly to suffer like that because you're too vain to wear glasses."

I butted in. "Look, darling, lots of actresses should and don't wear glasses. It's more than vanity; they're afraid."

The rain was letting up and the air was fresh and somehow one smelled spring in the air. Squeakie tucked her arm through mine and we followed Haley, who was following Gregory into 315.

"We can have coffee in our place," I said, "whenever you like," and Gregory nodded absently.

We rang Bob Morgan's bell a few times and Gregory made Haley thump on the door. At last we heard a door open somewhere inside and a lot of uncertain shuffling and groping.

When he opened the door and stood teetering, staring out vaguely, we all recoiled as if slapped. The odor of whisky filled the place and overflowed into the hall.

"Whar is it?" He spoke thickly and truculently.

"How long have you been at home?" asked Gregory.

The drunk looked helpless, and then he asked, "What time is it now?"

"About two o'clock," Haley told him, looking at his watch.

Morgan counted on wavering fingers, "Twelve o'clock, one o'clock, two o'clock. Been here two hours." Then he added slyly: "Came home drunk, sleeping it off now." He held his fingers to his lips and winked solemnly.

Gregory said, "May we come in? We want to talk to you."

"Sure." He swung away from the door and I noticed that though he was fully dressed he was in his stocking feet. Then he turned back and growled at us. "Say, who are you? What do you want?"

"We are the police," Gregory told him a trifle inaccurately. "Did you hear a scream when you came home tonight?"

"Nope. What do you police want with me? Is she a police?" He pointed at Squeakie in her air-raid-warden costume.

"She's a stenographer." Gregory was annoyed, but it was his own fault. "Did you know a Miss Perry living next door in apartment 3B?"

I thought the eyes in the doorway grew a little wary. "Sure, I know Judytha. What of it?"

Gregory pushed him inside as he spoke. "She's been murdered," he said quietly. "Would you know anything about that?"

"Oh, my God!" He jerked back as if he had been struck. He shivered and leaned against the wall; for a minute I thought he would be sick. Then his whole manner changed. "Come in," he said soberly and he led us across the hall into his bedroom.

The room was warm and in disorder. The tightly closed window kept the air foul with the smell of liquor. A depression showed in the rumpled bedspread where someone had been lying. A pair of hastily discarded shoes, laces not untied, lay in the middle of the rug.

"Just a minute," he said thickly. He vanished into the bathroom and I could hear him snorting under the cold water. He came out slicking his wet hair back from his face. He was a good-looking kid in a rather worn sort of way.

He apologized sheepishly and asked us to go into the living room. But Gregory preferred the bedroom and I could see why.

Morgan threw the windows wide open. "Sorry, but I came home pickled. I didn't open the window. Must have been in a state. I guess I passed out."

This was going to be pretty easy, I thought. He wasn't acting any too smart.

Haley saw it, too. The curtains of the window that hadn't been opened were wet! He went round the room making a perfunctory tour of inspection, then he peered out of the window and waited.

Still Gregory didn't speak, and after an awkward silence Morgan said, "How was she killed? When?" His voice was dry. He was dead sober now.

"She was lying in bed with her head bashed in. She screamed at midnight, was found a short time after. Where were you at that time, Mr. Morgan?"

"Still on the street drunk, I guess."

"Ah, well." Gregory dismissed it with a shrug. "How well did you know Miss Perry?"

He answered frankly enough. "Very well indeed, at one time—not lately."

"When did you last see her?"

"Two weeks ago."

Gregory leaned forward. "You don't seem sorry she's dead."

He considered that. "I'm shocked," he said, "naturally. I don't think I'm very sorry; she was such a malicious little . . ." He stopped short.

"Really? You resented her treatment of you, then?"

"I?" He raised his head. "No, I was thinking of Vera. Judytha was jealous of her work in the Theater. You see, Judytha had stage ambitions too. They met each other through theater work. She used to hound poor Vera."

"What did Miss Perry mean when she said she moved next door to keep an eye on you?"

I thought that had him, but he recovered and hurdled it easily enough. "Did she say that? Well, she may have been a bit jealous of me, but frankly I can't see her moving for that. She probably moved because she liked the apartment and then she said that to be mysterious. Mystery was her forte." He seemed to be puzzled. "I can't understand . . ."

"What?"

"Oh? The murder." But it was something else I thought that he couldn't understand.

Gregory's eyes roved around the room.

And then Squeakie spoke. She said, and I jumped at the familiarity, "Bob, tell them the truth. You're making it worse for yourself."

I thought Haley would put her out the door. He made a move but Gregory held him back. I couldn't understand that.

"The curtains," Squeakie said. "They were seen blowing. They know your window wasn't closed. They want to trap you. Look!" She pointed to the window. "They're wet!"

Bob Morgan stared at Squeakie as if he couldn't believe what she was saying to him. It was as if they were alone in the room. I could have throttled her. Even in the light of subsequent events it gives me the creeps to think of it. Just shows you what some people will risk when they have complete confidence in their own rightness.

"The whisky," Squeakie went on. "It was too fresh; you just spilled it around. And besides your eyes were too clear. The lieutenant wasn't fooled." She looked at a photograph on the dresser. "Is that the girl you want to marry? She looks sweet."

Gregory saw that Squeakie was off on a tangent again. He took over.

"Well?" he said.

Morgan straightened his shoulders and faced us boldly, but there was a slight tremulous twitch in his lips that he couldn't control. "All right," he said flatly. "I was there. But I left before she screamed. I know you won't believe me, and I can't prove it. I'll tell you what I did, just as I did it."

He sat and stared at the wall and talked a noose around his neck.

"Judy and I had a love affair a long time ago. After it was over she found out that I wanted to marry someone else. She made me pay for some letters that would have wrecked my life. She had something on me and she'd been smart enough to get letters from me referring to it." A bitter smile twisted his mouth. "I was innocent but I couldn't have proved it. I suppose it's an old story to you. Do I have to say what it was?" He held his head proudly as he pleaded not to be humiliated.

Gregory shook his head. "You don't have to say anything unless you want to," he said. "Let it go. Time for details when you make an official statement."

I don't think Morgan realized what a sinister forbearance this was.

"Thanks," he said and went on. "It kept me poor paying for the letters and I couldn't get married. This last year I went through hell. I tried to run from her; I didn't care what happened. But she followed me. Moved next door. That's what she meant. I'd have committed suicide to get away from her, but I thought I'd make one more try."

Haley said softly, "Murder?"

The young man blanched. "No," he said, "not murder. I'd managed to get a key to the chest where I thought she kept the letters. I went over there tonight, down the fire escape and up on her side. I went in the window. She was lying in bed asleep."

He reflected bitterly: "The only normal thing about Judytha was that she went to bed early; she thought it kept her young.

"I opened the chest and used a tiny blackout flashlight to get the letters. There were plenty of others I hadn't heard about there. I heard a key turning in the apartment door. I grabbed the key to the chest but didn't have time to lock it. Oh, I wore gloves—naturally. I went out the fire-escape window, and I didn't wait to see who came into the apartment either. I wasn't particularly surprised that there should have been someone. After all . . . !" He shrugged and went on.

"I didn't think she'd go to the police, considering the circumstances, yet I couldn't be sure of anything. She was a poisonous person to cross. I went down the fire escape cautiously. When I was in the middle of the courtyard I heard the scream. I didn't know what trick she'd pull. I couldn't go back up my fire escape for fear of being seen. I didn't like to go through the basement and risk meeting the superintendent. So I went out into the street through the little door in the fence and came in through the front door of the house. I acted drunk in case I met anyone. Then I came in here and set the stage just in case she tried to frame me for something. I burnt the letters in the living-room fireplace."

Gregory shook his head slowly. "Clever," he said, "clever of you to keep it close to the truth. But it won't do. She woke up and you killed her, didn't you?"

The misery and terror in his eyes made me feel sick.

"No," he said over and over again, "I didn't. I didn't kill her, I tell you I didn't."

In a casual tone Gregory asked, "How did you get the key to the chest?"

Bob Morgan shook his head.

"Miss Gaylord took an impression for you, didn't she? You told her about the letters. She pitied you, and when the opportunity presented itself she took an impression of the key for you. That's why she was so frightened tonight. She thought you had gone letter hunting and killed Judytha Perry. I'm going to arrest you for that murder, Mr. Morgan."

"Gregory, you can't!" It was Squeakie again.

I said, "Squeakie, shut up!"

But Gregory said, "Why can't I, Squeakie?"

"He didn't do it."

Gregory came over and looked at her closely. I believe he thinks she's psychic. "Can you prove that?" he asked.

She almost cried with vexation. "You know I can't, Gregory—but I can prove who did."

Gregory said, "Can you, Squeakie?"

She backed down. "Not yet, Gregory, but let me try. He won't run away." I was afraid she'd think she was Portia and that at any moment she'd break into "The quality of mercy," but I underestimated her.

She stopped dead and said, "Let's all have a cup of coffee." That is what is called a strategic retreat. We, including Bob Morgan, prisoner, went up to the apartment and drank Squeakie's coffee.

"You know," she said, sitting cross-legged on the floor (she always lives up to slacks), "for an actress, Miss Gaylord hasn't much taste."

We all opened our eyes. "That home-made wimple," she went on. "Her face is all wrong for it; she shouldn't wear one. Besides, she's too short."

"Home-made wimple! My God!" said Gregory. "I didn't see anything like that; she looked all right to me."

"I mean the hat," Squeakie told him scornfully. "She draped it herself."

"Look," I said, "leave her wimple alone. She probably had her reasons."

Squeakie set down her cup so hard that I thought it would split. She stared at me for a long time. I began to feel uncomfortable.

Suddenly she moaned and jumped up. "Oh, Gregory, oh, Gregory!" She said it in a way that made my flesh creep. "I've got to go," she said. "Wait for me, I'll be back."

"Well . . ." I began.

Gregory said, "Shut up. I'll stay here with Morgan and Haley. Go after her. See what she's up to."

I caught up with her on the stairs of 313. She went up to the third floor. But she didn't go into 3B; she went into the vacant apartment across the hall.

I followed her into the kitchen of the empty apartment. She opened the cupboards, looked on the shelves, sighed and went out. In every room she looked in the empty closets.

"Darling, what are you looking for?" I inquired as sweetly as I could.

"Cold cream, David."

What could I do? I looked, too.

We found Judytha Perry's cold cream in the bathroom medicine chest. Squeakie unscrewed the vermilion lid of the jar. She turned out the light and I heard her say with definite satisfaction, "There, I knew he didn't do it!"

"Good Lord," I said.

"Here!" She pushed the jar into my hands. "Take this to Gregory. Tell him to look at it under the bed, way under. And don't gape at me, David. Do it right away. It's important."

I did it. What the hell! I couldn't read her mind. I didn't know.

Gregory raised one eyebrow when I told him. There's one thing I'll always resent. He went into the guest room and shut the door behind him. I never did know whether he crawled under the bed to look at a jar of cold cream. But I heard the light switch go on and off.

His face was rigid when he came out. "Come on," he said. "Quick! Why didn't you stay with her, you chump?"

When we got there Vera Gray alias Vivian Gaylord was having hysterics and Squeakie was throwing cold water on her. When we had her calmed down Gregory arrested her for the murder of Judytha Perry. Squeakie spent some time telling him how it was really self-defense because the poor girl believed she was being made blind.

I got it all out of Squeakie the hard way later.

It was just getting light outside and we were in bed again.

"Squeakie?"

"Hmmmm?"

"Darling, how did you know?"

"Special knowledge, plus psychology."

I determined to be patient. "Yes, go on."

"Well, first of all, he hadn't, so she must have."

I gathered she meant, must have committed the murder.

"Then there was Vera's psychology. Something like *Macbeth:* 'And that which rather thou dost fear to do than wishest should be undone.' "

"Oh, my God," I said prayerfully.

"Silly, that only means she had the murder all thought out without ever admitting to herself that she was really going to do it. Even when the murder plan was in operation she told herself up to the last minute that all she was going to do was frighten Judytha into releasing her from the spell. Visiting Judytha in her glowing makeup and staging a mystic scene or something was her way of justifying herself. She was giving Judytha her chance to raise the spell she had put on her."

"Spell?"

"Yes. It wasn't a pin cushion, you know. It was a doll which represented Vera. The pins were sticking in the eyes. Vera believed she was making her blind."

I said, "People don't believe that stuff."

"Oh, yes they do. And if they believe it hard enough it sometimes happens. Ask a doctor. Of course, she needed glasses anyway. That made it easier for Judytha; she was exploiting a fear that was already there."

She went on enlightening me. "You see, there was the book, and the copper-handled sword which is an attribute of the magician. Judytha began her reign of terror for a lark, out of boredom. But when she saw how easy it was—Vera was a good subject—she went further. She was jealous of Vera's success and enjoyed making her suffer. It gave her a sense of power. She had no real understanding of the primitive fear she had aroused in Vera, nor how dangerous it was."

I said, "Tell me about the crime."

"Well, Vera thought of it first because of the opportunity she had of leaving the theater unnoticed. Last night she started home earlier than she said, and she did not remove her makeup at the theater. The wimple was draped to hide it, and remember she walked home in the rain through empty streets.

"It was her key that Bob heard. Judytha awakened just as she opened the door. They had a scene. Vera found the doll and begged her to do something about it. Judytha said some awful things to her. Vera wasn't very clear when she told me this part, but I think the plan in her mind was like a will that she had to obey. She killed her with the statue which she had seen as the weapon in her mind's eye. Diane isn't only the Huntress, you know, she's the Moon Goddess. People used to think there was such a thing as moon blindness. Perhaps Vera thought her a suitable goddess to administer justice.

"After she killed Judytha she went across the hall into the empty apartment and removed the makeup. If anyone had come through the halls she would have stayed there or gone down the back fire escape on the side of the house. But no one came, so she walked down, met the Cobalts and told her story of hearing the scream and trying to get into the apartment."

I said, "Why did you want Gregory to look at the cold cream under the bed? Why didn't you tell him to look at it in the dark if you wanted him to see the traces of phosphorescent makeup in it?"

She blushed. "Well, it is dark under a bed," she said weakly. And then, "Oh, David, did he really do it?"

I had to confess I didn't know.

"What do you think of it all?" she asked me.

I chose my words carefully. "Well," I said, "I really think a little knowledge is a dangerous thing, darling."

"Oh, David, I'm so glad that you realize your limitations. That's the most important step." Her face was radiant. "Now if you want to enroll for some of my courses, I'll . . . Oh, darling, this is grand!"

She kissed me. Now really! Could I bring it up again? Could I say that I wanted her to abandon the fascinating study of medieval witchcraft? Could I? I kissed her little pink thumb and let it go at that.

The Ipswich Phial
by Randall Garrett

*In an incredibly prolific career that began (except for
one story) in the early 1950s, Randall Garrett published several hundred science fiction stories. He was
also Walter Bupp, David Gordon, Darrel T. Langart,
and one half of Mark Phillips and Robert Randall, to
mention only a few of his many pseudonyms. During
one stretch in the 1960s he had more stories in*
Astounding/Analog *than any other writer. Unfortunately,
very few of these stories have been collected, although*
The Best of Randall Garrett *(1982) is an almost definitive volume. He is best known for his "Lord Darcy"
series about a detective in an alternate world where
England is still ruled by the Plantagenets and magic
has become a science. Perhaps his most popular
book,* Too Many Magicians *(1967), is part of the series,
as is the present selection.*

The pair-drawn brougham moved briskly along the Old Shore
Road, moving westward a few miles from the little village of
St.-Matthew's-Church, in the direction of Cherbourg.

The driver, a stocky man with a sleepy smile on his broad
face, was well bundled up in a gray driving cloak, and the hood
of his cowl was pulled up over his head and covered with a
wide-brimmed slouch hat. Even in early June, on a sunshiny
day, the Normandy coast can be chilly in the early morning,
especially with a stiff wind blowing.

"Stop here, Danglars," said a voice behind him. "This looks
like a good place for a walk along the beach."

"Yus, mistress." He reined in the horses, bringing the brougham
to an easy stop. "You sure it's safe down there, Mistress Jizelle?"
he asked, looking to his right, where the Channel stretched
across to the north, toward England.

"The tide is out, is it not?" she asked briskly.

258

Danglars looked at his wristwatch. "Yus. Just at the ebb now."

"Very well. Wait for me here. I may return here, or I may walk on. If I go far, I will signal you from down the road."

"Yus, mistress."

She nodded once, sharply, then strode off toward the beach.

She was a tall, not unhandsome woman, who appeared to be in late middle age. Her gray-silver hair was cut rather shorter than the usual, but was beautifully arranged. Her costume was that of an upper-middle-class Anglo-French woman on a walking tour, but it was more in the British style than the Norman: well-burnished knee-high boots; a Scottish woolen skirt, the hem of which just brushed the boot-tops; a matching jacket; and a soft sweater of white wool that covered her from waist to chin. She wore no hat. She carried herself with the brisk, no-nonsense air of a woman who knows what she is and who she is, and will brook no argument from anyone about it.

Mistress Jizelle de Ville found a pathway down to the beach. There was a low cliff, varying from fifteen to twenty feet high, which separated the upper downs from the beach itself, but there were slopes and washes here and there which could be maneuvered. The cliff itself was the ultimate high-tide mark, but only during great storms did the sea ever come up that high; the normal high tide never came within fifteen yards of the base of the cliff, and the intervening space was covered with soft, dry sand which was difficult to walk in. Mistress Jizelle crossed the dry sand to the damper, more solidly packed area, and began walking westward.

It was a beautiful morning, in spite of the slight chill; just the sort of morning one would choose for a brisk, healthful walk along a pleasant beach. Mistress Jizelle was a woman who liked exercise and long walks, and she was a great admirer of scenic beauty. To her right, the rushing wind made scudding whitecaps of the ebbing tide and brought the "smell of the sea"—an odor never found on the open expanse of the sea itself, for it is composed of the aroma of the sea things which dwell in the tidal basins and the shallow coastal waters and the faint smell of the decomposition of dead and dying things beached by the rhythmic ebb and flow of tide and wave.

Overhead, the floating gulls gave their plaintive, almost cat-like cries as they soared in search of the rich sustenance that the sea and shore gave them.

Not until she had walked nearly a hundred yards along the beach did Mistress Jizelle see anything out of the ordinary. When she did, she stopped and looked at it carefully. Ahead and to her left, some eight or nine yards from the base of the cliff, a man lay sprawled in the dry sand, twenty feet or so above the high-tide line.

After a moment, she walked toward the man, carefully and cautiously. He was certainly not dressed for bathing; he was wearing the evening dress of a gentleman. She walked up to the edge of the damp sand and stopped again, looking at the man carefully.

Then she saw something that made the hairs on the back of her neck rise.

Danglars was sitting placidly in the driver's seat of the brougham, smoking his clay pipe, when he saw the approaching trio. He eyed them carefully as they came toward the carriage. Two young men and an older one, all dressed in the work clothes typical of a Norman farmer. The eldest waved a hand and said something Danglars couldn't hear over the sound of the waves and the wind. Then they came close enough to be audible, and the eldest said: "Allo! Got dee any trouble here?"

Danglars shook his head. "Nup."

The farmer ignored that. "Me an' m'boys saw dee stop up here, an' thought mayap we could help. Name's Champtier. Samel Champtier. Dese two a my tads, Evrit an' Lorin. If dou hass need a aid, we do what we can."

Danglars nodded slowly, then took his pipe from his mouth. "Good o' ya, Goodman Samel. Grace to ya. But I got no problem. Mistress wanted to walk along the beach. Likes that sort of thing. We head on pretty soon."

Samel cleared his throat. "Hass dou broke dy fast, dou an' d' miss-lady? Wife fixin' breakfast now. Mayap we bring du somewhat?"

Danglars took another puff and sighed. Norman farmers were good, kindly folk, but sometimes they overdid it. "Broke fast, Goodman Samel. Grace to ya. Mistress comes back, we got to be gettin' on. Again, grace to ya."

"Caffe, then," Samel said decisively. He turned to the elder son. "Evrit! Go tell dy mama for a pot a caffe an' two mugs! Run it, now!"

Evrit took off like a turpentined ostrich.

Danglars cast his eyes toward heaven.

Mistress Jizelle swallowed and again looked closely at the dead man. There was a pistol in his right hand and an ugly hole in his right temple. There was blood all over the sand around his head. And there was no question about his being dead.

She looked up and down the beach while she rather dazedly brushed at her skirt with the palms of her hands. Then, bracing her shoulders, Mistress Jizelle turned herself about and walked back the way she had come, paralleling her own footprints. There were no others on the beach.

Three men were talking to Danglars, and Danglars did not seem to be agitated about it. Determinedly, she strode onward.

Not until she was within fifteen feet of the brougham did Danglars deign to notice her. Then he tugged his forelock and smiled his sleepy smile. "Greeting, mistress. Have a nice walk?" He had a mug of caffe in one hand. He gestured with the other. "Goodman Samel and his boys, mistress, from the near farm. Brought a pot o' caffe."

The three farmers were tugging at their forelocks, too.

"I appreciate that," she said. "Very much. But I fear we have an emergency to attend to. Come with me, all of you."

Danglars widened his eyes. "Emergency, mistress?"

"That's what I said, wasn't it? Now, all of you follow me, and I shall show you what I mean."

"But, mistress—" Danglars began.

"Follow me," she said imperatively.

Danglars got down from the brougham. He had no choice but to follow with the others.

Mistress Jizelle led them across the sparse grass to the edge of the cliff that overlooked the place where the dead man lay.

"Now look down there. There is a dead man down there. He has, I think, been shot to death. I am not much acquainted with such things, but that is what it looks like to me."

The four knelt and looked at the body below. There was silence for a moment, then Samel said, rather formally: "Dou be right, mistress. Dead he be."

"Who is he, goodman?" she asked.

Samel stood up slowly and brushed his trousers with calloused hands. "Don't rightly know, mistress." He looked at his two sons, who were still staring down with fascination. "Who be he, tads?"

They stood up, brushing their trousers as their father had. Evrit, the elder, spoke. "Don't know, papa. Ee not from hereabout." He nudged his younger brother with an elbow. "Lorin?"

Lorin shook his head, looking at his father.

"Well, that does not matter for the moment," Mistress Jizelle said firmly. "There is Imperial Law to follow in such cases as this, and we must do so. Danglars, get in the brougham and return to—"

"But, Mistress Jizelle," Danglars cut in, "I can't—"

"You must do exactly as I tell you, Danglars," she said forcefully. "It is most important. Go back to St.-Matthew's-Church and notify the Rector. Then go on to Caen and notify the Armsmen. Goodman Samel and his boys will wait here with me and make sure nobody disturbs anything. Do you understand?"

"Yus, mistress. Perfec'ly." And off he went.

She turned to Samel. "Goodman, can you spare some time? I am sure you have work to do, but I shouldn't like to be left here alone."

Samel smiled. "Mornin' chores all done, mistress. Eldest tad, Orval, can take care of all for a couple hours. Don't fret." He looked at the younger boy. "Lorin, go dou an tell dy mama an' dy brother what happen, but nobody else. An' say dey tell nobody. Hear?"

Lorin nodded and ran.

"And bring dou back somewat ta eat!" Evrit yelled after him.

Samel looked worried. "Mistress?"

"Yes, Goodman Samel?"

"Hass dou noticed somewat funny about d' man dere?"

"Funny?" She raised an eyebrow.

"Yea, mistress." He pointed down. "All around him, sand. Smooth. No footprints but dine own, an' dey come nowhere near him. Fresh dead, but—how he get dere?"

Five days later, Sir James le Lien, Special Agent of His Majesty's Secret Service, was seated in a comfortable chair in the studylike office of Lord Darcy, Chief Investigator for His Royal Highness, Richard, Duke of Normandy.

"And I still don't know where the Ipswich Phial is, Darcy," he was saying with some exasperation. "And neither do they."

Outside the open window, sounds of street traffic—the susurration of rubber-tired wheels on pavement, the clopping of horses' hooves, the footsteps and voices of a thousand people, and the myriad of other small noises that make up the song of a city—where wafted up from six floors below.

Lord Darcy leaned back in the chair behind his broad desk and held up a hand.

"Hold it, Sir James. You're leaping far ahead of yourself. I presume that by 'they' you mean the *Serka*—the Polish Secret Service. But what is this Phial, anyway?''

"I can't tell you for two reasons. First, you have no need to know. Second, neither do I, so I couldn't tell you if I wanted. Physically, it's a golden cylinder the size of your thumb, stoppered at one end with a golden stopper, which is sealed over with soft gold. Other than that, I know nothing but the code name: The Ipswich Phial.''

Sean O Lochlainn, Master Sorcerer, who had been sitting quietly in another chair with his hands folded over his stomach, his eyes half closed, and his ears wide open, said: "I'd give a pretty to know who assigned that code name; sure and I'd have him sacked for incompetence.''

"Oh?" said Sir James. "Why?''

Master Sean opened his eyes fully. "If the Poles don't know that the Ipswich Laboratories in Suffolk, under Master Sir Greer Davidson, is devoted to secret research in magic, then they are so incredibly stupid that we need not worry about them at all. With a name like 'Ipswich Phial' on it, the *Serka* would *have* to investigate, if they heard about it.''

"Maybe it's just a red herring designed to attract their attention while something else is going on," said Lord Darcy.

"Maybe," Master Sean admitted, "but if so, me lord, it's rather dear. What Sir James has just described is an auric-stabilized psychic shield. What would you put in such a container? Some Khemic concoction, like an explosive or a poison? Or a secret message? That'd be incompetence compounded, like writing your grocery list on vellum in gold. Conspicuous consumption.''

"I see," said Lord Darcy. He looked at Sir James. "What makes you think the *Serka* hasn't got it already?''

"If they had it," Sir James said, "they'd have cut and run. And they haven't; they're still swarming all over the place. There must be a dozen agents there.''

"I presume that your own men are all over the place, too?''

"We're trying to keep them covered," Sir James said.

"Then they know you don't have the Phial, either.''

"Probably.''

Lord Darcy sighed and began filling his silver-chased porcelain pipe. "You say the dead man is Noel Standish." He tapped a sheaf of papers with his pipestem. "These say he was identified as a man named Bourke. You say it was murder. These say that the court of His Majesty's Coroner was ready to call it suicide until you put pressure on to keep the decision open. I have the vague feeling, James, that I am being used. I should like to point out that I am Chief Criminal Investigator for the Duke of Normandy, not—repeat: *not*—an agent of His Majesty's Secret Service.''

''A crime has been committed,'' Sir James pointed out. ''It is your duty to investigate it.''

Lord Darcy calmly puffed his pipe alight. ''James, James.'' His lean, handsome face was utterly impassive as he blew out a long plume of smoke. ''You know perfectly well I am not obliged to investigate every homicide in the Duchy. Neither Standish nor Bourke was a member of the aristocracy. I don't *have* to investigate this mess unless and until I get a direct order from either His Highness the Duke or His Majesty the King. Come on, James—convince me.''

Master Sean did not smile, although it was somewhat of a strain to keep his face straight. The stout little Irish sorcerer knew perfectly well that his lordship was bluffing, Lord Darcy could no more resist a case like this than a bee can resist clover blossoms. But Sir James did not know that. He did know that by bringing the case before his superiors, he could eventually get an order from the King, but by then the whole thing would likely be over.

''What do you want, Darcy?'' the King's agent asked.

''Information,'' his lordship said flatly. ''You want me to go down to St.-Matthew's-Church and create a diversion while you and your men do your work. Fine. But I will not play the part of a dupe. I damn well want to know what's going on. I want the whole story.''

Sir James thought it over for ten or fifteen seconds, then said: ''All right, my lord. I'll give it to you straight.''

For centuries, the Kings of Poland had been expanding, in an ebb-and-flow fashion, the borders of their territories, primarily toward the east and south. In the south, they had been stopped by the Osmanlis. In the east, the last bite had been taken in the early 1930s, when the Ukraine was swallowed. King Casimir IX came to the throne in 1937 at the age of twenty, and two years later had plunged his country into a highly unsuccessful war with the Empire and her Scandinavian allies, and any further thought of expansion to the east was stopped by the threat of the unification of the Russian States.

Poland was now, quite literally, surrounded by enemies who hated her and neighbors who feared her. Casimir should have taken a few years to consolidate and conciliate, but it was apparent that the memory of his father and his own self-image as a conqueror were too strong for him. Knowing that any attempt to march his armies into the German buffer states that lay between his own western border and the eastern border of the Empire would be suicidal as things stood, Casimir decided to use his strongest nonmilitary weapon: the *Serka*.

The nickname comes from a phrase meaning roughly: "The king's Right Arm." For financial purposes, it is listed in the books as the Ministry of Security Control, making it sound as if it were a division of the King's Government. It is not; none of his Slavonic Majesty's ministers or advisors know anything about, or have any control over, its operation. It is composed of fanatically loyal men and women who have taken a solemn vow of obedience to the King himself, *not* to the Government. The *Serka* is responsible to no one but the King's Person.

It is composed of two main branches: The Secret Police (domestic), and the Secret Service (foreign). This separation, however, is far from rigid. An agent of one branch may at any time be assigned to the other.

The *Serka* is probably the most powerful, most ruthless instrument of government on the face of the Earth today. Its agents, many of them Talented sorcerers, infest every country in Europe, most especially the Anglo-French Empire.

Now, it is a historical fact that Plantagenet Kings do not take kindly to invasion of their domain by foreign sovereigns; for eight centuries they have successfully resisted such intrusive impudence.

There is a saying in Europe: "He who borrows from a Plantagenet may repay without interest; he who steals from a Plantagenet will repay at ruinous rates."

His present Majesty, John IV—by the Grace of God, King of England, Ireland, Scotland, and France; Emperor of the Romans and Germans; Premier Chief of the Moqtessumid Clan; Son of the Sun; Count of Anjou and Maine; Prince Donator of the Sovereign Order of St. John of Jerusalem; Sovereign of the Most Ancient Order of the Round Table, of the Order of the Leopard, of the Order of the Lily, of the Order of the Three Crowns, and of the Order of St. Andrew; Lord and Protector of the Western Continents of New England and New France; Defender of the Faith—was no exception to that rule.

Unlike his medieval predecessors, however, King John had no desire to increase Imperial holdings in Europe. The last Plantagenet to add to the Imperial domain in Europe was Harold I, who signed the original Treaty of København in 1420. The Empire was essentially frozen within its boundaries for more than a century until, during the reign of John III, the discovery of the continents of the Western Hemisphere opened a whole new world for Anglo-French explorers.

John IV no longer thought of European expansion, but he deeply resented the invasion of his realm by Polish *Serka* agents. Therefore, the theft of a small golden phial from the Ipswich Laboratories had provoked instant reaction from the King and from His Majesty's Secret Service.

"The man who actually stole it," Sir James explained, "is irrelevant. He was merely a shrewd biscuit who accidentally had a chance to get his hands on the Phial. Just how is immaterial, but rest assured that that hole has been plugged. The man saw an opportunity and grabbed it. He wasn't a Polish agent, but he knew how to get hold of one, and a deal was made."

"How much time did it take him to deal, after the Phial was stolen?" Lord Darcy asked.

"Three days, my lord. Sir Greer found it was missing within two hours of its being stolen, and notified us straight away. It was patently obvious who had taken it, but it took us three days to trace him down. As I said, he was a shrewd biscuit.

"By the time we'd found him, he'd made his deal and had the money. We were less than half an hour too late. A *Serka* agent already had the Phial and was gone.

"Fortunately, the thief was just that—a thief, not a real *Serka* agent. When he'd been caught, he freely told us everything he knew. That, plus other information received, convinced us our quarry was on a train for Portsmouth. We got hold of Noel Standish at the Portsmouth office by teleson, but . . ."

The plans of men do not necessarily coincide with those of the Universe. A three-minute delay in a traffic jam had ended with Noel Standish at the slip, watching the Cherbourg boat sliding out toward the Channel, with forty feet between himself and the vessel.

Two hours later, he was standing at the bow of H.I.M.S *Dart*, staring southward into the darkness, listening to the rushing of the Channel waters against the hull of the fast cutter. Standish was not in a good mood.

In the first place, the teleson message had caught him just as he was about to go out to dine with friends at the Bellefontaine, and he had had no chance to change; he felt silly as hell standing on the deck of a Navy cutter in full evening dress. Further, it had taken better than an hour to convince the Commanding Admiral at the Portsmouth Naval Docks that the use of a cutter was imperative—and then only at the cost of a teleson connection to London.

There was but one gem in these otherwise bleak surroundings: Standish had a firm psychic lock on his quarry.

He had already had a verbal description from London. *Young man, early to middle twenties. Five feet nine. Slender, but well-muscled. Thick, dark brown hair. Smooth shaven. Brown eyes. Well formed brows. Face handsome, almost pretty. Well-dressed. Conservative dark green coat, puce waistcoat, gold-brown trousers. Carrying a dark olive attaché case.*

And he had clearly seen the quarry standing on the deck of the cross-Channel boat as it had pulled out of Portsmouth, heading for Cherbourg.

Standish had a touch of the Talent. His own name for a rather specialized ability was "the Game of Hide and Seek," wherein Standish did both the hiding and the seeking. Once he got a lock on someone he could follow him anywhere. Further, Standish became psychically invisible to his quarry; even a Master Sorcerer would never notice him as long as Standish took care not to be located visually. Detection range, however, was only a matter of miles, and the man in the puce waistcoat, Standish know, was at the limit of that range.

Someone tapped Standish on the shoulder. "Excuse me, sir—" Standish jerked round nervously. "*What? What?*"

The young officer lifted his eyebrows, taken aback by the sudden reaction. This Standish fellow seemed to have every nerve on edge. "Begging your pardon, sir, but the Captain would have a word with you. Follow me, please."

Senior Lieutenant Malloix, commanding H.I.M.S. *Dart*, wearing his royal blue uniform, was waiting in his cabin with a glass of brandy in each hand. He gave one to Standish while the junior officer quietly disappeared. "Come in, Standish. Sit and relax. You've been staring off the starboard bow ever since we cast off, and that's no good. Won't get us there any the faster, you know."

Standish took the glass and forced a smile. "I know, Captain. Thanks." He sipped. "Still, do you think we'll make it?"

The captain frowned, sat down, and waved Standish to a chair while he said: "Hard to say, frankly. We're using all the power we have, but the sea and the wind don't always do what we'd like 'em to. There's not a damn thing we can do about it, so breathe deep and see what comes, eh?"

"Right you are, Captain." He took another swallow of brandy. "How good a bearing do we have on her?"

S/Lt Malloix patted the air with a hand. "Not to worry. Lieutenant Seamus Mac Lean, our navigator, has a Journeyman's rating in the Sorcerer's Guild, and this sort of thing is his speciality. The packet boat is two degrees off to starboard and, at our present speed, forty-one minutes ahead of us. That's the good news."

"And the bad news?"

Malloix shrugged. 'Wind variation. We haven't gained on her in fifteen minutes. Cheer up. Pour yourself another brandy."

Standish cheered up and drank more brandy, but it availed him nothing. The *Dart* pulled into the dock at Cherbourg one minute late, in spite of all she could do.

Nevertheless, Goodman Puce-Weskit was less than a hundred yards away as Standish ran down the gangplank of the *Dart*, and the distance rapidly closed as he walked briskly toward his quarry, following his psychic compass that pointed unerringly toward Puce-Weskit.

He was hoping that Puce-Weskit was still carrying the Phial; if he wasn't, if he had passed it on to some unknown person aboard the packet, the whole thing was blown. The thing would be in Krakowa before the month was out.

He tried not to think about that.

The only thing to do was follow his quarry until there came a chance to waylay and search him.

He had already given a letter to the captain of the *Dart*, to be delivered as soon as possible to a certain address on the Rue Queen Brigid, explaining to the agent in charge of the Cherbourg office what was going on. The trouble was, Standish was not carrying a tracer attuned to the Cherbourg office; there was no way to get in touch with them, and he didn't dare leave Puce-Weskit. He couldn't even set up a rendezvous, since he had no idea where Puce-Weskit would lead him.

And, naturally, when one needed an Armsman, there wasn't one in sight.

Twenty minutes later, Puce-Weskit turned on to the Rue Queen Brigid.

Don't tell me he's headed for the Service office, Standish thought. *My dear Puce-Weskit, surely you jest.*

No fear. A dozen squares from the Secret Service office, Goodman Puce-Weskit turned and went into a caffe-house called the Aden. There, he stopped.

Standish had been following on the opposite side of the street, so there was less chance of his being spotted. Dodging the early morning traffic, narrowly avoiding the lead horse of a beer lorry, he crossed the Rue Queen Brigid to the Aden.

Puce-Weskit was some forty feet away, toward the rear of the caffehouse. Could he be passing the Phial on to some confederate?

Standish was considering what to do next when the decision was made for him. He straightened up with a snap as his quarry suddenly began to move southward at a relatively high rate of speed.

He ran into the Aden. And saw his mistake.

The rear wall was only thirty feet away. Puce-Weskit had gone through the rear door, and had been standing *behind* the Aden.

He went right on through the large room, out the back door. There was a small alleyway there, but the man standing a few feet away was most certainly not his quarry.

"Quick!" Standish said breathlessly. "The man in the puce waistcoat! Where did he go?"

The man looked a little flustered. "Why—uh—I don't know, sir. As soon as his horse was brought—"

"Horse? Where did he get a horse?"

"Why, he left it in the proprietor's charge three or four days ago. Four days ago. Paid in advance for the keeping of it. He asked it to be fetched, and then he went. I don't know where."

"Where can I rent a horse?" Standish snapped.

"The proprietor—"

"Take me to him immediately!"

"And that," said Sir James le Lien, "is the last trace we were able to uncover until he reported in at Caen two days later. We wouldn't even know that much if one of our men hadn't been having breakfast at the Aden. He recognized Standish, of course, but didn't say anything to him, for obvious reasons."

Lord Darcy nodded. "And he turns up dead the following morning near St.-Matthew's-Church. Any conjecture on what he may have been doing during those two days?"

"It seems fairly clear. The proprietor of the Aden told us that our quarry—call him Bourke—had his saddlebags packed with food packets in protective-spell wrappers, enough for a three, maybe four-day trip. You know the Old Shore Road that runs southeast from Cherbourg to the Vire, crosses the river, then goes westward, over the Orne, and loops around to Harfleur?"

"Of course," Lord Darcy said.

"Well, then, you know it's mostly farming country, with only a few scattered villages, and no teleson connections. We think Bourke took that road, and that Standish followed him. We think Bourke was headed for Caen.''

Master Sean lifted an eyebrow. "Then why not take the train? 'Twould be a great deal easier and faster, Sir James.''

Sir James smiled. "It would be. But not safer. The trouble with public transportation is that you're essentially trapped on it. When you're fleeing, you want as much freedom of choice as possible. Once you're aboard a public conveyance, you're pretty much constrained to stay on it until it stops, and that isn't under your control.''

"Aye, that's clear,'' said Master Sean. He looked thoughtful. "This psychic lock-on you mentioned—you're sure Standish used it on Bourke?''

"Not absolutely certain, of course,'' Sir James admitted. "But he certainly had that Talent; he was tested by a board of Masters from your own Guild. Whether he used it or not at that particular time, I can only conjecture, but I think it's a pretty solid assumption.''

Lord Darcy carefully watched a column of pipesmoke rise toward the ceiling and said nothing.

"I'll agree with you,'' Master Sean said. "There's no doubt in me mind he did just that, and I'll not say he was wrong to do so. *De mortuis non disputandum est.* I just wonder if he knew how to handle it.''

"How do you mean?'' Sir James asked.

"Well, let's suppose a man could make himself perfectly transparent—'invisible,' in other words. The poor lad would have to be very careful, eh? In soft ground or in snow, he'll leave footprints; in a crowd, he may brush up against someone. Can you imagine what it would be like if you grabbed such a man? There you've got an armful of air that feels fleshy, smells sweaty, sounds excited, and would taste salty if you cared to try the experiment. You'll admit that such an object would be suspect?''

"Well, yes,'' Sir James admitted, "but—''

"Sir James,'' Master Sean continued, "you have no idea how conspicuous a psychically invisible person can be in the wrong circumstances. There he stands, visible to the eye, sensible to the touch, audible to the ear, and all the rest—*but there's nobody home!*

"The point I'm making, Sir James, is this: How competent was Noel Standish at handling his ability?''

Sir James opened his mouth, shut it, and frowned. After a

second, he said: "When you put it that way, Master Sean, I must admit I don't know. But he handled it successfully for twelve years."

"And failed once," said Master Sean. "Fatally."

"Now hold, my dear Sean," Lord Darcy said suddenly. "We have no evidence that he failed in that way. That he allowed himself to be killed is a matter of cold fact; that he did so in that way is pure conjecture. Let's not leap to totally unwarranted conclusions."

"Aye, me lord. Sorry."

Lord Darcy focused his gray eyes on Sir James. "Then I have not been called in merely to create a diversion, eh?"

Sir James blinked. "I beg your pardon, my lord?"

"I mean," said his lordship patiently, "that you actually want me to solve the problem of 'who killed Noel Standish?' "

"Of course! Didn't I make that clear?"

"Not very," Lord Darcy picked up the papers again. "Now let's get a few things straight. How did the body come to be identified as Bourke, and where is the real Bourke? Or whoever he was."

"The man Standish was following checked into the Green Seagull Inn under that name." Sir James said. "He'd used the same name in England. He was a great deal like Standish in height, weight, and coloring. He disappeared that night, and we've found no trace of him since."

Lord Darcy nodded thoughtfully. "It figures. Young gentleman arrives at village inn. Body of young gentleman found next morning. Since there is only one young gentleman in plain sight, they are the same young gentleman. Identifying a total stranger is a chancy thing at best."

"Exactly. That's why I held up my own identification."

"I understand. Now, exactly how did you happen to be in St.-Matthew's-Church that night?" Lord Darcy asked.

"Well, as soon as Standish was fairly certain that his quarry had settled down at the Green Seagull, he rode for Caen and sent a message to my office, here in Rouen. I took the first train, but by the time I got there, they were both missing."

"Yes," Lord Darcy sighed. "Well, I suppose we'd best be getting down there. I'll have to ask His Royal Highness to order me to, so you may as well come along with me and explain the whole thing all over again to Duke Richard."

Sir James looked pained. "I suppose so. We want to get there as soon as possible, or the whole situation will become impossible.

Their silly Midsummer Fair starts the day after tomorrow, and there are strangers showing up already.''

Lord Darcy closed his eyes. "That's all we need. Complications."

Master Sean went to the door of the office. "I'll have Ciardi pack our bags, me lord. Looks like a long stay."

The little village of St.-Matthew's-Church was transforming itself. The Fair proper was to be held in a huge field outside of town, and the tents were already collecting on the meadow. There was, of course, no room in the village itself for people to stay; certainly the little Green Seagull couldn't hold a hundredth of them. But a respectable tent-city had been erected in another big field, and there was plenty of parking space for horse-wagons and the like.

In the village, the storefronts were draped with bright bunting, and the shopkeepers were busy marking up all the prices. Both pubs had been stocking up on extra potables for weeks. For nine days, the village would be full of strangers going about their hectic business, disrupting the peace of the local inhabitants, bringing with them a strange sort of excitement. Then they would go, leaving behind acres of ugly rubbish and bushels of beautiful cash.

In the meanwhile, a glorious time would be had by all.

Lord Darcy cantered his horse along the River Road up from Caen and entered St.-Matthew's-Church at noon on that bright sunshiny day, dressed in the sort of riding clothes a well-to-do merchant might wear. He wasn't exactly incognito, but he didn't want to attract attention, either. Casually, he made his way through the already gathering throngs toward the huge old church dedicated to St. Matthew, which had given the village its name. He guided his mount over to the local muffin square, where the array of hitching posts stood, tethered his horse, and walked over to the church.

The Reverend Father Arthur Lyon, Rector of the Church of St.-Matthew, and *ipso facto*, Rector of St.-Matthew's-Church, was a broad-shouldered man in his fifties who stood a good two inches taller than six feet. His bald head was fringed with silvery hair, and his authoritative, pleasant face was usually smiling. He was sitting behind his desk in his office.

There came a rap at his office door. A middle-aged woman came in quickly and said: "Sorry to bodder dee, Fahder, but dere's a Lord Darcy to see dee."

"Show him in, Goodwife Anna."

Lord Darcy entered Father Art's office to find the priest waiting with outstretched hand. "It's been some time, my lord," he said with a broad smile. "Good to see you again."

"I may say the same. How have you been, old friend?"

"Not bad. Pray, sit down. May I offer you a drink?"

"Not just now, Father." He took the proffered seat. "I understand you have a bit of a problem here."

Father Art leaned back in his chair and folded his hands behind his head. "Ahh, yes. The so-called suicide. Bourke." He chuckled. "I thought higher authority would be in on that, sooner or later."

"Why do you say 'so-called suicide,' Father?"

"Because I know people, my lord. If a man's going to shoot himself, he doesn't go out to a lonely beach for it. If he goes to a beach, it's to drown himself. A walk into the sea. I don't say a man has never shot himself by the seaside, but it's so rare that when it happens I get suspicious."

"I agree," Lord Darcy said. He had known Arthur Lyon for some years, and knew that the man was an absolutely dedicated servant of his God and his King. His career had been unusual. During the '39 war, he had risen to the rank of Sergeant-Major in the Eighteenth Infantry. Afterwards, he had become an Officer of the King's Peace, and had returned as a Chief Master-at-Arms before taking up his vocation as a priest. He had shown himself to be not only a top-grade priest, but also a man with the Talent as a brilliant Healer, and had been admitted, with honors, to the Order of St. Luke.

"Old friend," Lord Darcy said, "I need your help. What I am about to tell you is most confidential; I will have to ask you to disclose none of it without official permission."

Father Art took his hands from behind his head and leaned forward with a gleam in his eyes. "As if it were under the Seal of the Confessional, my lord. Go ahead."

It took better than half an hour for Lord Darcy to give the good father the whole story as he knew it. Father Art had leaned back in his chair again with his hands locked behind his head, smiling seraphically at the ceiling. "Ah, yes, my lord. Utterly fascinating. I remember Friday, sixth June, very well. Yes, very well indeed." He continued to smile at the ceiling.

Lord Darcy closed his right eye and cocked his left eyebrow. "I trust you intend to tell me what incident stamped that day so indelibly on your mind."

"Certainly, my lord. I was just reveling in having made a deduction. When I tell my story, I dare say you'll make the same deduction." He brought his gaze down from the ceiling and his hands from behind his head. "You might say it began late Thursday night. Because of a sick call which had kept me up most of the previous night, I went to bed quite early Thursday evening. And, naturally, I woke up a little before midnight and couldn't get back to sleep. I decided I might as well make use of the time, so I did some paper work for a while and then went into the church to say the morning office before the altar. Then I decided to take a walk in the churchyard. I often do that; it's a pleasant place to meditate.

"There was no moon that night," the priest continued, "but the sky was cloudless and clear. It was about two hours before dawn. It was quite dark, naturally, but I know my way about those tombstones pretty well by now. I'd been out there perhaps a quarter of an hour when the stars went out."

Lord Darcy seemed to freeze for a full second. "When the *what?*"

"When the stars went out," Father Art repeated. "One moment, there they were, in their accustomed constellations—I was looking at Cygnus in particular—and the next moment the sky was black all over. Everywhere. All at once."

"I see," said Lord Darcy.

"Well, *I* couldn't," the priest said, flashing a smile. "It was black as the Pit. For a second or two, I confess, I was almost panicky. It's a weird feeling when the stars go out."

"I dare say," Lord Darcy murmured.

"But," the Father continued, "as a Sensitive, I knew that there was no threat close by, and, after a minute, I got my bearings again. I could have come back to the church, but I decided to wait for a while, just to find out what would happen next. I don't know how long I stood there. It seemed like an hour, but it was probably less than fifteen minutes. Then the stars came back on the same way they'd gone out—all at once, all over the sky."

"No dimming out?" Lord Darcy asked. "No slow brightening back on?"

"None, my lord. *Blink:* off. *Blink:* on."

"Not a sea fog, then."

"Impossible. No sea fog could move that fast."

Lord Darcy focused his eyes on a foot-high statue of St. Matthew that stood on a niche in the wall and stared at the Apostle without actually seeing him.

After a minute, Lord Darcy said: "I left Master Sean in Caen to make a final check of the body. He should be here within the hour. I'll talk to him, but . . ." His voice trailed off.

Father Art nodded. "Our speculation certainly needs to be confirmed, my lord, but I think we're on the right track. Now, how else can I help?"

"Oh, yes. That." Lord Darcy grinned. "Your revelation of the extinguished stars almost made me forget why I came to talk to you in the first place. What I'd like you to do, Father, is talk to the people that were at the Green Seagull on the afternoon and late evening of the fifth. I'm a stranger, and I probably wouldn't get much out of them—certainly not as much as you can. I want to know the whole pattern of comings and goings. I don't have to tell an old Armsman like yourself what to look for. Will you do it?"

Father Art's smile came back. "With pleasure, my lord."

"There's one other thing. Can you put up Master Sean and myself for a few days? There is, alas, no room at the inn."

Father Art's peal of laughter seemed to rock the bell tower.

Master Sean O Lochlainn had always been partial to mules. "The mule," he was fond of saying, "is as much smarter than a horse as a raven is smarter than a falcon. Neither a raven nor a mule will go charging into combat just because some human tells him to." Thus it was that the sorcerer came riding toward St.-Matthew's-Church, clad in plain brown, seated in a rather worn saddle, on the back of a very fine mule. He looked quite pleased with himself.

The River Road had plenty of traffic on it; half the population of the duchy seemed to be converging on the little coastal village of St.-Matthew's-Church. So Master Sean was mildly surprised to see someone headed toward him, but that feeling vanished when he saw that the approaching horseman was Lord Darcy.

"Not headed back to Caen, are you, me lord?" he asked when Lord Darcy came within speaking distance.

"Not at all, my dear Sean; I rode out to meet you. Let's take the cutoff road to the west; it's a shortcut that bypasses the village and takes us to the Old Shore Road, near where the body was found." He wheeled his horse around and rode beside Master Sean's mule. Together, they cantered briskly toward the Old Shore Road.

"Now," Lord Darcy said, "what did you find out at Caen?"

"Conflicting evidence, me lord; conflicting evidence. At least as far as the suicide theory is concerned. There was evidence at the cliff edge that he had fallen or been pushed over and tumbled down along the face of the cliff. But he was found twenty-five feet from the base of the cliff. He had two broken ribs and a badly sprained right wrist—to say nothing of several bad bruises. All of these had been inflicted some hours before death.''

Lord Darcy gave a rather bitter chuckle. ''Which leaves us with two possibilities. *Primus:* Goodman Standish stands on the edge of the cliff, shoots himself through the head, tumbles to the sand below, crawls twenty-five feet, and takes some hours to die of a wound that was obviously instantly fatal. Or, *secundus:* He falls off the cliff, crawls the twenty-five feet, does nothing for a few hours, then decides to shoot himself. I find the second hypothesis only slightly more likely than the first. That his right wrist was sprained badly is a fact that tops it all off. Not suicide; no, not suicide.'' Lord Darcy grinned. ''That leaves accident or murder. Which hypothesis do you prefer, my dear Sean.''

Master Sean frowned deeply, as if he were in the awful throes of concentration. Then his face brightened as if revelation had come. ''I have it, me lord! He was accidentally murdered!''

Lord Darcy laughed. ''Excellent! Now, having cleared that up, there is further evidence that I have not given you yet.''

He told Master Sean about Father Art's singular experience with the vanishing stars.

When he had finished, the two rode in silence for a minute or two. Then Master Sean said softly: ''So *that's* what it is.''

There was an Armsman standing off the road at the site of the death, and another seated, who stood up as Lord Darcy and Master Sean approached. The two riders dismounted and walked their mounts up to where the Armsmen were standing.

''I am sorry, gentlemen,'' said the first Armsman with an air of authority, ''but this area is off bounds, by order of His Royal Highness the Duke of Normandy.''

''Very good; I am happy to hear it,'' said his lordship, taking out his identification. ''I am Lord Darcy; this is Master Sorcerer Sean O Lochlainn.''

''Yes, my lord,'' said the Armsman. ''Sorry I didn't recognize you.''

''No problem. This is where the body was found?''

''Yes, my lord. Just below this cliff, here. Would you like to take a look, my lord?''

''Indeed I would. Thank you.''

Lord Darcy, under the respectful eyes of the two Armsmen, minutely examined the area around the cliff edge. Master Sean stayed with him, trying to see everything his lordship saw.

"Everything's a week old," Lord Darcy muttered bitterly. "Look at that grass, there. A week ago, I could have told you how many men were scuffing it up; today, I only know that it was more than two. I don't suppose there's any way of reconstructing it, my dear Sean?"

"No, me lord, I am a magician, not a miracle worker."

"Thought not. Look at the edge of this cliff. He fell, certainly. But was he pushed? Or thrown? No way of telling. Wind and weather have done their work too well. To quote my cousin de London: *'Pfui!'* "

"Yes, me lord."

"Well, let's go down to the beach and take a look from below."

That operation entailed walking fifty yards or so down the cliff edge to a steep draw which they could clamber down, then back again to where Standish had died.

There was a pleasant breeze from landward that brought the smell of growing crops. A dozen yards away, three gulls squabbled raucously over the remains of some dead sea-thing.

Lord Darcy was still in a bitter mood. "Nothing, damn it. *Nothing*. Footprints all washed away long ago. Or blown away by the wind. Damn, damn, *damn*! All we have to go by is the testimony of eyewitnesses, which is notoriously unreliable."

"You don't believe 'em, me lord?" Master Sean asked.

Lord Darcy was silent for several seconds. Then, in a calmer voice, he said: "Yes. Oddly enough, I do. I think the testimony of those farmers was absolutely accurate. They saw what they saw, and they reported what they saw. But they did not—they *could* not have seen everything!"

One of the Armsmen on the cliff above said: "That's the spot, right there, my lord. Near that flat rock." He pointed.

But Lord Darcy did not even look at the indicated spot. He had looked up when the Armsman spoke, and was staring at something on the cliff face about two feet below the Armsman's boot toes.

Master Sean followed his lordship's gaze and spotted the area immediately. "Looks like someone's been carving his initials, me lord."

"Indeed. How do you make them out?"

"Looks like S . . . S . . . O. Who do we know with the initials SSO?"

"Nobody connected with this case so far. The letters may have been up there for some time. But . . ."

"Aye, me lord," said Master Sean. "I see what you mean. I'll do a time check on them. Do you want 'em preserved?"

"Unless they're more than a week old, yes. By the by, did Standish have a knife on him when he was found?"

"Not so far as I know, me lord. Wasn't mentioned in the reports."

"Hmmm." Lord Darcy began prowling the whole area, reminding Master Sean of nothing so much as a leopard in search of his evening meal. He finally ended up at the base of the cliff, just below where the glyphs had been carved into the clay wall. He went down on his knees and began digging.

"It has to be here somewhere," he murmured.

"Might I ask what you're looking for, me lord?"

"A piece of steel, my dear Sean; a piece of steel."

Master Sean put his carpetbag on the sand and opened it, taking out a thin, dark, metallic-blue wand just as Lord Darcy said: "Aa*ha!*"

Master Sean, wand still in hand, said: "What is it, me lord?"

"As you see," Lord Darcy said, standing up and displaying the object in the palm of his hand. "Behold and observe, old friend: a man's pocketknife."

Master Sean smiled broadly. "Aye. I presume you'll be wanting a relationship test, me lord: Carving, cutter, and corpse?"

"Of course. No, don't put away your wand. That's your generalized metal detector, it is not?"

"Aye, me lord. It's been similarized to all things metallic."

"Good. Put this knife away for analysis, then let's go over to where the body was found. We'll see if there isn't something else to be dug up."

The Master Sorcerer pointed the wand in his right hand at the sand and moved back and forth across the area, his eyes almost closed, his left hand held above his head, fingers spread. Every time he stopped, Lord Darcy would dig into the soft sand and come up with a bit of metal—a rusty nail, a corroded brass belt buckle, a copper twelfth-bit, a bronze farthing, and even a silver half-sovereign—all of which showed evidence of having been there for some time.

While the two of them worked, the Armsmen on the cliff above watched in silence. It is not wise to disturb a magician at work.

Only one of the objects was of interest to Lord Darcy: a small lump of lead. He dropped it into a waistcoat pocket and went on digging.

At last, Master Sean, having covered an area of some eight by twelve feet, said: "That's it, me lord."

Lord Darcy stood up, brushed the sand from his hands and trousers, and looked at the collection of junk he had put on the big flat rock. "Too bad we couldn't have found a sixth-bit. We'd be an even solidus ahead. No gold in the lot, either."

Master Sean chuckled. "You can't expect to find a complete set of samples from the Imperial Mint, me lord."

"I suppose not. But here"—he took the small lump of lead from his waistcoat pocket—"is what I expected to find. Unless I am very much mistaken, this bullet came from the .36 Heron that the late Standish carried, and is the same bullet which passed through his head. Here; check on it, will you, my good Sean?"

Master Sean put the bullet in one of the carefully insulated pockets of his capacious carpetbag, and the two men trudged back across the sand, up the slope to the top of the cliff again.

Master Sean spread himself prone and looked over the edge of the cliff. After a minute inspection of the carving in the sandy clay of the cliff face, he got up, took some equipment from his carpetbag, and lay down again to go to work. A simple cohesion spell sufficed to set the clay so that it would not crumble. Then, he deftly began to cut out the brick of hardened clay defined by the spell.

In the meantime, Lord Darcy had called the senior of the two Armsmen to one side and had asked him a question.

"No, my lord, we ain't had any trouble," the Armsman said. "We been runnin' three eight-hour shifts out here ever since the body was found, and hardly nobody's come by. The local folk all know better. Wouldn't come near it, anyway, till the whole matter's been cleared up and the site's been blessed by a priest. 'Course, there was that thing this morning."

"This morning?" Lord Darcy lifted an eyebrow.

"Yes, my lord." He glanced at his wristwatch. "Just after we come on duty. Just on six hours ago—eight-twelve."

"And what happened?" his lordship asked with seemingly infinite patience.

"Well, these two folk come along the beach from the east. Romany, they was. Whole tribe of 'em come into St.-Matthew's-Church fairground early this morning. These two—man and a woman, they was—come along arm in arm. Dan—that's Armsman Danel, over there—warned 'em off, but they just smiled and

waved and kept coming. So Dan went down to the beach fast
and blocked 'em off. They pretended they didn't speak no
Anglo-French; you know how these Romany are. But Dan made
it clear they wasn't to come no farther, so off they went. No
trouble.''

"They went back without any argument, eh?"

"Yes, my lord, they did."

"Well, no harm done there, then. Carry on, Armsman."

"Yes, my lord."

Master Sean came back from the cliff edge with a chunk of
thaumaturgically hardened clay further loading his symbol-
decorated carpetbag. "Anything else, me lord?"

"I think not. Let's get some lunch."

In a tent near the fairgrounds, an agent of *Serka*, Mission
Commander for this particular operation, was opening what looked
on the outside like a battered, scuffed, worn, old leather suitcase.
The inside was new and in the best condition, and the contents
were startlingly similar to those of Master Sean's symbol-decorated
carpetbag.

Out came two small wands, scarcely six inches long, of
ruby-red crystal wound with oddly spaced helices of silver wire
that took exactly five turns around the ruby core. Each wand was
a mirror image of the other; one helix wound to the right, the
other to the left. Out came two small glass flacons, one containing a white, coarsely ground substance, the other an amber-
yellow mass of small granules. These were followed by a curiously
wrought golden candlestick some four inches high, an inch-thick
candle, and a small brazier.

Like any competent sorcerer, the Commander had hands that
were strong and yet capable of delicate work. The beeswax
candle was being fitted into the candlestick by those hands when
there came a scratching at the closed tent flap.

The Commander froze. "Yes?"

"One-three-seven comes," said a whispered voice.

The Commander relaxed. "Very well; send him in."

Seconds later, the tent flap opened, and another *Serka* agent
ducked into the tent. He glanced at the thaumaturgical equipment
on the table as he sat down on a stool. "It's come to that, eh?"
he said.

"I'm not certain yet," said the Commander. "It may. I don't
want it to. I want to avoid any entanglement with Master Sean O
Lochlainn. A man with his ability and power is a man to avoid
when he's on the other side."

"Your pardon, Mission Commander, but just how certain are you that the man you saw on the mule this morning was actually Master Sean?"

"Quite certain. I heard him lecture many times at the University at Buda-Pest when I was an undergraduate there in 'sixty-eight, 'sixty-nine, and 'seventy. He was taking his Th.D. in theoretics and analog math. His King paid for it from the Privy Purse, but he supplemented his income by giving undergrad lectures."

"Would he recognize you?"

"Highly unlikely. Who pays any attention to undergraduate students at a large University?"

The Commander waved an impatient hand. "Let's hear your report."

"Yes, Mission Commander," Agent 137 said briskly. "I followed the man on muleback, as you ordered. He met another man, ahorse, coming from the village. He was tall, lean but muscular, with handsome, rather English-looking features. He was dressed as a merchant, but I suspected . . ."

The Commander nodded. "Lord Darcy. Obviously. Continue."

"You said they'd go to the site of the death, and when they took the left-hand bypass I was sure of it. I left off following and galloped on to the village, where Number 202 was waiting with the boat. We had a good westerly breeze, so we made it to the cove before them. We anchored and lay some two hundred yards offshore. Number 202 did some fishing while I watched through field glasses.

"They talked to the Armsmen atop the cliff for a while, then went down to the beach. One of the Armsmen pointed to where the body had been. Darcy went on talking to him for a while. Then Darcy walked around, looking at things. He went over to the base of the cliff and began digging. He found something; I couldn't see what.

"Master Sean put it in his bag, then, for ten minutes or so, he quartered the area where the body'd been, using one of those long, blue-black metal wands—you know—"

"A metal detector," said the Commander. "Yes. Go on."

"Yes. Lord Darcy dug every time O Lochlainn pointed something out. Dug up an awful lot of stuff. But he found *some*thing interesting. Don't know what it was; couldn't see it. But he stuck it in his pocket and gave it to the sorcerer later."

"I know what it was," said the Commander in a hard voice. "Was that the only thing that seemed to interest him?"

"Yes, as far as I could tell," said 137.

"Then what happened?"

137 shrugged. "They went back topside. Darcy talked to one of the Armsmen; the other watched the sorcerer dig a hole in the cliff face."

The Mission Commander frowned. "Dig a hole? A *hole*?"

"That's right. Lay flat on his belly, reached down a couple of feet over the edge, and dug something out. Couldn't see what it was. Left a hole about the size of a man's two fists—maybe a bit bigger."

"Damn! Why couldn't you have watched more carefully?"

Agent 137's face stiffened. "It was very difficult to see well, Mission Commander. Any closer than two hundred yards, and we would have drawn attention. Did you ever try to focus six-by field glasses from a light boat bobbing up and down on the sea?"

"Calm down. I'm not angry with you. You did well. I just wish we had better information." The Commander looked thoughtful. "That tells us something. We can forget about the beach. Order the men to stay away; they are not to go there again for any reason.

"The Phial is not there now, if it ever was. If Master Sean did not find it, it wasn't there. If he *did* find it, it is gone now, and he and Lord Darcy know where it is. And that is a problem I must consider. Now get out of here and let me think."

Agent 137 got out.

The public room at the Green Seagull, as far as population went, looked like a London railway car at the rush hour.

Amidst all the hubbub, wine and beer crossed the bar in one direction, while copper and silver crossed it in the other, making everyone happy on both sides.

In the club bar, it was somewhat quieter, but the noise from the public bar was distinctly audible. The innkeeper himself was taking care of the customers in the club bar; he took a great deal of pride in his work. Besides, the tips were larger and the work easier.

"Would dere be anyting else for dee?" he asked as he set two pints of beer on one of the tables. "Someting to munch on, mayhap?"

"Not just now, Goodman Dreyque," said Father Art. "This will do us for a while."

"Very good, Fahder. Tank dee." He went quietly away.

Lord Darcy took a deep draught of his beer and sighed. "Cool beer is a great refresher on a midsummer evening. The Green Seagull keeps an excellent cellar. Food's good, too; Master Sean and I ate here this afternoon.''

"Where is Master Sean now?" the priest asked.

"In the rooms you assigned us in the Rectory, amidst his apparatus, doing lab work on some evidence we dug up." His voice became soft. "Did you find out what happened here that night?"

"Pretty much," Father Art replied in the same low tones. "There are a few things which are still a little hazy, but I think we can fill in most of those areas."

Standish's quarry had arrived at the Green Seagull late in the afternoon of the fifth, giving the name "Richard Bourke." He was carrying only an attaché case, but since he had a horse and saddle and saddlebags, they were considered surety against indebtedness.

There were only six rooms for hire in the inn, all on the upper floor of the two-storied building. Two of these were already occupied. At two-ten, the man Danglars had come in and registered for himself and his mistress, Jizelle de Ville.

"Bourke," said Father Art, "came in at five-fifteen. Nobody else at all checked in during that evening. And nobody saw a young man wearing evening clothes." He paused and smiled brightly. "How-*ev*-er . . ."

"Ahhh. I knew I could depend on you, my dear Arthur. What was it?"

Still smiling seraphically, the good father raised a finger and said: "The Case of the Sexton's Cloak."

"You fascinate me. Pray elucidate."

"My sexton," said Father Art, "has an old cloak, originally made from a couple of used horse blankets, so it wasn't exactly beautiful when new. But it *is* warm. He uses it when he has to work outside in winter. In summer, he hangs it in the stable behind the church. Claims it keeps the moths out—the smell, I mean.

"On the morning of sixth June, one of the men who works here in the inn brought it over to the church, asked my sexton if it were his. It was. Want to take a wild, silly guess where it was found?" Father Art asked.

"Does the room used by Bourke face the front or the rear?"

"The rear."

"Then it was found on the cobblestones at the rear of the building."

Smiling even more broadly, Father Art gently clapped his hands together once. "Precisely, my lord."

Lord Darcy smiled back. "Let's reconstruct. Bourke went to his room before five-thirty. Right?"

"Right. One of the maids went with him, let him in, and gave him the key."

"Was he ever seen again?"

"Only once. He ordered a light meal, and it was brought up about six. That's the last time he was seen."

"Were either of the other guests in the house at the time?"

"No. The man Danglars had left about four-thirty, and hadn't returned. No one saw Mistress Jizelle leave, but the girl who turns down the beds says that both rooms were empty at six. Bourke was still there at the time."

"Hmmmm."

Lord Darcy looked into the depths of his beer. After half a minute, he said: "Reverend Father, was a stranger in an old horse-blanket cloak actually seen in this inn, or are we speculating in insubstantial mist?"

Father Art's mouth twisted in a small grimace. "Not totally insubstantial, my lord, but not strong, either. The barmaid who was on duty that night says she remembers a couple of strangers who came in, but she doesn't remember anything about them. She's not terribly bright."

Lord Darcy chuckled. "All right, then. Let's assume that Standish actually came in here in a stolen—and uncomfortably warm—cloak. How did that come about, and what happened afterwards?"

Father Art fired up his old briar and took another sip from his seidel of beer. "Well, let's see. Standish comes into the village an hour after Bourke—perhaps a little more. But he doesn't come in directly; he circles round behind the church. Why? Not to steal the cloak. How would he know it was there?" He took two puffs from his pipe, then his eyes brightened. "Of course. To tether his horse. He didn't want it seen in the public square, and knew it would be safe in the church stable." Two more puffs.

"Hmmm. He sees the cloak on the stable wall and realizes that it will serve as a disguise, covering his evening dress. He borrows it and comes here to the inn. He makes sure that Bourke is firmly in place, then goes back to his horse and hightails it for Caen to send word to Sir James. Then he comes back here to the Green Seagull. He waits until nobody's looking, then sneaks up the stair to Bourke's room."

The priest stopped, scowled, and took a good, healthy drink from his seidel. "Some time later, he went out the window to the courtyard below, losing the cloak in the process." He shook his head. "But what happened between the time he went upstairs and the time he dropped the cloak, and what happened between then and his death, I haven't the foggiest conjecture."

"I have several," Lord Darcy said, "but they are all very, very foggy. We need more data. I have several questions." He ticked them off on his fingers.. "One: Where is Bourke? Two: Who shot Standish? Three: *Why* was he shot? Four: What happened here at the inn? Five: What happened on the beach? And, finally: *Where is the Ipswich Phial?*"

Father Art lifted his seidel, drained its contents on one extended draught, set it firmly on the table, and said: "I don't know. God does."

Lord Darcy nodded. "Indeed; and one of His greatest attributes is that if you ask Him the right question in the right way, He will always give you an answer."

"You intend to pray for answers to those questions, my lord?"

"That, yes. But I have found that the best way to ask God about questions like these is to go out and dig up the data yourself."

Father Art smiled. *"Dominus vobiscum."*

"Et cum spiritu tuo," Lord Darcy responded.

"Excavemus!" said the priest.

In his room in the Rectory, Master Sean had carefully set up his apparatus on the table. Noel Standish's .36 Heron was clamped securely into a padded vise which stood at one end of the table. Three feet in front of the muzzle, the bullet which Lord Darcy had dug from the sand had been carefully placed on a small pedestal, so that it was at exactly the same height as the muzzle. He was using certain instruments to make sure that the axis of the bullet was accurately aligned with the axis of the Heron's barrel when a rhythmic code knock came at the door. The sorcerer went over to the door, unbolted it, opened it, and said: "Come in, me lord."

"I hope I didn't interrupt anything," Lord Darcy said.

"Not at all, me lord." Master Sean carefully closed and bolted the door again. "I was just getting ready for the ballistics test. The similarity relationship tests have already assured me that the slug was the one that killed Standish. There's only to see if it came from his own gun. Have you found any further clues?"

"None," Lord Darcy admitted. "I managed to get a good look at the guest rooms in the Green Seagull. Nothing. Flat nothing. I have several ideas, but no evidence." Then he gestured at the handgun. "Pray proceed with your work. I will be most happy to wait."

"It'll only be a minute or so," Master Sean said apologetically. He went back to the table and continued his preparations while Lord Darcy watched in silence. His lordship was well aware of the principle involved; he had seen the test innumerable times. He recalled a lecture that Master Sean had once given on the subject.

"You see," the sorcerer had said, "the Principle of Relevance is important here. Most of the wear on a gun is purely mechanical. It don't matter *who* pulls the trigger, you see; the erosion caused by the gases produced in the chamber and the wear caused by the bullet's passing through the barrel will be the same. It's not relevant *to the gun* who pulled the trigger or what it was fired at. But, *to the bullet* it *is* relevant which gun it was fired from and what it hit. All this can be determined by the proper spells."

In spite of having seen it many times, Lord Darcy always liked to watch the test because it was rather spectacular when the test was positive. Master Sean sprinkled a small amount of previously charged powder on both the bullet and the gun. Then he raised his wand and said an incantation under his breath.

At the last syllable of the incantation, there was a sound as if someone had sharply struck a cracked bell as the bullet vanished. The .36 Heron shivered in its vise.

Master Sean let out his breath. "Just like a homing pigeon, me lord. Gun and bullet match."

"I've often wondered why the bullet does that," Lord Darcy said.

Master Sean chuckled. "Call it an induced return-to-the-womb fixation, my lord. Was there something you wanted?"

"A couple of things," Lord Darcy walked over to his suitcase, opened it, and took out a holstered handgun. It was a precision-made .40 caliber MacGregor—a heavy man-stopper.

While he checked out the MacGregor itself, he said: "This is one. The other is a question. How long before his body was found did Standish die?"

Master Sean rubbed the side of his nose with a thick finger. "Well, the investigative sorcerer at Caen, a good journeyman, placed the time as not more than fifteen minutes before the body was discovered. My own tests showed not more than twenty-five minutes, but not even the best preservative spell can keep something like that from blurring after a week has passed.''

Lord Darcy slid the MacGregor into its snugly-fitted holster and adjusted his jacket to cover it. "In other words, there's the usual hazy area. The bruises and fractures were definitely inflicted before death?"

"Definitely, my lord. About three hours before, give or take that same fifteen minutes."

"I see. Interesting. Very interesting." He looked in the wall mirror and adjusted his neckpiece. "Have you further work to do?"

"Only the analysis on the knife," Master Sean said.

Lord Darcy turned from the mirror. "Will you fix me up with a tracer? I'm going out to stroll about the village and possibly to the fairgrounds and the tent city. I anticipate no danger, but I don't want to get lost, either."

"Very well, me lord," the sorcerer said with resignation. He opened his symbol-decorated carpetbag and took out a little wooden box. It held what looked remarkably like one-inch toothpicks, except that they were evenly cylindrical, not tapered, and they were made of ash instead of pine. He selected one and put the box back in his bag. He handed the little cylinder to Lord Darcy, who took it between the thumb and forefinger of his right hand.

Then the master sorcerer took a little scented oil on his right thumb from a special golden oil stock and rubbed it along the sliver of ash, from Lord Darcy's thumb to the other end. Then he grasped that end in his own right thumb and forefinger.

A quick motion of both wrists, and the ashen splinter snapped.

But, psychically and symbolically, the halves were still part of an unbroken whole. As long as each man carried his half, the two of them were specially linked.

"Thank you, my dear Sean," Lord Darcy said. "And now I shall be off to enjoy the nightlife of the teeming metropolis surrounding us."

With that, he was gone, and Master Sean returned to his work.

The sun was a fat, squashed-looking, red-orange ellipsoid seated neatly on the horizon when Lord Darcy stepped out of the gate of the churchyard. It would be gone in a few minutes. The long shadow of the church spire reached out across the village and into the fields. The colors of the flags and banners and bunting around the village were altered in value by the reddish light. The weather had been beautiful and clear all day, and would continue to be, according to the Weather Bureau predictors. It would be a fine night.

"Please, my lord—are you Lord Darcy?"

Lord Darcy had noticed the woman come out of the church, but the village square was full of people, and he had paid little attention. Now he turned his full attention on her and was pleasantly surprised. She was quite the loveliest creature he had seen in a long time.

"I am, Damoselle," he said with a smile. "But I fear you have the advantage of me."

Her own smile was timid, almost frightened. "I am named Sharolta."

Her name, her slight accent, and her clothing all proclaimed her Romany. Her long, softly dark hair and her dark eyes, her well-formed nose and her full, almost too-perfect lips, along with her magnificently lush body, accentuated by the Romany costume, proclaimed her beautiful.

"May I be of help to you, Damoselle Sharolta?"

She shook her head. "No, no. I ask nothing. But perhaps I can be of help to you." Her smiled seemed to quaver. "Can we go somewhere to talk?"

"Where, for instance?" Lord Darcy asked carefully.

"Anywhere you say, my lord. Anywhere, so long as it is private." Then she flushed. "I—I mean, not *too much* private. I mean, where we can talk. You know."

"Of course. It is not yet time for Vespers; I suggest that we go into the church," Lord Darcy said.

"Yes, yes. That would be fine." She smiled. "There were not many folk in there. It should be fine."

The interior of the Church of St. Matthew was darkened, but far from being gloomy. The flickering clusters of candles around the statues and icons were like twinkling, multicolored star clusters.

Lord Darcy and the Damoselle Sharolta sat down in one of the rear pews. Most of a dozen or so people who were in the church were farther up toward the altar, praying; there was no one within earshot of the place Lord Darcy had chosen.

Lord Darcy waited in silence for the girl to speak. The Romany become silent under pressure; create a vacuum for them to fill, and the words come tumbling over each other in eloquent eagerness.

"You are the great Lord Darcy, the great Investigator," she began suddenly. "You are looking into the death of the poor Goodman Standish who was found on the beach a week ago. Is all this not so?"

Lord Darcy nodded silently.

"Well, then, there must be something wrong about that man's death, or you would not be here. So I must tell you what I know."

"A week ago, there came to our tribe a group of five men. They said they were from the tribe of Chanro—the Sword— which is in the area of Buda-Pest. Their leader, who calls himself Suv—the Needle—asked our chief for aid and sanctuary, as it is their right, and it was granted. But they are very secretive among themselves. They behave very well, mind you; I don't mean they are rude or boorish, or anything like that. But there is—how do I say it?—there is a *wrongness* about them.

"This morning, for instance. I must tell you of that. The man who calls himself Suv wanted me to walk along the beach with him. I did not want to, for I do not find him an attractive man—you understand?"

Again his lordship nodded. "Of course."

"But he said he meant nothing like that. He said he wanted to walk along the sea, but he did not want to walk alone. He said he would show me all the shore life—the birds, the things in the pools, the plants. I was interested, and I thought there would be no harm, so I went.

"He was true to his word. He did not try to make love to me. It was nice for a while. He showed me the tide pools and pointed out the different kinds of things in them. One had a jellyfish." She looked up from her hands, and there was a frown on her face.

"Then we got near to that little cove where the body was found. I wanted to turn back, but he said, no, he wanted to look at it. I said I wouldn't and started back. Then he told me that if I didn't, he'd break my arm. So I went." She seemed to shiver a little under her bright dress. "When the Armsman showed up, he kept on going, pretending he didn't understand Anglo-French. Then we saw that there were two of them, the Armsmen, I mean. So we turned around and went back. Suv was very furious."

She stopped and said no more.

"My dear," he asked gently, "why does one of the Romany come to the authorities with a story like this? Do not the Romany take care of their own?"

"Yes, my lord. But these men are not Rom."

"Oh?"

"Their tent is next to mine. I have heard them talking when they think no one is listening. I do not understand it very well, but I know it when I hear it; they were speaking *Burgdeutsch.*"

"I see," said Lord Darcy softly and thoughtfully. The German of Brandenburg was the court language of Poland, which suddenly made everything very interesting indeed.

"Do you suppose, Damoselle," he said, "that you could point out this Suv to me?"

She looked up at him with those great wonderful eyes and smiled. "I'm sure I could, my lord. Come; wrap your cloak about you and we shall walk through the village."

Outside the church, the darkness was relieved only by the regulation gaslamps of the various business places, and by the quarter moon hanging high in the sky, like a half-closed eye.

In the deeper darkness of the church porch, Lord Darcy, rather much to his surprise, took the girl in his arms and kissed her, with her warm cooperation. It was several wordless minutes before they went out to the street.

Master Sean woke to the six-o'clock Angelus bell feeling vaguely uneasy. A quick mental focus on his half of the tracer told him that Lord Darcy was in no danger. Actually, if he had been, Sean would have wakened immediately.

But he still had that odd feeling when he went down to Mass at seven; he had trouble keeping in his mind his prayers for the intercession of St. Basil the Great, and couldn't really bring his mind to focus until the Sanctus.

After Mass, he went up to Father Art's small parlor in the rectory, where he had been asked to break his fast, and was mildly surprised to find Sir James le Lien with the priest.

"Good morning, Master Sean," Sir James said calmly. "Have you found the Phial yet?"

The sorcerer shook his head. "Not so far as I know."

Sir James munched a buttered biscuit and sipped hot black caffe. Despite his calm expression Master Sean could tell that he was worried.

"I am afraid," Sir James said carefully, "we've been outfoxed."

"How so?" Father Art asked.

"Well, either the *Serka* have got it, or they think we have it safely away from them. They seem to have given the whole thing over." He drank more caffe. "Just after midnight, every known *Serka* agent in the area eluded our men and vanished. They dropped out of sight, and we haven't spotted a single one in over eight hours. We have reason to believe that some of them went south, toward Caen; some went west, toward Cherbourg; other are heading east, toward Harfleur."

Master Sean frowned. "And you think—"

"I think they found the Ipswich Phial and one of their men is carrying it to Krakowa. Or at least across the Polish border. I rode to Caen and made more teleson calls than I've ever made in so short a time in my life. There's a net out now, and we can only hope we can find the man with the Phial. Otherwise . . ." He closed his eyes. "Otherwise, we may be faced with an overland attack by the armies of His Slavonic Majesty, through one or more of the German states. God help us."

After what seemed like a terribly long time, Master Sean said: "Sir James, is there any likelihood that Noel Standish would have used a knife on the sealed Phial?"

"I don't know. Why do you ask?"

"We found a knife near where Standish's body was discovered. My tests show gold on the knife edge."

"May I see it?" Sir James asked.

"Certainly. I'll fetch it. Excuse me a minute."

He left the parlor and went down the rather narrow hallway of the rectory. From the nearby church came the soft chime of a small bell. The eight o'clock Mass was beginning.

Master Sean opened the door of his room . . .

. . . and stood stock still, staring, for a full fifteen seconds, while his eyes and other senses took in the room.

Then, without moving, he shouted: "Sir James! Father Art! Come here! Quickly!"

Both men came running. They stopped at the door.

"What's the matter?" Sir James snapped.

"Somebody," said Master Sean in an angry rumble, "has been prowlin' about in me room! And a trick like that is likely to be after gettin' me Irish up!" Master Sean's brogue varied with his mood. When he was calmly lecturing or discussing, it became almost nonexistent. But when he became angry . . .

He strode into the room for a closer look at the table which he had been using for his thaumaturgical analyses. In the center was a heap of crumbled clay. "They've destroyed me evidence! Look at that!" Master Sean pointed to the heap of crumbled clay on the table.

"And what is it, if I may ask?"

Master Sean explained about the letters that had been cut in the cliff face, and how he had taken the chunk of clay out for further examination.

"And this knife was used to cut the letters." He gestured toward the knife on the table nearby. "I haven't been able to check it against Standish's body yet."

"That's the one with the gold traces on the blade?" Sir James asked.

"It is."

"Well, it's Standish's knife, all right. I've seen it many times. I could even tell you how he got that deep cut in the ivory hilt." He looked thoughtful. "S . . . S . . . O . . ." After a moment, he shook his head. "Means nothing to me. Can't think what it might have meant to Standish."

"Means nothing to me, either," Father Art admitted.

"Well, now," said the stout little Irish sorcerer, "Standish must have been at the top of the cliff when he wrote it. What would be right side up to him would be inverted to anyone standing below. How about OSS?"

Again Sir James thought. Again he shook his head. "Still nothing, Master Sean. Father?"

The priest shook his head. "Nothing, I'm afraid."

Sir James said: "This was obviously done by a *Serka* agent. But why? And how did he get in here without your knowing it?"

Master Sean scowled. "To a sorcerer, that's obvious. First, whoever did it is an accomplished sorcerer himself, or he'd never have made it past that avoidance spell, which is keyed only to meself and to his lordship. Second, he picked exactly the right time—when I was at Mass and had me mind concentrated elsewhere so I wouldn't notice what he was up to. Were I doing it meself, I'd have started just as the Sanctus bell was rung. After that—no problem." He looked glum. "I just wasn't expecting it, that's all."

"I wish I could have seen that carving in the clay," Sir James said.

"Well, you can see the cast if they didn't—" Master Sean pulled open a desk drawer. "No, they didn't." He pulled out a thick slab of plaster. "I made this with quick-setting plaster. It's reversed, of course, but you can look at it in the mirror, over there."

Sir James took the slab, but didn't look at it immediately. His eyes were still on the heap of clay. "Do you suppose that Standish might have buried the Ipswich Phial in that clay to keep it from being found?"

Master Sean's eyes widened. "Great Heaven! It could be! With an auric-stabilized psychic shield around it, I'd not have perceived it at all!"

Sir James groaned. "That answers the question. *Why?*—doesn't it?"

"So it would seem," murmured Father Art.

Bleakly, Sir James held the plaster slab up to the mirror above the dresser. "SSO. No. Wait." He inverted it, and his lean face went pale. "Oh, no, God," he said softly. "Oh, please. No."

"What is it?" the priest asked. "Does OSS mean something?"

"Not OSS," Sir James said still more softly. "055. Number 055 of the *Serka*. Ólga Polovski, the most beautiful and the most dangerous woman in Europe."

It was at that moment that the sun went out.

The Reverend Father Mac Kennalty had turned to the congregation and asked them to lift up their hearts to the Lord that they might properly assist at the Holy Sacrifice of the Altar, when a cloud seemed to pass over the sun, dimming the light that streamed in through the stained glass windows. Even the candles on the Altar seemed to dim a little.

He hardly noticed it; it was a common enough occurrence. Without a pause, he asked the people to give thanks to the Lord God, and continued with the Mass.

In the utter blackness of the room, three men stood for a moment in silence.

"Well, that tears it," said Sir James's voice in the darkness. There was a noticeable lack of surprise or panic in his voice.

"So you lied to his lordship," said Master Sean.

"He did indeed," said Father Art.

"What do you mean?" Sir James asked testily.

"You said," Master Sean pointed out with more than a touch of acid in his voice, "that you didn't know what the Ipswich Phial is supposed to do."

"What makes you think I *do*?"

"In the first place, this darkness came as no surprise to you. In the second, you must have known what it was, because Noel Standish knew."

"I had my orders," Sir James le Lien said in a hard voice. "That's not the point now. The damned thing is being used. I—"

"*Listen!*" Father Art's voice cut in sharply. "*Listen!*"

In the blackness, all of them heard the sweet triple tone of the Sanctus bell.

Holy . . . Holy . . . Holy . . . Lord God Sabaoth . . .

"What—?" Sir James's low voice was querulous.

"Don't you understand?" Father Art asked. "The field of suppression doesn't extend as far as the church. Father Mac Kennalty could go on with the Mass in the dark, from memory. But the congregation wouldn't be likely to. They certainly don't sound upset."

"You're right, Father," Master Sean said. "That gives us the range, doesn't it? Let's see if we can feel our way out of here, toward the church. His lordship may be in trouble."

"Follow me," said the priest. "I know this church like I know my own face. Take my hand and follow me."

Cautiously, the three men moved from the darkness toward the light. They were still heading for the stairway when the sun came on again.

Lord Darcy rode into the stableyard behind the Church of St. Matthew, where four men were waiting for him. The sexton took his horse as he dismounted, and led it away to the stable. The other three just waited, expectantly.

"I could do with a cup of caffe, heavily laced with brandy, and a plate of ham and eggs, if they're available," said Lord Darcy with a rather dreamy smile. "If not, I'll just have the caffe and brandy."

"What's happened?" Sir James blurted abruptly.

Lord Darcy patted the air with a hand. "All in good time, my dear James; all in good time. Nothing's amiss, I assure you."

"I think a breakfast such as that could be arranged," Father Art said with a smile. "Come along."

The caffe and brandy came immediately, served by Father Art in a large mug. "The ham and eggs should be along pretty quickly," the priest said.

"Excellent! You're the perfect host, Father." Lord Darcy took a bracing jolt from the mug, then fished in his waistcoat pocket with thumb and forefinger. "Oh, by the by, Sir James, here's your play-pretty." He held up a small golden tube.

Sir James took it and looked at it while Master Sean scowled at it in a way that made him seem rather cross-eyed.

"The seal has been cut," Sir James said.

"Yes. By your man, Standish. I suggest you give the thing to Master Sean for resealing until you get it back to Ipswich."

Sir James gave the Phial to Master Sean. "How did you get it back from them?" the King's Agent asked.

"I didn't." Lord Darcy settled himself back in the big chair. "If you'll be patient, I'll explain. Last evening, I was approached by a young woman . . ."

His lordship repeated the entire conversation verbatim, and told them of her gestures and expressions while they were talking inside the church.

"And you went with her?" Sir James asked incredulously.

"Certainly. For two very good reasons. *Primus*: I had to find out what was behind her story. *Secundus*: I had fallen in love."

Sir James gawked. Master Sean's face became expressionless. Father Art cast his eyes toward Heaven.

Sir James found his voice first. "In *love*?" It was almost a squawk.

Lord Darcy nodded calmly. "In love. Deeply. Madly. Passionately."

Sir James shot to his feet. "Are you mad, Darcy? Don't you realize that that woman is a *Serka* agent?"

"So indeed I had surmised. Sit down, James; such outbursts are unseemly." Sir James sat down slowly. "Now pay attention," Lord Darcy continued. "Of course I knew she was a spy. If you had been listening closely when I quoted her words, you would have heard that she said I was investigating the death of *Standish*. And yet everyone here knows that the body was identified as *Bourke*. Obviously, she had recognized Standish and knew his name."

"Standish had recognized her, too," Sir James said. "Secret Agent Number 055, of *Serka*. Real name: Olga Polovski."

"Olga," Lord Darcy said, savoring the word. "That's a pretty name, isn't it?"

"Charming. Utterly enchanting. And in spite of the fact that she's a Polish agent, you love the wench?"

"I didn't say that, Sir James," said Lord Darcy. "I did not say I loved her; I said I was 'in love' with her. There is a fine distinction there, and I have had enough experience to be able to distinguish between the two states of mind. Your use of the word 'enchanting' is quite apropos, by the way. The emotion was artificially induced. The woman is a sorceress."

Master Sean suddenly snapped his fingers. "*That's* where I heard the name before! Olga Polovski! Six years ago, she was an undergraduate at the University in Buda-Pest. A good student, with high-grade Talent. No wonder you 'fell in love' with her."

Sir James narrowed his eyes. "I see. The purpose was to get information out of you. Did she succeed?"

"In a way," Lord Darcy chuckled. "I sang like a nightingale. Indeed, Darcy's *Mendacious Cantata,* sung *forte e claro,* may become one of the most acclaimed works of art of the twentieth century. Pardon me; I am euphoric."

"You have popped your parietals, my lord," Sir James said, with a slight edge to his voice. "What was the result of this baritone solo?"

"Actually, it was a duet. We alternated on the versicles and responses. The theme of my song was simply that I was a criminal investigator and nothing more. That I hadn't more than a vague notion of what His Imperial Majesty's Secret Service was up to. That, for some reason, the apprehension of this murderer was most important to the Secret Service, so their agents were hanging around to help me. That they were more hindrance than help." He paused to take another swallow of laced caffe, then continued: "And—oh, yes—that they must be going to England for more men, because, four days ago, a heavily armed group of four men took a Navy cutter from Harfleur for London."

Sir James frowned for a second, then his face lit up. "Ah, yes. You implied that we had already found the Phial and that it was safely in England."

"Precisely. And since she had not heard of that oh-so-secret departure, she was certain that it could not be a bluff. As a result, she scrubbed the entire mission. Around midnight, she excused herself for a moment and spoke to someone—I presume it was the second in command, the much-maligned Suv. Her men took off to three of the four winds."

"And she didn't?"

"Of course not. Why arouse my suspicions? Better to keep me under observation while her men made good their escape. I left her shortly after dawn, and—"

"You were there from sunset till dawn? What took you so long?"

Lord Darcy looked pained. "My dear James, surely you don't think I could simply hand her all that misinformation in half an hour without her becoming suspicious. I had to allow her to draw it from me, bit by bit. I had to allow her to give me more information than she intended to give in order to get the story out of me. And, of course, *she* had to be very careful in order not to arouse *my* suspicions. It was, I assure you, a very delicate and time-consuming series of negotiations."

Sir James did his best not to leer. "I can well imagine."

Father Art looked out the window, solemnly puffing his pipe as though he were in deep meditation and could hear nothing.

Rather hurriedly, Master Sean said: "Then it was you who broke the clay brick I dug out of the cliff, me lord."

"It was; I'm sorry I didn't tell you, but you were at Mass, and I was in somewhat of a hurry. You see, there were only two places where the Phial could possibly be, and I looked in the less likely place first—in that lump of clay. Standish *could* have hidden it there, but I thought it unlikely. Still, I had to look. It wasn't there."

"So I got my horse and rode out to where the body was found. You see, Standish *had* to have had it with him. He opened it to get away from his pursuers. I presume Master Sean knows how the thing works, but all I know is that it renders everyone blind for a radius of about a mile and a half."

Master Sean cleared his throat. "It's akin to what's called hysterical blindness. Nothing wrong with the eyes, ye see, but the mind blocks off the visual centers of the brain. The Phial contains a charged rod attached to the stopper. When you open it and expose the rod everything goes black. That's the reason for the auric-stabilized psychic shield which forms the Phial itself."

"Things don't go black for the person holding it," said Lord Darcy. "Everything becomes a colorless gray, but you can still see."

"That's the built-in safety spell in the stopper," said the little Irish sorcerer.

"Well, where *was* the blasted thing?" Sir James asked.

"Buried in the sand, almost under that big rock where his body was found. I just had to dig till I found it." Lord Darcy looked somber. "I fear my analytical powers are deserting me; otherwise, Master Sean and I would have found it yesterday. But I relied on his metal detector to find it. And yet, Master Sean clearly told me that a psychic shield renders anything psychically invisible. He was talking about Standish, of course, but I should have seen that the same logic applied to the Ipswich Phial as well."

"If ye'd told me what ye were looking for, me lord . . ." Master Sean said gently.

Lord Darcy chuckled mirthlessly. "After all our years together, my dear Sean, we still tend to overestimate each other. I assumed you had deduced what we were looking for, though you are no detective; you assumed I knew about psychic shielding, though I am no thaumaturge."

"I still can't quite see that entire chain of events," Father Art said. "Could you clarify it for us? What was Standish doing out on that beach, anyway?"

"Well, let's go back to the night before he was killed. He had been following the mysterious Bourke. When Bourke was firmly ensconced in the Green Seagull, Standish rode for Caen, notified you via teleson, then rode back. He borrowed the sexton's cloak and went over to the inn. When he saw his chance, he dodged upstairs fast and went to Bourke's room presumably to get the Phial.

"Now, you must keep in mind that all this is conjecture. I can't prove it, and I know of no way to prove it. I do not have, and cannot get, all the evidence I would need for *proof*. But all the data I *do* have leads inescapably to one line of action.

"Master Sean claims I have a touch of the Talent—the ability to leap from an unwarranted assumption to a foregone conclusion. That may be so. At any rate, I *know* what happened.

"Very well, then. Standish went into Bourke's room to arrest him. He *knew* Bourke was in that room because he was psychically locked on to Bourke.

"But when he broke into the room he was confronted by a woman—a woman he knew. The woman was just as surprised to see Standish.

"I don't know which of them recovered first, but I strongly suspect it was the woman. Number 055 is very quick on the uptake, believe me.

"But Standish was stronger. He sustained a few good bruises in the next several seconds, but he knocked her unconscious. I saw the bruise on her neck last night.

"He searched the room and found the Phial. Unfortunately, the noise had attracted two, possibly three, of her fellow *Serka* agents. He had to go out the window, losing his cloak in the process. The men followed him.

"He ran for the beach, and—"

"Wait a minute," Sir James interrupted. "You mean Bourke was actually Olga Polovski in disguise?"

"Certainly. She's a consummate actress. The idea was for Bourke to vanish completely. She knew the Secret Service would be after her, and she wanted to leave no trace. But she didn't realize that Standish was so close behind her because he was psychically invisible. That's why she was shocked when he came into her room.

"At any rate, he ran for the beach. There was no place else to go at that time of night, except for the church, and they'd have him trapped there.

"I must admit I'm very fuzzy about what happened during that chase, but remember he had ridden for two days without much rest, and he was battered a little by the blows Olga had landed. At any rate, he eventually found himself at the edge of that cliff, with *Serka* closing in around him. Remember, it was a moonless night, and there were only stars for him to see by. But at least one of the Polish agents had a lantern.

"Standish was trapped on the edge of a cliff, and he had no way to see how far down it went, nor what was at the bottom. He lay flat and kept quiet, but the others were getting close. He decided to get rid of the Phial. Better to lose it than have it fall into King Casimir's hands. He took out his knife and carved the '055' in the side of the cliff, to mark the spot and to make sure that someone else would see it if he were killed. I'm sure he intended to dig a hole and bury it there. I don't believe he was thinking too clearly by then.

"The *Serka* men were getting too close for comfort. He might be seen at any moment. So he cut the seal of the Phial and opened it. Blackout.

"Since he could see his pursuers—however dimly—and they couldn't see him, he decided to try to get past them, back to the village. If he had a time advantage, he could find a place to hide.

"He stood up.

"But as he turned, he made a misstep and fell twenty feet to the sand below." Lord Darcy paused.

Father Art, looking thoughtful, said: "He had a gun. Why didn't he use it?"

"Because they had guns, too, and he was outnumbered. He didn't want to betray his position by the muzzle flash unless he had to," Lord Darcy said. "To continue: The fall is what broke those ribs and sprained that wrist. It also very likely knocked him out for a few minutes. Not long. When he came to, he must have realized he had an advantage greater than he had thought at first. The *Serka* couldn't see the muzzle flash from his handgun. Badly hurt as he was, he waited for them."

"Admirable," said Father Art. "It's fantastic that he didn't lose the two parts of the Phial when he fell. Must have hung on for dear life."

"Standish would," said Sir James grimly. "Go on, my lord."

"Well, at that point, the *Serka* lads must have realized the same thing. They had no way of knowing how badly Standish was hurt, nor exactly where he was. He could be sneaking up on them, for all they knew. They got out of there. Slowly, of course, since they had to feel their way, but once they reached the Old Shore Road, they made better time.

"But by that time, Standish was close to passing out again. He still had to hide the Phial, so he buried it in the sand where I found it."

"Me lord," said Master Sean, "I still don't understand who killed Standish and why."

"Oh, that. Why that was patently obvious from the first. Wasn't it, Father Art?"

The good father stared at Lord Darcy. "Begging your pardon, my lord, but not to *me* it wasn't."

Lord Darcy turned his head. "Sir James?"

"No."

"Oh, dear. Well, I suppose I shall have to back up a bit, then. Consider: The Damoselle Olga, to cover her tracks, has to get rid of 'Bourke.' But if 'Bourke' disappears into nowhere, and someone else appears from nowhere, even a moron might suspect that the two were the same. So a cover must be arranged. Someone else, not connected in any way with 'Bourke,' must appear at the Green Seagull *before* 'Bourke' shows up.

"So, what happens? A coachman named Danglars shows up; a servant who registers for himself and his mistress, Jizelle de Ville. (Danglars and Suv were almost certainly the same man, by the way.) But who sees Mistress Jizelle? Nobody. *She is only a name in a register book until the next morning!*

"The original plan was to have Mistress Jizelle show up in the evening, then have Bourke show up again, and so on. The idea was to firmly establish that the two people were separate and not at all connected. The arrival and intrusion of Standish changed all that, but things worked out fairly well, nonetheless.

"It *had* to be 'Mistress Jizelle' who killed him. Look at the evidence. Standish died—correct me if I'm wrong, Master Sean—within plus or minus fifteen minutes of the time Standish was found."

Master Sean nodded.

"Naturally," his lordship continued, "we always assume a minus time. How could the person be killed *after* the body was found?"

"But there was no one else around who could have killed him! A farmer and his two sons were close enough to the road during that time to see anyone who came along unless that someone had walked along the beach. But there were no footprints in that damp sand except those of 'Mistress Jizelle'!

"Picture this, if you will: Number 055, still a little groggy, and suffering from a sore neck, is told by her returning henchmen that they have lost Standish. But she is clever enough to see what must have happened. As soon as possible, she puts on her 'Mistress Jizelle' *persona* and has her lieutenant drive her out to that section of the beach. She walks down to take a look. She sees Standish.

"Standish, meanwhile, has regained his senses. He opens his eyes and sees Olga Polovski. His gun is still in his hand. He tries to level it at her. She jumps him, in fear of her life. A struggle. The gun goes off. *Finis.*"

"Wouldn't the farmers have heard the shot?" Master Sean asked.

"At that distance, with a brisk wind blowing, the sea pounding, and a cliff to baffle the sound, it would be hard to hear a pistol shot. That one was further muffled by the fact that the muzzle was against Standish's head. No, it wouldn't have been heard."

"Why did her footprints only come up to some five yards from the body?" Sir James asked. "There were no prints in the dry sand."

"Partly because she smoothed her prints out, partly because of the wind, which blew enough to cover them. She was shaken and worried, but she did take time to search the body for the Phial. Naturally, she didn't want any evidence of that search around. She went back to consult Danglars-Suv about what to do next. When she saw the farmers, there was nothing she could do but bluff it through. Which, I must say, she did magnificently."

"Indeed." Sir James le Lien looked both cold and grim. "Where is she now?"

"By now, she has taken horse and departed."

"Riding sidesaddle, no doubt." His voice was as cold as his expression. "So you let her get away. Why didn't you arrest her?"

"On what evidence? Don't be a fool, Sir James. What would you charge her with? Could you swear in His Majesty's Court of High Justice that 'Mistress Jizelle' was actually Olga Polovski? If I had tried to arrest her, I would have been a corpse by now in that Romany camp, even it I'd had the evidence. Since I did not and do not have that evidence, there would be no point.

"I would not call it a satisfactory case, no. But you have the Phial, which was what you wanted. I'm afraid the death of Noel

Standish will have to be written off as enemy action during the course of a war. It was not first-degree murder; it was, as Master Sean put it yesterday, a case of accidental murder.''

"But—''

Lord Darcy leaned back in the chair and closed his eyes. "Drop it, Sir James. You'll get her eventually.''

Then, very quietly, he began to snore.

"I'll be damned!'' said Sir James. "I worked all night on my feet and found nothing. He spends all night in bed with the most beautiful woman in Europe and gets all the answers.''

"It all depends on your method of approach,'' Master Sean said. He opened his symbol-decorated carpetbag and took out a large, heavy book.

"Oh, certainly,'' said Sir James bitterly. "Some work vertically, some horizontally.''

Father Arthur Lyon continued to stare out the window, hearing nothing he didn't mean to hear.

"What are you looking up there, in that grimoire?'' he asked Master Sean after a moment.

"*Spells, infatuation; removal of,*'' said Master Sean calmly.

Black Heart and White Heart
by H. Rider Haggard

H. Rider Haggard (1856-1925) was the premier adventure story writer of the late nineteenth century, a man who single-handedly created the Great White Hunter and Lost Race branches of the genre. He did this primarily through the publication of two monumentally influential novels, King Solomon's Mines *(1885) and* She: A History of Adventure *(1887). Unfortunately, his later work never achieved the same high quality, although he wrote more than thirty additional novels. His much more limited short-fiction production can be found in* The Best Short Stories of H. Rider Haggard. *He was a devoted imperialist, and his now discredited politics may be responsible for his current lack of stature, but he certainly was one of the great storytellers of all time.*

I

A Zulu Idyll

At the date of our introduction to him, Philip Hadden was a transport-rider and a trader in "the Zulu." Still on the right side of forty, in appearance he was singularly handsome; tall, dark, upright, with keen eyes, short-pointed beard, curling hair and clear-cut features. His life had been varied, and there were passages in it which he did not narrate even to his most intimate friends. He was of gentle birth, however, and it was said that he had received a public school and university education in England. At any rate he could quote the classics with aptitude on occasion, an accomplishment which, coupled with his refined voice and a bearing not altogether common in the wild places of the world, had earned for him among his rough companions the *soubriquet* of "The Prince."

However these things may have been, it is certain that he had emigrated to Natal under a cloud, and equally certain that his relatives at home were content to take no further interest in his

303

fortunes. During the fifteen or sixteen years which he had spent in or about the colony, Hadden followed many trades, and did no good at any of them. A clever man, of agreeable and prepossessing manner, he always found it easy to form friendships and to secure a fresh start in life. But, by degrees, the friends were seized with a vague distrust of him; and, after a period of more or less application, he himself would close the opening that he had made by a sudden disappearance from the locality, leaving behind him a doubtful reputation and some bad debts.

Before the beginning of this story of the most remarkable episodes in his life, Philip Hadden was engaged for several years in transport-riding—that is, in carrying goods on ox waggons from Durban or Maritzburg to various points in the interior. A difficulty such as had more than once confronted him in the course of his career, led to his temporary abandonment of this means of earning a livelihood. On arriving at the little frontier town of Utrecht in the Transvaal, in charge of two waggon-loads of mixed goods consigned to a storekeeper there, it was discovered that out of six cases of brandy five were missing from his waggon. Hadden explained the matter by throwing the blame upon his Kaffir "boys," but the storekeeper, a rough-tongued man, openly called him a thief and refused to pay the freight on any of the load. From words the men came to blows, knives were drawn, and before anybody could interfere the storekeeper received a nasty wound in his side. That night, without waiting till the matter could be inquired into by the landdrost or magistrate, Hadden slipped away, and trekked back into Natal as quickly as his oxen would travel. Feeling that even here he was not safe, he left one of his waggons at Newcastle, loaded up the other with Kaffir goods—such as blankets, calico, and hardware—and crossed into Zululand, where in those days no sheriff's officer would be likely to follow him.

Being well acquainted with the language and customs of the natives, he did good trade with them, and soon found himself possessed of some cash and a small herd of cattle, which he received in exchange for his wares. Meanwhile news reached him that the man whom he had injured still vowed vengeance against him, and was in communication with the authorities in Natal. These reasons making his return to civilization undesirable for the moment, and further business being impossible until he could receive a fresh supply of trade stuff, Hadden like a wise man turned his thoughts to pleasure. Sending his cattle and waggon over the border to be left in charge of a native headman with whom he was friendly, he went on foot to Ulundi to obtain permission from the king, Cetywayo, to hunt game in his country. Somewhat to his surprise the Indunas, or headmen, received him courteously—for Hadden's visit took place within a few months of the outbreak of the Zulu war in 1878, when Cetywayo was already showing unfriendliness to the English traders and others, though why the king did so they knew not.

On the occasion of his first and last interview with Cetywayo, Hadden got a hint of the reason. It happened thus. On the second morning after his arrival at the royal kraal, a messenger came to inform him that "the Elephant whose tread shook the earth" had signified that it was his pleasure to see him. Accordingly he was led through the thousands of huts and across the Great Place to the little enclosure where Cetywayo, a royal-looking Zulu seated on a stool, and wearing a *Kaross* of leopard skins, was holding an *indaba,* or conference, surrounded by his counsellors. The Induna who had conducted him to the august presence went down upon his hands and knees, and, uttering the royal salute of *Bayéte,* crawled forward to announce that the white man was waiting.

"Let him wait," said the king angrily; and, turning, he continued the discussion with his counsellors.

Now, as has been said, Hadden thoroughly understood Zulu; and, when from time to time the king raised his voice, some of the words he spoke reached his ear.

"What!" Cetywayo said, to a wizened and aged man who seemed to be pleading with him earnestly; "am I a dog that these white hyenas should hunt me thus? Is not the land mine, and was it not my father's before me? Are not the people mine to save or to slay? I tell you that I will stamp out these little white men; my *impis* shall eat them up. I have said!"

Again the withered aged man interposed, evidently in the character of a peacemaker. Hadden could not hear his talk, but he rose and pointed towards the sea, while from his expressive gestures and sorrowful mien, he seemed to be prophesying disaster should a certain course of action be followed.

For a while the king listened to him, then he sprang from his seat, his eyes literally ablaze with rage.

"Hearken," he cried to the counsellor: "I have guessed it for long, and now I am sure of it. You are a traitor. You are Sompseu's[1] dog, and the dog of the Natal Government, and I will not keep another man's dog to bite me in my own house. Take him away!"

[1]Sir Theophilus Shepstone's.

A slight involuntary murmur rose from the ring of *indunas*, but the old man never flinched, not even when the soldiers, who presently would murder him, came and seized him roughly. For a few seconds, perhaps five, he covered his face with the corner of the *kaross* he wore, then he looked up and spoke to the king in a clear voice.

"O King," he said, "I am a very old man; as a youth I served under Chaka the Lion, and I heard his dying prophecy of the coming of the white man. Then the white men came, and I fought for Dingaan at the battle of the Blood River. They slew Dingaan, and for many years I was the counsellor of Panda, your father. I stood by you, O King, at the battle of the Tugela, when its grey waters were turned to red with the blood of Umbulazi your brother, and of the tens of thousands of his people. Afterwards I became your counsellor, O King, and I was with you when Sompseu set the crown upon your head and you made promises to Sompseu—promises that you have not kept. Now you are weary of me, and it is well; for I am very old, and doubtless my talk is foolish, as it chances to the old. Yet I think that the prophecy of Chaka, your great-uncle, will come true, and that the white men will prevail against you and that through them you shall find your death. I would that I might have stood in one more battle and fought for you, O King, since fight you will, but the end which you choose is for me the best end. Sleep in peace, O King, and farewell. *Bayétte!*"[1]

For a space there was silence, a silence of expectation while men waited to hear the tyrant reverse his judgment. But it did not please him to be merciful, or the needs of policy outweighed his pity.

"Take him away," he repeated. Then, with a slow smile on his face and one word, "Good-night," upon his lips, supported by the arm of a soldier, the old warrior and statesman shuffled forth to the place of death.

Hadden watched and listened in amazement not unmixed with fear. "If he treats his own servants like this, what will happen to me?" he reflected. "We English must have fallen out of favour since I left Natal. I wonder whether he means to make war on us or what? If so, this isn't my place."

Just then the king, who had been gazing moodily at the ground, chanced to look up. "Bring the stranger here," he said.

Hadden heard him, and coming forward offered Cetywayo his hand in as cool and nonchalant a manner as he could command.

[1]The royal salute of the Zulus.

Somewhat to his surprise it was accepted. "At least, White Man," said the king, glancing at his visitor's tall spare form and cleanly cut face, "you are no *umfagozan* (low fellow); you are of the blood of chiefs."

"Yes, King," answered Hadden, with a little sigh, "I am of the blood of chiefs."

"What do you want in my country, White Man?"

"Very little, King. I have been trading here, as I daresay you have heard, and have sold all my goods. Now I ask your leave to hunt buffalo, and other big game, for a while before I return to Natal."

"I cannot grant it," answered Cetywayo, "you are a spy sent by Sompseu, or by the Queen's Induna in Natal. Get you gone."

"Indeed," said Hadden, with a shrug of his shoulders; "then I hope that Sompseu, or the Queen's Induna, or both of them, will pay me when I return to my own country. Meanwhile I will obey you because I must, but I should first like to make you a present."

"What present?" asked the king. "I want no presents. We are rich here, White Man."

"So be it, King. It was nothing worthy of your taking, only a rifle."

"A rifle, White Man? Where is it?"

"Without. I would have brought it, but your servants told me that it is death to come armed before the 'Elephant who shakes the Earth.' "

Cetywayo frowned, for the note of sarcasm did not escape his quick ear.

"Let this white man's offering be brought; I will consider the thing."

Instantly the Induna who had accompanied Hadden darted to the gateway, running with his body bent so low that it seemed as though at every step he must fall upon his face. Presently he returned with the weapon in his hand and presented it to the king, holding it so that the muzzle was pointed straight at the royal breast.

"I crave leave to say, O Elephant," remarked Hadden in a drawling voice, "that it might be well to command your servant to lift the mouth of that gun from your heart."

"Why?" asked the king.

"Only because it is loaded, and at full cock, O Elephant, who probably desires to continue to shake the Earth."

At these words the "Elephant" uttered a sharp exclamation,

and rolled from his stool in a most unkingly manner, whilst the terrified Induna, springing backwards, contrived to touch the trigger of the rifle and discharge a bullet through the exact spot that a second before had been occupied by his monarch's head.

"Let him be taken away," shouted the incensed king from the ground, but long before the words had passed his lips the Induna, with a cry that the gun was bewitched, had cast it down and fled at full speed through the gate.

"He has already taken himself away," suggested Hadden, while the audience tittered. "No, King, do not touch it rashly; it is a repeating rifle. Look—" and lifting the Winchester, he fired the four remaining shots in quick succession into the air, striking the top of a tree at which he aimed with every one of them.

"*Wow*, it is wonderful!" said the company in astonishment.

"Has the thing finished?" asked the king.

"For the present it has," answered Hadden. "Look at it."

Cetywayo took the repeater in his hand, and examined it with caution, swinging the muzzle horizontally in an exact line with the stomachs of some of his most eminent Indunas, who shrank to this side and that as the barrel was brought to bear upon them.

"See what cowards they are, White Man," said the king with indignation; "they fear lest there should be another bullet in this gun."

"Yes," answered Hadden, "they are cowards indeed. I believe that if they were seated on stools they would tumble off them as it chanced to your Majesty to do just now."

"Do you understand the making of guns, White Man?" asked the king hastily, while the Indunas one and all turned their heads, and contemplated the fence behind them.

"No, King, I cannot make guns, but I can mend them."

"If I paid you well, White Man, would you stop here at my kraal, and mend guns for me?" asked Cetywayo anxiously.

"It might depend on the pay," answered Hadden; "but for a while I am tired of work, and wish to rest. If the king gives me the permission to hunt for which I asked, and men to go with me, then when I return perhaps we can bargain on the matter. If not, I will bid the king farewell, and journey to Natal."

"In order to make report of what he has seen and learned here," muttered Cetywayo.

At this moment the talk was interrupted, for the soldiers who had led away the old Induna returned at speed, and prostrated themselves before the king.

"Is he dead?" he asked.

"He has travelled the king's bridge," they answered grimly; "he died singing a song of praise to the king."

"Good," said Cetywayo, "that stone shall hurt my feet no more. Go, tell the tale of its casting away to Sompseu and to the Queen's Induna in Natal," he added with bitter emphasis.

"*Baba!* Hear our Father speak. Listen to the rumbling of the Elephant," said the Indunas taking the point, while one bolder than the rest added: "Soon we will tell them another tale, the white Talking Ones, a red tale, a tale of spears, and the regiments shall sing it in their ears."

At the words an enthusiasm caught hold of the listeners, as the sudden flame catches hold of dry grass. They sprand up, for the most of them were seated on their haunches, and stamping their feet upon the ground in unison, repeated:

> *Indaba ibomwu—indaba ye mikonto*
> *Lizo dunyiswa nge impi ndhlebeni yaho.*
> (A red tale! A red tale! A tale of spears,
> And the *impis* shall sing it in their ears.)

One of them, indeed, a great fierce-faced yellow, drew near to Hadden and shaking his fist before his eyes—fortunately being in the royal presence he had no assegai—shouted the sentences at him.

The king saw that the fire he had lit was burning too fiercely.

"Silence," he thundered in the deep voice for which he was remarkable, and instantly each man became as if he were turned to stone, only the echoes still answered back: "And the *impis* shall sing it in their ears—in their ears."

"I am growing certain that this is no place for me," thought Hadden; "if that scoundrel had been armed he might have temporarily forgotten himself. Hullo! who's this?"

Just then there appeared through the gate of the fence a splendid specimen of the Zulu race. The man, who was about thirty-five years of age, was arrayed in a full war dress of a captain of the Umcityu regiment. From the circlet of otter skin on his brow rose his crest of plumes, round his middle, arms and knees hung the long fringes of black oxtails, and in one hand he bore a little dancing shield, also black in colour. The other was empty, since he might not appear before the king bearing arms. In countenance the man was handsome, and though just now they betrayed some anxiety, his eyes were genial and honest, and his mouth sensitive. In height he must have measured six foot two inches, yet he did not strike the observer as being tall, perhaps because of his width of chest and the solidity of his limbs, that were in curious contrast to the delicate and almost womanish hands and feet which so often mark the Zulu of noble blood. In short the man was what he seemed to be, a savage gentleman of birth, dignity and courage.

In company with him was another man plainly dressed in a moocha and a blanket, whose grizzled hair showed him to be over fifty years of age. His face was pleasant and even refined, but the eyes were timorous, and the mouth lacked character.

"Who are these?" asked the king.

The two men fell on their knees before him, and bowed till their foreheads touched the ground—the while giving him his *sibonga* or titles of praise.

"Speak," he said impatiently.

"O King," said the young warrior, seating himself Zulu fashion, "I am Nahoon, the son of Zomba, a captain of the Umcityu, and this is my uncle, Umgona, the brother of one of my mothers, my father's youngest wife."

Cetywayo frowned. "What do you here away from your regiment, Nahoon?"

"May it please the king, I have leave of absence from the head captains, and I come to ask a boon of the king's bounty."

"Be swift, then, Nahoon."

"It is this, O King," said the captain with some embarrassment: "A while ago the king was pleased to make a *keshla* of me because of certain service that I did out yonder . . ." and he touched the black ring which he wore in the hair of his head. "Being now a ringed man and a captain, I crave the right of a man at the hands of the king—the right to marry."

"Right? Speak more humbly, son of Zomba; my soldiers and my cattle have no rights."

Nahoon bit his lip, for he had made a serious mistake.

"Pardon, O King. The matter stands thus: My uncle Umgona here has a fair daughter named Nanea, whom I desire to wife, and who desires me to husband. Awaiting the king's leave I am betrothed to her and in earnest of it I have paid to Umgona a *lobola* of fifteen head of cattle, cows and calves together. But Umgona has a powerful neighbour, an old chief named Maputa, the warden of the Crocodile Drift, who doubtless is known to the king, and this chief also seeks Nanea in marriage and harries Umgona, threatening him with many evils if he will not give the girl to him. But Umgona's heart is white towards me, and towards Maputa it is black, therefore together we come to crave this boon of the king.''

"It is so; he speaks the truth," said Umgona.

"Cease," answered Cetywayo angrily. "Is this a time that my soldiers should seek wives in marriage, wives to turn their hearts to water? Know that but yesterday for this crime I commanded that twenty girls who had dared without my leave to marry men of the Undi regiment, should be strangled and their bodies laid upon the crossroads and with them the bodies of their fathers, that all might know their sin and be warned thereby. Ay, Umgona, it is well for you and for your daughter that you sought my word before she was given in marriage to this man. Now this is my award: I refuse your prayer, Nahoon, and since you, Umgona, are troubled with one whom you would not take as son-in-law, the old chief Maputa, I will free you from his importunity. The girl, says Nahoon, is fair—good, I myself will be gracious to her, and she shall be numbered among the wives of the royal house. Within thirty days from now, in the week of the next new moon, let her be delivered into the *Sigodhla*, the royal house of the women, and with her those cattle, the cows and calves together, that Nahoon has given you, of which I fine him because he has dared to think of marriage without the leave of the king.''

II

The Bee Prophesies

"A Daniel come to judgment indeed," reflected Hadden, who had been watching this savage comedy with interest; "our love-sick friend has got more than he bargained for. Well, that comes of appealing to Caesar," and he turned to look at the two suppliants.

The old man, Umgona, merely started, then began to pour out sentences of conventional thanks and praise to the king for his goodness and condescension. Cetywayo listened to his talk in silence, and when he had done answered by reminding him tersely that if Nanea did not appear at the date named, both she and he, her father, would in due course certainly decorate a crossroad in their own immediate neighbourhood.

The captain, Nahoon, afforded a more curious study. As the fatal words crossed the king's lips, his face took on an expression of absolute astonishment, which was presently replaced by one of fury—the just fury of a man who suddenly has suffered an

unutterable wrong. His whole frame quivered, the veins stood
out in knots on his neck and forehead, and his fingers closed
convulsively as though they were grasping the handle of a spear.
Presently the rage passed away—for as well might a man be
wroth with fate as with a Zulu despot—to be succeeded by the
look of the most hopeless misery. The proud dark eyes grew
dull, the copper-coloured face sank in and turned ashen, the
mouth drooped, and down one corner of it there trickled a little
line of blood springing from the lip bitten through in the effort to
keep silence. Lifting his hand in salute to the king, the great man
rose and staggered rather than walked towards the gate.

As he reached it, the voice of Cetywayo commanded him to
stop. "Stay," he said, "I have a service for you, Nahoon, that
shall drive out of your head these thoughts of wives and marriage.
You see this white man here; he is my guest, and would hunt
buffalo and big game in the bush country. I put him in your
charge; take men with you, and see that he comes to no hurt.
See also that you bring him before me within a month, or your
life shall answer for it. Let him be here at my royal kraal in the
first week of the new moon—when Nanea comes—and then I
will tell you whether or no I agree with you that she is fair. Go
now, my child, and you, White Man, go also; those who are to
accompany you shall be with you at the dawn. Farewell, but
remember we meet again at the new moon, when we will settle
what pay you shall receive as keeper of my guns. Do not fail me,
White Man, or I shall send after you, and my messengers are
sometimes rough."

"This means that I am a prisoner," thought Hadden, "but it
will go hard if I cannot manage to give them the slip somehow. I
don't intend to stay in this country if war is declared, to be
pounded into *mouti* (medicine), or have my eyes put out, or any
little joke of that sort."

Ten days had passed, and one evening Hadden and his escort
were encamped in a wild stretch of mountainous country lying
between the Blood and Unvunyana Rivers, not more than eight
miles from that "Place of the Little Hand" which within a few
weeks was to become famous throughout the world by its native
name of Isandhlwana. For three days they had been tracking the
spoor of a small herd of buffalo that still inhabited the district,
but as yet they had not come up with them. The Zulu hunters had
suggested that they should follow the Unvunyana down towards
the sea where game was more plentiful, but this neither Hadden,

nor the captain, Nahoon, had been anxious to do, for reasons which each of them kept secret to himself. Hadden's object was to work gradually down to the Buffalo River across which he hoped to effect a retreat into Natal. That of Nahoon was to linger in the neighbourhood of the kraal of Umgona, which was situated not very far from their present camping place, in the vague hope that he might find an opportunity of speaking with or at least of seeing Nanea, the girl to whom he was affianced, who within a few weeks must be taken from him, and given over to the king.

A more eerie-looking spot than that where they were encamped Hadden had never seen. Behind them lay a tract of land—half-swamp and half-bush—in which the buffalo were supposed to be hiding. Beyond, in lonely grandeur, rose the mountain of Isandhlwana, while in front was an amphitheatre of the most gloomy forest, ringed round in the distance by sheer-sided hills. Into this forest there ran a river which drained the swamp, placidly enough upon the level. But it was not always level, for within three hundred yards of them it dashed suddenly over a precipice, of no great height but very steep, falling into a boiling rock-bound pool that the light of the sun never seemed to reach.

"What is the name of that forest, Nahoon?" asked Hadden.

"It is named *Emagudu*, The Home of the Dead," the Zulu replied absently, for he was looking towards the kraal of Nanea, which was situated an hour's walk away over the ridge to the right.

"The Home of the Dead! Why?"

"Because the dead live there, those whom we name the *Esemkofu*, the Speechless Ones, and with them other Spirits, the *Amahlosi*, from whom the breath of life has passed away, and who yet live on."

"Indeed," said Hadden, "and have you ever seen these ghosts?"

"Am I mad that I should go to look for them, White Man? Only the dead enter that forest, and it is on the borders of it that our people make offerings to the dead."

Followed by Nahoon, Hadden walked to the edge of the cliff and looked over it. To the left lay the deep and dreadful-looking pool, while close to the bank of it, placed upon a narrow strip of turf between the cliff and the commencement of the forest, was a hut.

"Who lives there?" asked Hadden.

"The great *Isanusi*—she who is named *Inyanga* or Doctoress; she who is named *Inyosi* (the Bee), because she gathers wisdom from the dead who grow in the forest."

"Do you think that she could gather enough wisdom to tell me whether I am going to kill any buffalo, Nahoon?"

"Mayhap, White Man, but," he added with a little smile, "those who visit the Bee's hive may hear nothing, or they may hear more than they wish for. The words of that Bee have a sting."

"Good; I will see if she can sting me."

"So be it," said Nahoon; and turning, he led the way along the cliff till he reached a native path which zig-zagged down its face.

By this path they climbed till they came to the sward at the foot of the descent, and walked up it to the hut which was surrounded by a low fence of reeds, enclosing a small courtyard paved with ant-heap earth beaten hard and polished. In this courtyard sat the Bee, her stool being placed almost at the mouth of the round opening that served as a doorway to the hut. At first all that Hadden could see of her, crouched as she was in the shadow, was a huddled shape wrapped round with a greasy and tattered catskin *kaross,* above the edge of which appeared two eyes, fierce and quick as those of a leopard. At her feet smouldered a little fire, and ranged around it in a semicircle were a number of human skulls, placed in pairs as though they were talking together, whilst other bones, to all appearance also human, were festooned about the hut and the fence of the courtyard.

"I see that the old lady is set up with the usual properties," thought Hadden, but he said nothing.

Nor did the witch-doctoress say anything; she only fixed her beady eyes upon his face. Hadden returned the compliment, staring at her with all his might, till suddenly he became aware that he was vanquished in this curious duel. His brain grew confused, and to his fancy it seemed that the woman before him had shifted shape into the likeness of a colossal and horrid spider sitting at the mouth of her trap, and that these bones were the relics of her victims.

"Why do you not speak, White Man?" she said at last in a slow clear voice. "Well, there is no need, since I can read your thoughts. You are thinking that I who am called the Bee should be better named the Spider. Have no fear; I did not kill these men. What would it profit me when the dead are so many? I suck the souls of men, not their bodies, White Man. It is their living hearts I love to look on, for therein I read much and thereby I grow wise. Now what would you of the Bee, White Man, the Bee that labours in this Garden of Death, and—what brings *you* here, son of Zomba? Why are you not with Umcityu now that they doctor themselves for the great war—the last war—the war of the white and the black—or if you have no stomach for fighting, why are you not at the side of Nanea the tall, Nanea the fair?''

Nahoon made no answer, but Hadden said:

"A small thing, mother. I would know if I shall prosper in my hunting.''

"In your hunting, White Man; what hunting? The hunting of game, of money, or of women? Well, one of them, for a-hunting you must ever be; that is your nature, to hunt and be hunted. Tell me now, how goes the wound of that trader who tasted of your steel yonder in the town of the Maboon (Boers)? No need to answer, White Man, but what fee, Chief, for the poor witch-doctress whose skill you seek,'' she added in a whining voice. "Surely you would not that an old woman should work without a fee?''

"I have none to offer you, mother, so I will be going," said Hadden, who began to feel himself satisfied with this display of the Bee's powers of observation and thought-reading.

"Nay," she answered with an unpleasant laugh, "would you ask a question, and not wait for the answer? I will take no fee from you at present, White Man; you shall pay me later on when we meet again," and once more she laughed. "Let me look in your face, let me look in your face," she continued, rising and standing before him.

Then of a sudden Hadden felt something cold at the back of his neck, and the next instant the Bee had sprung from him, holding between her thumb and finger a curl of dark hair which she had cut from his head. The action was so instantaneous that he had neither time to avoid nor to resent it, but stood still staring at her stupidly.

"That is all I need," she cried, "for like my heart my magic is white. Stay—son of Zomba, give me also of your hair, for those who visit the Bee must listen to her humming.''

Nahoon obeyed, cutting a little lock from his head with the sharp edge of his assegai, though it was very evident that he did this not because he wished to do so, but because he feared to refuse.

Then the Bee slipped back her *kaross,* and stood bending over the fire before them, into which she threw herbs taken from a pouch that was bound about her middle. She was still a finely-shaped woman, and she wore none of the abominations which

Hadden had been accustomed to see upon the persons of witch-doctoresses. About her neck, however, was a curious ornament, a small live snake, red and grey in hue, which her visitors recognised as one of the most deadly to be found in that part of the country. It is not unusual for Bantu witch-doctors thus to decorate themselves with snakes, though whether or not their fangs have first been extracted no one seems to know.

Presently the herbs began to smoulder, and the smoke of them rose up in a thin straight stream, that, striking upon the face of the Bee, clung about her head enveloping it as though with a strange blue veil. Then of a sudden she stretched out her hands, and let fall the two locks of hair upon the burning herbs, where they writhed themselves to ashes like things alive. Next she opened her mouth, and began to draw the fumes of the hair and herbs into her lungs in great gulps; while the snake, feeling the influence of the medicine, hissed and, uncoiling itself from about her neck, crept upwards and took refuge among the black *saccaboola* feathers of her head-dress.

Soon the vapours began to do their work; she swayed to and fro muttering, then sank back against the hut, upon the straw of which her head rested. Now the Bee's face was turned upwards towards the light, and it was ghastly to behold, for it had become blue in colour, and the open eyes were sunken like the eyes of one dead, whilst above her forehead the red snake wavered and hissed, reminding Hadden of the Uraeus crest on the brow of statues of Egyptian kings. For ten seconds or more she remained thus, then she spoke in a hollow and unnatural voice:

"O Black Heart and body that is white and beautiful, I look into your heart, and it is black as blood, and it shall be black with blood. Beautiful white body with a black heart, you shall find your game and hunt it, and it shall lead you into the House of the Homeless, into the Home of the Dead, and it shall be shaped as a bull, it shall be shaped as a tiger, it shall be shaped as a woman whom kings and waters cannot harm. Beautiful white body and black heart, you shall be paid your wages, money for money, and blow for blow. Think of my word when the spotted cat purrs above your breast; think of it when the battle roars about you; think of it when you grasp your great reward, and for the last time stand face to face with the ghost of the dead in the Home of the Dead.

"O White Heart and black body, I look into your heart and it is white as milk, and the milk of innocence shall save it. Fool, why do you strike that blow? Let him be who is loved of the tiger, and whose love is as the love of a tiger. Ah! what face is

that in the battle? Follow it, follow it, O swift of foot; but
follow warily, for the tongue that has lied will never plead for
mercy, and the hand that can betray is strong in war. White
Heart, what is death? In death life lives, and among the dead you
shall find the life you lost, for there awaits you she whom kings
and waters cannot harm."

As the Bee spoke, by degrees her voice sank lower and lower
till it was almost inaudible. Then it ceased altogether, and she
seemed to pass from trance to sleep. Hadden, who had been
listening to her with an amused and cynical smile, now laughed
aloud.

"Why do you laugh, White Man?" asked Nahoon angrily.

"I laugh at my own folly, in wasting time listening to the
nonsense of that lying fraud."

"It is no nonsense, White Man."

"Indeed? Then will you tell me what it means?"

"I cannot tell you what it means yet, but her words have to do
with a woman and a leopard, and with your fate and my fate."

Hadden shrugged his shoulders, not thinking the matter worth
further argument, and at that moment the Bee woke up shivering,
drew the red snake from her head-dress and coiling it about her
throat wrapped herself again in the greasy *kaross*.

"Are you satisfied with my wisdom, *Inkoos*?" she asked of
Hadden.

"I am satisfied that you are one of the cleverest cheats in
Zululand, mother," he answered coolly. "Now, what is there to
pay?"

The Bee took no offence at this rude speech, though for a
second or two the look in her eyes grew strangely like that which
they had seen in those of the snake when the fumes of the fire
made it angry.

"If the white lord says I am a cheat, it must be so," she
answered, "for he of all men should be able to discern a cheat. I
have said that I ask no fee—yet, give me a little tobacco from
your pouch."

Hadden opened the bag of antelope hide and drawing some
tobacco from it, gave it to her. In taking it she clasped his hand
and examined the gold ring that was upon the third finger, a ring
fashioned like a snake with two little rubies set in the head to
represent the eyes.

"I wear a snake about my neck, and you wear one upon your
hand, *Inkoos*. I should like to have this ring to wear upon my
hand, so that the snake about my neck may be less lonely
there."

"Then I am afraid you will have to wait till I am dead," said Hadden.

"Yes, yes," she answered in a pleased voice, "it is a good word. I will wait till you are dead and then I will take the ring, and none can say that I have stolen it, for Nahoon there will bear me witness that you gave me permission to do so."

For the first time Hadden started, since there was something about the Bee's tone that jarred upon him. Had she addressed him in her professional manner, he would have thought nothing of it; but in her cupidity she had become natural, and it was evident that she spoke from conviction, believing her own words.

She saw him start, and instantly changed her note.

"Let the white lord forgive the jest of a poor old witch-doctoress," she said in a whining voice. "I have so much to do with Death that his name leaps to my lips," and she glanced first at the circle of skulls about her, then towards the waterfall that fed the gloomy pool upon whose banks her hut was placed.

"Look," she said simply.

Following the line of her outstretched hand Hadden's eyes fell upon two withered mimosa trees which grew over the fall almost at right angles to its rocky edge. These trees were joined together by a rude platform made of logs of wood lashed down with *riems* of hide. Upon this platform stood three figures: notwithstanding the distance and the spray of the fall, he could see that they were those of two men and a girl, for their shapes stood out distinctly against the fiery red of the sunset sky. One instant there were three, the next there were two—for the girl had gone, and something dark rushing down the face of the fall struck the surface of the pool with a heavy thud, while a faint and piteous cry broke upon his ear.

"What is the meaning of that?" he asked, horrified and amazed.

"Nothing," answered the Bee with a laugh. "Do you not know, then, that this is the place where faithless women, or girls who have loved without the leave of the king, are brought to meet their death, and with them their accomplices? Oh! they die here thus each day, and I watch them die and keep the count of the number of them," and drawing a tally-stick from the thatch of the hut, she took a knife and added a notch to the many that appeared upon it, looking at Nahoon the while with a half-questioning, half-warning gaze.

"Yes, yes, it is a place of death," she muttered. "Up yonder the quick die day by day and down there"—and she pointed along the course of the river beyond the pool to where the forest began some two hundred yards from her hut—"the ghosts of them have their home. Listen!"

As she spoke, a sound reached their ears that seemed to swell from the dim skirts of the forests, a peculiar and unholy sound which it is impossible to define more accurately than by saying that it seemed beastlike, and almost inarticulate.

"Listen," repeated the Bee, "they are merry yonder."

"Who?" asked Hadden; "the baboons?"

"No, *Inkoos*, the *Amatongo*—the ghosts that welcome her who has just become of their number."

"Ghosts," said Hadden roughly, for he was angry at his own tremors, "I should like to see those ghosts. Do you think that I have never heard a troop of monkeys in the bush before, mother? Come, Nahoon, let us be going while there is light to climb the cliff. Farewell."

"Farewell, *Inkoos*, and doubt not that your wish will be fulfilled. Go in peace, *Inkoos*—to sleep in peace."

III

The End of the Hunt

The prayer of the Bee notwithstanding, Philip Hadden slept ill that night. He felt in the best of health, and his conscience was not troubling him more than usual, but rest he could not. Whenever he closed his eyes, his mind conjured up a picture of the grim witch-doctoress, so strangely named the Bee, and the sound of her evil-omened words as he had heard them that afternoon. He was neither a superstitious nor a timid man, and any supernatural beliefs that might linger in his mind were, to say the least of it, dormant. But do what he might, he could not shake off a certain eerie sensation of fear, lest there should be some grains of truth in the prophesyings of this hag. What if it were a fact that he was near his death, and that the heart which beat so strongly in his breast must soon be still for ever—no, he would not think of it. This gloomy place, and the dreadful sight which he saw that day, had upset his nerves. The domestic customs of these Zulus were not pleasant, and for his part he was determined to be clear of them so soon as he was able to escape the country.

In fact, if he could in any way manage it, it was his intention to make a dash for the border on the following night. To do this with a good prospect of success, however, it was necessary that he should kill a buffalo, or some other head of game. Then, as he knew well, the hunters with him would feast upon meat until they could scarcely stir, and that would be his opportunity. Nahoon, however, might not succumb to this temptation; therefore he must trust to luck to be rid of him. If it came to the worst, he could put a bullet through him, which he considered he would be justified in doing, seeing that in reality the man was his jailor. Should this necessity arise, he felt indeed that he could face it without undue compunction, for in truth he disliked Nahoon; at times he even hated him. Their natures were antagonistic, and he knew that the great Zulu distrusted and looked down upon him, and to be looked down upon by a savage "nigger" was more than his pride could stomach.

At the first break of dawn Hadden rose and roused his escort, who were still stretched in sleep around the dying fire, each man wrapped in his kaross or blanket. Nahoon stood up and shook himself, looking gigantic in the shadows of the morning.

"What is your will, *Umlungu* (white man), that you are up before the sun?"

"My will, *Muntumpofu* (yellow man), is to hunt buffalo," answered Hadden coolly. It irritated him that this savage should give him no title of any sort.

"Your pardon," said the Zulu reading his thoughts, "but I cannot call you *Inkoos* because you are not my chief, or any man's; still if the title 'white man' offends you, we will give you a name."

"As you wish," answered Hadden briefly.

Accordingly they gave him a name, *Inhlizin-mgama*, by which he was known among them thereafter, but Hadden was not best pleased when he found that the meaning of those soft-sounding syllables was "Black Heart." That was how the *inyanga* had addressed him—only she used different words.

An hour later, and they were in the swampy bush country that lay behind the encampment searching for their game. Within a very little while Nahoon held up his hand, then pointed to the ground. Hadden looked; there, pressed deep in the marshy soil, and to all appearance not ten minutes old, was the spoor of a small herd of buffalo.

"I knew that we should find game today," whispered Nahoon, "because the Bee said so."

"Curse the Bee," answered Hadden below his breath. "Come on."

For a quarter of an hour or more they followed the spoor

through thick reeds, till suddenly Nahoon whistled very softly and touched Hadden's arm. He looked up, and there, about two hundred yards away, feeding on some higher ground among a patch of mimosa trees, were the buffalos—six of them—an old bull with a splendid head, three cows, a heifer and a calf about four months old. Neither the wind nor the nature of the veldt were favourable for them to stalk the game from their present position, so they made a detour of half a mile and very carefully crept towards them up the wind, slipping from trunk to trunk of the mimosas and when these failed them, crawling on their stomachs under cover of the tall *tambuti* grass. At last they were within forty yards, and a further advance seemed impracticable; for although he could not smell them, it was evident from his movements that the old bull heard some unusual sound and was growing suspicious. Nearest to Hadden, who alone of the party had a rifle, stood the heifer broadside on—a beautiful shot. Remembering that she would make the best beef, he lifted his Martini, and aiming at her immediately behind the shoulder, gently squeezed the trigger. The rifle exploded, and the heifer fell dead, shot through the heart. Strangely enough the other buffaloes did not at once run away. On the contrary, they seemed puzzled to account for the sudden noise; and, not being able to wind anything, lifted their heads and stared round them.

The pause gave Hadden space to get in a fresh cartridge and to aim again, this time at the old bull. The bullet struck him somewhere in the neck or shoulder, for he came to his knees, but in another second was up and having caught sight of the cloud of smoke he charged straight at it. Because of the smoke, or for some other reason, Hadden did not see him coming, and in consequence would most certainly have been trampled or gored, had not Nahoon sprung forward, at the imminent risk of his own life, and dragged him down behind an ant-heap. A moment more and the great beast had thundered by, taking no further notice of them.

"Forward," said Hadden, and leaving most of the men to cut up the heifer and carry the best of her meat to camp, they started on the blood spoor.

For some hours they followed the bull, till at last they lost the trail on a patch of stony ground thickly covered with bush, and exhausted by the heat, sat down to rest and to eat some *biltong* or sun-dried flesh which they had with them. They finished their meal, and were preparing to return to camp, when one of the four Zulus who were with them went to drink at a little stream that ran at a distance of not more than ten paces away. Half a minute later they heard a hideous grunting noise and a splashing of water, and saw the Zulu fly into the air. All the while that they were eating, the wounded buffalo had been lying in wait for them under a thick bush on the banks of the streamlet, knowing—cunning brute' that he was—that sooner or later his turn would come. With a shout of consternation they rushed forward to see the bull vanish over the rise before Hadden could get a chance of firing at him, and to find their companion dying, for the great horn had pierced his lung.

"It is not a buffalo, it is a devil," the poor fellow gasped, and expired.

"Devil or not, I mean to kill it," exclaimed Hadden. So leaving the others to carry the body of their comrade to camp, he started on accompanied by Nahoon only. Now the ground was more open and the chase easier, for they sighted their quarry frequently, though they could not come near enough to fire. Presently they travelled down a steep cliff.

"Do you know where we are?" asked Nahoon, pointing to a belt of forest opposite. "That is *Emagudu*, the Home of the Dead—and look, the bull heads thither."

Hadden glanced round him. It was true; yonder to the left were the Fall, the Pool of Doom, and the hut of the Bee.

"Very well," he answered; "then we must head for it too."

Nahoon halted. "Surely you would not enter there," he exclaimed.

"Surely I will," replied Hadden, "but there is no need for you to do so if you are afraid."

"I am afraid—of ghosts," said the Zulu, "but I will come."

So they crossed the strip of turf, and entered the haunted wood. It was a gloomy place indeed; great wide-topped trees grew thick there shutting out the sight of the sky; moreover, the air in it which no breeze stirred, was heavy with the exhalations of rotting foliage. There seemed to be no life here and no sound—only now and again a loathsome spotted snake would uncoil itself and glide away, and now and again a heavy rotten bough fell with a crash.

Hadden was too intent upon the buffalo, however, to be much impressed by his surroundings. He only remarked that the light would be bad for shooting, and went on.

They must have penetrated a mile or more into the forest when the sudden increase of blood upon the spoor told them that the bull's wound was proving fatal to him.

"Run now," said Hadden cheerfully.

"Nay, *hamba gachle*—go softly—" answered Nahoon, "the devil is dying, but he will try to play us another trick before he dies." And he went on peering ahead of him cautiously.

"It is all right here, anyway," said Hadden, pointing to the spoor that ran straight forward printed deep in the marshy ground.

Nahoon did not answer, but stared steadily at the trunks of two trees a few paces in front of them and to their right. "Look," he whispered.

Hadden did so, and at length made out the outline of something brown that was crouched behind the trees.

"He is dead," he exclaimed.

"No," answered Nahoon, "he has come back on his own path and is waiting for us. He knows that we are following his spoor. Now if you stand here, I think that you can shoot him through the back between the tree trunks."

Hadden knelt down, and aiming very carefully at a point just below the bull's spine, he fired. There was an awful bellow, and the next instant the brute was up and at them. Nahoon flung his broad spear, which sank deep into its chest, then they fled this way and that. The buffalo stood still for a moment, its forelegs straddle wide and its head down, looking first after the one and then the other, till of a sudden it uttered a low moaning sound and rolled over dead, smashing Nahoon's assegai to fragments as it fell.

"There! he's finished," said Hadden, "and I believe it was your assegai that killed him. Hullo! what's that noise?"

Nahoon listened. In several quarters of the forest, but from how far away it was impossible to tell, there rose a curious sound, as of people calling to each other in fear but in no articulate language. Nahoon shivered.

"It is the *Esemkofu*," he said, "the ghosts who have no tongue, and who can only wail like infants. Let us be going; this place is bad for mortals."

"And worse for buffaloes," said Hadden, giving the dead bull a kick, "but I suppose that we must leave him here for your friends, the *Esemkofu*, as we have got meat enough, and can't carry his head."

So they started back towards the open country. As they threaded their way slowly through the tree trunks, a new idea came into Hadden's mind. Once out of this forest, he was within an hour's run of the Zulu border, and once over the Zulu border, he would feel a happier man than he did at that moment. As has been said, he had intended to attempt to escape in the darkness, but the plan was risky. All the Zulus might not over-eat themselves and go to sleep, especially after the death of their comrade; Nahoon, who watched him day and night, certainly would not. This was his opportunity—there remained the question of Nahoon.

Well, if it came to the worst, Nahoon must die; it would be easy—he had a loaded rifle, and now that his assegai was gone, Nahoon had only a kerry. He did not wish to kill the man, though it was clear to him, seeing that his own safety was at stake, that he would be amply justified in so doing. Why should he not put it to him—and then be guided by circumstances?

Nahoon was walking across a little open space about ten paces ahead of him where Hadden could see him very well, whilst he himself was under the shadow of a large tree with low horizontal branches running out from the trunk.

"Nahoon," he said.

The Zulu turned round, and took a step towards him.

"No, do not move, I pray. Stand where you are, or I shall be obliged to shoot you. Listen now: do not be afraid for I shall not fire without warning. I am your prisoner, and you are charged to take me back to the king to be his servant. But I believe that a war is going to break out between your people and mine; and this being so, you will understand that I do not wish to go to Cetywayo's kraal, because I should either come to a violent death there, or my own brothers will believe that I am a traitor and treat me accordingly. The Zulu border is not much more than an hour's journey away—let us say an hour and a half's: I mean to be across it before the moon is up. Now, Nahoon, will you lose me in the forest and give me this hour and a half's start—or will you stop here with that ghost people of whom you talk? Do you understand? No, please do not move."

"I understand you," answered the Zulu, in a perfectly composed voice, "and I think that was a good name which we gave you this morning, though, Black Heart, there is some justice in your words and more wisdom. Your opportunity is good, and one which a man named as you are should not let fall."

"I am glad to find that you take this view of the matter, Nahoon. And now will you be so kind as to lose me, and to promise not to look for me till the moon is up?"

"What do you mean, Black Heart?"

"What I say. Come, I have no time to spare."

"You are a strange men," said the Zulu reflectively. "You heard the king's order to me: would you have me disobey the order of the king?"

"Certainly, I would. You have no reason to love Cetywayo, and it does not matter to you whether or not I return to his kraal to mend guns there. If you think that he will be angry because I am missing, you had better cross the border also; we can go together."

"And leave my father and all my brethren to his vengeance? Black Heart, you do not understand. How can you, being so named? I am a soldier, and the king's word is the king's word. I hoped to have died fighting, but I am the bird in your noose. Come, shoot, or you will not reach the border before moonrise," and he opened his arms and smiled.

"If it must be, so let it be. Farewell, Nahoon, at least you are a brave man, but every one of us must cherish his own life," answered Hadden calmly.

Then with much deliberation he raised his rifle and covered the Zulu's breast.

Already—whilst his victim stood there still smiling, although a twitching of his lips betrayed the natural terrors that no bravery can banish—already his finger was contracting on the trigger, when of a sudden, as instantly indeed as though he had been struck by lightning, Hadden went down backwards, and behold! there stood upon him a great spotted beast that waved its long tail to and fro and glared down into his eyes.

It was a leopard—a tiger as they call it in Africa—which, crouched upon a bough of the tree above, had been unable to resist the temptation of satisfying its savage appetite on the man below. For a second or two there was silence, broken only by the purring, or rather the snoring sound made by the leopard. In those seconds, strangely enough, there sprang up before Hadden's mental vision a picture of the *inyanga* called *Inyosi* or the Bee, her death-like head resting against the thatch of the hut, and her death-like lips muttering "think of my word when the great cat purrs above your face."

Then the brute put out its strength. The claws of one paw it drove deep into the muscles of his left thigh, while with another it scratched at his breast, tearing the clothes from it and furrowing the flesh beneath. The sight of the white skin seemed to madden it, and in its fierce desire for blood it drooped its square muzzle and buried its fangs in its victim's shoulder. Next moment there was a sound of rushing feet and of a club falling heavily. Up reared the leopard with an angry snarl, up till it stood as high as the attacking Zulu. At him it came, striking out savagely and tearing the black man as it had torn the white.

Again the kerry fell full on its jaws, and down it went backwards. Before it could rise again, or rather as it was in the act of rising, the heavy knob-stick struck it once more, and with fearful force, this time as it chanced, full on the nape of the neck, and paralysing the brute. It writhed and bit and twisted, throwing up the earth and leaves, while blow after blow was rained upon it, till at length with a convulsive struggle and a stifled roar it lay still—the brains oozing from its shattered skull.

Hadden sat up, the blood running from his wounds.

"You have saved my life, Nahoon," he said faintly, "and I thank you."

"Do not thank me, Black Heart," answered the Zulu, "it was the king's word that I should keep you safely. Still this tiger has been hardly dealt with, for certainly *he* has saved *my* life," and lifting the Martini he unloaded the rifle.

At this juncture Hadden swooned away.

Twenty-four hours had gone by when, after what seemed to him to be but a little time of troubled and dreamful sleep, through which he could hear voices without understanding what they said, and feel himself borne he knew not whither, Hadden awoke to find himself lying upon a *kaross* in a large and beautifully clean Kaffir hut with a bundle of furs for a pillow. There was a bowl of milk at his side, and tortured as he was by thirst, he tried to stretch out his arm to lift it to his lips, only to find to his astonishment that his hand fell back to his side like that of a dead man. Looking round the hut impatiently, he found that there was nobody in it to assist him, so he did the only thing which remained for him to do—he lay still. He did not fall asleep, but his eyes closed, and a kind of gentle torpor crept over him, half obscuring his recovered senses. Presently he heard a soft voice speaking; it seemed far away, but he could clearly distinguish the words.

"Black Heart still sleeps," the voice said, "but there is colour in his face; I think that he will wake soon, and find his thoughts again."

"Have no fear, Nanea, he will surely wake, his hurts are not dangerous," answered another voice, that of Nahoon. "He fell heavily with the weight of the tiger on top of him, and that is why his senses have been shaken for so long. He went near to death, but certainly he will not die."

"It would have been a pity if he had died," answered the soft voice, "he is so beautiful; never have I seen a white man who was so beautiful."

"I did not think him beautiful when he stood with his rifle pointed at my heart," answered Nahoon sulkily.

"Well, there is this to be said," she replied, "he wished to escape from Cetywayo, and that is not to be wondered at," and she sighed. "Moreover he asked you to come with him, and it might have been well if you had done so, that is, if you would have taken me with you!"

"How could I have done it, girl?" he asked angrily. "Would you have me set at nothing the order of the king?"

"The king!" she replied raising her voice. "What do you owe to the king? You have served him faithfully, and your reward is that within a few days he will take me from you—me, who should have been your wife, and I must—I must . . ." And she began to weep softly, adding between her sobs, "If you loved me truly, you would think more of me and of yourself, and less of the Black One and his orders. Oh! let us fly, Nahoon, let us fly to Natal before this spear pierces me."

"Weep not, Nanea," he said; "why do you tear my heart in two between my duty and my love? You know that I am a soldier, and that I must walk the path whereon the king has set my feet. Soon I think I shall be dead, for I seek death, and then it will matter nothing."

"Nothing to you, Nahoon, who are at peace, but to me? Yet, you are right, and I know it, therefore forgive me, who am no warrior, but a woman who must also obey the will of the king." And she cast her arms about his neck, sobbing her fill upon his breast.

IV

Nanea

Presently, muttering something that the listener could not catch, Nahoon left Nanea, and crept out of the hut by its bee-hole entrance. Then Hadden opened his eyes and looked around him. The sun was sinking and a ray of its red light streaming through the little opening filled the place with a soft and crimson glow. In the centre of the hut—supporting it—stood a thorn-wood roof-tree coloured black by the smoke of the fire; and against this, the rich light falling full upon her, leaned the girl Nanea—a very picture of gentle despair.

As is occasionally the case among Zulu women, she was beautiful—so beautiful that the sight of her went straight to the white man's heart, for a moment causing the breath to catch in his throat. Her dress was very simple. On her shoulders, hanging open in front, lay a mantle of soft white stuff edged with blue beads, about her middle was a buck-skin moocha, also embroidered with blue beads, while round her forehead and left knee were strips of grey fur, and on her right wrist a shining bangle of copper. Her naked bronzed-hued figure was tall and perfect in its proportions; while her face had little in common with that of the ordinary native girl, showing as it did strong traces of ancestral Arabian or Semitic blood. It was oval in shape, with delicate aquiline features, arched eyebrows, a full mouth, that drooped a little at the corners, tiny ears, behind which the wavy coal-black hair hung down to the shoulders, and the very loveliest pair of dark and liquid eyes that it is possible to imagine.

For a minute or more Nanea stood thus, her sweet face bathed in the sunbeam, while Hadden feasted his eyes upon its beauty. Then sighing heavily, she turned, and seeing that he was awake, started, drew her mantle over her breast and came, or rather glided, towards him.

"The chief is awake," she said in her soft Zulu accents. "Does he need aught?"

"Yes, Lady," he answered; "I need to drink, but alas! I am too weak."

She knelt down beside him, and supporting him with her left arm, with her right held the gourd to his lips.

How it came about Hadden never knew, but before that draught was finished a change passed over him. Whether it was the savage girl's touch, or her strange and fawn-like loveliness, or the tender pity in her eyes, matters not—the issue was the same. She struck some chord in his turbulent uncurbed nature, and of a sudden it was filled full with passion for her—a passion which if not elevated, at least was real. He did not for a moment mistake the significance of the flood of feeling that surged through his veins. Hadden never shirked facts.

"By Heaven!" he said to himself, "I have fallen in love with a black beauty at first sight—more in love than I have ever been before. It's awkward, but there will be compensations. So much the worse for Nahoon, or for Cetywayo, or for both of them. After all, I can always get rid of her if she becomes a nuisance."

Then, in a fit of renewed weakness, brought about by the turmoil of his blood, he lay back upon the pillow of furs, watching Nanea's face while with a native salve of pounded leaves she busied herself dressing the wounds that the leopard had made.

It almost seemed as though something of what was passing in his mind communicated itself to that of the girl. At least, her hand shook a little at her task, and getting done with it as quickly as she could, she rose from her knees with a courteous "It is finished, *Inkoos*," and once more took up her position by the roof-tree.

"I thank you, Lady," he said; "your hand is kind."

"You must not call me lady, *Inkoos*," she answered, "I am no chieftainess, but only the daughter of a headman, Umgona."

"And named Nanea," he said. "Nay, do not be surprised, I have heard of you. Well, Nanea, perhaps you will soon become a chieftainess—up at the king's kraal yonder."

"Alas! and alas!" she said, covering her face with her hands.

"Do not grieve, Nanea, a hedge is never so tall and thick but that it can be climbed or crept through."

She let fall her hands and looked at him eagerly, but he did not pursue the subject.

"Tell me, how did I come here, Nanea?"

"Nahoon and his companions carried you, *Inkoos*."

"Indeed, I begin to be thankful to the leopard that struck me down. Well, Nahoon is a brave man, and he has done me a great service. I trust that I may be able to repay it—to you, Nanea."

This was the first meeting of Nanea and Hadden; but, although she did not seek them, the necessities of his sickness and of the situation brought about many another. Never for a moment did the white man waver in his determination to get into his keeping the native girl who had captivated him, and to attain his end he brought to bear all his powers and charm to detach her from Nahoon, and win her affections for himself. He was no rough wooer, however, but proceeded warily, weaving her about with a web of flattery and attention that must, he thought, produce the desired effect upon her mind. Without a doubt, indeed, it would have done so—for she was but a woman, and an untutored one—had it not been for a simple fact which dominated her whole nature. She loved Nahoon, and there was no room in her heart for any other man, white or black. To Hadden she was courteous and kindly but no more, nor did she appear to notice any of the subtle advances by which he attempted to win a foothold in her heart. For a while this puzzled him, but he remembered that the Zulu women do not usually permit themselves to show feeling towards an undeclared suitor. Therefore it became necessary that he should speak out.

His mind once made up, he had not to wait long for an opportunity. He was now quite recovered from his hurts, and accustomed to walk in the neighbourhood of the kraal. About two hundred yards from Umgona's huts rose a spring, and thither it was Nanea's habit to resort in the evening to bring back drinking-water for the use of her father's household. The path between this spring and the kraal ran through a patch of bush, where on a certain afternoon towards sundown Hadden took his seat under a tree, having first seen Nanea go down to the little stream as was her custom. A quarter of an hour later she reappeared carrying a large gourd upon her head. She wore no garment now except her moocha, for she had but one mantle and was afraid lest the water should splash it. He watched her advancing along the path, her hands resting on her hips, her splendid naked figure outlined against the westering sun, and wondered what excuse he could make to talk with her. As it chanced fortune favoured him, for when she was near him a snake glided across the path in front of the girl's feet, causing her to spring backwards in alarm and overset the gourd of water. He came forward, and picked it up.

"Wait here," he said laughing; "I will bring it to you full."

"Nay, *Inkoos*," she remonstrated, "that is a woman's work."

"Among my people," he said, "the men love to work for the women," and he started for the spring, leaving her wondering.

Before he reached her again, he regretted his gallantry, for it was necessary to carry the handleless gourd upon his shoulder, and the contents of it spilling over the edge soaked him. Of this, however, he said nothing to Nanea.

"There is your water, Nanea, shall I carry it for you to the kraal?"

"Nay, *Inkoos*, I thank you, but give it to me, you are weary with its weight."

"Stay awhile, and I will accompany you. Ah! Nanea, I am still weak, and had it not been for you I think that I should be dead."

"It was Nahoon who saved you—not I, *Inkoos*."

"Nahoon saved my body, but you, Nanea, you alone can save my heart."

"You talk darkly, *Inkoos*."

"Then I must make my meaning clear, Nanea. I love you." She opened her brown eyes wide.

"You, a white lord, love me, a Zulu girl? How can that be?"

"I do not know, Nanea, but it is so, and were you not blind you would have seen it. I love you, and I wish to take you to wife."

"Nay, *Inkoos*, it is impossible. I am already betrothed."

"Ay," he answered, "betrothed to the king."

"No, betrothed to Nahoon."

"But it is the king who will take you within a week; is it not so? And would you not rather that I should take you than the king?"

"It seems to be so, *Inkoos*, and I would rather go with you than with the king, but most of all I desire to marry Nahoon. It may be that I shall not be able to marry him, but if that is so, at least I will never become one of the king's women."

"How will you prevent it, Nanea?"

"There are waters in which a maid may drown, and trees upon which she can hang," she answered with a quick setting of the mouth.

"That were a pity, Nanea, you are too fair to die."

"Fair or foul, yet I die, *Inkoos*."

"No, no, come with me—I will find a way—and be my wife," and he put his arm about her waist, and strove to draw her to him.

Without any violence of movement, and with the most perfect dignity, the girl disengaged herself from his embrace.

"You have honoured me, and I thank you, *Inkoos*," she said quietly, "but you do not understand. I am the wife of Nahoon—I belong to Nahoon; therefore, I cannot look on any other man while Nahoon lives. It is not our custom, *Inkoos*, for we are not as the white women, but ignorant and simple, and when we vow ourselves to a man, we abide by that vow till death."

"Indeed," said Hadden; "and so now you go to tell Nahoon that I have offered to make you my wife."

"No, *Inkoos*, why should I tell Nahoon your secrets? I have said 'nay' to you, not 'yea,' therefore he has no right to know," and she stooped to lift the gourd of water.

Hadden considered the situation rapidly, for his repulse only made him the more determined to succeed. Of a sudden under the emergency he conceived a scheme, or rather its rough outline. It was not a nice scheme, and some men might have shrunk from it, but as he had no intention of suffering himself to be defeated by a Zulu girl, he decided—with regret, it is true—that having failed to attain his ends by means which he considered fair, he must resort to other of more doubtful character.

"Nanea," he said, "you are a good and honest woman, and I respect you. As I have told you, I love you also, but if you refuse to listen to me there is nothing more to be said, and after all, perhaps it would be better that you should marry one of your own people. But, Nanea, you will never marry him, for the king will take you; and, if he does not give you to some other man, either you will become one of his 'sisters,' or to be free of him, as you say, you will die. Now hear me, for it is because I love you and wish your welfare that I speak thus. Why do you not escape into Natal, taking Nahoon with you, for there as you know you may live in peace out of reach of the arm of Cetywayo?''

''That is my desire, *Inkoos*, but Nahoon will not consent. He says that there is to be war between us and you white men, and he will not break the command of the king and desert from his army.''

''Then he cannot love you much, Nanea, and at least you have to think of yourself. Whisper into the ear of your father and fly together, for be sure that Nahoon will soon follow you. Ay! and I myself will fly with you, for I too believe that there must be war, and then a white man in this country will be as a lamb among the eagles.''

''If Nahoon will come, I will go, *Inkoos*, but I cannot fly without Nahoon; it is better I should stay here and kill myself.''

''Surely then being so fair and loving him so well, you can teach him to forget his folly and to escape with you. In four days' time we must start for the king's kraal, and if you win over Nahoon, it will be easy for us to turn our faces southwards and cross the river that lies between the land of the Amazulu and Natal. For the sake of all of us, but most of all for your own sake, try to do this, Nanea, whom I have loved and whom I now would save. See him and plead with him as you know how, but as yet do not tell him that I dream of flight, for then I should be watched.''

''In truth, I will, *Inkoos*,'' she answered earnestly, ''and oh! I thank you for your goodness. Fear not that I will betray you— first would I die. Farewell.''

''Farewell, Nanea,'' and taking her hand he raised it to his lips.

Late that night, just as Hadden was beginning to prepare himself for sleep, he heard a gentle tapping at the board which closed the entrance to his hut.

''Enter,'' he said, unfastening the door, and presently by the light of the little lantern that he had with him, he saw Nanea creep into the hut, followed by the great form of Nahoon.

''*Inkoos*,'' she said in a whisper when the door was closed again, ''I have pleaded with Nahoon, and he has consented to fly; moreover, my father will come also.''

"Is it so, Nahoon?" asked Hadden.

"It is so," answered the Zulu, looking down shamefacedly; "to save this girl from the king, and because the love of her eats out my heart, I have bartered away my honour. But I tell you, Nanea, and you, White Man, as I told Umgona just now, that I think no good will come of this flight, and if we are caught or betrayed, we shall be killed every one of us."

"Caught we can scarcely be," broke in Nanea anxiously, "for who could betray us, except the *Inkoos* here—"

"Which he is not likely to do," said Hadden quietly, "seeing that he desires to escape with you, and that his life is also at stake."

"That is so, Black Heart," said Nahoon, "otherwise I tell you that I should not have trusted you."

Hadden took no notice of this outspoken saying, but until very late that night they sat there together making their plans.

On the following morning Hadden was awakened by sounds of violent altercation. Going out of his hut he found that the disputants were Umgona and a fat and evil-looking Kaffir chief who had arrived at the kraal on a pony. This chief, he soon discovered, was named Maputa, being none other than the man who had sought Nanea in marriage and brought about Nahoon's and Umgona's unfortunate appeal to the king. At present he was engaged in abusing Umgona furiously, charging him with having stolen certain of his oxen and bewitched his cows so that they would not give milk. The alleged theft it was comparatively easy to disprove, but the wizardry remained a matter of argument.

"You are a dog, and a son of a dog," shouted Maputa, shaking his fat fist in the face of the trembling but indignant Umgona. "You promised me your daughter in marriage, then having vowed her to that *umfagozan*—that low lout of a soldier, Nahoon, the son of Zomba—you went, the two of you, and poisoned the king's ear against me, bringing me into trouble with the king, and now you have bewitched my cattle. Well, wait, I will be even with you, Wizard; wait till you wake up in the cold morning to find your fence red with fire, and the slayers standing outside your gates to eat up you and yours with spears—"

At this juncture Nahoon, who till now had been listening in silence, intervened with effect.

"Good," he said, "we will wait, but not in your company, Chief Maputa. *Hamba!* (go)" and seizing the fat old ruffian by the scruff of his neck, he flung him backwards with such violence that he rolled over and over down the little slope.

Hadden laughed, and passed on towards the stream where he

proposed to bathe. Just as he reached it, he caught sight of
Maputa riding along the footpath, his head-ring covered with
mud, his lips purple and his black face livid with rage.

"There goes an angry man," he said to himself. "Now, how
would it be . . ." and he looked upwards like one seeking an
inspiration. It seemed to come; perhaps the devil finding it open
whispered in his ear, at any rate—in a few seconds his plan was
formed, and he was walking through the bush to meet Maputa.

"Go in peace, Chief," he said; "they seem to have treated
you roughly up yonder. Having no power to interfere, I came
away for I could not bear the sight. It is indeed shameful that an
old and venerable man of rank should be struck into the dirt, and
beaten by a soldier drunk with beer."

"Shameful, White Man!" gasped Maputa; "your words are
true indeed. But wait a while. I, Maputa, will roll that stone
over, I will throw that bull upon its back. When next the harvest
ripens, this I promise, that neither Nahoon nor Umgona, nor any
of his kraal shall be left to gather it."

"And how will you manage that, Maputa?"

"I do not know, but I will find a way. Oh! I tell you, a way
shall be found."

Hadden patted the pony's neck meditatively, then leaning
forward, he looked the chief in the eyes and said:

"What will you give me, Maputa, if I show you that way, a
sure and certain one, whereby you may be avenged to the death
upon Nahoon, whose violence I also have seen, and upon Umgona,
whose witchcraft brought sore sickness upon me?"

"What reward do you seek, White Man?" asked Maputa
eagerly.

"A little thing, Chief, a thing of no account, only the girl
Nanea, to whom as it chances I have taken a fancy."

"I wanted her for myself, White Man, but he who sits at
Ulundi has laid his hand upon her."

"That is nothing, Chief; I can arrange with him who 'sits at
Ulundi'. It is you who are great here that I wish to come to terms.
Listen: if you grant my desire, not only will I fulfil yours upon
your foes, but when the girl is delivered into my hands I will
give you this rifle and a hundred rounds of cartridges."

Maputa looked at the sporting Martini, and his eyes glistened.

"It is good," he said; "it is very good. Often have I wished
for such a gun that will enable me to shoot game, and to talk
with my enemies from far away. Promise it to me, White Man,
and you shall take the girl if I can give her to you."

"You swear it, Maputa?"

"I swear it by the head of Chaka, and the spirits of my fathers."

"Good. At dawn on the fourth day from now it is the purpose of Umgona, his daughter Nanea, and Nahoon, to cross the river into Natal by the drift that is called Crocodile Drift, taking their cattle with them and flying from the king. I also shall be of their company, for they know that I have learned their secret, and would murder me if I tried to leave them. Now you, who are chief of the border and guardian of that drift, must hide at night with some men among the rocks in the shallows of the drift and await our coming. First Nanea will cross driving the cows and calves, for so it is arranged, and I shall help her; then will follow Umgona and Nahoon with the oxen and heifers. On these two you must fall, killing them and capturing the cattle, and afterwards I will give you the rifle."

"What if the king ask for the girl, White Man?"

"Then you shall answer that in the uncertain light you did not recognise her and so she slipped away from you; moreover, that at first you feared to seize the girl lest her cries should alarm the men and they should escape you."

"Good, but how can I be sure that you will give me the gun once you are across the river?"

"Thus: before I enter the ford I will lay the rifle and cartridges upon a stone by the bank, telling Nanea that I shall return to fetch them when I have driven over the cattle."

"It is well, White Man; I will not fail you."

So the plot was made, and after some further conversation upon points of detail, the two conspirators shook hands and parted.

"That ought to come off all right," reflected Hadden to himself as he plunged and floated in the waters of the stream, "but somehow I don't quite trust our friend Maputa. It would have been better if I could have relied upon myself to get rid of Nahoon and his respected uncle—a couple of shots would do it in the water. But then that would be murder and murder is unpleasant; whereas the other thing is only the delivery to justice of two base deserters, a laudable action in a military country. Also personal interference upon my part might turn the girl against me; while after Umgona and Nahoon have been wiped out by Maputa, she *must* accept my escort. Of course there is a risk, but in every walk of life the most cautious have to take risks at times."

As it chanced, Philip Hadden was correct in his suspicions of his coadjutor, Maputa. Even before that worthy chief reached his own kraal, he had come to the conclusion that the white man's plan, though attractive in some ways, was too dangerous, since it was certain that if the girl Nanea escaped, the king would be indignant. Moreover, the men he took with him to do the killing in the drift would suspect something and talk. On the other hand he would earn much credit with his majesty by revealing the plot, saying that he had learned it from the lips of the white hunter, whom Umgona and Nahoon had forced to participate in it, and of whose coveted rifle he must trust to chance to possess himself.

An hour later two discreet messengers were bounding across the plains, bearing words from the Chief Maputa, the Warden of the Border, to the "great Black Elephant" at Ulundi.

V

The Doom Pool

Fortune showed itself strangely favourable to the plans of Nahoon and Nanea. One of the Zulu captain's perplexities was as to how he should lull the suspicions and evade the vigilance of his own companions, who together with himself had been detailed by the king to assist Hadden in his hunting and to guard against his escape. As it chanced, however, on the day after the incident of the visit of Maputa, a messenger arrived from no less a person than the great military Induna, Tvingwayo ka Marolo, who afterwards commanded the Zulu army at Isandhlwana; ordering these men to return to their regiment, the Umcityu Corps, which was to be placed upon full war footing. Accordingly Nahoon sent them, saying that he himself would follow with Black Heart in the course of a few days, as at present the white man was not sufficiently recovered from his hurts to allow of his travelling fast and far. So the soldiers went, doubting nothing.

Then Umgona gave it out that in obedience to the command of the king he was about to start for Ulundi, taking with him his daughter Nanea to be delivered over into the *Sigodhla,* and also those fifteen head of cattle that had been *lobola'd* by Nahoon in consideration of his forthcoming marriage, whereof he had been fined by Cetywayo. Under pretence that they required a change of veldt, the rest of his cattle he sent away in charge of a Basuto herd who knew nothing of their plans, telling him to keep them by the Crocodile Drift, as there the grass was good and sweet.

All preparations being completed, on the third day the party started, heading straight for Ulundi. After they had travelled some miles, however, they left the road and turning sharp to the right, passed unobserved of any through a great stretch of uninhabited bush. Their path now lay not far from the Pool of Doom, which, indeed, was close to Umgona's kraal, and the forest that was called Home of the Dead, but out of sight of these. It was their plan to travel by night, reaching the broken country near the Crocodile Drift on the following morning. Here they proposed to lie hid that day and through the night; then, having first collected the cattle which had preceded them, to cross the river at the break of dawn and escape into Natal. At least this was the plan of his companions; but, as we know, Hadden had another programme, wherein after one last appearance two of the party would play no part.

During that long afternoon's journey Umgona, who knew every inch of the country, walked ahead driving the fifteen cattle and carrying in his hand a long travelling stick of black and white *umzimbeet* wood, for in truth the old man was in a hurry to reach his journey's end. Next came Nahoon, armed with a broad assegai, but naked except for his moocha and necklet of baboon's teeth, and with him Nanea in her white bead-bordered mantle. Hadden, who brought up the rear, noticed that the girl seemed to be under the spell of an imminent apprehension, for from time to time she clasped her lover's arm, and looking into his face, addressed him with vehemence, almost with passion.

Curiously enough, the sight touched Hadden, and once or twice he was shaken by so sharp a pang of remorse at the thought of his share in this tragedy, that he cast about in his mind seeking a means to unravel the web of death which he himself had woven. But ever that evil voice was whispering in his ear. It reminded him that he, the white *Inkoos*, had been refused by this dusky beauty, and that if he found a way to save him, within some few hours she would be the wife of the savage gentleman at her side, the man who had named him Black Heart and who despised him, the man whom he had meant to murder and who immediately repaid his treachery by rescuing him from the jaws of the leopard at the risk of his own life. Moreover, it was a law of Hadden's existence never to deny himself anything that he desired if it lay within his power to take it—a law which had led him always deeper into sin. In other respects, indeed, it had not carried him far, for in the past he had desired much, and he had won little; but this particular flower was to his hand, and he would pluck it. If Nahoon stood between him and the flower, so much the worse for Nahoon, and if it should wither in his grasp, so much the worse for the flower; it could always be thrown away. Thus it came about that, not for the first time in his life, Philip Hadden discarded the somewhat spasmodic prickings of conscience and listened to that evil whispering at his ear.

About half-past five o'clock in the afternoon the four refugees passed the stream that a mile or so down fell over the little precipice into the Doom Pool; and, entering a patch of thorn trees on the further side, walked straight into the midst of two-and-twenty soldiers, who were beguiling the tedium of expectancy by the taking of snuff and the smoking of *dakka* or native hemp. With these soldiers, seated on his pony, for he was too fat to walk, waited the Chief Maputa.

Observing that their expected guests had arrived, the men knocked out the *dakka* pipe, replaced the snuff boxes in the slits made in the lobes of their ears, and secured the four of them.

"What is the meaning of this, O King's soldiers?" asked Umgona in a quavering voice. "We journey to the kraal of U'Cetywayo; why do you molest us?"

"Indeed. Wherefore then are your faces set towards the south? Does the Black One live in the south? Well, you will journey to another kraal presently," answered the jovial-looking captain of the party with a callous laugh.

"I do not understand," stammered Umgona.

"Then I will explain while you rest," said the captain. "The Chief Maputa yonder sent word to the Black One at Ulundi that he had learned of your intended flight to Natal from the lips of this white man, who had warned him of it. The Black One was angry, and despatched us to catch you and make an end of you. That is all. Come on now, quietly, and let us finish the matter. As the Doom Pool is near, your deaths will be easy."

Nahoon heard the words, and sprang straight at the throat of Hadden; but he did not reach it, for the soldiers pulled him down. Nanea heard them also, and turning, looked the traitor in the eye; she said nothing, she only looked, but he could never forget that look. The white man for his part was filled with a fiery indignation against Maputa.

"You wicked villain," he gasped, whereat the chief smiled in a sickly fashion, and turned away.

Then they were marched along the banks of the stream till they reached the waterfall that fell into the Pool of Doom.

Hadden was a brave man after his fashion, but his heart quailed as he gazed into that abyss.

"Are you going to throw me in there?" he asked of the Zulu captain in a thick voice.

"You, White Man?" replied the soldier unconcernedly. "No, our orders are to take you to the king, but what he will do with you I do not know. There is to be war between your people and ours, so perhaps he means to pound you into medicine for the use of the witch-doctors, or to peg you over an ant-heap as a warning to other white men."

Hadden received this information in silence, but its effect upon his brain was bracing, for instantfy he began to search out some means of escape.

By now the party had halted near the two thorn trees that hung over the waters of the pool.

"Who dives first?" asked the captain of the Chief Maputa.

"The old wizard," he replied, nodding at Umgona; "then his daughter after him, and last of all this fellow," and he struck Nahoon in the face with his open hand.

"Come on, Wizard," said the captain, grasping Umgona by the arm, "and let us see how you can swim."

At the words of doom Umgona seemed to recover his self-command, after the fashion of his race.

"No need to lead me, soldier," he said, shaking himself loose, "who am old and ready to die." Then he kissed his daughter at his side, wrung Nahoon by the hand, and turning from Hadden with a gesture of contempt walked out upon the platform that joined the two thorn trunks. Here he stood for a moment looking at the setting sun, then suddenly, and without a sound, he hurled himself into the abyss below and vanished.

"That was a brave one," said the captain with admiration. "Can you spring too, girl, or must we throw you?"

"I can walk my father's path," Nanea answered faintly, "but first I crave leave to say one word. It is true that we were escaping from the king, and therefore by the law we must die; but it was Black Heart here who made the plot, and he who has betrayed us. Would you know why he has betrayed us? Because he sought my favour, and I refused him, and this is the vengeance that he takes—a white man's vengeance."

"*Wow!*" broke in the Chief Maputa, "this pretty one speaks truth, for the white man would have made a bargain with me under which Umgona, the wizard, and Nahoon, the solider, were to be killed at the Crocodile Drift, and he himself suffered to escape with the girl. I spoke him softly and said 'yes,' and then like a loyal man I reported to the king."

"You hear," sighed Nanea. "Nahoon, fare you well, though presently perhaps we shall be together again. It was I who tempted you from your duty. For my sake you forgot your honour, and I am repaid. Farewell, my husband, it is better to die with you than to enter the house of the king's woman,'' and Nanea stepped on to the platform.

Here, holding to a bough of one of the thorn trees, she turned and addressed Hadden saying:

"Black Heart, you seem to have won the day, but me at least you lose and—the sun is not yet set. After sunset comes the night, Black Heart, and in the night I pray that you may wander eternally, and be given to drink of my blood and the blood of Umgona my father, and the blood of Nahoon my husband, who saved your life, and whom you have murdered. Perchance, Black Heart, we may yet meet yonder—in the House of the Dead.''

Then uttering a low cry Nanea clasped her hands and sprang upwards and outwards from the platform. The watchers bent their heads foward to look. They saw her rush headlong down the face of the fall to strike the water fifty feet below. A few seconds, and for the last time, they caught sight of her white garment glimmering on the surface of the gloomy pool. Then the shadows and mist-wreaths hid it, and she was gone.

"Now, husband,'' cried the cheerful voice of the captain, "yonder is your marriage bed, so be swift to follow a bride who is so ready to lead the way. *Wow!* but you are good people to kill; never have I had to do with any who gave less trouble. You—'' and he stopped, for mental agony had done its work, and suddenly Nahoon went mad before his eyes.

With a roar like that of a lion the great man cast off those who held him and seizing one of them round the waist and thigh, he put out all his terrible strength. Lifting him as though he had been an infant, he hurled him over the edge of the cliff to find his death on the rocks of the Pool of Doom. Then crying:

"Black Heart! your turn, Black Heart the traitor!'' he rushed at Hadden, his eyes rolling and foam flying from his lips, as he passed striking the Chief Maputa from his horse with a backward blow of his hand. Ill would it have gone with the white man if Nahoon had caught him. But he could not come at him, for the soliders sprang upon him and notwithstanding his fearful struggles they pulled him to the ground, as at certain festivals the Zulu regiments with their naked hands pull down a bull in the presence of the king.

"Cast him over before he can work more mischief,'' said a voice. But the captain cried out, "Nay, nay, he is sacred; the fire from Heaven has fallen on his brain, and we may not harm him, else evil would overtake us all. Bind him hand and foot, and bear him hence tenderly to where he can be cared for. Surely I thought that these evil-doers were giving us too little trouble, and thus it has proved.''

So they set themselves to make fast Nahoon's hands and wrists, using as much gentleness as they might, for among the Zulus a lunatic is accounted holy. It was no easy task, and it took time.

Hadden glanced around him, and saw his opportunity. On the ground close beside him lay his rifle, where one of the soldiers had placed it, and about a dozen yards away Maputa's pony was grazing. With a swift movement, he seized the Martini and five seconds later he was on the back of the pony, heading for the Crocodile Drift at a gallop. So quickly indeed did he execute his masterly retreat, that occupied as they all were in binding Nahoon, for half a minute or more none of the soldiers noticed what had happened. Then Maputa chanced to see, and waddled after him to the top of the rise, screaming:

''The white thief, he has stolen my horse, and the gun too, the gun that he promised to give me.''

Hadden, who by this time was a hundred yards away, heard him clearly, and a rage filled his heart. This man had made an open murderer of him; more, he had been the means of robbing him of the girl for whose sake he had dipped his hands in these iniquities. He glanced over his shoulder; Maputa was still running, and alone. Yes, there was time; at any rate he would risk it.

Pulling up the pony with a jerk, he leapt from its back, slipping his arms through the rein with an almost simultaneous movement. As it chanced, and as he had hoped would be the case, the animal was a trained shooting horse, and stood still. Hadden planted his feet firmly on the ground and drawing a deep breath, he cocked the rifle and covered the advancing chief. Now Maputa saw his purpose and with a yell of terror turned to fly. Hadden waited a second to get his sight fair on to his broad back, then just as the soldiers appeared above the rise he pressed the trigger. He was a noted shot, and in this instance his skill did not fail him; for, before he heard the bullet tell, Maputa flung his arms wide and plunged to the ground dead.

Three seconds more, and with a savage curse, Hadden had remounted the pony and was riding for his life towards the river, which a while later he crossed in safety.

VI

The Ghost of the Dead

When Nanea leapt from the dizzy platform that overhung the Pool of Doom, a strange fortune befell her. Close in the precipice were many jagged rocks, and on these the waters of the fall fell and thundered, bounding from them in spouts of spray into the troubled depths of the foss beyond. It was on these stones that the life was dashed out of the bodies of the wretched victims who were hurled from above. But Nanea, it will be remembered, had not waited to be treated thus, and as it chanced the strong spring with which she had leapt to death carried her clear of the rocks. By a very little she missed the edge of them and striking the deep water head first like some practised diver, she sank down and down till she thought that she would never rise again. Yet she did rise, at the end of the pool in the mouth of the rapid, along which she sped swiftly, carried down by the rush of the water. Fortunately there were no rocks here; and, since she was a skilful swimmer, she escaped the danger of being thrown against the banks.

For a long distance she was borne thus till at length she saw that she was in a forest, for trees cut off the light from the water, and their drooping branches swept its surface. One of these Nanea caught with her hand, and by the help of it she dragged herself from the River of Death whence none had escaped before. Now she stood upon the bank gasping but quite unharmed; there was not a scratch on her body; even her white garment was still fast about her neck.

But though she had suffered no hurt in her terrible voyage, so exhausted was Nanea that she could scarcely stand. Here the gloom was that of night, and shivering with cold she looked around helplessly to find some refuge. Close to the water's edge grew an enormous yellow-wood tree, and to this she staggered—thinking to climb it, and seek shelter in its boughs where, as she hoped, she would be safe from wild beasts. Again fortune befriended her, for at a distance of a few feet from the ground there was a great hole in the tree which, she discovered, was hollow. Into this hole she crept, taking her chance of its being the home of snakes or other evil creatures, to find that the interior was wide and warm. It was dry also, for at the bottom of the cavity lay a foot or more of rotten tinder and moss brought there by rats or birds. Upon this tinder she lay down, and covering herself with the moss and leaves soon sank into sleep or stupor.

How long Nanea slept she did not know, but at length she was awakened by a sound as of guttural human voices talking in a language that she could not understand. Rising to her knees she peered out of the hole in the tree. It was night, but the stars shone brilliantly, and their light fell upon an open circle of ground close by the edge of the river. In this circle there burned a great fire, and at a little distance from the fire were gathered eight or ten horrible-looking beings, who appeared to be rejoicing over something that lay upon the ground. They were small in stature, men and women together, but no children, and all of them were nearly naked. Their hair was long and thin, growing down almost to the eyes, their jaws and teeth protruded and the girth of their black bodies was out of all proportion to their height. In their hands they held sticks with sharp stones lashed on to them, or rude hatchet-like knives of the same material.

Now Nanea's heart shrank within her, and she nearly fainted with fear, for she knew that she was in the haunted forest, and without a doubt these were the *Esemkofu*, the evil ghosts that dwelt therein. Yes, that was what they were, and yet she could not take her eyes off them—the sight of them held her with a horrible fascination. But if they were ghosts, why did they sing and dance like men? Why did they wave those sharp stones aloft, and quarrel and strike each other? And why did they make a fire as men do when they wish to cook food? More, what was it that they rejoiced over, that long dark thing which lay so quiet upon the ground? It did not look like a head of game, and it could scarcely be a crocodile, yet clearly it was food of some sort, for they were sharpening the stone knives in order to cut it up.

While she wondered thus, one of the dreadful-looking little creatures advanced to the fire, and taking from it a burning bough, held it over the thing that lay upon the ground, to give light to a companion who was about to do something to it with a stone knife. Next instant Nanea drew back her head from the hole, a stifled shriek upon her lips. She saw what it was now—it was the body of a man. Yes, and these were not ghosts; they were cannibals of whom when she was little, her mother had told her tales to keep her from wandering away from home.

But who was the man they were about to eat? It could not be one of themselves, for his stature was much greater. Oh! now she knew; it must be Nahoon, who had been killed up yonder, and whose dead body the waters had brought down to the haunted forest as they had brought her alive. Yes, it must be Nahoon, and she would be forced to see her husband devoured before her eyes. The thought of it overwhelmed her. That he should die by order of the king was natural, but that he should be buried thus! Yet what could she do it prevent it? Well, if it cost her her life, it should be prevented. At the worst they could only kill and eat her also, and now that Nahoon and her father were gone, being untroubled by any religious or spiritual hopes and fears, she was not greatly concerned to keep her own breath in her.

Slipping through the hole in the tree, Nanea walked quietly towards the cannibals—not knowing in the least what she should do when she reached them. As she arrived in line with the fire this lack of programme came home to her mind forcibly, and she paused to reflect. Just then one of the cannibals looked up to see a tall and stately figure wrapped in a white garment which, as the flame-light flickered on it, seemed now to advance from the dense background of shadow, and now to recede into it. The poor savage wretch was holding a stone knife in his teeth when he beheld her, but it did not remain there long, for opening his great jaws he uttered the most terrified and piercing yell that Nanea had ever heard. Then the others saw her also, and presently the forest was ringing with shrieks of fear. For a few seconds the outcasts stood and gazed, then they were gone this way and that, bursting their path through the undergrowth like startled jackals. The *Esemkofu* of Zulu tradition had been routed in their own haunted home by what they took to be a spirit.

Poor *Esemkofu!* they were but miserable and starving bushmen who, driven into that place of ill omen many years ago, had adopted this means, the only one open to them, to keep the life in their wretched bodies. Here at least they were unmolested, and as there was little other food to be found amid the wilderness of trees, they took what the river brought them. When executions were few in the Pool of Doom, times were hard for them indeed—for then they were driven to eat each other. That is why there were no children.

As their inarticulate outcry died away in the distance, Nanea ran forward to look at the body that lay on the ground, and staggered back with a sigh of relief. It was not Nahoon, but she recognised the face for that of one of the party of executioners. How did he come here? Had Nahoon killed him? Had Nahoon escaped? She could not tell, and at the best it was improbable, but still the sight of this dead soldier lit her heart with a faint ray of hope, for how did he come to be dead if Nahoon had no hand in his death? She could not bear to leave him lying so near her hiding-place, however; therefore, with no small toil, she rolled the corpse back into the water, which carried it swiftly away. Then she returned to the tree, having first replenished the fire, and awaited the light.

At last it came—so much of it as ever penetrated this dark-some den—and Nanea, becoming aware that she was hungry, descended from the tree to search for food. All day long she searched, finding nothing, till towards sunset she remembered that on the outskirts of the forest there was a flat rock where it was the custom of those who had been in any way afflicted, or who considered themselves or their belongings to be bewitched, to place propitiatory offerings of food wherewith the *Esemkofu* and *Amalhosi* were supposed to satisfy their spiritual cravings. Urged by the pinch of starvation, to this spot Nanea journeyed rapidly, and found to her joy that some neighbouring kraal had evidently been in recent trouble, for the Rock of Offering was laden with cobs of corn, gourds of milk, porridge and even meat. Helping herself to as much as she could carry, she returned to her lair, where she drank of the milk and cooked meat and mealies at the fire. Then she crept back into the tree, and slept.

For nearly two months Nanea lived thus in the forest, since she could not venture out of it—fearing lest she should be seized, and for a second time taste of the judgement of the king. In the forest at least she was safe, for none dared enter there, nor did the *Esemkofu* give her further trouble. Once or twice she saw them, but on each occasion they fled shrieking from her presence— seeking some distant retreat, where they hid themselves or perished. Nor did food fail her, for finding that it was taken, the pious givers brought it in plenty to the Rock of Offering.

But, Oh! the life was dreadful, and the gloom and loneliness coupled with her sorrows at times drove her almost to insanity. Still she lived on, though often she desired to die, for if her father was dead, the corpse she had found was not the corpse of Nahoon, and in her heart there still shone that spark of hope. Yet what she hoped for she could not tell.

When Philip Hadden reached civilised regions, he found that war was about to be declared between the Queen and Cetywayo, King of the Amazulu; also that in the prevailing excitement his little adventure with the Utrecht store-keeper had been over-looked or forgotten. He was the owner of two good buck-waggons with spans of salted oxen, and at that time vehicles were much in request to carry military stores for the columns which were to advance into Zululand; indeed the transport authorities were glad to pay £90 a month for the hire of each waggon and to guarantee the owners against all loss of cattle. Although he was not desirous of returning to Zululand, this bait proved too much for Hadden, who accordingly leased out his waggons to the Commissariat, together with his own services as conductor and interpreter.

He was attached to No. 3 column of the invading force, which it may be remembered was under the immediate command of Lord Chelmsford, and on the 20 January, 1879, he marched with it by the road that runs from Rorke's Drift to the Indeni forest, and encamped that night beneath the shadow of the steep and desolate mountain known as Isandhlwana.

That day also a great army of King Cetywayo's, numbering twenty thousand men and more, moved down from the Upindo Hill and encamped upon the stony plain that lies a mile and a half to the east of Isandhlwana. No fires were lit, and it lay there in utter silence, for the warriors were "sleeping on their spears."

With that *impi* was the Umcityu regiment, three thousand five hundred strong. At the first break of dawn the Induna in command of the Umcityu looked up from beneath the shelter of the black shield with which he had covered his body, and through the thick mist he saw a great man standing before him, clothed only in a moocha, a gaunt wild-eyed man who held a rough club in his hand. When he was spoken to, the man made no answer; he only leaned upon his club looking from left to right along the dense array of innumerable shields.

"Who is this *Silwana* (wild creature)?" asked the Induna of his captains wondering.

The captains stared at the wanderer, and one of them replied, "This is Nahoon-ka-Zomba, it is the son of Zomba who not long ago held rank in this regiment of the Umcityu. His betrothed, Nanea, daughter of Umgona, was killed together with her father by order of the Black One, and Nahoon went mad with grief at the sight of it, for the fire of Heaven entered his brain, and mad he has wandered ever since."

"What would you here, Nahoon-ka-Zomba?" asked the Induna.

Then Nahoon spoke slowly. "My regiment goes down to war against the white men; give me a shield and a spear, O Captain of the king, that I may fight with my regiment, for I seek a face in the battle."

So they gave him a shield and a spear, for they dared not turn away one whose brain was alight with the fire of Heaven.

*   *   *

When the sun was high that day, bullets began to fall among the ranks of the Umcityu. Then the black-shielded, black-plumed Umcityu arose, company by company, and after them arose the whole vast Zulu army, breast and horns together, and swept down in silence upon the doomed British camp, a moving sheen of spears. The bullets pattered on the shields, the shells tore long lines through their array, but they never halted nor wavered. Forward on either side shot out the horns of armed men, clasping the camp in an embrace of steel. Then as these began to close, out burst the war cry of the Zulus, and with the roar of a torrent and the rush of a storm, with a sound like the humming of a billion bees, wave after wave the deep breast of the *impi* rolled down upon the white men. With it went the black-shielded Umcityu and with them went Nahoon, the son of Zomba. A bullet struck him in the side, glancing from his ribs, he did not heed; a white man fell from his horse before him, he did not stab, for he sought but one face in the battle.

He sought—and at last he found. There, among the waggons where the spears were busiest, there standing by his horse and firing rapidly was Black Heart, he who had given Nanea his betrothed to death. Three soldiers stood between them, one of them Nahoon stabbed, and two he brushed aside; then he rushed straight at Hadden.

But the white man saw him come, and even through the mask of his madness he knew Nahoon again, and terror took hold of him. Throwing away the empty rifle, for his ammunition was spent, he leaped upon his horse and drove his spurs into its flanks. Away it went among the carnage, springing over the dead and bursting through the lines of shields, and after it came Nahoon, running long and low with head stretched forward and trailing spear, running as a hound runs when the buck is at view.

Hadden's first plan was to head for Rorke's Drift, but a glance to the left showed him that the masses of the Undi barred that way, so he fled straight on, leaving his path to fortune. In five minutes he was over a ridge, and there was nothing of the battle to be seen, in ten all sounds of it had died away, for few guns were fired in the dread race to Fugitive's Drift, and the assegai makes no noise. In some strange fashion, even at this moment, the contract between the dreadful scene of blood and turmoil that he had left, and the peaceful face of Nature over which he was passing, came home to his brain vividly. Here birds sang and cattle grazed; here the sun shone undimmed by the smoke of cannon, only high up in the blue and silent air long streams of vultures could be seen winging their way to the Plain of Isandhlwana.

The ground was very rough, and Hadden's horse began to tire. He looked over his shoulder—there some two hundred yards behind came the Zulu, grim as Death, unswerving as Fate. He examined the pistol in his belt; there was but one undischarged cartridge left, all the rest had been fired and the pouch was empty. Well, one bullet should be enough for one savage: the question was should he stop and use it now? No, he might miss or fail to kill the man; he was on horseback and his foe on foot, surely he could tire him out.

A while passed, and they dashed through a little stream. It seemed familiar to Hadden. Yes, that was the pool where he used to bathe when he was the guest of Umgona, the father of Nanea; and there on the knoll to his right were the huts, or rather the remains of them, for they had been burnt with fire. What chance had brought him to this place, he wondered; then again he looked behind him at Nahoon, who seemed to read his thoughts, for he shook his spear and pointed to the ruined kraal.

On he went at speed for here the land was level, and to his joy he lost sight of his pursuer. But presently there came a mile of rocky ground, and when it was past, glancing back he saw that Nahoon was once more in his old place. His horse's strength was almost spent, but Hadden spurred it forward blindly, whither he knew not. Now he was travelling along a strip of turf and ahead of him he heard the music of a river, while to his left rose a high bank. Presently the turf bent inwards and there, not twenty yards away from him, was a Kaffir hut standing on the brink of a river. He looked at it, yes, it was the hut of that accursed *inyanga*, the Bee, and standing by the fence of it was none other than the Bee herself. At the sight of her the exhausted horse swerved violently, stumbled and came to the ground, where it lay panting. Hadden was thrown from the saddle but sprang to his feet unhurt.

"Ah! Black Heart, is it you? What news of the battle, Black Heart?" cried the Bee in a mocking voice.

"Help me, mother, I am pursued," he gasped.

"What of it, Black Heart, it is but by one tired man. Stand then and face him, for now Black Heart and White Heart are together again. You will not? Then away to the forest and seek shelter among the dead who await you there. Tell me, tell me, was it the face of Nanea that I saw beneath the waters a while ago? Good! bear my greetings to her when you two meet in the House of the Dead."

Hadden looked at the stream; it was in flood. He could not swim it, so followed by the evil laugh of the prophetess, he sped towards the forest. After him came Nahoon, his tongue hanging from his jaws like the tongue of a wolf.

Now he was in the shadow of the forest, but still he sped on following the course of the river, till at length his breath failed, and he halted on the further side of a little glade, beyond which a great tree grew. Nahoon was more than a spear's throw behind him: therefore he had time to draw his pistol and make ready.

"Halt, Nahoon," he cried, as once before he had cried; "I would speak with you."

The Zulu heard his voice, and obeyed.

"Listen," said Hadden. "We have run a long race and fought a long fight, you and I, and we are still alive both of us. Very soon, if you come on, one of us must be dead, and it will be you, Nahoon, for I am armed and as you know I can shoot straight. What do you say?"

Nahoon made no answer, but stood still at the edge of the glade, his wild and glowering eyes fixed on the white man's face and his breath coming in short gasps.

"Will you let me go, if *I* let *you* go?" Hadden asked once more. "I know why you hate me, but the past cannot be undone, nor can the dead be brought to earth again."

Still Nahoon made no answer, and his silence seemed more fateful and more crushing than any speech; no spoken accusation would have been so terrible in Hadden's ear. He made no answer, but lifting his assegai he stalked grimly toward his foe.

When he was within five paces Hadden covered him and fired. Nahoon sprang aside, but the bullet struck him somewhere, for his right arm dropped, and the stabbing spear that he held was jerked from it harmlessly over the white man's head. But still making no sound, the Zulu came on and gripped him by the throat with his left hand. For a space they struggled terribly, swaying to and fro, but Hadden was unhurt and fought with the fury of despair, while Nahoon had been twice wounded, and there remained to him but one sound arm wherewith to strike. Presently forced to earth by the white man's iron strength, the soldier was down, nor could he rise again.

"Now we will make an end," muttered Hadden savagely, and he turned to seek the assegai, then staggered slowly back with starting eyes and reeling gait. For there before him, still clad in her white robe, a spear in her hand, stood the spirit of Nanea!

"Think of it," he said to himself, dimly remembering the

words of the *inyanga*, "when you stand face to face with the ghost of the dead in the Home of the Dead."

There was a cry and a flash of steel; the broad spear leapt towards him to bury itself in his breast. He swayed, he fell, and presently Black Heart clasped that great reward which the word of the Bee had promised Him.

"Nahoon! Nahoon!" murmured a soft voice, "awake, it is no ghost, but I—Nanea—I, your living wife, to whom my *Ehlose*[1] has given it me to save you."

Nahoon heard and opened his eyes to look and his madness left him.

"Welcome, wife," he said faintly, "now I will live since Death has brought you back to me in the House of the Dead."

Today Nahoon is one of the Indunas of the English Government in Zululand, and there are children about his kraal. It was from the lips of none other than Nanea his wife that the teller of this tale heard its substance.

The Bee also lives and practises as much magic as she dares under the white man's rule. On her black hand shines a golden ring shaped like a snake with ruby eyes, and of this trinket the Bee is very proud.

[1]Guardian Spirit.

Volume Two

WIZARDS

Introduction

WIZARDS

by Isaac Asimov

There is nothing really mysterious about the word "wizard." The first syllable "wiz" is used, in common slang these days, for anyone or anything that is uncommonly smart or impressive, and it sounds very much like "wise." In fact, it *is* a form of "wise," and a "wizard" is simply a "wise man."

Of course there's the suffix "-ard," which, along with its variant "-art," is usually used to indicate an excessive amount of something. A "coward" is one who is too easily cowed; a "braggart" is one who brags entirely too much; a "drunkard" is one who is too frequently drunk.

And a "wizard," then? Presumably, a wizard is one who is too wise for anyone's comfort.

How is that possible? In general, we tend to honor wisdom, to deify it almost. How can one be too wise?

It depends on the kind of Universe we live in. To almost all people in every generation—even our own—the Universe is a frightening and dangerous place. It is operated on an entirely whimsical, capricious, and even clearly malevolent basis, and we are the helpless prey of forces enormously greater than we can handle.

How else can we explain the storms that strike without warning, the droughts, the sudden onset of disease and plagues, the mischances of every kind?

Surely, the Universe must be under the control of beings who are as irrational, as erratic, as irascible, as human beings are at their worst; who are incredibly powerful and yet incredibly childish as well; who, even if basically well-disposed, are apt to explode into uncontrollable anger at some small offense or meaningless slight.

Even if we picture the Universe as under the control of an all-good, as well as all-powerful, being, he is apt to lose his temper, and then—watch out. Or, if he is so good that never for an instant is his goodness in question, one can only suppose the additional existence of competing forces of evil, that the all-good being is forced to allow the existence of (or that he chooses, for some inscrutable reason of his own, to allow to exist).

However we may slice it, the Universe seems to be a horrible madhouse. Yet might it not be possible to behave in such a way as to keep all these supernatural beings in good temper? You might kill animals and burn them so that a delicious smoke rises to the sky where these beings live and feeds them into good-natured satiation. Or you might sing endless songs of praise to these beings, flattering them into benevolence. Or you might find magic chants that either lull them to kindness or bind them into impotence.

Everything, however, must be done *just so*. The words, the gestures, the exact order of events, the whole ritual, must be correct, or the result will surely be worse than if you had done nothing at all.

But how do you discover what the ritual must be? Clearly, the only sources are the supernatural beings themselves. If some human being learns the secrets, he can control the Universe by flattering, bamboozling, or overpowering the supernatural beings.

Does any human being actually learn the secret? Well, you and I, being very clever people who live in the twentieth century and have had an excellent scientific education, know that they don't, that there are no secrets of this sort, that there are, indeed, no supernatural beings of this sort, no demons, afreets, jinn, nymphs, satyrs—but that's just you and I. To others not so well placed in space and time, and not so learned and sophisticated as we are, it is enough if someone *says* he has the secrets. If he is clever enough and daring enough to make those who watch and listen think he is indeed controlling the Universe, they will believe him. (Why not? Think how many millions fall for all the hoary old tricks and flim-flams from astrology to spoon-bending, plus everything in between.)

There are various names one can give the people who know the secrets whereby the Universe might be controlled, but one of them is "wizard."

People might feel grateful to the controllers of fate, for surely it is to them that one must turn to make sure that the rains come and the infections don't; they are the saviors, the answerers of questions, the bringers of good fortune, the helpers in time of disappointment and sickness.

Think of Merlin, the archetypical wizard of legend and perhaps the most popular of all. Who has a bad word for him?

Then why that "-ard" ending?

Is not a wizard just as capable of irascibility and loss of temper as any supernatural being? Might not a wizard have his feelings hurt? Might he not hunger for more power? In short, are not wizards just as dangerous as the beings they control?

Of course.

Wizardry is a double-edged sword, then, and if we deal with stories of wizards, which edge are we likely to harp on? Remember that catastrophe is more dramatic than peace; danger more dramatic than sleep; and—yes—evil is more dramatic than good. Writers, being human, and wanting to go where the readers are, are apt therefore to stress the evils and dangers of wizardry.

What you have in this book, then, are a group of stories that are full of drama, of danger, and of heart-stopping action. That's the best kind of stories to have as long as you're sitting comfortably in your favorite armchair or cuddled cozily in bed—so best wishes to you, and good reading.

MAZIRIAN THE MAGICIAN

by
Jack Vance

Jack Vance first appeared in the science fiction maga-
zines in the late 1940s and quickly established a loyal
following, both for his sf and for his fantasy. Among his
many notable books are THE DYING EARTH (1950),
SHOWBOAT WORLD (1975), WYST: ALASTOR 1716
(1978), and THE BOOK OF DREAMS (1981), the
latter part of his popular "Demon Princes" series. He
is one of very few writers to have won the Edgar Award
of the Mystery Writers of America, the Hugo Award for
outstanding sf, and the Nebula Award of the Science
Fiction Writers of America. A writer's writer, he is highly
regarded by his peers and by his still-growing readership.
* From his classic collection THE DYING EARTH,*
"Mazirian the Magician" is an enchanting example of
Jack Vance's ability to write future fairy tales.

Deep in thought, Mazirian the Magician walked his garden.
Trees fruited with many intoxications overhung his path, and
flowers bowed obsequiously as he passed. An inch above the

357

ground, dull as agates, the eyes of mandrakes followed the tread
of his black-slippered feet. Such was Mazirian's garden—three
terraces growing with strange and wonderful vegetations. Certain
plants swam with changing iridescences; others held up blooms
pulsing like sea-anemones, purple, green, lilac, pink, yellow.
Here grew trees like feather parasols, trees with transparent
trunks threaded with red and yellow veins, trees with foliage like
metal foil, each leaf a different metal—copper, silver, blue
tantalum, bronze, green iridium. Here blooms like bubbles tugged
gently upward from glazed green leaves, there a shrub bore a
thousand pipe-shaped blossoms, each whistling softly to make
music of the ancient Earth, of the ruby-red sunlight, water
seeping through black soil, the languid winds. And beyond the
roqual hedge the trees of the forest made a tall wall of mystery.
In this waning hour of Earth's life no man could count himself
familiar with the glens, the glades, the dells and deeps, the
secluded clearings, the ruined pavilions, the sun-dappled pleas-
aunces, the gullys and heights, the various brooks, freshets,
ponds, the meadows, thickets, brakes and rocky outcrops.

Mazirian paced his garden with a brow frowning in thought.
His step was slow and his arms were clenched behind his back.
There was one who had brought him puzzlement, doubt, and a
great desire: a delightful woman-creature who dwelt in the woods.
She came to his garden half-laughing and always wary, riding a
black horse with eyes like golden crystals. Many times had
Mazirian tried to take her; always her horse had borne her from
his varied enticements, threats, and subterfuges.

Agonized screaming jarred the garden. Mazirian, hastening his
step, found a mole chewing the stalk of a plant-animal hybrid.
He killed the marauder, and the screams subsided to a dull
gasping. Mazirian stroked a furry leaf and the red mouth hissed
in pleasure.

Then: "K-k-k-k-k-k," spoke the plant. Mazirian stooped,
held the rodent to the red mouth. The mouth sucked, the small
body slid into the stomach-bladder underground. The plant gurgled,
eructated, and Mazirian watched with satisfaction.

The sun had swung low in the sky, so dim and red that the
stars could be seen. And now Mazirian felt a watching presence.
It would be the woman of the forest, for thus had she disturbed
him before. He paused in his stride, feeling for the direction of
the gaze.

He shouted a spell of immobilization. Behind him the plant-
animal froze to rigidity and a great green moth wafted to the

ground. He whirled around. There she was, at the edge of the forest, closer than ever she had approached before. Nor did she move as he advanced. Mazirian's young-old eyes shone. He would take her to his manse and keep her in a prison of green glass. He would test her brain with fire, with cold, with pain and with joy. She should serve him with wine and make the eighteen motions of allurement by yellow lamp-light. Perhaps she was spying on him; if so, the Magician would discover immediately, for he could call no man friend and had forever to guard his garden.

She was but twenty paces distant—then there was a thud and pound of black hooves as she wheeled her mount and fled into the forest.

The Magician flung down his cloak in rage. She held a guard—a counter-spell, a rune of protection—and always she came when he was ill-prepared to follow. He peered into the murky depths, glimpsed the wanness of her body flitting through a shaft of red light, then black shade and she was gone . . . Was she a witch? Did she come of her own volition, or—more likely—had an enemy sent her to deal him inquietude? If so, who might be guiding her? There was Prince Kandive the Golden, of Kaiin, whom Mazirian had bilked of his secret of renewed youth. There was Azvan the Astronomer, there was Turjan— hardly Turjan, and here Mazirian's face lit in a pleasing recollection . . . He put the thought aside. Azvan, at least, he could test. He turned his steps to his workshop, went to a table where rested a cube of clear crystal, shimmering with a red and blue aureole. From a cabinet he brought a bronze gong and a silver hammer. He tapped on the gong and the mellow tone sang through the room and out, away and beyond. He tapped again and again. Suddenly Azvan's face shone from the crystal, beaded with pain and great terror.

"Stay the strokes, Mazirian!" cried Azvan. "Strike no more on the gong of my life!"

Mazirian paused, his hand poised over the gong.

"Do you spy on me, Azvan? Do you send a woman to regain the gong?"

"Not I, Master, not I. I fear you too well."

"You must deliver me the woman, Azvan; I insist."

"Impossible, Master! I know not who or what she is!"

Mazirian made as if to strike. Azvan poured forth such a torrent of supplication that Mazirian with a gesture of disgust threw down the hammer and restored the gong to its place.

Azvan's face drifted slowly away, and the fine cube of crystal shone blank as before.

Mazirian stroked his chin. Apparently he must capture the girl himself. Later, when black night lay across the forest, he would seek through his books for spells to guard him through the unpredictable glades. They would be poignant corrosive spells, of such a nature that one would daunt the brain of an ordinary man and two render him mad. Mazirian, by dint of stringent exercise, could encompass four of the most formidable, or six of the lesser spells.

He put the project from his mind and went to a long vat bathed in a flood of green light. Under a wash of clear fluid lay the body of a man, ghastly below the green glare, but of great physical beauty. His torso tapered from wide shoulders through lean flanks to long strong legs and arched feet; his face was clean and cold with hard flat features. Dusty golden hair clung about his head.

Mazirian stared at the thing, which he had cultivated from a single cell. It needed only intelligence, and this he knew not how to provide. Turjan of Miir held the knowledge, and Turjan—Mazirian glanced with a grim narrowing of the eyes at a trap in the floor—refused to part with his secret.

Mazirian pondered the creature in the vat. It was a perfect body; therefore might not the brain be ordered and pliant? He would discover. He set in motion a device to draw off the liquid and presently the body lay stark to the direct rays. Mazirian injected a minim of drug into the neck. The body twitched. The eyes opened, winced in the glare. Mazirian turned away the projector.

Feebly the creature in the vat moved its arms and feet, as if unaware of their use. Mazirian watched intently: perhaps he had stumbled on the right synthesis for the brain.

"Sit up!" commanded the Magician.

The creature fixed its eyes upon him, and reflexes joined muscle to muscle. It gave a throaty roar and sprang from the vat at Mazirian's throat. In spite of Mazirian's strength it caught him and shook him like a doll.

For all Mazirian's magic he was helpless. The mesmeric spell had been expended, and he had none other in his brain. In any event he could not have uttered the space-twisting syllables with that mindless clutch at his throat.

His hand closed on the neck of a leaden carboy. He swung and struck the head of his creature, which slumped to the floor.

Mazirian, not entirely dissatisfied, studied the glistening body at his feet. The spinal coordination had functioned well. At his table he mixed a white potion, and, lifting the golden head, poured the fluid into the lax mouth. The creature stirred, opened its eyes, propped itself on its elbows. The madness had left its face—but Mazirian sought in vain for the glimmer of intelligence. The eyes were as vacant as those of a lizard.

The Magician shook his head in annoyance. He went to the window and his brooding profile was cut black against the oval panes . . . Turjan once more? Under the most dire inquiry Turjan had kept his secret close. Mazirian's thin mouth curved wryly. Perhaps if he inserted another angle in the passage . . .

The sun had gone from the sky and there was dimness in Mazirian's garden. His white night-blossoms opened and their captive gray moths fluttered from bloom to bloom. Mazirian pulled open the trap in the floor and descended stone stairs. Down, down, down . . . At last a passage intercepted at right angles, lit with the yellow light of eternal lamps. To the left were his fungus beds, to the right a stout oak and iron door, locked with three locks. Down and ahead the stone steps continued, dropping into blackness.

Mazirian unlocked the three locks, flung wide the door. The room within was bare except for a stone pedestal supporting a glass-topped box. The box measured a yard on a side and was four or five inches high. Within the box—actually a squared passageway, a run with four right angles—moved two small creatures, one seeking, the other evading. The predator was a small dragon with furious red eyes and a monstrous fanged mouth. It waddled along the passage on six splayed legs, twitching its tail as it went. The other stood only half the size of the dragon—a strong-featured man, stark naked, with a copper fillet binding his long black hair. He moved slightly faster than his pursuer, which still kept relentless chase, using a measure of craft, speeding, doubling back, lurking at the angle in case the man should unwarily step around. By holding himself continually alert, the man was able to stay beyond the reach of the fangs. The man was Turjan, whom Mazirian by trickery had captured several weeks before, reduced in size and thus imprisoned.

Mazirian watched with pleasure as the reptile sprang upon the momentarily relaxing man, who jerked himself clear by the thickness of his skin. It was time, Mazirian thought, to give both rest and nourishment. He dropped panels across the passage,

separating it into halves, isolating man from beast. To both he
gave meat and pannikins of water.

Turjan slumped in the passage.

"Ah," said Mazirian, "you are fatigued. You desire rest?"

Turjan remained silent, his eyes closed. Time and the world
had lost meaning for him. The only realities were the gray
passage and the interminable flight. At unknown intervals came
food and a few hours rest.

"Think of the blue sky," said Mazirian, "the white stars,
your castle Miir by the river Derna; think of wandering free in
the meadows."

The muscles at Turjan's mouth twitched.

"Consider, you might crush the little dragon under your heel."

Turjan looked up. "I would prefer to crush your neck,
Mazirian."

Mazirian was unperturbed. "Tell me, how do you invest your
vat creatures with intelligence? Speak, and you go free."

Turjan laughed, and there was madness in his laughter.

"Tell you? And then? You would kill me with hot oil in a
moment."

Mazirian's thin mouth drooped petulantly.

"Wretched man, I know how to make you speak. If your
mouth were stuffed, waxed and sealed, you would speak! Tomorrow I take a nerve from your arm and draw coarse cloth along its
length."

The small Turjan, sitting with his legs across the passageway,
drank his water and said nothing.

"Tonight," said Mazirian with studied malevolence, "I add
an angle and change your run to a pentagon."

Turjan paused and looked up through the glass cover at his
enemy. Then he slowly sipped his water. With five angles there
would be less time to evade the charge of the monster, less of the
hall in view from one angle.

"Tomorrow," said Mazirian, "you will need all your agility."
But another matter occurred to him. He eyed Turjan speculatively.
"Yet even this I spare you if you assist me with another problem."

"What is your difficulty, febrile Magician?"

"The image of a woman-creature haunts my brain, and I
would capture her." Mazirian's eyes went misty at the thought.
"Late afternoon she comes to the edge of my garden riding a
great black horse—you know her, Turjan?"

"Not I, Mazirian." Turjan sipped his water.

Mazirian continued. "She has sorcery enough to ward away

Felojun's Second Hypnotic Spell—or perhaps she has some protective rune. When I approach, she flees into the forest."

"So then?" asked Turjan, nibbling the meat Mazirian had provided.

"Who may this woman be?" demanded Mazirian, peering down his long nose at the tiny captive.

"How can I say?"

"I must capture her," said Mazirian abstractedly: "What spells, what spells?"

Turjan looked up, although he could see the Magician only indistinctly through the cover of glass.

"Release me, Mazirian, and on my word as a Chosen Hierarch of the Maram-Or, I will deliver you this girl."

"How would you do this?" asked the suspicious Mazirian.

"Pursue her into the forest with my best Live Boots and a headful of spells."

"You would fare no better than I," retorted the Magician. "I give you freedom when I know the synthesis of your vat-things. I myself will pursue the woman."

Turjan lowered his head that the Magician might not read his eyes.

"And as for me, Mazirian?" he inquired after a moment.

"I will treat with you when I return."

"And if you do not return?"

Mazirian stroked his chin and smiled, revealing fine white teeth. "The dragon could devour you now, if it were not for your cursed secret."

The Magician climbed the stairs. Midnight found him in his study, poring through leather-bound tomes and untidy portfolios . . . At one time a thousand or more runes, spells, incantations, curses, and sorceries had been known. The reach of Grand Motholam—Ascolais, the Ide of Kauchique, Almery to the South, the Land of the Falling Wall to the East—swarmed with sorcerers of every description, of whom the chief was the Arch-Necromancer Phandaal. A hundred spells Phandaal personally had formulated—though rumor said that demons whispered at his ear when he wrought magic. Pontecilla the Pious, then ruler of Grand Motholam, put Phandaal to torment, and after a terrible night, he killed Phandaal and outlawed sorcery throughout the land. The wizards of Grand Motholam fled like beetles under a strong light; the lore was dispersed and forgotten, until now, at this dim time, with the sun dark, wilderness obscuring Ascolais, and the white city Kaiin half in ruins, only a few more than a hundred spells remained to the knowledge of man. Of these, Mazirian had access to seventy-three, and gradually, by stratagem and negotiation, was securing the others.

Mazirian made a selection from his books and with great effort forced five spells upon his brain: Phandaal's Gyrator, Felojun's Second Hypnotic Spell, The Excellent Prismatic Spray, The Charm of Untiring Nourishment, and the Spell of the Omnipotent Sphere. This accomplished, Mazirian drank wine and retired to his couch.

The following day, when the sun hung low, Mazirian went to walk in his garden. He had but short time to wait. As he loosened the earth at the roots of his moon-geraniums a soft rustle and stamp told that the object of his desire had appeared.

She sat upright in the saddle, a young woman of exquisite configuration. Mazirian slowly stooped, as not to startle her, put his feet into the Live Boots and secured them above the knee.

He stood up. "Ho, girl," he cried, "you have come again. Why are you here of evenings? Do you admire the roses? They are vividly red because live red blood flows in their petals. If today you do not flee, I will make you the gift of one."

Mazirian plucked a rose from the shuddering bush and advanced toward her, fighting the surge of the Live Boots. He had taken but four steps when the woman dug her knees into the ribs of her mount and so plunged off through the trees.

Mazirian allowed full scope to the life in his boots. They gave a great bound, and another, and another, and he was off in full chase.

So Mazirian entered the forest of fable. On all sides mossy boles twisted up to support the high panoply of leaves. At intervals shafts of sunshine drifted through to lay carmine blots on the turf. In the shade long-stemmed flowers and fragile fungi sprang from the humus; in this ebbing hour of Earth nature was mild and relaxed.

Mazirian in his Live Boots bounded with great speed through the forest, yet the black horse, running with no strain, stayed easily ahead.

For several leagues the woman rode, her hair flying behind like a pennon. She looked back and Mazirian saw the face over her shoulder as a face in a dream. Then she bent forward; the golden-eyed horse thundered ahead and soon was lost to sight. Mazirian followed by tracing the trail in the sod.

The spring and drive began to leave the Live Boots, for they had come far and at great speed. The monstrous leaps became shorter and heavier, but the strides of the horse, shown by the

tracks, were also shorter and slower. Presently Mazirian entered
a meadow and saw the horse, riderless, cropping grass. He
stopped short. The entire expanse of tender herbiage lay before
him. The trail of the horse leading into the glade was clear, but
there was no trail leaving. The woman therefore had dismounted
somewhere behind—how far he had no means of knowing. He
walked toward the horse, but the creature shied and bolted
through the trees. Mazirian made one effort to follow, and
discovered that his Boots hung lax and flaccid—dead.

He kicked them away, cursing the day and his ill-fortune.
Shaking the cloak free behind him, a baleful tension shining on
his face, he started back along the trail.

In this section of the forest, outcroppings of black and green
rock, basalt and serpentine, were frequent—forerunners of the
crags over the River Derna. On one of these rocks Mazirian saw
a tiny man-thing mounted on a dragon-fly. He had skin of a
greenish cast; he wore a gauzy smock and carried a lance twice
his own length.

Mazirian stopped. The Twk-man looked down stolidly.

"Have you seen a woman of my race passing by, Twk-man?"

"I have seen such a woman," responded the Twk-man after a
moment of deliberation.

"Where may she be found?"

"What may I expect for the information?"

"Salt—as much as you can bear away."

The Twk-man flourished his lance. "Salt? No. Liane the
Wayfarer provides the chieftain Dandanflores salt for all the
tribe."

Mazirian could surmise the services for which the bandit-
troubadour paid salt. The Twk-men, flying fast on their dragon-
flies, saw all that happened in the forest.

"A vial of oil from my telanxis blooms?"

"Good," said the Twk-man. "Show me the vial."

Mazirian did so.

"She left the trail at the lightning-blasted oak lying a little
before you. She made directly for the river valley, the shortest
route to the lake."

Mazirian laid the vial beside the dragon-fly and went off
toward the river oak. The Twk-man watched him go, then
dismounted and lashed the vial to the underside of the dragon-
fly, next to the skein of fine haft the woman had given him thus
to direct Mazirian.

The Magician turned at the oak and soon discovered the trail

over the dead leaves. A long open glade lay before him, sloping
gently to the river. Trees towered to either side and the long
sundown rays steeped one side in blood, left the other deep in
black shadow. So deep was the shade that Mazirian did not see
the creature seated on a fallen tree; and he sensed it only as it
prepared to leap on his back.

Mazirian sprang about to face the thing, which subsided again
to sitting posture. It was a Deodand, formed and featured like a
handsome man, finely muscled, but with a dead black lusterless
skin and long slit eyes.

"Ah, Mazirian, you roam the woods far from home," the
black thing's soft voice rose through the glade.

The Deodand, Mazirian knew, craved his body for meat. How
had the girl escaped? Her trail led directly past.

"I come seeking, Deodand. Answer my questions, and I
undertake to feed you much flesh."

The Deodand's eyes glinted, flitting over Mazirian's body.
"You may in any event, Mazirian. Are you with powerful spells
today?"

"I am. Tell me, how long has it been since the girl passed?
Went she fast, slow, alone or in company? Answer, and I give
you meat at such time as you desire."

The Deodand's lips curled mockingly. "Blind Magician! She
has not left the glade." He pointed, and Mazirian followed the
direction of the dead black arm. But he jumped back as the
Deodand sprang. From his mouth gushed the syllables of
Phandaal's Gyrator Spell. The Deodand was jerked off his feet
and flung high in the air, where he hung whirling, high and low,
faster and slower, up to the tree-tops, low to the ground. Mazirian
watched with a half-smile. After a moment he brought the
Deodand low and caused the rotations to slacken.

"Will you die quickly or slow?" asked Mazirian. "Help me
and I kill you at once. Otherwise you shall rise high where the
pelgrane fly."

Fury and fear choked the Deodand.

"May dark Thial spike your eyes! May Kraan hold your living
brain in acid!" And it added such charges that Mazirian felt
forced to mutter countercurses.

"Up then," said Mazirian at last, with a wave of his hand.
The black sprawling body jerked high above the tree-tops to
revolve slowly in the crimson bask of setting sun. In a moment a
mottled bat-shaped thing with hooked snout swept close and its

beak tore the black leg before the crying Deodand could kick it away. Another and another of the shapes flitted across the sun.

"Down, Mazirian!" came the faint call. "I tell what I know."

Mazirian brought him close to earth.

"She passed alone before you came. I made to attack her but she repelled me with a handful of thyle-dust. She went to the end of the glade and took the trail to the river. This trail leads also past the lair of Thrang. So is she lost, for he will sate himself on her till she dies."

Mazirian rubbed his chin. "Had she spells with her?"

"I know not. She will need strong magic to escape the demon Thrang."

"Is there anything else to tell?"

"Nothing."

"Then you may die." And Mazirian caused the creature to revolve at ever greater speed, faster and faster, until there was only a blur. A strangled wailing came and presently the Deodand's frame parted. The head shot like a bullet far down the glade; arms, legs, viscera flew in all directions.

Mazirian went his way. At the end of the glade the trail led steeply down ledges of dark green serpentine to the River Derna. The sun had set and shade filled the valley. Mazirian gained the riverside and set off downstream toward a far shimmer known as Sanra Water, the Lake of Dreams.

An evil odor came to the air, a stink of putrescence and filth. Mazirian went ahead more cautiously, for the lair of Thrang the ghoul-bear was near, and in the air was the feel of magic—strong brutal sorcery his own more subtle spells might not contain.

The sound of voices reached him, the throaty tones of Thrang and gasping cries of terror. Mazirian stepped around a shoulder of rock, inspected the origin of the sounds.

Thrang's lair was an alcove in the rock, where a fetid pile of grass and skins served him for a couch. He had built a rude pen to cage three women, these wearing many bruises on their bodies and the effects of much horror on their faces. Thrang had taken them from the tribe that dwelt in silk-hung barges along the lake-shore. Now they watched as he struggled to subdue the woman he had just captured. His round gray man's face was contorted and he tore away her jerkin with his human hands. But she held away the great sweating body with an amazing dexterity. Mazirian's eyes narrowed. Magic, magic!

So he stood watching, considering how to destroy Thrang with no harm to the woman. But she spied him over Thrang's shoulder.

"See," she panted, "Mazirian has come to kill you."

Thrang twisted about. He saw Mazirian and came charging on all fours, venting roars of wild passion. Mazirian later wondered if the ghoul had cast some sort of spell, for a strange paralysis strove to bind his brain. Perhaps the spell lay in the sight of Thrang's raging graywhite face, the great arms thrust out to grasp.

Mazirian shook off the spell, if such it were, and uttered a spell of his own, and all the valley was lit by streaming darts of fire, lashing in from all directions to spit Thrang's blundering body in a thousand places. This was the Excellent Prismatic Spray—many-colored stabbing lines. Thrang was dead almost at once, purple blood flowing from countless holes where the radiant rain had pierced him.

But Mazirian heeded little. The girl had fled. Mazirian saw her white form running along the river toward the lake, and took up the chase, heedless of the piteous cries of the three women in the pen.

The lake presently lay before him, a great sheet of water whose further rim was but dimly visible. Mazirian came down to the sandy shore and stood seeking across the dark face of Sanra Water, the Lake of Dreams. Deep night with only a verge of afterglow ruled the sky, and stars glistened on the smooth surface. The water lay cool and still, tideless as all Earth's waters had been since the moon had departed the sky.

Where was the woman? There, a pale white form, quiet in the shadow across the river. Mazirian stood on the riverbank, tall and commanding, a light breeze ruffling the cloak around his legs.

"Ho, girl," he called. "It is I, Mazirian, who saved you from Thrang. Come close, that I may speak to you."

"At this distance I hear you well, Magician," she replied. "The closer I approach the farther I must flee."

"Why then do you flee? Return with me and you shall be mistress of many secrets and hold much power."

She laughed. "If I wanted these, Mazirian, would I have fled so far?"

"Who are you then that you desire not the secrets of magic?"

"To you, Mazirian, I am nameless, lest you curse me. Now I go where you may not come." She ran down the shore, waded slowly out till the water circled her waist, then sank out of sight. She was gone.

Mazirian paused indecisively. It was not good to use so many

spells and thus shear himself of power. What might exist below
the lake? The sense of quiet magic was there, and though he was
not at enmity with the Lake Lord, other beings might resent a
trespass. However, when the figure of the girl did not break the
surface, he uttered the Charm of Untiring Nourishment and
entered the cool waters.

He plunged deep through the Lake of Dreams, and as he stood
on the bottom, his lungs at ease by virtue of the charm, he
marveled at the fey place he had come upon. Instead of blackness a green light glowed everywhere and the water was but little
less clear than air. Plants undulated to the current and with them
moved the lake flowers, soft with blossoms of red, blue and
yellow. In and out swam large-eyed fish of many shapes.

The bottom dropped by rocky steps to a wide plain where trees
of the underlake floated up from slender stalks to elaborate
fronds and purple water-fruits, and so till the misty wet distance
veiled all. He saw the woman, a white water nymph now,
her hair like dark fog. She half-swam, half-ran across the sandy
floor of the water-world, occasionally looking back over her
shoulder. Mazirian came after, his cloak streaming out behind.

He drew nearer to her, exulting. He must punish her for
leading him so far . . . The ancient stone stairs below his workroom led deep and at last opened into chambers that grew ever
vaster as one went deeper. Mazirian had found a rusted cage in
one of these chambers. A week or two locked in the blackness
would curb her willfulness. And once he had dwindled a woman
small as his thumb and kept her in a little glass bottle with two
buzzing flies . . .

A ruined white temple showed through the green. There were
many columns, some toppled, some still upholding the pediment.
The woman entered the great portico under the shadow of the
architrave. Perhaps she was attempting to elude him; he must
follow closely. The white body glimmered at the far end of the
nave, swimming now over the rostrum and into a semi-circular
alcove behind.

Mazirian followed as fast as he was able, half-swimming,
half-walking through the solemn dimness. He peered across the
murk. Smaller columns here precariously upheld a dome from
which the keystone had dropped. A sudden fear smote him, then
realization as he saw the flash of movement from above. On all
sides the columns toppled in, and an avalanche of marble blocks
tumbled at his head. He jumped frantically back.

The commotion ceased, the white dust of the ancient mortar

drifted away. On the pediment of the main temple the woman kneeled on slender knees, staring down to see how well she had killed Mazirian.

She had failed. Two columns, by sheerest luck, had crashed to either side of him, and a slab had protected his body from the blocks. He moved his head painfully. Through a chink in the tumbled marble he could see the woman, leaning to discern his body. So she would kill him? He, Mazirian, who had already lived more years than he could easily reckon? So much more would she hate and fear him later. He called his charm, the Spell of the Omnipotent Sphere. A film of force formed around his body, expanding to push aside all that resisted. When the marble ruins had been thrust back, he destroyed the sphere, regained his feet, and glared about for the woman. She was almost out of sight, behind a brake of long purple kelp, climbing the slope to the shore. With all his power he set out in pursuit.

T'sain dragged herself up on the beach. Still behind her came Mazirian the Magician, whose power had defeated each of her plans. The memory of his face passed before her and she shivered. He must not take her now.

Fatigue and despair slowed her feet. She had set out with but two spells, the Charm of Untiring Nourishment and a spell affording strength to her arms—the last permitting her to hold off Thrang and tumble the temple upon Mazirian. These were exhausted; she was bare of protection; but, on the other hand, Mazirian could have nothing left.

Perhaps he was ignorant of the vampire-weed. She ran up the slope and stood behind a patch of pale, wind-beaten grass. And now Mazirian came from the lake, a spare form visible against the shimmer of the water.

She retreated, keeping the innocent patch of grass between them. If the grass failed—her mind quailed at the thought of what she must do.

Mazirian strode into the grass. The sickly blades became sinewy fingers. They twined about his ankles, holding him in an unbreakable grip, while others sought to find his skin.

So Mazirian chanted his last spell—the incantation of paralysis, and the vampire grass grew lax and slid limply to earth. T'sain watched with dead hope. He was now close upon her, his cloak flapping behind. Had he no weakness? Did not his fibers ache, did not his breath come short? She whirled and fled across the meadow, toward a grove of black trees. Her skin chilled at the deep shadows, the somber frames. But the thud of the Magician's feet was loud. She plunged into the dread shade. Before all in the grove awoke she must go as far as possible.

Snap! A thong lashed at her. She continued to run. Another and another—she fell. Another great whip and another beat at her. She staggered up, and on, holding her arms before her face. Snap! The flails whistled through the air, and the last blow twisted her around. So she saw Mazirian.

He fought. As the blows rained on him, he tried to seize the whips and break them. But they were supple and springy beyond his powers, and jerked away to beat at him again. Infuriated by his resistance, they concentrated on the unfortunate Magician, who foamed and fought with transcendent fury, and T'sain was permitted to crawl to the edge of the grove with her life.

She looked back in awe at the expression of Mazirian's lust for life. He staggered about in a cloud of whips, his furious obstinate figure dimly silhouetted. He weakened and tried to flee, and then he fell. The blows pelted at him—on his head, shoulders, the long legs. He tried to rise but fell back.

T'sain closed her eyes in lassitude. She felt the blood oozing from her broken flesh. But the most vital mission yet remained. She reached her feet, and reelingly set forth. For a long time the thunder of many blows reached her ears.

Mazirian's garden was surpassingly beautiful by night. The star-blossoms spread wide, each of magic perfection, and the captive half-vegetable moths flew back and forth. Phosphorescent water-lilies floated like charming faces on the pond and the bush which Mazirian had brought from far Almery in the south tinctured the air with sweet fruity perfume.

T'sain, weaving and gasping, now came groping through the garden. Certain of the flowers awoke and regarded her curiously. The half-animal hybrid sleepily chittered at her, thinking to recognize Mazirian's step. Faintly to be heard was the wistful music of the blue-cupped flowers singing of ancient nights when a white moon swam the sky, and great storms and clouds and thunder ruled the seasons.

T'sain passed unheeding. She entered Mazirian's house, found the workroom where glowed the eternal yellow lamps. Mazirian's golden-haired vat-thing sat up suddenly and stared at her with his beautiful vacant eyes.

She found Mazirian's keys in the cabinet, and managed to claw open the trap door. Here she slumped to rest and let the pink gloom pass from her eyes. Visions began to come—Mazirian, tall and arrogant, stepping out to kill Thrang; the strange-hued flowers under the lake; Mazirian, his magic lost, fighting the whips . . . She was brought from the half-trance by the vat-thing timidly fumbling with her hair.

She shook herself awake, and half-walked, half-fell down the stairs. She unlocked the thrice-bound door, thrust it open with almost the last desperate urge of her body. She wandered in to clutch at the pedestal where the glass-topped box stood and Turjan and the dragon were playing their desperate game. She flung the glass crashing to the floor, gently lifted Turjan out and set him down.

The spell was disrupted by the touch of the rune at her wrist, and Turjan became a man again. He looked aghast at the nearly unrecognizable T'sain.

She tried to smile up at him.

"Turjan—you are free—"

"And Mazirian?"

"He is dead." She slumped wearily to the stone floor and lay limp. Turjan surveyed her with an odd emotion in his eyes.

"T'sain, dear creature of my mind," he whispered, "more noble are you than I, who used the only life you knew for my freedom."

He lifted her body in his arms.

"But I shall restore you to the vats. With your brain I build another T'sain, as lovely as you. We go."

He bore her up the stone stairs.

PLEASE STAND BY

by
Ron Goulart

*Ron Goulart has published scores of novels and hun-
dreds of short stories, the vast majority wonderful, zany
tales bursting with social satire. Goulart is sf's premier
humorist, and once addicted to his work, the reader is
hooked for life. Among his best books are AFTER
THINGS FELL APART (1970), GADGET MAN (1971),
SKYROCKET STEELE (1980), and the story collections
WHAT'S BECOME OF SCREWLOOSE? AND OTHER
INQUIRIES (1971) and NUTZENBOLTS AND MORE
TROUBLES WITH MACHINES (1975). He is even better at the shorter lengths, and a BEST OF GOULART
would be a treasure.*

*Perhaps the funniest story Ron Goulart ever wrote,
"Please Stand By" recounts the difficulties of being
transformed into an elephant on national holidays!*

The art department secretary put her Christmas tree down and
kissed Max Kearny. "There's somebody to see you," she said,
getting her coat the rest of the way on and picking up the tree again.

Max shifted on his stool. "On the last working day before Christmas?"

"Pile those packages in my arms," the secretary said. "He says it's an emergency."

Moving away from his drawing board Max arranged the gift packages in the girl's arms. "Who is it? A rep?"

"Somebody named Dan Padgett."

"Oh, sure. He's a friend of mine from another agency. Tell him to come on back."

"Will do. You'll have a nice Christmas, won't you, Max?"

"I think the Salvation Army has something nice planned."

"No, seriously, Max. Don't sit around some cold bar. Well, Merry Christmas."

"Same to you." Max looked at the rough layout on his board for a moment and then Dan Padgett came in. "Hi, Dan. What is it?"

Dan Padgett rubbed his palms together. "You still have your hobby?"

Max shook out a cigarette from his pack. "The ghost detective stuff? Sure."

"But you don't specialize in ghosts only?" Dan went around the room once, then closed the door.

"No. I'm interested in most of the occult field. The last case I worked on involved a free-lance resurrectionist. Why?"

"You remember Anne Clemens, the blonde?"

"Yeah. You used to go out with her when we worked at Bryan-Josephs and Associates. Skinny girl."

"Slender. Fashion model type." Dan sat in the room's chair and unbuttoned his coat. "I want to marry her."

"Right now?"

"I asked her two weeks ago but she hasn't given me an answer yet. One reason is Kenneth Westerland."

"The animator?"

"Yes. The guy who created Major Bowser. He's seeing Anne, too."

"Well," said Max, dragging his stool back from the drawing board. "I don't do lovelorn work, Dan. Now if Westerland were a vampire or a warlock I might be able to help."

"He's not the main problem. It's if Anne says yes."

"What is?"

"I can't marry her."

"Change of heart?"

"No." Dan tilted to his feet. "No." He rubbed his hands

together. "No, I love her. The thing is there's something wrong with me. I hate to bother you so close to Christmas, but that's part of it."

Max lit a fresh cigarette from the old one. "I still don't have a clear idea of the problem, Dan."

"I change into an elephant on all national holidays."

Max leaned forward and squinted one eye at Dan. "An elephant?"

"Middle-sized gray elephant."

"On national holidays?"

"More or less. It started on Halloween. It didn't happen again till Thanksgiving. Fortunately I can talk during it and I was able to explain to my folks that I wouldn't get home for our traditional Thanksgiving get-together."

"How do you dial the phone?"

"I waited till they called me. You can pick up a phone with your trunk. I found that out."

"Usually people change into cats or wolves."

"I wouldn't mind that," Dan said, sitting. "A wolf, that's acceptable. It has a certain appeal. I'd even settle for a giant cockroach, for the symbolic value. But a middle-sized gray elephant. I can't expect Anne to marry me when I do things like that."

"You don't think," said Max, crossing to the window and looking down at the late afternoon crowds, "that you're simply having hallucinations?"

"If I am they are pretty authentic. Thanksgiving Day I ate a bale of hay " Dan tapped his fingers on his knees. "See, the first time I changed I got hungry after a while. But I couldn't work the damned can opener with my trunk. So I figured I'd get a bale of hay and keep it handy if I ever changed again."

"You seemed to stay an elephant for how long?"

"Twenty-four hours. The first time—both times I've been in my apartment, which has a nice solid floor—I got worried. I trumpeted and stomped around. Then the guy upstairs, the queer ceramacist, started pounding on the floor. I figured I'd better keep quiet so nobody would call the cops and take me off to a zoo or animal shelter. Well, I waited around and tried to figure things out and then right on the nose at midnight I was myself again."

Max ground his cigarette into the small metal pie plate on his workstand. "You're not putting me on, are you?"

"No, Max." Dan looked up hopefully. "Is this in your line? I don't know anyone else to ask. I tried to forget it. Now, though, Christmas is nearly here. Both other times I changed was on a holiday. I'm worried.''

"Lycanthropy," said Max. "That can't be it. Have you been near any elephants lately?''

"I was at the zoo a couple of years ago. None of them bit me or even looked at me funny.''

"This is something else. Look, Dan, I've got a date with a girl down in Palo Alto on Christmas Day. But Christmas Eve I can be free. Do you change right on the dot?''

"If it happens I should switch over right at midnight on the twenty-fourth. I already told my folks I was going to spend these holidays with Anne. And I told her I'd be with them.''

"Which leaves her free to see Westerland.''

"That son of a bitch.''

"Major Bowser's not a bad cartoon show.''

"Successful anyway. That dog's voice is what makes the show. I hate Westerland and I've laughed at it.'' Dan rose. "Maybe nothing will happen.''

"If anything does it may give me a lead.''

"Hope so. Well, Merry Christmas, Max. See you tomorrow night.''

Max nodded and Dan Padgett left. Leaning over his drawing board Max wrote *Hex?* on the margin of his layout.

He listened to the piped in music play Christmas carols for a few minutes and then started drawing again.

The bale of hay crackled as Max sat down on it. He lit a cigarette carefully and checked his watch again. "Half hour to go," he said.

Dan Padgett poured some scotch into a cup marked Tom & Jerry and closed the venetian blinds. "I felt silly carrying that bale of hay up here. People expect to see you with a tree this time of year.''

"You could have hung tinsel on it.''

"That'd hurt my fillings when I eat the hay.'' Dan poured some more scotch and walked to the heater outlet. He kicked it once. "Getting cold in here. I'm afraid to complain to the landlady. She'd probably say—'Who else would let you keep an elephant in your rooms? A little chill you shouldn't mind.' ''

"You know," said Max, "I've been reading up on lycanthropy. A friend of mine runs an occult bookshop.''

"Non-fiction seems to be doing better and better.''

"There doesn't seem to be any recorded case of were-elephants."

"Maybe the others didn't want any publicity."

"Maybe. It's more likely somebody has put a spell on you. In that case you could change into most anything."

Dan frowned. "I hadn't thought of that. What time is it?"

"Quarter to."

"A spell, huh? Would I have to meet the person who did it? Or is it done from a distance?"

"Usually there has to be some kind of contact."

"Say," said Dan, lowering his head and stroking his nose, "you'd better not sit on the bale of hay. Animals don't like people fooling with their food." He was standing with his feet wide apart, his legs stiff.

Max carefully got up and moved back across the room. "Something?"

"No," said Dan. He leaned far forward, reaching for the floor with his hands. "I just have an itch. My stomach."

Max watched as Dan scratched his stomach with his trunk. "Damn."

Raising his head, the middle-sized gray elephant squinted at Max. "Hell, I thought it wouldn't happen again."

"Can I come closer?"

Dan beckoned with his trunk. "I won't trample you."

Max reached out and touched the side of the elephant. "You're a real elephant sure enough."

"I should have thought to get some cabbages, too. This stuff is pretty bland." He was tearing trunkfuls of hay from the bale and stuffing them into his mouth.

Max remembered the cigarette in his hand and lit it. He walked twice around the elephant and said, "Think back now, Dan. To the first time this happened. When was it?"

"I told you. Halloween."

"But that's not really a holiday. Was it the day after Halloween? Or the night itself?"

"Wait. It was before. It was the day after the party at Eando Carawan's. In the Beach."

"Where?"

"North Beach. There was a party. Anne knows Eando's wife. Her name is Eando, too."

"Why?"

"His name is Ernest and hers is Olivia. E-and-O. So they both called themselves Eando. They paint those pictures of bug-eyed children you can buy in all the stores down there. You should know them, being an artist yourself.''

Max grunted. ''Ernie Carawan. Sure, he used to be a freelance artist, specializing in dogs. We stopped using him because all his dogs started having bug-eyes.''

''You ought to see Olivia.''

''What happened at the party?''

''Well,'' said Dan, tearing off more hay, ''I get the idea that there was some guy at this party. A little round fat guy. About your height. Around thirty-five. Somebody said he was a stage magician or something.''

''Come on,'' said Max, ''elephants are supposed to have good memories.''

''I think I was sort of drunk at the time. I can't remember all he said. Something about doing me a favor. And a flash.''

''A flash?''

''The flash came to him like that. I told him to—to do whatever he did.'' Dan stopped eating the hay. ''That would be magic, though, Max. That's impossible.''

''Shut up and eat your hay. Anything is possible.''

''You're right. Who'd have thought I'd be spending Christmas as an elephant.''

''That magician for one,'' said Max. ''What's his name? He may know something.''

''His name?''

''That's right.''

''I don't know. He didn't tell me.''

''Just came up and put a spell on you.''

''You know how it is at parties.''

Max found the phone on a black table near the bookshelves. ''Where's the phone book?''

''Oh, yeah.''

''What?''

''It's not here. The last time I was an elephant I ate it.''

''I'll get Carawan's number from information and see if he knows who this wizard is.''

Carawan didn't. But someone at his Christmas Eve party did. The magician ran a sandal shop in North Beach. His name was Claude Waller. As far as anyone knew he was visiting his ex-wife in Los Angeles for Christmas and wouldn't be back until Monday or Tuesday.

*   *   *

Max reached for the price tag on a pair of orange leather slippers. The beaded screen at the back of the shop clattered.

"You a fagot or something, buddy?" asked the heavy-set man who came into the room.

"No, sir. Sorry."

"Then you don't want that pair of slippers. That's my fagot special. Also comes in light green. Who are you?"

"Max Kearny. Are you Claude Waller?"

Waller was wearing a loose brown suit. He unbuttoned the coat and sat down on a stool in front of the counter. "That's who I am. The little old shoemaker."

Max nodded.

"That's a switch on the wine commercial with the little old winemaker."

"I know."

"My humor always bombs. It's like my life. A big bomb. What do you want?"

"I hear you're a magician."

"No."

"You aren't?"

"Not anymore. My ex-wife, that flat-chested bitch, and I have reunited. I don't know what happened. I'm a tough guy. I don't take any crap."

"I'd say so."

"Then why'd I send her two hundred bucks to come up here?"

"Is there time to stop the check?"

"I sent cash."

"You're stuck then, I guess."

"She's not that bad."

"Do you know a guy named Dan Padgett?"

"No."

"How about Ernie Carawan?"

"Eando? Yeah."

"On Halloween you met Dan Padgett and a girl named Anne Clemens at the party the Carawans gave."

"That's a good act. Can you tell me what it says on the slip of paper in my pocket?"

"Do you remember talking to Dan? Could you have put some kind of spell on him?"

Waller slid forward off the stool. "That guy. I'll be damned. I did do it then."

"Do what?"

"I was whacked out of my mind. Juiced out of my skull, you know. I got this flash. Some guy was in trouble. This Padgett it was. I didn't think I'd really done anything. Did I?"

"He turns into an elephant on national holidays."

Waller looked at his feet. Then laughed. "He does. That's great. Why'd I do that do you suppose?"

"Tell me."

Waller stopped laughing. "I get these flashes all the time. It bugs my wife. She doesn't know who to sleep with. I might get a flash about it. Wait now." He picked up a hammer from his workbench and tapped the palm of his hand. "That girl. The blonde girl. What's her name?"

"Anne Clemens."

"There's something. Trouble. Has it happened yet?"

"What's supposed to happen?"

"Ouch," said Waller. He'd brought the hammer down hard enough to start a bruise. "I can't remember. But I know I put a spell on your friend so he could save her when the time came."

Max lit a cigarette. "It would be simpler just to tell us what sort of trouble is coming."

Waller reached out behind him to set the hammer down. He missed the bench and the hammer smashed through the top of a shoe box. "Look, Kearny. I'm not a professional wizard. It's like in baseball. Sometimes a guy's just a natural. That's the way I am. A natural, I'm sorry, buddy. I can't tell you anything else. And I can't take that spell off your friend. I don't even remember how I did it."

"There's nothing else you can remember about what kind of trouble Anne is going to have?"

Frowning, Waller said, "Dogs. A pack of dogs. Dogs barking in the rain. No, that's not right. I can't get it. I don't know. This Dan Padgett will save her." Waller bent to pick up the hammer. "I'm pretty sure of that."

"This is Tuesday. On Saturday he's due to change again. Will the trouble come on New Year's Eve?"

"Buddy, if I get another flash I'll let you know."

At the door Max said, "I'll give you my number."

"Skip it," said Waller. "When I need it, I'll know it."

The door of the old Victorian house buzzed and Max caught the doorknob and turned it. The stairway leading upstairs was lined with brown paintings of little girls with ponies and dogs. The light from the door opening upstairs flashed down across the bright gilt frames on which eagles and flowers twisted and curled together.

"Max Kearny?" said Anne Clemens over the stair railing.

"Hi, Anne. Are you busy?"

"Not at the moment. I'm going out later. I just got home from work a little while ago."

This was Wednesday night. Max hadn't been able to find Anne at home until now. "I was driving by and I thought I'd stop."

"It's been several months since we've seen each other," said the girl as Max reached the doorway to her apartment. "Come in."

She was wearing a white blouse and what looked like a pair of black leotards. She wasn't as thin as Max had remembered. Her blonde hair was held back with a thin black ribbon.

"I won't hold you up?" Max asked.

Anne shook her head. "I won't have to start getting ready for a while yet."

"Fine." Max got out his cigarettes and sat down in the old sofa chair Anne gestured at.

"Is it something about Dan, Max?" The single overhead light was soft and it touched her hair gently.

"In a way."

"Is it some trouble?" She was sitting opposite Max, straight up on the sofa bed.

"No," said Max. "Dan's got the idea, though, that you might be in trouble of some sort."

The girl moistened her lips. "Dan's too sensitive in some areas. I think I know what he means."

Max held his pack of cigarettes to her.

"No, thanks. Dan's worried about Ken Westerland, isn't he?"

"That's part of it."

"Max," said Anne, "I worked for Ken a couple of years ago. We've gone out off and on since then. Dan shouldn't worry about that."

"Westerland isn't causing you any trouble?"

"Ken? Of course not. If I seem hesitant to Dan it's only that I don't want Ken to be hurt either." She frowned, turning away. She turned back to Max and studied him as though he had suddenly appeared across from her. "What was I saying? Well, never mind. I really should be getting ready."

"If you need anything," said Max, "let me know."

"What?"

"I said that—"

"Oh, yes. If I need anything. Fine. If I'm going to dinner I should get started."

"You studying modern dance?"

Anne opened the door. "The leotards. No. They're comfortable. I don't have any show business leanings." She smiled quickly. "Thank you for dropping by, Max."

The door closed and he was in the hall. Max stood there long enough to light a cigarette and then went downstairs and outside.

It was dark now. The street lights were on and the night cold was coming. Max got in his car and sat back, watching the front steps of Anne's building across the street. Next to his car was a narrow empty lot, high with dark grass. A house had been there once and when it was torn down the stone stairs had been left. Max's eyes went up, stopping in nothing beyond the last step. Shaking his head and lighting a new cigarette he turned to watch Anne's apartment house.

The front of the building was covered with yards and yards of white wooden gingerbread. It wound around and around the house. There was a wide porch across the building front. One with a peaked roof over it.

About an hour later Kenneth Westerland parked his gray Mercedes sedan at the corner. He was a tall thin man of about thirty-five. He had a fat man's face, too round and plump-cheeked for his body. He was carrying a small suitcase.

After Westerland had gone inside Max left his car and walked casually to the corner. He crossed the street. He stepped suddenly across a lawn and into the row of darkness alongside Anne's building. Using a garbage can to stand on Max pulled himself up onto the first landing of the fire escape without use of the noisy ladder.

Max sat on the fire escape rail and, concealing the match flame, lit a cigarette. When he'd finished smoking it he ground out the butt against the ladder. Then he swung out around the edge of the building and onto the top of the porch roof. Flat on his stomach he worked up the slight incline. In a profusion of ivy and hollyhock Max concealed himself and let his left eye look up into the window.

This was the window of her living room and he could see Anne sitting in the chair he'd been sitting in. She was wearing a black cocktail dress now and her hair was down, touching her shoulders. She was watching Westerland. The suitcase was sitting on the rug between Max and the animator.

Westerland had a silver chain held between his thumb and forefinger. On the end of the chain a bright silver medallion spun.

Max blinked and ducked back into the vines. Westerland was hypnotizing Anne. It was like an illustration from a pulp magazine.

Looking in again Max saw Westerland let the medallion drop into his suit pocket. Westerland came toward the window and Max eased down.

After a moment he looked in. Westerland had opened the suitcase. It held a tape recorder. The mike was in Anne's hand. In her other she held several stapled together sheets of paper.

Westerland pushed her coffee table in front of Anne and she set the papers on it. Her eyes seemed focused still on the spot where the spinning disc had been.

On his knees by the tape machine Westerland fitted on a spool of tape. After speaking a few words into the mike he gave it back to the girl. They began recording what had to be a script of some kind.

From the way Westerland used his face he was doing different voices. Anne's expression never changed as she spoke. Max couldn't hear anything.

Letting himself go flat he slid back to the edge of the old house and swung onto the fire escape. He waited to make sure no one had seen him and went to work on the window that led to the escape. It wasn't much work because there was no lock on it. It hadn't been opened for quite a while and it creaked. Max stepped into the hall and closed the window. Then he went slowly to the door of Anne's apartment and put his ear against it.

He could hear the voices faintly now. Westerland speaking as various characters. Anne using only one voice, not her own. Max sensed something behind him and turned to see the door of the next apartment opening. A big girl with black-rimmed glasses was looking at him.

"What is it?" she said.

Max smiled and came to her door. "Nobody home I guess. Perhaps you'd like to subscribe to the *Seditionist Daily*. If I sell eight more subscriptions I get a stuffed panda."

The girl poked her chin. "A panda? A grown man like you shouldn't want a stuffed panda."

Max watched her for a second. "It is sort of foolish. To hell with them then. It's not much of a paper anyway. No comics and only fifteen words in the crossword puzzle. Good night, miss. Sorry to bother you. You've opened my eyes." He went down the stairs as the door closed behind him.

What he'd learned tonight gave him no clues as to Dan's problem. But it was interesting. For some reason Anne Clemens was the voice of Westerland's animated cartoon character, Major Bowser.

By Friday Max had found out that Westerland had once worked in night clubs as a hypnotist. That gave him no leads about why Dan Padgett periodically turned into an elephant.

Early in the afternoon Dan called him. "Max. Something's wrong."

"Have you changed already?"

"No, I'm okay. But I can't find Anne."

"What do you mean?"

"She hasn't showed up at work today. And I can't get an answer at her place."

"Did you tell her about Westerland? About what I found out the other night?"

"I know you said not to. But you also said I was due to save her from some trouble. I thought maybe telling her about Westerland was the way to do it."

"You're supposed to save her while you're an elephant. Damn it. I didn't want her to know what Westerland was doing yet."

"If it's any help Anne didn't know she was Major Bowser. And she thinks she went to dinner with Westerland on Wednesday."

"No wonder she's so skinny. Okay. What else did she say?"

"She thought I was kidding. Then she seemed to become convinced. Even asked me how much Westerland probably made off the series."

"Great," said Max, making heavy lines on his memo pad. "Now she's probably gone to him and asked him for her back salary or something."

"Is that so bad?"

"We don't know." Max looked at his watch. "I can take off right now. I'll go out to her place and look around. Then check at Westerland's apartment. He lives out on California Street. I'll call you as soon as I find out anything."

"In the meantime," said Dan, "I'd better see about getting another bale of hay."

*   *   *

There was no lead on Anne's whereabouts at her apartment, which Max broke into. Or at Westerland's, where he came in through the skylight.

At noon on Saturday Max was wondering if he should sit back and trust to Waller's prediction that Dan would save Anne when the time came.

He lit a new cigarette and wandered about his apartment. He looked through quite a few of the occult books he'd collected.

The phone rang.

"Yes?"

"This is Waller's Sandal Shop."

"The magician?"

"Right, buddy. That is you, Kearny?"

"Yes. What's happening?"

"I got a flash."

"So?"

"Go to Sausalito."

"And?"

"That's all the flash told me. You and your friend get over to Sausalito. Today. Before midnight."

"You haven't got any more details?"

"Sorry. My ex-wife got in last night and I've been too unsettled to get any full scale flashes." The line went dead.

"Sausalito?" said Dan when Max called him.

"That's what Waller says."

"Hey," said Dan. "Westerland's ex-wife."

"He's got one, too?"

"His wife had a place over there. I remember going to a party with Anne there once. Before Westerland got divorced. Could Anne be there?"

"Wouldn't Mrs. Westerland complain?"

"No, she's in Europe. It was in Herb Caen and—Max! The house would be empty now. Anne must be there. And in trouble."

The house was far back from the road that ran up through the low hills of Sausalito, the town just across the Golden Gate Bridge from San Francisco. It was a flat scattered house of redwood and glass.

Max and Dan had driven by it and parked the car. Max in the lead, they came downhill through a stretch of trees, descending toward the back of the Westerland house. It was late afternoon now and the great flat windows sparkled and went black and sparkled again as they came near. A high hedge circled the patio and when Max and Dan came close their view of the house was cut off.

"Think she's here?" Dan asked.

"We should be able to spot some signs of life," Max said. "I'm turning into a first class peeping tom. All I do is watch people's houses."

"I guess detective work's like that," said Dan. "Even the occult stuff."

"Hold it," said Max. "Listen."

"To what?"

"I heard a dog barking."

"In the house?"

"Yep."

"Means there's somebody in there."

"It means Anne's in there probably. Pretty sure that was Major Bowser."

"Hi, pals," said a high-pitched voice.

"Hello," said Max, turning to face the wide bald man behind them.

"Geese Louise," the man said, pointing his police special at them, "this sure saves me a lot of work. The boss had me out looking for you all day. And just when I was giving up and coming back here with my tail between my legs—well, here you are."

"Who's your boss?"

"Him. Westerland. I'm a full-time pro gunman. Hired to get you."

"You got us," said Max.

"Look, would you let me tell him I caught you over in Frisco? Makes me seem more efficient."

"We will," said Max, "if you'll let us go. Tell him we used karate on you. We can even break your arm to make it look good."

"No," said the bald man. "Let it pass. You guys want too many concessions. Go on inside."

Westerland was opening the refrigerator when his gunman brought Max and Dan into the kitchen.

"You brought it off, Lloyd," said Westerland, taking a popsicle from the freezer compartment.

"I studied those pictures you gave me."

"Where's Anne?" Dan asked.

Westerland squeezed the wrapper off the popsicle. "Here. We've only this minute finished a recording session. Sit down."

When the four of them were around the white wooden table Westerland said, "You, Mr. Kearny."

Max took out his pack of cigarettes and put them on the table in front of him. "Sir?"

"Your detective work will be the ruin of you."

"All I did was look through a few windows. It's more acrobatics than detection."

"Nevertheless, you're on to me. Your overprotective attitude toward Miss Clemens has caused you to stumble on one of the most closely guarded secrets of the entertainment industry."

"You mean Anne's being the voice of Major Bowser?"

"Exactly," said Westerland, his round cheeks caving as he sucked the popsicle. "But it's too late. Residuals and reruns."

Dan tapped the tabletop. "What's that mean?"

"What else? I've completed taping the sound track for episode 78 F Major Bowser. I have a new series in the works. Within a few months the major will be released to secondary markets. That means I don't need Anne Clemens anymore."

Dan clenched his fists. "So let her go."

"Why did you ever need her?" Max asked, looking at Westerland.

"She's an unconscious talent," said Westerland, catching the last fragment of the popsicle off the stick. "She first did that voice one night over two years ago. After a party I'd taken her to. She'd had too much to drink. I thought it was funny. The next day she'd forgotten about it. Couldn't even remember the voice. Instead of pressing her I used my hypnotic ability. I had a whole sketch book full of drawings of that damned dog. The voice clicked. It matched. I used it."

"And made $100,000," said Dan.

"The writing is mine. And quite a bit of the drawing."

"And now?" said Max.

"She knows about it. She has thoughts of marrying and settling down. She asked me if $5,000 would be a fair share of the profits from the major."

"Is that scale for 78 shows?" Max said.

"I could look it up," said Westerland. He was at the refrigerator again. "Lemon, lime, grape, watermelon. How's grape sound? Fine. Grape it is." He stood at the head of the table and unwrapped the purple popsicle. "I've come up with an alternative. I intend to eliminate all of you. Much cheaper way of settling things."

"You're kidding," said Dan.

"Animators are supposed to be lovable guys like Walt Disney,'' said Max.

"I'm a businessman first. I can't use Anne Clemens anymore. We'll fix her first and you two at some later date. Lloyd, put these detectives in the cellar and lock it up."

Lloyd grinned and pointed to a door beyond the stove. Max and Dan were made to go down a long flight of wooden stairs and into a room that was filled with the smell of old newspapers and unused furniture. There were small dusty windows high up around the beamed ceiling.

"Not a very tough cellar," Dan whispered to Max.

"But you won't be staying here," said Lloyd. He kept his gun aimed at them and stepped around a fallen tricycle to a wide oak door in the cement wall. A padlock and chain hung down from a hook on the wall. Lloyd slid the bolt and opened the door. "The wine cellar. He showed it to me this morning. No wine left, but it's homey. You'll come to like it."

He got them inside and bolted the door. The chains rattled and the padlock snapped.

Max blinked. He lit a match and looked around the cement room. It was about twelve feet high and ten feet wide.

Dan made his way to an old cobbler's bench in the corner. "Does your watch glow in the dark?" he asked as the match went out.

"It's five thirty."

"The magician was right. We're in trouble."

"I'm wondering," said Max, striking another match.

"You're wondering what the son of a bitch is going to do to Anne."

"Yes," Max said, spotting an empty wine barrel. He turned it upside down and sat on it.

"And what'll he do with us?"

Max started a cigarette from the dying match flames. "Drop gas pellets through the ceiling, fill the room with water, make the walls squeeze in."

"Westerland's trickier than that. He'll probably hypnotize us into thinking we're pheasants and then turn us loose the day the hunting season opens."

"Wonder how Lloyd knew what we looked like."

"Anne's got my picture in her purse. And one I think we all took at some beach party once."

Max leaned back against the dark wall. "This is about a middle-sized room, isn't it?"

"I don't know. The only architecture course I took at school was in water color painting."

"In six hours you'll be a middle-sized elephant."

Dan's bench clattered. "You think this is it?"

"Should be. How else are we going to get out of here?"

"I smash the door like a real elephant would." He snapped his fingers. "That's great."

"You should be able to do it."

"But Max?"

"Yeah?"

"Suppose I don't change?"

"You will."

"We only have the word of an alcoholic shoemaker."

"He knew about Sausalito."

"He could be a fink."

"He's a real magician. You're proof of that."

"Max?"

"Huh?"

"Maybe Westerland hypnotized us into thinking I was an elephant."

"How could he hypnotize me? I haven't seen him for years."

"He could hypnotize you and then make you forget you were."

"Dan," said Max, "relax. After midnight if we're still in here we can think up excuses."

"How do we know he won't harm Anne before midnight?"

"We don't."

"Let's try to break out now."

Max lit a match and stood up. "I don't think these barrel staves will do it. See anything else?"

"Legs off this bench. We can unscrew them and bang the door down."

They got the wooden legs loose and taking one each began hammering at the bolt with them.

After a few minutes a voice echoed in. "Stop that ruckus."

"The hell with you," said Dan.

"Wait now," said Westerland's voice. "You can't break down the door. And even if you could Lloyd would shoot you. I'm sending him down to sit guard. Last night at Playland he won four Betty Boop dolls at the shooting gallery. Be rational."

"How come we can hear you?"

"I'm talking through an air vent."

"Where's Anne?" shouted Dan.

"Still in a trance. If you behave I may let her bark for you before we leave."

"You louse."

Max found Dan in the dark and caught his arm. "Take it easy." Raising his voice he said, "Westerland, how long do we stay down here?"

"Well, my ex-wife will be in Rome until next April. I hope to have a plan worked out by then. At the moment, however, I can't spare the time. I have to get ready for the party."

"What party?"

"The New Year's Eve party at the Leversons'. It's the one where Anne Clemens will drink too much."

"What?"

"She'll drink too much and get the idea she's an acrobat. She'll borrow a car and drive to the Golden Gate Bridge. While trying out her act on the top rail she'll discover she's not an acrobat at all and actually has a severe dread of heights. When I hear about it I'll still be at the Leversons' party. I'll be saddened that she was able to see so little of the New Year."

"You can't make her do that. Hypnotism doesn't work that way."

"That's what you say now, Padgett. In the morning I'll have Lloyd slip the papers under the door."

The pipe stopped talking.

Dan slammed his fist into the cement wall. "He can't do it."

"Who are the Leversons?"

Dan was silent for a moment. "Leverson. Joe and Jackie. Isn't that the art director at BBDO? He and his wife live over here. Just up from Sally Stanford's restaurant. It could be them."

"It's a long way to midnight," said Max. "But I have a feeling we'll make it."

"We have to save Anne," said Dan, "and there doesn't seem to be anything to do but wait."

"What's the damn time, Max?"

"Six thirty."

"Must be nearly eight by now."

"Seven fifteen."

"I think I still hear them up there."

*   *   *

"Now?"

"Little after nine."

"Only ten? Is that watch going?"

"Yeah, it's ticking."

"Eleven yet, Max?"

"In five minutes."

"They've gone, I'm sure."

"Relax."

"Look," said Dan, when Max told him it was quarter to twelve, "I don't want to step on you if I change."

"I'll duck down on the floor by your feet. Your present feet. Then when you've changed I should be under your stomach."

"Okay. After I do you hop on my back."

At five to twelve Max sat down on the stone floor. "Happy New Year."

Dan's feet shuffled, moved farther apart. "My stomach is starting to itch."

Max ducked a little. In the darkness a darker shadow seemed to grow overhead. "Dan?"

"I did it, Max." Dan laughed. "I did it right on time."

Max edged up and climbed on top of the elephant. "I'm aboard."

"Hang on. I'm going to push the door with my head."

Max hung on and waited. The door creaked and began to give.

"Watch it, you guys!" shouted Lloyd from outside.

"Trumpet at him," said Max.

"Good idea." Dan gave a violent angry elephant roar.

"Jesus!" Lloyd said.

The door exploded out and Dan's trunk slapped Lloyd into the side of the furnace. His gun sailed into a clothes basket. Max jumped down and retrieved it.

"Go away," he said to Lloyd.

Lloyd blew his nose. "What kind of prank is this?"

"If he doesn't go," said Max, "trample him."

"Let's trample him no matter what," said Dan.

Lloyd left.

"Hell," said Dan. "How do I get up those stairs?"

"You don't," said Max, pointing. "See there, behind that stack of papers. A door. I'll see if it's open."

"Who cares. I'll push it open."

"Okay. I'll go find a phone book and look up Leversons. Meet you in the patio."

Dan trumpeted and Max ran up the narrow wooden stairs.

The elephant careened down the grassy hillside. All around now New Year's horns were sounding.

"Only two Leversons, huh?" Dan asked again.

"It's most likely the art director. He's nearest the bridge."

They came out on Bridgeway, which ran along the water.

Dan trumpeted cars and people out of the way and Max ducked down, holding onto the big elephant ears.

They turned as the road curved and headed them for the Leverson home. "It better be this one," Dan said.

The old two story house was filled with lighted windows, the windows spotted with people. "A party sure enough," said Max.

In the long twisted driveway a motor started. "A car," said Dan, running up the gravel.

Max jumped free as Dan made himself a road block in the driveway.

Red tail lights tinted the exhaust of a small gray Jaguar convertible. Max ran to the car. Anne Clemens jerked the wheel and spun it. Max dived over the back of the car and, teetering on his stomach, jerked the ignition key off and out. Anne kept turning the wheel.

Max caught her by the shoulders, swung around off the car and pulled her up so that she was now kneeling in the driver's seat.

The girl shook her head twice, looking beyond Max.

He got the door open and helped her out. The gravel seemed to slide away from them in all directions.

"Duck," yelled Dan, still an elephant.

Max didn't turn. He dropped, pulling the girl with him.

A shot smashed a cobweb pattern across the windshield.

"You've spoiled it for sure," cried Westerland. "You and your silly damn elephant have spoiled my plan for sure."

The parking area lights were on and a circle of people was forming behind Westerland. He was standing twenty feet away from Max and Anne.

Then he fell over as Dan's trunk flipped his gun away from him.

Dan caught up the fallen animator and shook him.

Max got Anne to her feet and held onto her. "Bring her out of this, Westerland."

"In a pig's valise."

Dan tossed him up and caught him.

"Come on."

"Since you're so belligerent," said Westerland. "Dangle me closer to her."

Max had Lloyd's gun in his coat pocket. He took it out now and pointed it up at the swinging Westerland. "No wise stuff."

Westerland snapped his fingers near Anne's pale face.

She shivered once and fell against Max. He put his arms under hers and held her.

Dan suddenly dropped Westerland and, trumpeting once at the silent guests, galloped away into the night.

As his trumpet faded a siren filled the night.

"Real detectives," said Max.

Both Anne and Westerland were out. The guests were too far away to hear him.

A bush crackled behind him and Max turned his head.

Dan, himself again, came up to them. "Would it be okay if I held Anne?"

Max carefully transferred her. "She should be fine when she comes to."

"What'll we tell the law?"

"The truth. Except for the elephant."

"How'd we get from his place here?"

"My car wouldn't start. We figured he'd tampered with it. We hailed a passing motorist who dropped us here."

"People saw the elephant."

"It escaped from a zoo."

"What zoo?"

"Look," said Max, dropping the gun back into his pocket, "don't be so practical about this. We don't have to explain it. Okay?"

"Okay. Thanks, Max."

Max lit a cigarette.

"I changed back in only an hour. I don't think it will happen again, Max. Do you?"

"If it would make you feel any better I'll spend the night before Lincoln's Birthday with you and Anne."

"How about what?" said Anne. She looked up at Dan. "Dan? What is it?"

"Nothing much. A little trouble with Westerland. I'll explain."

Max nodded at them and went up the driveway to meet the approaching police. Somewhere in the night a final New Year's horn sounded.

WHAT GOOD IS A GLASS DAGGER?

by
Larry Niven

*Larry Niven is simply amazing. Renowned for his
"hard" science fiction like RINGWORLD (1970) and
its sequel THE RINGWORLD ENGINEERS (1980), he
is also a master of fantasy, and such books as THE
FLYING SORCERERS (1971; with David Gerrold) and
THE MAGIC GOES AWAY (1978) are tremendously
popular. He has also teamed with Jerry Pournelle to
form one of science fiction's most successful collabora-
tive pairs. A frequent guest at sf conventions, he has
won five Hugo Awards and one Nebula to date.*

*"What Good Is a Glass Dagger?" is the second of a
series of stories in which Larry Niven tries to give a
scientific explanation for magic. And as a bonus, he
also throws in a new rationale for lycanthropy.*

I

Twelve thousand years before the birth of Christ, in an age
when miracles were somewhat more common, a warlock used
an ancient secret to save his life.

In later years he regretted that. He had kept the secret of the

Warlock's Wheel for several normal lifetimes. The demon-sword Glirendree and its stupid barbarian captive would have killed him, no question of that. But no mere demon could have been as dangerous as that secret.

Now it was out, spreading like ripples on a pond. The battle between Glirendree and the Warlock was too good a tale not to tell. Soon no man would call himself a magician who did not know that magic could be used up. So simple, so dangerous a secret. The wonder was that nobody had noticed it before.

A year after the battle with Glirendree, near the end of a summer day, Aran the Peacemonger came to Shayl Village to steal the Warlock's Wheel.

Aran was a skinny eighteen-year-old, lightly built. His face was lean and long, with a pointed chin. His dark eyes peered out from under a prominent shelf of bone. His short, straight dark hair dropped almost to his brows in a pronounced widow's peak. What he was was no secret; and anyone who touched hands with him would have known at once, for there was short fine hair on his palms. But had anyone known his mission, he would have been thought mad.

For the Warlock was a leader in the Sorcerer's Guild. It was known that he had a name; but no human throat could pronounce it. The shadow demon who had been his name-father had later been imprisoned in tattooed runes on the Warlock's own back: an uncommonly dangerous bodyguard.

Yet Aran came well protected. The leather wallet that hung from his shoulder was old and scarred, and the seams were loose. By its look it held nuts and hard cheese and bread and almost no money. What it actually held was charms. Magic would serve him better than nuts and cheese, and Aran could feed himself as he traveled, at night.

He reached the Warlock's cave shortly after sunset. He had been told how to use his magic to circumvent the Warlock's safeguards. His need for magic implied a need for voice and hands, so that Aran was forced to keep the human shape; and this made him doubly nervous. At moonrise he chanted the words he had been taught, and drew a live bat from his pouch and tossed it gently through the barred entrance to the cave.

The bat exploded into a mist of blood that drifted slant-wise across the stone floor. Aran's stomach lurched. He almost ran then; but he quelled his fear and followed it in, squeezing between the bars.

Those who had sent him had repeatedly diagrammed the cave for him. He could have robbed it blindfolded. He would have preferred darkness to the flickering blue light from what seemed to be a captured lightning bolt tethered in the middle of the cavern. He moved quickly, scrupulously tracing what he had been told was a path of safety.

Though Aran had seen sorcerous tools in the training laboratory in the School for Mercantile Grammaree in Atlantis, most of the Warlock's tools were unfamiliar. It was not an age of mass production. He paused by a workbench, wondering. Why would the Warlock be grinding a glass dagger?

But Aran found a tarnish-blackened metal disc hanging above the workbench, and the runes inscribed around its rim convinced him that it was what he had come for. He took it down and quickly strapped it against his thigh, leaving his hands free to fight if need be. He was turning to go, when a laughing voice spoke out of the air.

"Put that down, you mangy son of a bitch—"

Aran converted to wolf.

Agony seared his thigh!

In human form Aran was a lightly built boy. As a wolf he was formidably large and dangerous. It did him little good this time. The pain was blinding, stupefying. Aran the wolf screamed and tried to run from the pain.

He woke gradually, with an ache in his head and a greater agony in his thigh and a tightness at his wrists and ankles. It came to him that he must have knocked himself out against a wall.

He lay on his side with his eyes closed, giving no sign that he was awake. Gently he tried to pull his hands apart. He was bound, wrists and ankles. Well, he had been taught a word for unbinding ropes.

Best not to use it until he knew more.

He opened his eyes a slit.

The Warlock was beside him, seated in lotus position, studying Aran with a slight smile. In one hand he held a slender willow rod.

The Warlock was a tall man in robust good health. He was deeply tanned. Legend said that the Warlock never wore anything above the waist. The years seemed to blur on him; he might have been twenty or fifty. In fact he was one hundred and ninety years old, and bragged of it. His condition indicated the power of his magic.

Behind him, Aran saw that the Warlock's Wheel had been returned to its place on the wall.

Waiting for its next victim? The real Warlock's Wheel was of copper; those who had sent Aran had known that much. But this decoy must be tarnished silver, to have seared him so.

The Warlock wore a dreamy, absent look. There might still be a chance, if he could be taken by surprise. Aran said, "Kplir—"

The Warlock lashed him across the throat.

The willow wand had plenty of spring in it. Aran choked and gagged; he tossed his head, fighting for air.

"That word has four syllables," the Warlock informed him in a voice he recognized. "You'll never get it out."

"Gluck," said Aran.

"I want to know who sent you."

Aran did not answer, though he had his wind back.

"You're no ordinary thief. But you're no magician either," the Warlock said almost musingly. "I heard you. You were chanting by rote. You used basic spells, spells that are easy to get right, but they were the right spells each time.

"Somebody's been using prescience and farsight to spy on me. Someone knows too many of my defenses," the ancient magician said gently. "I don't like that. I want to know who, and why."

When Aran did not reply, the Warlock said, "He had all the knowledge, and he knew what he was after, but he had better sense than to come himself. He sent a fool." The Warlock was watching Aran's eyes. "Or perhaps he thought a werewolf would have a better chance at me. By the way, there's silver braid in those cords, so you'd best stay human for the nonce."

"You knew I was coming."

"Oh, I had ample warning. Didn't it occur to you that I've got prescience and farsight too? It occurred to your master," said the Warlock. "He set up protections around you, a moving region where prescience doesn't work."

"Then what went wrong?"

"I foresaw the dead region, you ninny. I couldn't get a glimpse of what was stealing into my cave. But I could look around it. I could follow its path through the cavern. That path was most direct. I knew what you were after.

"Then, there were bare footprints left behind. I could study them before they were made. You waited for moonrise instead of trying to get in after dusk. On a night of the full moon, too.

"Other than that, it wasn't a bad try. Sending a werewolf was bright. It would take a kid your size to squeeze between the bars, and then a kid your size couldn't win a fight if something went wrong. A wolf your size could."

"A lot of good it did me."

"What I want to know is, how did they talk an Atlantean into this? They must have known what they were after. Didn't they tell you what the Wheel does?"

"Sucks up magic," said Aran. He was chagrined, but not surprised, that the Warlock had placed his accent.

"Sucks up *mana*," the Warlock corrected him. "Do you know what *mana* is?"

"The power behind magic."

"So they taught you that much. Did they also tell you that when the *mana* is gone from a region, it doesn't come back? Ever?"

Aran rolled on his side. Being convinced that he was about to die, he felt he had nothing to lose by speaking boldly. "I don't understand why you'd want to keep it a secret. A thing like the Warlock's Wheel, it could make war obsolete! It's the greatest purely defensive weapon ever invented!"

The Warlock didn't seem to understand. Aran said, "You *must* have thought of that. Why, no enemy's curses could touch Atlantis, if the Warlock's Wheel were there to absorb it!"

"Obviously you weren't sent by the Atlantean Minister of Offense. He'd know better." The Warlock watched him shrewdly. "Or were you sent by the Greek Isles?"

"I don't understand."

"Don't you know that Atlantis is tectonically unstable? For the last half a thousand years, the only thing that's kept Atlantis above the waves has been the spells of the sorcerer-kings."

"You're lying."

"You obviously aren't." The Warlock made a gesture of dismissal. "But the Wheel would be bad for any nation, not just Atlantis. Spin the Wheel, and a wide area is dead to magic for—as far as I've been able to tell—the rest of eternity. Who would want to bring about such a thing?"

"I would."

"You would. Why?"

"We're sick of war," Aran said roughly. Unaware that he had said *we*. "The Warlock's Wheel would end war. Can you imagine an army trying to fight with nothing but swords and daggers? No hurling of death spells. No prescients spying out the enemy's battle plans. No killer demons beating at unseen protective walls."

Aran's eyes glowed. "Man to man, sword against sword, blood and bronze, and no healing spells. Why, no king would ever fight on such terms! We'd give up war forever!"

"Some basic pessimism deep within me forces me to doubt it."

"You're laughing at me. You don't *want* to believe it," Aran said scornfully. "No more *mana* means the end of your youth spells. You'd be an old man, too old to live!"

"That must be it. Well, let's see who you are." The Warlock touched Aran's wallet with the willow wand, let it rest there a few moments. Aran wondered frantically what the Warlock could learn from his wallet. If the lockspells didn't hold, then—

They didn't, of course. The Warlock reached in, pulled out another live bat, then several sheets of parchment marked with what might have been geometry lessons and with script printed in a large, precise hand.

"Schoolboy script," he commented. "Lines drawn with painful accuracy, mistakes scraped out and redrawn . . . The idiot! He forgot the hooked tail on the Whirlpool design. A wonder it didn't eat him." The Warlock looked up. "Am I being attacked by children? These spells were prepared by half a dozen apprentices!"

Aran didn't answer; but he lost hope of concealing anything further.

"They have talent, though. So. You're a member of the Peacemongers, aren't you? All the army-age youngsters. I'll wager you're backed by half the graduating class of the School of Mercantile Grammaree. They must have been watching me for months now, to have my defenses down so pat.

"And you want to end the war against the Greek Isles. Did you think you'd help matters by taking the Warlock's Wheel to Atlantis? Why, I'm half minded to let you walk out with the thing. It would serve you right for trying to rob me."

He looked hard into Aran's eyes. "Why, you'd do it, wouldn't you? Why? I said *why?*"

"We could still use it."

"You'd sink Atlantis. Are the Peacemongers traitors now?"

"I'm no traitor." Aran spoke low and furious. "We want to change Atlantis, not destroy it. But if we owned the Warlock's Wheel, the Palace would listen to us!"

He wriggled in his tight bonds, and thought once again of the word that would free him. Then, convert to werewolf and run! Between the bars, down the hill, into the woods and freedom.

"I think I'll make a conservative of you," the Warlock said suddenly.

He stood up. He brushed the willow wand lightly across Aran's lips. Aran found that he could not open his mouth. He remembered now that he was entirely in the Warlock's power— and that he was a captured thief.

The Warlock turned, and Aran saw the design on his back. It was an elaborately curlicued five-sided tattoo in red and green and gold inks. Aran remembered what he had been told of the Warlock's bodyguard.

"Recently I dreamed," said the Warlock. "I dreamed that I would find a use for a glass dagger. I thought that the dream might be prophetic, and so I carved—"

"That's silly," Aran broke in. "What good is a glass dagger?"

He had noticed the dagger on the way in. It had a honed square point and honed edges and a fused-looking hilt with a guard. Two clamps padded with fox leather held it in place on the work table. The uppermost cutting edge was not yet finished.

Now the Warlock removed the dagger from its clamps. While Aran watched, the Warlock scratched designs on the blade with a pointed chunk of diamond that must have cost him dearly. He spoke low and softly to it, words that Aran couldn't hear. Then he picked it up like—a dagger.

Frightened as he was, Aran could not quite believe what the Warlock was doing. He felt like a sacrificial goat. There was *mana* in sacrifice . . . and more *mana* in human sacrifice . . . but he wouldn't. He wouldn't!

The Warlock raised the knife high, and brought it down hard in Aran's chest.

Aran screamed. He had felt it! A whisper of sensation, a slight ghostly tug—the knife was an insubstantial shadow. But there was a knife in Aran the Peacemonger's heart! The hilt stood up out of his chest!

The Warlock muttered low and fast. The glass hilt faded and was gone, apparently.

"It's easy to make glass invisible. Glass is half invisible already. It's still in your heart," said the Warlock. "But don't worry about it. Don't give it a thought. Nobody will notice. Only, be sure to spend the rest of your life in *mana*-rich territory. Because if you ever walk into a place where magic doesn't work—well, it'll reappear, that's all."

Aran struggled to open his mouth.

"Now, you came for the secret of the Warlock's Wheel, so

you might as well have it. It's just a simple kinetic sorcery, but open-ended.'' He gave it. ''The Wheel spins faster and faster until it's used up all the *mana* in the area. It tends to tear itself apart, so you need another spell to hold it together—'' and he gave that, speaking slowly and distinctly. Then he seemed to notice that Aran was flopping about like a fish. He said, ''Kplirapranthry.''

The ropes fell away. Aran stood up shakily. He found he could speak again, and what he said was, ''Take it out. Please.''

''Now, there's one thing about taking that secret back to Atlantis. I assume you still want to? But you'd have to describe it before you could use it as a threat. You can see how easy it is to make. A big nation like Atlantis tends to have enemies, doesn't it? And you'd be telling them how to sink Atlantis in a single night.''

Aran pawed at his chest, but he could feel nothing. ''Take it out.''

''I don't think so. Now we face the same death, wolf boy. Goodby, and give my best to the School for Mercantile Grammaree. And, oh yes, don't go back by way of Hvirin Gap.''

''Grandson of an ape!'' Aran screamed. He would not beg again. He was wolf by the time he reached the bars, and he did not touch them going through. With his mind he felt the knife in his chest, and he heard the Warlock's laughter following him down the hill and into the trees.

When next he saw the Warlock, it was thirty years later and a thousand miles away.

II

Aran traveled as a wolf, when he could. It was an age of greater magic; a werewolf could change shape whenever the moon was in the sky. In the wolf shape Aran could forage, reserving his remaining coins to buy his way home.

His thoughts were a running curse against the Warlock.

Once he turned about on a small hill, and stood facing north toward Shayl Village. He bristled, remembering the Warlock's laugh; but he remembered the glass dagger. He visualized the Warlock's throat, and imagined the taste of arterial blood; but the glowing, twisting design on the Warlock's back flashed at the back of Aran's eyes, and Aran tasted defeat. He could not fight a shadow demon. Aran howled, once, and turned south.

Nildiss Range, the backbone of a continent, rose before him as
he traveled. Beyond the Range was the sea, and a choice of
boats to take him home with what he had learned of the Warlock.
Perhaps the next thief would have better luck . . .

And so he came to Hvirin Gap.

Once the range had been a formidable barrier to trade. Then,
almost a thousand years ago, a sorcerer of Rynildissen had
worked an impressive magic. The Range had been split as if by a
cleaver. Where the mountains to either side sloped precipitously
upward, Hvirin Gap sloped smoothly down to the coast, between
rock walls flat enough to have a polished look.

Periodically the bandits had to be cleaned out of Hvirin Gap.
This was more difficult every year; for the spells against banditry
didn't work well there, and swords had to be used instead. The
only compensation was that the dangerous mountain dragons had
disappeared too.

Aran stopped at the opening. He sat on his haunches,
considering.

For the Warlock might have been lying. He might have thought
it funny to send Aran the long way over Nildiss Range.

But the dragon bones. Where magic didn't work, dragons
died. The bones were there, huge and reptilian. They had fused
with the rock of the pass somehow, so that they looked tens of
millions of years old.

Aran had traveled the Gap in wolf form. If Hvirin Gap was
dead of magic, he should have been forced into the man form.
Or would he find it impossible to change at all?

"But I can go through as a wolf," Aran thought. "That way I
can't be killed by anything but silver and platinum. The glass
dagger should hurt, but—

"Damn! I'm invulnerable, but is it *magic?* If it doesn't work
in Hvirin Gap—" and he shuddered.

The dagger had never been more than a whisper of sensation,
that had faded in half an hour and never returned. But Aran
knew it was there. Invisible, a knife in his heart, waiting.

It might reappear in his chest, and he could still survive—as a
wolf. But it would hurt! And he could never be human again.

Aran turned and padded away from Hvirin Gap. He had passed
a village yesterday. Perhaps the resident magician could help
him.

"A glass dagger!" the magician chortled. He was a portly,
jolly, balding man, clearly used to good living. "Now I've heard

everything. Well, what were you worried about? It's got a handle, doesn't it? Was it a complex spell?''

"I don't think so. He wrote runes on the blade, then stabbed me with it.''

"Fine. You pay in advance. And you'd better convert to wolf, just to play safe.'' He named a sum that would have left Aran without money for passage home. Aran managed to argue him down to something not far above reason, and they went to work.

The magician gave up some six hours later. His voice was hoarse, his eyes were red from oddly colored, oddly scented smokes, and his hands were discolored with dyes. ''I can't touch the hilt, I can't make it visible, I can't get any sign that it's there at all. If I use any stronger spell, it's likely to kill you. I quit, wolf boy. Whoever put this spell on you, he knows more than a simple village magician.''

Aran rubbed his chest where the skin was stained by mildly corrosive dyes. ''They call him the Warlock.''

The portly magician stiffened. ''The Warlock? *The* Warlock? And you didn't think to tell me. Get out.''

"What about my money?''

"I wouldn't have tried it for ten times the fee! Me, a mere hedge-magician, and you turned me loose against the Warlock! We might both have been killed. If you think you're entitled to your money, let's go to the headman and state our case. Otherwise, get out.''

Aran left, shouting insults.

"Try other magicians if you like,'' the other shouted after him. ''Try Rynildissen City! But tell them what they're doing first!''

III

It had been a difficult decision for the Warlock. But his secret was out and spreading. The best he could do was see to it that world sorcery understood the implications.

The Warlock addressed the Sorcerers' Guild on the subject of *mana* depletion and the Warlock's Wheel.

"Think of it every time you work magic,'' he thundered in what amounted to baby talk after his severely technical description of the Wheel. ''Only finite *mana* in the world, and less of it every year, as a thousand magicians drain it away. There were beings who ruled the world as gods, long ago, until the raging power of their own being used up the *mana* that kept them alive.

"One day it'll all be gone. Then all the demons and dragons and unicorns, trolls and rocs and centaurs will vanish quite away, because their metabolism is partly based on magic. Then all the dream-castles will evaporate, and nobody will ever know they were there. Then all the magicians will become tinkers and smiths, and the world will be a dull place to live. You have the power to bring that day nearer!"

That night he dreamed.

A duel between magicians makes a fascinating tale. Such tales are common—and rarely true. The winner of such a duel is not likely to give up trade secrets. The loser is dead, at the very least.

Novices in sorcery are constantly amazed at how much preparation goes into a duel, and how little action. The duel with the Hill Magician started with a dream, the night after the Warlock's speech made that duel inevitable. It ended thirty years later.

In that dream the enemy did not appear. But the Warlock saw a cheerful, harmless-looking fairy castle perched on an impossible hill. From a fertile, hummocky landscape, the hill rose like a breaking wave, leaning so far that the castle at its crest had empty space below it.

In his sleep the Warlock frowned. Such a hill would topple without magic. The fool who built it was wasting *mana*.

And in his sleep he concentrated, memorizing details. A narrow path curled up the hillside. Facts twisted, dreamlike. There was a companion with him; or there wasn't. The Warlock lived until he passed through the gate; or he died at the gate, in agony, with great ivory teeth grinding together through his rib cage.

He woke himself up trying to sort it out.

The shadowy companion was necessary, at least as far as the gate. Beyond the enemy's gate he could see nothing. A Warlock's Wheel must have been used there, to block his magic so thoroughly.

Poetic justice?

He spent three full days working spells to block the Hill Magician's prescient sense. During that time his own sleep was dreamless. The other's magic was as effective as his own.

IV

Great ships floated at anchor in the harbor.

There were cargo ships whose strange demonic figureheads had limited power of movement, just enough to reach the rats that tried to swarm up the mooring lines. A large Atlantean passenger liner was equipped with twin outriggers made from whole tree trunks. By the nearest dock a magician's slender yacht floated eerily above the water. Aran watched them all rather wistfully.

He had spent too much money traveling over the mountains. A week after his arrival in Rynildissen City he had taken a post as bodyguard/watchdog to a rug merchant. He had been down to his last coin, and hungry.

Now Lloraginezee the rug merchant and Ra-Harroo his secretary talked trade secrets with the captain of a Nile cargo ship. Aran waited on the dock, watching ships with indifferent patience.

His ears came to point. The bearded man walking past him wore a captain's kilt. Aran hailed him: "Ho, Captain! Are you sailing to Atlantis?"

The bearded man frowned. "And what's that to you?"

"I would send a message there."

"Deal with a magician."

"I'd rather not," said Aran. He could hardly tell a magician that he wanted to send instructions on how to rob a magician. Otherwise the message would have gone months ago.

"I'll charge you more, and it will take longer," the bearded man said with some satisfaction. "Who in Atlantis, and where?"

Aran gave him an address in the city. He passed over the sealed message pouch he had been carrying for three months now.

Aran too had made some difficult decisions. In final draft his message warned of the tectonic instability of the continent, and suggested steps the Peacemongers could take to learn if the Warlock had lied. Aran had not included instructions for making a Warlock's Wheel.

Far out in the harbor, dolphins and mermen played rough and complicated games. The Atlantean craft hoisted sail. A wind rose from nowhere to fill the sails. It died slowly, following the passenger craft out to sea.

Soon enough, Aran would have the fare. He would almost have it now, except that he had twice paid out sorcerer's fees, with the result that the money was gone and the glass dagger was not. Meanwhile, Lloraginezee did not give trade secrets to his bodyguard. He knew that Aran would be on his way as soon as he had the money.

Here they came down the gangplank: Lloraginezee with less waddle than might be expected of a man of his girth; the girl walking with quiet grace, balancing the rug samples on her head. Ra-Harroo was saying something as Aran joined them, something Aran may have been intended to hear.

"Beginning tomorrow, I'll be off work for five days. *You* know," she told Lloraginezee—and blushed.

"Fine, fine," said Lloraginezee, nodding absently.

Aran knew too. He smiled but did not look at her. He might embarrass her . . . and he knew well enough what Ra-Harroo looked like. Her hair was black and short and coarse. Her nose was large but flat, almost merging into her face. Her eyes were brown and soft, her brows dark and thick. Her ears were delicately formed and convoluted, and came to a point. She was a lovely girl, especially to another of the wolf people.

They held hands as they walked. Her nails were narrow and strong, and the fine hair on her palm tickled.

In Atlantis he would have considered marrying her, had he the money to support her. Here, it was out of the question. For most of the month they were friends and co-workers. The night life of Rynildissen City was more convenient for a couple, and there were times when Lloraginezee could spare them both.

Perhaps Lloraginezee made such occasions. He was not of the wolf people. He probably enjoyed thinking that sex had reared its lovely, disturbing head. But sex could not be involved—except at a certain time of the month. Aran didn't see her then. She was locked up in her father's house. He didn't even know where she lived.

He found out five nights later.

He had guarded Lloraginezee's way to Adrienne's House of Pleasures. Lloraginezee would spend the night . . . on an air mattress floating on mercury, a bed Aran had only heard described. A pleasant sleep was not the least of pleasures.

The night was warm and balmy. Aran took a long way home, walking wide of the vacant lot behind Adrienne's. That broad, flat plot of ground had housed the palace of Shilbree the Dreamer, three hundred years ago. The palace had been all magic, and quite an achievement even in its day. Eventually it had . . . worn out, Shilbree would have said.

One day it was gone. And not even the simplest of spells would work in that vacant lot.

Someone had told Aran that households of wolf people occupied several blocks of the residential district. It seemed to be true, for he caught identifying smells as he crossed certain paths.

He followed one, curious to see what kind of house a wealthy
werewolf would build in Rynildissen.

The elusive scent led him past a high, angular house with a
brass door . . . and then it was too late, for another scent was in
his nostrils and in his blood and brain. He spent that whole night
howling at the door. Nobody tried to stop him. The neighbors
must have been used to it; or they may have known that he
would kill rather than be driven away.

More than once he heard a yearning voice answering from
high up in the house. It was Ra-Harroo's voice. With what
remained of his mind, Aran knew that he would be finding
apologies in a few days. She would think he had come deliberately

Aran howled a song of sadness and deprivation and shame.

V

The first was a small village called Gath, and a Guild 'prentice
who came seeking black opals. He found them, and free for the
taking too, for Gath was dead empty. The 'prentice sorcerer
wondered about that, and he looked about him, and presently he
found a dead spot with a crumbled castle in it. It might have
been centuries fallen. Or it might have been raised by magic, and
collapsed when the *mana* went out of it, yesterday or last week.

It was a queer tale, and it got around. The 'prentice grew rich
on the opals, for black opals are very useful for cursing. But the
empty village bothered him.

"I thought it was slavers at first," he said once, in the
Warlock's hearing as it turned out. "There were no corpses,
none anywhere. Slave traders don't kill if they can help it.

"But why would a troop of slavers leave valuables lying
where they were? The opals were all over the street, mixed with
hay. I think a jeweler must have been moving them in secret
when—*something* smashed his wagon. But why didn't they pick
up the jewels?"

It was the crumbled castle the Warlock remembered three
years later, when he heard about Shiskabil. He heard of that one
directly, from a magpie that fluttered out of the sky onto his
shoulder and whispered, "Warlock?"

And when he had heard, he went.

Shiskabil was a village of stone houses within a stone wall. It
must have been abandoned suddenly. Dinners had dried or rotted
on their plates; meat had been burnt to ash in ovens. There were
no living inhabitants, and no dead. The wall had not been

breeched. But there were signs of violence everywhere: broken furniture, doors with broken locks or splintered hinges, crusted spears and swords and makeshift clubs, and blood. Dried black blood everywhere, as if it had rained blood.

Clubfoot was a younger Guild member, thin and earnest. Though talented, he was still a little afraid of the power he commanded through magic. He was not happy in Shiskabil. He walked with shoulders hunched, trying to avoid the places where blood had pooled.

"Weird, isn't it? But I had a special reason to send for you," he said. "There's a dead region outside the wall. I had the idea someone might have used a Warlock's Wheel there."

A rectangular plot of fertile ground, utterly dead, a foretaste of a world dead to magic. In the center were crumbled stones with green plants growing between.

The Warlock circled the place, unwilling to step where magic did not work. He had used the Wheel once before, against Glirendree, after the demon-sword had killed his shadow demon. The Wheel had sucked the youth from him, left the Warlock two hundred years old in a few seconds.

"There was magic worked in the village," said Clubfoot. "I tried a few simple spells. The *mana* level's very low. I don't remember any famous sorcerers from Shiskabil; do you?"

"No."

"Then whatever happened here was done by magic." Clubfoot almost whispered the word. Magic could be very evil—as he knew.

They found a zigzag path through the dead borderline, and a faintly live region inside. At a gesture from the Warlock, the crumbled stones stirred feebly, trying to rise.

"So it was somebody's castle," said Clubfoot. "I wonder how he got this effect?"

"I thought of something like it once. Say you put a heavy kinetic spell on a smaller Wheel. The Wheel would spin very fast, would use up mana in a very tight area—"

Clubfoot was nodding. "I see it. He could have run it on a track, a close path. It would give him a kind of hedge against magic around a live region."

"And he left the border open so he could get his tools in and out. He zigzagged the entrance so no spells could get through. Nobody could use farsight on him. I wonder . . ."

"I wonder what he had to hide?"

"I wonder what happened in Shiskabil," said the Warlock.

And he remembered the dead barrier that hid the Hill Magician's castle. His leisurely duel with a faceless enemy was twelve years old.

It was twenty-three years old before they found the third village.

Hathzoril was bigger than Shiskabil, and better known. When a shipment of carvings in ivory and gem woods did not arrive, the Warlock heard of it.

The village could not have been abandoned more than a few days when the Warlock arrived. He and Clubfoot found meals half cooked, meals half eaten, broken furniture, weapons that had been taken from their racks, broken doors—

"But no blood. I wonder why?"

Clubfoot was jittery. "Otherwise it's just the same. The whole population gone in an instant, probably against their will. Ten whole years; no, more. I'd half forgotten . . . You got here before I did. Did you find a dead area and a crumbled castle?"

"No. I looked."

The younger magician rubbed his birth-maimed foot—which he could have cured in half an hour, but it would have robbed him of half his powers. "We could be wrong. If it's him, he's changed his techniques."

That night the Warlock dreamed a scrambled dream in pyrotechnic colors. He woke thinking of the Hill Magician.

"Let's climb some hills," he told Clubfoot in the morning. "I've got to know if the Hill Magician has something to do with these empty villages. We're looking for a dead spot on top of a hill."

That mistake almost killed him.

The last hill Clubfoot tried to climb was tumbled, crumbled soil and rock that slid and rolled under his feet. He tried it near sunset, in sheer desperation, for they had run out of hills and patience.

He was still near the base when the Warlock came clambering to join him. "Come down from there!" he laughed. "Nobody would build on this sand heap."

Clubfoot looked around, and shouted, "Get out of here! You're older!"

The Warlock rubbed his face and felt the wrinkles. He picked his way back in haste and in care, wanting to hurry, but fearful of breaking fragile bones. He left a trail of fallen silver hair.

Once beyond the *mana*-poor region, he cackled in falsetto.

"My mistake. I know what he did now. Clubfoot, we'll find the dead spot inside the hill."

"First we'll work you a rejuvenation spell." Clubfoot laid his tools out on a rock. A charcoal block, a silver knife, packets of leaves . . .

"That border's bad. It sucks up *mana* from inside. He must have to move pretty often. So he raised up a hill like a breaking wave. When the magic ran out the hill just rolled over the castle and covered up everything. He'll do it again, too."

"Clever. What do you think happened in Hathzoril Village?"

"We may never know." The Warlock rubbed new wrinkles at the corners of his eyes. "Something bad, I think. Something very bad."

VI

He was strolling through the merchants' quarter that afternoon, looking at rugs.

Normally this was a cheerful task. Hanging rugs formed a brightly colored maze through this part of the quarter. As Aran the rug merchant moved through the maze, well-known voices would call his name. Then there would be gossip and canny trading.

He had traded in Rynildissen City for nearly thirty years, first as Lloraginezee's apprentice, later as his own man. The finest rugs and the cheapest, from all over this continent and nearby islands, came by ship and camel's back to Rynildissen City. Wholesalers, retailers, and the odd nobleman who wished to furnish a palace would travel to Rynildissen City to buy. Today they glowed in the hot sunlight . . . but today they only depressed him. Aran was thinking of moving away.

A bald man stepped into view from behind a block of cured sphinx pelts.

Bald as a roc's egg he was, yet young, and in the prime of muscular good health. He was shirtless like a stevedore, but his pantaloons were of high quality and his walk was pure arrogance. Aran felt he was staring rather rudely. Yet there was something familiar about the man.

He passed Aran without a glance.

Aran glanced back once, and was jolted. The design seemed to leap out at him: a five-sided multicolored tattoo on the man's back.

Aran called, "Warlock!"

Larry Niven

He regretted it the next moment. The Warlock turned on him the look one gives a presumptuous stranger.

The Warlock had not changed at all, except for the loss of his hair. But Aran remembered that thirty years had passed; that he himself was a man of fifty, with the hollows of his face filled out by rich living. He remembered that his greying hair had receded, leaving his widow's peak as a shock of hair all alone on his forehead. And he remembered, in great detail, the circumstances under which he had met the Warlock.

He had spent a thousand nights plotting vengeance against the Warlock; yet now his only thought was to get away. He said, "Your pardon, sir—"

But something else occurred to him, so that he said firmly, "But we *have* met."

"Under what circumstance? I do not recall it," the Warlock said coldly.

Aran's answer was a measure of the self-confidence that comes with wealth and respect. He said, "I was robbing your cave."

"Were you!" The Warlock came closer. "Ah, the boy from Atlantis. Have you robbed any magicians lately?"

"I have adopted a somewhat safer way of life," Aran said equably. "And I do have reason for presuming on our brief acquaintance."

"Our brief—" The Warlock laughed so that heads turned all over the marketplace. Still laughing, he took Aran's arm and led him away.

They strolled slowly through the merchants' quarter, the Warlock leading. "I have to follow a certain path," he explained. "A project of my own. Well, my boy, what have you been doing for thirty years?"

"Trying to get rid of your glass dagger."

"Glass dagger? . . . Oh, yes, I remember. Surely you found time for other hobbies?"

Aran almost struck the Warlock then. But there was something he wanted from the Warlock; and so he held his temper.

"My whole life has been warped by your damned glass dagger," he said. "I had to circle Hvirin Gap on my way home. When I finally got here I was out of money. No money for passage to Atlantis, and no money to pay for a magician, which meant that I couldn't get the glass knife removed.

"So I hired out to Lloraginezee the rug merchant as a bodyguard/watchdog. Now I'm the leading rug merchant in

Rynildissen City, I've got two wives and eight children and a few grandchildren, and I don't suppose I'll ever get back to Atlantis."

They bought wine from a peddler carrying two fat wineskins on his shoulders. They took turns drinking from the great copper goblet the man carried.

The Warlock asked, "Did you ever get rid of the knife?"

"No, and you ought to know it! What kind of a spell did you *put* on that thing? The best magicians in this continent haven't been able to so much as *touch* that knife, let alone pull it out. I wouldn't be a rug merchant if they had."

"Why not?"

"Well, I'd have earned my passage to Atlantis soon enough, except that every time I heard about a new magician in the vicinity I'd go to him to see if he could take that knife out. Selling rugs was a way to get the money to pay the magicians. Eventually I gave up on the magicians and kept the money. All I'd accomplished was to spread your reputation in all directions."

"Thank you," the Warlock said politely.

Aran did not like the Warlock's amusement. He decided to end the conversation quickly. "I'm glad we ran into each other," he said, "because I have a problem that is really in your province. Can you tell me something about a magician named Wavyhill?"

It may be that the Warlock stiffened. "What is it that you want to know?"

"Whether his spells use excessive power."

The Warlock lifted an interrogatory eyebrow.

"You see, we try to restrict the use of magic in Rynildissen City. The whole nation could suffer if a key region like Rynildissen City went dead to magic. There'd be no way to stop a flood, or a hurricane, or an invasion of barbarians. Do you find something amusing?"

"No, no. But could a glass dagger possibly have anything to do with your conservative attitude?"

"That's entirely my own business, Warlock. Unless you'd care to read my mind?"

"No, thank you. My apologies."

"I'd like to point out that more than just the welfare of Rynildissen City is involved. If this region went dead to magic, the harbor mermen would have to move away. They have quite an extensive city of their own, down there beyond the docks. Furthermore, they run most of the docking facilities and the *entire* fishing industry—"

"Relax. I agree with you completely. You know that," the magician laughed. "You ought to!"

"Sorry. I preach at the drop of a hat. It's been ten years since anyone saw a dragon near Rynildissen City. Even further out, they're warped, changed. When I first came here the dragons had a mercenary's booth in the city itself! What are you doing?"

The Warlock had handed the empty goblet back to the vendor and was pulling at Aran's arm. "Come this way, please. Quickly, before I lose the path."

"Path?"

"I'm following a fogged prescient vision. I could get killed if I lose the path—or if I don't, for that matter. Now, just what was your problem?"

"That," said Aran, pointing among the fruit stalls.

The troll was an ape's head on a human body, covered from head to toe in coarse brown hair. From its size it was probably female, but it had no more breasts than a female ape. It held a wicker basket in one quite human hand. Its bright brown eyes glanced up at Aran's pointing finger—startlingly human eyes— then dropped to the melon it was considering.

Perhaps the sight should have roused reverence. A troll was ancestral to humanity: *Homo habilis*, long extinct. But they were too common. Millions of the species had been fossilized in the drylands of Africa. Magicians of a few centuries ago had learned that they could be reconstituted by magic.

"I think you've just solved one of my own problems," the Warlock said quietly. He no longer showed any trace of amusement.

"Wonderful," Aran said without sincerity. "My own problem is, how much *mana* are Wavyhill's trolls using up? The *mana* level in Rynildissen City was never high to start with. Wavyhill must be using terrifically powerful spells just to keep them walking." Aran's fingertips brushed his chest in an unconscious gesture. "I'd hate to leave Rynildissen City, but if magic stops working here I won't have any choice."

"I'd have to know the spells involved. Tell me something about Wavyhill, will you? Everything you can remember."

To most of Rynildissen City the advent of Wavyhill the magician was very welcome.

Once upon a time troll servants had been common. They were terrifically strong. Suffering no pain, they could use hysterical strength for the most mundane tasks. Being inhuman, they could work on official holidays. They needed no sleep. They did not steal.

But Rynildissen City was old, and the *mana* was running low. For many years no troll had walked in Rynildissen City. At the gate they turned to blowing dust.

Then came Wavyhill with a seemingly endless supply of trolls, which did *not* disintegrate at the gate. The people paid him high prices in gold and in honors.

"For half a century thieves have worked freely on holidays," Aran told the Warlock. "Now we've got a trollish police force again. Can you blame people for being grateful? They made him a Councilman—over my objections. Which means that there's very little short of murder that Wavyhill can't do in Rynildissen City."

"I'm sorry to hear that. Why did you say *over your objections?* Are you on the Council?"

"Yes. I'm the one who rammed through the laws restricting magic in Rynildissen City. And failed to ram through some others, I might add. The trouble is that Wavyhill doesn't make the trolls in the city. Nobody knows where they come from. If he's depleting the *mana* level, he's doing it somewhere else."

"Then what's your problem?"

"Suppose the trolls use up *mana* just by existing? . . . I should be asking, *do they?*"

"I think so," said the Warlock.

"I *knew* it. Warlock, will you testify before the Council? Because—"

"No, I won't."

"But you've got to! I'll never convince anyone by myself. Wavyhill is the most respected magician around, and he'll be testifying against me! Besides which, the Council all own trolls themselves. They won't want to believe they've been suckered, and they have been if we're right. The trolls will collapse as soon as they've lowered the *mana* level enough."

At that point Aran ran down, for he had seen with what stony patience the Warlock was waiting for him to finish.

The Warlock waited three seconds longer, using silence as an exclamation point. Then he said, "It's gone beyond that. Talking to the Council would be like shouting obscenities at a forest fire. I could get results that way. You couldn't."

"Is he *that* dangerous?"

"I think so."

Aran wondered if he was being had. But the Warlock's face

was so grave . . . and Aran had seen that face in too many
nightmares. *What am I doing here?* he wondered. *I had a
technical question about trolls. So I asked a magician . . . and
now . . .*

"Keep talking. I need to know more about Wavyhill. And
walk faster," said the Warlock. "How long has he been here?"

"Wavyhill came to Rynildissen City seven years ago. Nobody
knows where he came from; he doesn't have any particular
accent. His palace sits on a hill that looks like it's about to fall
over. What are you nodding at?"

"I know that hill. Keep talking."

"We don't see him often. He comes with a troupe of trolls, to
sell them; or he comes to vote with the Council on important
matters. He's short and dark—."

"That could be a seeming. Never mind, describe him anyway.
I've never seen him."

"Short and dark, with a pointed nose and a pointed chin and
very curly dark hair. He wears a dark robe of some soft material,
a tall pointed hat, and sandals, and he carries a sword."

"Does he!" The Warlock laughed out loud.

"What's the joke? I carry a sword myself sometimes.—Oh,
that's right, magicians have a *thing* about swordsmen."

"That's not why I laughed. It's a trade joke. A sword can be a
symbol of masculine virility."

"Oh?"

"You see the point, don't you? A sorcerer doesn't need a
sword. He knows more powerful protections. When a sorcerer
takes to carrying a sword, it's pretty plain he's using it as a cure
for impotence."

"And it works?"

"Of course it works. It's straight one-for-one similarity magic,
isn't it? But you've got to take the sword to bed with you!"
laughed the Warlock. But his eyes found a troll servant, and his
laughter slipped oddly.

He watched as the troll hurried through a gate in a high white
wall. They had passed out of the merchants' quarter.

"I think Wavyhill's a necromancer," he said abruptly.

"Necromancer. What is it? It sounds ugly."

"A technical term for a new branch of magic. And it is ugly.
Turn sharp left here."

They ducked into a narrow alley. Two- and three-story houses
leaned over them from both sides. The floor of the alley was

filthy, until the Warlock snarled and gestured. Then the dirt and garbage flowed to both sides.

The Warlock hurried them deep into the alley. "We can stop here, I think. Sit down if you like. We'll be here for some time—or I will."

"Warlock, are you playing games with me? What does this new dance have to do with a duel of sorcery?"

"A fair question. Do you know what lies that way?"

Aran's sense of direction was good, and he knew the city. "The Judging Place?"

"Right. And that way, the vacant lot just this side of Adrienne's House of Pleasures—you know it? The deadest spot in Rynildissen City. The palace of Shilbree the Dreamer once stood there."

"*Might* I ask—"

"The courthouse is void of *mana* too, naturally. Ten thousand defendants and thirty thousand lawyers all praying for conviction or acquittal doesn't leave much magic in *any* courthouse. If I can keep either of those spots between me and Wavyhill, I can keep him from using farsight on me."

Aran thought about it. "But you have to know where he is."

"No. I only have to know where I ought to be. Most of the time, I don't. Wavyhill and I have managed to fog each other's prescient senses pretty well. But I'm supposed to be meeting an unknown ally along about now, and I've taken great care that Wavyhill can't spy on me.

"You see, I invented the Wheel. Wavyhill has taken the Wheel concept and improved it in at least two ways that I know of. Naturally he uses up *mana* at a ferocious rate.

"He may also be a mass murderer. And he's my fault. That's why I've got to kill him."

Aran remembered then that his wives were waiting dinner. He remembered that he had decided to end this conversation hours ago. And he remembered a story he had been told, of a layman caught in a sorcerer's duel, and what had befallen him.

"Well, I've got to be going," he said, standing up. "I wish you the best of luck in your duel, Warlock. And if there's anything I can do to help . . ."

"Fight with me," the Warlock said instantly.

Aran gaped. Then he burst out laughing.

The Warlock waited with his own abnormal patience. When he had some chance of being heard, he said, "I dreamed that an ally would meet me during this time. That ally would accompany me to the gate of Wavyhill's castle. I don't have many of those dreams to help me, Aran. Wavyhill's good. If I go alone, my forecast is that I'll be killed.''

"Another ally," Aran suggested.

"No. Too late. The time has passed."

"Look." Aran slapped his belly with the flat of his hand. The flesh rippled. "It's not that much extra weight," he said, "for a man. I'm not *unsightly*. But as a wolf I'd look ten years pregnant! I haven't turned wolf in years.

"What am I doing? I don't have to convince you of anything," Aran said abruptly. And he walked away fast.

The Warlock caught him up at the mouth of the alley. "I swear you won't regret staying. There's something you don't know yet."

"Don't follow me too far, Warlock. You'll lose your path." Aran laughed in the magician's face. "Why should I fight by your side? If you really need me to win, I couldn't be more delighted! I've seen your face in a thousand nightmares, you and your glass dagger! So die, Warlock. It's my dinner time."

"Shh," said the Warlock. And Aran saw that the Warlock was not looking at him, but over his shoulder.

Aran felt the urge to murder. But his eyes flicked to follow the Warlock's gaze, and the imprecations died in his throat.

It was a troll. Only a troll, a male, with a tremendous pack on its back. Coming toward them.

And the Warlock was gesturing to it. Or were those magical passes?

"Good," he said. "Now, I could tell you that it's futile to fight fate, and you might even believe me, because I'm an expert. But I'd be lying. Or I could offer you a chance to get rid of the dagger—"

"Go to Hell. I learned to live with that dagger—"

"Wolf man, if you never learn anything else from me, learn never to blaspheme in the presence of a magician! Excuse me." The troll had walked straight to the mouth of the alley. Now the Warlock took it by the arm and led it inside. "Will you help me? I want to get the pack off its back."

They lifted it down, while Aran wondered at himself. Had he been bewitched into obedience? The pack was very heavy. It took all of Aran's strength, even though the Warlock bore the brunt of the load. The troll watched them with blank brown eyes.

"Good. If I tried this anywhere else in the city, Wavyhill would know it. But this time I know where he is. He's in

Adrienne's House of Pleasures, searching for me, the fool! He's already searched the courthouse.

"Never mind that. Do you know of a village named Gath?"

"No."

"Or Shiskabil?"

"No. Wait." A Shiska had bought six matching green rugs from him once. "Yes. A small village north of here. Something . . . happened to it . . ."

"The population walked out one night, leaving all their valuables and a good deal of unexplained blood."

"That's right." Aran felt sudden horrible doubt. "It was never explained."

"Gath was first. Then Shiskabil, then Hathzoril. Bigger cities each time. At Hathzoril he was clever. He found a way to hide where his palace had been, and he didn't leave any blood."

"But what does he *do?* Where do the people go?"

"What do you know about *mana*, Aran? You know that it's the power behind magic, and you know it can be used up. What else?"

"I'm not a magician. I sell rugs."

"*Mana* can be used for good or evil; it can be drained, or transferred from one object to another, or from one man to another. Some men seem to carry *mana* with them. You can find concentrations in oddly shaped stones, or in objects of reverence, or in meteoroids.

"There is much *mana* associated with murder," said the Warlock. "Too much for safety, in my day. My teacher used to warn us against working near the site of a murder, or the corpse of a murdered man, or murder weapons—as opposed to weapons of war, I might add. War and murder are different in intent.

"Necromancy uses murder as a source of magic. It's the most powerful form of magic—so powerful that it could never have developed until now, when the *mana* level everywhere in the world is so low.

"I think Wavyhill is a necromancer," said the Warlock. And he turned to the troll. "We'll know in a moment."

The troll stood passive, its long arms relaxed at its sides, watching the Warlock with strangely human brown eyes and with a human dignity that contrasted oddly with its low animal brow and hairy body. It did not flinch as the Warlock dropped a kind of necklace over its head.

The change came instantly. Aran backed away, sucking air. The Warlock's necklace hung around a man's neck—a man in his middle thirties, blond-haired and bearded, wearing a porter's kilt—and that man's belly had been cut wide open by one clean swing of a sword or scimitar. Aran caught the smell of him: he had been dead for three or four days, plus whatever time the preserving effects of magic had been at work on him. Yet he stood, passively waiting, and his expression had not changed.

"Wavyhill has invented a kind of perpetual motion," the Warlock said dryly; but he backed away hastily from the smell of the dead man. "There's enough power in a murdered man to make him an obedient slave, and plenty left over to cast on him the seeming of a troll. He takes more *mana* from the environment, but what of that? When the *mana* runs out in Gath, Wavyhill's trolls kill their masters. Then twice as many trolls move on to Shiskabil. In Hathzoril they probably used strangling cords; they wouldn't spill any blood that way, and they wouldn't bleed themselves. I wonder where he'll go after Rynildissen?"

"Nowhere! We'll tell the Council!"

"And Wavyhill a Councilman? No. And you can't spread the word to individual members, because eventually one of them would tip Wavyhill that you're slandering him."

"They'd believe *you.*"

"All it takes is one who doesn't. Then he tells Wavyhill, and Wavyhill turns loose the trolls. No. You'll do three things," said the Warlock in tones not of command but of prophecy. "You'll go home. You'll spend the next week getting your wives and children out of Rynildissen City."

"My gods, yes!"

"I swore you wouldn't regret hearing me out. The third thing, if you so decide, is to join me at dawn, at the north gate, a week from today. Come by way of Adrienne's House of Pleasures," the Warlock ordered, "and stay awhile. The dead area will break your trail.

"Do that today, too. I don't want Wavyhill to follow you by prescience. Go *now*," said the Warlock.

"I can't decide!"

"Take a week."

"I may not be here. How can I contact you?"

"You can't. It doesn't matter. I'll go with you or without you." Abruptly the Warlock stripped the necklace from the neck of the standing corpse, turned and strode off down the alley. Following the path.

The dead man was a troll again. It followed Aran with large, disturbingly human brown eyes.

VII

That predawn morning, Adrienne's House of Pleasures was wrapped in thick black fog. Aran the rug merchant hesitated at the door; then, shivering, squared his shoulders and walked out into it.

He walked with his sword ready for tapping or killing. The fog grew lighter as he went, but no less dense. Several times he thought he saw monstrous vague shapes pacing him. But there was no attack. At dawn he was at the north gate.

The Warlock's mounts were either lizards enlarged by magic or dragons mutated by no magic. They were freaks, big as twin bungalows. One carried baggage; the other, two saddles in tandem.

"Mount up," the Warlock urged. "We want to get there before nightfall." Despite the chill of morning he was bare to the waist. He turned in his saddle as Aran settled behind him. "Have you lost weight?"

"I fasted for six days, and exercised too. And my wives and children are four days on their way to Atlantis by sea. You can guess what pleasures I chose at Adrienne's."

"I wouldn't have believed it. Your belly's as flat as a board."

"A wolf can fast for a long time. I ate an unbelievable meal last night. Today I won't eat at all."

The fog cleared as they left Rynildissen, and the morning turned clear and bright and hot. When Aran mentioned it, the Warlock said, "That fog was mine. I wanted to blur things for Wavyhill."

"I thought I saw shapes in the fog. Were those yours too?"

"No."

"Thanks."

"Wavyhill meant to frighten you, Aran. He wouldn't attack you. He *knows* you won't be killed before we reach the gate."

"That explains the pack lizards. I wondered how you could possibly expect to sneak up on him."

"I don't. He knows we're coming. He's waiting."

The land was rich in magic near Wavyhill's castle. You could tell by the vegetation: giant mushrooms, vying for variety of shape and color; lichens growing in the shapes of men or beasts; trees with contorted trunks and branches, trees that moved menacingly as the pack-lizards came near.

"I could make them talk," said the Warlock. "But I couldn't trust them. They'll be Wavyhill's allies."

In the red light of sunset, Wavyhill's castle seemed all rose marble, perched at the top of a fairy mountain. The slender tower seemed made for kidnapped damsels. The mountain itself, as Aran saw it now for the first time, was less a breaking wave than a fist raised to the sky in defiance.

"We couldn't use the Wheel here," said the Warlock. "The whole mountain would fall on us."

"I wouldn't have let you use the Wheel."

"I didn't bring one."

"Which way?"

"Up the path. He knows we're coming."

"Is your shadow demon ready?"

"Shadow demon?" The Warlock seemed to think. "Oh. For a moment I didn't know what you were talking about. That shadow demon was killed in the battle with Glirendree, thirty years ago."

Words caught in Aran's throat, then broke loose in a snarl. *"Then why don't you put on a shirt?"*

"Habit. I've got lots of strange habits. Why so vehement?"

"I don't know. I've been staring at your back since morning. I guess I was counting on the shadow demon." Aran swallowed. "It's just us, then?"

"Just us."

"Aren't you even going to take a sword? Or a dagger?"

"No. Shall we go?"

The other side of the hill was a sixty degree slope. The narrow, meandering path could not support the lizard beasts. Aran and the Warlock dismounted and began to climb.

The Warlock said, "There's no point in subtlety. We know we'll get as far as the gate. So does Wavyhill . . . excuse me." He threw a handful of silver dust ahead of them. "The road was about to throw us off. Apparently Wavyhill doesn't take anything for granted."

But Aran had only the Warlock's word for it; and that was the only danger that threatened their climb.

There was a rectangular pond blocking the solid copper gates. An arched bridge led across the pond. They were approaching the bridge when their first challenger pushed between the gates.

"What is it?" Aran whispered. "I've never *heard* of anything like it."

"There isn't. It's a changed one. Call it a snail dragon . . ."

. . . A snail dragon. Its spiral shell was just wide enough to block the gate completely. Its slender, supple body was fully exposed, reared high to study the intruders. Shiny leaflike scales covered the head and neck; but the rest of the body was naked, a soft greyish-brown. Its eyes were like black marbles. Its teeth were white and pointed, and the longest pair had been polished to a liquid glow.

From the other side of the small arched bridge, the Warlock called, "Ho, guardian! Were you told of our coming?"

"No," said the dragon. "Were you welcome, I would have been told."

"Welcome!" The Warlock guffawed. "We came to kill your master. Now, the interesting thing is that he knows of our coming. Why did he not warn you?"

The snail dragon tilted its mailed head.

The Warlock answered himself. "He knows that we will pass this gate. He suspects that we must pass over your dead body. He chose not to tell you so."

"That was kind of him." The dragon's voice was low and very gravelly, a sound like rocks being crushed.

"Kind, yes. But since we are foredoomed to pass, why not step aside? Or make for the hills, and we will keep your secret."

"It cannot be."

"You're a changed one, snail dragon. Beasts whose energy of life is partly magical, breed oddly where the *mana* is low. Most changed ones are not viable. So it is with you," said the Warlock. "The shell could not protect you from a determined and patient enemy. Or were you counting on speed to save you?"

"You raise a salient point," said the guardian. "If I were to leave now, what then? My master will very probably kill you when you reach his sanctum. Then, by and by, this week or the next, he will wonder how you came to pass his guardian. Then, next week or the week following, he will come to see, or to remove the discarded shell. By then, with luck and a good tail wind, I could be halfway to the woods. Perchance he will miss me in the tall grass," said the bungalow-sized beast. "No. Better to take my chances here in the gate. At least I know the direction of attack."

"Damn, you're right," said the Warlock. "My sympathies, snail dragon."

And he set about fixing the bridge into solidity. Half of it, the half on the side away from the gate, really was solid. The other half was a reflected illusion, until the Warlock—did things.

"The dead border runs under the water," he told Aran. "Don't fall into it."

The snail dragon withdrew most of itself into its shell. Only his scaly head showed now, as Aran and the Warlock crossed.

Aran came running.

He was still a man. It was not certain that Wavyhill knew that Aran was a werewolf. It *was* certain that they would pass the gate. So he reserved his last defense, and came at the dragon with a naked sword.

The dragon blew fire.

Aran went through it. He carried a charm against dragon fire.

But he couldn't *see* through it. It shocked hell out of him when teeth closed on his shoulder. The dragon had stretched incredibly. Aran screamed and bounced his blade off the metallic scales and—the teeth loosed him, snapped ineffectually at the Warlock, who danced back laughing, waving—

But the Warlock had been unarmed!

The dragon collapsed. His thick neck was cut half in two, behind the scales. The Warlock wiped his weapon on his pantaloons and held it up.

Aran felt suddenly queasy.

The Warlock laughed again. " 'What good is a glass dagger?' The fun thing about being a magician is that everyone always expects you to use magic."

"But, but—"

"It's just a glass dagger. No spells on it, nothing Wavyhill could detect. I had a friend drop it in the pond two days ago. Glass in water is near enough to invisible to fool the likes of Wavyhill."

"Excuse my open mouth. I just don't like glass daggers. Now what?"

The corpse and shell of the snail dragon still blocked the gate.

"If we try to squeeze around, we could be trapped. I suppose we'll have to go over."

"Fast," said Aran.

"Right, fast. Keep in mind that he could be *anywhere*." The Warlock took a running start and ran/climbed up the curve of the shell.

Aran followed almost as quickly.

In his sanctum, the snail dragon had said. The picture he had evoked was still with Aran as he went up the shell. Wavyhill would be hidden in his basement or his tower room, in some place of safety. Aran and the Warlock would have to fight their way through whatever the enemy could raise against them, while Wavyhill watched to gauge their defenses. There were similar tales of magicians' battles . . .

Aran was ravenously hungry. It gave him a driving energy he hadn't had in years, decades. His pumping legs drove a body that seemed feather-light. He reached the top of the shell just as the Warlock was turning full about in apparent panic.

Then he saw them: a horde of armed and armored skeletons coming at them up a wooden plank. There must have been several score of them. Aran shouted and drew his sword. *How do you kill a skeleton?*

The Warlock shouted too. Strange words, in the Guild language.

The skeletons howled. A whirlwind seemed to grip them and lift them and fling them forward. Already they were losing form, like smoke rings. Aran turned to see the last of them vanishing into the Warlock's back.

My name is legion. They must have been animated by a single demon. And the Warlock had pulled that demon into a demon trap, empty and waiting for thirty years.

The problem was that both Aran and the Warlock had been concentrating on the plural demon.

The Warlock's back was turned, and Aran could do nothing. He spotted Wavyhill gesticulating from across the courtyard, in the instant before Wavyhill completed his spell.

Aran turned to shout a warning; and so he saw what the spell did to the Warlock. The Warlock was old in an instant. The flesh seemed to fade into his bones. He looked bewildered, spat a mouthful of blackened pebbles—no, teeth—closed his eyes and started to fall.

Aran caught him.

It was like catching an armload of bones. He eased the Warlock onto his back on the great snail shell. The Warlock's breathing was stertorous; he could not have long to live.

"Aran the Merchant!"

Aran looked down. "What did you do to him?"

The magician Wavyhill was dressed as usual, in dark robe and sandals and pointed hat. A belt with a shoulder loop held his big-hilted sword just clear of the ground. He called, "That is precisely what I wish to discuss. I have found an incantation that behaves as the Warlock's Wheel behaves, but directionally. Is this over your head?"

"I understand you."

"In layman's terms, I've sucked the magic from him. That leaves him two hundred and twenty-six years old. I believe that gives me the win.

"My problem is whether to let you live. Aran, do you understand what my spell will do to you?"

Aran did, but—"Tell me anyway. Then tell me how you found out."

"From some of my colleagues, of course, after I determined that you were my enemy. You must have consulted an incredible number of magicians regarding the ghostly knife in your heart."

"More than a dozen. Well?"

"Leave in peace. Don't come back."

"I have to take the Warlock."

"He is my enemy."

"He's my ally. I won't leave him," said Aran.

"Take him then."

Aran stooped. He was forty-eight years old, and the bitterness of defeat had replaced the manic energy of battle. But the Warlock was little more than a snoring mummy, dry and light. The problem would be to get the fragile old man down from the snail shell.

Wavyhill was chanting!

Aran stood—in time to see the final gesture. Then the spell hit him.

For an instant he thought that the knife had truly reappeared in his heart. But the pain was all through him! like a million taut strings snapping inside him! The shape of his neck changed grindingly; all of his legs snapped forward; his skull flattened, his eyes lost color vision, his nose stretched, his lips pulled back from bared teeth.

The change had never come so fast, had never been more complete. A blackness fell on Aran's mind. It was a wolf that rolled helplessly off the giant snail shell and into the courtyard. A wolf bounced heavily and rolled to its feet, snarled deep in its throat and began walking stiff-legged toward Wavyhill.

Wavyhill was amazed! He started the incantation over, speaking very fast, as Aran approached. He finished as Aran came within leaping distance.

This time there was no change at all. Except that Aran leapt, and Wavyhill jumped back just short of far enough, and Aran tore his throat out.

*   *   *

For Aran the nightmare began then. What had gone before was as sweet dreams.

Wavyhill should have been dead. His severed carotid arteries pumped frantically, his windpipe made horrid bubbling sounds, and—Wavyhill drew his sword and attacked.

Aran the wolf circled and moved in and slashed—and backed away howling, for Wavyhill's sword had run him through the heart. The wound healed instantly. Aran the wolf was not surprised. He leapt away, and circled, and slashed and was stabbed again, and circled . . .

It went on and on.

Wavyhill's blood had stopped flowing. He'd run out. Yet he was still alive. So was his sword, or so it seemed. Aran never attacked unless it seemed safe, but the sword bit him every time. And every time he attacked, he came away with a mouthful of Wavyhill.

He was going to win. He could not help but win. His wounds healed as fast as they were made. Wavyhill's did not. Aran was stripping the flesh from the magician's bones.

There was a darkness on his brain. He moved by animal cunning. Again and again he herded Wavyhill back onto the slippery flagstones where Wavyhill had spilled five quarts of his blood. Four feet were surer than two. It was that cunning that led him to bar Wavyhill from leaving the courtyard. He tried. He must have stored healing magic somewhere in the castle. But Aran would not let him reach it.

He had done something to himself that would not let him die. He must be regretting it terribly. Aran the wolf had crippled him now, slashing at his ankles until there was not a shred of muscle left to work the bones. Wavyhill was fighting on his knees. Now Aran came closer, suffering the bite of the sword to reach the magician . . .

Nightmare.

Aran the Peacemonger had been wrong. If Aran the rug merchant could work on and on, stripping the living flesh from a man in agony, taking a stab wound for every bite—if Aran could suffer such agonies to do this to *anyone,* for *any* cause—

Then neither the end of magic, nor anything else, would ever persuade men to give up war. They would fight on, with swords and stones and whatever they could find, for as long as there were men.

The blackness had lifted from Aran's brain. It must have been the sword: the *mana* in an enchanted sword had replaced the *mana* sucked from him by Wavyhill's variant of the Warlock's Wheel.

And, finally, he realized that the sword was fighting alone.

Wavyhill was little more than bloody bones. He might not be dead, but he certainly couldn't move. The sword waved itself at the end of the stripped bones of his arm, still trying to keep Aran away.

Aran slid past the blade. He gripped the hilt in his teeth and pulled it from the magician's still-fleshy hand. The hand fought back with a senseless determined grip, but it wasn't enough.

He had to convert to human to climb the dragon shell.

The Warlock was still alive, but his breathing was a thing of desperation. Aran laid the blade across the Warlock's body and waited.

The Warlock grew young. Not as young as he had been, But he no longer looked—dead. He was in the neighborhood of seventy years old when he opened his eyes, blinked, and asked, "What happened?"

"You missed all the excitement," said Aran.

"I take it you beat him. My apologies. It's been thirty years since I fought Glirendree. With every magician in the civilized world trying to duplicate the Warlock's Wheel, one or another was bound to improve on the design."

"He used it on me, too."

"Oh?" The Warlock chuckled. "I suppose you're wondering about the knife."

"It did come to mind. Where is it?"

"In my belt. Did you think I'd leave it in your chest? I'd had a dream that I would need it. So I kept it. And sure enough—"

"But it was in my heart!"

"I made an image of it. I put the image in your heart, then faded it out."

Aran's fingernails raked his chest. "You miserable son of an ape! You let me think that knife was in me for thirty years!"

"You came to my house as a thief," the Warlock reminded him. "Not an invited guest."

Aran the merchant had acquired somewhat the same attitude toward thieves. With diminished bitterness he said, "Just a little magician's joke, was it? No wonder nobody could get it out. All right. Now tell me why Wavyhill's spell turned me into a wolf."

The Warlock sat up carefully. He said, "What?"

"He waved his arms at me and sucked all the *mana* out of me, and I turned into a wolf. I even lost my human intelligence. Probably my invulnerability too. If he hadn't been using an enchanted sword he'd have cut me to ribbons."

"I don't understand that. You should have been frozen into human form. Unless . . ."

Then, visibly, the answer hit him. His pale cheeks paled further. Presently he said, "You're not going to like this, Aran."

Aran could see it in the Warlock's face, seventy years old and very tired and full of pity. "Go on," he said.

"The Wheel is a new thing. Even the dead spots aren't *that* old. The situation has never come up before, that's all. People automatically assume that werewolves are people who can turn themselves into wolves.

"It seems obvious enough. You can't even make the change without moonlight. You keep your human intelligence. But there's never been proof, one way or another, until now."

"You're saying I'm a wolf."

"Without magic, you're a wolf," the Warlock agreed.

"Does it matter? I've spent most of my life as a man," Aran whispered. "What difference does it make—oh. Oh, yes."

"It wouldn't matter if you didn't have children."

"Eight. And they'll have children. And one day the *mana* will be gone everywhere on Earth. Then what, Warlock?"

"You know already."

"They'll be wild dogs for the rest of eternity!"

"And nothing anyone can do about it."

"Oh, yes, there is! I'm going to see to it that no magician ever enters Rynildissen again!" Aran stood up on the dragon's shell. "Do you hear me, Warlock? Your kind will be barred. Magic will be barred. We'll save the *mana* for the sea people and the dragons!"

It may be that he succeeded. Fourteen thousand years later, there are still tales of werewolves where Rynildissen City once stood. Certainly there are no magicians.

THE EYE OF TANDYLA

by
L. Sprague de Camp

L. Sprague de Camp has been entertaining science fiction and fantasy readers for more than forty-five years. Although he is proficient at all types of speculative fiction, one of his characteristics is a well-developed sense of humor that has earned him a devoted following. His major works have spanned the decades from sf's "Golden Age" to the present: LEST DARKNESS FALL (1941), ROGUE QUEEN (1951), THE INCOMPLETE ENCHANTER (1942; with Fletcher Pratt), TALES FROM GAVAGAN'S BAR (1953, with Pratt), THE WHEELS OF IF (1948), THE BEST OF L. SPRAGUE DE CAMP (1977), and THE GREAT FETISH (1978), among many others. In addition, he has co-written a large number of Conan the Barbarian tales, some from short stories and fragments left to us by Conan's creator, Robert E. Howard.

A droll parody of sword and sorcery quest, "The Eye of Tandyla" is an enjoyable story which might make an even more enjoyable movie.

One day—so long ago that mountains have arisen since. with cities on their flanks—

Derezong Taash, sorcerer to King Vuar the capricious, sat in his library reading the Collected Fragments of Lontang and drinking the green wine of Zhysk. He was at peace with himself and the world, for nobody had tried to murder him for ten whole days, by natural means or otherwise. When tired of puzzling out the cryptic glyphs, Derezong would gaze over the rim of his goblet at his demon-screen, on which the great Shuazid (before King Vuar took a capricious dislike to him) had depicted Derezong's entire stable of demons, from the fearful Fernazot down to the slightest sprite that submitted to his summons.

One wondered, on seeing Derezong, why even a sprite should bother. For Derezong Taash was a chubby little man (little for a Lorska, that is) with white hair framing a round youthful face. When he had undergone the zompur-treatment, he had carelessly forgotten to name his hair among the things for which he wanted eternal youth—an omission which had furnished his fellow magicians with fair scope for ribald ridicule.

On this occasion, Derezong Taash planned, when drunk enough, to heave his pudgy form out of the reading-chair and totter in to dinner with his assistant, Zhamel Seh. Four of Derezong's sons should serve the food as a precaution against Derezong's ill-wishers, and Zhamel Seh should taste it first as a further precaution.

And then the knock upon the door and the high voice of King Vuar's most insolent page: "My lord sorcerer, the king will see you forthwith!"

"What about?" grumbled Derezong Taash.

"Do I know where the storks go in winter? Am I privy to the secrets of the living dead of Sedo? Has the North Wind confided to me what lies beyond the ramparts of the Riphai?"

"I suppose not." Derezong yawned, rose, and toddled throneward. He glanced back over his shoulders as he went, disliking to walk through the halls of the palace without Zhamel to guard his back against a sudden stab.

The lamplight gleamed upon King Vuar's glabrous pate, and the king looked up at Derezong Taash from under his hedge of heavy brows. He sat upon his throne in the audience chamber, and over his head upon the wall was fastened the hunting-horn of the great King Zynah, Vuar's father.

After his preliminary prostration, Derezong Taash observed something else that had escaped his original notice: that on a small table in front of the throne, which usually bore a vase of flowers, there now reposed a silver plate, and on the plate the head of the Minister of Commerce, wearing that witlessly blank expression that heads are wont to do when separated from their proper bodies.

Evidently King Vuar was not in his jolliest mood.

"Yes, O King?" said Derezong Taash, his eyes swivelling nervously from the head of the late minister to that of his sovereign.

King Vuar said: "Good my lord, my wife Ilepro, whom I think you know, has a desire that you alone can satisfy."

"Yes, Sire?"

The king said: "She wishes that jewel that forms the third eye of the goddess Tandyla. You know that temple in Lotor?"

"Yes, Sire."

"This small-souled buckster," said Vuar, indicating the head, "said, when I put the proposal to him, that the gem could not be bought, wherefore I caused his length to be lessened. This hasty act I now regret, for it transpires that he was right. Therefore, our only remaining course is to steal the thing."

"Y-yes, Sire."

The king rested his long chin upon his fist and his agate eyes saw distant things. The lamplight gleamed upon the ring of gray metal on his finger, a ring made from the heart of a falling star, and of such might as a magic-repellant that not even the sendings of the wizards of Lotor had power to harm its wearer.

He continued: "We can either essay to seize it openly, which would mean war, or by stealth. Now, although I will go to some trouble to gratify the whims of Ilepro, my plans do not include a Lotrian war. At least, not until all other expedients have been attempted. You, therefore, are hereby commissioned to go to Lotor and obtain this jewel."

"Yes indeed, Sire," said Derezong with a heartiness that was, to say the least, a bit forced. Any thoughts of protest that he might have entertained had some minutes since been banished by the sight of the unlucky minister's head.

"Of course," said Vuar in tones of friendly consideration, "should you feel your own powers inadequate, I'm sure the King of Zhysk will lend me his wizard to assist you. . . ."

"Never, Sire!" cried Derezong, drawing himself up to his full five-five. "That bungling beetlehead, far from helping, would be but an anchor stone about my neck!"

King Vuar smiled a lupine smile, though Derezong could not perceive the reason. "So be it, then."

Back in his own quarters Derezong Taash rang for his assistant. After the third ring Zhamel Seh sauntered in, balancing his big bronze sword by the pommel on his palm.

"Some day," said Derezong, "you'll amputate some poor wight's toe showing off that trick, and I only hope it will be yours. We leave tomorrow on a mission."

Zhamel Seh grasped his sword securely by the hilt and grinned down upon his employer. "Good! Whither?"

Derezong Taash told him.

"Better yet! Action! Excitement!" Zhamel swished the air with his sword. "Since you put the geas upon the queen's mother have we sat in these apartments like barnacles on a pile, doing nought to earn King Vuar's bounty."

"What's wrong with that? I plague none and nobody plagues me. And now with winter coming on, we must journey forth to the ends of rocky Lotor to try to lift this worthless bauble the king's sack of a favorite has set her silly heart upon."

"I wonder why?" said Zhamel. "Since she's Lotri by birth, you'd think she'd wish to ward her land's religious symbols instead of stealing them away for her own adornment."

"One never knows. Our own women are unpredictable enough, and as for Lotris . . . But let's to the task of planning our course and equipage."

They rode east to fertile Zhysk on the shores of the Tritonian Sea, and in the city of Bienkar sought out Derezong's friend, Goshap Tuzh the lapidary, from whom they solicited information to forearm them against adversity.

"This jewel," said Goshap Tuzh, "is about the size of a small fist, egg-shaped without facets, and of a dark purple hue. When seen from one end, it displays rays like a sapphire, but seven instead of six. It forms the pupil of the central eye of the statue of Tandyla, being held in place by leaden prongs. As to what other means, natural or otherwise, the priests of Tandyla employ to guard their treasure, I know not, save that they are both effective and unpleasing. Twenty-three attempts have been made to pilfer the stone in the last five centuries, all terminating fatally for the thieves. The last time I, Goshap Tuzh, saw the body of the thief . . ."

As Goshap told the manner in which the unsuccessful thief had been used, Zhamel gagged and Derezong looked into his wine with an expression of distaste, as if some many-legged creeping thing swam therein—although he and his assistant were by no means the softest characters in a hard age.

"Its properties?" said Derezong Taash.

"Considerable, though perhaps over-rated by distant rumor. It is the world's most sovereign antidemonic, repelling even the dread Tr'lang himself, who is of all demons the deadliest."

"Is it even stronger than King Vuar's ring of starmetal?"

"Much. However, for our old friendship, let me advise you to change your name and take service with some less exacting liege lord. There's no profit in seeking to snatch this Eye."

Derezong Taash ran his fingers through his silky-white hair and beard. "True, he ever wounds me by his brutally voiced suspicions of my competence, but to relinquish such luxe as I enjoy were not so simple. Where else can I obtain such priceless books and enrapturing women for the asking? Nay, save when he becomes seized of these whimsies, King Vuar's a very good master indeed."

"But that's my point. When do you know his caprice notorious may not be turned against you?"

"I know not; betimes I think it must be easier to serve a barbarian king. Barbarians, being wrapped in a mummy-cloth of custom and ritual, are more predictable."

"Then why not flee? Across the Tritonian Sea lies lordly Torrutseish, where one of your worth would soon rise—"

"You forget," said Derezong, "King Vuar holds hostages: my not inconsiderable family. And for them I must stick it out, though the Western Sea swallow the entire land of Pusaad as it predicted in the prophecies."

Goshap shrugged. " 'Tis your affair. I do but indigitate that you are one of these awkward intermediates: Too tub-like ever to make a prow swordsman, and unable to attain the highest grade of magical adeptry because you'll not forswear the delights of your zenana."

"Thank you, good Goshap," said Derezong, sipping the green wine. "Howsoever, I live not to attain preeminence in some austere regimen disciplinary, but to enjoy life. And now who's a reliable apothecary in Bienkar from whom I can obtain a packet of syr-powder of highest grade and purity?"

"Dualor can furnish you. What semblance do you propose upon yourselves to cast?"

"I thought we'd go as a pair of traders from Parsk. So, if you hear of a couple traversing Lotor accompanied by vast uproar and vociferation, fail not to show the due surprise."

Derezong Taash bought his syr-powder with squares of gold bearing the stamp of King Vuar, then returned to their inn where he drew his pentacles and cast his powder and recited the Incantation of the Nines. At the end, both he and Zhamel Seh were both lying helpless on the floor, with their appearance changed to that of a pair of dark hawk-nosed fellows in the fluttery garb of Parsk, with rings in their ears.

When they recovered their strength, they rode forth. They crossed the desert of Reshape without suffering excessively either from thirst, or from the bites of venomous serpents, or from attacks of spirits of the waste. They passed through the Forest of Antro without being assailed by brigands, swordtoothed cats, or the Witch of Antro. And at last they wound among the iron hills of Lator.

As they stopped for one night, Derezong said: "By my reckoning and according to what passersby have told us, the temple should lie not more than one day's journey ahead. Hence, it were time to try whether we can effect our direption by surrogate instead of in our own vulnerable persons." And he began drawing pentacles in the dirt.

"You mean to call up Feranzot?" asked Zhamel Seh.

"The same."

Zhamel shuddered. "Some day you'll leave an angle of a pentacle unclosed, and that will be the end of us."

"No doubt. But to assail this stronghold of powers chthonian by any but the mightiest means were an even surer passport to extinction. So light the rushes and begin."

"I can fancy nothing riskier than dealing with Feranzot," grumbled Zhamel, "save perhaps invoking the terrible Tr'lang himself." But he did as he was bid.

They went through the Incantation of Br'tong, as reconstructed by Derezong Taash from the Fragments of Lontang, and the dark shape of Feranzot appeared outside the main pentacle, wavering and rippling. Derezong felt the heat of his body sucked forth by the cold of the daev, and felt the overwhelming depression the thing's presence engendered. Zhamel Seh, for all his thews, cowered.

"What would you?" whispered Feranzot.

Derezong Taash gathered his weakened forces and replied: "You shall steal the jewel in the middle eye of the statue of the goddess Tandyla in the nearby temple thereof and render it to me."

"That I cannot."

"And why not?"

"First, because the priests of Tandyla have traced around their temple a circle of such puissance that no sending or semblance or spirit, save the great Tr'lang, can cross it. Second, because the Eye itself is surrounded by an aura of such baleful influence that not I, nor any other of my kind, nor even Tr'lang himself, can exert a purchase upon it on this plane. May I return to my own dimension now?"

"Depart, depart, depart . . . Well, Zhamel, it looks as though we should be compelled to essay this undelightsome task ourselves."

Next day they continued their ride. The hills became mountains of uncommon ruggedness, and the road a mere trail cut into cliffs of excessive steepness. The horses, more accustomed to the bison-swarming plains of windy Lorsk, misliked the new topography, and rubbed their riders' legs painfully against the cliffside in their endeavor to keep away from the edge.

Little sun penetrated these gorges of black rock, which began to darken almost immediately after noon. Then the sky clouded over and the rocks became shiny with cold mist. The trail crossed the gorge by a spidery bridge suspended from ropes. The horses balked.

"Not that I blame them," said Derezong Taash, dismounting. "By the red-hot talons of Vrazh, it takes the thought of my fairest concubine to nerve me to cross!"

When led in line with Zhamel belaboring their rumps from the rear, the animals crossed, though unwillingly. Derezong, towing them, took one brief look over the side of the bridge at the white thread of water foaming far below and decided not to do that again. Feet and hooves resounded hollowly on the planking and echoed from the cliffsides, and the wind played with the ropes as with the strings of a great harp.

On the other side of the gorge, the road continued its winding upward way. They passed another pair, a man and a woman, riding down the trail, and had to back around a bend to find a place with room enough to pass. The man and the woman went by looking somberly at the ground, barely acknowledging with the grunt the cheerful greeting Derezong tossed at them.

Then the road turned sharply into a great cleft in the cliff, wherein their hooffalls echoed thrice as loud as life and they could scarcely see to pick their way. The bottom of the cleft sloped upward, so that in time they came out upon an area of tumbled stones with a few dwarfed trees. The road ran dimly on through the stones until it ended in a flight of steps, which in turn led up to the Temple of Tandyla itself. Of this temple of ill repute, the travellers could see only the lower parts, for the upper ones disappeared into the cloud floor. What they could see of it was all black and shiny and rising to sharp peaks.

Derezong remembered the unpleasant attributes ascribed to the goddess, and the even more disagreeable habits credited to her priests. It was said, for instance, that the worship of Tandyla, surely a sinister enough figure in the Pusaadian pantheon, was a mere blind to cover dark rites concerning the demon Tr'lang, who in elder days had been a god in his own right. That was before the towering Lorskas, driven from the mainland by the conquering Hauskirik, had swarmed across the Tritonian Sea to Pusaad, before that land had begun its ominous subsidence.

Derezong Taash assured himself that gods and demons alike were not usually so formidable as their priests, from base motives of gain, tried to make them out. Also, that wild tales of the habits of priests usually turned out to be at least somewhat exaggerated. Although he did not fully believe his own assurances, they would have to suffice for want of better.

In front of the half-hidden temple, Derezong Taash pulled up, dismounted, and with Zhamel's help weighted down the reins of their beasts with heavy stones to hinder them from straying.

As they started for the steps Zhamel cried: "Master!"

"What is't?"

"Look upon us!"

Derezong looked and saw that the semblance of traders from Parsk had vanished, and that they were again King Vuar's court magician and his assistant, plain for all to see. They must have stepped across that line that Fernazot had warned them of.

Derezong took a sharp look at the entrance, and half-hidden in the inadequate light he saw two men flanking the doorway. His eye caught the gleam of polished bronze. But if these doorkeepers had observed the change in the looks of the visitors, they gave no sign.

Derezong Taash drove his short legs up the shiny black steps. The guards came into full view, thick-bodied Lotris with beetling brows. Men said they were akin to the savages of Ierarne in the far Northeast, who knew not horse-taming and fought with sharpened stone. These stood staring straight ahead, each facing the other like statues. Derezong and Zhamel passed between them.

They found themselves in a vestibule where a pair of young Lotri girls said: "Your boots and swords, sirs."

Derezong lifted off his baldric and handed it to the nearest, scabbard and all; then pulled off his boots and stood barefoot with the grass he had stuffed into them to keep them from chafing sticking out from between his toes. He was glad to feel the second sword hanging down his back inside his shirt.

"Come on," said Derezong Taash, and led the way into the naos of the temple.

It was much like other temples: a big rectangular room smelling of incense, with a third of the area partitioned off by a railing, behind which rose the huge black squat statue of Tandyla. The smooth basalt of which it was carved reflected feebly the highlights from the few lamps, and up at the top, where its head disappeared into the shadows, a point of purple light showed where the jewel in its forehead caught the rays.

A couple of Lotris knelt before the railing, mumbling prayers. A priest appeared from the shadows on one side, waddled across the naos behind the railing. Derezong half expected the priest to turn on him with a demand that he and Zhamel follow him into the sanctum of the high priest, but the priest kept on walking and disappeared into the darkness on the other side.

Derezong Taash and his companion advanced, a slow step at a time, towards the railing. As they neared it, the two Lotris completed their devotions and rose. One of them dropped something that jingled into a large tub-like receptacle behind the railing, and the two squat figures walked quickly out.

For the moment, Derezong and Zhamel were entirely alone in the big room, though in the silence they could hear faint motions and voices from other parts of the temple. Derezong brought out his container of syr-powder and sprinkled it while racing through the Incantation of Ansuan. When he finished, there stood between himself and Zhamel a replica of himself.

Derezong Taash climbed over the railing and trotted on the tips of his plump toes around behind the statue. Here in the shadows, he could see doors in the walls. The statue sat with its back almost but not quite touching the wall behind it, so that an active man, by bracing his back against the statue and his feet against the wall, could lever himself up. Though Derezong was "active" only in a qualified sense, he slipped into the gap and squirmed into a snugly-fitting fold in the goddess's stone draperies. Here he lay, hardly breathing, until he heard Zhamel's footfalls die away.

The plan was that Zhamel should walk out of the temple, accompanied by the double of Derezong. The guards, believing that the temple was now deserted of visitors, would relax. Derezong would steal the stone; Zhamel should raise a haro outside, urging the guards to "Come quickly!" and while their attention was thus distracted, Derezong would rush out.

Derezong Taash began to worm his way up between the statue and the wall. It was hard going for one of his girth, and sweat ran out from under his cap of fisher-fur and down his face. Still no interruption.

He arrived on a level with the shoulder and squirmed out on to that projection, holding the right ear for safety. The slick stone was cold under his bare feet. By craning his neck, he could see the ill-favored face of the goddess in profile, and by stretching he could reach the jewel in her forehead.

Derezong Taash took out of his tunic a small bronze pry-bar he had brought along for this purpose. With it he began to pry up the leaden prongs that held the gem in place, carefully lest he mar the stone or cause it to fall to the floor below. Every few pries, he tested it with his finger. Soon it felt loose.

The temple was quiet.

Around the clock he went with his little bar, prying. Then the stone came out, rubbing gently against the smooth inner surfaces of the bent-out leaden prongs. Derezong Taash reached for the inside of his tunic, to hide the stone and the bar. But the two objects proved too much for his pudgy fingers to handle at once. The bar came loose and fell with a loud ping—ping down the front of the statue, bouncing from breast to belly to lap, to end with a sonorous clank on the stone floor in front of the image.

Derezong Taash froze rigid. Seconds passed and nothing happened. Surely the guards had heard . . .

But still there was silence.

Derezong Taash secured the jewel in his tunic and squirmed back over the shoulder to the darkness behind the statue. Little by little, he slid down the space between statue and wall. He reached the floor. Still no noise save an occasional faint sound such as might have been made by the temple servants preparing dinner for their masters. He waited for the diversion promised by Zhamel Seh.

He waited and waited. From somewhere came the screech of a man in the last agonies.

At last, giving up, Derezong Taash hurried around the hip of the statue. He scooped up the pry-bar with one quick motion, climbed back over the railing, and tiptoed toward the exit.

There stood the guards with swords out, ready for him.

Derezong Taash reached back over his shoulder and pulled out
his second sword. In a real fight, he knew he would have little
hope against one hardened and experienced swordfighter, let
alone two. His one slim chance lay in bursting through them by a
sudden berserk attack and keeping on running.

He expected such adroit and skillful warriors to separate and
come at him from opposite sides. Instead, one of them stepped
forward and took an awkward swipe at him. Derezong parried
with a clash of bronze and struck back. Clang! clang! went the
blades, and then his foe staggered back, dropped his sword with
a clatter, clutched both hands to his chest, and folded up in a
heap on the floor. Derezong was astonished; he could have
sworn he had not gotten home.

Then the other man was upon him. At the second clash of
blades, that of the guard spun out of his hand, to fall ringingly to
the stone pave. The guard leaped back, turned and ran, disappearing through one of the many ambient doors.

Derezong Taash glanced at his sword, wondering if he had not
known his own strength all this time. The whole exchange had
taken perhaps ten seconds, and so far as he could tell in the dim
light, no blood besmeared his blade. He was tempted to test the
deadness of the fallen guard by poking him, but lacked both time
and ruthlessness to do so. Instead, he ran out of the vestibule and
looked for Zhamel and the double of himself.

No sign of either. The four horses were still tethered a score of
paces from the steps of the temple. The stones were sharp under
Derezong's bare and unhardened soles.

Derezong hesitated, but only for a flash. He was in a way fond
of Zhamel Seh, and his assistant's brawn had gotten him out of
trouble about as often as Zhamel's lack of insight had gotten
them into it. On the other hand, to plunge back into the temple in
search of his erratic aide would be rash to the point of madness.
And he did have definite orders from the king.

He sheathed his sword, scrambled on to the back of his horse,
and cantered off, leading the other three beasts by their bridles.

During the ride down the narrow deft, Derezong had time to
think, and the more he thought the less he liked what he thought.
The behavior of the guards was inexplicable on any grounds but
their being drunk or crazy, and he did not believe either. Their
failure to attack him simultaneously; their failure to note the fall
of the pry-bar; the ease with which he, an indifferent swordsman,
had bested them; the fact that one fell down without being
touched; their failure to yell for help . . .

Unless they planned it that way. The whole thing had been too easy to account for by any other hypothesis. Maybe they wanted him to steal the accursed bauble.

At the lower end of the cleft, where the road turned out on to the side of the cliff forming the main gorge, he pulled up, dismounted, and tied the animals, keeping an ear cocked for the sound of pursuers echoing down the cleft. He took out the Eye of Tandyla and looked at it. Yes, when seen end-on it showed the rayed effect promised by Goshap Tuzh. Otherwise, it exhibited no special odd or unnatural properties. So far.

Derezong Taash set it carefully on the ground and backed away from it to see it from a greater distance. As he backed, the stone moved slightly and started to roll towards him.

At first he thought he had not laid it down on a level enough place, and leaped to seize it before it should roll over the edge into the gulf. He put it back and heaped a little barrier of pebbles and dust around it. Now it should not roll!

But when he backed again it did, right over his little rampart. Derezong Taash began to sweat anew, and not, this time, from physical exertion. The stone rolled toward him, faster and faster. He tried to dodge by shrinking into a recess in the cliff-wall. The stone swerved and came to rest at the toe of one of his bare feet, like a pet animal asking for a pat on the head.

He scooped out a small hole, laid the gem in it, placed a large stone over the hole, and walked away. The large stone shook and the purple egg appeared, pushing aside the pebbles in its path as if it were being pulled out from under the rock by an invisible cord. It rolled to his feet again and stopped.

Derezong Taash picked up the stone and looked at it again. It did not seem to have been scratched. He remembered that the demand for the stone originated with an Ilepro, the King's wife.

With a sudden burst of emotion, Derezong Taash threw the stone from him, towards the far side of the gorge.

By all calculation, the gem should have followed a curved path, arching downward to shatter against the opposite cliff. Instead, it slowed in midflight over the gorge, looped back, and flew into the hand that had just thrown it.

Derezong Taash did not doubt that the priests of Tandyla had laid a subtle trap for King Vuar in the form of this jewel. What it would do to the king and to the kingdom of Lorsk if Derezong carried out his mission, he had no idea. So far as he knew, it was merely an antidemonic, and therefore should protect Vuar instead of harming him. Nevertheless, he was sure something unpleasant was planned, of which he was less than eager to be the agency. He placed the gem on a flat rock, found a stone the size of his head, raised it in both hands, and brought it down upon the jewel.

Or so he intended. On the way down, the stone struck a projecting shelf of rock, and a second later Derezong was capering about like a devil-dancer of Dzen, sucking his mashed fingers and cursing the priests of Tandyla in the names of the most fearful demons in his repertory. The stone lay unharmed.

For, Derezong reasoned, these priests must have put upon the gem not only a following-spell, but also the Incantation of Duzhateng, so that every effort on the part of Derezong to destroy the object would rebound to his own damage. If he essayed some more elaborate scheme of destruction, he would probably end up with a broken leg. The Incantation of Duzhateng could be lifted only by a complicated spell for which Derezong did not have the materials, which included some very odd and repellant substances indeed.

Now, Derezong Taash knew that there was only one way in which he could both neutralize these spells and secure the jewel so that it should plague him no more, and that was to put it back in the hole in the forehead of the statue of Tandyla and hammer down the leaden prongs that held it in its setting. Which task, however, promised to present more difficulties than the original theft. For if the priests of Tandyla had meant Derezong to steal the object, they might show greater acumen in thwarting his attempt to return it, than they had in guarding it in the first place.

One could but try. Derezong Taash put the jewel into his tunic, mounted his horse (leaving the other three still tethered) and rode back up the echoing cleft. When he came out upon the little plateau upon which squatted the temple of Tandyla, he saw that he had indeed been forestalled. Around the entrance to the temple stood a double row of guards, the bronze scales of their cuirasses glimmering faintly in the fading light. The front rank carried shields of mammoth hide and big bronze swords, while those in the rear bore long pikes which they held in both hands and thrust between the men of the front rank. They thus presented a formidable hedge to any attacker, who had first to get past the spear-points and then deal with the swords.

One possibility was to gallop at them in the hope that one or two directly in one's way would flinch aside, opening a path by which one could burst through the serried line. Then, one could ride on into the temple and perhaps get the gem back into place before being caught up with. If not, there would be a great smash, some battered guards, a wounded horse, and a thoroughly skewered and sliced sorcerer all tangled in a kicking heap.

Derezong Taash hesitated, then thought of his precious manuscripts awaiting him in King Vuar's palace, which he could never safely enter again unless he brought either the gem or an acceptable excuse for not having it. He kicked his mount into motion.

As the animal cantered toward the line, the spear-points got closer and larger and sharper-looking, and Derezong Taash saw that the guards were not going to flinch aside and obligingly let him through. Then, a figure came out of the temple and ran down the steps to the rear of the guards. It wore a priest's robe, but just before the shock of impact Derezong recognized the rugged features of Zhamel Seh.

Derezong Taash hauled on his reins, and the horse skidded to a halt with its nose a scant span from the nearest point. Derezong—living in a stirrupless age—slid forward until he bestrode the animal's neck. Clutching its mane with his left hand, he felt for the gem with his right.

"Zhamel!" he called. "Catch!"

He threw. Zhamel leaped high and caught the stone before it had time to loop back.

"Now put it back!" cried Derezong.

"What? Art mad?"

"Put it back, speedily, and secure it!"

Zhamel, trained to obey commands no matter how bizarre, dashed back into the temple, albeit wagging his head as if in sorrow for his master's loss of sanity. Derezong Taash untangled himself from his horse's mane and pulled the beast back out of reach of the spears. Under their lacquered helmets, the heads of the guards turned this way and that in evident perplexity. Derezong surmised that they had been given one simple order—to keep him out—and that they had not been told how to cope with fraternization between the stranger and one of their own priests.

As the guards did not seem to be coming after him, Derezong sat on his horse, eyes on the portal. He'd given Zhamel a fair chance to accomplish his mission and escape, though he thought little of the youth's chances. If Zhamel tried to push or cut his way through the guards, they would make mincemeat of him, unarmored as he was. And he, Derezong, would have to find and train another assistant, who would probably prove as unsatisfac-

tory as his predecessor. Still, Derezong could not leave the boy
utterly to his fate.

Then, Zhamel Seh ran down the steps carrying a long pike of
the kind held by the rear-rank guards. Holding this pike level, he
ran at the guards as though he were about to spear one in the
back. Derezong, knowing that such a scheme would not work,
shut his eyes.

But just before he reached the guards, Zhamel Seh dug the
point of the pike into the ground and pole-vaulted. Up he went,
legs jerking and dangling like those of a man being hanged, over
the lacquered helmets and the bronze swords and the mammoth
hide shields. He came down in front of the guards, breaking one
of their pikes with a loud snap, rolled to his feet, and ran
towards Derezong Taash. The latter had already turned his horse
around.

As Zhamel caught hold of the edge of the saddle pad, an
uproar arose behind them as priests ran out of the temple shouting.
Derezong drummed with his bare heels on the stallion's ribs and
set off at a canter, Zhamel swinging along in great leaps beside
him. They wended their way down the cleft while the sound of
hooves wafted after them.

Derezong Taash wasted no breath in questions while picking
his way down the trail. At the bottom, where the cleft ended on
one side of the great gorge, they halted for Zhamel to mount his
own horse, then continued as fast as they dared. The echoes of
the pursuers' hooves came down the cleft with a deafening
clatter.

At the suspension-bridge, the horses balked again, but Derezong
mercilessly pricked and slapped his mount with his sword until
the beast trotted out upon the swaying walkway. The cold wind
hummed through the ropes and the daylight was almost gone.

At the far end, with a great sigh of relief, Derezong Taash
looked back. Down the cliffside road came a line of pursuers,
riding at reckless speed.

He said: "Had I but time and materials, I'd cast a spell on
yonder bridge that should make it look as 'twere broken and
dangling useless."

"What's wrong with making it broken and useless in very
truth?" cried Zhamel, pulling his horse up against the cliffside
and hoisting himself so that he stood upon his saddle.

He swung his sword at the cables. As the first of the pursuers
reached the far side of the bridge, the structure sagged and fell
away with a great swish of ropes and clatter of planks. The men

from the temple set up an outcry, and an arrow whizzed across the gap to shatter against the rock. Derezong and Zhamel resumed their journey.

A fortnight later, they sat in the garden back of the shop of Goshap Tuzh the lapidary in sunny Bienkar. Zhamel Seh told his part of the tale:

". . . so on my way out, this little Lotri cast her orbs upon me once again. Now, thought I, there'll be time in plenty to perform the Master's work and make myself agreeable in this quarter as well—"

"Young cullion!" growled Derezong into his wine.

"—so I followed her. And in truth all was going in most propitious and agreeable wise, when who should come in but one of these chinless wonders in cowl and robe, and went for me with a knife. I tried to fend the fellow off, and fear that in the fracas his neck by ill hap got broke. So, knowing there might be trouble, I borrowed his habit and sallied forth therein, to find that Master, horses, and Master's double had all gone."

"And how time had flown!" said Derezong Taash in sarcastic tones. "I trust at least that the young Lotri has cause to remember this episode with pleasure. The double no doubt being a mere thing of shadow and not a being rational, walked straight out and vanished when it crossed the magical barrier erected by the priests."

"And," continued Zhamel, "there were priests and guards rushing about chittering like a pack of monkeys. I rushed about as if I were one of them, saw them range the guards around the portal, and then the Master returned and threw me the stone. I grasped the situation, swarmed up the statue, popped Tandyla's third eye back into its socket, and hammered the prongs in upon it with the pommel of my dagger. Then I fetched a pike from the armory, pausing but to knock senseless a couple of Lotris who sought to detain me for interrogation, and you know the rest."

Derezong Taash rounded out the story and said: "Good Goshap, perchance you can advise our next course, for I fear that should we present ourselves before King Vuar in proper persons, without the gem, he'd have our heads set tastefully on silver platters ere were our explanation finished. No doubt, remorse would afterwards o'erwhelm him, but that would help us not."

"Since he holds you in despite, why not leave him, as I've urged before?" said Goshap.

Derezong Taash shrugged. "Others, alas, show a like lack of appreciation, and would prove no easier masters. For had these priests of Tandyla confided in my ability to perform a simple task like carrying their gemstone from Lotor to Lorsk, their plot would doubtless have borne its intended fruit. But fearing lest I should lose or sell it on the way, they put a supernumerary spell upon it—''

"How could they, when the stone has anti-magical properties?''

"Its anti-magical properties comprise simple antidemonism, whereas the following-spell and the Incantation of Duzhateng are sympathetic magic, not sorcerous. At any rate, they caused it to follow me hither and thither, thus arousing my already awakened suspicions to the feverpitch." He sighed and took a pull on the green wine. "What this sorry world needs is more confidence. But say on, Goshap.''

"Well, then, why not write him a letter setting forth the circumstances? I'll lend you a slave to convey it to Lorsk in advance of your persons, so that when you arrive, King Vuar's wrath shall have subsided."

Derezong pondered. "Sage though I deem your suggestion, it faces one obstacle insurmountable. Namely: That of all the men at the court of Lorsk, but six can read; and among these King Vuar is not numbered. Whereas of the six, at least five are among my enemies who'd like nought better than to see me tumbled from my place. And should the task of reading my missive to the king devolve on one of these, you can fancy how he'd distort my harmless pictographs to my discredit. Could we trick old Vuar into thinking we'd performed our task, as by passing off on him a stone similar to that he expects of us? Know you of such?''

"Now there," said Goshap, "is a proposal indeed. Let me cogitate . . . Last year, when the bony specter of want came upon the land, King Daior placed his best crown in pawn to the Temple of Kelk, for treasure wherewith to still the clamorings of his people. Now, this crown bears at its apex a purple star sapphire of wondrous size and fineness, said to have been shaped by the gods before the Creation for their own enjoyment, and being in magnitude and hue not unlike that which forms the Eye of Tandyla. And the gem has never been redeemed, wherefore the priests of Kelk have set the crown on exhibition, thereby mulcting the curious of further offerings. But as to how this well-guarded gem shall be transferred from this crown to your possession, ask me not, and in truth I had liefer know nought of the matter.''

Next day, Derezong Taash cast upon himself and Zhamel Seh

the likeness of Atlantes, from the misty mountain range in the desert of Gautha, far to the East across the Tritonian Sea, where it was said in Pusaad that there were men with snakes for legs and others with no heads but faces in their chests.

Zhamel Seh grumbled: "What are we, magicians or thieves? Perhaps if we succeed in this, the King of Torrutseish across the Tritonian Sea has some bauble he specially fancies, that we could rob him of."

Derezong Taash did not argue the point, but led the way to the square fronted by the Temple of Kelk. They strode up to the temple with the Atlantean swagger, and into where the crown lay upon a cushion on a table with a lamp to illuminate it and two seven-foot Lorskas to guard it, one with a drawn sword and the other with a nocked arrow. The guards looked down over their great black beards at the red-haired Atlanteans in their blue cloaks and armlets of orichalc who pointed and jabbered as they saw the crown. And then the shorter Atlantean, that was Derezong Taash beneath the illusion, wandered out, leaving the other to gape.

Scarcely had the shorter Atlas passed the portal than he gave a loud squawk. The guards, looking that way, saw his head in profile projecting past the edge of the doorway and looking upward as though his body were being bent backward, while a pair of hands gripped his throat.

The guards, not knowing that Derezong was strangling himself, rushed to the portal. As they neared it, the head of the assailed Atlantean disappeared from view, and they arrived to find Derezong Taash in his proper form strolling up to the entrance. All the while behind them the powerful fingers of Zhamel Seh pried loose the stone from King Daior's crown.

"Is aught amiss, sirs?" said Derezong to the guards, who stared about wildly as Zhamel Seh came out of the temple behind them. As he did so, he also dropped his Atlantean disguise and became another Lorska like the guards, though not quite so tall and bushy-bearded.

"If you seek an Atlas," said Derezong in answer to their questions, "I saw two such issue from your fane and slink off into yonder alley with furtive gait. Perhaps it behooves you to see whether they have committed some depredation in your hallowed precincts?"

As the guards rushed back into the temple to see, Derezong Taash and his assistant made off briskly in the opposite direction.

Zhamel Seh muttered: "At least, let's hope we shall not have
to return this jewel to the place whence we obtained it!"

Derezong and Zhamel reached Lezohtr late at night, but had
not even finished greeting their loving concubines when a messenger informed Derezong Taash that the king wanted him at
once.

Derezong Taash found King Vuar in the audience room, evidently freshrisen from his bed for he wore nought but his crown
and bearskin wrapped about his bony body. Ilepro was there,
too, clad with like informality, and with her were her ever-
present Lotrian quartet.

"You have it?" said King Vuar, lifting a bushy brow that
boded no good for a negative answer.

"Here, Sire," said Derezong, heaving himself up off the floor
and advancing with the jewel from the crown of King Daior.

King Vuar took it in his finger-tips and looked at it in the light
of the single lamp. Derezong Taash wondered if the king would
think to count the rays to see if there were six or seven; but he
reassured himself with the thought that King Vuar was notoriously weak in higher mathematics.

The king extended the jewel towards Ilepro. "Here, Madam,"
he said. "And let us hope that with this transaction ends your
incessant plaint."

"My lord is as generous as the sun," said Ilepro in her thick
Lotrian accent. "'Tis true I have a little more to say, but not for
servile ears." She spoke in Lotrian to her four attendants, who
scuttled out.

"Well?" said the king.

Ilepro stared into the sapphire and made a motion with her free
hand, meanwhile reciting something in her native tongue. Although she went too fast for Derezong Taash to understand, he
caught a word several times repeated, that shook him to the core.
The word was "Tr'lang".

"Sire!" he cried. "I fear this northern witch is up to no
good—"

"What?" roared King Vuar. "You hlipend my wife, and
before my very optics? I'll have your head—"

"But Sire! King! Look!"

The king broke into his tirade long enough to look, and never
resumed it. For the flame of the lamp had shrunk to a bare spark.
Cold eddies stirred the air of the room, in the midst of which the
gloom thickened into shadow and the shadow into substance. At
first, it seemed a shapeless darkness, a sable fog, but then a pair

of glowing points appeared, palpable eyes, at twice the height of a man.

Derezong's mind sought for exorcisms while his tongue clove to the roof of his mouth with terror. For his own Ferenzot was but a kitten compared to this, and no pentacle protected him.

The eyes grew plainer, and lower down horny talons threw back faint highlights from the feeble flame of the lamp. The cold in the room was as if an iceberg had walked in, and Derezong smelt an odor as of burning feathers.

Ilepro pointed at the king and cried something in her own language. Derezong thought he saw fangs as a great mouth opened and Tr'lang swept forward towards Ilepro. She held the jewel in front of her, as if to ward off the daev. But it paid no attention. As the blackness settled around her, she gave a piercing scream.

The door now flew open again and the four Lotri women rushed back in. Ilepro's screams continued, diminuendo, with a curious effect of distance, as if Tr'lang were dragging her far away. All that could be seen was a dwindling shapeless shape of shadow in the middle of the floor.

The foremost of the Lotris cried "Ilepro!" and sprang towards the shape, shedding wraps with one hand while tugging out a great bronze sword with the other. As the other three did likewise, Derezong Taash realized that they were not women at all, but burly male Lotris given a superficially feminine look by shaving their beards and padding their clothes in appropriate places.

The first of the four swung his sword through the place where the shape of Tr'lang had been, but without meeting resistance other than that of air. Then he turned toward the king and Derezong.

"Take these alive!" he said in Lotrian. "They shall stand surety for our safe departure."

The four moved forward, their swords ready and their free hands spread to clutch like the talons of the just-departed demon. Then the opposite door opened and in came Zhamel Seh with an armful of swords. Two he tossed to Derezong Taash and King Vuar, who caught them by the hilts; the third he gripped in his own large fist as he took his place beside the other two.

"Too late," said another Lotri. "Slay them and run's our only chance."

Suiting the deed to the declaration, he rushed upon the three Lorskas. Clang! Clang! went the swords as the seven men slashed and parried in the gloom. King Vuar had whirled his bearskin around his left arm for a shield and fought naked save for his crown. While the Lorskas had an advantage of reach, they were handicapped by the king's age and Derezong's embonpoint and mediocrity of swordsmanship.

Though Derezong cut and thrust nobly, he found himself pushed back towards a corner, and felt the sting of a flesh-wound in the shoulder. And whatever the ignorant might think of a wizard's powers, it was quite impossible to fight physically for one's life and cast a spell at the same time.

The king bellowed for help, but no answer came, for in these inner chambers the thick stone walls and hangings deadened sound before it reached the outer rooms of the palace where King Vuar's guards had their stations. Like the others, he, too, was driven back until the three were fighting shoulder to shoulder in the corner. A blade hit Derezong's head flatsides and made him dizzy, while a metallic sound told that another blow had gotten home on the king's crown, and a yelp from Zhamel Seh revealed that he also had been hurt.

Derezong Taash found himself fast tiring. Each breath was a labor, and the hilt was slippery in his aching fingers. Soon they'd beat down his guard and finish him, unless he found some more indirect shift by which to make head against them.

He threw his sword, not at the Lotri in front of him, but at the little lamp that flickered on the table. The lamp flew off with a clatter and went out as Derezong Taash dropped on all fours and crept after his sword. Behind him in the darkness he could hear the footsteps and the hard breathing of men, afraid to strike for fear of smiting a friend and afraid to speak lest they reveal themselves to a foe.

Derezong Taash felt along the wall until he came to the hunting-horn of King Zynah. Wrenching the relic from the wall he filled his lungs and blew a tremendous blast.

The blast of the horn resounded deafeningly in the confined space. Derezong took several steps, lest one of the Lotris locate him by sound and cut him down in the dark, and blew again. With loud tramplings and clankings, the guards of King Vuar approached. The door burst open and in they came with weapons ready and torches high.

"Take them!" said King Vuar, pointing at the Lotris.

One of the Lotris tried to resist, but a guardsman's sword sheared the hand from his arm as he swung, and the Lotri yelled and sank to the floor to bleed to death. The others were subdued with little trouble.

"Now," said the king, "I can give you the boon of a quick

death, or I can turn you over to the tormentors for a slower and much more interesting one. Do you confess your plans and purposes in full, the former alternative shall be permitted you. Speak.''

The Lotri who had led the others when they entered the room said: ''Know, King, that I am Paanuvel, the husband of Ilepro. The others are gentlemen of the court of Ilepro's brother Konesp, High Chief of Lotor.''

''Gentlemen!'' snorted King Vuar.

''As my brother-in-law has no sons of his own, he and I concocted this sublime scheme for bringing his kingdom and yours under the eventual united rule of my son Pendetr. This magician of yours was to steal the Eye of Tandyla, so that, when Ilepro conjured up the daev Tr'lang, the monster would not assail her as she'd be protected by the gem's powers; it would, instead, dispose of you. For she knew that no lesser creature of the outer dimensions could assail you whilst you wear the ring of starmetal. Then she'd proclaim the child Pendetr king, as you've already named him heir, with herself as regent till he comes of age. But the antisorcellarious virtues of this jewel are evidently not what they once were, for Tr'lang engulfed my wife though she thrust the gem in its maw.''

''You have spoken well and frankly,'' said King Vuar, ''though I question the morality of turning your wife over to me, yourself being not only alive but present here in disguise. However, the customs of the Lotris are not ours. Lead them out, guards, and take off their heads.''

''One more word, King,'' said Paanuvel. ''For myself I care little, now that my beloved Ilepro's gone. But I ask that you make not the child Pendetr suffer for his father's faulty schemes.''

''I will think on't. Now, off with you and with your heads.'' The king turned to Derezong Taash, who was mopping at his flesh-wound. ''What is the cause of the failure of the Eye of Tandyla?''

Derezong, in fear and trembling, told the true tale of their foray into Lotor and their subsequent theft of the sapphire in Bienkar.

''Aha!'' said King Vuar. ''So that's what we get for not counting the rays seen in the stone!''

He paused to pick up the jewel from where it lay upon the floor, and the quaking Derezong foresaw his own severance, like that which the Lotris were even now experiencing.

Then Vuar smiled thinly. ''A fortunate failure, it seems,'' said the king. "I am indebted to you both, first for your shrewdness in penetrating the plans of the Lotris to usurp the throne of Lorsk, second for fighting beside me to such good purpose this night.

"Howsoever, we have here a situation fraught with some slight embarrassment. For King Daior is a good friend of mine, which friendship I would not willingly forego. And even though I should return the gem to him with explanation and apology, the fact that my servants purloined it in the first place would not sit well with him. My command to you, therefore, is to return at once to Bienkar—"

"Oh, no!" cried Derezong Taash, the words escaping involuntarily from him under the impetus of strong emotion.

"—return to Bienkar," continued the king as if he had not heard, "and smuggle the jewel back to its original position in the crown of the King of Zhysk, without letting anyone know that you are involved either in the disappearance of the stone or in its eventual restoration. For such accomplished rogues as you and your apprentice have shown yourselves to be, this slight feat will pose no serious obstacle. And so goodnight, my lord sorcerer."

King Vuar threw his bearskin about him and tramped off to his apartments, leaving Derezong and Zhamel staring at one another with expressions of mingled horror and a vast dismay.

THE WHITE HORSE CHILD

by
Greg Bear

Greg Bear is a young (born in 1951) American writer who is rapidly achieving recognition as an excellent storyteller and craftsman. His novels include HEGIRA (1979), PSYCHLONE (1979), and the very interesting BEYOND HEAVEN'S RIVER (1980). His short stories have appeared in such publications as ANALOG, UNIVERSE, and NEW DIMENSIONS. Mr. Bear lives in California and has worked as a planetarium operator, a most fitting occupation for a science fiction writer.

"The White Horse Child" is a memorable story about the wizardry of writing, normality, and children, and how the three often don't mix.

When I was seven years old, I met an old man by the side of the dusty road between school and farm. The late afternoon sun had cooled and he was sitting on a rock, hat off, hands held out to the gentle warmth, whistling a pretty song. He nodded at me as I walked past. I nodded back. I was curious, but I knew better than to get involved with strangers. Nameless evils seemed to attach themselves to strangers, as if they might turn into lions when no one but a little kid was around.

"Hello, boy," he said.

I stopped and shuffled my feet. He looked more like a hawk than a lion. His clothes were brown and gray and russet, and his hands were pink like the flesh of some rabbit a hawk had just plucked up. His face was brown except around the eyes, where he might have worn glasses; around the eyes he was white, and this intensified his gaze. "Hello," I said.

"Was a hot day. Must have been hot in school," he said.

"They got air conditioning."

"So they do, now. How old are you?"

"Seven," I said. "Well, almost eight."

"Mother told you never to talk to strangers?"

"And Dad, too."

"Good advice. But haven't you seen me around here before?" I looked him over. "No."

"Closely. Look at my clothes. What color are they?"

His shirt was gray, like the rock he was sitting on. The cuffs, where they peeped from under a russet jacket, where white. He didn't smell bad, but he didn't look particularly clean. He was smooth-shaven, though. His hair was white and his pants were the color of the dirt below the rock. "All kinds of colors," I said.

"But mostly I partake of the landscape, no?"

"I guess so," I said.

"That's because I'm not here. You're imagining me, at least part of me. Don't I look like somebody you might have heard of?"

"Who are you supposed to look like?" I asked.

"Well, I'm full of stories," he said. "Have lots of stories to tell little boys, little girls, even big folk, if they'll listen."

I started to walk away.

"But only if they'll listen," he said. I ran. When I got home, I told my older sister about the man on the road, but she only got a worried look and told me to stay away from strangers. I took her advice. For some time afterward, into my eighth year, I avoided that road and did not speak with strangers more than I had to.

The house that I lived in, with the five other members of my family and two dogs and one beleaguered cat, was white and square and comfortable. The stairs were rich, dark wood overlaid with worn carpet. The walls were dark oak paneling up to a foot above my head, then white plaster, with a white plaster ceiling. The air was full of smells—bacon when I woke up, bread and soup and dinner when I came home from school, dust on weekends when we helped clean.

Sometimes my parents argued, and not just about money, and those were bad times; but usually we were happy. There was talk about selling the farm and the house and going to Mitchell where Dad could work in a computerized feed-mixing plant, but it was only talk.

It was early summer when I took the dirt road again. I'd forgotten about the old man. But in almost the same way, when the sun was cooling and the air was haunted by lazy bees, I saw an old woman. Women strangers are less malevolent than men, and rarer. She was sitting on the gray rock, in a long green skirt summer-dusty, with a daisy-colored shawl and a blouse the precise hue of cottonwoods seen in a late hazy day's muted light. "Hello, boy," she said.

"I don't recognize you, either," I blurted, and she smiled.

"Of course not. If you didn't recognize him, you'd hardly know me."

"Do you know him?" I asked. She nodded. "Who was he? Who are you?"

"We're both full of stories. Just tell them from different angles. You aren't afraid of us, are you?"

I was, but having a woman ask the question made all the difference. "No," I said. "But what are you doing here? And how do you know—?"

"Ask for a story," she said. "One you've never heard of before." Her eyes were the color of baked chestnuts, and she squinted into the sun so that I couldn't see her whites. When she opened them wider to look at me, she didn't have any whites.

"I don't want to hear stories," I said softly.

"Sure you do. Just ask."

"It's late. I got to be home."

"I knew a man who became a house," she said. "He didn't like it. He stayed quiet for thirty years, and watched all the people inside grow up, and be just like their folks, all nasty and dirty and leaving his walls to flake, and the bathrooms were unbearable. So he spit them out one morning, furniture and all, and shut his doors and locked them."

"What?"

"You heard me. Upchucked. The poor house was so disgusted he changed back into a man, but he was older and he had a

cancer and his heart was bad because of all the abuse he had
lived with. He died soon after.''

I laughed, not because the man had died but because I knew
such things were lies. ''That's silly,'' I said.

''Then here's another. There was a cat who wanted to eat
butterflies. Nothing finer in the world for a cat than to stalk the
grass, waiting for black and pumpkin butterflies. It crouches
down and wriggles its rump to dig in the hind paws, then it
jumps. But a butterfly is no sustenance for a cat. It's practice.
There was a little girl about your age—might have been your
sister, but she won't admit it—who saw the cat and decided to
teach it a lesson. She hid in the taller grass with two old kites
under each arm and waited for the cat to come by stalking. When
it got real close, she put on her mother's dark glasses, to look all
bug-eyed, and she jumped up flapping the kites. Well, it was just
a little too real, because in a trice she found herself flying, and
she was much smaller than she had been, and the cat jumped at
her. Almost got her, too. Ask your sister about that sometime.
See if she doesn't deny it.''

''How'd she get back to be my sister again?''

''She became too scared to fly. She lit on a flower and found
herself crushing it. The glasses broke, too.''

''My sister did break a pair of Mom's glasses once.''

The woman smiled.

''I got to be going home.''

''Tomorrow you bring me a story, okay?''

I ran off without answering. But in my head, monsters were
already rising. If she thought I was scared, wait until she heard
the story I had to tell! When I got home my oldest sister,
Barbara, was fixing lemonade in the kitchen. She was a year
older than I, but acted as if she were grown-up. She was a good
six inches taller and I could beat her if I got in a lucky punch, but
no other way—so her power over me was awesome. But we
were usually friendly.

''Where you been?'' she asked, like a mother.

''Somebody tattled on you,'' I said.

Her eyes went doe-scared, then wizened down to slits. ''What're
you talking about?''

''Somebody tattled about what you did to Mom's sunglasses.''

''I already been whipped for that,'' she said nonchalantly.
''Not much more to tell.''

''Oh, but *I* know more.''

''Was *not* playing doctor,'' she said. The youngest, Sue-Ann,

weakest and most full of guile, had a habit of telling the folks
somebody or other was playing doctor. She didn't know what it
meant—I just barely did—but it had been true once, and she
held it over everybody as her only vestige of power.

"No," I said, "but I know what you were doing. And I won't
tell anybody."

"You don't know nothing," she said. Then she accidentally
poured half a pitcher of lemonade across the side of my head and
down my front. When Mom came in I was screaming and
swearing like Dad did when he fixed the cars, and I was put
away for life plus ninety years in the bedroom I shared with
younger brother Michael. Dinner smelled better than usual that
evening, but I had none of it. Somehow, I wasn't brokenhearted.
It gave me time to think of a scary story for the country-colored
woman on the rock.

School was the usual mix of hell and purgatory the next day.
Then the hot, dry winds cooled and the bells rang and I was on
the dirt road again, across the southern hundred acres, walking in
the lees and shadows of the big cottonwoods. I carried my
Road-Runner lunch pail and my pencil box and one book—a
handwriting manual I hated so much I tore pieces out of it at
night, to shorten its lifetime—and I walked slowly, to give my
story time to gel.

She was leaning up against a tree, not far from the rock.
Looking back, I can see she was not so old as a boy of eight
years thought. Now I see her lissome beauty and grace, despite
the dominance of gray in her reddish hair, despite the crow's-feet
around her eyes and the smile-haunts around her lips. But to the
eight-year-old she was simply a peculiar crone. And he had a
story to tell her, he thought, that would age her unto graveside.

"Hello, boy," she said.

"Hi." I sat on the rock.

"I can see you've been thinking," she said.

I squinted into the tree shadow to make her out better. "How'd
you know?"

"You have the look of a boy that's been thinking. Are you
here to listen to another story?"

"Got one to tell, this time," I said.

"Who goes first?"

It was always polite to let the woman go first so I quelled my
haste and told her she could. She motioned me to come by the
tree and sit on a smaller rock, half-hidden by grass. And while the
crickets in the shadow tuned up for the evening, she said, "Once

there was a dog. This dog was a pretty usual dog, like the ones
that would chase you around home if they thought they could get
away with it—if they didn't know you, or thought you were up
to something the big people might disapprove of. But this dog
lived in a graveyard. That is, he belonged to the caretaker.
You've seen a graveyard before, haven't you?"

"Like where they took Grandpa."

"Exactly," she said. "With pretty lawns, and big white and
gray stones, and for those who've died recently, smaller gray
stones with names and flowers and years cut into them. And
trees in some places, with a mortuary nearby made of brick, and
a garage full of black cars, and a place behind the garage where
you wonder what goes on." She knew the place, all right. "This
dog had a pretty good life. It was his job to keep the grounds
clear of animals at night. After the gates were locked, he'd be set
loose, and he wandered all night long. He was almost white, you
see. Anybody human who wasn't supposed to be there would
think he was a ghost, and they'd run away.

"But this dog had a problem. His problem was, there were
rats that didn't pay much attention to him. A whole gang of rats.
The leader was a big one, a good yard from nose to tail. These
rats made their living by burrowing under the ground in the old
section of the cemetery."

That did it. I didn't want to hear any more. The air was a lot
colder than it should have been, and I wanted to get home in
time for dinner and still be able to eat it. But I couldn't go just
then.

"Now the dog didn't know what the rats did, and just like you
and I, probably, he didn't much care to know. But it was his job
to keep them under control. So one day he made a truce with a
couple of cats that he normally tormented and told them about
the rats. These cats were scrappy old toms and they'd long since
cleared out the competition of other cats, but they were friends
themselves. So the dog made them a proposition. He said he'd
let them use the cemetery any time they wanted, to prowl or hunt
in or whatever, if they would put the fear of God into a few of
the rats. The cats took him up on it. 'We get to do whatever we
want,' they said, 'whenever we want, and you won't bother us.'
The dog agreed.

"That night the dog waited for the sounds of battle. But they
never came. Nary a yowl." She glared at me for emphasis. "Not
a claw scratch. Not even a twitch of tail in the wind." She took
a deep breath, and so did I. "Round about midnight the dog

went out into the graveyard. It was very dark and there wasn't wind, or bird, or speck of star to relieve the quiet and the dismal, inside-of-a-box-camera blackness. He sniffed his way to the old part of the graveyard, and met with the head rat, who was sitting on a slanty, cracked wooden grave marker. Only his eyes and a tip of tail showed in the dark, but the dog could smell him. 'What happened to the cats?' he asked. The rat shrugged his haunches. 'Ain't seen any cats,' he said. 'What did you think—that you could scare us out with a couple of cats? Ha. Listen—if there had been any cats here tonight, they'd have been strung and hung like meat in a shed, and my youn'uns would have grown fat on—' "

"No-o-o!" I screamed, and I ran away from the woman and the tree until I couldn't hear the story any more.

"What's the matter?" she called after me. "Aren't you going to tell me your story?" Her voice followed me as I ran.

It was funny. That night, I wanted to know what happened to the cats. Maybe nothing had happened to them. Not knowing made my visions even worse—and I didn't sleep well. But my brain worked like it had never worked before.

The next day, a Saturday, I had an ending—not a very good one in retrospect—but it served to frighten Michael so badly he threatened to tell Mom on me.

"What would you want to do that for?" I asked. "Cripes, I won't ever tell you a story again if you tell Mom!"

Michael was a year younger and didn't worry about the future. "You never told me stories before," he said, "and everything was fine. I won't miss them."

He ran down the stairs to the living room. Dad was smoking a pipe and reading the paper, relaxing before checking the irrigation on the north thirty. Michael stood at the foot of the stairs, thinking. I was almost down to grab him and haul him upstairs when he made his decision and headed for the kitchen. I knew exactly what he was considering—that Dad would probably laugh and call him a little scaredy cat. But Mom would get upset and do me in proper.

She was putting a paper form over the kitchen table to mark it for fitting a tablecloth. Michael ran up to her and hung onto a pants leg while I halted at the kitchen door, breathing hard, eyes threatening eternal torture if he so much as peeped. But Michael didn't worry about the future much.

"Mom," he said.

"Cripes!" I shouted, high-pitching on the *i*. Refuge awaited

me in the tractor shed. It was an agreed-upon hiding place. Mom
didn't know I'd be there, but Dad did, and he could mediate.

It took him a half-hour to get to me. I sat in the dark behind a
workbench, practicing my pouts. He stood in the shaft of light
falling from the unpatched chink in the roof. Dust motes May-
poled around his legs. "Son," he said. "Mom wants to know
where you got that story."

Now, this was a peculiar thing to be asked. The question I'd
expected had been, "Why did you scare Michael?" or maybe,
"What made you think of such a thing?" But no. Somehow, she
had plumbed the problem, planted the words in Dad's mouth, and
impressed upon him that father-son relationships were temporarily suspended.

"I made it up," I said.

"You've never made up that kind of story before."

"I just started.

He took a deep breath. "Son, we get along real good, except
when you lie to me. We know better. Who told you that story?"

This was uncanny. There was more going on than I could
understand—there was a mysterious, adult thing happening. I
had no way around the truth. "An old woman," I said.

Dad sighed even deeper. "What was she wearing?"

"Green dress," I said.

"Was there an old man?"

I nodded.

"Christ," he said softly. He turned and walked out of the
shed. From outside, he called me to come into the house. I
dusted off my overalls and followed him. Michael sneered at me.

" 'Locked them in coffins with old dead bodies,' " he
mimicked. "Phhht! You're going to get it."

The folks closed the folding door to the kitchen with both of
us outside. This disturbed Michael, who'd expected instant
vengeance. I was too curious and worried to take revenge on
him, so he skulked out the screen door and chased the cat around
the house. "Lock you in a coffin!" he screamed.

Mom's voice drifted from behind the louvred doors. "Do you
hear that? The poor child's going to have nightmares. It'll warp
him."

"Don't exaggerate," Dad said.

"Exaggerate what? That those filthy people are back? Ben,
they must be a hundred years old now! They're trying to do the
same thing to your son that they did to your brother . . . and just

look at *him!* Living in sin, writing for those hell-spawned girlie magazines.''

"He ain't living in sin, he's living alone in an apartment in New York City. And he writes for all kinds of places."

"They tried to do it to you, too! Just thank God your aunt saved you."

"Margie, I hope you don't intend—"

"Certainly do. She knows all about them kind of people. She chased them off once, she can sure do it again!"

All hell had broken loose. I didn't understand half of it, but I could feel the presence of Great Aunt Sybil Danser. I could almost hear her crackling voice and the shustle of her satchel of Billy Grahams and Zondervans and little tiny pamphlets with shining light in blue offset on their covers.

I knew there was no way to get the full story from the folks short of listening in, but they'd stopped talking and were sitting in that stony kind of silence that indicated Dad's disgust and Mom's determination. I was mad that nobody was blaming me, as if I were some idiot child not capable of being bad on my own. I was mad at Michael for precipitating the whole mess.

And I was curious. Were the man and woman more than a hundred years old? Why hadn't I seen them before, in town, or heard about them from other kids? Surely I wasn't the only one they'd seen on the road and told stories to. I decided to get to the source. I walked up to the louvred doors and leaned my cheek against them. "Can I go play at George's?"

"Yes," Mom said. "Be back for evening chores."

George lived on the next farm, a mile and a half east. I took my bike and rode down the old dirt road going south.

They were both under the tree, eating a picnic lunch from a wicker basket. I pulled my bike over and leaned it against the gray rock, shading my eyes to see them more clearly.

"Hello, boy," the old man said. "Ain't seen you in a while."

I couldn't think of anything to say. The woman offered me a cookie and I refused with a muttered, "No, thank you, ma'am."

"Well then, perhaps you'd like to tell us your story."

"No, ma'am."

"No story to tell us? That's odd. Meg was sure you had a story in you someplace. Peeking out from behind your ears maybe, thumbing its nose at us."

The woman smiled ingratiatingly. "Tea?"

"There's going to be trouble," I said.

"Already?" The woman smoothed the skirt in her lap and set

a plate of nut bread into it. "Well, it comes sooner or later, this time sooner. What do you think of it, boy?"

"I think I got into a lot of trouble for not much being bad," I said. "I don't know why."

"Sit down then," the old man said. "Listen to a tale, then tell us what's going on."

I sat down, not too keen about hearing another story but out of politeness. I took a piece of nut bread and nibbled on it as the woman sipped her tea and cleared her throat. "Once there was a city on the shore of a broad, blue sea. In the city lived five hundred children and nobody else, because the wind from the sea wouldn't let anyone grow old. Well, children don't have kids of their own, of course, so when the wind came up in the first year the city never grew any larger."

"Where'd all the grownups go?" I asked. The old man held his fingers to his lips and shook his head.

"The children tried to play all day, but it wasn't enough. They became frightened at night and had bad dreams. There was nobody to comfort them because only grownups are really good at making nightmares go away. Now, sometimes nightmares are white horses that come out of the sea, so they set up guards along the beaches, and fought them back with wands made of blackthorn. But there was another kind of nightmare, one that was black and rose out of the ground, and those were impossible to guard against. So the children got together one day and decided to tell all the scary stories there were to tell, to prepare themselves for all the nightmares. They found it was pretty easy to think up scary stories, and every one of them had a story or two to tell. They stayed up all night spinning yarns about ghosts and dead things, and live things that shouldn't have been, and things that were neither. They talked about death and about monsters that suck blood, about things that live way deep in the earth and long, thin things that sneak through cracks in doors to lean over the beds at night and speak in tongues no one could understand. They talked about eyes without heads, and vice versa, and little blue shoes that walk across a cold empty white room, with no one in them, and a bunk bed that creaks when it's empty, and a printing press that produces newspapers from a city that never was. Pretty soon, by morning, they'd told all the scary stories. When the black horses came out of the ground the next night, and the white horses from the sea, the children greeted them with cakes and ginger ale, and they held a big party. They also invited the pale sheet-things from the clouds, and everyone ate hearty and had a good time. One white horse let a little boy ride on it, and took him wherever he wanted to go. So there were no more bad dreams in the city of children by the sea.''

I finished the piece of bread and wiped my hands on my crossed legs. "So that's why you tried to scare me," I said.

She shook her head. "No. I never had a reason for telling a story, and neither should you."

"I don't think I'm going to tell stories any more," I said. "The folks get too upset."

"Philistines," the old man said, looking off across the fields.

"Listen, young man. There is nothing finer in the world than the telling of tales. Split atoms if you wish, but splitting an infinitive—and getting away with it—is far nobler. Lance boils if you wish, but pricking pretensions is often cleaner and always more fun."

"Then why are Mom and Dad so mad?"

The old man shook his head. "An eternal mystery."

"Well, I'm not so sure," I said. "I scared my little brother pretty bad and that's not nice."

"Being scared is nothing," the old woman said. "Being bored, or ignorant—now that's a crime."

"I still don't know. My folks say you have to be a hundred years old. You did something to my uncle they didn't like, and that was a long time ago. What kind of people are you, anyway?"

The old man smiled. "Old, yes. But not a hundred."

"I just came out here to warn you. Mom and Dad are bringing out my great aunt, and she's no fun for anyone. You better go away." With that said, I ran back to my bike and rode off, pumping for all I was worth. I was between a rock and a hard place. I loved my folks but I itched to hear more stories. Why wasn't it easier to make decisions?

That night I slept restlessly. I didn't have any dreams, but I kept waking up with something pounding at the back of my head, like it wanted to be let in. I scrunched my face up and pressed it back.

At Sunday breakfast, Mom looked across the table at me and put on a kind face. "We're going to pick up Auntie Danser this afternoon, at the airport," she said.

My face went like warm butter.

"You'll come with us, won't you?" she asked. "You always did like the airport."

"All the way from where she lives?" I asked.

"From Omaha," Dad said.

I didn't want to go, but it was more a command than a request. I nodded and Dad smiled at me around his pipe.

"Don't eat too many biscuits," Mom warned him. "You're putting on weight again."

"I'll wear it off come harvest. You cook as if the whole crew was here, anyway."

"Auntie Danser will straighten it all out," Mom said, her mind elsewhere. I caught the suggestion of a grimace on Dad's face, and the pipe wriggled as he bit down on it harder.

The airport was something out of a TV space movie. It went on forever, with stairways going up to restaurants and big smoky windows which looked out on the screaming jets, and crowds of people, all leaving, except for one pear-shaped figure in a cotton print dress with fat ankles and glasses thick as headlamps. I knew her from a hundred yards.

When we met, she shook hands with Mom, hugged Dad as if she didn't want to, then bent down and gave me a smile. Her teeth were yellow and even, sound as a horse's. She was the ugliest woman I'd ever seen. She smelled of lilacs. To this day lilacs take my appetite away.

She carried a bag. Part of it was filled with knitting, part with books and pamphlets. I always wondered why she never carried a Bible—just Billy Grahams and Zondervans. One pamphlet fell out and Dad bent to pick it up.

"Keep it, read it," Auntie Danser instructed him. "Do you good." She turned to Mom and scrutinized her from the bottom of a swimming pool. "You're looking good. He must be treating you right."

Dad ushered us out the automatic doors into the dry heat. Her one suitcase was light as a mummy and probably just as empty. I carried it and it didn't even bring sweat to my brow. Her life was not in clothes and toiletry but in the plastic knitting bag.

We drove back to the farm in the big white station wagon. I leaned my head against the cool glass of the rear seat window and considered puking. Auntie Danser, I told myself, was like a mental dose of castor oil. Or like a visit to the dentist. Even if nothing was going to happen her smell presaged disaster, and like a horse sniffing a storm, my entrails worried.

Mom looked across the seat at me—Auntie Danser was riding up front with Dad—and asked, "You feeling okay? Did they give you anything to eat? Anything funny?"

I said they'd given me a piece of nut bread. Mom went, "Oh, Lord."

"Margie, they don't work like that. They got other ways." Auntie Danser leaned over the back seat and goggled at me. "Boy's just worried. I know all about it. These people and I have had it out before."

Through those murky glasses, her flat eyes knew me to my young, pithy core. I didn't like being known so well. I could see that Auntie Danser's life was firm and predictable, and I made a sudden commitment. I liked the man and woman. They caused trouble, but they were the exact opposite of my great-aunt. I felt better, and I gave her a reassuring grin. "Boy will be okay," she said. "Just a colic of the upset mind."

Michael and Barbara sat on the front porch as the car drove up. Somehow a visit by Auntie Danser didn't bother them as much as it did me. They didn't fawn over her but they accepted her without complaining—even out of adult earshot. That made me think more carefully about them. I decided I didn't love them any the less, but I couldn't trust them, either. The world was taking sides and so far on my side I was very lonely. I didn't count the two old people on my side, because I wasn't sure they were—but they came a lot closer than anybody in the family.

Auntie Danser wanted to read Billy Graham books to us after dinner, but Dad snuck us out before Mom could gather us together—all but Barbara, who stayed to listen. We watched the sunset from the loft of the old wood barn, then tried to catch the little birds that live in the rafters. By dark and bedtime I was hungry, but not for food. I asked Dad if he'd tell me a story before bed.

"You know your Mom doesn't approve of all that fairy-tale stuff," he said.

"Then no fairy tales. Just a story."

"I'm out of practice, son," he confided. He looked very sad. "Your mom says we should concentrate on things that are real and not waste our time with make-believe. Life's hard. I may have to sell the farm, you know, and work for that feed-mixer in Mitchell."

I went to bed and felt like crying. A whole lot of my family had died that night, I didn't know exactly how, or why. But I was mad.

I didn't go to school the next day. During the night I'd had a dream, which came so true and whole to me that I had to rush to the stand of cottonwoods and tell the old people. I took my lunch box and walked rapidly down the road.

They weren't there. On a piece of wire braided to the biggest tree they'd left a note on faded brown paper. It was in a strong, feminine hand, sepia-inked, delicately scribed with what could have been a goose-quill pen. It said: ''We're at the old Hauskopf farm. Come if you must.''

Not ''Come if you can.'' I felt a twinge. The Hauskopf farm, abandoned fifteen years ago and never sold, was three miles farther down the road and left on a deep-rutted fork. It took me an hour to get there.

The house still looked deserted. All the white paint was flaking, leaving dead gray wood. The windows stared. I walked up the porch steps and knocked on the heavy oak door. For a moment I thought no one was going to answer. Then I heard what sounded like a gust of wind, but inside the house, and the old woman opened the door. ''Hello, boy,'' she said. ''Come for more stories?''

She invited me in. Wildflowers were growing along the baseboards and tiny roses peered from the brambles that covered the walls. A quail led her train of inch-and-a-half fluffball chicks from under the stairs, into the living room. The floor was carpeted but the flowers in the weave seemed more than patterns. I could stare down and keep picking out detail for minutes. ''This way, boy,'' the woman said. She took my hand. Hers was smooth and warm but I had the impression it was also hard as wood.

A tree stood in the living room, growing out of the floor and sending its branches up to support the ceiling. Rabbits and quail and a lazy-looking brindle cat looked at me from tangles of roots. A wooden bench surrounded the base of the tree. On the side away from us, I heard someone breathing. The old man poked his head around, and smiled at me, lifting his long pipe in greeting. ''Hello, boy,'' he said.

''The boy looks like he's ready to tell us a story, this time,'' the woman said.

''Of course, Meg. Have a seat, boy. Cup of cider for you? Tea? Herb biscuit?''

''Cider, please,'' I said.

The old man stood and went down the hall to the kitchen. He came back with a wooden tray and three steaming cups of mulled cider. The cinnamon tickled my nose as I sipped.

''Now. What's your story?''

''It's about two hawks,'' I said. I hesitated.

''Go on.''

"Brother hawks. Never did like each other. Fought for a strip of land where they could hunt."

"Yes?"

"Finally, one hawk met an old, crippled bobcat that had set up a place for itself in a rockpile. The bobcat was learning itself magic so it wouldn't have to go out and catch dinner, which was awful hard for it now. The hawk landed near the bobcat and told it about his brother, and how cruel he was. So the bobcat said, 'Why not give him the land for the day? Here's what you can do.' The bobcat told him how he could turn into a rabbit, but a very strong rabbit no hawk could hurt."

"Wily bobcat," the old man said, smiling.

" 'You mean, my brother wouldn't be able to catch me?' the hawk asked. 'Course not,' the bobcat said. 'And you can teach him a lesson. You'll tussle with him, scare him real bad—show him what tough animals there are on the land he wants. Then he'll go away and hunt somewhere else.' The hawk thought that sounded like a fine idea. So he let the bobcat turn him into a rabbit and he hopped back to the land and waited in a patch of grass. Sure enough, his brother's shadow passed by soon, and then he heard a swoop and saw the claws held out. So he filled himself with being mad and jumped up and practically bit the tail feathers off his brother. The hawk just flapped up and rolled over on the ground, blinking and gawking with his beak wide. 'Rabbit,' he said, 'that's not natural. Rabbits don't act that way.'

" 'Round here they do,' the hawk-rabbit said. 'This is a tough old land, and all the animals here know the tricks of escaping from bad birds like you.' This scared the brother hawk, and he flew away as best he could, and never came back again. The hawk-rabbit hopped to the rockpile and stood up before the bobcat, saying, 'It worked real fine. I thank you. Now turn me back and I'll go hunt my land.' But the bobcat only grinned and reached out with a paw and broke the rabbit's neck. Then he ate him, and said, 'Now the land's mine, and no hawks can take away the easy game.' And that's how the greed of two hawks turned their land over to a bobcat."

The old woman looked at me with wide, baked-chestnut eyes and smiled. "You've got it," she said. "Just like your uncle. Hasn't he got it, Jack?" The old man nodded and took his pipe from his mouth. "He's got it fine. He'll make a good one."

"Now, boy, why did you make up that story?"

I thought for a moment, then shook my head. "I don't know," I said. "It just came up."

"What are you going to do with the story?"

I didn't have an answer for that question, either.

"Got any other stories in you?"

I considered, then said. "Think so."

A car drove up outside and Mom called my name. The old woman stood and straightened her dress. "Follow me," she said. "Go out the back door, walk around the house. Return home with them. Tomorrow, go to school like you're supposed to do. Next Saturday, come back and we'll talk some more."

"Son? You in there?"

I walked out the back and came around to the front of the house. Mom and Auntie Danser waited in the station wagon. "You aren't allowed out here. Were you in that house?" Mom asked. I shook my head.

My great aunt looked at me with her glassed-in flat eyes and lifted the corners of her lips a little. "Margie," she said, "go have a look in the windows."

Mom got out of the car and walked up the porch to peer through the dusty panes. "It's empty, Sybil."

"Empty, boy, right?"

"I don't know," I said. "I wasn't inside."

"I could hear you, boy," she said. "Last night. Talking in your sleep. Rabbits and hawks don't behave that way. You know it, and I know it. So it ain't no good thinking about them that way, is it?"

"I don't remember talking in my sleep," I said.

"Margie, let's go home. This boy needs some pamphlets read into him."

Mom got into the car and looked back at me before starting the engine. "You ever skip school again, I'll strap you black and blue. It's real embarrassing having the school call, and not knowing where you are. Hear me?"

I nodded.

Everything was quiet that week. I went to school and tried not to dream at night, and did everything boys are supposed to do. But I didn't feel like a boy. I felt something big inside, and no amount of Billy Grahams and Zondervans read at me could change that feeling.

I made one mistake, though. I asked Auntie Danser why she never read the Bible. This was in the parlor one evening after dinner and cleaning up the dishes. "Why do you want to know, boy?" she asked.

"Well, the Bible seems to be full of fine stories, but you don't carry it around with you. I just wondered why."

"Bible is a good book," she said. "The only good book. But it's difficult. It has lots of camouflage. Sometimes—" She stopped. "Who put you up to asking that question?"

"Nobody," I said.

"I heard that question before, you know," she said. "Ain't the first time I been asked. Somebody else asked me, once."

I sat in my chair, stiff as a ham.

"Your father's brother asked me that once. But we won't talk about him, will we?"

I shook my head.

Next Saturday I waited until it was dark and everyone was in bed. The night air was warm but I was sweating more than the warm could cause as I rode my bike down the dirt road, lamp beam swinging back and forth. The sky was crawling with stars, all of them looking at me. The Milky Way seemed to touch down just beyond the road, like I might ride straight up it if I went far enough.

I knocked on the heavy door. There were no lights in the windows and it was late for old folks to be up, but I knew these two didn't behave like normal people. And I knew that just because the house looked empty from the outside didn't mean it was empty within. The wind rose up and beat against the door, making me shiver. Then it opened. It was dark for a moment and the breath went out of me. Two pairs of eyes stared from the black. They seemed a lot taller this time. "Come in, boy," Jack whispered.

Fireflies lit up the tree in the living room. The brambles and wildflowers glowed like weeds on a sea floor. The carpet crawled, but not to my feet. I was shivering in earnest now and my teeth chattered.

I only saw their shadows as they sat on the bench in front of me. "Sit," Meg said. "Listen close. You've taken the fire and it glows bright. You're only a boy but you're just like a pregnant woman now. For the rest of your life you'll be cursed with the worst affliction known to humans. Your skin will twitch at night. Your eyes will see things in the dark. Beasts will come to you and beg to be ridden. You'll never know one truth from another. You might starve, because few will want to encourage you. And if you do make good in this world, you might lose the gift and search forever after, in vain. Some will say the gift isn't special.

Beware them. Some will say it is special and beware them, too. And some—''

There was a scratching at the door. I thought it was an animal for a moment. Then it cleared its throat. It was my great-aunt.

''Some will say you're damned. Perhaps they're right. But you're also enthused. Carry it lightly, and responsibly.''

''Listen in there. This is Sybil Danser. You know me. Open up.''

''Now stand by the stairs, in the dark where she can't see,'' Jack said. I did as I was told. One of them—I couldn't tell which—opened the door and the lights went out in the tree, the carpet stilled, and the brambles were snuffed. Auntie Danser stood in the doorway, outlined by star glow, carrying her knitting bag. ''Boy?'' she asked. I held my breath.

''And you others, too.''

The wind in the house seemed to answer. ''I'm not too late,'' she said. ''Damn you, in truth, damn you to hell! You come to our towns, and you plague us with thoughts no decent person wants to think. Not just fairy stories, but telling the way people live, and why they shouldn't live that way! Your very breath is tainted! Hear me?'' She walked slowly into the empty living room, feet clonking on the wooden floor. ''You make them write about us, and make others laugh at us. Question the way we think. Condemn our deepest prides. Pull out our mistakes and amplify them beyond all truth. What right do you have to take young children and twist their minds?''

The wind sang through the cracks in the walls. I tried to see if Jack or Meg was there, but only shadows remained.

''I know where you come from, don't forget that! Out of the ground! Out of the bones of old, wicked Indians! Shamans and pagan dances and worshiping dirt and filth! I heard about you from the old squaws on the reservation. Frost and Spring, they called you, signs of the turning year. Well, now you got a different name! Death and demons, I call you, hear me?''

She seemed to jump at a sound but I couldn't hear it. ''Don't you argue with me!'' she shrieked. She took her glasses off and held out both hands. ''Think I'm a weak old woman, do you? You don't know how deep I run in these communities! I'm the one who had them books taken off the shelves. Remember me? Oh, you hated it—not being able to fill young minds with your pestilence. Took them off high school shelves, and out of lists—burned them for junk! Remember? That was me. I'm not dead yet! Boy, where are you?''

"Enchant her," I whispered to the air. "Magic her. Make her go away. Let me live here with you."

"Is that you, boy? Come with your aunt, now. Come with, come away!"

"Go with her," the wind told me. "Send your children this way, years from now. But go with her."

I felt a kind of tingly warmth and knew it was time to get home. I snuck out the back way and came around to the front of the house. There was no car. She'd followed me on foot all the way from the farm. I wanted to leave her there in the old house, shouting at the dead rafters, but instead I called her name and waited.

She came out crying. She knew.

"You poor, sinning boy," she said, pulling me to her lilac bosom.

SEMLEY'S NECKLACE

by
Ursula K. Le Guin

Ursula K. Le Guin is one of science fiction's most renowned and honored writers—she has won (to date) three Nebulas, four Hugos, the National Book Award, two Jupiters, and the Gandalf Life Award, among others. She was also the Guest of Honor at the 1975 World Science Fiction Convention in Australia. Her classic works include THE LEFT HAND OF DARKNESS (1969), THE LATHE OF HEAVEN (1971), and THE DIS-POSSESSED: AN AMBIGUOUS UTOPIA (1974). Some of her finest short stories can be found in THE WIND'S TWELVE QUARTERS (1975). She is also a leading critic of the field.

A poignant fairy tale, "Semley's Necklace" exempli-fies Arthur C. Clarke's first law—to the beholder an advanced science appears to be magic.

How can you tell the legend from the fact on these worlds that lie so many years away?—planets without names, called by their people simply The World, planets without history, where the past is the matter of myth, and a returning explorer finds his own doings of a few years back have become the gestures of a god. Unreason darkens that gap of time bridged by our lightspeed ships, and in the darkness uncertainty and disproportion grow like weeds.

In trying to tell the story of a man, an ordinary League scientist, who went to such a nameless half-known world not many years ago, one feels like an archaeologist amid millennial ruins, now struggling through choked tangles of leaf, flower, branch and vine to the sudden bright geometry of a wheel or a polished cornerstone, and now entering some commonplace, sunlit doorway to find inside it the darkness, the impossible flicker of a flame, the glitter of a jewel, the half-glimpsed movement of a woman's arm.

How can you tell fact from legend, truth from truth?

Through Rocannon's story the jewel, the blue glitter seen briefly, returns. With it let us begin, here:

Galactic Area 8, No. 62: FOMALHAUT II.
High-Intelligence Life Forms: Species Contacted:
Species I.

A. Gdemiar (singular Gdem): Highly intelligent, fully hominoid nocturnal troglodytes, 120–135 cm. in height, light skin, dark head-hair. When contacted these cave-dwellers possessed a rigidly stratified oligarchic urban society modified by partial colonial telepathy, and a technologically oriented Early Steel culture. Technology enhanced to Industrial, Point C, during League Mission of 252–254. In 254 an Automatic Drive ship (to-from New South Georgia) was presented to oligarchs of the Kiriensea Area community. Status C-Prime.

B. Fiia (singular Fian): Highly intelligent, fully hominoid, diurnal, av. ca. 130 cm. in height, observed individuals generally light in skin and hair. Brief contacts indicated village and nomadic communal societies, partial colonial telepathy, also some indication of short-range TK. The race appears a-technological and evasive, with minimal and fluid culture-patterns. Currently untaxable. Status E-Query.

Species II.
Liuar (singular Liu): Highly intelligent, fully hominoid, diurnal, av. height above 170 cm., this species possesses a fortress/village, clan-descent society, a blocked technology (Bronze), a feudal-

heroic culture. Note horizontal social cleavage into 2 pseudo-races: (a) Olgyior, "midmen," light-skinned and dark-haired; (b) Angyar, "lords," very tall, dark-skinned, yellow-haired—

"That's her," said Rocannon, looking up from the *Abridged Handy Pocket Guide to Intelligent Life-forms* at the very tall, dark-skinned, yellow-haired woman who stood halfway down the long museum hall. She stood still and erect, crowned with bright hair, gazing at something in a display case. Around her fidgeted four uneasy and unattractive dwarves.

"I didn't know Fomalhaut II had all those people besides the trogs," said Ketho, the curator.

"I didn't either. There are even some 'Unconfirmed' species listed here, that they never contacted. Sounds like time for a more thorough survey mission to the place. Well, now at least we know what she is."

"I wish there were some way of knowing *who* she is. . . ."

She was of an ancient family, a descendant of the first kings of the Angyar, and for all her poverty her hair shone with the pure, steadfast gold of her inheritance. The little people, the Fiia, bowed when she passed them, even when she was a barefoot child running in the fields, the light and fiery comet of her hair brightening the troubled winds of Kirien.

She was still very young when Durhal of Hallan saw her, courted her, and carried her away from the ruined towers and windy halls of her childhood to his own high home. In Hallan on the mountainside there was no comfort either, though splendor endured. The windows were unglassed, the stone floors bare; in coldyear one might wake to see the night's snow in long, low drifts beneath each window. Durhal's bride stood with narrow bare feet on the snowy floor, braiding up the fire of her hair and laughing at her young husband in the silver mirror that hung in their room. That mirror, and his mother's bridal-gown sewn with a thousand tiny crystals, were all his wealth. Some of his lesser kinfolk of Hallan still possessed wardrobes of brocaded clothing, furniture of gilded wood, silver harness for their steeds, armor and silver mounted swords, jewels and jewelry—and on these last Durhal's bride looked enviously, glancing back at a gemmed coronet or a golden brooch even when the wearer of the ornament stood aside to let her pass, deferent to her birth and marriage-rank.

Fourth from the High Seat of Hallan Revel sat Durhal and his

bride Semley, so close to Hallanlord that the old man often
poured wine for Semley with his own hand, and spoke of
hunting with his nephew and heir Durhal, looking on the young
pair with a grim, unhopeful love. Hope came hard to the Angyar
of Hallan and all the Western Lands, since the Starlords had
appeared with their houses that leaped about on pillars of fire and
their awful weapons that could level hills. They had interfered
with all the old ways and wars, and though the sums were small
there was terrible shame to the Angyar in having to pay a tax to
them, a tribute for the Starlords' war that was to be fought with
some strange enemy, somewhere in the hollow places between
the stars, at the end of years. "It will be your war too," they
said, but for a generation now the Angyar had sat in idle shame
in their revel-halls, watching their double swords rust, their sons
grow up without ever striking a blow in battle, their daughters
marry poor men, even midmen, having no dowry of heroic loot
to bring a noble husband. Hallanlord's face was bleak when he
watched the fair-haired couple and heard their laughter as they
drank bitter wine and joked together in the cold, ruinous, resplendent fortress of their race.

Semley's own face hardened when she looked down the hall
and saw, in seats far below hers, even down among the half
breeds and the midmen, against white skins and black hair, the
gleam and flash of precious stones. She herself had brought
nothing in dowry to her husband, not even a silver hairpin. The
dress of a thousand crystals she had put away in a chest for the
wedding-day of her daughter, if daughter it was to be.

It was, and they called her Haldre, and when the fuzz on her
little brown skull grew longer it shone with steadfast gold, the
inheritance of the lordly generations, the only gold she would
ever possess. . . .

Semley did not speak to her husband of her discontent. For all
his gentleness to her, Durhal in his pride had only contempt for
envy, for vain wishing, and she dreaded his contempt. But she
spoke to Durhal's sister Durossa.

"My family had a great treasure once," she said. "It was a
necklace all of gold, with the blue jewel set in the center—
sapphire?"

Durossa shook her head, smiling, not sure of the name either.
It was late in warmyear, as these Northern Angyar called the
summer of the eight-hundred-day year, beginning the cycle of
months anew at each equinox; to Semley it seemed an outlandish
calendar, a mid-mannish reckoning. Her family was at an end,

but it had been older and purer than the race of any of these northwestern marchlanders, who mixed too freely with the Olgyior. She sat with Durossa in the sunlight on a stone windowseat high up in the Great Tower, where the older woman's apartment was. Widowed young, childless, Durossa had been given in second marriage to Hallanlord, who was her father's brother. Since it was a kinmarriage and a second marriage on both sides she had not taken the title of Hallanlady, which Semley would some day bear; but she sat with the old lord in the High Seat and ruled with him his domains. Older than her brother Durhal, she was fond of his young wife, and delighted in the bright-haired baby Haldre.

"It was bought," Semley went on, "with all the money my forebear Leynen got when he conquered the Southern Fiefs—all the money from a whole kingdom, think of it, for one jewel! Oh, it would outshine anything here in Hallan, surely, even those crystals like koob-eggs your cousin Issar wears. It was so beautiful they gave it a name of its own; they called it the Eye of the Sea. My great-grandmother wore it."

"You never saw it?" the older woman asked lazily, gazing down at the green mountainslopes where long, long summer sent its hot and restless winds straying among the forests and whirling down white roads to the seacoast far away.

"It was lost before I was born.

"No, my father said it was stolen before the Starlords ever came to our realm. He wouldn't talk of it, but there was an old midwoman full of tales who always told me the Fiia would know where it was."

"Ah, the Fiia I should like to see!" said Durossa. "They're in so many songs and tales; why do they never come to the Western Lands?"

"Too high, too cold in winter, I think. They like the sunlight of the valleys of the south."

"Are they like the Clayfolk?"

"Those I've never seen; they keep away from us in the south. Aren't they white like midmen, and misformed? The Fiia are fair; they look like children, only thinner, and wiser. Oh, I wonder if they know where the necklace is, who stole it and where he hid it! Think, Durossa—if I could come into Hallan Revel and sit down by my husband with the wealth of a kingdom round my neck, and outshine the other women as he outshines all men!"

Durossa bent her head above the baby, who sat studying her own brown toes on a fur rug between her mother and aunt.

"Semley is foolish," she murmured to the baby; "Semley who shines like a falling star, Semley whose husband loves no gold but the gold of her hair. . . ."

And Semley, looking out over the green slopes of summer toward the distant sea, was silent.

But when another coldyear had passed, and the Starlords had come again to collect their taxes for the war against the world's end—this time using a couple of dwarfish Clayfolk as interpreters, and so leaving all the Angyar humiliated to the point of rebellion—and another warmyear too was gone, and Haldre had grown into a lovely, chattering child, Semley brought her one morning to Durossa's sunlit room in the tower. Semley wore an old cloak of blue, and the hood covered her hair.

"Keep Haldre for me these few days, Durossa," she said, quick and calm. "I'm going south to Kirien."

"To see your father?"

"To find my inheritance. Your cousins of Harget Fief have been taunting Durhal. Even that halfbreed Parna can torment him, because Parna's wife has a satin coverlet for her bed, and a diamond earring, and three gowns, the dough-faced black-haired trollop! while Durhal's wife must patch her gown—"

"Is Durhal's pride in his wife, or what she wears?"

But Semley was not to be moved. "The Lords of Hallan are becoming poor men in their own hall. I am going to bring my dowry to my lord, as one of my lineage should."

"Semley! Does Durhal know you're going?"

"My return will be a happy one—that much let him know," said young Semley, breaking for a moment into her joyful laugh; then she bent to kiss her daughter, turned, and before Durossa could speak, was gone like a quick wind over the floors of sunlit stone.

Married women of the Angyar never rode for sport, and Semley had not been from Hallan since her marriage; so now, mounting the high saddle of a windsteed, she felt like a girl again, like the wild maiden she had been, riding half-broken steeds on the north wind over the fields of Kirien. The beast that bore her now down from the hills of Hallan was of finer breed, striped coat fitting sleek over hollow, buoyant bones, green eyes slitted against the wind, light and mighty wings sweeping up and down to either side of Semley, revealing and hiding, revealing and hiding the clouds above her and the hills below.

On the third morning she came to Kirien and stood again in the ruined courts. Her father had been drinking all night, and, just as in the old days, the morning sunlight poking through his fallen ceilings annoyed him, and the sight of his daughter only increased his annoyance. "What are you back for?" he growled, his swollen eyes glancing at her and away. The fiery hair of his youth was quenched, grey strands tangled on his skull. "Did the young Halla not marry you, and you've come sneaking home?"

"I am Durhal's wife. I came to get my dowry, father."

The drunkard growled in disgust; but she laughed at him so gently that he had to look at her again, wincing.

"It is true, father, that the Fiia stole the necklace Eye of the Sea?"

"How do I know? Old tales. The thing was lost before I was born, I think. I wish I never had been. Ask the Fiia if you want to know. Go to them, go back to your husband. Leave me alone here. There's no room at Kirien for girls and gold and all the rest of the story. The story's over here; this is the fallen place, this is the empty hall. The sons of Leynen all are dead, their treasures are all lost. Go on your way, girl."

Grey and swollen as the web-spinner of ruined houses, he turned and went blundering toward the cellars where he hid from daylight.

Leading the striped windsteed of Hallan, Semley left her old home and walked down the steep hill, past the village of the midmen, who greeted her with sullen respect, on over fields and pastures where the great, wing-clipped, half-wild herilor grazed, to a valley that was green as a painted bowl and full to the brim with sunlight. In the deep of the valley lay the village of the Fiia, and as she descended leading her steed the little, slight people ran up toward her from their huts and gardens, laughing, calling out in faint, thin voices.

"Hail Halla's bride, Kirienlady, Windborne, Semley the Fair!"

They gave her lovely names and she liked to hear them, minding not at all their laughter; for they laughed at all they said. That was her own way, to speak and laugh. She stood tall in her long blue cloak among their swirling welcome.

"Hail Lightfolk, Sundwellers, Fiia friends of men!"

They took her down into the village and brought her into one of their airy houses, the tiny children chasing along behind. There was no telling the age of a Fian once he was grown; it was hard even to tell one from another and be sure, as they moved about quick as moths around a candle, that she spoke always to the same one. But it seemed that one of them talked with her for a while, as the others fed and petted her steed, and brought water for her to drink, and bowls of fruit from their gardens of little trees. "It was never the Fiia that stole the necklace of the Lords of Kirien!" cried the little man. "What would the Fiia do with gold, Lady? For us there is sunlight in warmyear, and in coldyear the remembrance of sunlight; the yellow fruit, the yellow leaves in endseason, the yellow hair of our lady of Kirien; no other gold."

"Then it was some midman stole the thing?"

Laughter rang long and faint about her. "How would a midman dare? O Lady of Kirien, how the great jewel was stolen no mortal knows, not man nor midman nor Fian nor any among the Seven Folk. Only dead minds know how it was lost, long ago when Kireley the Proud whose great-granddaughter is Semley walked alone by the caves of the sea. But it may be found perhaps among the Sunhaters."

"The Clayfolk?"

A louder burst of laughter, nervous.

"Sit with us, Semley, sunhaired, returned to us from the north." She sat with them to eat, and they were as pleased with her graciousness as she with theirs. But when they heard her repeat that she would go to the Clayfolk to find her inheritance, if it was there, they began not to laugh; and little by little there were fewer of them around her. She was alone at last with perhaps the one she had spoken with before the meal. "Do not go among the Clayfolk, Semley," he said, and for a moment her heart failed her. The Fian, drawing his hand down slowly over his eyes, had darkened all the air about him. Fruit lay ash-white on the plate; all the bowls of clear water were empty.

"In the mountains of the far land the Fiia and the Gdemiar parted. Long ago we parted," said the slight, still man of the Fiia. "Longer ago we were one. What we are not, they are. What we are, they are not. Think of the sunlight and the grass and the trees that bear fruit, Semley; think that not all roads that lead down lead up as well."

"Mine leads neither down nor up, kind host, but only straight on to my inheritance. I will go to it where it is, and return with it."

The Fian bowed, laughing a little.

Outside the village she mounted her striped windsteed, and, calling farewell in answer to their calling, rose up into the wind of afternoon and flew southwestward toward the caves down by the rocky shores of Kiriensea.

She feared she might have to walk far into those tunnel-caves to find the people she sought, for it was said the Clayfolk never came out of their caves into the light of the sun, and feared even the Greatstar and the moons. It was a long ride; she landed once to let her steed hunt tree-rats while she ate a little bread from her saddlebag. The bread was hard and dry by now and tasted of leather, yet kept a faint savor of its making, so that for a moment, eating it alone in a glade of the southern forests, she heard the quiet tone of a voice and saw Durhal's face turned to her in the light of the candles of Hallan. For a while she sat daydreaming of that stern and vivid young face, and of what she would say to him when she came home with a kingdom's ransom around her neck: "I wanted a gift worthy of my husband, Lord. . . ." Then she pressed on, but when she reached the coast the sun had set, with the Greatstar sinking behind it. A mean wind had come up from the west, starting and gusting and veering, and her windsteed was weary fighting it. She let him glide down on the sand. At once he folded his wings and curled his thick, light limbs under him with a thrum of purring. Semley stood holding her cloak close at her throat, stroking the steed's neck so that he flicked his ears and purred again. The warm fur comforted her hand, but all that met her eyes was grey sky full of smears of cloud, grey sea, dark sand. And then running over the sand a low, dark creature—another—a group of them, squatting and running and stopping.

She called aloud to them. Though they had not seemed to see her, now in a moment they were all around her. They kept a distance from her windsteed; he had stopped purring, and his fur rose a little under Semley's hand. She took up the reins, glad of his protection but afraid of the nervous ferocity he might display. The strange folk stood silent, staring, their thick bare feet planted in the sand. There was no mistaking them: they were the height of the Fiia and in all else a shadow, a black image of those laughing people. Naked, squat, stiff, with lank hair and grey-white skins, dampish-looking like the skins of grubs; eyes like rocks.

"You are the Clayfolk?"

"Gdemiar are we, people of the Lords of the Realms of Night." The voice was unexpectedly loud and deep, and rang out pompous through the salt, blowing dusk; but, as with the Fiia, Semley was not sure which one had spoken.

"I greet you, Nightlords. I am Semley of Kirien, Durhal's wife of Hallan. I come to you seeking my inheritance, the necklace called Eye of the Sea, lost long ago."

"Why do you seek it here, Angya? Here is only sand and salt and night."

"Because lost things are known of in deep places," said Semley, quite ready for a play of wits, "and gold that came from earth has a way of going back to the earth. And sometimes the made, they say, returns to the maker." This last was a guess; it hit the mark.

"It is true the necklace Eye of the Sea is known to us by name. It was made in our caves long ago, and sold by us to the Angyar. And the blue stone came from the Clayfields of our kin to the east. But these are very old tales, Angya."

"May I listen to them in the places where they are told?"

The squat people were silent a while, as if in doubt. The grey wind blew by over the sand, darkening as the Greatstar set; the sound of the sea loudened and lessened. The deep voice spoke again: "Yes, lady of the Angyar. You may enter the Deep Halls. Come with us now." There was a changed note in his voice, wheedling. Semley would not hear it. She followed the Claymen over the sand, leading on a short rein her sharp-taloned steed.

At the cave-mouth, a toothless, yawning mouth from which a stinking warmth sighed out, one of the Claymen said, "The air-beast cannot come in."

"Yes," said Semley.

"No," said the squat people.

"Yes. I will not leave him here. He is not mine to leave. He will not harm you, so long as I hold the reins."

"No," deep voices repeated; but others broke in, "As you will," and after a moment of hesitation they went on. The cave-mouth seemed to snap shut behind them, so dark was it under the stone. They went in single file, Semley last.

The darkness of the tunnel lightened, and they came under a ball of weak white fire hanging from the roof. Farther on was another, and another; between them long black worms hung in festoons from the rock. As they went on these fire-globes were set closer, so that all the tunnel was lit with a bright, cold light.

Semley's guides stopped at a parting of three tunnels, all blocked by doors that looked to be of iron. "We shall wait, Angya," they said, and eight of them stayed with her, while three others unlocked one of the doors and passed through. It fell to behind them with a clash.

Straight and still stood the daughter of the Angyar in the white, blank light of the lamps; her windsteed crouched beside her, flicking the tip of his striped tail, his great folded wings stirring again and again with the checked impulse to fly. In the tunnel behind Semley the eight Claymen squatted on their hams, muttering to one another in their deep voices, in their own tongue.

The central door swung clanging open. "Let the Angya enter the Realm of Night!" cried a new voice, booming and boastful. A Clayman who wore some clothing on his thick grey body stood in the doorway, beckoning to her. "Enter and behold the wonders of our lands, the marvels made by hands, the works of the Nightlords!"

Silent, with a tug at her steed's reins, Semley bowed her head and followed him under the low doorway made for dwarfish folk. Another glaring tunnel stretched ahead, dank walls dazzling in the white light, but, instead of a way to walk upon, its floor carried two bars of polished iron stretching off side by side as far as she could see. On the bars rested some kind of cart with metal wheels. Obeying her new guide's gestures, with no hesitation and no trace of wonder on her face, Semley stepped into the cart and made the windsteed crouch beside her. The Clayman got in and sat down in front of her, moving bars and wheels about. A loud grinding noise arose, and a screaming of metal on metal, and then the walls of the tunnel began to jerk by. Faster and faster the walls slid past, till the fireglobes overhead ran into a blur, and the stale warm air became a foul wind blowing the hood back off her hair.

The cart stopped. Semley followed the guide up basalt steps into a vast anteroom and then a still vaster hall, carved by ancient waters or by the burrowing Clayfolk out of the rock, its darkness that had never known sunlight lit with the uncanny cold brilliance of the globes. In grilles cut in the walls huge blades turned and turned, changing the stale air. The great closed space hummed and boomed with noise, the loud voices of the Clayfolk, the grinding and shrill buzzing and vibration of turning blades and wheels, the echoes and re-echoes of all this from the rock. Here all the stumpy figures of the Claymen were clothed in garments imitating those of the Starlords—divided trousers, soft boots, and hooded tunics—though the few women to be seen, hurrying servile dwarves, were naked. Of the males many were soldiers, bearing at their sides weapons shaped like the terrible light-throwers of the Starlords, though even Semley could see these were merely shaped iron clubs. What she saw, she saw without looking. She followed where she was led, turning her head neither to left nor right. When she came before a group of

Claymen who wore iron circlets on their black hair her guide halted, bowed, boomed out, "The High Lords of the Gdemiar!"

There were seven of them, and all looked up at her with such arrogance on their lumpy grey faces that she wanted to laugh.

"I come among you seeking the lost treasure of my family, O Lords of the Dark Realm," she said gravely to them. "I seek Leynen's prize, the Eye of the Sea." Her voice was faint in the racket of the huge vault.

"So said our messengers, Lady Semley." This time she could pick out the one who spoke, one even shorter than the others, hardly reaching Semley's breast, with a white, fierce face. "We do not have this thing you seek."

"Once you had it, it is said."

"Much is said, up there where the sun blinks."

"And words are borne off by the winds, where there are winds to blow. I do not ask how the necklace was lost to us and returned to you, its makers of old. Those are old tales, old grudges. I only seek to find it now. You do not have it now; but it may be you know where it is."

"It is not here."

"Then it is elsewhere."

"It is where you cannot come to it. Never, unless we help you."

"Then help me. I ask this as your guest."

"It is said, *The Angyar take; the Fiia give; the Gdemiar give and take*. If we do this for you, what will you give us?"

"My thanks, Nightlord."

She stood tall and bright among them, smiling. They all stared at her with a heavy, grudging wonder, a sullen yearning.

"Listen, Angya, this is a great favor you ask of us. You do not know how great a favor. You cannot understand. You are of a race that will not understand, that cares for nothing but wind-riding and crop-raising and sword-fighting and shouting together. But who made your swords of the bright steel? We, the Gdemiar! Your lords come to us here and in the Clayfields and buy their swords and go away, not looking, not understanding. But you are here now, you will look, you can see a few of our endless marvels, the lights that burn forever, the car that pulls itself, the machines that make our clothes and cook our food and sweeten our air and serve us in all things. Know that all these things are beyond your understanding. And know this: we, the Gdemiar, are the friends of those you call the Starlords! We came with them to Hallan, to Reohan, to Hul-Orren, to all your castles, to

help them speak to you. The lords to whom you, the proud
Angyar, pay tribute, are our friends. They do us favors as we do
them favors! Now, what do your thanks mean to us?''

"That is your question to answer," said Semley, ''not mine. I
have asked my question. Answer it, Lord.''

For a while the seven conferred together, by word and silence.
They would glance at her and look away, and mutter and be still.
A crowd grew around them, drawn slowly and silently, one after
another till Semley was encircled by hundreds of the matted
black heads, and all the great booming cavern floor was covered
with people, except a little space directly around her. Her windsteed
was quivering with fear and irritation too long controlled, and his
eyes had gone very wide and pale, like the eyes of a steed forced
to fly at night. She stroked the warm fur of his head, whispering,
"Quietly now, brave one, bright one, windlord. . . .''

"Angya, we will take you to the place where the treasure
lies.'' The Clayman with the white face and iron crown had
turned to her once more. "More than that we cannot do. You
must come with us to claim the necklace where it lies, from
those who keep it. The airbeast cannot come with us. You must
come alone.''

"How far a journey, Lord?''

His lips drew back and back. "A very far journey, Lady. Yet it
will last only one long night.''

"I thank you for your courtesy. Will my steed be well cared
for this night? No ill must come to him.''

"He will sleep till you return. A greater windsteed you will
have ridden, when you see that beast again! Will you not ask
where we take you?''

"Can we go soon on this journey? I would not stay long away
from my home.''

"Yes. Soon.'' Again the grey lips widened as he stared up
into her face.

What was done in those next hours Semley could not have
retold; it was all haste, jumble, noise, strangeness. While she
held her steed's head a Clayman stuck a long needle into the
golden-striped haunch. She nearly cried out at the sight, but her
steed merely twitched and then, purring, fell asleep. He was
carried off by a group of Clayfolk who clearly had to summon up
their courage to touch his warm fur. Later on she had to see a
needle driven into her own arm—perhaps to test her courage, she
thought, for it did not seem to make her sleep; though she was
not quite sure. There were times she had to travel in the rail-

carts, passing iron doors and vaulted caverns by the hundred and hundred; once the rail-cart ran through a cavern that stretched off on either hand measureless into the dark, and all that darkness was full of great flocks of herilor. She could hear their cooing, husky calls, and glimpse the flocks in the front-lights of the cart; then she saw some more clearly in the white light, and saw that they were all wingless, and all blind. At that she shut her eyes. But there were more tunnels to go through, and always more caverns, more grey lumpy bodies and fierce faces and booming boasting voices, until at last they led her suddenly out into the open air. It was full night; she raised her eyes joyfully to the stars and the single moon shining, little Heliki brightening in the west. But the Clayfolk were all about her still, making her climb now into some new kind of cart or cave, she did not know which. It was small, full of little blinking lights like rushlights, very narrow and shining after the great dank caverns and the starlit night. Now another needle was stuck in her, and they told her she would have to be tied down in a sort of flat chair, tied down head and hand and foot.

"I will not," said Semley.

But when she saw that the four Claymen who were to be her guides let themselves be tied down first, she submitted. The others left. There was a roaring sound, and a long silence; a great weight that could not be seen pressed upon her. Then there was no weight; no sound; nothing at all.

"Am I dead?" asked Semley.

"Oh no, Lady," said a voice she did not like.

Opening her eyes, she saw the white face bent over her, the wide lips pulled back, the eyes like little stones. Her bonds had fallen away from her, and she leaped up. She was weightless, bodiless; she felt herself only a gust of terror on the wind.

"We will not hurt you," said the sullen voice or voices. "Only let us touch you, Lady. We would like to touch your hair. Let us touch your hair. . . ."

The round cart they were in trembled a little. Outside its one window lay blank night, or was it mist, or nothing at all? One long night, they had said. Very long. She sat motionless and endured the touch of their heavy grey hands on her hair. Later they would touch her hands and feet and arms, and once her throat: at that she set her teeth and stood up, and they drew back.

"We have not hurt you, Lady," they said. She shook her head.

When they bade her, she lay down again in the chair that

bound her down; and when light flashed golden, at the window, she would have wept at the sight, but fainted first.

"Well," said Rocannon, "now at least we know what she is."

"I wish there were some way of knowing *who* she is," the curator mumbled. "She wants something we've got here in the Museum, is that what the trogs say?"

"Now, don't call 'em trogs," Rocannon said conscientiously; as a hilfer, an ethnologist of the High Intelligence Life-forms, he was supposed to resist such words. "They're not pretty, but they're Status C Allies. . . . I wonder why the Commission picked them to develop? Before even contacting all the HILF species? I'll bet the survey was from Centaurus—Centaurans always like nocturnals and cave dwellers. I'd have backed Species II, here, I think."

"The troglodytes seem to be rather in awe of her."

"Aren't you?"

Ketho glanced at the tall woman again, then reddened and laughed. "Well, in a way. I never saw such a beautiful alien type in eighteen years here on New South Georgia. I never saw such a beautiful woman anywhere, in fact. She looks like a goddess." The red now reached the top of his bald head, for Ketho was a shy curator, not given to hyperbole. But Rocannon nodded soberly, agreeing.

"I wish we could talk to her without those tr—Gdemiar as interpreters. But there's no help for it." Rocannon went toward their visitor, and when she turned her splendid face to him he bowed down very deeply, going right down to the floor on one knee, his head bowed and his eyes shut. This was what he called his All-Purpose Intercultural Curtsey, and he performed it with some grace. When he came erect again the beautiful woman smiled and spoke.

"She say, Hail, Lord of Stars," growled one of her squat escorts in Pidgin-Galactic.

"Hail, Lady of the Angyar," Rocannon replied. "In what way can we of the Museum serve the lady?"

Across the troglodytes' growling her voice ran like a brief silver wind.

"She say, Please give her necklace which treasure her blood-kin-forebears long long."

"Which necklace?" he asked, and understanding him, she pointed to the central display of the case before them, a magnificent thing, a chain of yellow gold, massive but very delicate in workmanship, set with one big hot-blue sapphire. Rocannon's eyebrows went up, and Ketho at his shoulder murmured, "She's got good taste. That's the Fomalhaut Necklace—famous bit of work."

She smiled at the two men, and again spoke to them over the heads of the troglodytes.

"She say, O Starlords, Elder and Younger Dwellers in House of Treasures, this treasure her one. Long long time. Thank you."

"How did we get the thing, Ketho?"

"Wait; let me look it up in the catalogue. I've got it here. Here. It came from these trogs—trolls—whatever they are: Gdemiar. They have a bargain-obsession, it says; we had to let 'em buy the ship they came here on, an AD-4. This was part payment. It's their own handiwork."

"And I'll bet they can't do this kind of work anymore, since they've been steered to Industrial."

"But they seem to feel the thing is hers, not theirs or ours. It must be important, Rocannon, or they wouldn't have given up this time-span to her errand. Why, the objective lapse between here and Fomalhaut must be considerable!"

"Several years, no doubt," said the hilfer, who was used to star-jumping. "Not very far. Well, neither the *Handbook* nor the *Guide* gives me enough data to base a decent guess on. These species obviously haven't been properly studied at all. The little fellows may be showing her simple courtesy. Or an interspecies war may depend on this damn sapphire. Perhaps her desire rules them, because they consider themselves totally inferior to her. Or despite appearances she may be their prisoner, their decoy. How can we tell? . . . Can you give the thing away, Ketho?"

"Oh, yes. All the Exotica are technically on loan, not our property, since these claims come up now and then. We seldom argue. Peace above all, until the War comes. . . ."

"Then I'd say give it to her."

Ketho smiled. "It's a privilege," he said. Unlocking the case, he lifted out the great golden chain; then, in his shyness, he held it out to Rocannon, saying, "You give it to her."

So the blue jewel first lay, for a moment, in Rocannon's hand.

His mind was not on it; he turned straight to the beautiful, alien woman, with his handful of blue fire and gold. She did not raise her hands to take it, but bent her head, and he slipped the necklace over her hair. It lay like a burning fuse along her

golden-brown throat. She looked up from it with such pride,
delight, and gratitude in her face that Rocannon stood wordless,
and the little curator murmured hurriedly in his own language,
"You're welcome, you're very welcome." She bowed her golden
head to him and to Rocannon. Then, turning, she nodded to her
squat guards—or captors?—and, drawing her worn blue cloak
about her, paced down the long hall and was gone. Ketho and
Rocannon stood looking after her.

"What I feel . . ." Rocannon began.

"Well?" Ketho inquired hoarsely, after a long pause.

"What I feel sometimes is that I . . . meeting these people
from worlds we know so little of, you know, sometimes . . . that
I have as it were blundered through the corner of a legend, or a
tragic myth, maybe, which I do not understand. . . ."

"Yes," said the curator, clearing his throat. "I wonder . . . I
wonder what her name is."

Semley the Fair, Semley the Golden, Semley of the Necklace.
The Clayfolk had bent to her will, and so had even the Starlords
in that terrible place where the Clayfolk had taken her, the city at
the end of the night. They had bowed to her, and given her
gladly her treasure from amongst their own.

But she could not yet shake off the feeling of those caverns
about her where rock lowered overhead, where you could not tell
who spoke or what they did, where voices boomed and grey
hands reached out—Enough of that. She had paid for the necklace;
very well. Now it was hers. The price was paid, the past was the
past.

Her windsteed had crept out of some kind of box, with his
eyes filmy and his fur rimed with ice, and at first when they had
left the caves of the Gdemiar he would not fly. Now he seemed
all right again, riding a smooth south wind through the bright sky
toward Hallan. "Go quick, go quick," she told him, beginning
to laugh as the wind cleared away her mind's darkness. "I want
to see Durhal soon, soon. . . ."

And swiftly they flew, coming to Hallan by dusk of the
second day. Now the caves of the Clayfolk seemed no more than
last year's nightmare, as the steed swooped with her up the
thousand steps of Hallan and across the Chasmbridge where the
forests fell away for a thousand feet. In the gold light of evening
in the flightcourt she dismounted and walked up the last steps
between the stiff cavern figures of heroes and the two gatewards,

who bowed to her, staring at the beautiful, fiery thing around her neck.

In the Forehall she stopped a passing girl, a very pretty girl, by her looks one of Durhal's close kin, though Semley could not call to mind her name. "Do you know me, maiden? I am Semley, Durhal's wife. Will you go tell the Lady Durossa that I have come back?"

For she was afraid to go on in and perhaps face Durhal at once, alone; she wanted Durossa's support.

The girl was gazing at her, her face very strange. But she murmured, "Yes, Lady," and darted off toward the Tower.

Semley stood waiting in the gilt, ruinous hall. No one came by; were they all at table in the Revel-hall? The silence was uneasy. After a minute Semley started toward the stairs to the Tower. But an old woman was coming to her across the stone floor, holding her arms out, weeping.

"O Semley, Semley!"

She had never seen the grey-haired woman, and shrank back.

"But Lady, who are you?"

"I am Durossa, Semley."

She was quiet and still, all the time that Durossa embraced her and wept, and asked if it were true the Clayfolk had captured her and kept her under a spell all these long years, or had it been the Fiia with their strange arts? Then, drawing back a little, Durossa ceased to weep.

"You're still young, Semley. Young as the day you left here. And you wear round your neck the necklace. . . ."

"I have brought my gift to my husband Durhal. Where is he?"

"Durhal is dead."

Semley stood unmoving.

"Your husband, my brother, Durhal Hallanlord was killed seven years ago in battle. Nine years you had been gone. The Starlords came no more. We fell to warring with the Eastern Halls, with the Angyar of Log and Hull-Orren. Durhal, fighting, was killed by a midman's spear, for he had little armor for his body, and none at all for his spirit. He lies buried in the fields above Orren Marsh."

Semley turned away. "I will go to him, then," she said, putting her hand on the gold chain that weighed down her neck. "I will give him my gift."

"Wait, Semley! Durhal's daughter, your daughter, see her now, Haldre the Beautiful!"

It was the girl she had first spoken to and sent to Durossa, a girl of nineteen or so, with eyes like Durhal's eyes, dark blue. She stood beside Durossa, gazing with those steady eyes at this woman Semley who was her mother and was her own age. Their age was the same, and their gold hair, and their beauty. Only Semley was a little taller, and wore the blue stone on her breast.

"Take it, take it. It was for Durhal and Haldre that I brought it from the end of the long night!" Semley cried this aloud, twisting and bowing her head to get the heavy chain off, dropping the necklace so it fell on the stones with a cold, liquid clash. "O take it, Haldre!" she cried again, and then, weeping aloud, turned and ran from Hallan, over the bridge and down the long, broad steps, and, darting off eastward into the forest of the mountainside like some wild thing escaping, was gone.

AND THE MONSTERS WALK

by
John Jakes

John Jakes is known to millions of readers as the author of the best-selling BICENTENNIAL SERIES of novels about America's past. However, before his current successes, he was an excellent writer of suspense, Western, fantasy, and science fiction stories for the genre magazines. Especially noteworthy novels in the sf field are BLACK IN TIME (1970), ON WHEELS (1973) and SIX-GUN PLANET (1970). A definitive sf collection of his shorter stories is THE BEST OF JOHN JAKES (1977). He is also fondly remembered in the fantasy field for his tales of "Brak the Barbarian."

"And the Monsters Walk" is a superior hardboiled supernatural thriller which, oddly enough, has never been anthologized. An oversight which we are pleased to correct.

We were somewhere in the Channel, with France lying to starboard and the country of England on the other hand. Both were lost in the fog and darkness of that impenetrable night. The

freighter *Queen of Madagascar* rolled on the oily swells, and
hundreds of gallons of water thundered across the lonely decks
with each rise and fall.

The ship was a ship of strangers. The men were not English or
American or even European. They were odd hues: swarthy, some
of them, others yellowish with the cast of the Orient. At mess I
sat alone, an Englishman working my way homeward by the
only trade I knew—the sea.

And here we were, that strange, murderous crew with the
slashed scarred faces, the dark furtive eyes, the pistols and the
knives. One day out from England. Twenty-four hours. And
my curiosity had risen to a fever pitch. I had to know what
we carried in that sealed main hold. Once, off Algiers, when the
hatch was open, I caught a whiff from down there. Standing in
the bright sun, I swore it was a smell of bones and age. A
smell of dead men. The vague thought of our being a monstrous
coffin-ship intrigued me, played on my curiosity—a characteris-
tic in me which, if not particularly worthy, provided for a life
that was far from dull.

There was an opening into the main hold from a lower deck.
Not a regular entrance-way or anything of the like. A makeshift
iron door, probably cut from the bulkhead by a torch and refitted
into its original frame.

No one guarded that door, you see. On our first day out,
Captain Bezahrov had informed the crew that the penalty for
entering the hold was instantaneous death. But there I was, crazy
with curiosity, and yet lucky, too. Because what I found gave me
knowledge that more important men longed for—later. Lucky, in
a hellish sort of a way.

I stole through the rocking corridors, finished with my watch.
From the faraway forecastle, echoing down the dismal metal
companionways, came a wordless primitive song. One of the
crewmen singing of his homeland, probably. It counterpointed
the thunder of the waves in the black sea outside, and made my
spine crawl.

I listened for a few moments, hesitating before the door. No
footsteps sounded. No voices spoke anywhere near. Carefully, I
eased the crude handle upward and inched the bulkhead door
open. It was well oiled. It made no sound.

The hold was dark. At once, that overpowering stench of age
and evil decay struck me. I stepped inside, inserting my penknife
to keep the door ajar. I had nothing to lose. I don't mean that in
a bragging sense. A life is certainly something to part with. But

no wife, no children to care for. And curiosity burned high and insistent. There was just enough of an element of chance. I just *might* get away with it—

I flicked on my pocket torch and looked around, excited. They *did* look like coffins! Row on row of rough wooden boxes. I stepped closer and peered at the markings. *T. Nedros. Importer, 8 Ryster Lane, London, England.* I checked several of the strange packing cases. The address was always the same. All of them to this mysterious T. Nedros, Importer.

The boxes had lids, and those lids were only fastened down with cheap wire. What more could I ask? Holding my torch steady, I unwound the twists of wire and pushed back the lid. I leaned forward to peer at the contents.

And then the nightmare began.

I looked into that box for perhaps forty-five seconds. It couldn't have been longer. But what I saw could easily drive a man mad. A . . . a *shape*—could I call it that?—lay within. Nearly seven feet in length, I realized, estimating the length of the box. A shape in human form, but not human at all. A shadow shape, with monstrous furred hands and a blur of darkness for the head, in which burned two smoky red eyes, wide open, staring up blankly at the roof of the hold.

A . . . a *thing*, it was. A creature from some more ancient world, when spirits of evil trod the earth. A creature not of our time, not of the world of civilized men. A demon reshaped in human mold, dug from God knows what sorcerer's burying ground and boxed up and—this was the most horrible—loaded on a ship for London! The others must contain the same sort of monstrosity, I realized.

I retched. The death-smell filled my nostrils.

All in the forty-five seconds or less, flashing through my brain like flickering pictures on a screen. Like a man seeing his entire life in the moment before he dies. And I was dying then, in a sense. Dying and being re-born into a world of terrors unfit for humans to endure.

Quickly, then, the rest happened. I heard the sounds of the door, of feet clanging on the metal plates, of harsh foreign curses. Hands threw me quickly to the floor. I peered up. Lights had come on in the hold.

Captain Bezahrov stood over me, hands clenched in fury. "Marlow," he said quietly, holding his teeth together in rage, "you are a fool. You should have known that we would be wise enough to prepare an alarm system on the bridge for something as important as this.''

I said nothing. From far away came the wild and lonely drumming of the sea. My only chance was to make a break for it. With an effort, I sprang to my feet.

Bezahrov caught me when I was only half-risen. He towered above me, his round face jerked awry by the livid scar lying alongside his nose. A light far above him threw a dim halo around his cap, and I wondered how the angel Satan had looked when he fell from Paradise.

Bezahrov's pistol came sweeping down, butt first. I tried to dodge, but it was no use. He hit me several times and, in a pain-filled delirium, I felt hands lift me and carry me. Upward. *The deck!*

But I had known the penalty. I had known, and they did not have to speak of it. Abruptly, I felt wind lashing my face, and a fine rain. The waves thundered more loudly. A few more steps. The hands lifted me. *Lifted* . . .

And then the hands were gone. I hung in space for a moment and then I fell like a plummet, without thought, straight down to the black raging waters of the Channel. I struck the water and my mind went dark.

Slowly, I began to drift back into consciousness, stripes of gray light creeping across my eyes. I awoke as if from a pleasant sleep. I kept my eyes closed as the first coherent thoughts crossed my mind. I had no knowledge of how I managed to come out of that angry sea alive.

I recalled the thing in the box, and that same feeling of dread and loathing swept over me. And then I remembered the nightmare fall into the depths of the Channel. *By God, Marlow,* my mind said, *you have no right to be alive.*

But I was alive. That, or hell was a place to lie quietly between blankets. I opened my eyes. I felt no pain. My head was clear and my thoughts orderly. Or as orderly as they could be, with the vision of what I had seen gnawing at the back of my mind.

The room was bleak, with only the bed, a washstand, a chair and a writing desk. I blinked with astonishment. Neat and dry, my clothes, complete to cap and pea jacket, hung on the back of the chair.

I got out of bed, feeling chill air on my naked body. Dressing hastily, I approached the window under the slanting roof and raised the blind. Outside lay a gray and dismal sky brooding over the desolate roofs and docks of London's East End.

Then I was in London, and alive! But *how?* Already the nightmare had begun to take shape. I started walking back and forth across the room, trying to find an answer. But there was no answer. Not even a logical puzzle. Just a series of mad, frightening events—random, inexplicable.

After a few moments I saw the piece of paper on the writing desk. I snatched it up and read the lines inked in a small, almost childish hand. The words only added to the madness surrounding me.

We are your friends, it ran. *Do not question the fact that you are alive. We will contact you.*

I stared at the paper and questions flooded over me again. I stopped after a moment. It was futile. Two immediate things could be done. I was in London. I could find out exactly where I was, and I could go to Scotland Yard and tell them of the things I had seen.

I left the room, went down a short chilly hall, and downstairs into the main room of the lodging house. In the dim light, a fat, blowzy red-haired woman dozed at the desk.

"I'd like to know how I got here," I said to her, almost afraid to learn.

She looked at me out of eyes surrounded by wrinkles, and laughed coarsely. "Don't ask me, mate. I suppose you like your nip too much, like most of them. Blind when they come in, and afterwards they all want to know how they arrived."

"I wasn't drunk," I insisted. "Someone brought me here. When was it?"

"What's your name?"

"Marlow. Steven Marlow."

She consulted the spotted pages of the register. "Two nights ago. Monday."

"Who brought me?" I repeated.

"How should I know that?" she said, irritated. "I wasn't working then. Mr. Sudbury was here Monday night. He'd know who brought you in, I suppose." I could see from her face that she was still convinced I had come to the lodging house in a stupor.

"Then when can I talk to Mr. Sudbury?" I persisted.

"You can't," she said triumphantly. "He quit last night."

"Q—quit?" I stammered. The thing was becoming too confused even to think about.

"Yes, quit! Listen, matey, we don't ask questions around here. Mr. Sudbury only worked here three weeks. How do I know he wasn't wanted by the coppers? How do I know he didn't have some girl in trouble?" She threw up her hands. "I don't. But we don't ask questions, see. Why don't you just forget it and start off where you were before you got hold of the stuff?"

Angrily, I turned from the desk and walked out of the place. A sign above the door read *Bane's Rest*. Well, there wasn't any information to be had from the woman. I glared at her through the window, leaning on her elbows, her frowzy red hair bobbing as she nodded off to sleep.

I started off down the narrow street. I needed sanity. A touch of it, just a tiny bit of it.

Scotland Yard brought sanity to me. The office of Inspector Rohm, to whom I was sent after I gave many evasive answers to the question—for what did I need the Yard?—proved to be a bare little cubbyhole, not much more cheerful than the bedroom in which I had awakened.

Inspector Rohm was a thin, scholarly-looking man with sandy hair, erect posture, and sharp blue eyes. He sat in his chair and listened to my story. I poured it all out, incoherently, even wildly, while he sat there as if listening to a learned paper on physics. The only part I omitted concerned the note from my rescuers, whoever they were.

When I finished, Inspector Rohm peered at me with his blue eyes and said, "Is that *all?*"

"Yes," I said, "and it's the truth."

Rohm laughed. "I doubt that," he said gently. "My friend, we are bothered with many cranks and lunatics here, but I have never heard such a fantastic story."

"But I saw the thing!"

"Granted such creatures existed," he continued, "why would you come to us?"

And there he had me stopped. Why indeed? Except that I had sensed terrible evil in that thing on the ship, in all the cases in the hold, in fact. And evil had its opposite in good, and the law represented the most accessible source of that good.

I could not convey to him in words the impending sense of danger and unearthly evil I had felt on the *Queen of Madagascar*. I sat there, helpless under his critical gaze, twisting my cap in my hands.

"I . . . I don't know," I said. "I'm only a seaman, sir. I . . .

well . . . I felt that it meant trouble for us, somehow . . . for England . . . for the world. Evil, you understand . . ."

Rohm laughed again. "No, I'm afraid we'll have to have something a bit more concrete than that."

"But can't you check my story?" I pleaded. "Can't you check on the ship and her cargo?"

He thought a minute, and I suppose he finally decided to accept my suggestion, because he was a man who was meticulous about his duty, leaving no alternative open, no matter how impossible.

"All right. I'll ring up Customs."

After a few minutes on the phone, talking in clipped monosyllables, he turned back to me, pulling out a cigarette and lighting it. "Well, Marlow, the cargo from the *Queen of Madagascar* arrived all right, consigned to a perfectly legitimate importer named Nedros in Ryster Lane."

"What was the cargo?" I asked quietly.

"The usual run of Oriental stuff. Carpets, cloth goods, wines, water pipes." He smiled a bit sardonically. "For the curio shops. Items to give your parlor that odd touch, you know." When he laughed this time, it was in appreciation of his own humor.

"I saw that thing in the box," I insisted.

He shook his head. "No," he said with finality, "the cargo was as stated. That has been verified."

'But I knew the name of the person it was being sent to," I said. "I was on that ship!"

"Very true. But as for the rest, Mr. Marlow, you are either lying or in need of help from a psychiatrist. And now, I'm rather busy. If that's all, I'd appreciate your leaving."

"All right," I said, rising. "That's all, I suppose."

I walked out, feeling his eyes in my back, branding me a liar and a madman. The world had gone insane. Somehow, those *things* had left the *Queen of Madagascar* before she reached port. I knew there were many of them. I had looked into that box, and smelled the hold. I knew they threatened danger, vast and terrible danger, but no one cared. I knew they were somewhere in England now, in London, perhaps. And no one would pay any attention . . .

But I had that note in my pocket! I had come back out of the sea. And even if I had not, no one could have looked into the blank, hellish red eyes of that thing lying there in the iron hold

of that storm-lashed ship and not known that here was greater evil
than mankind had seen for centuries.

I went to a pub and tried to drink. Amid the laughter and the
clink of mugs, I tried to sop up nightmare in alcohol. But it
didn't work. I would drink for a bit, concentrating on the warm,
light-headed feeling it produced. And then, I'd think of the shape
in the box, and I would be sober again, as if I had not touched a
drop.

I went back to Bane's Rest in the East End that night. I had no
place else to go. The room was dark and chill, and I stared at the
ceiling all night. I could not sleep.

Next morning my head was filled with a buzzing born of
weariness, and my arms and legs felt as though they were lead.
A little after seven I put on my cap and jacket and left the Rest to
get some breakfast. An ample supply of pound notes had been
left in the pocket of my coat by those responsible for the note, it
seemed.

As I walked along I couldn't help noticing the early-morning
mist and the rooftops against the sky beyond. Gray—all gray—
suggestive of a hideous dead quality, as if a malignant living
mold shrouded London. I bought several newspapers and proceeded to find an inexpensive restaurant. Black taxis and other
traffic moved briskly on the streets, and well-dressed men in
bowlers, carrying umbrellas, moved on the walks, looking very
content and complacent. I envied them in their security.

Over an egg and tea in the dimly lit white tile interior of the
restaurant, I examined the newspapers. The huge headline of the
first paper jerked my attention away from my food and filled me
with fresh dread.

Lord Wolters Slain, the words shouted. *Harley Square Home
Devastated. Mysterious Killers Still at Large.*

Lord Wolters. I knew the name, of course. Everyone did. In
the Cabinet he was perhaps the most important man, particularly
valuable to England in these times of stress because of his
military experience. Defense needed an able guiding hand, and
Lord Wolters provided it. Or he had. Now he was dead. And
somehow it formed a link in my mind with the horror on the
Queen of Madagascar.

I read the other accounts. They said much the same thing. But
the third paper gave a bit of news that made me grow cold again.
An unofficial report, it said, from servants of Lord Wolters,
hinted that the corpse was mangled and dismembered, and that

whole sections of the house had been demolished, including several walls.

There must be a connection. There *had* to be. Madness was slowly breaking loose in the streets of London. In such a time of world crisis, the death of Lord Wolters and the strange cargo out of the East united to form—what?

I could not say, exactly. But I knew some meaning lurked there. A dreadful meaning.

Another item on a back page confirmed my suspicions. A fisherman had been killed in a little village on the Channel coast. Before he died, he babbled insanely of monstrous, gigantic shapes coming out of the water, rising from the waves at night, and overwhelming him. A back page! No one would notice it.

This was two nights ago, the same night I was dropped over the side of the *Queen*. Those . . . *things* . . . came ashore and Captain Bezahrov loaded the long boxes with the regular cargo Inspector Rohm had named as checked by Customs. The things made their way to London, and Lord Wolters died. I had to see Harley Square. Every moment drew me deeper into the pattern, all the more frightening because I knew only vaguely what it was, and not why, or from where.

I left the papers on the table and hurried from the restaurant. A few minutes after eight o'clock I stood in the center of a crowd of the curious outside of the iron fence before the home of Lord Wolters. Scotland Yard was already on duty, guarding the doors. I could see nothing of the ruined interior of the house.

"Have they taken him away?" I asked a man next to me.

"Yes, a few minutes ago." The man scowled harshly and sucked on his pipe. "Only he wasn't on a stretcher. The hospital men brought out a big canvas sack. I hear he was in small pieces, all torn up. Devil's work, it sounds like."

I turned away, feeling the chill of the morning fog on me. *Devil's work*. Yes, living devils. My nose twitched, and I finally took conscious thought of the odor hanging over the whole square. Decay and festering rot. The smell in the ship's hold. The smell of the things. They *had* been here!

I listened for a bit and heard people talking about the odor. It puzzled them, but not one ventured a guess as to what it was. I wanted to seize them one by one; scream at them that I knew. But they never would have believed me, and the police would probably have run me off, less politely than Inspector Rohm had done.

Someone tugged at my sleeve. I turned, half-expecting to see the man with the pipe I had spoken to only a moment before. But another man stood there, a wizened, rat-like little man in filthy clothes and a checked cap. One milky blue eye peered at me from a stubbled triangular face. The other was covered by a dirty black patch. The man leaned close to me.

"Mr. Marlow," he said in a wheezing voice. His breath reeked of alcohol.

"Yes, my name's Marlow."

"I got a message for you."

Perhaps they were contacting me at last. "Who's it from?" I asked quickly.

The man with the patch cackled softly. "Him Who Doesn't Walk."

"Him—" The words stuck in my mouth. "Look here," I said angrily, "who are you and who's this man you're talking about?"

"Him Who Doesn't Walk," the fellow repeated in his shrill whisper. "He says to tell you he knows you're alive when you're not supposed to be. He says it won't be long, though. He says you haven't got much more time."

"Time? Time for what?"

The blue eye winked at me. "Time to live, Mr. Marlow. Time to live."

Angrily I reached out for him, intending to grab him and haul him off to some alley and beat the truth out of him about this incoherent babble of someone called Him Who Doesn't Walk. But as if it were a perfectly timed signal, the man turned away and someone to the rear of the crowd shoved abruptly.

I stumbled forward, bumping against two ladies who were in turn pushed against the iron fence. I fought to get my balance, and finally pulled myself erect. One of the women was adjusting her hat and glaring at me as she pinned it in place.

"Look here, sonny—" she exclaimed loudly.

"I'm sorry, madam," I blurted back, and turned again to where I had been standing. I searched the crowd, but I didn't see the man. I pushed my way out and stood in the middle of the square, surrounded by the gloomy gray fronts of the old houses. The man with the patch was nowhere in sight.

I started walking. One more incident, one more name on the role of horror and impossibility. Him Who Doesn't Walk. And not much time for me to live. Evidently these men weren't connected with my rescuers. Evidently they did not want me to remain alive because I knew of the cargo of the ship, and linked it with the slaying of Lord Wolters. And by some means, they could watch my every move, as my rescuers could evidently also do. I walked on, smoking a cigarette thoughtfully.

What could I do? Where could I run? I had so little information, and yet it was enough to warrant my dying. And how soon would the attack come? And from where?

I stopped at a news kiosk to light another cigarette. A man approached me, this time well-dressed, in a gray overcoat and bowler. He had a slender, scholarly face with intense black eyes, a straight nose, thin lips and a deeply bronzed complexion. He could have been any age from forty to seventy. His face was strange, decidedly not English.

"Excuse me," he said. "Do you have a light?" I nodded, holding the match to his cigarette. I had a wild desire to run. He might be the very killer with orders to put a knife in my back.

"Let's walk a bit," he said softly. His voice was accented with strange, resonant tones, as if an Oriental were trying to speak perfect English. He put his hand on my elbow and piloted me down a side street. Then he relaxed his grip and puffed his cigarette. I waited ready to turn on him at the first sign of danger.

"I sent you that note, Marlow," he said quietly, staring straight ahead. "I dragged you out of the sea and put you up at *Bane's Rest*. My name is Gerasmin."

The name meant nothing to me. "Can . . . can you explain anything about what's going on?" I stammered. "You said in the note you . . . you were my friends. Where are the others?"

"There is only one other," Gerasmin said, with a hint of sadness in his voice. "Her name is Angela. If you will come to my rooms, we will explain a few things to you."

"How do I know you don't want to kill me once you get me there?"

"You don't," he replied. "You must take that chance. But I can only say we trusted you and kept you from dying. You could do the same for us."

"All right," I said. "To your rooms." I wanted, more than anything, to get at the roots of the situation, and I determined to keep alert for trouble while I learned as much as possible.

Gerasmin had rooms in one of the better West End hotels. I felt out of place in my sailor's jacket and cap as we rode the lift to the fifth floor. He led me down a dim, thickly-carpeted hallway and into a spacious, well-furnished suite. Large glass windows, stretching from ceiling to floor, looked out upon the street.

The girl he had called Angela stood by the window, smoking and staring out at the gray sky. She was slender and nicely built, with dark hair drawn tightly back over her head. A very lovely young woman as she turned and looked at me with frank brown eyes.

"This must be Mr. Marlow," she said warmly. Her smile was weary, though, as if from strain. "How are you?" I heard the click as the door was locked behind me.

"Fine, thanks," I said, feeling awkward. Gerasmin threw his hat and topcoat onto a chair and moved to the liquor cabinet. "Sit down, Marlow, I'll fix us drinks. Scotch do for you?"

"Yes, that'll be fine." I twisted my cap in my hands. I wanted answers. The curiosity was pulsing through me again, almost eclipsing the terrors of the last thirty-six hours.

We said nothing until Gerasmin handed out the drinks. Then he lit another cigarette with a steady hand and said, "Marlow, we pulled you out of the sea two nights ago."

"How?"

"Perhaps I can explain by telling you a little about Angela and me. I am an Indian by birth, and I spent much time in Tibet. Consequently, I have studied certain realms of knowledge that would not be recognized as valid at Oxford." He tapped his skull, smiling. "Spirit matters, Marlow. Movement of matter by thought. It can be done. And second sight, if you want to call it that. I can see anywhere, at any time."

His words were calm and quiet, and yet the meaning struck home with the force of blows. Here he was, this dark-skinned man with the ageless face, in a hotel room in London, telling me in clipped British accents that he had powers that I never knew existed; powers only hinted at in ancient legends.

"I'm afraid I can't believe you," I said weakly, like a man in shock.

He smiled. "No, I imagine not. You see that?" He was pointing to a small blue vase standing on top of a radio-phonograph console. "Watch it, Marlow. Watch it carefully." He closed his eyes and drew his lips together tightly. His ageless face assumed a rigid quality. I turned my eyes to the vase.

And suddenly—*it vanished.*

Amazed, I turned back to Gerasmin. His eyes were open again and a lazy smile lay on his lips. He weighed an object in his left hand. The blue vase.

"That," he said, "was relatively easy. I saw you on the *Queen of Madagascar*, saw you dropped over the rail. I brought you out of the sea, to this room, and took you by cab to the Rest."

What was the man saying? A sorcerer . . . he must be that, an ancient sorcerer reborn. This was not the modern world of London. And yet it was, with a new and frightening dimension added, a dimension of magic and witchcraft—the supernatural.

"Why did you rescue me?" I stammered. "And how did you know about me in the first place?"

"We, or rather Gerasmin here, had been watching the *Queen*," Angela explained, "ever since she set out from India with her cargo of demons. That's what they are, Marlow. Creations of sorcery."

"And I just happened to be on board. Is that it?"

"Yes." She nodded. "The *Queen* needed one more crewman. They were undermanned as it was, since all of them but you were hirelings in the scheme. Only Captain Bezahrov and his mates, though, knew what the cargo was. And when Gerasmin saw you about to die, he decided to save you, in the hope that you would join us."

The questions were coming faster. "Where . . . where did those things come from?"

"The monsters?" Gerasmin said quietly. "From India, Tibet, Russia—all the dark corners of the East. They have been in the process of creation for ten years or so, by men who still practice the black arts. In a hundred shops in a hundred cities, men worked to fashion and animate them. They are actual demons, Mr. Marlow, children of what you call Hell. They were common in ancient times. The men who created them did not know their purpose in the Plan. They were paid, and they did their evil work."

"But what for?" I asked. "I still don't see that."

"It's a scheme that's been under way for years," Angela said, almost in a whisper. The smoke from her cigarette made a filmy halo around her head. "A scheme to take over the western world. My father and Gerasmin unearthed it in India twelve years ago. My father was Colonel Hilary St. Giles Saunders."

I nodded. The name was famous in the Indian Colonial Regiments.

Her face grew strained and harsh. "The leader of the organization discovered my father and Gerasmin. Father was killed in

Bombay. Gerasmin escaped and we are the only two people who
now have full knowledge of the organization.''

"To take over the Western world?" I choked. "That seems
incredible."

"It's possible," Gerasmin breathed. "It's too possible, with
their power. Marlow, the secrets of the East are undreamed of.
Those things have monstrous strength. They cannot easily be
killed. We have been alone, Angela and I. Now, if you'll join
us, there'll be three. There's not a great deal we can do, but we
can at least try. We must try! Angela and I have been waiting for
years for the scheme to come off. And now it's under way, and
London is the starting point."

"From the East," I murmured. "Russia?"

Gerasmin smiled. "Yes, partly. They're even blatant about
the fact. It's been written in their books for years. Captain
Bezahrov is perhaps the second most important man in the
organization. He is pure Russian. The real leader is a mixture of
the worst elements in all the Eastern races."

"Would that have anything to do with Him Who Doesn't
Walk?" I said.

Angela started. "How did you know that name?"

I explained about the incident in Harley Square, and the man
with the patch over his eye.

Gerasmin snapped his fingers and got to his feet. "Then
they're on to you. It was only a matter of time, since they can
see anywhere just as easily as I can. Yes, Him Who Doesn't
Walk is the leader. I've never seen him, but I know he is a
cripple and can't use his legs, if he has any legs at all."

"Where is he?" I said. The thing was beginning to fall
together, damnably, horribly, and I realized that I was now
alone, cut off—almost forced into alliance with these two. I had
little choice, even though they seemed hopelessly pitiful in their
efforts, just the two of them.

"He's somewhere under London," Angela said, gesturing.
"In sewers, deep underground, in hidden rooms—everywhere.
We've picked up bits of information here and there, and evidently London is honeycombed with tunnels and subterranean
chambers he and his followers have made over the years."

"Can't you get Scotland Yard to work?" I said, forgetting for
a moment my own experience.

Gerasmin smiled grimly. "You tried it, Marlow. We saw you
try, and we let you go ahead because we knew what would
happen. They called you insane. We face the same problem.

And now that Him Who Doesn't Walk is on to you, we may not have much time to work.''

He said it calmly, impassively. And I realized that they were bound to me now, instead of the other way around. They had taken me in on a chance of my joining them, and had thereby exposed themselves to a heightened possibility of sudden death. I felt instinctively closer to them, and I couldn't help watching Angela. She was a very beautiful woman to find in such a lunatic's game.

"Look, Marlow," Gerasmin said, "we don't have much chance, I admit. Lord Wolters is already out of the way. God knows who is next. That item about the dead fisherman went unnoticed. Nobody will listen to us, and we're entirely alone. But we'd like to have you in.''

I gazed at him closely, at those ageless black eyes and the fine dark hair resting sleekly on his head. A gentleman of this and other worlds, fighting against an army of hellish creatures born of magic. Then I looked at Angela.

"I'm in, if you want me.''

I walked to the liquor cabinet to refill my drink, gesturing as I moved. "And you don't look so bad from here. You seem to take care of everything. I suppose you even had Mr. Sudbury move on, as a precaution.''

Angela laughed softly again and moved to the window. "He's a very intelligent fellow, Gerasmin, this Mr. Marlow.''

"Where can we start?" I asked. "Or can we start—do anything at all?''

"Now that you are with us," Gerasmin said briskly, "there will be two of us for the actual work. I never wanted to operate alone, and I did not want to expose Angela to danger. She's too valuable.''

"I'm afraid I won't be much help," I told them. "I don't have any power—''

"We won't worry about that. I think the first thing is to find out how we get into the underground and see if we can scout some of the rooms belonging to Him Who Doesn't Walk. We'll ask around in the pubs. I have a few friends, although I have a strong hunch the entrance to the underground is through the shop of T. Nedros in Ryster Lane. He—''

"*Gerasmin!*" Angela spoke sharply at the window. We hurried over and looked down. Two cabs had pulled up before the hotel, and half a dozen men were getting out. Their heads were covered and we could not see their faces. I felt sweat run down my armpits, and for some reason I remembered the words of the man with the patch.

"Can you go into their minds?" Angela whispered.

Gerasmin nodded, closing his eyes. A moment later he opened them. "They're from the organization, all right. Him Who Doesn't Walk has seen us together and has decided to finish us all at one time. Come on!"

He ran to the closet, pulled it open, and took two large pistols from the top shelf. He gave one to Angela and one to me. Unbuttoning his suit coat, he loosened the brass hilts of the two knives in his waistband. Then, after a minute's thought, he took the pistol from Angela and dropped it into his own pocket.

"They're coming fast," he said. "We'll try the regular way out." He headed for the hall, jerked the door open and started down the fire escape. I ran ahead and pulled the door open, but I stopped short, seeing the figure in the coat and bowler two flights below.

"One's coming up here." I looked out again and caught a glimpse of a dark, upraised face glaring at me as the man climbed. "They look human enough. But there's another one down in the alley."

Gerasmin started back toward the rooms, with Angela and me close behind. Gerasmin indicated the open door from which we had just come. "In here. We'll try—"

There was a thunderous explosion, and a shot tore past my ear. Angela screamed softly and I whirled, pistol in hand. The quartet of killers had come around the bend of the hall and was closing in.

I dropped to one knee, sighted and fired. One of the men fell but the other three came on, coats thrown open and hands bringing out knives. They were men with dark, alien features, like the crew on the *Queen of Madagascar*. They were perhaps fifty yards down the hall, which was already filled with ropes of acrid smoke and echoes of shots. A woman screamed in the distance. I remember two heads popping out of doors and drawing back hastily.

Gerasmin fired over my shoulder, carefully and steadily. The second of the killers fell. Almost immediately I fired again, and the third staggered and bumped against the wall, screeching in an unfamiliar singsong language, clutching his arm where a dark, ugly stain began to grow. Abruptly, Angela cried out and we whirled in time to see the fire escape door come open. The first of the men from the alley flung his knife at us, his mouth twisted into a thick-lipped snarl.

I shoved Gerasmin roughly and he tumbled into the open door of the suite. I flattened myself out, feeling the rough carpet slam into my face as the knife whispered by overhead. From the corner of my eye, I saw it bury itself in the woodwork a dozen inches above my head, whirring.

We were holding our own; they hadn't been expecting us to be prepared, I suppose. This had evidently been the first move to eliminate Gerasmin, as well as me. The Indian leaned around the doorframe and triggered another shot. The knife-thrower was blown backwards through the fire escape door. He slammed into the railing, was thrown off balance, and went tumbling over the guard rail. His shriek dwindled as he fell toward the stones of the alley.

An alarm bell jangled down the corridor. I started to get to my feet, and just as I did Angela jerked the knife from the wall, her eyes wide with fright. She lashed out over my head. I ducked instinctively and heard a savage groan. When I turned again, I saw the fourth man of the quartet staggering back, an expression of bewilderment on his dark, primitive face. His head tilted back and the bowler fell off. He turned around, took a few steps, fell incongruously like a graceful ballet dancer, and lay still.

Angela's shoulders were shaking. She stared down at the knife with its blade stained a bright liquid red. Her left hand was pressed to her cheek, white-knuckled. "I had to," she breathed, not to us but to some great invisible jury of righteous men. "I had to kill him. He was almost on you . . ." She managed to glance at me, and then she began to sob, her shoulders slumping. "I've never killed anyone before. I've never . . ." Her words were obliterated by the crying.

Gerasmin put his arm around her and led her back into the apartment. I followed, the smoking gun hanging from my hand. I was beginning to relax, feeling the strain seep out of my muscles. The three of us were in the vestibule, Gerasmin in the lead, when he stepped back suddenly and faced us. His dark eyes were those of a man who had looked into the pit. I caught that hideous odor again. Death . . . decay . . .

"Him Who Doesn't Walk has been watching his agents die," Gerasmin breathed with harsh intensity. "Now he's sent—"

"What's wrong?" I snapped.

"Don't waste words. Stand close to me. We'll have to leave here. The thing's been transported right into the sitting room."

He drew the sobbing girl closer and I moved in toward them. Thank God she was too upset to realize what was going on.

Something tore the vestibule curtains aside and I saw it, towering there, its red smoky eyes glaring with dull fires of infinite evil, its body a thing of shadow, misshapen and vile in form, its great furred hands reaching out for us, its mouth emitting snuffling sounds. Again the power of Him Who Doesn't Walk struck home as I realized that this thing had been transported *by thought* to this very room, to destroy us.

It took a step forward. Its hands stretched toward us. I looked frantically to Gerasmin, but his eyes were closed, his lips clamped together tightly, and that vacant mindless expression lay on his face. Tiny dots of sweat glistened on his dark forehead. Angela sobbed wordlessly. *Hurry up*, my mind screamed, *for God's sake, hurry up!*

My flesh crawled. The thing took another step. Gerasmin groaned loudly. The furry hands reached for us and the stench grew overpowering. My mind swam, blank and incoherent, and I wanted to fall forward in weak helplessness. I wanted to stop the terrible effort and let myself be drawn into that thing of ancient evil. Dimly, I heard Gerasmin's whispered words and I held on for a moment longer.

"*We're going . . .*"

Then my mind whirled all the more. The room tilted crazily. Gerasmin and Angela fell away, and I swam over and over in a swirling gray vacuum where a furious wind shrieked. I moved my arms wildly, trying to catch hold of something. My stomach pushed toward my throat and the wind tearing at my skin brought real pain.

Gradually, a kind of sea-sick rocking sensation filled me. The grayness broke apart and portions of a scene sifted through. The gray vanished bit by bit, and I stared at the brick wall across the tiny alleyway, watching it heave from side to side and gradually come to rest.

Gerasmin was looking around, examining the alleyway. A hundred yards to our right lay a street. "We are five or six blocks from the hotel," he mused, staring at the crowds passing on the street. "That should do. We'll get a cab."

Angela gazed at me, quiet now, only her eyes showing the agony she had experienced. They were reddish and raw-looking. Gerasmin seized my hand. "Put your gun away, Marlow. You too, Angela. We must get out of here."

Angela dropped the knife, still clutched in her hand, into her purse. I nodded and clumsily put my pistol into the pocket of my pea jacket. Without a word we started toward the alley mouth. "That wasn't easy," Gerasmin said as we walked. "Three humans a distance of six blocks . . ." He shook his head and closed his eyes tightly. "I get a ferocious pain in my head . . ."

I wondered about the effort it must have been to lift me from the Channel, miles away, and bring me all the way to London. Evidently he had thought me valuable to do such a thing, and it drew me closer to them.

We stepped out onto the street and began walking toward the corner. The crowd eddied around us, oblivious of the things we had seen and been through. It made me laugh inwardly, a bit crazily. If they knew, what would any one of them do? It was hard to say, but I wondered how long they would remain sane.

"What was in the room?" Angela asked wearily.

"One of *them*," Gerasmin answered.

"From the ship?"

Gerasmin nodded, and I saw her shudder.

"Look," I said, pointing. "There's a cab. Shall we get it?"

They indicated that we should, and minutes later we were cruising through London streets, relatively safe from attack. Only the watching mind of Him Who Doesn't Walk could be on us now. We still had to be careful.

"Now," Gerasmin said, adjusting his necktie, "we'll start getting information about the entrance to the underground."

"It seems pretty risky going in there now," I countered. "We'd be in greater danger of being killed."

"He's right," Angela said softly.

"They will keep trying to kill us," Gerasmin said, staring at the panel closing the driver off from us, "no matter what we do or where we are. We can at least make some effort to find out more about their plans. Perhaps we might run across something. You see, Marlow—" He stared at me with those incredibly ancient eyes. "We don't have much chance to live anyway. We might as well make our remaining hours count."

I thought about that a minute. I tried to smile. "All right. We'll see for how much it'll count, then."

"Good. The pubs. We'll start there, so . . ."

I didn't need the end of the sentence. I leaned forward, slid the panel back and spoke to the driver. "We want to go somewhere near Ryster Lane."

"Whereabouts, guv'nor?" he said, not turning his head. "What number in the Lane?"

"Not *in* the Lane," I corrected. "A few blocks from it."

"All right, guv'nor. Where?"

"Any place. You pick the spot."

He turned around and stared at me in a peculiar manner. "Suit yourself," he said, shaking his head. They all thought we were insane. We, Gerasmin, Angela Saunders and I—mad, and removed from society. Yet we saw horrible realities where supposedly saner men could not.

I slid the panel shut and leaned back, lighting a cigarette. Gerasmin had closed his eyes and was resting his head in his hands. He'd been at it a long time, and I supposed every effort of his mind put on the strain a bit more.

Angela sat between us. Her head was nodding in exhaustion, dropping slowly toward my shoulder. Once she awoke with a start and smiled hazily, questioningly. I said, "Go ahead. Rest." Her expression was one of grateful weariness as she dropped off, her hair fanning out on the shoulder of my jacket.

I leaned back deeper into the seat and shut my eyes. A little rest, even in the joggling cab, would do me good.

Twenty minutes later the cabby let us out in a narrow street four blocks from Ryster Lane. Gerasmin paid him. I glanced at my watch. A few minutes past noon. We looked around. The houses were old, falling into ruin. Here and there newer facades intruded among these ancient moldering wrecks. A greengrocer in one place, a phonograph shop in another. Somewhere in the distance a boat horn hooted on the Thames. Not too far away, I decided.

"Down there." I pointed to the left, to a pub in the next block. We started walking, our heels clicking on the stone sidewalks. A strange trio we were as we went into that smoky, beery place. The bartender glanced at us sleepily, moved away from the two seedy-looking customers, men of middle age in the garb of workmen, and came to wait on us.

We each ordered a lager, Angela with obvious distaste. Gerasmin called the barkeep by name, and they exchanged a few words of greeting. Then the barkeep moved away to fetch the drinks. I leaned closer to Gerasmin, fidgeting, wanting to get some concrete action.

"Why can't you send your mind up to Nedros's place," I asked, "and take a look around? It would save a lot of time, and we're short of that."

"And Him Who Doesn't Walk would know somebody was

spying. He can feel other minds watching him," Gerasmin replied in a whisper.

"Well, then, I suspect he can probably see us right here, too, and find out what we're doing."

"No." The dark head shook back and forth. "There's been a mental shield around us, the three of us, ever since we came out in that alley. It's hard to keep up, but Him Who Doesn't Walk can't see or hear us. That's one trick we've got over him, I think. As far as he's concerned, Claud has been talking to empty air."

"Careful," Angela whispered suddenly. Claud, the barkeep, was returning with three pints of beer. He set them down with great precision, so that none of the fluffy white foam spilled.

"There you are, chum," he said to Gerasmin, rumbling the words loudly. Gerasmin paid him and leaned across the bar in a confidential manner. He crooked his finger and Claud caught on, glancing at the two working men, then drawing in close.

"I want to ask you a couple of questions, Claud. If you answer the last one right, there's ten quid in it for you."

Claud laughed under his breath, his thick red face spreading itself into a grin. "Go ahead, chum. Let's have your questions."

"This one is a point of information," Gerasmin said. "How far is Ryster Lane from here?"

Claud jerked a thick thumb. "Three blocks. Towards the river."

"Good." Gerasmin took a sip of the lager and I followed suit. Angela left hers untouched, watching the barkeep Claud intently. "Here's the next," Gerasmin said. "Have you ever heard of a person called Him Who Doesn't Walk?"

Claud blanched. His eyes grew wide and round; his hands clutched the edge of the bar. I had a strange eerie feeling, as if some strange force, or power, or *mind* were trying, straining to peer at us, but could not. As if it were fighting a barrier, smashing wrathfully against it to see what was going on beyond.

"Look, chum," Claud breathed in terror, "I don't want no trouble. Why don't you and your friends go someplace else?"

Gerasmin fingered the notes. In my growing impatience, I wanted to reach out and grab the barkeep's throat and shake the truth out of him. But Gerasmin remained cool and careful, displaying the pound notes only a few inches from Claud's florid face.

"Have you heard that name?" Gerasmin repeated.

Claud licked his lips and eyed the notes. "Yes."

"This is the important question," Gerasmin said smoothly. "Answer it and the money's yours."

"Let's hear it first."

"There's an importer in Ryster Lane. Nedros. Is that shop the entrance to . . ." Gerasmin hesitated. His eyes and voice grew hard. ". . . *the underground?*"

Claud breathed heavily, not answering. His eyes darted around the room, and I could see him taking in the tawdriness of his pub, thinking of the tawdriness and the struggle in his existence. He looked at the money again.

"I don't—" he began.

"Ten pounds," Gerasmin murmured, "is ten pounds."

"Sure," Claud blurted out suddenly. "Nedros's place is the entrance. But I only *heard* that. I don't know for sure. Remember that—I just heard it." He snatched the money from Gerasmin, his tone growing strident. "You and your friends better go."

Gerasmin smiled thinly and motioned to Angela and me. We walked out of the pub, leaving Claud staring down at the notes in his hand. Poor devil, I thought. He'll be wondering when he's going to get a knife in the back every day for the next five years.

Angela glanced at the clouds, darker now. It was only early afternoon, but it might as well have been the deep of night. We stood on the walk, clearing the stuffy smell of the pub from our heads. Angela spoke abruptly.

"Look, you two. Wherever we go from here, I'm coming along."

"Don't be foolish," Gerasmin said.

"I'm perfectly serious."

"We've seen things no man should," I said to her, "let alone a woman."

"You forget, Mr. Marlow," she replied, her tone hardening, "my father died in India because of what is going on now. I have a right to be part of your work. I've got a score to settle. Woman or not, my father died because of Him Who Doesn't Walk."

"This doesn't seem like a good place to argue about it," I said, glancing back into the pub. The two working men were staring curiously.

"You're right," Gerasmin put in. "We'll find a place to stay until after dark. And then we'll try our luck at getting into the shop of Mr. Nedros."

"I'm going with you," Angela said again, determined.

We did not reply as we moved off along the walk. The room

we rented was in a rooming house two blocks from the pub. We sat in the chill, dismal place all afternoon, playing cards with a pack we had been lucky enough to find at the desk. None of us said much. The ominous sky beyond the cheap yellowed window curtains threw a pall over our spirits, and now and again we heard the mournful sound of a hooter, on the river.

About six I went out for some food and the latest papers. I read them hastily on my way back to the rooming house, my throat growing tight and dry, my stomach growing cold. I raced up the stairs, forgetting about the sacks of food, and threw the papers down in front of Angela and Gerasmin. "More of it," was all I could say.

They glanced at me worriedly and bent over the papers. One lead story covered the killings in the hotel under a headline that began: *Mass Slaying*. But the most terrible piece of news concerned Sir Guy Folversham, Minister of the Exchequer. He had been slain around noon on his country estate. Torn to bits and left dead and mutilated in his eight-car garage. A gardener reported having seen something fleeing across the fields that looked like, ". . . *a great shadow*," the story said.

Gerasmin ground out his cigarette with deliberate anger. "Again," he breathed savagely. "They'll have the country wrecked in a week, at this rate. All the leaders being murdered." He slammed his fist into his palm.

"To Nedros," I said. "Let's get started."

He nodded, rising and checking his pistol. Angela once again brought up the subject of her accompanying us, and Gerasmin argued with her briefly.

"I'm going," she insisted.

"All right," he said, irritably, slipping into his topcoat. "We must stop wasting time. Come with us, but if we signal for you to turn back, return here and don't question us. Is that clear?"

She nodded, silent and stern-faced.

We set off through a heavy fog. I felt depressed, overwhelmed by the odds facing us. Our heels clicked on the cobbles, and the bellow of fog horns sounded dismally in our ears. A flickering street lamp illuminated the sign indicating Ryster Lane. We moved down the crooked little way, examining each of the shadowed doorways.

Finally I tugged at Gerasmin's arm and pointed. "Here." A numeral above the door said *8*. We stepped into the doorway. The shop lay in darkness, its two windows curtained top to bottom. Heavy gold lettering on the glass proclaimed, *T. Nedros, Importer.*

"Not much of a shop," Angela whispered.

"Doesn't need to be," I said, "for what's behind it."

Gerasmin tried the door. It was locked, of course. Without a word he closed his eyes, his lips drew tight and his brow wrinkled with strain. Angela seized my arm, staring at the Indian in the shadowed gloom. Gerasmin groaned and we heard a faint click. He sighed and relaxed, his shoulders slumping as he leaned forward to test the door again. It swung open imperceptibly.

"Come on," he said. "The lock's broken."

We had no sooner stepped into the darkened interior, reeking of incense and the smell of musty cloth and wood, than a bare bulb in the ceiling flared on, revealing the angular glare of dust-covered glass cases, empty of goods. Evidently T. Nedros did no importing at all to speak of. I snatched my gun from my pocket and shoved Angela behind me.

A voice cut through the silence. "Do not use the weapons, gentlemen."

We whirled around.

A section of empty wall shelving stood aside. The entrance framed a monstrously gross man in dirty gray trousers and filthy white shirt. His head was round and laden with fold upon pendulous fold of yellowish fat. Small eyes darted nervously at us, and a tiny pink tongue, like a snake's, flicked over his lips. The naked light bulb shone on his damp black hair, and I smelled the sickening odor of lemon cologne. His fat fingers were curled around a heavy .45 caliber automatic.

"I have a warning system set up," he said tonelessly. "It arouses me when anyone steps through my front door."

"You're Nedros?" I questioned.

"That is correct. But I have not had the pleasure of meeting *you.*"

"We'll forego that pleasure," Gerasmin said, coldly.

"I will be quick about it," Nedros said, his cheeks quivering. "I do not know you, but I can guess why you are here. No one would come here who did not belong to the organization, unless they were spies. You could not be here on business of a commercial nature, since I do not actually carry on that kind of business." He laughed ponderously, then sobered again. "I must, of course, kill you."

My stomach twisted and coiled into writhing knots. Suddenly, I felt something cold touch my free hand, which hung at my side. Nedros could not see that hand, and I felt experimentally. A cold, sharp edge. A *knife!* One from the hotel! I wanted to turn and speak to Angela, to burst out my thanks. But instead I slid the knife up my sleeve and waited tensely.

"Let me have your weapons," Nedros ordered. He indicated Gerasmin. "You first."

Gerasmin took one cat-like step forward and started to bring his pistol up. Nedros reached out, smashing down with the barrel of his weapon and knocking the gun to the floor with a clatter. His thick lips quivered. "If I were not going to kill you," he breathed, "I would punish you for being so foolish. I would punish you painfully. You!" he snarled in my direction. "Your weapon!"

I began walking forward, feeling the knife pressing against my fingertips, up inside my sleeve. Nedros shifted his gun to his left hand and extended his right to take the pistol. I took more steps, as if I were out for a Sunday walk.

"That's far enough," he said, not knowing whether to expect an attack or not. His one moment of hesitation, thrown off guard by my feigned carelessness, was enough. His trigger finger began to whiten. I whipped up my gun, striking the barrel of his weapon aside. It roared loudly and one of the glass cases tinkled and smashed. By that time I had slipped the knife out, and as quickly as I could I drove it into his chest.

He gasped, his tiny eyes widening. His gun exploded again as his finger jerked spasmodically, but the bullet buried itself in the floor. He peered down curiously at the ugly red blotch widening on his dirty white shirt. Abruptly, his eyes closed, as if he had fallen asleep. His legs collapsed. His whole fleshy body quivered once in obscene ripples, and lay still.

Angela watched with a terrified expression. I pulled her gently forward, and she shielded her eyes as we stepped across the corpse of the gross and very dead Mr. Nedros and into the room beyond.

It was a plain room, with only a bed, a table and chairs and a lavatory behind a screen painted with Japanese figures. A green light bulb was set high in one wall. Evidently the alarm. In the opposite wall was a heavy gray iron door studded with large round rivets.

Gerasmin breathed deeply. "This looks like the entrance. From now on we've got to be more careful than ever." I stepped forward and pulled up the massive handle. The door swung open noiselessly.

Stairs descended, shrouded in darkness. Far, far down in the distance was a vague gleam of light.

I turned to Angela. "Do you feel up to it?"

She nodded. "Of course." I could see that her hands were trembling though. "Go on," she said.

I took the lead, my heart pounding at triphammer speed as we started down those stairs that led into a pit of darkness and God knows what unnamed horrors.

The steps were narrow and steep, so that we had to go down them almost sideways. We tried to make as little noise as possible, holding our pistols ready. The gleam of lights grew larger, but with terrible slowness. It seemed as though we were going downward for hour after hour. My legs began to tire. Once, Angela stumbled and almost fell. I turned in time, catching my balance in time to keep her from going down and sending me tumbling with her. She breathed tensely a moment, clutching my arms, her face quite near mine. Then she said, "I'm all right. Let's keep going."

We were like three heroes from ancient legend making the traditional descent into hell, except that we were not heroic. We were frightened; even Gerasmin had been edgy since the encounter with the killers at the hotel. What lay down where the light beckoned, we couldn't tell. One thing was certain, however. We were in the underground. The horrible stench of those *things* filled the air.

The light turned out to be a small blue bulb set in the wall at the bottom of the stairs. I turned back to them and whispered, "We're almost at the bottom. A tunnel runs on from here."

"Let's wait a minute and get our breath," Gerasmin replied. I nodded, stepping off the lowest step and helping Angela down. She leaned against me. We examined the corridor ahead, our nostrils filled with that timeless reek of dead life reborn.

The corridor stretched into the distance, lit every hundred yards or so by one of those blue bulbs. They shone like blurred rows of streetlamps. The corridor evidently had no end. It stretched away into shadows.

Gerasmin and Angela indicated that they were ready. We started out again. We tramped on down that hall for another long space of time, the blue bulbs marching past, one after another. At last Gerasmin whispered, "Look up ahead, Marlow. The corridor ends!"

Perhaps we had stumbled into some by-way designed to throw

prowlers off the track. But how could that be? There had been no cross corridors anywhere along the passage. "No," I replied, "there must be a door." I walked faster, conscious of the fact that we were deep in the earth; above us lay London, where perhaps, even now, more hideous crimes were taking place. We were in the stronghold of Him Who Doesn't Walk, and though Gerasmin's mind kept a shield around us, I had the feeling that we were close to death.

The corridor did not end with a door. It turned abruptly to the right for a few feet, and to the left again. As I rounded the first turn, I jammed myself back against the wall. Gerasmin and Angela pulled up short. Light spilled down the corridor, evidently from a room a few feet to the left of the next turning. I listened and heard the harsh tones of a voice I recognized.

"*All right, old boy,*" the voice said, "*so you do argue with him, wot does it get you? A berth in the river, is all.*"

A heavier, deeper voice mumbled something in reply; I could not make it out.

"That voice belongs to the man with the patch on his eye," I whispered to the two behind me. "You remember—the one who gave me the message from Him Who Doesn't Walk, in Harley Square?"

"Hear anything else?" Gerasmin asked.

"Another voice. This must be a stop on the route to the center of operations."

"We'll have to rush them," Gerasmin said.

I nodded. "Angela, you stay here until we get them cleaned out." I silenced her with a wave of my hand. "You ready?"

Gerasmin said that he was. He hesitated only a moment. Here again, beyond the bend of the tunnel, lay possible death. I was becoming numb with the thought of it; I think I had counted myself a dead man soon after waking up in *Bane's Rest*. I brought my pistol up, feeling the sweat on my palms, and started along the corridor at a dead run. Gerasmin kept pace behind me.

As we rounded the turn, an alarm bell began to ring. I cursed myself. Of course they'd have them. And the corridor was thirty feet long! I was halfway down it when the alarm went off. They'd have plenty of time to get ready. I broke into the room and slid out flat on the floor, firing. Two men crouched behind a large table, firing back. One was the man with the patch, who recognized me and cackled with laughter, because he thought we were trapped. The other, a swarthy, thick-set man wearing gold earrings and a thin black moustache, fired at us with one hand. His other was frantically pressing an alarm switch on the table.

The few moments that it lasted were filled with noise and smoke. I aimed and shot, and the swarthy man's hand, pressing hard on the buzzer, disappeared in a welter of blood. He reared up above the table top, and Gerasmin's shot sheared half his head away.

The man with the patch screamed and tossed his gun down. "Don't kill me," he begged. "Give a lad a sporting chance." He raised his hands over his head, but I watched his one milk-blue eye rolling wildly. He was listening for someone—

The room contained doorways to half a dozen corridors leading off in all directions. From down one of them, I knew, would come men to finish us. Gerasmin pressed forward and shoved his gun against the one-eyed man's neck.

"I want you to talk," he whispered, "and immediately. The friends you signaled won't be here in time to save your life."

"I don't know much, your honor," the man whined. "Honest to living Jesus, I don't, your honor."

Gerasmin jammed the barrel tight against the man's throat. "The next attack. When will it be? The next killing. What will it be?"

The man writhed against the wall. "Please, your honor . . ." His one eye blinked wildly.

"Tell me!" Gerasmin snarled. I caught a whiff of fetid air from a corridor at the opposite side of the room. Not the smell of the beasts. The river smell. Perhaps that corridor was a way out, leading to the Thames. I noted it quickly in my mind and turned back to Gerasmin and the one-eyed man who was cringing now, trembling against the wall. In the distance, down another corridor, I heard footsteps running. Still far away, though.

"I'll kill you before they get here," Gerasmin raged. "Tell me! The next attack!"

"Tomorrow . . ." the man wheezed. "Tomorrow, I think that's it, your honor."

"You'd better be sure."

"That's it," the man fairly screamed. "Don't shoot, your honor, I'm sure. Captain Bezahrov himself told me, just an hour or so ago."

"What time?"

"Ten o'clock, tomorrow morning."

"Where?"

"Number . . . Number Ten, Downing Street . . ."

"Good God!" I exclaimed. *"The Prime Minister!"*

"That's what we wanted to know," Gerasmin said. "You'd better get Angela."

I had completely forgotten about her. I went back into the corridor, softly calling her name. And then I stopped. The tunnel was filled with that overpowering stench—and a section of the floor was gone.

I knelt down and found an iron ladder leading down into darkness. The smell rising from the hole made me choke. Angela was gone! Fear raced through me. I started down the ladder, but heard Gerasmin call me.

"Marlow! They're coming!"

"Angela's gone!" I shouted back. "She's—"

A volley of shouts cut off the rest. I stood for a moment, my mind raging, torn in two directions. Angela, lovely, frightened Angela was gone into the darkness, gone with the monster taint lingering in the air behind her. Someone watched the corridor, not with his mind but in actuality. Something had risen up out of the dark ground and *taken* Angela—

Shots were roaring back in the tiny room. I heard Gerasmin's anguished scream: *"Marlow!"*

I raced back. The man with the black patch had fled. Gerasmin was crouched behind the table, firing down a corridor. Answering shots filled the room, bullets smacking into the walls.

I ran across the room on my knees and dropped down beside him, triggering a couple of shots.

"We've got to get word back about the Prime Minister," he whispered. "We've got to go back *now*."

I indicated the corridor directly behind of us. "Do you smell the river there, or is it my imagination?"

His teeth were clenched together. "I smell it. We'll have to run for it. I'm—I'm too tired to try with my mind." The corridor from which the shots had come was silent now. But we heard a soft rustling of feet. They were stealing closer . . . closer . . . Gerasmin pulled at my sleeve and, bent over, we ran toward the corridor.

Bullets whispered in the air around us, but we got safely into the darkness and we kept running. They came after us, but our shots kept them off. No blue bulbs lit this corridor. Finally we slammed into another iron door. The strong odor of the river filtered through a thick wire grill.

My hands moved over the door; I found a wheel. "Here," I whispered, and began to turn it. Gradually the door swung open.

We stepped out onto the slippery mud bank of the river. I let go of the door and it closed automatically. Breathing hard, we pulled ourselves up the slope until we were directly above the door, and we lay there with our guns ready, waiting.

The killers did not come out.

Finally I began to breathe more easily. I looked around. The embankment stretched away in either direction. Lights lined the opposite shore, and a tug moved past us in the stream, its whistle sounding. My mind relaxed a little then. We were out of that hellish underground—out of the nightmare world of dark corridors and death at every turn. Two thoughts struck me suddenly. The assassination scheduled for tomorrow at ten, and Angela. I turned to Gerasmin quickly.

He lay stretched out on his stomach, as if tired. I spoke to him. He didn't answer. I spoke again, and again silence. My back grew cold. I reached out and touched him. I turned him over, and saw with horror the dark ugly stains on the front of his coat. He stared at me, his eyes wide open.

He was dead.

I heard the tug's whistle cry out mournfully a second time.

The night closed upon me, and I felt death and horror creeping near. I realized now just how alone I was. Gerasmin lay dead, all that strange ancient power gone—cut off. Mighty as he was, his mind had not been quick enough to stop the bullets that tore life out of him. The shield was down, too. No longer could I move unobserved. Him Who Doesn't Walk could watch me any hour of the day or night.

And Angela. The frightening thoughts struck me, one after another. She was down there in the underground, perhaps already dead. I had a wild urge to go back, and I started scrabbling on the bank to find the entrance. But I couldn't locate it anywhere. Perfectly concealed. The wet clay of the slope was everywhere the same.

Marlow alone. Marlow against them, the unseen ones, all the more terrible because they *were* unseen. I realized dimly that there was only one way for me to stay alive; one way for me to be strong enough and quick enough to elude them for a time. I had to hate them. I had to hate them with every anguished fiber of my soul. Hate would make me move faster, and even though I might move into a rain of bullets or the arms of one of those shadowy things, still, on the other hand, I might spend my time deliberating and die all the sooner.

Slowly, methodically, I began to think about them. I concentrated on Gerasmin's corpse, stared at the blood thickening and darkening on his coat. I remembered Angela. I pictured her writhing under a hundred obscene tortures; pictured her starving; pictured her dead, that lovely face racked by fear and unspeakable sights. I felt tension gathering in my body; focusing. The thoughts sang loud and clear as I pictured the man with the patch and his sly, lecherous warning in Harley Square, and the news of next morning's proposed slaughter.

My hate bubbled up, seethed and became a constant fire of anger within me. It was personal now, very personal. I had forgotten the other men who had died. I wanted to be there when Bezahrov arrived at 10 Downing Street. I wanted to stand up to Bezahrov and fight him and kill him for the beast he was, he and all of them.

But a bit of rationality got through to me, thank God. I went away from the bank, much as I did not want to. With one last look at Gerasmin's corpse and a promise uttered silently to him, I walked away from the river. I had one person to turn to now; one—whether he wanted to help me or not. I would force him to help me. I would transfuse my hate into his body and his mind and show him that he had no other choice.

I checked a phone directory for the address of Inspector Rohm. A cab carried me to his flat. Two flights up dingy red-carpeted stairs, three doors down the hall smelling of tobacco and liquor and sweat, and I knocked on his door. I heard his voice from within saying, "Just a moment." I took out my pistol again.

The pistol greeted him when he opened the door. His sharp blue eyes took it in, and darted to my face. "Do you remember me?" I said. "Steven Marlow. The man with the insane story?"

"I remember you, certainly," he replied, his scholarly face a bit pale.

I gestured with the gun. "Let me in."

He stepped back and I went into the flat, closing the door behind me. Rohm blinked and I gestured again. "Get your coat on."

"Where are we going?"

"Number 10, Downing Street."

"*Number 10—*" he choked. "You are mad!"

"This is part of my story," I said evenly. "A story that is not mad, a story that is not insane or unbelievable. If you don't come with me, the Prime Minister will die at ten tomorrow morning, exactly as Lord Wolters and Sir Guy Folversham died. I'm forcing you to come with me so that others will eventually believe what I say. I'm forcing you because it's the only way you'll see that what I say is true."

"What if I don't?" he asked quietly.

"I'll kill you, Inspector. Do you believe me?"

He stared at me from those probing eyes for a long minute. "No," he said finally. "But I'll get my coat."

We hailed another cab. I pushed the pistol toward the driver and told him I was taking over. With Inspector Rohm beside me, we drove to Downing Street and parked the cab. Then I began talking, while the dark hours of night raced by and the stars lay hidden behind mourning-robes of clouds. I poured out the story, the part he had heard and the part he had not heard. I told it all, every detail, every instant.

And then I said, "Now do you believe me?"

"No," he said quietly. "I don't. Are you going to kill me for thinking it's too incredible?"

"Damn you!" I shouted at him. "It won't stop here. They'll burn Europe and they'll destroy America, systematically, because it will be too incredible that such a thing could ever happen. And then they'll pour out of the East, out of Russia, and the few poor devils left alive won't ever have a chance to live like decent human beings again!"

"I am willing to take one precaution," he said as dawn began to etch itself gray on the eastern sky. A horn honked in the distance. "Lord Wolters and Folversham have died, so we can't really afford to take chances. I'd like to ring up the Yard and get a squad of men."

"Machine guns," I insisted. "Get machine guns."

"And I'll have to ring up my superior to request that the Prime Minister be removed from here for the morning. I'll need a telephone for that. I'll believe you that much Marlow—do that much for you. You haven't committed any crime *yet*."

"Get to the phone," I said, thanking God for his sense of duty; his determination to leave none of the possibilities unaccounted for. If he couldn't see the greater danger, he could at least provide for the one at hand.

I began to sweat. The morning grew brighter, or as bright as another of those lead-gray days could be. The Prime Minister was no longer at 10 Downing Street when the appointed hour came. I had seen him leave, quiet, impressive, dignified. We had to keep off those obscene things! Men like this were worth it. Ordinary men, everywhere, were worth it.

Officers were stationed in every room. The officers were armed with machine guns. I stood with Rohm, smoking nervously, wishing that I were somewhere else, wishing I could wake up from this hell's dream. From another room came the metallic chime of a clock. The hour was ten.

They came up through the floor, six of them, materializing like foul black shadows, swirling, tumbling, roiling up. Captain Bezahrov came that way too, into our room, and it was madly incredible to see a human *coming up from the underground.*

The machine guns exploded in a roaring thunder and the things broke apart in blood and screams and decaying filth. Bezahrov whirled around once and sprawled on the floor, spilling out his life. They had been transported up through the ground, *thought* into this building on their mission of destruction, only to meet quick, furious death.

We bent over Bezahrov, dying, his scarred face twitching convulsively. There were rapid questions and whispered desperate answers. A bomb. Under London. Demolish half the city. Noon. Two days from now. Noon.

"Rohm?" I whispered, "we've got to get into the underground."

He turned to me. His voice suddenly faded away into the distance and I saw his horrible sharp eyes peering into mine. *"Yes, Marlow,"* he whispered, so the others could not hear, *"into the underground."* His voice died suddenly and he stared at me.

I tried to say something. I could not. I could not speak. My throat was tight and dry and I could not say a word. In a sick horror, I heard Rohm dismiss his men, sending them back to Scotland Yard. And then I heard a voice whisper in my brain:

"Come, Marlow. Into the underground. I want to kill you before I go. You have caused me much trouble. I want to kill you *myself.*"

The voice of Inspector Rohm. The *mind* of Inspector Rohm taking me over, holding me speechless, immobile. Holding, gripping. *The bomb*—I wanted to scream. Dimly I saw the officers moving toward the street. Inspector Rohm stared at me. Inspector Rohm—

Him Who Doesn't Walk.

I heard the wild laughter of the man who called himself Inspector Rohm. It echoed a dirge in my brain until I lost consciousness.

The pattern became clear as I awoke. Somehow, in a period of half-consciousness before I opened my eyes, a mind seemed to be telling me things I wanted to know, telling me in order to torment me before I reached the end. Why did I think I had been sent to him especially, out of all others, at Scotland Yard? He had willed it. Then he had sent me away. When I returned again, he had been forced to protect the Prime Minister, because he did not want me to suspect. Did I understand?

A laugh.

He had allowed Bezahrov to die, he had not cancelled the attack even though he knew it would fail, in order to take me. He did his duty as Inspector Rohm and the Prime Minister lived. And Him Who Doesn't Walk dismissed the officers. They had not been close enough to hear Bezahrov's whispered words, you see. Thus he took me into the underground, to kill me before the bomb went off. All along, he had been watching, been waiting at certain points along the trail. Damnably clever.

The thoughts came faster now, vengeful. *Where now?* Paris, Berlin, America, anywhere. Step by step. The high ones commanded it.

Where were they? I felt my muscles aching as if some monstrous thought-hand held them. The masters were in Russia; in the East. The masters wanted the world. Had not they told us that so many times?

We were alone in the underground and no one would know about the bomb to go off in two days. Inspector Rohm could arrange to die as a hero. Strange, eh? But I did not understand him, quite . . . the Prime Minister allowed to live that I might die . . . once again I caught a conception of the violent, gigantic force of evil in Him Who Doesn't Walk. It was vindictive; personal—

Wake up, Marlow!

I opened my eyes. I was standing in a room similar to the one in which we had fought with the man with the patch. There before me floated the torso of Inspector Rohm, alive, peering at me. But—but—Great God—*he had no legs!*

From the waist down there was nothing but emptiness— invisibility. I saw the trousers, socks, shoes and shorts on the floor. The monstrous vision hung before me, grinning at me. Him Who Doesn't Walk held a pistol.

"Now, Mr. Marlow," he said quietly, "you have thirty seconds before I shoot you down." His voice was soft. "You're peering so intently at my legs." He laughed at the last word. "Thought, Mr. Marlow. The power of brain. Life where there is no life. Inspector Rohm walked on legs of *mind.*"

Mind . . . desperately, I sought for the answer. I felt it gnawing at my brain, another voice, trying to get through, trying to break the wall. I felt the weight of the pistol still in my pocket. Him Who Doesn't Walk did not think I could use it. Could I? If the voice . . . if the voice . . .

"Thirty seconds, Mr. Marlow—counting from *now*."

I felt the sweat standing out on my face. The voice . . . the voice was coming closer, rushing with a sound of other ancient voices flying on the wind from lonely temples on snowy peaks. The spirits of men who had touched holiness, goodness, coming toward me, summoned by that prime voice to add their strength, coming, if only I could let them in. But how? I was not calling them. Who was?

"Twenty seconds. Prepare yourself, Mr. Marlow. Pray to God who does not exist." He laughed shortly and cocked the pistol. "I am going to enjoy slaying you, Mr. Marlow. You have interfered so much . . ."

Come! Come! From a thousand ancient lands someone is calling for strength. Strength and a moment of life . . . straining, fighting . . . screaming his thoughts in an effort to penetrate . . .

"Fifteen seconds, Mr. Marlow."

I am coming . . . I am trying . . . I am coming . . . call me by name . . .

I can't, I thought wildly, I don't know of these things. I don't know of powers like this.

"Ten seconds."

You must call me by name.

I can't.

Can you hear me?

Yes.

Call me by name. It rests with you. You are afraid.

Yes, I am.

Do not listen to your fear. Think of me . . . think of me . . . who am I? I am here for a moment in eternity, waiting, watching. Call me . . . the spirits of good men have filled me . . . I am yours . . . call me, the desperate voice shrieked.

"Five seconds. Goodbye, Mr. Marlow." Him Who Doesn't Walk laughed.

His finger whitened upon the trigger.

No . . . no . . . I thought. *No* . . . I waited for the bullet, and in that instant I pushed down the nauseous fear flooding over me and thought clearly . . . of course . . . of course . . . the one . . .

"*Gerasmin!*" I screamed, throwing myself forward.

Him Who Doesn't Walk started and cursed. "You fool! Gerasmin is de—"

But he was not. I had thought his name and summoned him and he stood in the room, pale, shadowy, filmy of body, one hand pointing accusingly at Him Who Doesn't Walk, and the blood still running on his chest. His lips were tight, and his eyes were closed, and that ageless face seemed to radiate a kind of unearthly light.

Him Who Doesn't Walk turned on the apparition and started firing. Wildly. It vanished as quickly as it had come, like a puff of magician's smoke. By that time, though, I had my pistol out. I shot with hateful accuracy, aiming at the figure before me, wanting to tear the legless horror to bits. Finally the smoke and the noise diminished and I looked down. I knew I would never see his true face. Inspector Rohm's face had certainly not been his.

And I had blown his head away.

I heard a rushing of wind in my mind, of the spirits, of the entities, going back to their temples against the roof of the world, back to their ancient books of goodness and truth and wisdom and light. Another sound mingled in—the voice of Gerasmin returning to the mystic realm of the dead, with a syllable of farewell. It was no word I could utter or write down, yet I understood it. He had given me the strength to call upon him, and the ancient forgotten power.

I glanced at my watch. Ten-thirty. I began to walk through the underground. At fifteen minutes before eleven, I found the bomb mechanism and broke the wires. At eleven-eight, I found Angela locked in a cell off one of the main corridors, sleeping drugged and her hair disheveled, her face thin and pale. Perhaps Him Who Doesn't Walk had forgotten her in his fury to get me. Not stopping to wonder why, I thanked God she was still alive and carried her out of the underground, up through the shop of T. Nedros into the daylight. Behind me as I walked, I heard countless scurryings. The servants, the lackeys of hell were leaving, returning to their holes, their driving life force gone. The master was dead and I hoped that another would not call them forth for ten thousand years.

They put our story in the newspapers. Not with our names, because I did not want that, and the government supported me. They told how the real Inspector Rohm—his corpse—was found by the landlady in a closet in his flat the afternoon after I destroyed Him Who Doesn't Walk. They burned out the underground with flame throwers, too, destroying the last remnants of the things I first saw that night on the *Queen of Madagascar*.

And for us, then, Angela and me, it was over. We were free. I gave up the sea and took up a landsman's trade. We married a year later, and now we have our own home and a small son growing up. Once a year we go down to the cliffs of England and stand looking out at the dark Channel and the dark sky and the darker world beyond. We remember that it came once. We remember that it is written in their books. We stand on the cliffs in the wind once a year and watch the East.

We must not forget.

THE SEEKER IN THE FORTRESS

by
Manly Wade Wellman

Manly Wade Wellman is one of the great veterans of the science fiction/fantasy field, appearing in the sf magazines as early as 1927. He is best known for his stories featuring John the Ballad Singer, but the bulk of his writing has consisted of excellent novels for younger readers. His best work has been at the shorter lengths and can be found in his collections WHO FEARS THE DEVIL? (1963) and WORSE THINGS WAITING (1973). A noted historian of the state of North Carolina, he is still going strong and producing quality work at (as these words are written) the age of seventy-nine.

One of a series of stories about the last Atlantean, "The Seeker in the Fortress" pits wizard against warrior in an exciting tale of rescue.

Trombroll the wizard had set his fortress in what had been a small, jagged crater, rather like an ornate stopper in the crumpled neck of a wineskin. Up to it on all sides came the tumbled, clotted lips of the cone. Above and within them it lodged, a sheaf of round towers with, on the tallest, a fluttering banner of red, purple and black. At the lower center, where the fitted gray rocks of the walls fused with the jumbled gray rocks of the crater, stood a mighty double door of black metal. Slits in the towers seemed ready to rain point-blanked missiles, smoking floods of boiling oil. In the distance rose greater heights, none close enough to command the fortress. On the slope below the door, Prince Feothro of Deribana stood among his captains and councillors and shrugged inside his elegant armor. The plain behind him was thronged with his horsemen and footmen, his heavy engines of war. But just then he could not think of how to use them.

"What is there to do?" he almost whined into the gilded face-bars of his helmet and, as though in answer, a mighty voice boomed from a speaking trumpet on the battlement.

"Greetings, Prince, and shortly farewell. Do you give your princely pledge to a parley?"

"It is given," called back Feothro.

The black gates opened ringingly. Out paced a figure in elaborate ceremonial mail, to halt halfway down.

"I am a herald speaking with the voice of mighty Trombroll," said this man. "Trombroll is supreme in magic. The winds and the thunder fight his battles."

"Trombroll has plagued the world long enough," returned Feothro, sternly enough. "He threatens plague and famine, and demands tribute to hold them back. Tell him we've come to destroy him. These armies are the allied might of Deribana and Varlo, sworn to end Trombroll's reign of evil. Varlo's King Zapaun who is as my father, has pledged his thrice lovely daughter, the Princess Yann, to be my consort. Let Trombroll come out and fight."

"Why should he?" inquired the herald. "We have wells of water, stores of provisions. And we have also that exemplary triumph of beauty, the Princess Yann herself."

"Princess Yann!" howled Feothro. "You lie!"

"Cast your eyes upward to where our banner flies."

All looked aloft. Two guards were visible, escorting between them a slender figure in a bright red garment. Then all three drew back out of sight.

"That was Yann," babbled Feothro. "How possibly—"

"Trombroll's accomplished spies brought word of your advance against him, also word that Princess Yann was being sent to you. Her escort was ambushed, and she was brought here." A pause, to let it sink in. "Prince Feothro, you see how impossible your situation is. If you storm us, if you seek to enter this one gateway, the unhappy Princess will die an intricate death even now being invented for her. You wouldn't let that happen to her. We give you until sunrise tomorrow to lead your host away."

With which, the herald returned through the gate. The black portals clashed shut behind him.

Feothro called upon the names of half a dozen gods, in hope that at least one would hear him. "We must do something!" he half wailed to his chieftains to both sides. "Do something, I say!"

"Do what?" asked a silver-mailed subordinate, not very helpfully.

If Feothro had a reply to that, which is highly improbable, he did not give it. He looked to where two spearmen marched an upstanding stranger toward him.

"My Lord," said one of the two, saluting, "this man has been prowling here and there among the various commands, and he only laughs at questions."

Feothro regarded the stranger with what he hoped was a terrifying scowl. He saw one as tall as himself, but broader-shouldered, deeper-chested, leaner-waisted. The fellow wore dusty sandals and a shabby blue tunic with points of white. He carried a long sword at his belt, and behind his shoulder rode a gold-mounted harp. His features were saturnine and his hair tumbled in a dark mane.

"A spy for Trombroll, no doubt," Feothro snarled.

A shake of the head. "Not I. I was passing through and saw your army gathered. I strolled over to see what was afoot."

"Looking for trouble, were you?" suggested Feothro.

"I never look for trouble. It's everywhere."

"What's your name and people, and lie no more than you can help."

Amused white teeth flashed. "I'm an Atlantean—"

"A lie at once," charged Feothro. "Atlantis is drowned, and all Atlanteans with it."

"Except for me," said the other easily. "I was swept over the sea, with a broken gate for raft, came ashore, and have wandered ever since. My name's Kardios."

A chief leaned to Feothro. "My Lord, that name is known to me. Kardios is much talked of, as an adventurer among monsters."

Again Feothro surveyed Kardios. "If that's true, if you came here only to see what we do, what then?"

Kardios shrugged, and the strings of his harp whispered. "I heard your problem. Trombroll defies you in his fortress, and you don't dare attack for fear of what he'll do to your princess. Maybe I happened along in good time to help you."

"Then you know we can't storm their gate," said Feothro testily. "How would you mount the siege?"

"That's a good question," said Kardios, using the locution for perhaps the first time in the history of the world. "I hesitate to answer it, since you know that Trombroll's spies are apt to be listening. Maybe I wouldn't exactly mount a siege?"

"If you bring Princess Yann back safely, name your reward," said Feothro, not very graciously. "If you fail—"

"Oh," said Kardios, "if I come back, I'll have her with me. Have I leave to begin?"

"Don't go beyond this host," said Feothro. "Not beyond sight of this fortress."

"Naturally." Kardios turned on his heel and headed down slope among the gathered armed bands.

As he did so, he twitched his harp forward and swept its strings. He made up words to sing, no louder than he himself could hear:

> *"The keep is strong, the keep is tall,*
> *Its gates are black as sin,*
> *It bids defiance unto all*
> *Who seek to enter in."*

He liked that, and played and sang it again as he strode on past the rearmost elements of Feothro's besieging myriad. Some distance behind him followed the two spearmen, obviously told off to keep him in sight. Kardios headed around the foot of the slope, to where he could see the other side of the fortress. No gates there, only more slits for arrows and darts and lances to be cast down. Pondering this, Kardios smiled. Again he twanged the harp:

> *"Here, mysteries are grim and deep,*
> *Here, secrets men may shun,*
> *But never have I known a keep*
> *Without more gates than one."*

Something twitched beside his sandal, and he looked down. A frog, only a frog, prettily patterned in green. Kardios nodded to

it. "Thank you, little brother," he said. "You may have solved
a problem."

The frog hopped into some coarse green bush, the only vegetation Kardios had seen on the whole rocky crater. Dropping to
one knee, he poked into the matted growth. Sure enough, it was
damp where roots delved into earth. He glanced around, to see
that his two escorting guardsmen were gazing, not at him, but up
at the towers. Swiftly he dived into the brush as into a pool.
Crouching low, he crept along the way the frog had shown him.

A tunnel of sorts was there, with water trickling on its floor.
It was not too narrow for his shoulders. As he entered on hands
and knees, he was encouraged by a patch of dim light ahead. On
and on he worked his way, many times his own length, until his
head came out into a gloomy upright shaft, with golden radiance
above. He nodded congratulations to himself. The channel joined
one of the wells of which he had heard Trombroll's herald boast.

It was faced with smooth, damp stones. Climbing them would
be a dire danger, even for as active a climber as Kardios. He
studied the shaft narrowly and saw that a rope dangled into it.
Presumably a bucket hung below. Kardios drew his sword,
reached out to the point, and pulled a loop of the rope to him. He
tugged at it experimentally. Perhaps it would bear his weight. It
must. He sheathed the sword, caught the rope in both hands, and
swung out upon it.

Up he swarmed, hand over hand, helping himself now and
then with a toe in a crevice of the stone-faced wall. It was not far
to the top. He caught the lip of the curb, drew himself upon it,
and found himself looking into the beady eyes of a squat,
puffy-faced fellow in scale armor.

"What are you doing in the well?" challenged this one.

"Weren't you told about it, you fool?" snapped Kardios in his
turn. "I did the bidding of our master Trombroll, I fetch news of
the besiegers. Here, help me out."

A fat hand caught his wrist and Kardios sprang out upon stone
flagging. Above them rose the torchlit roof of a cavern. The man
glowered at Kardios.

"I don't know you," he said. "You're not of the garrison."

"I'm Trombroll's spy captain, noddlehead," said Kardios.
"Since you saw me come in, you'll bear me witness with him.
Now, look down into the well. See what treasure I brought with
me, lashed to the rope below."

The man bent to look down. Kardios caught him by elbow and

ankle and flung him headlong into the shaft. So swiftly did he fall that he had no time to howl. He only splashed, far below.

Now Kardios had time to see the cave into which he had won. Against the rough walls were bracketed blazing torches of pitchy wood. He saw bins and trestles piled with stores, he saw rows of tall earthenware jars of oil and wine. Plainly, this was one of Trombroll's well-stored larders. He dipped his hand into a wine jar, then another and another, drinking appreciatively of the best of them. He tore a barley loaf in two, bit into it, and helped it along with a morsel from a huge mottled cheese. Feeling refreshed, he moved along toward where must be a door.

He found it, made of heavy wooden slabs and iron bolts. He tried it. It was locked.

"Is that you, Smar?" challenged someone from the other side. "Your tour of duty has long to run before I let you out."

"Help in here, friend," said Kardios at once. "Smar fell down the well."

"Who's in yonder?" demanded the one outside.

Kardios heard a key grate in a lock. As the door swung inward, Kardios ducked behind it. In came another armored sentry, sword in hand. Kardios kicked the door shut again. As he did so, his own blade flashed out and he pushed the point close to the sentry's hairy throat.

"One sound or move without my leave and you're off duty forever," Kardios warned. "Drop that sword. Thank you. Now, where are we here?"

"Where but in Trombroll's deepest cellar?" gulped the sentry.

"Deepest cellar, eh? What's above here?"

"The guard chamber, and, above that, the concourse. Higher still, defenses and Trombroll's quarters."

Kardios's extended sword was pale and keen. The sentry sweated as he looked at it.

"How many men in the guard chamber?" Kardios inquired.

"Men?" repeated his captive. "Just now, no men." Almost a smile with that.

"A guard chamber unguarded?" said Kardios, scowling.

"No men are there, none at all."

"You wouldn't say that curious thing if it hadn't an element of truth," judged Kardios. "Turn your back."

The sentry obeyed. Kardios yanked open the fastening of the coat of mail and dragged it free. He lifted off the combed helmet and set it on his own head. "Now, cross your hands behind you."

Kardios bound the wrists with the man's own belt. He made a gag of a dagger sheath from that belt, and took a bunch of keys.

"I don't kill unless I must, and so you may live if you stay here without struggling free for, say, an hour," said Kardios, and cautiously opened the door. He saw a passage, heavily faced with cut stones and lighted by more torches but with no sign of life. Into the passage he stepped and closed the door behind him.

He donned the mail jacket. It fit loosely, but that was better than tightness. He left the door unlocked behind him and went onward.

Steps led into a dark niche, and Kardios mounted them. At the top was another locked door. He found a key for it and went through into what must be that guard chamber where, he had been assured, no men would be found just then.

It was a square, lofty apartment, with arms of all sorts racked against its walls and dangling from its beams. There were rows of shields, barred with Trombroll's garish colors of red, purple and black. Lances were clumped in sheafs, swords hung in bunches like gleaming soup vegetables. There were bales of armored jackets such as Kardios himself had captured to wear, and heaps of helmets, combed and plumed. If Trombroll had followers enough to bear all these arms, his fortress was well garrisoned.

Light shone from a cluster of lamps upon a great table of polished black wood, and on benches and chairs around this lounged, not men but women, young women. A dozen of them, variously and attractively clad in gold-mounted breastplates and greaves, with shining helmets bracketing their flowerlike faces. They had weapons, too—curved swords, short-handled axes. One held in her hand a stout, polished pole to which was attached by a chain a lethal-seeming globe studded with fanglike spikes. This one rose from her seat. She was tall, cleanly symmetrical, and her blue eyes flashed loftily.

"Sentry, have you forgotten that we are not to be intruded upon without order from Lord Trombroll?" she addressed him. "We know your sort, and the unsoldierly motives that bring you here. Speak your business, if any, and get out."

"And be glad you're able to get out," added another, almost as tall and fully as beautiful. The armor the girls wore might have protected them, here and there, against attack, but not very thoroughly against admiration. All of them had their shapely hands on their weapons.

"Shall I go before I sing you a song?" asked Kardios, summoning the most agreeable smile of which he was capable. He took his harp in his hands and touched the strings. He hoped words would come:

> *"Each is armored, each has a blade,*
> *Whetted and bright and keen,*
> *Each is a splendid warrior maid,*
> *Fair as a gracious queen. . . ."*

He deplored the scanning of that, but not so his audience. They squealed applause.

"Beautiful!" cried the one who had first addressed him. "We were so bored here. We don't know you, do we? What's your name, harp-striker?"

"Call me Kardios."

"If I call you Kardios, call me Elwa. I'm under-officer of this guard force. We're here because Trombroll won't put men on guard over Princess Yann. He fears they'll fall in love with her and help her escape, though I don't see why."

"Princess Yann?" said Kardios, as though the name were strange to him. "I'm new in this fortress—"

"And welcome, at least to us," beamed one of the girls.

"I didn't know she was here, in this guard chamber."

"We'd call you stupid if you weren't so handsome and melodious a singer," said Elwa, with a smile. "What's the rest of your song? For there must be more."

"Of course," said Kardios, who had been making up a second verse. He struck tender chords and sang again:

> *"Who dares face them with dauntless heart?*
> *A smile or a tender glance*
> *Would strike him down like a deadly dart,*
> *A trenchant sword or a lance."*

More applause, far more than Kardios thought his effort deserved. The girls flocked around him like doves to a handful of bread crumbs. Their smiles and tender glances might well accomplish the fate he had sung about. Elwa poured wine from a patterned jug into a silver-banded cup.

"Drink, Kardios," she bade, handing it to him. "I think I can guess why you came here—to see if we're as appetizing as rumored."

He drank. The wine was better than that in the cellars. "Far more appetizing," he made haste to assure her.

"More, do you think, than Yann in the cage yonder?"

She gestured toward the far end of the chamber. It was closed off with bars that seemed forged of gold. In the shadows within lurked something, somebody. Kardios took a step that way.

"No," warned Elwa, lifting her flaillike mace across his chest. "Trombroll wants no man of his following to look at her or speak to her. If we have to kill you, we'll sorrow, but we must."

"Which hardly encourages me to try speech with her," said Kardios, sitting on a bench to sip more wine. "Of course, if Trombroll should find me here—"

"We'll see he doesn't find you," promised a girl whose armor seemed uncomfortably tight on her splendid, tawny body. "Sing some more, it's prosy on duty down here."

"Prosy on duty," repeated Kardios, with his most agreeable smile. "That's like poetry, my dear. I'll dedicate this song to you."

He swept the strings and began:

> *"If Trombroll's wise, as people say,*
> *And shrewd, as people guess,*
> *Then why does Trombroll stay away*
> *From all this loveliness?"*

> *"Why does he keep to his towers*
> *When he could enter here,*
> *All among these lovely flowers—"*

Three loud thumps rang from the ceiling overhead.

"He's coming," breathed Elwa. "Quick, Kardios, get behind these cloaks."

She hustled him to a corner behind a garment-hung rack. Peeping out, Kardios saw a strangely spiny figure descend, as on an invisible cord, from a trapdoor above. All the girls snapped becomingly to attention.

"What report of my prisoner?" asked a deep, dull voice, like water flowing under snow.

"She stays quiet, says nothing, noble Lord Trombroll," said Elwa.

"I've come to take her away for an important interview," croaked Trombroll.

Peering between two cloaks, Kardios studied the wizard. Trombroll was in armor from toe to neck, a bizarre armor indeed. It was of drab metal and it bristled all over with ugly spikes and blades, so that Trombroll looked like a profusely spiny lizard. Even the backs of his gauntlets sprouted points. No sane man would grapple Trombroll.

Only his face was bare and, in Kardios's opinion, Trombroll would have done well to cover that, too. The nose stuck out like one of the armor spikes, and beneath it was a wide, taut-lipped mouth and a chin that slanted so far back as to be almost no chin at all. By contrast, Trombroll's brow bulged as though ready to burst. His gloomily gray hair fell to his shoulders and was bound with a fillet studded ostentatiously with many-colored jewels. Trombroll's eyes, pale as a crocodile's, fixed on the cage at the far end of the room.

"Bring her out," he ordered.

Two of the prettiest hastened to obey. One of them opened the cage door with a huge key. There was a murmur of argument, and then both the warrior maids reached in and fetched the prisoner out, holding her by the wrists. They marched her toward where Trombroll waited.

At once Kardios saw why Elwa and the others had spoken so disparagingly of Yann. She was smaller than the smallest of them, and considerably fairer than the fairest. Her flaming red gown was snug enough to accentuate every contour of her supple, dainty figure. Her lustrous dark hair was dressed in two winglike sweeps. Her blue eyes were large, though not large enough to be out of proportion to her rosy, round-chinned face. As she was led up to Trombroll, those eyes regarded him with concentrated dislike.

He laughed gratingly. One of his gloved hands took her by the chin. It looked like a sea urchin on a pink seashell.

"Princess," he said, "that fool who says you're betrothed to him lingers outside, not knowing whether to go or stay. It would be discourteous to leave you shut up here while you wait for him to make up his mind. I thought to offer you some entertainment."

"You'll please let me go," she said, in a voice that would, as Kardios thought, sing delightfully. She shrank from Trombroll's spiny person.

"I venture to assure you of the contrary. Wait until you see what is prepared for you, above here."

He shifted his grip to her elbow. "Relax in my hold," he said, "and here we go."

With that, he rose in the air, carrying Yann with him. They soared like leaves in a gale. They vanished through the trapdoor in the ceiling. All the warrior maids gazed upward after them, so intently that they were not aware that Kardios had come out from hiding.

"What Trombroll sees in her I can't understand," said Elwa acidly. She turned and saw Kardios. "It's all right, he's gone."

Kardios looked up at the trap. It was closed from above, apparently by a simple lid. "Where did he take her?"

"None of us knows that," said Elwa. "His apartments are far above here—this guard room is in the cellar of the fortress, and the towers reach high, high above us."

"I'd like to see," said Kardios, tossing aside the captured helmet and shucking off the shirt of mail.

All gazed with admiration at his revealed muscles of chest and arm. "Armor is so cumbersome," said one. "Shall we take off ours?"

"If my duty did not call me away, that would be delightful," smiled Kardios as he sprang lightly upon the table.

The trap door was at arm's length above his head. He prodded upward with his sword point. The lid shifted at the pressure, and he edged it clear of the opening. Pallid light was visible above him. Quickly he sheathed his sword and bestowed his harp at his back.

"Lovely ladies," he said, "I'd stay with you for hours if it weren't for that duty, but—"

With that, he leaped upward. His hand clutched through the trap and hooked on its rim. He heard them all gasp as he hauled himself powerfully upward, got hold with his other hand, and dragged his body to where he could get a knee upon the surface overhead. Next moment, he had hoisted himself clear of the trap and upon a paved floor.

His first sensation was of space, vast space, enough for an arena such as some nations used for bloody contests between armed men and fierce beasts. As he stood up, he half expected to see some great, abhorrent creature stealing toward him. But he was all alone on that bare, broad floor, with pale, plastered walls distantly all around him, up to a ceiling that gave off flickers of light. No sight of Trombroll or Yann. He looked this way and that.

He saw an uneven line slanting up the wall nearest him. It was a flight of railless stairs mounting to a corner, where another flight went across the adjacent wall to meet yet another. Those stairs mounted all the way around, and at the upper end of the highest flight appeared a dark blotch, a cavelike passage of some sort. That was the only hint of a way out of this mighty enclosure.

Kardios headed for the stairs. His feet struck sound from the floor and it echoed back to him. He hoped nobody was listening. He reached the bottom of the stairs. They were of cut stone, and narrow—room for only one to mount them. If he met somebody coming down, there would be no passing. As he walked up, the floor below dropped away. It would be a considerable fall down there. Kardios asked himself how he would accomplish the mission for which he had so lightly volunteered.

So close did he press to the wall, his hand against it and his eyes on those narrow steps, that he was not aware of other movement until it was almost upon him from above. Then he looked, to where four armored men descended, one behind the other. They bore jagged weapons that combined deadly features of both sword and axe.

"Who are you?" one of them growled. "Give the watchword."

"Never mind watchwords," replied Kardios. "I'm on special duty, I have a message for Trombroll."

"He went sailing from below, up to his own place," said another. "Had somebody with him, I thought. What's your message?"

"It's not for underlings," said Kardios.

"We know our orders," blustered the first speaker, burly and shaggy-jawed. "And we don't know you." He descended close and held out a big hand. "Give me your sword, you're under arrest until you can account for yourself."

"Arrest me if you dare," said Kardios, sliding his own weapon into view.

A grumbling laugh. "You fool, we're four to your one."

"Not as many as that, my friend," said Kardios, and shot out his point, swift as the head of a snake. It drove between joints of armor, and he cleared it as the big man tumbled from the stairs.

"Only three to one now," said Kardios, flashing his teeth.

The others came down toward him, but two of them could not stand side by side on the stairs. One slashed at Kardios, who parried expertly. Another dropped to his knees just behind his fellow and tried to stab past him at Kardios.

That made things difficult enough for laughter on the part of Kardios. He fended off a blow from the man standing erect, disengaged and lunged at the kneeling one. A howl of pain told him he had struck home. Up whirled his sword to pierce the belly of the other. He pushed close to the wall and let both of them go slamming overside in a fall many times a man's height.

"And now," said Kardios, his eyes twinkling at the remaining adversary, "it's only one against one. I never counted that as serious odds at all."

But that fourth man had seen three of his comrades perish in almost as many breaths. He turned and fled up the steps. Kardios followed, shaking drops of blood from his sword.

Where the steps turned at a corner was a door. The fugitive dragged it open and darted through like a frightened rabbit, slamming the door behind him. When Kardios came to that point, he could barely see the crack where the door closed. There was no knob or latch, and he could not pry it open with his sword. He negotiated the turn of the stairs and went on upward. The stairs at this new angle seemed narrower, if anything. Kardios forebore to look down.

There was movement, off there in the broad emptiness above the floor so far beneath. He spared a glance.

It flew. It was something woolly white, as big, perhaps, as a man, sliding here and there on outflung ribbed wings. It made a graceful arc as it headed toward Kardios. He saw that it had a face of some sort, bright black eyes anyway, and flaps of ears like a donkey's. As it came winging close, he saw that it had claws, too, both on its drawn-up legs and at the knuckle ends of its wings.

It swooped in at him, like a bat after a beetle.

Kardios ducked low, one knee to a stair. As the fluffy bulk struck the wall against which he had just stood, he smelled its stale odor. A thin shriek buzzed his ears. The flying thing retreated with a clumsy flip-flop of wings, Kardios glimpsed a splash of blood, like a ribbon across its bushy white chest. It recovered, dipped its wings right and left, and came at him again.

"You learn slowly, don't you?" Kardios addressed it, rising with his back pressed to the wall, his sword dancing before him.

It flew upon him. He saw the jaws gape, the rows of gleaming, daggerlike teeth. A bite from them might take off a man's arm or leg. The head craned forward in flight, driving close.

And Kardios reaped that head from its neck, as a harvester fells a tussock of grain with his sickle. Blood spurted into his own face as he watched his enemy go down, its wings not even fluttering.

Kardios mopped his lean, bloody cheeks. He wondered what that thing had been, where it had come from and why. Then he told himself that wondering was profitless. He resumed his climb of the stairs.

They grew ever narrower and steeper. Or they seemed to, which just now amounted to much the same thing. He felt like a spider that crept along a crack in a rock. The steps made a turn at another corner, and he took the new direction. Above him the ceiling glowed. If he looked at it, his vision would blur. On he went, on, on. He turned at the next corner. Three corners, he was on the ascent's last stage. There above him would be the way out of this dizzying ordeal.

A rumble above. Down the steps jumped and rolled something. A great stone cylinder, as big as a barrel, straight at him.

There was only one thing to do, and Kardios did it. As the rushing, whirling weight almost reached and struck him, he leaped high and let it thunder beneath him. He had a sense that its sides were inscribed with characters or diagrams, but could not be sure. As he came down on the stairs he almost lost footing, but dropped to his knees and one hand, while the cylinder tumbled away below him.

Instantly he was up again. Without pausing to think, he charged up the remaining stairs to the opening above, and into it. A figure crouched there. It tried to turn and flee into shadows beyond, but Kardios clutched at a shaggy neck. Powerfully he slammed the captive against the rocky wall and set his sword point at the fellow's throat.

"Were you supposed to kill me?" he inquired softly. "Make ready to depart into whatever reward waits for tricksters."

"No, don't!" cried the other. It was the survivor of the quartet that had challenged Kardios on his way up. "Have mercy—you must be someone great and powerful, and I'm just a minor servitor of Trombroll."

"True on all counts," said Kardios. "You've picked the most unlucky day of your life to ignore Trombroll's orders." And he made his sword point dance against the jugular.

"Wh-what orders?"

"Now you confess to negligence and defective hearing. I'm entrusted with the most vitally important information from outside, I'm directed to bring it to Trombroll. He left those lower levels before I could reach him, but he must have said I was coming.''

"Maybe he told the under-officer.'' A submissive cringing in Kardios's grasp. "You killed him on the stairs. I'm only a common warder, I thought you were invading. I turned the Flying Fear loose upon you, then tried to crush you with a stone from up here.'' The voice shook miserably. "It's plain from how you handle your sword that you're important. I ask mercy.''

Kardios let him go. "Very well, if you prove trustworthy. Begin by conducting me to Trombroll.''

"To Trombroll?'' a helpless wave of the hands. "Yes, but I won't go in where he is, I'd never dare call myself to his attention.''

"Then take me to his door,'' commanded Kardios. "If you do that promptly and courteously, perhaps I'll say a good word for you when we examine your blundering treatment of me.''

The man led him along a corridor lighted with small crumbs of radiance in its vaulted roof. Other passages showed to either side, but Kardios's guide led him straight ahead, up a ramp, and to where a door stood at the end of the corridor. It was a dark door, of a material hard to identify, without latch or knob in sight.

"Here is where Trombroll makes his quarters,'' said the guardsman. "How is it you do not know?''

"I knew all the time, I wondered if you did,'' Kardios replied readily. "Now go back to your post. If you're lonely without your three companions, perhaps you'll have time to think things over.''

Gladly the man trotted away. Kardios studied the door, wondering how to enter.

It might swing open outward or inward, but he saw no indication of where hinges might be. He gave his attention to its snug-fitting edge, all the way around. At the bottom appeared a slight gap. Stooping, Kardios investigated the space with his fingers, then got those fingers under the door and dragged upward.

The door rose like a curtain, barely whispering in its grooves. He looked into a soft dimness. Then he walked in and drew the door down again behind him.

For an instant he thought he had stepped into some sort of grove or thicket. Then he saw that the throng of trees had trunks of enamelled bronze, with golden leaves set closely with emeralds. Underfoot, a gravelly mass of rubies crunched beneath his sandals. Walking with the utmost care to keep his feet silent, he moved among those jewelled trees toward light beyond. At the edge of them, with convenient artificial foliage to mask him, he looked into a spacious compartment, lighted by brilliant lamps.

It was a hall ornamented so richly as to bring into question the owner's taste. What the walls were made of Kardios could not see, for they were draped and swaddled in showily embroidered hangings. The ceiling beams were each of a different sort of rare wood, carved in intricate designs and polished to metallic brightness. The floor was a glowing white stone, pretentiously studded with stars, whorls and rings of coins of all sizes and devices. At the very center stood a table, apparently fashioned from a single green gem—if it were an emerald, then that had been the biggest emerald in all the world. Upon it were golden and silver dishes of appetizing foods, flagons for wine and goblets in which to pour it. On two elaborate gold-mounted benches sat Trombroll and the Princess Yann.

Naturally, Kardios first looked at Yann. At that close, clear view, she was even more splendidly beautiful than she had been in the guard chamber. She held her red gown close to her delectable bosom with a white hand sparkling with rings. The rays of the lamps struck blue lights from her heavy hair. Her eyes gleamed the brighter for disdain of Trombroll.

As for Trombroll, he had doffed his unbecoming spiny armor and gloves, and sat in an over-decorated tunic and tights. His legs looked amusingly bandy. One hand held the brownly roasted drumstick of a fowl. He eyed Yann fixedly.

"You won't flourish without eating well, and this dinner is excellent," he droned out as he chewed.

"I urge you to better manners and better sense," smirked Trombroll unpleasantly. "That fool Geothro knows he must lead his army away, to save your life. If your life is saved, you must decide what to do with it."

"You're fantastic," Yann told him.

"True," and Trombroll bowed, "for a wizard deals in fantastics. I'm a distinguished figure in my profession, respected by many and feared wherever I'm known. My fortress is stocked with wealth and power enough to persuade your father, Zapaun of Varlo, that I'd be a proper son-in-law. I'm personally attracted to you. We'd do well together."

She turned her lovely face away.

"Consider me without prejudice," Trombroll urged, biting into the drumstick. "I was considered handsome in my younger days. Many now think me impressive."

"You look like an anteater," pronounced Yann accurately.

"I put off my armor to please you—"

"You put it off because you don't fear that any of your men will venture here and assassinate you." As Yann spoke, her magnificent eyes fixed themselves on Kardios where he lurked. "If one came here, you'd scream with fright."

"I put off my armor," said Trombroll again, "so that I could embrace you without hurting your tender skin. Why don't you look at me?"

Yann's eyes were fixed upon Kardios. She winked one of them, in a fashion dazzlingly conspiratorial.

"Enter the assassin, Trombroll," she said brightly.

Kardios stepped into the open, sword drawn. Trombroll sprang up and whirled around. His eyes popped wide and his nose twitched.

"I've been watching as he stole upon you, Trombroll," said Yann's triumphant voice. "Now I'll watch as he kills you."

Trombroll's face twisted. "I suppose this means another of those conspiracies," he growled. "But I can count on a faithful servant. If I but make the proper sound—"

"You have no servants at hand," said Kardios. "There would have been one at the door to this place. Even if there were any, you wouldn't live to see him answer your call. The business here can best be settled among us three."

"I don't recognize you, you must be one of the least important of my garrison, and one of the most ignorant," said Trombroll. "I keep my men at a distance. The servant on whose faithfulness I count isn't of your sort."

He snapped his fingers. From under the emerald table, a shaggy mass humped itself into view.

Kardios's first impression was of something that might have developed into a wolf, a tiger, or a big ape, and had stopped developing before it had chosen which. It rose on ungainly hind legs, with its forelimbs slightly lifted and handlike paws hooked, talon fashion. Its muscular body was tufted over with dark, coarse hair. It showed unpleasantly dingy fangs, and its gray features writhed and furrowed repulsively. It shuffled toward Kardios, as tall as he and more powerfully built.

"I can trust him," declared Trombroll.

"Can he trust you?" asked Kardios.

He advanced his right foot and lifted his sword. The motion made the strings of his harp whisper at his shoulder. The bizarre creature stopped its advance, staring with eyes like cold pink fire.

"If you're a music lover, I truly hate to do this," said Kardios.

He did it, a swift lunge with the point that gashed the hairy shoulder. The creature retreated with a grating cry of pain.

Trombroll, watching, snapped his fingers twice. His grotesque servitor charged at a crouch, strangely swift.

Kardios sidestepped and slashed. His edge drove into the shallow skull, and the beast went into an uncouth, flopping fall. It writhed its forelimbs, clenched its paws, and lay motionless. Kardios faced toward Trombroll and Yann at the table.

Yann sat at ease. She smiled, as though in applause of sprightly music. Trombroll lounged erect. "I'm amazed that he didn't stand against your blade," he said.

"He was wide open to a drawing cut," said Kardios.

"Something failed of my charm that should have shielded him from you," said Trombroll, drawing his own long sword. "I'll be more careful in shielding myself." He lifted hilt to jaw in salute. "Shall we make sport for the lady?"

"Since she seems to enjoy it," said Kardios, crossing his weapon upon Trombroll's.

Then there was fierce, swift fencing. Kardios wondered if he should not have kept the mail shirt. His own sword seemed to glance away from a cut at Trombroll, who made no effort to parry. It was slice, counter, jab, dodge.

"Ha!" cried Trombroll, lunging. Kardios struck the point out of line and extended his own blade in a swift return. That thrust, too, glided off. Trombroll gave him a lopsided smile.

"A very minor charm, my poor foolish adversary," he mocked. "It keeps metal from approaching me."

Yann watched raptly. If she worried about Kardios, it was not evident in her expression.

"If you're so protected, why fear your own followers?" asked Kardios, dancing clear.

"They know the charm; they might try something other than sword or axe." Trombroll grinned more broadly. He licked his thin lips with a thinner tongue. Suddenly he flung out his arms, sword well out of line.

"Strike at me," he invited. "At the throat, if you like."

Kardios darted his point. It slid harmlessly to the side, as though from an invisible solidity, and he whipped it back only just in time to parry Trombroll's slicing edge.

"You're indeed under magical protection," said Kardios. "Congratulations."

He dropped his own sword. It rang on the floor, close to the silent form of the dead guardian-monster.

"Congratulations accepted," jeered Trombroll, "but not capitulation. I think," and he glanced sidelong at Yann, "that her gracious highness wants to see more bloodshed. I'll shed it, naturally."

"Hardly naturally," amended Kardios, sliding leftward. Trombroll also shifted position. The hairy body lay between them.

"Now," he said, and slid his right foot forward as he extended his arm.

Kardios beat the blade aside with a slap of his left hand. As Trombroll followed the lunge, his foot found a pool of blood. He shambled forward. Kardios spun in close. Down came his spread right hand, its tensed edge striking like a hatchet. It drove against Trombroll's exposed nape, with a sound like that of a shattering stick. Yann cried out in amazement or applause. Trombroll smashed down on his face and lay as motionless as his slain servitor.

Kardios wrung the hand with which he had struck, then stooped and recovered his sword. He wiped it with an embroidered napkin from the table.

"That was a gamble," he said quietly. "Maybe with the odds in my favor, but a gamble anyway. His magic guarded him only from metal. My hand is of flesh and blood and bone."

Yann rose to her feet, her eyes bewitchingly wide. "You killed him," she whispered.

"I always kill when I strike them like that," said Kardios. "It breaks the neck every time."

"You were magnificent," she was saying. "You—but I don't even know your name."

"It's Kardios," he said. "We can go now. But let's take a souvenir to Prince Feothro."

Straddling the body of Trombroll, he smote with the edge of Trombroll's sword. Trombroll's head rolled away from the severed neck.

"Ah," said Kardios. "His magic died with him."

He stooped to lift the head, but Yann was before him. "Let me," she said, and picked it up by the gray locks. "It's a comfort to look at, without hearing his disgusting addresses. But how shall we get out?"

"It can't be far to the door. We won't have to go to those cellars again."

He took her arm, which trembled at his touch. They went out at an inner door. Halfway down a stairway an armored guardsman came hurrying up to them. Kardios set his hand to hilt, but the fellow only goggled at Trombroll's head in Yann's grasp.

"Then it's true," he cried. "He's dead—Trombroll who made us fear him, serve him, steal and kill for him!"

"He's dead enough, yes," Kardios assured him. "If it brings you happiness, that's good."

The guardsman went running back downstairs. "Did you hear, comrades?" he whooped. "Trombroll's dead, we're free! He can't order us any more, and all that treasure we gathered for him is ours now!"

A many-voiced howl of joy rose from below. The guardsman turned and gestured at Kardios.

"We owe you everything," he said happily. "Come on, take your pick of anything in all those treasure rooms."

"No, thank you," said Kardios. "I promised to bring this lady out to where her friends are waiting for her."

They paced along a great hall at the bottom of the stairs. Doors stood open to both sides. In the chambers within these, Kardios saw happy members of the garrison, off duty at last and snatching at things of considerable value.

"Surely you're one of the world's highest heroes," Yann said. "Heedless of peril, heedless of wealth. Kardios is there nothing of reward you want, nothing I can grant you?"

She bestowed upon him her most winning smile. It was very winning indeed.

"Princess, when I left Feothro outside, he was of half a mind to lead his men away," said Kardios. "If we don't hurry, we may find that he hasn't waited for us."

"Feothro?" repeated Yann, as though the name were strange to her.

"Up ahead yonder is what looks like the gate."

They went there together. It was closed with a mighty bar of wrought metal, which Kardios lifted from its brackets. With a push of his foot, he drove one wing of the gate wide open and led Yann out into the last of the afternoon light.

As they emerged side by side, Kardios felt a myriad eyes fixed upon him. Feothro's hosts waited on the plain at the foot of the slope, phalanxes of spearmen, squadrons of cavalry, trains of siege equipment. All those thousands stared upward as sunset dimmed into twilight.

Then a wild chorus of cheers shook the earth and sky. Weapons and banners waved. Kardios escorted Yann down from the doorway.

Resplendent officers surrounded them. Eagerly these questioned, and Kardios told, in as few words as he could manage, of his entry into the fortress and his destruction of Trombroll.

"His men are left leaderless, disorganized," he finished. "They can't plan or act without him. You can round them up before they go away with all the plunder."

"Your Highness," a young officer addressed Yann, "our gracious Prince Feothro will be overjoyed to see you safe."

"I'll take the Princess to him," said Kardios, and led her in the direction the officer pointed.

Feothro came at an undignified run, several commanders following at his heels. He flung wide his arms. "Yann, my beloved," he quavered.

Yann threw Trombroll's head at Feothro's feet. It rolled there like a pumpkin fallen from a shelf. "Kardios, do you know Feothro?" she asked.

"Never mind Kardios, my dearest one," said Feothro. "You and I are together again—"

"Kardios," said Yann again, turning to look for him.

Kardios was gone.

"I want Kardios," said Yann, as one who was used to having whatever she wanted.

Feothro grimaced, for those commanders were listening intently. "Why do you want Kardios, my beloved?" he asked.

"He saved me," she replied. "Single-handed, he saved me, single-handed against all the fortress yonder. He killed Trombroll and I don't know how many others. Find him, I want him."

Feothro tried to take her hand. "But this Kardios is only a vagabond adventurer," he argued. "He doesn't even have a country, his kingdom of Atlantis was swallowed by the sea."

"He shall have a new kingdom," announced Yann authoritatively. "My father, Zapaun of Varlo, will welcome him as a son-in-law. He'll be the handsomest man at our court. All other women will envy me." She turned from Feothro. "Where did he go? Bring him back."

Feothro scowled among those artless listeners.

"Yes, bring Kardios back," he shrilled suddenly. "I'll have a

few words with him, a very few words, and then the executioner."
His voice rose like a scream. "Send my bodyguard to fetch
him!"

Men scurried obediently in the twilight. Shouts answered shouts.
There were orders and inquiries, to little purpose.

Kardios had strode swiftly away through more distant ranks,
and headed around the slope of the crater. He was thankful for
the coming of darkness. The voices of the searchers bellowed
behind him. Usually he enjoyed the admiration of women. But
just now, what with the way Feothro was acting, the situation
might turn out to be awkward; even for Kardios.

Far away to the east, the moon's rim peeped above the
horizon. Kardios pointed his feet in that direction, for he had no
other guide away from where both Yann and Feothro wanted
him, for widely different reasons.

THE WALL AROUND THE WORLD

by
Theodore Cogswell

*A professor of English at Keystone Junior College in
Pennsylvania since 1965, Ted Cogswell has produced a
brace of outstanding short stories in the sf magazines
since the 1950s. These can be found in two collections—
THE WALL AROUND THE WORLD (1962) and THE
THIRD EYE (1968)—and combine creative ideas with
frequent good humor. Unfortunately, his stories do not
appear often enough, and his many admirers wish that
he would give us more. Professor Cogswell has been an
active member of the Science Fiction Writers of America from its founding, serving as editor of its FORUM
and as secretary of the organization.*

*A story about an attempt to discover the nature of
one's own world, "The Wall Around the World" also
illustrates the concept of the self-fulfilling prophecy.*

The wall that went all the way around the World had always
been there, so nobody paid much attention to it—except Porgie.
Porgie was going to find out what was on the other side of

it—assuming there was another side—or break his neck trying. He was going on fourteen, an age that tends to view the word *impossible* as a meaningless term invented by adults for their own peculiar purposes. But he recognized that there were certain practical difficulties involved in scaling a glassy-smooth surface that rose over a thousand feet straight up. That's why he spent a lot of time watching the eagles.

This morning, as usual, he was late for school. He lost time finding a spot for his broomstick in the crowded rack in the school yard, and it was exactly six minutes after the hour as he slipped guiltily into the classroom.

For a moment, he thought he was safe. Old Mr. Wickens had his back to him and was chalking a pentagram on the blackboard.

But just as Porgie started to slide into his seat, the schoolmaster turned and drawled, "I see Mr. Mills has finally decided to join us."

The class laughed, and Porgie flushed.

"What's your excuse this time, Mr. Mills?"

"I was watching an eagle," said Porgie lamely.

"How nice for the eagle. And what was he doing that was of such great interest?"

"He was riding up on the wind. His wings weren't flapping or anything. He was over the box canyon that runs into the East wall, where the wind hits the Wall and goes up. The eagle just floated in circles, going higher all the time. You know, Mr. Wickens, I'll bet if you caught a whole bunch of eagles and tied ropes to them, they could lift you right up to the top of the wall!"

"That," said Mr. Wickens, "is possible—if you could catch the eagles. Now, if you'll excuse me, I'll continue with the lecture. When invoking Elementals of the Fifth Order, care must be taken to . . ."

Porgie glazed his eyes and began to think up ways and means to catch some eagles.

The next period, Mr. Wickens gave them a problem in Practical Astrology. Porgie chewed his pencil and tried to work on it, but couldn't concentrate. Nothing came out right—and when he found he had accidentally transposed a couple of signs of the zodiac at the very beginning, he gave up and began to draw plans for eagle traps. He tried one, decided it wouldn't work, started another—

"Porgie!"

He jumped. Mr. Wickens, instead of being in front of the

class, was standing right beside him. The schoolmaster reached down, picked up the paper Porgie had been drawing on, and looked at it. Then he grabbed Porgie by the arm and jerked him from his seat.

"Go to my study!"

As Porgie went out the door, he heard Mr. Wickens say, "The class is dismissed until I return!"

There was a sudden rush of large, medium, and small-sized boys out of the classroom. Down the corridor to the front door they pelted, and out into the bright sunshine. As they ran past Porgie, his cousin Homer skidded to a stop and accidentally on purpose jabbed an elbow into his ribs. Homer, usually called "Bull Pup" by the kids because of his squat build and pugnacious face, was a year older than Porgie and took his seniority seriously.

"Wait'll I tell Dad about this. You'll catch it tonight!" He gave Porgie another jab and then ran out into the schoolyard to take command of a game of Warlock.

Mr. Wickens unlocked the door to his study and motioned Porgie inside. Then he shut and locked it carefully behind him. He sat down in the high-backed chair behind his desk and folded his hands.

Porgie stood silently, hanging his head, filled with that helpless guilty anger that comes from conflict with superior authority.

"What were you doing instead of your lesson?" Mr. Wickens demanded.

Porgie didn't answer.

Mr. Wickens narrowed his eyes. The large hazel switch that rested on top of the bookcase beside the stuffed owl lifted lightly into the air, drifted across the room, and dropped into his hand.

"Well?" he said, tapping the switch on the desk.

"Eagle traps," admitted Porgie. "I was drawing eagle traps. I couldn't help it. The Wall made me do it."

"Proceed."

Porgie hesitated for a moment. The switch tapped. Porgie burst out, "I want to see what's on the other side! There's no magic that will get me over, so I've got to find something else!"

Tap, went the switch. "Something else?"

"If a magic way was in the old books, somebody would have found it already!"

Mr. Wickens rose to his feet and stabbed one bony finger accusingly at Porgie. "Doubt is the mother of damnation!"

Porgie dropped his eyes to the floor and wished he was someplace else.

"I see doubt in you. Doubt is evil, Porgie, *evil!* There are ways permitted to men and ways forbidden. You stand on the brink of the fatal choice. Beware that the Black Man does not come for you as he did for your father before you. Now, bend over!"

Porgie bent. He wished he'd worn a heavier pair of pants.

"Are you ready?"

"Yes, sir," said Porgie sadly.

Mr. Wickens raised the switch over his head. Porgie waited. The switch slammed—but on the desk.

"Straighten up," Mr. Wickens said wearily. He sat down again. "I've tried pounding things into your head, and I've tried pounding things on your bottom, and one end is as insensitive as the other. Porgie, can't you understand that you aren't supposed to try and find out new things? The Books contain everything there is to know. Year by year, what is written in them becomes clearer to us."

He pointed out the window at the distant towering face of the Wall that went around the World. "Don't worry about what is on the other side of that! It may be a place of angels or a place of demons—the Books do not tell us. But no man will know until he is ready for that knowledge. Our broomsticks won't climb that high, our charms aren't strong enough. We need more skill at magic, more understanding of the strange unseen forces that surround us. In my grandfather's time, the best of the broomsticks wouldn't climb over a hundred feet in the air. But Adepts in the Great Tower worked and worked until now, when the clouds are low, we can ride right up among them. Someday we will be able to soar all the way to the top of the Wall—"

"Why not now?" Porgie asked stubbornly. "With eagles."

"Because we're not *ready*," Mr. Wickens snapped. "Look at mind-talk. It was only thirty years ago that the proper incantations were worked out, and even now there are only a few who have the skill to talk across the miles by just thinking out their words. Time, Porgie—it's going to take time. We were placed here to learn the Way, and everything that might divert us from the search is evil. Man can't walk two roads at once. If he tries, he'll split himself in half."

"Maybe so," said Porgie. "But birds get over the Wall, and they don't know any spells. Look, Mr. Wickens, if everything is magic, how come magic won't work on everything? Like this, for instance—''

He took a shiny quartz pebble out of his pocket and laid it on the desk.

Nudging it with his finger, he said:

> *"Stone fly,*
> *Rise on high,*
> *Over cloud*
> *And into sky."*

The stone didn't move.

"You see, sir? If words work on broomsticks, they should work on stones, too."

Mr. Wickens stared at the stone. Suddenly it quivered and jumped into the air.

"That's different," said Porgie. "You took hold of it with your mind. Anybody can do that with little things. What I want to know is why the words won't work by themselves."

"We just don't know enough yet," said Mr. Wickens impatiently. He released the stone and it clicked on the desktop. "Every year we learn a little more. Maybe by your children's time we'll find the incantation that will make everything lift." He sniffed. "What do you want to make stones fly for, anyhow? You get into enough trouble just throwing them."

Porgie's brow furrowed. "There's a difference between *making* a thing do something, like when I lift it with my hand or mind, and putting a spell on it so it does the work by itself, like a broomstick."

There was a long silence in the study as each thought his own thoughts.

Finally Mr. Wickens said, "I don't want to bring up the unpleasant past, Porgie, but it would be well to remember what happened to your father. His doubts came later than yours—for a while he was my most promising student—but they were just as strong."

He opened a dark drawer, fumbled in it for a moment, and brought out a sheaf of papers yellow with age. "This is the paper that damned him—*An Enquiry into Non-Magical Methods of Levitation*. He wrote it to qualify for his Junior Adeptship." He threw the paper down in front of Porgie as if the touch of it defiled his fingers.

Porgie started to pick it up.

Mr. Wickens roared, "Don't touch it! It contains blasphemy!"

Porgie snatched back his hand. He looked at the top paper and saw a neat sketch of something that looked like a bird—except that it had two sets of wings, one in front and one in back.

Mr. Wickens put the papers back in the desk drawer. His disapproving eyes caught and held Porgie's as he said, "If you want to go the way of your father, none of *us* can stop you." His voice rose sternly, "But there is one who can . . . Remember the Black Man, Porgie, for his walk is terrible! There are fires in his eyes and no spell may defend you against him. When he came for your father, there was darkness at noon and a high screaming. When the sunlight came back, they were gone—and it is not good to think where."

Mr. Wickens shook his head as if overcome at the memory and pointed toward the door. "Think before you act. Porgie. Think well!"

Porgie was thinking as he left, but more about the sketch in his father's paper than about the Black Man.

The orange crate with the two boards across it for wings had looked something like his father's drawing, but appearances had been deceiving. Porgie sat on the back steps of his house feeling sorry for himself and alternately rubbing two tender spots on his anatomy. Though they were at opposite ends, and had different immediate causes, they both grew out of the same thing. His bottom was sore as a result of a liberal application of his uncle's hand. His swollen nose came from an aerial crack-up.

He'd hoisted his laboriously contrived machine to the top of the woodshed and taken a flying leap in it. The expected soaring glide hadn't materialized. Instead, there had been a sickening fall, a splintering crash, a momentary whirling of stars as his nose banged into something hard.

He wished now he hadn't invited Bull Pup to witness his triumph, because the story'd gotten right back to his uncle—with the usual results.

Just to be sure the lesson was pounded home, his uncle had taken away his broomstick for a week—and just so Porgie wouldn't sneak out, he'd put a spell on it before locking it away in the closet.

"Didn't feel like flying, anyway," Porgie said sulkily to himself, but the pretense wasn't strong enough to cover up the loss. The gang was going over to Red Rocks to chase bats as soon as the sun went down, and he wanted to go along.

He shaded his eyes and looked toward the western Wall as he
heard a distant halloo of laughing voices. They were coming in
high and fast on their broomsticks. He went back to the woodshed so they wouldn't see him. He was glad he had when they
swung low and began to circle the house yelling for him and Bull
Pup. They kept hooting and shouting until Homer flew out of his
bedroom window to join them.

"Porgie can't come," he yelled. "He got licked and Dad took
his broom away from him. Come on, gang!"

With a quick looping climb, he took the lead and they went
hedge-hopping off toward Red Rocks. Bull Pup had been top
dog ever since he got his big stick. He'd zoom up to five
hundred feet, hang from his broom by his knees and then let go.
Down he'd plummet, his arms spread and body arched as if he
were making a swan dive—and then, when the ground wasn't
more than a hundred feet away, he'd call and his broomstick
would arrow down after him and slide between his legs, lifting
him up in a great sweeping arc that barely cleared the treetops.

"Showoff!" muttered Porgie and shut the woodshed door on
the vanishing stick-riders.

Over on the work bench sat the little model of paper and sticks
that had got him into trouble in the first place. He picked it up
and gave it a quick shove into the air with his hands. It dove
toward the floor and then, as it picked up speed, tilted its nose
toward the ceiling and made a graceful loop in the air. Leveling
off, it made a sudden veer to the left and crashed against the
woodshed wall. A wing splintered.

Porgie went to pick it up. "Maybe what works for little things
doesn't work for big ones," he thought sourly. The orange crate
and the crossed boards had been as close an approximation of the
model as he had been able to make. Listlessly, he put the broken
glider back on his work bench and went outside. Maybe Mr.
Wickens and his uncle and all the rest were right. Maybe there
was only one road to follow.

He did a little thinking about it and came to a conclusion that
brought forth a secret grin. He'd do it their way—but there
wasn't any reason why he couldn't hurry things up a bit. Waiting
for his grandchildren to work things out wasn't getting *him* over
the wall.

Tomorrow, after school, he'd start working on his new idea,
and this time maybe he'd find the way.

In the kitchen, his uncle and aunt were arguing about him.
Porgie paused in the hall that led to the front room and listened.

"Do you think I like to lick the kid? I'm not some kind of an ogre. It hurt me more than it hurt him."

"I notice you were able to sit down afterward," said Aunt Olga dryly.

"Well, what else could I do? Mr. Wickens didn't come right out and say so, but he hinted that if Porgie didn't stop mooning around, he might be dropped from school altogether. He's having an unsettling effect on the other kids. Damn it, Olga, I've done everything for that boy I've done for my own son. What do you want me to do, stand back and let him end up like your brother?"

"You leave my brother out of this! No matter what Porgie does, you don't have to beat him. He's still only a little boy."

There was a loud snort. "In case you've forgotten, dear, he had his thirteenth birthday last March. He'll be a man pretty soon."

"Then why don't you have a man-to-man talk with him?"

"Haven't I tried? You know what happens everytime. He gets off with these crazy questions and ideas of his and I lose my temper and pretty soon we're back where we started." He threw up his hands. "I don't know what to do with him. Maybe that fall he had this afternoon will do some good. I think he had a scare thrown into him that he won't forget for a long time. Where's Bull Pup?"

"Can't you call him Homer? It's bad enough having his friends call him by that horrible name. He went out to Red Rocks with the other kids. They're having a bat hunt or something."

Porgie's uncle grunted and got up. "I don't see why that kid can't stay at home at night for a change. I'm going in the front room and read the paper."

Porgie was already there, flipping the pages of his schoolbooks and looking studious. His uncle settled down in his easy chair, opened his paper, and lit his pipe. He reached out to put the charred match in the ashtray, and as usual the ashtray wasn't there.

"Damn that woman," he muttered to himself and raised his voice: "Porgie."

"Yes, Uncle Veryl?"

"Bring me an ashtray from the kitchen, will you please? Your aunt has them all out there again."

"Sure thing," said Porgie and shut his eyes. He thought of the kitchen until a picture of it was crystal-clear in his mind. The beaten copper ashtray was sitting beside the sink where his aunt had left it after she had washed it out. He squinted the little eye inside his head, stared hard at the copper bowl, and whispered:

> *"Ashtray fly,*
> *Follow eye."*

Simultaneously he lifted with his mind. The ashtray quivered and rose slowly into the air.

Keeping it firmly suspended, Porgie quickly visualized the kitchen door and the hallway and drifted it through.

"Porgie!" came his uncle's angry voice.

Porgie jumped, and there was a crash in the hallway outside as the bowl was suddenly released and crashed to the floor.

"How many times have I told you not to levitate around the house? If it's too much work to go out to the kitchen, tell me and I'll do it myself."

"I was just practicing," mumbled Porgie defensively.

"Well, practice outside. You've got the walls all scratched up from banging things against them. You know you shouldn't fool around with telekinesis outside sight range until you've mastered full visualization. Now go and get me that ashtray."

Crestfallen, Porgie went out the door into the hall. When he saw where the ashtray had fallen, he gave a silent whistle. Instead of coming down the center of the hall, it had been three feet off course and heading directly for the hall table when he let it fall. In another second, it would have smashed into his aunt's precious black alabaster vase.

"Here it is, Uncle," he said, taking it into the front room. "I'm sorry."

His uncle looked at his unhappy face, sighed and reached out and tousled his head affectionately.

"Buck up, Porgie. I'm sorry I had to paddle you this afternoon. It was for your own good. Your aunt and I don't want you to get into any serious trouble. You know what folks think about machines." He screwed up his face as if he'd said a dirty word. "Now, back to your books—we'll forget all about what happened today. Just remember this, Porgie: If there's anything you want to know, don't go fooling around on your own. Come and ask me, and we'll have a man-to-man talk."

Porgie brightened. "There's something I have been wondering about."

"Yes?" said his uncle encouragingly.

"How many eagles would it take to lift a fellow high enough to see what was on the other side of the Wall?"

Uncle Veryl counted to ten—very slowly.

The next day Porgie went to work on his new project. As soon as school was out, he went over to the Public Library and climbed upstairs to the main circulation room.

"Little boys are not allowed in this section," the librarian said. "The children's division is downstairs."

"But I need a book," protested Porgie. "A book on how to fly."

"This section is only for adults."

Porgie did some fast thinking. "My uncle can take books from here, can't he?"

"I suppose so."

"And he could send me over to get something for him, couldn't he?"

The librarian nodded reluctantly.

Porgie prided himself on never lying. If the librarian chose to misconstrue his questions, it was her fault, not his.

"Well, then," he said, "do you have any books on how to make things fly in the air?"

"What kind of things?"

"Things like birds."

"Birds don't have to be made to fly. They're born that way."

"I don't mean real birds," said Porgie. "I mean birds you make."

"Oh, Animation. Just a second, let me visualize." She shut her eyes and a card catalogue across the room opened and shut one drawer after another. "Ah, that might be what he's looking for," she murmured after a moment, and concentrated again. A large brass-bound book came flying out of the stacks and came to rest on the desk in front of her. She pulled the index card out of the pocket in the back and shoved it toward Porgie. "Sign your uncle's name here."

He did and then, hugging the book to his chest, got out of the library as quickly as he could.

By the time Porgie had worked three-quarters of the way through the book, he was about ready to give up in despair. It was all grown-up magic. Each set of instructions he ran into either used words he didn't understand or called for unobtainable ingredients like powdered unicorn horns and the blood of red-headed female virgins.

During the next three months, there was room in Porgie's mind for only one thing—the machine he was building in the roomy old cave at the top of the long hill on the other side of Arnett's grove. As a result, he kept slipping further and further behind at school.

Things at home weren't too pleasant, either—Bull Pup felt it was his duty to keep his parents fully informed of Porgie's short-comings. Porgie didn't care, though. He was too busy. Every minute he could steal was spent in either collecting materials or putting them together.

The afternoon the machine was finally finished, he could hardly tear himself away from it long enough to go home for dinner. He was barely able to choke down his food, and didn't even wait for dessert.

He sat on the grass in front of the cave, waiting for darkness. Below, little twinkling lights marked the villages that stretched across the plain for a full forty miles. Enclosing them like encircling arms stretched the dark and forbidding mass of the Wall. No matter where he looked, it stood high against the night. He followed its curve with his eyes until he had turned completely around, and then he shook his fist at it.

Patting the ungainly mass of the machine that rested on the grass beside him, he whispered fiercely, "I'll get over you yet. Old *Eagle* here will take me!"

Old *Eagle* was an awkward, boxkite-like affair; but to Porgie she was a thing of beauty. She had an uncovered fuselage composed of four long poles braced together to make a rectangular frame, at each end of which was fastened a large wing.

When it was dark enough, he climbed into the open frame and reached down and grabbed hold of the two lower members. Grunting, he lifted until the two upper ones rested under his armpits. There was padding there to support his weight comfortably once he was airborne. The bottom of the machine was level with his waist and the rest of him hung free. According to his thinking, he should be able to control his flight by swinging his legs. If he swung forward, the shifting weight should tilt the nose down; if he swung back, it should go up.

There was only one way to find out if his ifs were right. The *Eagle* was a heavy contraption. He walked awkwardly to the top of the hill, the cords standing out on his neck. He was scared as he looked down the long steep slope that stretched out before him—so scared that he was having trouble breathing. He swallowed twice in a vain attempt to moisten his dry throat, and then lunged forward, fighting desperately to keep his balance as his wobbling steps gradually picked up speed.

Faster he went, and faster, his steps turning into leaps as the wing surfaces gradually took hold. His toes scraped through the long grass and then they were dangling in free air.

He was aloft.

Not daring to even move his head, he slanted his eyes down and to the left. The earth was slipping rapidly by a dozen feet below him. Slowly and cautiously, he swung his feet back. As the weight shifted, the nose of the glider rose. Up, up he went, until he felt a sudden slowing down and a clumsiness of motion. Almost instinctively, he leaned forward again, pointing the nose down in a swift dip to regain flying speed.

By the time he reached the bottom of the hill, he was a hundred and fifty feet up. Experimentally, he swung his feet a little to the left. The glider dipped slightly and turned. Soaring over a clump of trees, he felt a sudden lifting as an updraft caught him.

Up he went—ten, twenty, thirty feet—and then slowly began to settle again.

The landing wasn't easy. More by luck than by skill, he came down in the long grass of the meadow with no more damage than a few bruises. He sat for a moment and rested, his head spinning with excitement. He had flown like a bird, without his stick, without uttering a word. There *were* other ways than magic!

His elation suddenly faded with the realization that, while gliding down was fun, the way over the Wall was *up*. Also, and of more immediate importance, he was half a mile from the cave with a contraption so heavy and unwieldy that he could never hope to haul it all the way back up the hill by himself. If he didn't get it out of sight by morning, there was going to be trouble, serious trouble. People took an unpleasant view of machines and those who built them.

Broomsticks, he decided, had certain advantages, after all. They might not fly very high, but at least you didn't have to walk home from a ride.

"If I just had a great big broomstick," he thought, "I could lift the *Eagle* up with it and fly her home."

He jumped to his feet. It might work!

He ran back up the hill as fast as he could and finally, very much out of breath, reached the entrance of the cave. Without waiting to get back his wind, he jumped on his stick and flew down to the stranded glider.

Five minutes later, he stepped back and said:

> *"Broomstick fly,*
> *Rise on high,*
> *Over cloud*
> *And into sky."*

It didn't fly. It couldn't. Porgie had lashed it to the framework of the *Eagle*. When he grabbed hold of the machine and lifted, nine-tenths of its weight was gone, canceled out by the broomstick's lifting power.

He towed it back up the hill and shoved it into the cave. Then he looked uneasily at the sky. It was later than he had thought. He should be home and in bed—but when he thought of the feeling of power he had had in his flight, he couldn't resist hauling the *Eagle* back out again.

After checking the broomstick to be sure it was still fastened tightly to the frame, he went swooping down the hill again. This time when he hit the thermal over the clump of trees, he was pushed up a hundred feet before he lost it. He curved through the darkness until he found it again and then circled tightly within it.

Higher he went and higher, higher than any broomstick had ever gone!

When he started to head back, though, he didn't have such an easy time of it. Twice he was caught in downdrafts that almost grounded him before he was able to break loose from the tugging winds. Only the lifting power of his broomstick enabled him to stay aloft. With it bearing most of the load, the *Eagle* was so light that it took just a flutter of air to sweep her up again.

He landed the glider a stone's throw from the mouth of his cave.

"Tomorrow night!" he thought exultantly as he unleashed his broomstick. "Tomorrow night!"

There was a tomorrow night, and many nights after that. The *Eagle* was sensitive to every updraft, and with care he found he could remain aloft for hours, riding from thermal to thermal. It was hard to keep his secret, hard to keep from shouting the news, but he had to. He slipped out at night to practice, slipping back in again before sunrise to get what sleep he could.

He circled the day of his fourteenth birthday in red and waited. He had a reason for waiting.

In the World within the Wall, fourteenth birthdays marked the boundary between the little and the big, between being a big child and a small man. Most important, they marked the time when one was taken to the Great Tower where the Adepts lived and given a full-sized broomstick powered by the most potent of spells, sticks that would climb to a full six hundred feet, twice the height that could be reached by the smaller ones the youngsters rode.

Porgie needed a man-sized stick, needed that extra power, for he had found that only the strongest of updrafts would lift him past the three-hundred-foot ceiling where the lifting power of his little broomstick gave out. He had to get up almost as high as the Wall before he could make it across the wide expanse of flat plain that separated him from the box canyon where the great wind waited.

So he counted the slowly passing days and practiced flying during the rapidly passing nights.

The afternoon of his fourteenth birthday found Porgie sitting on the front steps expectantly, dressed in his best and waiting for his uncle to come out of the house. Bull Pup came out and sat down beside him.

"The gang's having a coven up on top of old Baldy tonight," he said. "Too bad you can't come."

"I can go if I want to," said Porgie.

"How?" said Bull Pup and snickered. "You going to grow wings and fly? Old Baldy's five hundred feet up and your kid stick won't lift you that high."

"Today's my birthday."

"You think you're going to get a new stick?"

Porgie nodded.

"Well, you ain't. I heard Mom and Dad talking. Dad's mad because you flunked Alchemy. He said you had to be taught a lesson."

Porgie felt sick inside, but he wouldn't let Bull Pup have the satisfaction of knowing it.

"I don't care," he said. "I'll go to the coven if I want to. You just wait and see."

Bull Pup was laughing when he hopped on his stick and took off down the street. Porgie waited an hour, but his uncle didn't come out.

He went into the house. Nobody said anything about his new broomstick until after supper. Then his uncle called him into the living room and told him he wasn't getting it.

"But, Uncle Veryl, you promised!"

"It was a conditional promise, Porgie. There was a big if attached to it. Do you remember what it was?"

Porgie looked down at the floor and scuffed one toe on the worn carpet. "I tried."

"Did you really, son?" His uncle's eyes were stern but compassionate. "Were you trying when you fell asleep in school today? I've tried talking with you and I've tried whipping you and neither seems to work. Maybe this will. Now you run upstairs and get started on your studies. When you can show me that your marks are improving, we'll talk about getting you a new broomstick. Until then, the old one will have to do."

Porgie knew that he was too big to cry, but when he got to his room, he couldn't help it. He was stretched out on his bed with his face buried in the pillows when he heard a hiss from the window. He looked up to see Bull Pup sitting on his stick, grinning malevolently at him.

"What do you want?" sniffed Porgie.

"Only little kids cry," said Bull Pup.

"I wasn't crying. I got a cold."

"I just saw Mr. Wickens. He was coming out of that old cave back of Arnett's grove. He's going to get the Black Man, I'll bet."

"I don't know anything about that old cave," said Porgie, sitting bolt upright on his bed.

"Oh, yes, you do. I followed you up there one day. You got a machine in there. I told Mr. Wickens and he gave me a quarter. He was real interested."

Porgie jumped from his bed and ran toward the window, his face red and his fists doubled. "I'll fix you!"

Bull Pup backed his broomstick just out of Porgie's reach, and then stuck his thumbs in his ears and waggled his fingers. When Porgie started to throw things, he gave a final taunt and swooped away toward old Baldy and the coven.

Porgie's uncle was just about to go out in the kitchen and fix himself a sandwich when the doorbell rang. Grumbling, he went out into the front hall. Mr. Wickens was at the door. He came into the house and stood blinking in the light. He seemed uncertain as to just how to begin.

"I've got bad news for you," he said finally. "It's about Porgie. Is your wife still up?"

Porgie's uncle nodded anxiously.

"She'd better hear this, too."

Aunt Olga put down her knitting when they came into the living room.

"You're out late, Mr. Wickens."

"It's not of my own choosing."

"Porgie's done something again," said his uncle.

Aunt Olga sighed. "What is it this time?"

Mr. Wickens hesitated, cleared his throat, and finally spoke in a low, hushed voice: "Porgie's built a machine. The Black Man told me. He's coming after the boy tonight."

Uncle Veryl dashed up the stairs to find Porgie. He wasn't in his room.

Aunt Olga just sat in her chair and cried shrilly.

The moon stood high and silver-lit the whole countryside. Porgie could make out the world far below him almost as if it were day. Miles to his left, he saw the little flickering fires on top of old Baldy where the kids were holding their coven. He fought an impulse and then succumbed to it. He circled the *Eagle* over a clump of trees until the strong rising currents lifted him almost to the height of the Wall. Then he twisted his body and banked over toward the distant red glowing fires.

Minutes later, he went silently over them at eight hundred feet, feeling out the air currents around the rocks. There was a sharp downdraft on the far side of Baldy that dropped him suddenly when he glided into it, but he made a quick turn and found untroubled air before he fell too far. On the other side, toward the box canyon, he found what he wanted, a strong, rising current that seemed to have no upward limits.

He fixed its location carefully in his mind and then began to circle down toward the coven. Soon he was close enough to make out individual forms sitting silently around their little fires.

"Hey, Bull Pup," he yelled at the top of his lungs.

A stocky figure jumped to its feet and looked wildly around for the source of the ghostly voice.

"Up here!"

Porgie reached in his pocket, pulled out a small pebble and chucked it down. It cracked against a shelf of rock four feet from Bull Pup. Porgie's cousin let out a howl of fear. The rest of the kids jumped up and reared back their heads at the night sky, their eyes blinded by firelight.

"I told you I could come to the coven if I wanted to," yelled Porgie, "but now I don't. I don't have any time for kid stuff; I'm going over the Wall!"

During his last pass over the plateau he wasn't more than thirty feet up. As he leaned over, his face was clearly visible in the firelight.

Placing one thumb to his nose, he waggled his fingers and chanted, "nyah, nyah, nyah, you can't catch me!"

His feet were almost scraping the ground as he glided over the drop-off. There was an anxious second of waiting and then he felt the sure, steady thrust of the up-current against his wings.

He looked back. The gang was milling around, trying to figure out what had happened. There was an angry shout of command from Bull Pup, and after a moment of confused hesitation they all made for their brooms and swooped up into the air.

Porgie mentally gauged his altitude and then relaxed. He was almost at their ceiling and would be above it before they reached him.

He flattened out his glide and yelled, "Come on up! Only little kids play that low!"

Bull Pup's stick wouldn't rise any higher. He circled impotently, shaking his fist at the machine that rode serenely above him.

"You just wait," he yelled. "You can't stay up there all night. You got to come down some time, and when you do, we'll be waiting for you."

"Nyah, nyah, nyah," chanted Porgie and mounted higher into the moonlit night.

When the updraft gave out, he wasn't as high as he wanted to be, but there wasn't anything he could do about it. He turned and started a flat glide across the level plain toward the box canyon. He wished now that he had left Bull Pup and the other kids alone. They were following along below him. If he dropped down to their level before the canyon winds caught him, he was in trouble.

He tried to flatten his glide still more, but instead of saving altitude, he went into a stall that dropped him a hundred feet before he was able to regain control. He saw now that he could never make it without dropping to Bull Pup's level.

Bull Pup saw it, too, and let out an exultant yell: "Just you wait! You're going to get it good!"

Porgie peered over the side into the darkness where his cousin rode, his pug face gleaming palely in the moonlight.

"Leave him alone, gang," Bull Pup shouted. "He's mine!"

The rest pulled back and circled slowly as the *Eagle* glided quietly down among them. Bull Pup darted in and rode right alongside Porgie.

He pointed savagely toward the ground: "Go down or I'll knock you down!"

Porgie kicked at him, almost upsetting his machine. He wasn't fast enough. Bull Pup dodged easily. He made a wide circle and came back, reaching out and grabbing the far end of the *Eagle's* front wing. Slowly and maliciously, he began to jerk it up and down, twisting violently as he did so.

"Get down," he yelled, "or I'll break it off!"

Porgie almost lost his head as the wrenching threatened to throw him out of control.

"Let go!" he screamed, his voice cracking.

Bull Pup's face had a strange excited look on it as he gave the wing another jerk. The rest of the boys were becoming frightened as they saw what was happening.

"Quit it, Bull Pup!" somebody called. "Do you want to kill him?"

"Shut up or you'll get a dose of the same!"

Porgie fought to clear his head. His broomstick was tied to the frame of the *Eagle* so securely that he would never be able to free it in time to save himself. He stared into the darkness until he caught the picture of Bull Pup's broomstick sharply in his mind. He'd never tried to handle anything that big before, but it was that or nothing.

Tensing suddenly, he clamped his mind down on the picture and held it hard. He knew that words didn't help, but he uttered them anyway:

"Broomstick stop,
Flip and Flop!"

There was a sharp tearing pain in his head. He gritted his teeth and held on, fighting desperately against the red haze that threatened to swallow him. Suddenly there was a half-startled, half-frightened squawk from his left wingtip, and Bull Pup's stick jerked to an abrupt halt, gyrating so madly that its rider could hardly hang on.

"All right, the rest of you," screamed Porgie. "Get going or I'll do the same thing to you!"

They got, arcing away in terrified disorder. Porgie watched as they formed a frightened semicircle around the blubbering Bull Pup. With a sigh of relief, he let go with his mind.

As he left them behind in the night, he turned his head back and yelled weakly, "Nyah, nyah, nyah, you can't catch me!"

He was only fifty feet off the ground when he glided into the far end of the box canyon and was suddenly caught by the strong updraft. As he soared in a tight spiral, he slumped down against the arm-rests, his whole body shaking in delayed reaction.

The lashings that held the front wing to the frame were dangerously loose from the manhandling they had received. One more tug and the whole wing might have twisted back, dumping him down on the sharp rocks below. Shudders ran through the *Eagle* as the supports shook in their loose bonds. He clamped both hands around the place where the rear wing spar crossed the frame and tried to steady it.

He felt his stick's lifting power give out at three hundred feet. The *Eagle* felt clumsy and heavy, but the current was still enough to carry him slowly upward. Foot by foot he rose toward the top of the Wall, losing a precious hundred feet once when he spiraled out of the updraft and had to circle to find it. A wisp of cloud curled down from the top of the Wall and he felt a moment of panic as he climbed into it.

Momentarily, there was no left or right or up or down. Only damp whiteness. He had the feeling the *Eagle* was falling out of control; but he kept steady, relying on the feel for the air he had gotten during his many practice flights.

The lashings had loosened more. The full strength of his hands wasn't enough to keep the wing from shuddering and trembling. He struggled resolutely to maintain control of ship and self against the strong temptation to lean forward and throw the *Eagle* into a shallow dive that would take him back to normalcy and safety.

He was almost at the end of his resolution when with dramatic suddenness he glided out of the cloud into the clear moon-touched night. The up-current under him seemed to have lessened. He banked in a gentle arc, trying to find the center of it again.

As he turned, he became aware of something strange, something different, something almost frightening. For the first time in his life, there was no Wall to block his vision, no vast black line stretching through the night.

He was above it!

There was no time for looking. With a loud *ping*, one of the lashings parted and the leading edge of the front wing flapped violently. The glider began to pitch and yaw, threatening to nose over into a plummeting dive. He fought for mastery, swinging his legs like desperate pendulums as he tried to correct the erratic side swings that threatened to throw him out of control. As he fought, he headed for the Wall.

If he were to fall, it would be on the other side. At least he would cheat old Mr. Wickens and the Black Man.

Now he was directly over the Wall. It stretched like a wide road underneath him, its smooth top black and shining in the moonlight. Acting on quick impulse, he threw his body savagely forward and to the right. The ungainly machine dipped abruptly and dove toward the black surface beneath it.

Eighty feet, seventy, sixty, fifty—he had no room to maneuver, there would be no second chance—thirty, twenty—

He threw his weight back, jerking the nose of the *Eagle* suddenly up. For a precious second the wings held, there was a sharp breaking of his fall; then, with a loud, cracking noise, the front wing buckled back in his face. There was a moment of blind whirling fall and a splintering crash that threw him into darkness.

Slowly, groggily, Porgie pulled himself up out of the broken wreckage. The *Eagle* had made her last flight. She perched precariously, so near the outside edge of the wall that part of her rear wing stretched out over nothingness.

Porgie crawled cautiously across the slippery wet surface of the top of the Wall until he reached the center. There he crouched down to wait for morning. He was exhausted, his body so drained of energy that in spite of himself he kept slipping into an uneasy sleep.

Each time he did, he'd struggle back to consciousness trying to escape the nightmare figures that scampered through his brain. He was falling, pursued by wheeling, batlike figures with pug faces. He was in a tiny room and the walls were inching in toward him and he could hear the voice of Bull Pup in the distance chanting, "You're going to get it." And then the room turned into a long, dark corridor and he was running. Mr. Wickens was close behind him, and he had long, sharp teeth and he kept yelling, "Porgie! Porgie!"

He shuddered back to wakefulness, crawled to the far edge of the Wall and, hanging his head over, tried to look down at the Outside World. The clouds had boiled up and there was nothing underneath him but gray blankness hiding the sheer thousand foot drop. He crawled back to his old spot and looked toward the east, praying for the first sign of dawn. There was only blackness there.

He started to doze off again and once more he heard the voice:
"Porgie! Porgie!"

He opened his eyes and sat up. The voice was still calling,
even though he was awake. It seemed to be coming from high up
and far away.

It came closer, closer, and suddenly he saw it in the darkness—a
black figure wheeling above the Wall like a giant crow. Down it
came, nearer and nearer, a man in black with arms outstretched
and long fingers hooked like talons!

Porgie scrambled to his feet and ran, his feet skidding on the
slippery surface. He looked back over his shoulder. The black
figure was almost on top of him. Porgie dodged desperately and
slipped.

He felt himself shoot across the slippery surface toward the
edge of the Wall. He clawed, scrabbling for purchase. He couldn't
stop. One moment he felt wet coldness slipping away under him;
the next, nothingness as he shot out into the dark and empty air.

He spun slowly as he fell. First the clouds were under him and
they tipped and the star-flecked sky took their places. He felt
cradled, suspended in time. There was no terror. There was
nothing.

Nothing—until suddenly the sky above him was blotted out by
a plummeting black figure that swooped down on him, hawk-like
and horrible.

Porgie kicked wildly. One foot slammed into something solid
and for an instant he was free. Then strong arms circled him
from behind and he was jerked out of the nothingness into a
world of falling and fear.

There was a sudden strain on his chest and then he felt himself
being lifted. He was set down gently on the top of the Wall.

He stood defiant, head erect, and faced the black figure.

"I won't go back. You can't make me go back."

"You don't have to go back, Porgie."

He couldn't see the hooded face, but the voice sounded strangely
familiar.

"You've earned your right to see what's on the other side," it
said. Then the figure laughed and threw back the hood that
partially covered his face.

In the bright moonlight, Porgie saw Mr. Wickens!

The schoolmaster nodded cheerfully. "Yes, Porgie, I'm the
Black Man. Bit of a shock, isn't it?"

Porgie sat down suddenly.

"I'm from the Outside," said Mr. Wickens, seating himself

carefully on the slick black surface. "I guess you could call me a sort of observer."

Porgie's spinning mind couldn't catch up with the new ideas that were being thrown at him. "Observer?" he said uncomprehendingly. "Outside?"

"Outside. That's where you'll be spending your next few years. I don't think you'll find life better there, and I don't think you'll find it worse. It'll be different, though, I can guarantee that." He chuckled. "Do you remember what I said to you in my office that day—that Man can't follow two paths at once, that Mind and Nature are bound to conflict? That's true, but it's also false. You can have both, but it takes two worlds to do it.

"Outside, where you're going, is the world of the machines. It's a good world, too. But the men who live there saw a long time ago that they were paying a price for it; that control over Nature meant that the forces of the Mind were neglected, for the machine is a thing of logic and reason, but miracles aren't. Not yet. So they built the Wall and they placed people within it and gave them such books and such laws as would insure development of the powers of the Mind. At least they hoped it would work that way—and it did."

"But—but why the Wall?" asked Porgie.

"Because their guess was right. There is magic." He pulled a bunch of keys from his pocket. "Lift it, Porgie."

Porgie stared at it until he had the picture in his mind and then let his mind take hold, pulling with invisible hands until the keys hung high in the air. Then he dropped them back into Mr. Wickens' hand.

"What was that for?"

"Outsiders can't do that," said the schoolmaster. "And they can't do conscious telepathy—what you call mind-talk—either. They can't because they really don't believe such things can be done. The people inside the Wall do, for they live in an atmosphere of magic. But once these things are worked out, and become simply a matter of training and method, then the ritual, the mumbo-jumbo, the deeply ingrained belief in the existence of supernatural forces will be no longer necessary.

"These phenomena will be only tools that anybody can be trained to use, and the crutches can be thrown away. Then the Wall will come tumbling down. But until then—" he stopped and frowned in mock severity—"there will always be a Black

Man around to see that the people inside don't split themselves up the middle trying to walk down two roads at once.''

There was a lingering doubt in Porgie's eyes. "But you flew without a machine.''

The Black Man opened his cloak and displayed a small, gleaming disk that was strapped to his chest. He tapped it. "A machine, Porgie. A machine, just like your glider, only of a different sort and much better. It's almost as good as levitation. Mind and Nature . . . magic and science . . . they'll get together eventually.''

He wrapped his cloak about him again. "It's cold up here. Shall we go? Tomorrow is time enough to find out what is Outside the Wall that goes around the World.''

"Can't we wait until the clouds lift?'' asked Porgie wistfully. "I'd sort of like to see it for the first time from up here.''

"We could,'' said Mr. Wickens, "but there is somebody you haven't seen for a long time waiting for you down there. If we stay up here, he'll be worried.''

Porgie looked up blankly. "I don't know anybody Outside. I—'' He stopped suddenly. He felt as if he were about to explode. "Not my father!''

"Who else? He came out the easy way. Come, now, let's go and show him what kind of man his son has grown up to be. Are you ready?''

"I'm ready,'' said Porgie.

"Then help me drag your contraption over to the other side of the Wall so we can drop it inside. When the folk find the wreckage in the morning, they'll know what the Black Man does to those who build machines instead of tending to their proper business. It should have a salutary effect on Bull Pup and the others.''

He walked over to the wreckage of the *Eagle* and began to tug at it.

"Wait,'' said Porgie. "Let me.'' He stared at the broken glider until his eyes began to burn. Then he gripped and pulled.

Slowly, with an increasing consciousness of mastery, he lifted until the glider floated free and was rocking gently in the slight breeze that rippled across the top of the great Wall. Then, with a sudden shove, he swung it far out over the abyss and released it.

The two stood silently, side by side, watching the *Eagle* pitch downward on broken wings. When it was lost in the darkness below, Mr. Wickens took Porgie in his strong arms and stepped confidently to the edge of the Wall.

"Wait a second," said Porgie, remembering a day in the schoolmaster's study and a switch that had come floating obediently down through the air. "If you're from Outside, how come you can do lifting?"

Mr. Wickens grinned. "Oh, I was born Inside. I went over the Wall for the first time when I was just a little older than you are now."

"In a glider?" asked Porgie.

"No," said the Black Man, his face perfectly sober. "I went out and caught myself a half-dozen eagles."

THE PEOPLE OF THE BLACK CIRCLE

by
Robert E. Howard

The story of Robert E. Howard is truly stranger than fiction. A physically robust young man, he could not cope with the death of his mother in 1936 and killed himself. He was thirty years old. Before his tragic death he had produced a considerable body of fiction which has been undergoing an enormous revival in recent years. Howard wrote many different kinds of fiction and poetry, but his fame rests largely on his creation of Conan the Barbarian, a muscular axe-man who has become one of the most popular characters in the fantasy field, single-handedly creating the sub-genre of "heroic fantasy." The Conan character has been continued by such authors as Lin Carter and L. Sprague de Camp, and he was the subject of a major motion picture in 1982.

One of the longest and most memorable of the Conan stories, "The People of the Black Circle" deals with a royal family's attempts to revenge themselves against an attack by wizardry.

*   *   *

In another part of the city, a man stood in a latticed balcony overlooking a long street in which torches tossed luridly, smokily revealing upturned dark faces and the whites of gleaming eyes. A long-drawn wailing rose from the multitude.

The man shrugged his broad shoulders and turned back into the arabesqued chamber. He was a tall man, compactly built and richly clad.

"The king is not yet dead, but the dirge is sounded," he said to another man who sat cross-legged on a mat in a corner. This man was clad in a brown camel-hair robe and sandals, and a green turban was on his head. His expression was tranquil, his gaze impersonal.

"The people know he will never see another dawn," this man answered.

The first speaker favored him with a long, searching stare.

"What I can not understand," he said, "is why I have had to wait so long for your masters to strike. If they have slain the king now, why could they not have slain him months ago?"

"Even the arts you call sorcery are governed by cosmic laws," answered the man in the green turban. "The stars direct these actions, as in other affairs. Not even my masters can alter the stars. Not until the heavens were in the proper order could they perform this necromancy." With a long, stained fingernail he mapped the constellations on the marble-tiled floor. "The slant of the moon presaged evil for the king of Vendhya; the stars are in turmoil, the Serpent in the House of the Elephant. During such juxtaposition, the invisible guardians are removed from the spirit of Bhunda Chand. A path is opened in the unseen realms, and once a point of contact was established, mighty powers were put in play along that path."

"Point of contact?" inquired the other. "Do you mean that lock of Bhunda Chand's hair?"

"Yes. All discarded portions of the human body still remain part of it, attached to it by intangible connections. The priests of Asura have a dim inkling of this truth, and so all nail-trimmings, hair, and other waste products of the persons of the royal family are carefully reduced to ashes and the ashes hidden. But at the urgent entreaty of the princess of Kosala, who loved Bhunda Chand vainly, he gave her a lock of his long black hair as a token of remembrance. When my masters decided upon his doom, the lock, in its golden, jewel-crusted case, was stolen from under her pillow while she slept, and another substituted,

1. Death Strikes a King

The king of Vendhya was dying. Through the hot, stifling ni
the temple gongs boomed and the conchs roared. Their clar
was a faint echo in the gold-domed chamber where Bhu
Chand struggled on the velvet-cushioned dais. Beads of sw
glistened on his dark skin; his fingers twisted the gold-worl
fabric beneath him. He was young; no spear had touched him,
poison lurked in his wine. But his veins stood out like blue co
on his temples, and his eyes dilated with the nearness of dea
Trembling slave-girls knelt at the foot of the dais, and lean
down on him, watching him with passionate intensity, was
sister, the Devi Yasmina. With her was the *wazam*, a no
grown old in the royal court.

She threw up her head in a gusty gesture of wrath and desp
as the thunder of the distant drums reached her ears.

"The priests and their clamor!" she exclaimed. "They are
wiser than the leeches, who are helpless! Nay, he dies and no
can say why. He is dying now—and I stand here helpless, w
would burn the whole city and spill the blood of thousands
save him."

"Not a man of Ayodhya but would die in his place, if it mig
be, Devi," answered the *wazam*. "This poison———"

"I tell you it is not poison!" she cried. "Since his birth he h
been guarded so closely that the cleverest poisoners of the Ea
could not reach him. Five skulls bleaching on the Tower of t
Kites can testify to attempts which were made—and which faile
As you well know, there are ten men and ten women whose so
duty is to taste his food and wine, and fifty armed warriors guard h
chambers as they guard it now. No, it is not poison; it
sorcery—black, ghastly magic———"

She ceased as the king spoke; his livid lips did not move, ar
there was no recognition in his glassy eyes. But his voice rose i
an eery call, indistinct and far away, as if he called to her fro
beyond vast, wind-blown gulfs.

"Yasmina! Yasmina! My sister, where are you? I can not fin
you. All is darkness, and the roaring of great winds!"

"Brother!" cried Yasmina, catching his limp hand in a convul
sive grasp. "I am here! Do you not know me———"

Her voice died at the utter vacancy of his face. A low
confused moaning waned from his mouth. The slave-girls at th
foot of the dais whimpered with fear, and Yasmina beat he
breast in her anguish.

so like the first that she never knew the difference. Then the genuine lock traveled by camel-caravan up the long, long road to Peshkhauri, thence up the Zhaibar Pass, until it reached the hands of those for whom it was intended.''

"Only a lock of hair," murmured the nobleman.

"By which a soul is drawn from its body and across gulfs of echoing space," returned the man on the mat.

The nobleman studied him curiously.

"I do not know if you are a man or a demon, Khemsa," he said at last. "Few of us are what we seem. I, whom the Kshatriyas know as Kerim Shah, a prince from Iranistan, am no greater a masquerader than most men. They are all traitors in the one way or another, and half of them know not whom they serve. There at least I have no doubts; for I serve King Yezdigerd of Turan.''

"And I the Black Seers of Yimsha," said Khemsa; "and my masters are greater than yours, for they have accomplished by their arts what Yezdigerd could not with a hundred thousand swords.''

Outside, the moan of the tortured thousands shuddered up to the stars which crusted the sweating Vendhyan night, and the conchs bellowed like oxen in pain.

In the gardens of the palace the torches glinted on polished helmets and curved swords and gold-chased corselets. All the noble-born fighting-men of Ayodhya were gathered in the great palace or about it, and at each broad-arched gate and door fifty archers stood on guard, with bows in their hands. But Death stalked through the royal palace and none could stay his ghostly tread.

On the dais under the golden dome the king cried out again, racked by awful paroxysms. Again his voice came faintly and far away, and again the Devi bent to him, trembling with a fear that was darker than the terror of death.

"Yasmina!" Again that far, weirdly dreeing cry, from realms immeasurable. "Aid me! I am far from my mortal house! Wizards have drawn my soul through the wind-blown darkness. They seek to snap the silver cord that binds me to my dying body. They cluster around me; their hands are taloned, their eyes are red like flame burning in darkness. *Aie*, save me, my sister! Their fingers sear me like fire! They would slay my body and damn my soul! What is this they bring before me?—*Aie!*''

At the terror in his hopeless cry Yasmina screamed uncontrollably and threw herself bodily upon him in the abandon of her anguish. He was torn by a terrible convulsion; foam flew from his contorted lips and his writhing fingers left their marks on the girl's shoulders. But the glassy blankness passed from his eyes like smoke blown from a fire, and he looked up at his sister with recognition.

"Brother!" she sobbed. "Brother——"

"Swift!" he gasped, and his weakening voice was rational. "I know now what brings me to the pyre. I have been on a far journey and I understand. I have been ensorceled by the wizards of the Himelians. They drew my soul out of my body and far away, into a stone room. There they strove to break the silver cord of life, and thrust my soul into the body of a foul night-weird their sorcery summoned up from Hell. Ah! I feel their pull upon me now! Your cry and the grip of your fingers brought me back, but I am going fast. My soul clings to my body, but its hold weakens. Quick—kill me, before they can trap my soul for ever!"

"I can not!" she wailed, smiting her naked breasts.

"Swiftly, I command you!" There was the old imperious note in his flailing whisper. "You have never disobeyed me—obey my last command! Send my soul clean to Asura! Haste, lest you damn me to spend eternity as a filthy gaunt of darkness. Strike, I command you! *Strike!*"

Sobbing wildly, Yasmina plucked a jeweled dagger from her girdle and plunged it to the hilt in his breast. He stiffened and then went limp, a grim smile curving his dead lips. Yasmina hurled herself face-down on the rush-covered floor, beating the reeds with her clenched hands. Outside, the gongs and conchs brayed and thundered and the priests gashed themselves with copper knives.

2. A Barbarian from the Hills

Chunder Shan, governor of Peshkhauri, laid down his golden pen and carefully scanned that which he had written on parchment that bore his official seal. He had ruled Peshkhauri so long only because he weighed his every word, spoken or written. Danger breeds caution, and only a wary man lives long in that wild country where the hot Vendhyan plains meet the crags of the Himelians. An hour's ride westward or northward and one crossed the border and was among the Hills where men lived by the law of the knife.

The governor was alone in his chamber, seated at his ornately-carven table of inlaid ebony. Through the wide window, open for the coolness, he could see a square of the blue Himelian night, dotted with great white stars. An adjacent parapet was a shadowy line, and further crenelles and embrasures were barely hinted at in the dim starlight. The governor's fortress was strong, and situated outside the walls of the city it guarded. The breeze that stirred the tapestries on the wall brought faint noises from the streets of Peshkhauri—occasional snatches of wailing song, or the thrum of a cithern.

The governor read what he had written, slowly, with his open hand shading his eyes from the bronze butter-lamp, his lips moving. Absently, as he read, he heard the drum of horses' hoofs outside the barbican, the sharp staccato of the guards' challenge. He did not heed, intent upon his letter. It was addressed to the *wazam* of Vendhya, at the royal court of Ayodhya, and it stated, after the customary salutations:

> Let it be known to your Excellency that I have faithfully carried out your Excellency's instructions. The seven tribesmen are well guarded in their prison, and I have repeatedly sent word into the hills that their chief come in person to bargain for their release. But he has made no move, except to send word that unless they are freed he will burn Peshkhauri and cover his saddle with my hide, begging your Excellency's indulgence. This he is quite capable of attempting, and I have tripled the numbers of the lance guards. The man is not a native of Ghulistan. I can not with certainty predict his next move. But since it is the wish of the Devi——

He was out of his ivory chair and on his feet facing the arched door, all in one instant. He snatched at the curved sword lying in its ornate scabbard on the table, and then checked the movement.

It was a woman who had entered unannounced, a woman whose gossamer robes did not conceal the rich garments beneath any more than they concealed the suppleness and beauty of her tall, slender figure. A filmy veil fell below her breasts, supported by a flowing headdress bound about with a triple gold braid and adorned with a golden crescent. Her dark eyes regarded the astonished governor over the veil, and then with an imperious gesture of her white hand, she uncovered her face.

"Devi!" The governor dropped to his knee before her, his

surprise and confusion somewhat spoiling the stateliness of his obeisance. With a gesture she motioned him to rise, and he hastened to lead her to the ivory chair, all the while bowing level with his girdle. But his first words were of reproof.

"Your Majesty! This was most unwise! The border is unsettled. Raids from the hills are incessant. You came with a large attendance?"

"An ample retinue followed me to Peshkhauri," she answered. "I lodged my people there and came on to the fort with my maid, Gitara."

Chunder Shan groaned in horror.

"Devi! You do not understand the peril. An hour's ride from this spot, the hills swarm with barbarians who make a profession of murder and rapine. Women have been stolen and men stabbed between the fort and the city. Peshkhauri is not like your southern provinces——"

"But I am here, and unharmed," she interrupted with a trace of impatience. "I showed my signet ring to the guard at the gate, and to the one outside your door, and they admitted me unannounced, not knowing me, but supposing me to be a secret courier from Ayodhya. Let us not now waste time. You have received no word from the chief of the barbarians?"

"None save threats and curses, Devi. He is wary and suspicious. He deems it a trap, and perhaps he is not to be blamed. The Kshatriyas have not always kept their promises to the hill people."

"He must be brought to terms!" broke in Yasmina, the knuckles of her clenched hands showing white.

"I do not understand." The governor shook his head. "When I chanced to capture these seven hillmen, I reported their capture to the *wazam*, as the custom, and then, before I could hang them, there came an order to hold them and communicate with their chief. This I did, but the man holds aloof, as I have said. These men are of the tribe of Afghulis, but he is a foreigner from the West, and he is called Conan. I have threatened to hang them tomorrow at dawn, if he does not come."

"Good!" exclaimed the Devi. "You have done well. And I will tell you why I have given these orders. My brother——" she faltered, choking, and the governor bowed his head, with the customary gesture of respect for a departed sovereign.

"The king of Vendhya was destroyed by magic," she said at last. "I have devoted my life to the destruction of his murderers. As he died he gave me a clue, and I have followed it. I have read the Book of Skelos, and talked with nameless hermits in the caves below Jhelai. I learned how, and by whom, he was destroyed. His enemies were the Black Seers of Mount Yimsha.''

"Asura!'' whispered Chunder Shan, paling.

Her eyes knifed him through. ''Do you fear them?''

"Who does not, your Majesty?'' he replied. ''They are black devils, haunting the uninhabited hills beyond the Zhaibar. But the sages say that they seldom interfere in the lives of mortal men.''

"Why they slew my brother I do not know,'' she answered. ''But I have sworn on the altar of Asura to destroy them! And I need the aid of a man beyond the border. A Kshatriya army, unaided, would never reach Yimsha.''

"Aye,'' muttered Chunder Shan. ''You speak the truth there. It would be a fight every step of the way, with hairy hillmen hurling down boulders from every height, and rushing us with their long knives in every valley. The Turanians fought their way through the Himelians once, but how many returned to Khurusun? Few of those who escaped the swords of the Kshatriyas, after the king, your brother, defeated their host on the Jhumda River, ever saw Secunderam again.''

"And so I must control men across the border,'' she said, ''men who know the way to Mount Yimsha——''

"But the tribes fear the Black Seers and shun the unholy mountain,'' broke in the governor.

"Does the chief, Conan, fear them?'' she asked.

"Well, as to that,'' muttered the governor, ''I doubt if there is anything that devil fears.''

"So I have been told. Therefore he is the man I must deal with. He wishes the release of his seven men. Very well; their ransom shall be the heads of the Black Seers!'' Her voice thrummed with hate as she uttered the last words, and her hands clenched at her sides. She looked an image of incarnate passion as she stood there with her head thrown high and her bosom heaving.

Again the governor knelt, for part of his wisdom was the knowledge that a woman in such an emotional tempest is as perilous as a blind cobra to any about her.

"It shall be as you wish, your Majesty.'' Then as she presented a calmer aspect, he rose and ventured to drop a word of warning. ''I can not predict what the chief Conan's action will be. The tribesmen are always turbulent, and I have reason to believe that emissaries from the Turanians are stirring them up to raid our borders. As your majesty knows, the Turanians have established themselves in Secunderam and other northern cities, though the hill tribes remain unconquered. King Yezdigerd has long looked southward with greedy lust and perhaps is seeking to gain by treachery what he could not win by force of arms. I have thought that Conan might well be one of his spies.''

"We shall see," she answered. "If he loves his followers, he will be at the gates at dawn, to parley. I shall spend the night in the fortress. I came in disguise to Peshkhauri, and lodged my retinue at an inn instead of the palace. Besides my people, only yourself knows of my presence here."

"I shall escort you to your quarters, your Majesty," said the governor, and as they emerged from the doorway, he beckoned the warrior on guard there, and the man fell in behind them, spear held at a salute.

The maid waited, veiled like her mistress, outside the door, and the group traversed a wide, winding corridor, lighted by smoky torches, and reached the quarters reserved for visiting notables—generals and viceroys, mostly; none of the royal family had ever honored the fortress before. Chunder Shan had a perturbed feeling that the suite was not suitable to such an exalted personage as the Devi, and though she sought to make him feel at ease in her presence, he was glad when she dismissed him and he bowed himself out. All the menials of the fort had been summoned to serve his royal guest—though he did not divulge her identity—and he stationed a squad of spearmen before her doors, among them the warrior who had guarded his own chamber. In his preoccupation he forgot to replace the man.

The governor had not been gone long from her when Yasmina suddenly remembered something else which she had wished to discuss with him, but had forgotten until that moment. It concerned the past actions of one Kerim Shah, a nobleman from Iranistan, who had dwelt for a while in Peshkhauri before coming on to the court at Ayodhya. A vague suspicion concerning the man had been stirred by a glimpse of him in Peshkhauri that night. She wondered if he had followed her from Ayodhya. Being a truly remarkable Devi, she did not summon the governor to her again, but hurried out into the corridor, and hastened toward his chamber.

Chunder Shan, entering his chamber, closed the door and went to his table. There he took the letter he had been writing and tore it to bits. Scarcely had he finished when he heard something drop softly onto the parapet adjacent to the window. He looked up to see a figure loom briefly against the stars, and then a man dropped lightly into the room. The light glinted on a long sheen of steel in his hand.

"Shhhh!" he warned. "Don't make a noise, or I'll send the Devil a henchman!"

The governor checked his motion toward the sword on the table. He was within reach of the yard-long Zhaibar knife that glittered in the intruder's fist, and he knew the desperate quickness of a hillman.

The invader was a tall man, at once strong and supple. He was dressed like a hillman, but his dark features and blazing blue eyes did not match his garb. Chunder Shan had never seen a man like him; he was not an Easterner, but some barbarian from the West. But his aspect was as untamed and formidable as any of the hairy tribesmen who haunt the hills of Ghulistan.

"You come like a thief in the night," commented the governor, recovering some of his composure, although he remembered that there was no guard within call. Still, the hillman could not know that.

"I climbed a bastion," snarled the intruder. "A guard thrust his head over the battlement in time for me to rap it with my knife-hilt."

"You are Conan?"

"Who else? You sent word into the hills that you wished for me to come and parley with you. Well, by Crom, I've come! Keep away from that table or I'll gut you."

"I merely wish to seat myself," answered the governor, carefully sinking into the ivory chair, which he wheeled away from the table. Conan moved restlessly before him, glancing suspiciously at the door, thumbing the razor edge of his three-foot knife. He did not walk like an Afghuli, and was bluntly direct where the East is subtle.

"You have seven of my men," he said abruptly. "You refused the ransom I offered. What the devil do you want?"

"Let us discuss terms," answered Chunder Shan cautiously.

"Terms?" There was a timbre of dangerous anger in his voice. "What do you mean? Haven't I offered you gold?"

Chunder Shan laughed.

"Gold? There is more gold in Peshkhauri than you ever saw."

"You're a liar," retorted Conan. "I've seen the *suk* of the goldsmiths in Khurusun."

"Well, more than any Afghuli ever saw," amended Chunder Shan. "And it is but a drop of all the treasure of Vendhya. Why should we desire gold? It would be more to our advantage to hang these seven thieves.''

Conan ripped out a sulfurous oath and the long blade quivered in his grip as the muscles rose in ridges on his brown arm.

''I'll split your head like a ripe melon!''

A wild blue flame flickered in the hillman's eyes, but Chunder Shan shrugged his shoulders, though keeping an eye on the keen steel.

''You can kill me easily, and probably escape over the wall afterward. But that would not save the seven tribesmen. My men would surely hang them. And these men are headmen among the Afghulis.''

''I know it,'' snarled Conan. ''The tribe is baying like wolves at my heels because I have not procured their release. Tell me in plain words what you want, because, by Crom! if there's no other way, I'll raise a horde and lead it to the very gates of Peshkhauri!''

Looking at the man as he stood squarely, knife in fist and eyes glaring, Chunder Shan did not doubt that he was capable of it. The governor did not believe any hill-horde could take Peshkhauri, but he did not wish a devastated countryside.

''There is a mission you must perform,'' he said, choosing his words with as much care as if they had been razors. ''There——''

Conan had sprung back, wheeling to face the door at the same instant, lips asnarl. His barbarian ears had caught the quick tread of soft slippers outside the door. The next instant the door was thrown open and a slim, silk-robed form entered hastily, pulling the door shut—then stopping short at sight of the hillman.

Chunder Shan sprang up, his heart jumping into his mouth.

''Devi!'' he cried involuntarily, losing his head momentarily in his fright.

''*Devi!*'' It was like an explosive echo from the hillman's lips. Chander Shan saw recognition and intent flame up in the fierce blue eyes.

The governor shouted desperately and caught at his sword, but the hillman moved with the devastating speed of a hurricane. He sprang, knocked the governor sprawling with a savage blow of his knife-hilt, swept up the astounded Devi in one brawny arm and leaped for the window. Chunder Shan, struggling frantically to his feet, saw the man poise an instant on the sill in a flutter of silken skirts and white limbs that was his royal captive, and heard his fierce, exultant snarl: ''*Now* dare to hang my men!''

and then Conan leaped to the parapet and was gone. A wild scream floated back to the governor's ears.

"Guard! *Guard!*" screamed the governor, struggling up and running drunkenly to the door. He tore it open and reeled into the hall. His shouts re-echoed along the corridors, and warriors came running, gaping to see the governor holding his broken head, from which the blood streamed.

"Turn out the lancers!" he roared. "There has been an abduction!" Even in his frenzy he had enough sense left to withhold the full truth. He stopped short as he heard a sudden drum of hoofs outside, a frantic scream and a wild yell of barbaric exultation.

Followed by the bewildered guardsmen, the governor raced for the stair. In the courtyard of the fort a force of lancers always stood by saddled steeds, ready to ride at an instant's notice. Chunder Shan led his squadron flying after the fugitive, though his head swam so he had to hold with both hands to the saddle. He did not divulge the identity of the victim, but said merely that the noblewoman who had borne the royal signet ring had been carried away by the chief of the Afghulis. The abductor was out of sight and hearing, but they knew the path he would strike— the road that runs straight to the mouth of the Zhaibar. There was no moon; peasant huts rose dimly in the starlight. Behind them fell away the grim bastion of the fort, and the towers of Peshkhauri. Ahead of them loomed the black walls of the Himelians.

3. Khemsa Uses Magic

In the confusion that reigned in the fortress while the guard was being turned out, no one noticed that the girl who had accompanied the Devi slipped out the great arched gate and vanished in the darkness. She ran straight for the city, her garments tucked high. She did not follow the open road, but cut straight through fields and over slopes, avoiding fences and leaping irrigation ditches as surely as if it were broad daylight, and as easily as if she were a trained masculine runner. The hoof-drum of the guardsmen had faded away up the hill road before she reached the city wall. She did not go to the great gate, beneath whose arch men leaned on spears and craned their necks into the darkness, discussing the unwonted activity about the fortress. She skirted the wall until she reached a certain point where the spire of a tower was visible above the battlements. Then she placed her hands to her mouth and voiced a low, weird call that carried strangely.

Almost instantly a head appeared at an embrasure and a rope came wriggling down the wall. She seized it, placed a foot in the loop at the end, and waved her arm. Then quickly and smoothly she was drawn up the sheer stone curtain. An instant later she scrambled over the merlons and stood up on a flat roof which covered a house that was built against the wall. There was an open trap there, and a man in a camel-hair robe who silently coiled the rope, not showing in any way the strain of hauling a full-grown woman up a forty-foot wall.

"Where is Kerim Shah?" she gasped, panting after a long run.

"Asleep in the house below. You have news?"

"Conan has stolen the Devi out of the fortress and carried her away into the hills!" She blurted out her news in a rush, the words stumbling over one another.

Khemsa showed no emotion, but merely nodded his turbaned head. "Kerim Shah will be glad to hear that," he said.

"Wait!" The girl threw her supple arms about his neck. She was panting hard, but not only from exertion. Her eyes blazed like black jewels in the starlight. Her upturned face was close to Khemsa's, but though he submitted to her embrace, he did not return it.

"Do not tell the Hyrkanian!" she panted. "Let us use this knowledge ourselves! The governor has gone into the hills with his riders, but he might as well chase a ghost. He has not told anyone that it was the Devi who was kidnapped. None in Peshkhauri or the fort knows it except us."

"But what good does it do us?" the man expostulated. "My masters sent me with Kerim Shah to aid him in every way——"

"Aid yourself!" she cried fiercely. "Shake off your yoke!"

"You mean—disobey my masters?" he gasped, and she felt his whole body turn cold under her arms.

"Aye!" she shook him in the fury of her emotion. "You too are a magician! Why will you be a slave, using your powers only to elevate others? Use your arts for yourself!"

"That is forbidden!" He was shaking as if with an ague. "I am not one of the Black Circle. Only by the command of the masters do I dare to use the knowledge they have taught me."

"But you *can* use it!" she argued passionately. "Do as I beg you! Of course Conan has taken the Devi to hold as hostage against the seven tribesmen in the governor's prison. Destroy

them, so Chunder Shan can not use them to buy back the Devi.
Then let us go into the mountains and take her from the Afghulis.
They can not stand against your sorcery with their knives. The
treasure of the Vendhyan kings will be ours as ransom—and then
when we have it in our hands, we can trick them, and sell her to
the king of Turan. We shall have wealth beyond our maddest
dreams. With it we can buy warriors. We will take Khorbhul,
oust the Turanians from the hills, and send our hosts southward;
become king and queen of an empire!''

Khemsa too was panting, shaking like a leaf in her grasp; his
face showed gray in the starlight, beaded with great drops of
perspiration.

"I love you!'' she cried fiercely, writhing her body against
his, almost strangling him in her wild embrace, shaking him in
her abandon. "I will make a king of you! For love of you I
betrayed my mistress; for love of me betray your masters! Why
fear the Black Seers? By your love for me you have broken one
of their laws already! Break the rest! You are as strong as they!''

A man of ice could not have withstood the searing heat of her
passion and fury. With an inarticulate cry he crushed her to him,
bending her backward and showering gasping kisses on her eyes,
face, and lips.

"I'll do it!'' His voice was thick with laboring emotions. He
staggered like a drunken man. "The arts they have taught me
shall work for me, not for my masters. We shall be rulers of the
world—of the world——''

"Come then!'' Twisting lithely out of his embrace, she seized
his hand and led him toward the trap-door. "First we must make
sure that the governor does not exchange those seven Afghulis
for the Devi.''

He moved like a man in a daze, until they had descended a
ladder and she paused in the chamber below. Kerim Shah lay on
a couch motionless, an arm across his face as though to shield
his sleeping eyes from the soft light of a brass lamp. She plucked
Khemsa's arm and made a quick gesture across her own throat.
Khemsa lifted his hand; then his expression changed and he drew
away.

"I have eaten his salt,'' he muttered. "Besides, he can not
interfere with us.''

He led the girl through a door that opened on a winding stair.
After their soft tread had faded into silence, the man on the
couch sat up. Kerim Shah wiped the sweat from his face. A

knife-thrust he did not dread, but he feared Khemsa as a man fears a poisonous reptile.

"People who plot on roofs should remember to lower their voices," he muttered. "But as Khemsa has turned against his masters, and as he was my only contact with them, I can count on their aid no longer. From now on I play the game in my own way."

Rising to his feet he went quickly to a table, drew pen and parchment from his girdle, and scribbled a few succinct lines:

> To Khosru Khan, governor of Secunderam: the Cimmerian Conan has carried the Devi Yasmina to the villages of the Afghulis. It is an opportunity to get the Devi into our hands, as the king has so long desired. Send three thousand horsemen at once. I will meet them in the Valley of Gurashah with native guides.

And he signed it with a name that was not in the least like Kerim Shah.

Then from a golden cage he drew forth a carrier pigeon, to whose leg he made fast the parchment, rolled into a tiny cylinder and secured with gold wire. Then he went quickly to a casement and tossed the bird into the night. It wavered on fluttering wings, balanced, and was gone like a flitting shadow. Catching up helmet, sword, and cloak, Kerim Shah hurried out of the chamber and down the winding stair.

The prison quarters of Peshkhauri were separated from the rest of the city by a massive wall, in which was set a single iron-bound door under an arch. Over the arch burned a lurid red cresset, and beside the door squatted a warrior with spear and shield.

This warrior, leaning on his spear, and yawning from time to time, started suddenly to his feet. He had not thought he had dozed, but a man was standing before him, a man he had not heard approach. The man wore a camel-hair robe and a green turban. In the flickering light of the cresset his features were shadowy, but a pair of lambent eyes shone surprisingly in the lurid glow.

"Who comes?" demanded the warrior, presenting his spear. "Who are you?"

The stranger did not seem perturbed, though the spear-point

touched his bosom. His eyes held the warrior's with strange intensity.

"What are you obliged to do?" he asked, strangely.

"To guard the gate!" The warrior spoke thickly and mechanically; he stood rigid as a statue, his eyes slowly glazing.

"You lie! You are obliged to obey me! You have looked into my eyes, and your soul is no longer your own. Open that door!"

Stiffly, with the wooden features of an image, the guard wheeled about, drew a great key from his girdle, turned it in the massive lock, and swung open the door. Then he stood at attention, his unseeing stare straight ahead of him.

A woman glided from the shadows and laid an eager hand on the mesmerist's arm.

"Bid him fetch us horses, Khemsa," she whispered.

"No need of that," answered the Rakhsha. Lifting his voice slightly he spoke to the guardsman. "I have no more use for you. Kill yourself!"

Like a man in a trance, the warrior thrust the butt of his spear against the base of the wall and placed the keen head against his body, just below the ribs. Then slowly, stolidly, he leaned against it with all his weight, so that it transfixed his body and came out between his shoulders. Sliding down the shaft he lay still, the spear jutting above him its full length, like a horrible stalk growing out of his back.

The girl stared down at him in morbid fascination, until Khemsa took her arm and led her through the gate. Torches lighted a narrow space between the outer wall and a lower inner one, in which were arched doors at regular intervals. A warrior paced this enclosure, and when the gate opened he came sauntering up, so secure in his knowledge of the prison's strength that he was not suspicious until Khemsa and the girl emerged from the archway. Then it was too late. The Rahksha did not waste time in hypnotism, though his action savored of magic to the girl. The guard lowered his spear threateningly, opening his mouth to shout an alarm that would bring spearmen swarming out of the guardrooms at either end of the alleyway. Khemsa flicked the spear aside with his left hand, as a man might flick a straw, and his right flashed out and back, seeming gently to caress the warrior's neck in passing. And the guard pitched on his face without a sound, his head lolling on a broken neck.

Khemsa did not glance at him, but went straight to one of the arched doors and placed his open hand against the heavy bronze lock. With a rending shudder the portal buckled inward. As the girl followed him through, she saw that the thick teakwood hung in splinters, the bronze bolts were bent and twisted from their sockets, and the great hinges broken and disjointed. A thousand-pound battering-ram with forty men to swing it could have shattered the barrier no more completely. Khemsa was drunk with freedom and the exercise of his power, glorying in his might and flinging his strength about as a young giant exercises his thews with unnecessary vigor in the exultant pride of his prowess.

The broken door let them into a small courtyard, lit by a cresset. Opposite the door was a wide grille of iron bars. A hairy hand was visible, gripping one of these bars, and in the darkness behind them glimmered the whites of eyes.

Khemsa stood silent for a space, gazing into the shadows from which those glimmering eyes gave back his stare with burning intensity. Then his hand went into his robe and came out again, and from his opening fingers a shimmering feather of sparkling dust shifted to the flags. Instantly a flare of green fire lighted the enclosure. In the brief glare the forms of seven men, standing motionless behind the bars, were limned in vivid detail; tall, hairy men in ragged hillmen's garments. They did not speak, but in their eyes blazed the fear of death, and their hairy fingers gripped the bars.

The fire died out but the glow remained, a quivering ball of lambent green that pulsed and shimmered on the flags before Khemsa's feet. The wide gaze of the tribesmen was fixed upon it. It wavered, elongated; it turned into a luminous green smoke spiraling upward. It twisted and writhed like a great shadowy serpent, then broadened and billowed out in shining folds and whirls. It grew to a cloud moving silently over the flags—straight toward the grille. The men watching its coming with dilated eyes; the bars quivered with the grip of their desperate fingers. Bearded lips parted but no sound came forth. The green cloud rolled on the bars and blotted them from sight. Like a fog it oozed through the grille and hid the men within. From the enveloping folds came a strangled gasp, as of a man plunged suddenly under the surface of water. That was all.

Khemsa touched the girl's arm, as she stood with parted lips and dilated eyes. Mechanically she turned away with him, looking back over her shoulder. Already the mist was thinning; close to the bars she saw a pair of sandaled feet, the toes turned upward—she glimpsed the indistinct outlines of seven still, prostrate shapes.

"And now for a steed swifter than the fastest horse ever bred in a mortal stable," Khemsa was saying. "We will be in Afghulistan before dawn."

4. An Encounter in the Pass

Yasmina Devi could never clearly remember the details of her abduction. The unexpectedness and violence stunned her; she had only a confused impression of a whirl of happenings—the terrifying grip of a mighty arm, the blazing eyes of her abductor, and his hot breath burning on her flesh. The leap through the window to the parapet, the mad race across battlements and roofs when the fear of falling froze her, the reckless descent of a rope bound to a merlon—he went down almost at a run, his captive folded limply over his brawny shoulder—all this was a befuddled tangle in the Devi's mind. She retained a more vivid memory of him running fleetly into the shadows of the trees, carrying her like a child, and vaulting into the saddle of a fierce Bhalkhana stallion which reared and snorted. Then there was a sensation of flying, and the racing hoofs were striking sparks of fire from the flinty road as the stallion swept up the slopes.

As the girl's mind cleared, her first sensations were furious rage and shame. She was appalled. The rulers of the golden kingdoms south of the Himelians were considered little short of divine; and she was the Devi of Vendyha! Fright was submerged in regal wrath. She cried out furiously and began struggling. She, Yasmina, to be carried on the saddle-bow of a hill chief, like a common wench of the market place! He merely hardened his massive thews slightly against her writhings, and for the first time in her life she experienced the coercion of superior physical strength. His arms felt like iron about her slender limbs. He glanced down at her and grinned hugely. His teeth glimmered whitely in the starlight. The reins lay loose on the stallion's flowing mane, and every thew and fiber of the great beast strained as he hurtled along the boulder-strew trail. But Conan sat easily, almost carelessly, in the saddle, riding like a centaur.

"You hill-bred dog!" she panted, quivering with the impact of shame, anger, and the realization of helplessness. "You dare—you *dare!* Your life shall pay for this! Where are you taking me?"

"To the villages of Afghulistan," he answered, casting a glance over his shoulder.

Behind them, beyond the slopes they had traversed, torches

were tossing on the walls of the fortress, and he glimpsed a flare of light that meant the great gate had been opened. And he laughed a deep-throated boom gusty as the hill wind.

"The Governor has sent his riders after us," he laughed. "By Crom, we will lead him a merry chase! What do you think, Devi—will they pay seven lives for a Kshatriya princess?"

"They will send an army to hang you and your spawn of devils," she promised him with conviction.

He laughed gustily and shifted her to a more comfortable position in his arms. But she took this as a fresh outrage, and renewed her vain struggles, until she saw that her efforts were only amusing him. Besides, her light silken garments, floating on the wind, were being outrageously disarranged by her struggles. She concluded that a scornful submission was the better part of dignity, and lapsed into a smoldering quiescence.

She felt even her anger being submerged by awe as they entered the mouth of the Pass, lowering like a black well mouth in the blacker walls that rose like colossal ramparts to bar their way. It was as if a gigantic knife had cut the Zhaibar out of walls of solid rock. On either hand sheer slopes pitched up for thousands of feet, and the mouth of the Pass was dark as hate. Even Conan could not see with any accuracy, but he knew the road, even by night. And knowing that armed men were racing through the starlight after him, he did not check the stallion's speed. The great brute was not yet showing fatigue. He thundered along the road that followed the valley bed, labored up a slope, swept along a low ridge where treacherous shale on either hand lurked for the unwary, and came upon a trail that followed the lap of the left-hand wall.

Not even Conan could spy, in that darkness, an ambush set by Zhaibar tribesmen. As they swept past the black mouth of a gorge that opened into the Pass, a javelin swished through the air and thudded home behind the stallion's straining shoulder. The great beast let out his life in a shuddering sob and stumbled, going headlong in mid-stride. But Conan had recognized the flight and stroke of the javelin, and he acted with spring-steel quickness.

As the horse fell he leaped clear, holding the girl aloft to guard her from striking boulders. He lit on his feet like a cat, thrust her into a cleft of rock, and wheeled toward the outer darkness, drawing his knife.

Yasmina, confused by the rapidity of events, not quite sure just what had happened, saw a vague shape rush out of the darkness, bare feet slapping softly on the rock, ragged garments whipping on the wind of his haste. She glimpsed the flicker of steel, heard the lightning crack of stroke, parry, and counter-stroke, and the crunch of bone as Conan's long knife split the other's skull.

Conan sprang back, crouching in the shelter of the rocks. Out in the night men were moving and a stentorian voice roared: "What, you dogs! Do you flinch? In, curse you, and take them!"

Conan started, peered into the darkness and lifted his voice.

"Yar Afzal! Is it you?"

There sounded a startled imprecation, and the voice called warily.

"Conan? Is that you, Conan?"

"Aye!" The Cimmerian laughed. "Come forth, you old war-dog. I've slain one of your men."

There was movement among the rocks, a light flared dimly, and then a flame appeared and came bobbing toward him, and as it approached, a fierce bearded countenance grew out of the darkness. The man who carried it held it high, thrust forward, and craned his neck to peer among the boulders it lighted; the other hand gripped a great curved tulwar. Conan stepped forward, sheathing his knife, and the other roared a greeting.

"Aye, it is Conan! Come out of your rocks, dogs! It is Conan!"

Others pressed into the wavering circle of light—wild, ragged, bearded men, with eyes like wolves, and long blades in their fists. They did not see Yasmina, for she was hidden by Conan's massive body. But peeping from her covert, she knew icy fear for the first time that night. These men were more like wolves than human beings.

"What are you hunting in the Zhaibar by night, Yar Afzal?" Conan demanded of the burly chief, who grinned like a bearded ghoul.

"Who knows what might come up the Pass after dark? We Wazulis are nighthawks. But what of you, Conan?"

"I have a prisoner," answered the Cimmerian. And moving aside he disclosed the cowering girl. Reaching a long arm into the crevice he drew her trembling forth.

Her imperious bearing was gone. She stared timidly at the ring of bearded faces that hemmed her in, and was grateful for the strong arm that clasped her possessively. The torch was thrust close to her, and there was a sucking intake of breath about the ring.

"She is my captive," Conan warned, glancing pointedly at the feet of the man he had slain, just visible within the ring of light. "I was taking her to Afghulistan, but now you have slain my horse, and the Kshatriyas are close behind me."

"Come with us to my village," suggested Yar Afzal. "We have horses hidden in the gorge. They can never follow us in the darkness. They are close behind you, you say?"

"So close that I hear now the clink of their hoofs on the flint," answered Conan grimly.

Instantly there was movement; the torch was dashed out and the ragged shapes melted like phantoms into the darkness. Conan swept up the Devi in his arms, and she did not resist. The rocky ground hurt her slim feet in their soft slippers and she felt very small and helpless in that brutish, primordial blackness among those colossal, nighted crags.

Feeling her shiver in the wind that moaned down the defiles, Conan jerked a ragged cloak from its owner's shoulders and wrapped it about her. He also hissed a warning in her ear, ordering her to make no sound. She did not hear the distant clink of shod hoofs on rock that warned the keen-eared hillmen; but she was far too frightened to disobey, in any event.

She could see nothing but a few faint stars far above, but she knew by the deepening darkness when they entered the gorge mouth. There was a stir about them, the uneasy movement of horses. A few muttered words, and Conan mounted the horse of the man he had killed, lifting the girl up in front of him. Like phantoms except for the click of their hoofs, the band swept away up the shadowy gorge. Behind them on the trail they left the dead horse and the dead man, which were found less than half an hour later by the riders from the fortress, who recognized the man as a Wazuli and drew their own conclusions accordingly.

Yasmina, snuggled warmly in her captor's arms, grew drowsy in spite of herself. The motion of the horse, though it was uneven, uphill and down, yet possessed a certain rhythm which combined with weariness and emotional exhaustion to force sleep on her. She had lost all sense of time or direction. They moved in soft thick darkness, in which she sometimes glimpsed vaguely gigantic walls sweeping up like black ramparts, or great crags shouldering the stars; at times she sensed echoing depths beneath them, or felt the wind of dizzy heights blowing cold about her. Gradually these things faded into a dreamy unwakefulness in which the clink of hoofs and the creak of saddles were like the irrelevant sounds in a dream.

She was vaguely aware when the motion ceased and she was lifted down and carried a few steps. There she was laid down on something soft and rustling, and something—a folded coat, perhaps—was thrust under her head, and the cloak in which she was wrapped was carefully tucked about her. She heard Yar Afzal laugh.

"A rare prize, Conan; fit mate for a chief of the Afghulis."

"Not for me," came Conan's answering rumble. "This wench will buy the lives of my seven headmen, blast their souls."

That was the last she heard as she sank into dreamless slumber.

She slept while armed men rode through the dark hills; and the fate of kingdoms hung in the balance. Through the shadowy gorges and defiles that night there rang the hoofs of galloping horses, and the starlight glimmered on helmets and curved blades, until the ghoulish shapes that haunt the crags stared into the darkness from ravine and boulder and wondered what things were afoot.

A band of these sat gaunt horses in the black pit-mouth of a gorge as the hurrying hoofs swept past. Their leader, a well-built man in a helmet and gilt-braided cloak, held up his hand warningly, until the riders had sped on. Then he laughed softly.

"They must have lost the trail! Or else they have found that Conan has already reached the Afghuli villages. It will take many riders to smoke out that hive. There will be squadrons riding up the Zhaibar by dawn."

"If there is fighting in the hills there will be looting," muttered a voice behind him, in the dialect of the Irakzai.

"There will be looting," answered the man with the helmet. "But first it is our business to reach the valley of Gurashah and await the riders that will be galloping southward from Secunderam before daylight."

He lifted his reins and rode out of the defile, his men falling in behind him—thirty ragged phantoms in the starlight.

5. The Black Stallion

The sun was well up when Yasmina awoke. She did not start and stare blankly, wondering where she was. She awoke with full knowledge of all that had occurred. Her supple limbs were stiff from her long ride, and her firm flesh still seemed to feel the contact of the muscular arm that had borne her so far.

She was lying on a sheepskin covering a pallet of leaves on a
hard-beaten dirt floor. A folded sheepskin coat was under her
head, and she was wrapped in a ragged cloak. She was in a large
room, the walls of which were crudely but strongly built of uncut
rocks, plastered with sun-baked mud. Heavy beams supported a
roof of the same kind, in which showed a trap-door up to which
led a ladder. There were no windows in the thick walls, only
loopholes. There was one door, a sturdy bronze affair that must
have been looted from some Vendhyan border tower. Opposite
it was a wide opening in the wall, with no door, but several
strong wooden bars in place. Beyond them Yasmina saw a
magnificent black stallion munching a pile of dried grass. The
building was fort, dwelling place, and stable in one.

At the other end of the room a girl in the vest and baggy
trousers of a hillwoman squatted beside a small fire, cooking
strips of meat on an iron grid laid over blocks of stone. There
was a sooty cleft in the wall a few feet from the floor, and some
of the smoke found its way out there. The rest floated in blue
wisps about the room.

The hill girl glanced at Yasmina over her shoulder, displaying
a bold, handsome face, and then continued her cooking. Voices
boomed outside; then the door was kicked open, and Conan
strode in. He looked more enormous than ever with the morning
sunlight behind him, and Yasmina noted some details that had
escaped her the night before. His garments were clean and not
ragged. The broad Bakhariot girdle that supported his knife in its
ornamented scabbard would have matched the robes of a prince,
and there was a glint of fine Turanian mail under his shirt.

"Your captive is awake, Conan," said the Wazuli girl, and he
grunted, strode up to the fire, and swept the strips of mutton off
into a stone dish.

The squatting girl laughed up at him, with some spicy jest,
and he grinned wolfishly, and hooking a toe under her haunches,
tumbled her sprawling onto the floor. She seemed to derive
considerable amusement from this bit of rough horseplay, but
Conan paid no more heed to her. Producing a great hunk of
bread from somewhere, with a copper jug of wine, he carried the
lot to Yasmina, who had risen from her pallet and was regarding
him doubtfully.

"Rough fare for a Devi, girl, but our best," he grunted. "It
will fill your belly, at least."

He set the platter on the floor, and she was suddenly aware of
a ravenous hunger. Making no comment, she seated herself

cross-legged on the floor, and taking the dish in her lap, she began to eat, using her fingers, which were all she had in the way of table utensils. After all, adaptability is one of the tests of true aristocracy. Conan stood looking down at her, his thumbs hooked in his girdle. He never sat cross-legged, after the Eastern fashion.

"Where am I?" she asked abruptly.

"In the hut of Yar Afzal, the chief of the Khurum Wazulis," he answered. "Afghulistan lies a good many miles farther on to the west. We'll hide here awhile. The Kshatriyas are beating up the hills for you—several of their squads have been cut up by the tribes already."

"What are you going to do?" she asked.

"Keep you until Chundar Shan is willing to trade back my seven cow-thieves," he grunted. "Women of the Wazulis are crushing ink out of *shoki* leaves, and after a while you can write a letter to the governor."

A touch of her old imperious wrath shook her, as she thought how maddeningly her plans had gone awry, leaving her captive of the very man she had plotted to get into her power. She flung down the dish, with the remnants of her meal, and sprang to her feet, tense with anger.

"I will not write a letter! If you do not take me back, they will hang your seven men, and a thousand more besides!"

The Wazuli girl laughed mockingly, Conan scowled, and then the door opened and Yar Afzal came swaggering in. The Wazuli chief was as tall as Conan, and of greater girth, but he looked fat and slow beside his hard compactness of the Cimmerian. He plucked his red-stained beard and stared meaningly at the Wazuli girl, and that wench rose and scurried out without delay. Then Yar Afzal turned to his guest.

"The damnable people murmur, Conan," quoth he. "They wish me to murder you and take the girl to hold for ransom. They say that anyone can tell by her garments that she is a noble lady. They say why should the Afghuli dogs profit by her, when it is the people who take the risk of guarding her?"

"Lend me your horse," said Conan. "I'll take her and go."

"Pish!" boomed Yar Afzal. "Do you think I can't handle my own people? I'll have them dancing in their shirts if they cross me! They don't love you—or any other outlander—but you saved my life once, and I will not forget. Come out, though, Conan; a scout has returned."

Conan hitched at his girdle and followed the chief outside.

They closed the door after them, and Yasmina peeped through a loop-hole. She looked out on a level space before the hut. At the farther end of that space there was a cluster of mud and stone huts, and she saw naked children playing among the boulders, and the slim erect women of the hills going about their tasks.

Directly before the chief's hut a circle of hairy, ragged men squatted, facing the door. Conan and Yar Afzal stood a few paces before the door, and between them and the ring of warriors another man sat cross-legged. This one was addressing his chief in the harsh accents of the Wazuli which Yasmina could scarcely understand, though as part of her royal education she had been taught the languages of Iranistan and the kindred tongues of Ghulistan.

"I talked with a Dagozai who saw the riders last night," said the scout. "He was lurking near when they came to the spot where we ambushed the lord Conan. He overheard their speech. Chunder Shan was with them. They found the dead horse, and one of the men recognized it as Conan's. Then they found the man Conan slew, and knew him for a Wazuli. It seemed to them that Conan had been slain and the girl taken by the Wazuli; so they turned aside from their purpose of following to Afghulistan. But they did not know from which village the dead man was come, and we had left no trail a Kshatriya could follow.

"So they rode to the nearest Wazuli village, which was the village of Jugra, and burnt it and slew many of the people. But the men of Khojur came upon them in darkness and slew some of them, and wounded the governor. So the survivors retired down the Zhaibar in the darkness before dawn, but they returned with reinforcements before sunrise, and there has been skirmishing and fighting in the hills all morning. It is said that a great army is being raised to sweep the hills about the Zhaibar. The tribes are whetting their knives and laying ambushes in every pass from here to Gurashah valley. Moreover, Kerim Shah has returned to the hills."

A grunt went around the circle, and Yasmina leaned closer to the loop-hole at the name she had begun to mistrust.

"Where went he?" demanded Yar Afzal.

"The Dagozai did not know; with him were thirty Irakzai of the lower villages. They rode into the hills and disappeared."

"These Irakzai are jackals that follow a lion for crumbs," growled Yar Afzal. "They have been lapping up the coins Kerim Shah scatters among the border tribes to buy men like horses. I like him not, for all he is our kinsman from Iranistan."

"He's not even that," said Conan. "I know him of old. He's an Hyrkanian, a spy of Yezdigerd's. If I catch him I'll hang his hide to a tamarisk."

"But the Kshatriyas!" clamored the men in the semi-circle. "Are we to squat on our haunches until they smoke us out? They will learn at last in which Wazuli village the wench is held. We are not loved by the Zhaibari; they will help the Kshatriyas hunt us out."

"Let them come," grunted Yar Afzal. "We can hold the defiles against a host."

One of the men leaped up and shook his fist at Conan.

"Are we to take all the risks while he reaps the rewards?" he howled. "Are we to fight his battles for him?"

With a stride Conan reached him and bent slightly to stare full into his hairy face. The Cimmerian had not drawn his long knife, but his left hand grasped the scabbard, jutting the hilt suggestively forward.

"I ask no man to fight my battles," he said softly. "Draw your blade if you dare, you yapping dog!"

The Wazuli started back, snarling like a cat.

"Dare to touch me and here are fifty men to rend you apart!" he screeched.

"What!" roared Yar Afzal, his face purpling with wrath. His whiskers bristled, his belly swelled with his rage. "Are you chief of Khurum? Do the Wazulis take orders from Yar Afzal, or from a low-bred cur?"

The man cringed before his invincible chief, and Yar Afzal, striding up to him, seized him by the throat and choked him until his face was turning black. Then he hurled the man savagely against the ground and stood over him with his tulwar in his hand.

"Is there any who questions my authority?" he roared, and his warriors looked down sullenly as his bellicose glare swept their semicircle. Yar Afzal grunted scornfully and sheathed his weapon with a gesture that was the apex of insult. Then he kicked the fallen agitator with a concentrated vindictiveness that brought howls from his victim.

"Get down the valley to the watchers on the heights and bring word if they have seen anything," commanded Yar Afzal, and the man went, shaking with fear and grinding his teeth with fury.

Yar Afzal then seated himself ponderously on a stone, growling in his beard. Conan stood near him, legs braced apart, thumbs hooked in his girdle, narrowly watching the assembled warriors. They stared at him sullenly, not daring to brave Yar Afzal's fury, but hating the foreigner as only a hillman can hate.

"Now listen to me, you sons of nameless dogs, while I tell you what the lord Conan and I have planned to fool the Kshatriyas" —the boom of Yar Afzal's bull-like voice followed the discomfited warrior as he slunk away from the assembly.

The man passed by the cluster of huts, where women who had seen his defeat laughed at him and called stinging comments, and hastened on along the trail that wound among spurs and rocks toward the valley head.

Just as he rounded the first turn that took him out of sight of the village, he stopped short, gaping stupidly. He had not believed it possible for a stranger to enter the valley of Khurum without being detected by the hawk-eyed watchers along the heights; yet a man sat cross-legged on a low ledge beside the path—a man in a camel-hair robe and a green turban.

The Wazuli's mouth gaped for a yell, and his hand leaped to his knife-hilt. But at that instant his eyes met those of the stranger and the cry died in his throat, his fingers went limp. He stood like a statue, his own eyes glazed and vacant.

For minutes the scene held motionless; then the man on the ledge drew a cryptic symbol in the dust on the rock with his forefinger. The Wazuli did not see him place anything within the compass of that emblem, but presently something gleamed there—a round, shiny black ball that looked like polished jet. The man in the green turban took this up and tossed it the Wazuli, who mechanically caught it.

"Carry this to Yar Afzal," he said, and the Wazuli turned like an automaton and went back along the path, holding the black jet ball in his outstretched hand. He did not even turn his head to the renewed jeers of the women as he passed the huts. He did not seem to hear.

The man on the ledge gazed after him with a cryptic smile. A girl's head rose above the rim of the ledge and she looked at him with admiration and a touch of fear that had not been present the night before.

"Why did you do that?" she asked.

He ran his fingers through her dark locks caressingly.

"Are you still dizzy from your flight on the horse-of-air, that you doubt my wisdom?" he laughed. "As long as Yar Afzal lives, Conan will bide safe among the Wazuli fighting-men. Their knives are sharp, and there are many of them. What I plot will be safer, even for me, than to seek to slay him and take her

from among them. It takes no wizard to predict what the Wazulis
will do, and what Conan will do, when my victim hands the
globe of Yezud to the chief of Khurum.''

Back before the hut, Yar Afzal halted in the midst of some
tirade, surprised and displeased to see the man he had sent up the
valley, pushing his way through the throng.

''I bade you go to the watchers!'' the chief bellowed. ''You
have not had time to come from them.''

The other did not reply; he stood woodenly, staring vacantly
into the chief's face, his palm outstretched holding the jet ball.
Conan, looking over Yar Afzal's shoulder, murmured something
and reached to touch the chief's arm, but as he did so, Yar
Afzal, in a paroxysm of anger, struck the man with his clenched
fist and felled him like an ox. As he fell, the jet sphere rolled to
Yar Afzal's foot, and the chief, seeming to see it for the first
time, bent and picked it up. The men, staring perplexedly at their
senseless comrade, saw their chief bend, but they did not see
what he picked up from the ground.

Yar Afzal straightened, glanced at the jet, and made a motion
to thrust it into his girdle.

''Carry that fool to his hut,'' he growled. ''He has the look of
a lotus-eater. He returned me a blank stare. I—*aie!*''

In his right hand, moving toward his girdle, he had suddenly
felt movement where movement should not be. His voice died
away as he stood and glared at nothing; and inside his clenched
right hand he felt the quivering of *change*, of *motion*, of *life*. He
no longer held a smooth shining sphere in his fingers. And he
dared not look; his tongue clove to the roof of his mouth, and he
could not open his hand. His astonished warriors saw Yar Afzal's
eyes distend, the color ebb from his face. Then suddenly a
bellow of agony burst from his bearded lips; he swayed and fell
as if struck by lightning, his right arm tossed out in front of him.
Face down, he lay, and from between his opening fingers crawled
a spider—a hideous, black, hairy-legged monster whose body
shone like black jet. The men yelled and gave back suddenly,
and the creature scuttled into a crevice of the rocks and disappeared.

The warriors started up, glaring wildly, and a voice rose above
their clamor, a far-carrying voice of command which came from
none knew where. Afterward each man there—who still lived—
denied that he had shouted, but all there heard it.

''Yar Afzal is dead! Kill the outlander!''

That shout focused their whirling minds as one. Doubt, bewil-

derment and fear vanished in the uproaring surge of the blood-
lust. A furious yell rent the skies as the tribesmen responded
instantly to the suggestion. They came headlong across the open
space, cloaks flapping, eyes blazing, knives lifted.

Conan's action was as quick as theirs. As the voice shouted he
sprang·for the hut door. But they were closer to him than he was
to the door, and with one foot on the sill he had to wheel and
parry the swipe of a yard-long blade. He split the man's skull—
ducked another swinging knife and gutted the wielder—felled a
man with his left fist and stabbed another in the belly—and
heaved back mightily against the closed door with his shoulders.
Hacking blades were nicking chips out of the jambs about his
ears, but the door flew open under the impact of his shoulders,
and he went stumbling backward into the room. A bearded
tribesman, thrusting with all his fury as Conan sprang back,
over-reached and pitched headfirst through the doorway. Conan
stooped, grasped the slack of his garments and hauled him clear,
and slammed the door in the faces of the men who came surging
into it. Bones snapped under the impact, and the next instant
Conan slammed the bolts into place and whirled with desperate
haste to meet the man, who sprang from the floor and tore into
action like a madman.

Yasmina cowered in a corner, staring in horror as the two men
fought back and forth across the room, almost trampling her at
times; the flash and clangor of their blades filled the room, and
outside the mob clamored like a wolf-pack, hacking deafeningly
at the bronze door with their long knives, and dashing huge
rocks against it. Somebody fetched a tree trunk, and the door
began to stagger under the thunderous assault. Yasmina clasped
her ears, staring wildly. Violence and fury within, cataclysmic
madness without. The stallion in his stall neighed and reared,
thundering with his heels against the walls. He wheeled and
launched his hoofs through the bars just as the tribesman, back-
ing away from Conan's murderous swipes, stumbled against
them. His spine cracked in three places like a rotten branch and
he was hurled headlong against the Cimmerian, bearing him
backward so that they both crashed to the beaten floor.

Yasmina cried out and ran forward; to her dazed sight it
seemed that both were slain. She reached them just as Conan
threw aside the corpse and rose. She caught his arm, trembling
from head to foot.

"Oh, you live! I thought—I thought you were dead!"

He glanced down at her quickly, into the pale, upturned face and the wide staring dark eyes.

"Why are you trembling?" he demanded. "Why should you care if I live or die?"

A vestige of her poise returned to her, and she drew away, making a rather pitiful attempt at playing the Devi.

"You are preferable to those wolves howling without," she answered, gesturing toward the door, the stone sill of which was beginning to splinter away.

"That won't hold long," he muttered, then turned and went swiftly to the stall of the stallion.

Yasmina clenched her hands and caught her breath as she saw him tear aside the splintered bars and go into the stall with the maddened beast. The stallion reared above him, neighing terribly, hoofs lifted, eyes and teeth flashing and ears laid back, but Conan leaped and caught his mane with a display of sheer strength that seemed impossible, and dragged the beast down on his forelegs. The steed snorted and quivered, but stood still while the man bridled him and clapped on the gold-worked saddle, with the wide silver stirrups.

Wheeling the beast around in the stall, Conan called quickly to Yasmina, and the girl came, sidling nervously past the stallion's heels. Conan was working at the stone wall, talking swiftly as he worked.

"A secret door in the wall here, that not even the Wazuli know about. Yar Afzal showed it to me once when he was drunk. It opens out into the mouth of the ravine behind the hut. Ha!"

As he tugged at a projection that seemed casual, a whole section of the wall slid back on oiled iron runners. Looking through, the girl saw a narrow defile opening in a sheer stone cliff within a few feet of the hut's back wall. Then Conan sprang into the saddle and hauled her up before him. Behind them the great door groaned like a living thing and crashed in, and a yell rang to the roof as the entrance was instantly flooded with hairy faces and knives in hairy fists. And then the great stallion went through the wall like a javelin from a catapult, and thundered into the defile, running low, foam flying from the bit-rings.

That move came as an absolute surprise to the Wazulis. It was a surprise, too, to those stealing down the ravine. It happened so quickly—the hurricane-like charge of the great horse—that a man in a green turban was unable to get out of the way. He went down under the frantic hoofs, and a girl screamed. Conan got one

glimpse of her as they thundered by—a slim, dark girl in silk
trousers and a jeweled breast-band, flattening herself against the
ravine wall. Then the black horse and his riders were gone up the
gorge like the spume blown before a storm, and the men who
came tumbling through the wall into the defile after them met
that which changed their yells of bloodlust to shrill screams of
fear and death.

6. The Mountain of the Black Seers

"Where now?" Yasmina was trying to sit erect on the rocking
saddlebow, clutching her captor. She was conscious of a recognition of shame that she should not find unpleasant the feel of his
muscular flesh under her fingers.

"To Afghulistan," he answered. "It's a perilous road, but the
stallion will carry us easily, unless we fall in with some of your
friends, or my tribal enemies. Now that Yar Afzal is dead, those
damned Wazulis will be on our heels. I'm surprised we haven't
sighted them behind us already."

"Who was that man you rode down?" she asked.

"I don't know. I never saw him before. He's no Ghuli, that's
certain. What the devil he was doing there is more than I can
say. There was a girl with him, too."

"Yes." Her gaze was shadowed. "I can not understand that.
That girl was my maid, Gitara. Do you suppose she was coming
to aid me? That the man was a friend? If so, the Wazulis have
captured them both."

"Well," he answered, "there's nothing we can do. If we go
back, they'll skin us both. I can't understand how a girl like that
could get this far into the mountains with only one man—and he
a robed scholar, for that's what he looked like. There's something infernally queer in all this. That fellow Yar Afzal beat and
sent away—he moved like a man walking in his sleep. I've seen
the priests of Zamora perform their abominable rituals in their
forbidden temples, and their victims had a stare like that man.
The priests looked into their eyes and muttered incantations, and
then the people became like walking dead men, with glassy eyes,
doing as they ordered.

"And then I saw what the fellow had in his hand, which Yar
Afzal picked up. It was like a big black jet bead, such as the
temple girls of Yezud wear when they dance before the black
stone spider which is their god. Yar Afzal held it in his hand,
and he didn't pick up anything else. Yet when he fell dead, a

spider, like the god at Yezud, only smaller, ran out of his fingers. And then, when the Wazulis stood uncertain there, a voice cried out for them to kill me, and I know that voice didn't come from any of the warriors, nor from the women who watched by the huts. It seemed to come from *above*."

Yasmina did not reply. She glanced at the stark outlines of the mountains all about them and shuddered. Her soul shrank from their gaunt brutality. This was a grim, naked land where anything might happen. Age-old traditions invested it with shuddery horror for anyone born in the hot, luxuriant southern plains.

The sun was high, beating down with fierce heat, yet the wind that blew in fitful gusts seemed to sweep off slopes of ice. Once she heard a strange rushing above them that was not the sweep of the wind, and from the way Conan looked up, she knew it was not a common sound to him, either. She thought that a strip of the cold blue sky was momentarily blurred, as if some all but invisible object had swept between it and herself, but she could not be sure. Neither made any comment, but Conan loosened his knife in his scabbard.

They were following a faintly marked path dipping down into ravines so deep the sun never struck bottom, laboring up steep slopes where loose shale threatened to slide from beneath their feet, and following knife-edge ridges with blue-hazed echoing depths on either hand.

The sun had passed its zenith when they crossed a narrow trail winding among the crags. Conan reined the horse aside and followed it southward, going almost at right angles to their former course.

"A Galzai village is at one end of the trail," he explained. "Their women follow it to a well, for water. You need new garments."

Glancing down at her filmy attire, Yasmina agreed with him. Her cloth-of-gold slippers were in tatters, her robes and silken under-garments torn to shreds that scarcely held together decently. Garments meant for the streets of Peshkhauri were scarcely appropriate for the crags of the Himelians.

Coming to a crook in the trail, Conan dismounted, helped Yasmina down and waited. Presently he nodded, though she heard nothing.

"A woman coming along the trail," he remarked. In sudden panic she clutched his arm.

"You will not—not kill her?"

"I don't kill women ordinarily," he grunted; "though some of these hillwomen are she-wolves. No," he grinned as at a huge jest. "By Crom, I'll *pay* for her clothes! How is that?" He displayed a handful of gold coins, and replaced all but the largest. She nodded, much relieved. It was perhaps natural for men to slay and die; her flesh crawled at the thought of watching the butchery of a woman

Presently, a woman appeared around the crook of the trail—a tall, slim Galzai girl, straight as a young sapling, bearing a great empty gourd. She stopped short and the gourd fell from her hands when she saw them; she wavered as though to run, then realized that Conan was too close to her to allow her to escape, and so stood still, staring at them with a mixed expression of fear and curiosity.

Conan displayed the gold coin.

"If you will give this woman your garments," he said, "I will give you this money."

The response was instant. The girl smiled broadly with surprise and delight, and, with the disdain of a hillwoman for prudish conventions, promptly yanked off her sleeveless embroidered vest, slipped down her wide trousers and stepped out of them, twitched off her wide-sleeved shirt, and kicked off her sandals. Bundling them all in a bunch, she proffered them to Conan, who handed them to the astonished Devi.

"Get behind that rock and put these on," he directed, further proving himself no native hillman. "Fold your robes up into a bundle and bring them to me when you come out."

"The money!" clamored the hill girl, stretching out her hands eagerly. "The gold you promised me!"

Conan flipped the coin to her, she caught it, bit, then thrust it into her hair, bent and caught up the gourd and went on down the path, as devoid of self-consciousness as of garments. Conan waited with some impatience while the Devi, for the first time in her pampered life, dressed herself. When she stepped from behind the rock he swore in surprise, and she felt a curious rush of emotions at the unrestrained admiration burning in his fierce blue eyes. She felt shame, embarrassment, yet a stimulation of vanity she had never before experienced, and a tingling when meeting the impact of his eyes. He laid a heavy hand on her shoulder and turned her about, staring avidly at her from all angles.

"By Crom!" said he. "In those smoky, mystic robes you were aloof and cold and far off as a star! Now you are a woman of warm flesh and blood! You went behind that rock as the Devi of Vendhya; you come out as a hill girl—though a thousand times more beautiful than any wench of the Zhaibar! You were a goddess—now you are real!''

He spanked her resoundingly, and she, recognizing this as merely another expression of admiration, did not feel outraged. It was indeed as if the changing of her garments had wrought a change in her personality. The feelings and sensations she had suppressed rose to domination in her now, as if the queenly robes she had cast off had been material shackles and inhibitions.

But Conan, in his renewed admiration, did not forget that peril lurked all about them. The farther they drew away from the region of the Zhaibar, the less likely he was to encounter any Kshatriya troops. On the other hand, he had been listening all throughout their flight for sounds that would tell him the vengeful Wazulis of Khurum were on their heels.

Swinging the Devi up, he followed her into the saddle and again reined the stallion westward. The bundle of garments she had given him, he hurled over a cliff, to fall into the depths of a thousand-foot gorge.

"Why did you do that?" she asked. "Why did you not give them to the girl?"

"The riders from Peshkhauri are combing these hills," he said. "They'll be ambushed and harried at every turn, and by way of reprisal they'll destroy every village they can take. They may turn westward any time. If they found a girl wearing your garments, they'd torture her into talking, and she might put them on my trail."

"What will she do?" asked Yasmina.

"Go back to her village and tell her people that a stranger attacked her," he answered. "She'll have them on our track, all right. But she had to go on and get the water first; if she dared go back without it, they'd whip the skin off her. That gives us a long start. They'll never catch us. By nightfall we'll cross the Afghuli border."

"There are no paths or signs of human habitation in these parts," she commented. "Even for the Himelians this region seems singularly deserted. We have not seen a trail since we left the one where we met the Galzai woman."

For answer he pointed to the northwest, where she glimpsed a peak in a notch of the crags.

"Yimsha," grunted Conan. "The tribes build their villages as far from that mountain as they can."

She was instantly rigid with attention.

"Yimsha!" she whispered. "The mountain of the Black Seers!"

"So they say," he answered. "This is as near as I ever approached it. I have swung north to avoid any Kshatriya troops that might be prowling through the hills. The regular trail from Khurum to Afghulistan lies farther south. This is an ancient one, and seldom used."

She was staring intently at the distant peak. Her nails bit into her pink palms.

"How long would it take to reach Yimsha from this point?"

"All the rest of the day, and all night," he answered, and grinned. "Do you want to go there? By Crom, it's no place for an ordinary human, from what the hill people say."

"Why do they not gather and destroy the devils that inhabit it?" she demanded.

"Wipe out wizards with swords? Anyway, they never interfere with people, unless the people interfere with them. I never saw one of them, though I've talked with men who swore they had. They say they've glimpsed people from the tower among the crags at sunset or sunrise—tall, silent men in black robes."

"Would you be afraid to attack them?"

"I?" The idea seemed a new one to him. "Why, if they imposed upon me, it would be my life or theirs. But I have nothing to do with them. I came to these mountains to raise a following of human beings, not to war with wizards."

Yasmina did not at once reply. She stared at the peak as at a human enemy, feeling all her anger and hatred stir in her bosom anew. And another feeling began to take dim shape. She had plotted to hurl against the masters of Yimsha the man in whose arms she was now carried. Perhaps there was another way, besides the method she had planned, to accomplish her purpose. She could not mistake the look that was beginning to dawn in this wild man's eyes as they rested on her. Kingdoms have fallen when a woman's slim white hands pulled the strings of destiny. Suddenly she stiffened, pointing.

"Look!"

Just visible on the distant peak there hung a cloud of peculiar aspect. It was a frosty crimson in color, veined with sparkling gold. This cloud was in motion; it rotated, and as it whirled it contracted. It dwindled to a spinning taper that flashed in the sun. And suddenly it detached itself from the snow-tipped peak, floated out over the void like a gay-hued feather, and became invisible against the cerulean sky.

"What could that have been?" asked the girl uneasily, as a shoulder of rock shut the distant mountain from view; the phenomenon had been disturbing, even its beauty.

"The hillmen call it Yimsha's Carpet, whatever that means," answered Conan. "I've seen five hundred of them running as if the devil were at their heels, to hide themselves in caves and crags, because they saw that crimson cloud float up from the peak. What in——"

They had advanced through a narrow, knife-cut gash between turreted walls and emerged upon a broad ledge, flanked by a series of rugged slopes on one hand, and a gigantic precipice on the other. The dim trail followed this ledge, bent around a shoulder and reappeared at intervals far below, working a tedious way downward. And emerging from the gut that opened upon the ledge, the black stallion halted short, snorting. Conan urged him on impatiently, and the horse snorted and threw his head up and down, quivering and straining as if against an invisible barrier.

Conan swore and swung off, lifting Yasmina down with him. He went forward, with a hand thrown out before him as if expecting to encounter unseen resistance, but there was nothing to hinder him, though when he tried to lead the horse, it neighed shrilly and jerked back. Then Yasmina cried out, and Conan wheeled, hand starting to knife-hilt.

Neither of them had seen him come, but he stood there, with his arms folded, a man in a camel-hair robe and a green turban. Conan grunted with surprise to recognize the man the stallion had spurned in the ravine outside the Wazuli village.

"Who the devil are you?" he demanded.

The man did not answer. Conan noticed that his eyes were wide, fixed, and of a peculiar luminous quality. And those eyes held his like a magnet.

Khemsa's sorcery was based on hypnotism, as is the case with most Eastern magic. The way has been prepared for the hypnotist for untold centuries of generations who have lived and died in the firm conviction of the reality and power of hypnotism, building up, by mass thought and practice, a colossal though intangible atmosphere against which the individual, steeped in the traditions of the land, finds himself helpless.

But Conan was not a son of the East. Its traditions were meaningless to him; he was the product of an utterly alien atmosphere. Hypnotism was not even a myth in Cimmeria. The heritage that prepared a native of the East for submission to the mesmerist was not his.

He was aware of what Khemsa was trying to do to him; but he felt the impact of the man's uncanny power only as a vague impulsion, a tugging and pulling that he could shake off as a man shakes spider webs from his garments.

Aware of hostility and black magic, he ripped out his long knife and lunged, as quick on his feet as a mountain lion.

But hypnotism was not all of Khemsa's magic. Yasmina, watching, did not see by what roguery of movement or illusion the man in the green turban avoided the terrible disemboweling thrust. But the keen blade whickered between side and lifted arm, and to Yasmina it seemed that Khemsa merely brushed his open palm lightly against Conan's bullneck. But the Cimmerian went down like a slain ox.

Yet Conan was not dead; breaking his fall with his left hand, he slashed at Khemsa's legs even as he went down, and the Rakhsha avoided the scythe-like swipe only by a most unwizardly bound backward. Then Yasmina cried out sharply as she saw a woman she recognized as Gitara glide out from among the rocks and come up to the man. The greeting died in the Devi's throat as she saw the malevolence in the girl's beautiful face.

Conan was rising slowly, shaken and dazed by the cruel craft of that blow which, delivered with an art forgotten of men before Atlantis sank, would have broken like a rotten twig the neck of a lesser man. Khemsa gazed at him cautiously and a trifle uncertainly. The Rakhsha had learned the full flood of his own power when he faced at bay the knives of the maddened Wazulis in the ravine behind Khurum village; but the Cimmerian's resistance had perhaps shaken his newfound confidence a trifle. Sorcery thrives on success, not on failure.

He stepped forward, lifting his hand—then halted as if frozen, head tilted back, eyes wide open, hand raised. In spite of himself Conan followed his gaze, and so did the women—the girl cowering by the trembling stallion, and the girl beside Khemsa.

Down the mountain slopes, like a whirl of shining dust blown before the wind, a crimson, conoid cloud came dancing. Khemsa's dark face turned ashen; his hand began to tremble, then sank to his side. The girl beside him, sensing the change in him, stared at him inquiringly.

The crimson shape left the mountain slope and came down in a long arching swoop. It struck the ledge between Conan and Khemsa, and the Rakhsha gave back with a stifled cry. He backed away, pushing the girl Gitara back with groping, fending hands.

The crimson cloud balanced like a spinning top for an instant, whirling in a dazzling sheen on its point. Then without warning it was gone, vanished as a bubble vanishes when burst. There on the ledge stood four men. It was miraculous, incredible, impossible, yet it was true. They were not ghosts or phantoms. They were four tall men, with shaven, vulture-like heads, and black robes that hid their feet. Their hands were concealed by their wide sleeves. They stood in silence, their naked heads nodding slightly in unison. They were facing Khemsa, but behind them Conan felt his own blood turning to ice in his veins. Rising, he backed stealthily away, until he felt the stallion's shoulder trembling against his back, and the Devi crept into the shelter of his arm. There was no word spoken. Silence hung like a stifling pall.

All four of the men in black robes stared at Khemsa. Their vulture-like faces were immobile, their eyes introspective and contemplative. But Khemsa shook like a man in an ague. His feet were braced on the rock, his calves straining as if in physical combat. Sweat ran in streams down his dark face. His right hand locked on something under his brown robe so desperately that the blood ebbed from that hand and left it white. His left hand fell on the shoulder of Gitara and clutched in agony like the grasp of a drowning man. She did not flinch or whimper, though his fingers dug like talons into her firm flesh.

Conan had witnessed hundreds of battles in his wild life, but never one like this, wherein four diabolical wills sought to beat down one lesser but equally devilish will that opposed them. But he only faintly sensed the monstrous quality of that hideous struggle. With his back to the wall, driven to bay by his former masters, Khemsa was fighting for his life with all the dark power, all the frightful knowledge they had taught him through long, grim years of neophytism and vassalage.

He was stronger than even he had guessed, and the free exercise of his powers in his own behalf had tapped unsuspected reservoirs of forces. And he was nerved to super-energy by frantic fear and desperation. He reeled before the merciless impact of those hypnotic eyes, but he held his ground. His features were distorted into a bestial grin of agony, and his limbs were twisted as in a rack. It was a war of souls, of frightful brains steeped in lore forbidden to men for a million years, of mentalities which had plumbed the abysses and explored the dark stars where spawn the shadows.

Yasmina understood this better than did Conan. And she dimly understood why Khemsa could withstand the concentrated impact of those four hellish wills which might have blasted into atoms the very rock on which he stood. The reason was the girl that he clutched with the strength of his despair. She was like an anchor to his staggering soul, battered by the waves of those psychic emanations. His weakness was now his strength. His love for the girl, violent and evil though it might be, was yet a tie that bound him to the rest of humanity, providing an earthly leverage for his will, a chain that his inhuman enemies could not break; at least not break through Khemsa.

They realized that before he did. And one of them turned his gaze from the Rakhsha full upon Gitara. There was no battle there. The girl shrank and wilted like a leaf in the drought. Irresistibly impelled, she tore herself from her lover's arms before he realized what was happening. Then a hideous thing came to pass. She began to back toward the precipice, facing her tormentors, her eyes wide and blank as dark gleaming glass from behind which a lamp has been blown out. Khemsa groaned and staggered toward her, falling into the trap set for him. A divided mind could not maintain the unequal battle. He was beaten, a straw in their hands. The girl went backward, walking like an automaton, and Khemsa reeled drunkenly after her, hands vainly outstretched, groaning, slobbering in his pain, his feet moving heavily like dead things.

On the very brink she paused, standing stiffly, her heels on the edge, and he fell on his knees and crawled whimpering toward her, groping for her, to drag her back from destruction. And just before his clumsy fingers touched her, one of the wizards laughed, like the sudden, bronze note of a bell in Hell. The girl reeled suddenly and, consummate climax of exquisite cruelty, reason and understanding flooded back into her eyes, which flared with awful fear. She screamed, clutched wildly at her lover's straining hands, and then, unable to save herself, fell headlong with a moaning cry.

Khemsa hauled himself to the edge and stared over, haggardly, his lips working as he mumbled to himself. Then he turned and stared for a long minute at his torturers, with wide eyes that held no human light. And then with a cry that almost burst the rocks, he reeled up and came rushing toward them, a knife lifted in his hand.

One of the Rakhshas stepped forward and stamped his foot, and as he stamped, there came a rumbling that grew swiftly to a grinding roar. Where his foot struck, a crevice opened in the solid rock that widened instantly. Then, with a deafening crash, a whole section of the ledge gave way. There was a last glimpse of Khemsa, with arms wildly upflung, and then he vanished amidst the roar of the avalanche that thundered down into the abyss.

The four looked contemplatively at the ragged edge of the rock that formed the new rim of the precipice, and then turned suddenly. Conan, thrown off his feet by the shudder of the mountain, was rising, lifting Yasmina. He seemed to move as slowly as his brain was working. He was befogged and stupid. He realized that there was desperate need for him to lift the Devi on the black stallion, and ride like the wind, but an unaccountable sluggishness weighed his every thought and action.

And now the wizards had turned toward him; they raised their arms, and to his horrified sight, he saw their outlines fading, dimming, becoming hazy and nebulous, as a crimson smoke billowed around their feet and rose about them. They were blotted out by a sudden whirling cloud—and then he realized that he too was enveloped in a blinding crimson mist—he heard Yasmina scream, and the stallion cried out like a woman in pain. The Devi was torn from his arm, and as he lashed out with his knife blindly, a terrific blow like a gust of storm wind knocked him sprawling against a rock. Dazedly he saw a crimson conoid cloud spinning up and over the mountain slopes. Yasmina was gone, and so were the four men in black. Only the terrified stallion shared the ledge with him.

7. On to Yimsha

As mists vanish before a strong wind, the cobwebs vanished from Conan's brain. With a searing curse he leaped into the saddle and the stallion reared neighing beneath him. He glared up the slopes, hesitated, and then turned down the trail in the direction he had been going when halted by Khemsa's trickery. But now he did not ride at a measured gait. He shook loose the reins and the stallion went like a thunderbolt, as if frantic to lose hysteria in violent physical exertion. Across the ledge and around the crag and down the narrow trail threading the great steep they plunged at breakneck speed. The path followed a fold of rock, winding interminably down from tier to tier of striated escarpment, and once, far below, Conan got a glimpse of the ruin that had fallen—a mighty pile of broken stone and boulders at the foot of a gigantic cliff.

The valley floor was still far below him when he reached a

long and lofty ridge that led out from the slope like a natural causeway. Out upon this he rode, with an almost sheer drop on either hand. He could trace ahead of him the trail he had to follow; far ahead it dropped down from the ridge and made a great horseshoe back into the river bed at his left hand. He cursed the necessity of traversing those miles, but it was the only way. To try to descend to the lower lap of the trail here would be to attempt the impossible. Only a bird could get to the river-bed with a whole neck.

So he urged on the wearying stallion, until a clink of hoofs reached his ears, welling up from below. Pulling up short and reining to the lip of the cliff, he stared down into the dry river-bed that wound along the foot of the ridge. Along that gorge rode a motley throng—bearded men on half-wild horses, five hundred strong, bristling with weapons. And Conan shouted suddenly, leaning over the edge of the cliff, three hundred feet above them.

At his shout they reined back, and five hundred bearded faces were tilted up toward him; a deep, clamorous roar filled the canyon. Conan did not waste words.

"I was riding for Ghor!" he roared. "I had not hoped to meet you dogs on the trail. Follow me as fast as your nags can push! I'm going to Yimsha, and——"

"Traitor!" The howl was like a dash of ice-water in his face.

"What?" He glared down at them, jolted speechless. He saw wild eyes blazing up at him, faces contorted with fury, fists brandishing blades.

"Traitor!" they roared back, wholeheartedly. "Where are the seven chiefs held captive in Peshkhauri?"

"Why, in the governor's prison, I suppose," he answered.

A bloodthirsty yell from a hundred throats answered him with such a waving of weapons and a clamor that he could not understand what they were saying. He beat down the din with a bull-like roar, and bellowed: "What devil's play is this? Let one of you speak, so I can understand what you mean!"

A gaunt old chief elected himself to this position, shook his tulwar at Conan as a preamble, and shouted accusingly: "You would not let us go raiding Peshkhauri to rescue our brothers!"

"No, you fools!" roared the exasperated Cimmerian. "Even if you'd breached the wall, which is unlikely, they'd have hanged the prisoners before you could reach them."

"And you went alone to traffic with the governor!" yelled the Afghuli, working himself into a frothing frenzy.

"Well?"

"Where are the seven chiefs?" howled the old chief, making his tulwar into a glimmering wheel of steel about his head. "Where are they? Dead!"

"What!" Conan nearly fell off his horse in his surprise.

"Aye, dead!" five hundred bloodthirsty voices assured him.

The old chief brandished his arms and got the floor again. "They were not hanged!" he screeched. "A Wazuli in another cell saw them die! The governor sent a wizard to slay them by craft!"

"That must be a lie," said Conan. "The governor would not dare. Last night I talked with him——"

The admission was unfortunate. A yell of hate and accusation split the skies.

"Aye! You went to him alone! To betray us! It is no lie. The Wazuli escaped through the doors the wizard burst in his entry, and told the tale to our scouts whom he met in the Zhaibar. They had been sent forth to search for you, when you did not return. When they heard the Wazuli's tale, they returned with all haste to Ghor, and we saddled our steeds and girt our swords!"

"And what do you fools mean to do?" demanded the Cimmerian.

"To avenge our brothers!" they howled. "Death to the Kshatriyas! Slay him, brothers, he is a traitor!"

Arrows began to rattle around him. Conan rose in his stirrups, striving to make himself heard above the tumult, and then, with a roar of mingled rage, defiance, and disgust, he wheeled and galloped back up the trail. Behind him and below him the Afghulis came pelting, mouthing their rage, too furious even to remember that the only way they could reach the height whereon he rode was to traverse the river-bed in the other direction, make the broad bend, and follow the twisting trail up over the ridge. When they did remember this, and turned back, their repudiated chief had almost reached the point where the ridge joined the escarpment.

At the cliff he did not take the trail by which he had descended, but turned off on another, a mere trace along a rock-fault, where the stallion scrambled for footing. He had not ridden far when the stallion snorted and shied back from something lying in the trail. Conan stared down on the travesty of a man, a broken, shredded, bloody heap that gibbered and gnashed splintered teeth.

Only the dark gods that rule over the grim destinies of wizards know how Khemsa dragged his shattered body from beneath that awful cairn of fallen rocks and up the steep slope to the trail.

Impelled by some obscure reason, Conan dismounted and stood looking down at the ghastly shape, knowing that he was witness of a thing miraculous and opposed to nature. The Rakhsha lifted his gory head, and his strange eyes, glazed with agony and approaching death, rested on Conan with recognition.

"Where are they?" It was a racking croak not even remotely resembling a human voice.

"Gone back to their damnable castle on Yimsha," grunted Conan. "They took the Devi with them."

"I will go!" muttered the man. "I will follow them! They killed Gitara; I will kill them—the acolytes, the Four of the Black Circle, the Master himself! Kill—kill them all!" He strove to drag his mutilated frame along the rock, but not even his indomitable will could animate that gory mass longer, where the splintered bones hung together only by torn tissue and ruptured fiber.

"Follow them!" raved Khemsa, drooling a bloody slaver. "Follow!"

"I'm going to," growled Conan. "I went to fetch my Afghulis, but they've turned on me. I'm going on to Yimsha alone. I'll have the Devi back if I have to tear down that damned mountain with my bare hands. I didn't think the governor would dare kill my headmen, when I had the Devi, but it seems he did. I'll have his head for that. She's no use to me now as a hostage, but——"

"The curse of Yizil on them!" gasped Khemsa. "Go! I—Khemsa—am dying. Wait—take my girdle."

He tried to fumble with a mangled hand at his tatters, and Conan, understanding what he sought to convey, bent and drew from about his gory waist a girdle of curious aspect.

"Follow the golden vein through the abyss," muttered Khemsa. "Wear the girdle. I had it from a Stygian priest. It will aid you, though it failed me at last. Break the crystal globe with the four golden pomegranates. Beware of the Master's transmutations—I am going to Gitara—she is waiting for me in Hell—*aie, ya Skelos yar!*" And so he died.

Conan stared down at the girdle. The hair of which it was woven was not horsehair. He was convinced that it was woven of the thick black tresses of a woman. Set in the thick mesh were tiny jewels such as he had never seen before. The buckle was strangely made, in the form of a golden serpent head, flat, wedge-shaped, and scaled with curious art. A strong shudder

shook Conan as he handled it, and he turned as though to cast it
over the precipice; then he hesitated, and finally buckled it about
his waist, under the Bakhariot girdle. Then he mounted and
pushed on.

The sun had sunk behind the crags. He climbed the trail in the
vast shadow of the cliffs that was thrown out like a dark blue
mantle over valleys and ridges far below. He was not far from
the crest when, edging around the shoulder of a jutting crag, he
heard the clink of shod hoofs ahead of him. He did not turn
back. Indeed, so narrow was the path that the stallion could not
have wheeled his great body upon it. He rounded the jut of the
rock and came upon a portion of the path that broadened somewhat.
A chorus of threatening yells broke on his ear, but his stallion
pinned a terrified horse hard against the rock, and Conan caught
the arm of the rider in an iron grip, checking the lifted sword in
midair.

"Kerim Shah!" muttered Conan, red glints smoldering luridly
in his eyes. The Turanian did not struggle; they sat their horses
almost breast to breast, Conan's fingers locking the other's
sword arm. Behind Kerim Shah filed a group of lean Irakzai on
gaunt horses. They glared like wolves, fingering bows and knives,
but rendered uncertain because of the narrowness of the path and
the perilous proximity of the abyss that yawned beneath them.

"Where is the Devi?" demanded Kerim Shah.

"What's it to you, you Hyrkanian spy?" snarled Conan.

"I know you have her," answered Kerim Shah. "I was on
my way northward with some tribesmen when we were ambushed by enemies in Shalizah Pass. Many of my men were
slain, and the rest of us harried through the hills like jackals.
When we had beaten off our pursuers, we turned westward,
toward Amir Jehun Pass, and this morning we came upon a
Wazuli wandering through the hills. He was quite mad, but I
learned much from his incoherent gibberings before he died. I
learned that he was the sole survivor of a band which followed a
chief of the Afghulis and a captive Kshatriya woman into a gorge
behind Khurum village. He babbled much of a man in a green
turban whom the Afghuli rode down, but who, when attacked by
the Wazulis who pursued, smote them with a nameless doom
that wiped them out as a gust of wind-driven fire wipes out a
cluster of locusts.

"How that one man escaped, I do not know, nor did he; but I
knew from his maunderings that Conan of Ghor had been in

Khurum with his royal captive. And as we made our way through the hills, we overtook a naked Galzai girl bearing a gourd of water, who told us a tale of having been stripped and ravished by a giant foreigner in the garb of an Afghuli chief, who, she said, gave her garments to a Vendhyan woman who accompanied him. She said you rode westward."

Kerim Shah did not consider it necessary to explain that he had been on his way to keep his rendezvous with the expected troops from Secunderam when he found his way barred by hostile tribesmen. The road to Gurashah valley through Shalizah Pass was longer than the road that wound through Amir Jehun Pass, but the latter traversed part of the Afghuli country, which Kerim Shah had been anxious to avoid until he came with an army. Barred from the Shalizah road, however, he had turned to the forbidden route, until news that Conan had not yet reached Afghulistan with his captive had caused him to turn southward and push on recklessly in the hope of overtaking the Cimmerian in the hills.

"So you had better tell me where the Devi is," suggested Kerim Shah. "We outnumber you—"

"Let one of your dogs nock a shaft and I'll throw you over the cliff," Conan promised. "It wouldn't do you any good to kill me, anyhow. Five hundred Afghulis are on my trail, and if they find you've cheated them, they'll flay you alive. Anyway, I haven't got the Devi. She's in the hands of the Black Seers of Yimsha."

"*Tarim!*" swore Kerim Shah softly, shaken out of his poise for the first time. "Khemsa—"

"Khemsa's dead," grunted Conan. "His masters sent him to Hell on a landslide. And now get out of my way. I'd be glad to kill you if I had the time, but I'm on my way to Yimsha."

"I'll go with you," said the Turanian abruptly.

Conan laughed at him. "Do you think I'd trust you, you Hyrkanian dog?"

"I don't ask you to," returned Kerim Shah. "We both want the Devi. You know my reason; King Yezdigerd desires to add her kingdom to his empire, and herself in his seraglio. And I knew you, in the days when you were a hetman of the *kozak* steppes; so I know your ambition is wholesale plunder. You want to loot Vendhya, and to twist out a huge ransom for Yasmina. Well, let us for the time being, without any illusion about each other, unite our forces, and try to rescue the Devi from the Seers. If we succeed, and live, we can fight it out to see who keeps her."

Conan narrowly scrutinized the other for a moment, and then nodded, releasing the Turanian's arm. "Agreed; what about your men?"

Kerim Shah turned to the silent Irakzai and spoke briefly: "This chief and I are going to Yimsha to fight the wizards. Will you go with us, or stay here to be flayed by the Afghulis who are following this man?"

They looked at him with eyes grimly fatalistic. They were doomed and they knew it—had known it ever since the singing arrows of the ambushed Dagozai had driven them back from the pass of Shalizah. The men of the lower Zhaibar had too many reeking blood-feuds among the crag-dwellers. They were too small a band to fight their way back through the hills to the villages of the border, without the guidance of the crafty Turanian. They counted themselves as dead already, so they made the reply that only dead men would make: "We will go with thee and die on Yimsha."

"Then in Crom's name let us be gone," grunted Conan, fidgeting with impatience as he stared into the blue gulfs of the deepening twilight. "My wolves were hours behind me, but we've lost a devilish lot of time."

Kerim Shah backed his steed from between the black stallion and the cliff, sheathed his sword and cautiously turned the horse. Presently the band was filing up the path as swiftly as they dared. They came out upon the crest nearly a mile east of the spot where Khemsa had halted the Cimmerian and the Devi. The path they had traversed was a perilous one, even for hillmen, and for that reason Conan had avoided it that day when carrying Yasmina, though Kerim Shah, following him, had taken it supposing the Cimmerian had done likewise. Even Conan sighed with relief when the horses scrambled up over the last rim. They moved like phantom riders through an enchanted realm of shadows. The soft creak of leather, the clink of steel marked their passing, then again the dark mountain slopes lay naked and silent in the starlight.

8. *Yasmina Knows Stark Terror*

Yasmina had time but for one scream when she felt herself enveloped in that crimson whirl and torn from her protector with appalling force. She screamed once, and then she had no breath to scream. She was blinded, deafened, rendered mute and eventually senseless by the terrific rushing of the air about her. There was a dazed consciousness of dizzy height and numbing speed, a confused impression of natural sensations gone mad, and then vertigo and oblivion.

A vestige of these sensations clung to her as she recovered consciousness; so she cried out and clutched wildly as though to stay a headlong and involuntary flight. Her fingers closed on soft fabric, and a relieving sense of stability pervaded her. She took cognizance of her surroundings.

She was lying on a dais covered with black velvet. This dais stood in a great, dim room whose walls were hung with dusky tapestries across which crawled dragons reproduced with repellent realism. Floating shadows merely hinted at the lofty ceiling, and gloom that lent itself to illusion lurked in the corners. There seemed to be neither windows nor doors in the walls, or else they were concealed by the nighted tapestries. Where the dim light came from, Yasmina could not determine. The great room was a realm of mysteries, of shadows, and shadowy shapes in which she could not have sworn to observe movement, yet which invaded her mind with a dim and formless terror.

But her gaze fixed itself on a tangible object. On another, smaller dais of jet, a few feet away, a man sat cross-legged, gazing contemplatively at her. His long black velvet robe, embroidered with gold thread, fell loosely about him, masking his figure. His hands were folded in his sleeves. There was a velvet cap upon his head. His face was calm, placid, not unhandsome, his eyes lambent and slightly oblique. He did not move a muscle as he sat regarding her, nor did his expression alter when he saw she was conscious.

Yasmina felt fear crawl like a trickle of ice-water down her supple spine. She lifted herself on her elbows and stared apprehensively at the stranger.

"Who are you?" she demanded. Her voice sounded brittle and inadequate.

"I am Master of Yimsha." The tone was rich and resonant, like the mellow notes of a temple bell.

"Why did you bring me here?" she demanded.

"Were you not seeking me?"

"If you are one of the Black Seers—yes!" she answered recklessly, believing that he could read her thoughts anyway.

He laughed softly, and chills crawled up and down her spine again.

"You would turn the wild children of the hills against the Seers of Yimsha!" he smiled. "I have read it in your mind, princess. Your weak, human mind, filled with petty dreams of hate and revenge.''

"You slew my brother!'' A rising tide of anger was vying with her fear; her hands were clenched, her lithe body rigid. "Why did you persecute him? He never harmed you. The priests say the Seers are above meddling in human affairs. Why did you destroy the king of Vendhya?''

"How can an ordinary human understand the motives of a Seer?'' returned the Master calmly. "My acolytes in the temples of Turan, who are the priests behind the priests of Tarim, urged me to bestir myself in behalf of Yezdigerd. For reasons of my own, I complied. How can I explain my mystic reasons to your puny intellect? You could not understand.''

"I understand this: my brother died!'' Tears of grief and rage shook in her voice. She rose upon her knees and stared at him with wide blazing eyes, as supple and dangerous in that moment as a she-panther.

"As Yezdigerd desired,'' agreed the Master calmly. "For a while it was my whim to further his ambitions.''

"Is Yezdigerd your vassal?'' Yasmina tried to keep the timbre of her voice unaltered. She had felt her knee pressing something hard and symmetrical under a fold of velvet. Subtly she shifted her position, moving her hand under the fold.

"Is the dog that licks up the offal in the temple yard the vassal of the god?'' returned the Master.

He did not seem to notice the actions she sought to dissemble. Concealed by the velvet, her fingers closed on what she knew was the golden hilt of a dagger. She bent her head to hide the light of triumph in her eyes.

"I am weary of Yezdigerd,'' said the Master. "I have turned to other amusements—ha!''

With a fierce cry Yasmina sprang like a jungle cat, stabbing murderously. Then she stumbled and slid to the floor, where she cowered, staring up at the man on the dais. He had not moved; his cryptic smile was unchanged. Tremblingly she lifted her hand and stared at it with dilated eyes. There was no dagger in her fingers; they grasped a stalk of golden lotus, the crushed blossoms drooping on the bruised stem.

She dropped it as if it had been a viper, and scrambled away from the proximity of her tormenter. She returned to her own dais, because that was at least more dignified for a queen than groveling on the floor at the feet of a sorcerer, and eyed him apprehensively, expecting reprisals.

guish her feeble flicker of animate life like a candle blown out in
a storm.

Then there came a period of blind impulse and movement,
when the atom that was she mingled and merged with myraid
other atoms of spawning life in the yeasty morass of existence,
molded by formative forces until she emerged again a conscious
individual, whirling down an endless spiral of lives.

In a mist of terror she relived all her former existences, recognized and *was* again all the bodies that had carried her ego
throughout the changing ages. She bruised her feet again over
the long, weary road of life that stretched out behind her into the
immemorial Past. Back beyond the dimmest dawns of Time she
crouched shuddering in primordial jungles, hunted by slavering
beasts of prey. Skin-clad, she waded thigh-deep in rice-swamps,
battling with squawking waterfowl for the precious grains. She
labored with the oxen to drag the pointed stick through the
stubborn soil, and she crouched endlessly over looms in peasant
huts.

She saw walled cities burst into flame, and fled screaming
before the slayers. She reeled naked and bleeding over burning
sands, dragged at the slaver's stirrup, and she knew the grip of
hot, fierce hands on her writhing flesh, the shame and agony of
brutal lust. She screamed under the bite of the lash, and moaned
on the rack; mad with terror she fought against the hands that
forced her head inexorably down on the bloody block.

She knew the agonies of childbirth, and the bitterness of love
betrayed. She suffered all the woes and wrongs and brutalities
that man has inflicted on woman throughout the eons; and she
endured all the spite and malice of woman for woman. And like
the flick of a fiery whip throughout was the consciousness she
retained of her Devi-ship. She was all the women she had ever
been, yet in her knowing she was Yasmina. This consciousness
was not lost in the throes of reincarnation. At one and the same
time she was a naked slave-wench groveling under the whip, and
the proud Devi of Vendhya. And she suffered not only as the
slave-girl suffered, but as Yasmina, to whose pride the whip was
like a white-hot brand.

Life merged into life in flying chaos, each with its burden of
woe and shame and agony, until she dimly heard her own voice
screaming unbearably, like one long-drawn cry of suffering echoing down the ages.

Then she awakened on the velvet-covered dais in the mystic
room.

In a ghostly gray light she saw again the dais and the cryptic robed figure seated upon it. The hooded head was bent, the high shoulders faintly etched against the uncertain dimness. She could make out no details clearly, but the hood, where the velvet cap had been, stirred a formless uneasiness in her. As she stared, there stole over her a nameless fear that froze her tongue to her palate—a feeling that it was not the Master who sat so silently on that black dais.

Then the figure moved and rose upright, towering above her. It stooped over her and the long arms in their wide black sleeves bent about her. She fought against them in speechless fright, surprised by their lean hardness. The hooded head bent down toward her averted face. And she screamed, and screamed again in poignant fear and loathing. Bony arms gripped her lithe body, and from that hood looked forth a countenance of death and decay—features like rotting parchment on a moldering skull.

She screamed again, and then, as those champing, grinning jaws bent toward her lips, she lost consciousness. . . .

9. *The Castle of the Wizards*

The sun had risen over the white Himelian peaks. At the foot of a long slope, a group of horsemen halted and stared upward. High above them a stone tower poised on the pitch of the mountainside. Beyond and above that gleamed the walls of a greater keep, near the line where the snow began that capped Yimsha's pinnacle. There was a touch of unreality about the whole—purple slopes pitching up to that fantastic castle, toy-like with distance, and above it the white glistening peak shouldering the cold blue.

"We'll leave the horses here," grunted Conan. "That treacherous slope is safer for a man on foot. Besides, they're done."

He swung down from the black stallion which stood with wide-braced legs and drooping head. They had pushed hard throughout the night, gnawing at scraps from saddle-bags, and pausing only to give the horses the rests they had to have.

"That first tower is held by the acolytes of the Black Seers," said Conan. "Or so men say; watch-dogs for their masters—lesser sorcerers. They won't sit sucking their thumbs as we climb this slope."

Kerim Shah glanced up the mountain, then back the way they had come; they were already far up on Yimsha's side, and a vast expanse of lesser peaks and crags spread out beneath them.

Among those labyrinths the Turanian sought in vain for a movement of color that would betray men. Evidently the pursuing Afghulis had lost their chief's trail in the night.

"Let us go, then."

They tied the weary horses in a clump of tamarisk and without further comment turned up the slope. There was no cover. It was a naked incline, strewn with boulders not big enough to conceal a man. But they did conceal something else.

The party had not gone fifty steps when a snarling shape burst from behind a rock. It was one of the gaunt savage dogs that infested the hill villages, and its eyes glared redly, its jaws dripped foam. Conan was leading, but it did not attack him. It dashed past him and leaped at Kerim Shah. The Turanian leaped aside, and the great dog flung itself upon the Irakzai behind him. The man yelled and threw up his arm, which was torn by the brute's fangs as it bore him backward, and the next instant half a dozen tulwars were hacking at the beast. Yet not until it was literally dismembered did the hideous creature cease its efforts to seize and rend its attackers.

Kerim Shah bound up the wounded warrior's gashed arm, looked at him narrowly, and then turned away without a word. He rejoined Conan, and they renewed the climb in silence.

Presently Kerim Shah said: "Strange to find a village dog in this place."

"There's no offal here," grunted Conan.

Both turned their heads to glance back at the wounded warrior toiling after them among his companions. Sweat glistened on his dark face and his lips were drawn back from his teeth in a grimace of pain. Then both looked again at the stone tower squatting above them.

A slumberous quiet lay over the uplands. The tower showed no sign of life, nor did the strange pyramidal structure beyond it. But the men who toiled upward went with the tenseness of men walking on the edge of a crater. Kerim Shah had unslung the powerful Turanian bow that killed at five hundred paces, and the Irakzai looked to their own lighter and less lethal bows.

But they were not within bow-shot of the tower when something shot down out of the sky without warning. It passed so close to Conan that he felt the wind of the rushing wings, but it was an Irakzai who staggered and fell, blood jetting from a severed jugular. A hawk with wings like burnished steel shot up again, blood dripping from the scimitar-beak, to reel against the sky as Kerim Shah's bowstring twanged. It dropped like a plummet, but no man saw where it struck the earth.

Conan bent over the victim of the attack, but the man was already dead. No one spoke; useless to comment on the fact that never before had a hawk been known to swoop on a man. Red rage began to vie with fatalistic lethargy in the wild souls of the Irakzai. Hairy fingers nocked arrows and men glared vengefully at the tower whose very silence mocked them.

But the next attack came swiftly. They all saw it—a white puffball of smoke that tumbled over the tower-rim and came drifting and rolling down the slope toward them. Others followed it. They seemed harmless, mere woolly globes of cloudy foam, but Conan stepped aside to avoid contact with the first. Behind him one of the Irakzai reached out and thrust his sword into the unstable mass. Instantly a sharp report shook the mountainside. There was a burst of blinding flame, and then the puffball had vanished, and of the too-curious warrior remained only a heap of charred and blackened bones. The crisped hand still gripped the ivory sword-hilt, but the blade was gone—melted and destroyed by that awful heat. Yet men standing almost within reach of the victim had not suffered except to be dazzled and half blinded by the sudden flare.

"Steel touches it off," grunted Conan. "Look out—here they come!"

The slope above them was almost covered by the billowing spheres. Kerim Shah bent his bow and sent a shaft into the mass, and those touched by the arrow burst like bubbles in spurting flame. His men followed his example and for the next few minutes it was as if a thunderstorm raged on the mountain slope, with bolts of lightning striking and bursting in showers of flame. When the barrage ceased, only a few arrows were left in the quivers of the archers.

They pushed on grimly, over soil charred and blackened, where the naked rock had in places been turned to lava by the explosion of those diabolical bombs.

Now they were almost within arrowflight of the silent tower, and they spread their line, nerves taut, ready for any horror that might descend upon them.

On the tower appeared a single figure, lifting a ten-foot bronze horn. Its strident bellow roared out across the echoing slopes, like the blare of trumpets on Judgment Day. And it began to be fearfully answered. The ground trembled under the feet of the invaders, and the rumblings and grindings welled up from the subterranean depths.

The Irakzai screamed, reeling like drunken men on the shuddering slope, and Conan, eyes glaring, charged recklessly up the incline, knife in hand, straight at the door that showed in the tower-wall. Above him the great horn roared and bellowed in brutish mockery. And then Kerim Shah drew a shaft to his ear and loosed.

Only a Turanian could have made that shot. The bellowing of the horn ceased suddenly, and a high, thin scream shrilled in its place. The green-robed figure on the tower staggered, clutching at the long shaft which quivered in its bosom, and then pitched across the parapet. The great horn tumbled upon the battlement and hung precariously, and another robed figure rushed to seize it, shrieking in horror. Again the Turanian bow twanged, and again it was answered by a death-howl. The second acolyte, in falling, struck the horn with his elbow and knocked it clattering over the parapet to shatter on the rocks far below.

At such headlong speed had Conan covered the ground that before the clattering echoes of that fall had died away, he was hacking at the door. Warned by his savage instinct, he gave back suddenly as a tide of molten lead splashed down from above. But the next instant he was back again, attacking the panels with redoubled fury. He was galvanized by the fact that his enemies had resorted to earthly weapons. The sorcery of the acolytes was limited. Their necromantic resources might well be exhausted.

Kerim Shah was hurrying up the slope, his hillmen behind him in a straggling crescent. They loosed as they ran, their arrows splintering against the walls or arching over the parapet.

The heavy teak portal gave way beneath the Cimmerian's assault, and he peered inside warily, expecting anything. He was looking into a circular chamber from which a stair wound upward. On the opposite side of the chamber a door gaped open, revealing the outer slope—and the backs of half a dozen green-robed figures in full retreat.

Conan yelled, took a step into the tower, and then native caution jerked him back, just as a great block of stone fell crashing to the floor where his foot had been an instant before. Shouting to his followers, he raced around the tower.

The acolytes had evacuated their first line of defense. As Conan rounded the tower he saw their green robes twinkling up the mountain ahead of him. He gave chase, panting with earnest blood-lust, and behind him Kerim Shah and the Irakzai came pelting, the latter yelling like wolves at the flight of their enemies, their fatalism momentarily submerged by temporary triumph.

The tower stood on the lower edge of a narrow plateau whose upward slant was barely perceptible. A few hundred yards away, this plateau ended abruptly in a chasm, which had been invisible farther down the mountain. Into this chasm the acolytes apparently leaped without checking their speed. Their pursuers saw the green robes flutter and disappear over the edge.

A few moments later they themselves were standing on the brink of the mighty moat that cut them off from the castle of the Black Seers. It was a sheer-walled ravine that extended in either direction as far as they could see, apparently girdling the mountain, some four hundred yards in width and five hundred feet deep. And in it, from rim to rim, a strange, translucent mist sparkled and shimmered.

Looking down, Conan grunted. Far below him, moving across the glimmering floor, which shone like burnished silver, he saw the forms of the green-robed acolytes. Their outline was wavering and indistinct, like figures seen under deep water. They walked in single file, moving toward the opposite wall.

Kerim Shah nocked an arrow and sent it singing downward. But when it struck the mist that filled the chasm it seemed to lose momentum and direction, wandering widely from its course.

"If they went down, so can we!" grunted Conan, while Kerim Shah stared after his shaft in amazement. "I saw them last at this spot——"

Squinting down he saw something shining like a golden thread across the canyon floor far below. The acolytes seemed to be following this thread, and there suddenly came to him Khemsa's cryptic words—"Follow the golden vein!" On the brink, under his very hand as he crouched, he found it, a thin vein of sparkling gold running from an outcropping of ore to the edge and down across the silvery floor. And he found something else, which had before been invisible to him because of the peculiar refraction of the light. The gold vein followed a narrow ramp which slanted down into the ravine, fitted with niches for hand and foot hold.

"Here's where they went down," he grunted to Kerim Shah. "They're no adepts, to waft themselves through the air! We'll follow them——"

It was at that instant that the man who had been bitten by the mad dog cried out horribly and leaped at Kerim Shah, foaming and gnashing his teeth. The Turanian, quick as a cat on his feet,

sprang aside and the madman pitched head-first over the brink.
The others rushed to the edge and glared after him in amazement.
The maniac did not fall plummetlike. He floated slowly down
through the rosy haze like a man sinking in deep water. His
limbs moved like a man trying to swim, and his features were
purple and convulsed beyond the contortions of his madness. Far
down at last on the shining floor his body settled and lay still.

"There's death in that chasm," muttered Kerim Shah, drawing back from the rosy mist that shimmered almost at his feet.
"What now, Conan?"

"On!" answered the Cimmerian grimly. "Those acolytes are
human; if the mist doesn't kill them, it won't kill me."

He hitched his belt, and his hands touched the girdle Khemsa
had given him; he scowled, then smiled bleakly. He had forgotten that girdle; yet thrice had death passed him by to strike
another victim.

The acolytes had reached the farther wall and were moving up
it like great green flies. Letting himself upon the ramp, he
descended warily. The rosy cloud lapped about his ankles, as-
cending as he lowered himself. It reached his knees, his thighs,
his waist, his armpits. He felt it as one feels a thick heavy fog on
a damp night. With it lapping about his chin he hesitated, and
then ducked under. Instantly his breath ceased; all air was shut
off from him and he felt his ribs caving in on his vitals. With a
frantic effort he heaved himself up, fighting for life. His head
rose above the surface and he drank air in great gulps.

Kerim Shah leaned down toward him, spoke to him, but
Conan neither heard nor heeded. Stubbornly, his mind fixed on
what the dying Khemsa had told him, the Cimmerian groped for
the gold vein, and found that he had moved off it in his descent.
Several series of hand-holds were niched in the ramp. Placing
himself directly over the thread, he began climbing down once
more. The rosy mist rose about him, engulfed him. Now his head
was under, but he was still drinking pure air. Above him he saw
his companions staring down at him, their features blurred by the
haze that shimmered over his head. He gestured for them to
follow and went down swiftly, without waiting to see whether
they complied or not.

Kerim Shah sheathed his sword without comment and followed,
and the Irakzai, more fearful of being left alone than of the
terrors that might lurk below, scrambled after him. Each man
clung to the golden thread as they saw the Cimmerian do.
Down the slanting ramp they went to the ravine floor and

moved out across the shining level, treading the gold vein like rope-walkers. It was as if they walked along an invisible tunnel through which air circulated freely. They felt death pressing in on them above and on either hand, but it did not touch them.

The vein crawled up a similar ramp on the other wall up which the acolytes had disappeared, and up it they went with taut nerves, not knowing what might be waiting for them among the jutting spurs of rock that fanged the lip of the precipice.

It was the green-robed acolytes who awaited them, with knives in their hands. Perhaps they had reached the limits to which they could retreat. Perhaps the Stygian girdle about Conan's waist could have told why their necromantic spells had proven so weak and so quickly exhausted. Perhaps it was a knowledge of death decreed for failure that sent them leaping from among the rocks, eyes glaring and knives glittering, resorting in their desperation to material weapons.

There among the rocky fangs on the precipice lip was no war of wizard craft. It was a whirl of blades, where real steel bit and real blood spurted, where sinewy arms dealt forthright blows that severed quivering flesh, and men went down to be trodden under foot as the fight raged over them.

One of the Irakzai bled to death among the rocks, but the acolytes were down—slashed and hacked asunder or hurled over the edge to float sluggishly down to the silver floor that shone so far below.

Then the conquerors shook blood and sweat from their eyes, and looked at one another. Conan and Kerim Shah still stood upright and four of the Irakzai.

They stood among the rocky teeth that serrated the precipice brink, and from that spot a path wound up a gentle slope to a broad stair, consisting of half a dozen steps, a hundred feet across, cut out of a green jade-like substance. They led up to a broad stage or roofless gallery of the same polished stone, and above it rose, tier upon tier, the castle of the Black Seers. It seemed to have been carved out of the sheer stone of the mountain. The architecture was faultless, but unadorned. The many casements were barred and masked with curtains within. There was no sign of life, friendly or hostile.

They went up the path in silence, and warily as men treading the lair of a serpent. The Irakzai were dumb, like men marching to a certain doom. Even Kerim Shah was silent. Only Conan seemed unaware what a monstrous dislocating and uprooting of accepted thought and action their invasion constituted, what an unprecedented violation of tradition. He was not of the East; and he came of a breed who fought devils and wizards as promptly and matter-of-factly as they battled human foes.

He strode up the shining stairs and across the wide green gallery straight toward the great golden-bound teak door that opened upon it. He cast but a single glance upward at the higher tiers of the great pryamidal structure towering above him. He reached a hand for the bronze prong that jutted like a handle from the door—then checked himself, grinning hardly. The handle was made in the shape of a serpent, head lifted on arched neck; and Conan had a suspicion that that metal head would come to grisly life under his hand.

He struck it from the door with one blow, and its bronze clink on the glassy floor did not lessen his caution. He flipped it aside with his knife-point, and again turned to the door. Utter silence reigned over the towers. Far below them the mountain slopes fell away into a purple haze of distance. The sun glittered on snow-clad peaks on either hand. High above, a vulture hung like a black dot in the cold blue of the sky. But for it, the men before thg gold-bound door were the only evidence of life, tiny figures on a green jade gallery poised on the dizzy height, with that fantastic pile of stone towering above them.

A sharp wind off the snow slashed them, whipping their tatters about. Conan's long knife splintering through the teak panels roused the startled echoes. Again and again he struck, hewing through polished wood and metal bands alike. Through the sundered ruins he glared into the interior, alert and suspicious as a wolf. He saw a broad chamber, the polished stone walls untapestried, the mosaic floor uncarpeted. Square, polished ebon stools and a stone dais formed the only furnishings. The room was empty of human life. Another door showed in the opposite wall.

"Leave a man on guard outside," grunted Conan. "I'm going in."

Kerim Shah designated a warrior for that duty, and the man fell back toward the middle of the gallery, bow in hand. Conan strode into the castle, followed by the Turanian and the three remaining Irakzai. The one outside spat, grumbled in his beard, and started suddenly as a low mocking laugh reached his ears.

He lifted his head and saw, on the tier above him, a tall, black-robed figure, naked head nodding slightly as he stared down. His whole attitude suggested mockery and malignity.

Quick as a flash the Irakzai bent his bow and loosed, and the arrow streaked upward to strike full in the black-robbed breast. The mocking smile did not alter. The Seer plucked out the missile and threw it back at the bowman, not as a weapon is hurled, but with a contemptuous gesture. The Irakzai dodged, instinctively throwing up his arm. His fingers closed on the revolving shaft.

Then he shrieked. In his hand the wooden shaft suddenly *writhed*. Its rigid outline became pliant, melting in his grasp. He tried to throw it from him, but it was too late. He held a living serpent in his naked hand, and already it had coiled about his wrist and its wicked wedge-shaped head darted at his muscular arm. He screamed again and his eyes became distended, his features purple. He went to his knees shaken by an awful convulsion, and then lay still.

The men inside had wheeled at his first cry. Conan took a swift stride toward the open doorway, and then halted short, baffled. To the men behind him it seemed that he strained against empty air. But though he could see nothing, there was a slick, smooth, hard surface under his hands, and he knew that a sheet of crystal had been let down in the doorway. Through it he saw the Irakzai lying motionless on the glassy gallery, an ordinary arrow sticking in his arm.

Conan lifted his knife and smote, and the watchers were dumbfounded to see his blow checked apparently in midair, with the loud clang of steel that meets an unyielding substance. He wasted no more effort. He knew that not even the legendary tulwar of Amir Khurum could shatter that invisible curtain.

In a few words he explained the matter to Kerim Shah, and the Turanian shrugged his shoulders. "Well, if our exit is barred, we must find another. In the meanwhile our way lies forward, does it not?"

With a grunt the Cimmerian turned and strode across the chamber to the opposite door, with a feeling of treading on the threshold of doom. As he lifted his knife to shatter the door, it swung silently open as if of its own accord. He strode into a great hall, flanked with tall glassy columns. A hundred feet from the door began the broad jade-green steps of a stair that tapered toward the top like the side of a pyramid. What lay beyond that stair he could not tell. But between him and its shimmering foot stood a curious altar of gleaming black jet. Four great golden serpents twined their tails about this altar and reared their wedge-shaped heads in the air, facing the four quarters of the compass like the enchanted guardians of a fabled treasure. But on the altar, between the arching necks, stood only a crystal globe filled with a cloudy smoke-like substance, in which floated four golden pomegranates.

The sight stirred some dim recollection in his mind; then Conan heeded the altar no longer, for on the lower steps of the stair stood four black-robed figures. He had not seen them come. They were simply there, tall, gaunt, their vulture-heads nodding in unison, their feet and hands hidden by their flowing garments.

One lifted his arm and the sleeve fell away revealing his hand—and it was not a hand at all. Conan halted in midstride, compelled against his will. He had encountered a force differing subtly from Khemsa's mesmerism, and he could not advance, though he felt it in his power to retreat if he wished. His companions had likewise halted, and they seemed even more helpless than he, unable to move in either direction.

The Seer whose arm was lifted beckoned to one of the Irakzai, and the man moved toward him like one in a trance, eyes staring and fixed, blade hanging in limp fingers. As he pushed past Conan, the Cimmerian threw an arm across his breast to arrest him. Conan was so much stronger than the Irakzai that in ordinary circumstances he could have broken his spine between his hands. But now the muscular arm was brushed aside like a straw and the Irakzai, moved toward the stair, treading jerkily and mechanically. He reached the steps and knelt stiffly, proffering his blade and bending his head. The Seer took the sword. It flashed as he swung it up and down. The Irakzai's head tumbled from his shoulders and thudded heavily on the black marble floor. An arch of blood jetted from the severed arteries and the body slumped over and lay with arms spread wide.

Again a malformed hand lifted and beckoned, and another Irakzai stumbled stiffly to his doom. The ghastly drama was re-enacted and another headless form lay beside the first.

As the third tribesman clumped his way past Conan to his death, the Cimmerian, his veins bulging in his temples with his efforts to break past the unseen barrier that held him, was suddenly aware of allied forces, unseen, but waking into life about him. This realization came without warning, but so power-fully that he could not doubt his instinct. His left hand slid involuntarily under his Bakhariot belt and closed on the Stygian girdle. And as he gripped it he felt new strength flood his numbed limbs; the will to live was a pulsing white-hot fire, matched by the intensity of his burning rage.

The third Irakzai was a decapitated corpse, and the hideous finger was lifting again when Conan felt the bursting of the invisible barrier. A fierce, involuntary cry burst from his lips as he leaped with the explosive suddenness of pent-up ferocity. His left hand gripped the sorcerer's girdle as a drowning man grips a floating log, and the long knife was a sheen of light in his right. The men on the steps did not move. They watched calmly, cynically; if they felt surprise they did not show it. Conan did not allow himself to think what might chance when he came within knife-reach of them. His blood was pounding in his temples, a mist of crimson swam before his sight. He was afire with the urge to kill—to drive his knife deep into flesh and bone, and twist the blade in blood and entrails.

Another dozen strides would carry him to the steps where the sneering demons stood. He drew his breath deep, his fury rising redly as his charge gathered momentum. He was hurtling past the altar with its golden serpents when like a levin-flash there shot across his mind again as vividly as if spoken in his external ear, the cryptic words of Khemsa: *"Break the crystal ball!"*

His reaction was almost without his own volition. Execution followed impulse so spontaneously that the greatest sorcerer of the age would not have had time to read his mind and prevent his action. Wheeling like a cat from his headlong charge, he brought his knife crashing down upon the crystal. Instantly the air vibrated with a peal of terror, whether from the stairs, the altar, or the crystal itself he could not tell. Hisses filled his ears as the golden serpents, suddenly vibrant with hideous life, writhed and smote at him. But he was fired to the speed of a maddened tiger. A whirl of steel sheared through the hideous trunks that waved toward him, and he smote the crystal sphere again and yet again. And the globe burst with a noise like a thunder-clap, raining fiery shards on the black marble, and the gold pomegranates, as if released from captivity, shot upward toward the lofty roof and were gone.

A mad screaming, bestial and ghastly, was echoing through the great hall. On the steps wirthed four black-robed figures, twisting in convulsions, froth dripping from their livid mouths. Then with one frenzied crescendo of inhuman ululation they stiffened and lay still, and Conan knew that they were dead. He stared down at the altar and the crystal shards. Four headless golden serpents still coiled about the altar, but no alien life now animated the dully gleaming metal.

Kerim Shah was rising slowly from his knees, whither he had

been dashed by some unseen force. He shook his head to clear the ringing from his ears.

"Did you hear that crash when you struck? It was as if a thousand crystal panels shattered all over the castle as that globe burst. Were the souls of the wizards imprisoned in those golden balls?—Ha!"

Conan wheeled as Kerim Shah drew his sword and pointed.

Another figure stood at the head of the stair. His robe, too, was black, but of richly embroidered velvet, and there was a velvet cap on his head. His face was calm, and not unhandsome.

"Who the devil are you?" demanded Conan, staring up at him, knife in hand.

"I am the Master of Yimsha!" His voice was like the chime of a temple bell, but a note of cruel mirth ran through it.

"Where is Yasmina?" demanded Kerim Shah.

The Master laughed down at him.

"What is that to you, dead man? Have you so quickly forgotten my strength, once lent to you, that you come armed against me, you poor fool? I think I will take your heart, Kerim Shah!"

He held out his hand as if to receive something, and the Turanian cried out sharply like a man in mortal agony. He reeled drunkenly, and then, with a splintering of bones, a rending of flesh and muscle, and a snapping of mail-links, his breast burst outward with a shower of blood, and through the ghastly aperture something red and dripping shot through the air into the Master's outstretched hand, as a bit of steel leaps to the magnet. The Turanian slumped to the floor and lay motionless, and the Master laughed and hurled the object to fall before Conan's feet—a still-quivering human heart.

With a roar and a curse Conan charged the stair. From Khemsa's girdle he felt strength and deathless hate flow into him to combat the terrible emanation of power that met him on the steps. The air filled with a shimmering steely haze through which he plunged like a swimmer, head lowered, left arm bent about his face, knife gripped low in his right hand. His half-blinded eyes, glaring over the crook of his elbow, made out the hated shape of the Seer before and above him, the outline wavering as a reflection wavers in disturbed water.

He was racked and torn by forces beyond his comprehension, but he felt a driving power outside and beyond his own lifting him inexorably upward and onward, despite the wizard's strength and his own agony.

Now he had reached the head of the stairs, and the Master's

face floated in the steely haze before him, and a strange fear shadowed the inscrutable eyes. Conan waded through the mist as through a surf, and his knife lunged upward like a live thing. The keen point ripped the Master's robe as he sprang back with a low cry. Then before Conan's gaze, the wizard vanished—simply disappeared like a burst bubble, and something long and undulating darted up one of the smaller stairs that led up to the left and right from the landing.

Conan charged after it, up the left-hand stair, uncertain as to just what he had seen whip up those steps, but in a berserk mood that drowned the nausea and horror whispering at the back of his consciousness.

He plunged out into a broad corridor whose uncarpeted floor and untapestried walls were of polished jade, and something long and swift whisked down the corridor ahead of him, and into a curtained door. From within the chamber rose a scream of urgent terror. The sound lent wings to Conan's flying feet, and he hurtled through the curtains and headlong into the chamber within.

A frightful scene met his glare. Yasmina cowered on the farther edge of a velvet-covered dais, screaming her loathing and horror, an arm lifted as if to ward off attack, while before her swayed the hideous head of a giant serpent, shining neck arching up from dark-gleaming coils. With a choked cry Conan threw his knife.

Instantly the monster whirled and was upon him like the rush of wind through tall grass. The long knife quivered in its neck, point and a foot of blade showing on one side, and the hilt and a hand's-breadth of steel on the other, but it only seemed to madden the giant reptile. The great head towered above the man who faced it, and then darted down, the venom-dripping jaws gaping wide. But Conan had plucked a dagger from his girdle and he stabbed upward as the head dipped down. The point tore through the lower jaw and transfixed the upper, pinning them together. The next instant, the great trunk had looped itself about the Cimmerian as the snake, unable to use its fangs, employed its remaining form of attack.

Conan's left arm was pinioned among the bone-crushing folds, but his right was free. Bracing his feet to keep upright, he stretched forth his hand, gripped the hilt of the long knife jutting from the serpent's neck, and tore it free in a shower of blood. As if divining his purpose with more than bestial intelligence, the snake writhed and knotted, seeking to cast its loops about his right arm. But with the speed of light the long knife rose and fell, shearing half-way through the reptile's giant trunk.

Before he could strike again, the great, pliant loops fell from him and the monster dragged itself across the floor, gushing blood from its ghastly wounds. Conan sprang after it, knife lifted, but his vicious swipe cut empty air as the serpent writhed away from him and struck its blunt nose against a paneled screen of sandalwood. One of the panels gave inward and the long, bleeding barrel whipped through it and was gone.

Conan instantly attacked the screen. A few blows rent it apart and he glared into the dim alcove beyond. No horrific shape coiled there; there was blood on the marble floor, and bloody tracks led to a cryptic arched door. Those tracks were of a man's bare feet. . . .

"*Conan!*" He wheeled back into the chamber just in time to catch the Devi of Vendhya in his arms as she rushed across the room and threw herself upon him, catching him about the neck with a frantic clasp, half hysterical with terror and gratitude and relief.

His wild blood had been stirred to its uttermost by all that had passed. He caught her to him in a grasp that would have made her wince at another time, and crushed her lips with his. She made no resistance; the Devi was drowned in the elemental woman. She closed her eyes and drank in his fierce, hot, lawless kisses with all the abandon of passionate thirst. She was panting with his violence when he ceased for breath, and glared down at her lying limp in his mighty arms.

"I knew you'd come for me," she murmured. "You would not leave me in this den of devils."

At her words, recollection of their environment came to him suddenly. He lifted his head and listened intently. Silence reigned over the castle of Yimsha, but it was a silence impregnated with menace. Peril crouched in every corner, leered invisibly from every hanging.

"We'd better go while we can," he muttered. "Those cuts were enough to kill any common beast—or *man*—but a wizard has a dozen lives. Wound one, and he writhes away like a crippled snake to soak up fresh venom from some source of sorcery."

He picked up the girl and, carrying her in his arms like a child, he strode out into the gleaming jade corridor and down the stairs, nerves tautly alert for any sign or sound.

"I met the Master," she whispered, clinging to him and shuddering. "He worked his spells on me to break my will. The most awful was a moldering corpse which seized me in its arms—I fainted then and lay as one dead, I do not know how long. Shortly after I regained consciousness I heard sounds of strife below, and cries, and then that snake came slithering through the curtains—ah!" She shook at the memory of that horror. "I knew somehow that it was not an illusion, but a real serpent that sought my life."

"It was not a shadow, at least," answered Conan cryptically. "He knew he was beaten, and chose to slay you rather than let you be rescued."

"What do you mean, *he?*" she asked uneasily, and then shrank against him, crying out, and forgetting her question. She had seen the corpses at the foot of the stairs. Those of the Seers were not good to look at, as they lay twisted and contorted, their hands and feet exposed to view, and at the sight Yasmina went livid and hid her face against Conan's powerful shoulder.

10. Yasmina and Conan

Conan passed through the hall quickly enough, traversed the outer chamber, and approached the door that led upon the gallery. Then he saw the floor sprinkled with tiny, glittering shards. The crystal sheet that had covered the doorway had been shivered to bits, and he remembered the crash that had accompanied the shattering of the crystal globe. He believed that every piece of crystal in the castle had broken at that instant, and some dim instinct or memory of esoteric lore vaguely suggested the truth of the monstrous connection between the Lords of the Black Circle and the golden pomegranates. He felt the short hair bristle chilly at the back of his neck and put the matter hastily out of his mind.

He breathed a deep sigh of relief as he stepped out upon the green jade gallery. There was still the gorge to cross, but at least he could see the white peaks glistening in the sun, and the long slopes falling away into the distant blue hazes.

The Irakzai lay where he had fallen, an ugly blotch on the glassy smoothness. As Conan strode down the winding path, he was surprised to note the position of the sun. It had not yet passed its zenith; and yet it seemed to him that hours had passed since he plunged into the castle of the Black Seers.

He felt an urge to hasten, not a mere blind panic, but an instinct of peril growing behind his back. He said nothing to

Yasmina, and she seemed content to nestle her dark head against his arching breast and find security in the clasp of his iron arms. He paused an instant on the brink of the chasm, frowning down. The haze which danced in the gorge was no longer rose-hued and sparkling. It was smoky, dim, ghostly, like the life-tide that flickered thinly in a wounded man. The thought came vaguely to Conan that the spells of magicians were more closely bound to their personal beings than were the actions of common men to the actors.

But far below, the floor shone like tarnished silver, and the gold thread sparkled undimmed. Conan shifted Yasmina across his shoulder, where she lay docilely, and began the descent. Hurriedly he descended the ramp, and hurriedly he fled across the echoing floor. He had a conviction that they were racing with time, that their chances of survival depended upon crossing that gorge of horrors before the wounded Master of the castle should regain enough power to loose some other doom upon them.

When he toiled up the farther ramp and came out upon the crest, he breathed a gusty sigh of relief and stood Yasmina upon her feet.

"You walk from here," he told her; "it's downhill all the way."

She stole a glance at the gleaming pyramid across the chasm; it reared up against the snowy slope like the citadel of silence and immemorial evil.

"Are you a magician, that you have conquered the Black Seers of Yimsha, Conan of Ghor?" she asked, as they went down the path, with his heavy arm about her supple waist.

"It was a girdle Khemsa gave me before he died," Conan answered. "Yes, I found him on the trail. It is a curious one, which I'll show you when I have time. Against some spells it was weak, but against others it was strong, and a good knife is always a hearty incantation."

"But if the girdle aided you in conquering the Master," she argued, "why did it not aid Khemsa?"

He shook his head. "Who knows? But Khemsa had been the Master's slave; perhaps that weakened its magic. He had no hold on me as he had on Khemsa. Yet I can't say that I conquered him. He retreated, but I have a feeling that we haven't seen the last of him. I want to put as many miles between us and his lair as we can."

He was further relieved to find horses tethered among the

tamarisks as he had left them. He loosed them swiftly and mounted the black stallion, swinging the girl up before him. The others followed, freshened by their rest.

"And what now?" she asked. "To Afghulistan?"

"Not just now!" He grinned hardly. "Somebody—maybe the governor—killed my seven headmen. My idiotic followers think I had something to do with it, and unless I am able to convince them otherwise, they'll hunt me like a wounded jackal."

"Then what of me? If the headmen are dead, I am useless to you as a hostage. Will you slay me to avenge them?"

He looked down at her, with eyes fiercely aglow, and laughed at the suggestion.

"Then let us ride to the border," she said. "You'll be safe from the Afghulis there——"

"Yes, on a Vendhyan gibbet."

"I am queen of Vendhya," she reminded him with a touch of her old imperiousness. "You have saved my life. You shall be rewarded."

She did not intend it as it sounded, but he growled in his throat, ill pleased.

"Keep your bounty for your city-bred dogs, princess! If you're a queen of the plains, I'm chief of the hills, and not one foot toward the border will I take you!"

"But you would be safe——" she began bewilderedly.

"And you'd be the Devi again," he broke in. "No, girl; I prefer you as you are now—a woman of flesh and blood, riding on my saddle bow."

"But you can't *keep* me!" she cried. "You can't——"

"Watch and see!" he advised grimly.

"But I will pay you a vast ransom——"

"Devil take your ransom!" he answered roughly, his arms hardening around her supple figure. "The kingdom of Vendhya could give me nothing I desire half so much as I desire you. I took you at the risk of my neck; if your courtiers want you back, let them come up the Zhaibar and fight for you."

"But you have no followers now!" she protested. "You are hunted! How can you preserve your own life, much less mine?"

"I still have friends in the hills," he answered. "There is a chief of the Khurakzai who will keep you safely while I bicker with the Afghulis. If they will have none of me, by Crom! I will ride northward with you to the steppes of the *kozaki*. I was a

hetman among the Free Companions before I rode southward.
I'll make you a queen on the Zaporoska River!''

"But I can not!'' she objected. "You must not hold me———''

"If the idea's so repulsive,'' he demanded, "why did you
yield your lips to me so willingly?''

"Even a queen is human,'' she answered, coloring. "But
because I am a queen, I must consider my kingdom. Do not carry
me away into some foreign country. Come back to Vendhya with
me!''

"Would you make me your king?'' he asked sardonically.

"Well, there are customs———'' she stammered, and he interrupted her with a hard laugh.

"Yes, civilized customs that won't let you do as you wish.
You'll marry some withered old king of the plains, and I can go
my way with only the memory of a few kisses snatched from
your lips. Ha!''

"But I must return to my kingdom!'' she repeated helplessly.

"Why?'' he demanded angrily. "To chafe your rump on gold
thrones, and listen to the plaudits of smirking, velvet-skirted
fools? Where is the gain? Listen: I was born in the Cimmerian
hills where the people are all barbarians. I have been a mercenary soldier, a corsair, a *kozak*, and a hundred other things.
What king has roamed the countries, fought the battles, loved the
women, and won the plunder that I have?

"I came into Ghulistan to raise a horde and plunder the
kingdoms to the south—your own among them. Being chief of the
Afghulis was only a start. If I can conciliate them, I'll have a
dozen tribes following me within a year. But if I can't, I'll ride
back to the steppes and loot the Turanian borders with the
kozaki. And you'll go with me. To the devil with your kingdom;
they fended for themselves before you were born.''

She lay in his arms looking up at him, and she felt a tug at her
spirit, a lawless, reckless urge that matched his own and was by
it called into being. But a thousand generations of sovereignship
rode heavy upon her.

"I can't! I can't!'' she repeated helplessly.

"You haven't any choice,'' he assured her. "You—what the
devil!''

They had left Yimsha some miles behind them, and were
riding along a high ridge that separated two deep valleys. They
had just topped a steep crest where they could gaze down into
the valley on their right hand. And there a running fight was in
progress. A strong wind was blowing away from them, carrying

the sound from their ears, but even so the clashing of steel and thunder of hoofs welled up from far below.

They saw the glint of the sun on lancetip and spired helmet. Three thousand mailed horsemen were driving before them a ragged band of turbaned riders, who fled snarling and striking like fleeing wolves.

"Turanians!" muttered Conan. "Squadrons from Secunderam. What the devil are they doing here?"

"Who are the men they pursue?" asked Yasmina. "And why do they fall back so stubbornly? They can not stand against such odds."

"Five hundred of my mad Afghulis," he growled, scowling down into the vale. "They're in a trap, and they know it."

The valley was indeed a cul-de-sac at the end. It narrowed to a high-walled gorge, opening out further into a round bowl, completely rimmed with lofty, unscalable walls.

The turbaned riders were being forced into this gorge, because there was nowhere else for them to go, and they went reluctantly, in a shower of arrows and a whirl of swords. The helmeted riders harried them, but did not press in too rashly. They knew the desperate fury of the hill tribes, and they knew too that they had their prey in a trap from which there was no escape. They had recognized the hillmen as Afghulis, and they wished to hem them in and force a surrender. They needed hostages for the purpose they had in mind.

Their emir was a man of decision and initiative. When he reached Gurashah valley, and found neither guides nor emissary waiting for him, he pushed on, trusting to his own knowledge of the country. All the way from Secunderam there had been fighting, and tribesmen were licking their wounds in many a crag-perched village. He knew there was a good chance that neither he nor any of his helmeted spearmen would ever ride through the gates of Secunderam again, for the tribes would all be up behind him now, but he was determined to carry out his orders—which were to take Yasmina Devi from the Afghulis at all costs, and to bring her captive to Secunderam or, if confronted by impossibility, to strike off her head before he himself died.

Of all this, of course, the watchers on the ridge were not aware. But Conan fidgeted with nervousness.

"Why the devil did they get themselves trapped?" he demanded of the universe at large. "I know what they're doing in these parts—they were hunting me, the dogs! Poking into every valley—and found themselves penned in before they knew it.

The poor fools! They're making a stand in the gorge, but they can't hold out for long. When the Turanians have pushed them back into the bowl, they'll slaughter them at their leisure."

The din welling up from below increased in volume and intensity. In the strait of the narrow gut, the Afghulis, fighting desperately, were for the time holding their own against the mailed riders, who could not throw their whole weight against them.

Conan scowled darkly, moved restlessly, fingering his hilt, and finally spoke bluntly: "Devi, I must go down to them. I'll find a place for you to hide until I come back to you. You spoke of your kingdom—well, I don't pretend to look on those hairy devils as my children, but after all, such as they are, they're my henchmen. A chief should never desert his followers, even if they desert him first. They think they were right in kicking me out—Hell, I won't be cast off! I'm still chief of the Afghulis, and I'll prove it! I can climb down on foot into the gorge."

"But what of me?" she queried. "You carried me away forcibly from *my* people; now will you leave me to die in the hills alone while you go down and sacrifice yourself uselessly?"

His veins swelled with the conflict of his emotions.

"That's right," he muttered helplessly. "Crom knows what I *can* do."

She turned her head slightly, a curious expression dawning on her beautiful face. Then:

"Listen!" she cried. "Listen!"

A distant fanfare of trumpets was borne faintly to their ears. They stared into the deep valley on the left and caught a glint of steel on the farther side. A long line of lances and polished helmets moved along the vale, gleaming in the sunlight.

"The riders of Vendhya!" she cried exultingly.

"There are thousands of them!" muttered Conan. "It has been long since a Kshatriya host has ridden this far into the hills."

"They are searching for me!" she exclaimed. "Give me your horse! I will ride to my warriors! The ridge is not so precipitous on the left, and I can reach the valley floor. Go to your men and make them hold out a little longer. I will lead my horsemen into the valley at the upper end and fall upon the Turanians! We will crush them in the vise! Quick, Conan! Will you sacrifice your men to your own desire?"

The burning hunger of the steppes and the wintry forests glared out of his eyes, but he shook his head and swung off the stallion, placing the reins in her hands.

"You win!" he grunted. "Ride like the devil!"

She wheeled away down the left-hand slope, and he ran swiftly along the ridge until he reached the long ragged cleft that was the defile in which the fight raged. Down the rugged wall he scrambled like an ape, clinging to projections and crevices, to fall at last, feet first, into the mêlée that raged in the mouth of the gorge. Blades were whickering and clanging about him, horses rearing and stamping, helmet plumes nodding among turbans that were stained crimson.

As he hit, he yelled like a wolf, caught a gold-worked rein, and dodging the sweep of a scimitar, drove his long knife upward through the rider's vitals. In another instant he was in the saddle, yelling ferocious orders to the Afghulis. They stared at him stupidly for an instant; then as they saw the havoc his steel was wreaking among their enemies, they fell to their work again, accepting him without comment. In that inferno of licking blades and spurting blood there was no time to ask or answer questions.

The riders in their spired helmets and gold-worked hauberks swarmed about the gorge mouth, thrusting and slashing, and the narrow defile was packed and jammed with horses and men, the warriors crushed breast to breast, stabbing with shortened blades, slashing murderously when there was an instant's room to swing a sword. When a man went down he did not get up from beneath the stamping, swirling hoofs. Weight and sheer strength counted heavily there, and the chief of the Afghulis did the work of ten. At such times accustomed habits sway men strongly, and the warriors, who were used to seeing Conan in their vanguard, were heartened mightily, despite their distrust of him.

But superior numbers counted too. The pressure of the men behind forced the horsemen of Turan deeper and deeper into the gorge, in the teeth of the flickering tulwars. Foot by foot the Afgulis were shoved back, leaving the defile-floor carpeted with dead, on which the riders trampled. As he hacked and smote like a man possessed, Conan had time for some chilling doubts—would Yasmina keep her word? She had but to join her warriors, turn southward, and leave him and his band to perish.

But at last, what seemed centuries of desperate battling, in the valley outside there rose another sound above the clash of steel and yells of slaughter. And then with a burst of trumpets that shook the walls, and rushing thunder of hoofs, five thousand riders of Vendhya smote the hosts of Secunderam.

That stroke split the Turanian squadrons asunder, shattered, tore, and rent them and scattered their fragments all over the valley. In an instant the surge had ebbed back out of the gorge; there was a chaotic, confused swirl of fighting, horsemen wheeling and smiting singly and in clusters, and then the emir went down with a Kshatirya lance through his breast, and the riders in their spired helmets turned their horses down the valley, spurring like mad and seeking to slash a way through the swarms which had come upon them from the rear. As they scattered in flight, the conquerors scattered in pursuit, and all across the valley floor, and up on the slopes near the mouth and over the crests streamed the fugitives and the pursuers. The Afghulis, those left to ride, rushed out of the gorge and joined in the harrying of their foes, accepting the unexpected alliance as unquestionably as they had accepted the return of their repudiated chief.

The sun was sinking toward the distant crags when Conan, his garments hacked to tatters and the mail under them reeking and clotted with blood, his knife dripping and crusted to the hilt, strode over the corpses to where Yasmina Devi sat her horse among her nobles on the crest of the ridge, near a lofty precipice.

"You kept your word, Devi!" he roared. "By Crom, though, I had some bad seconds down in that gorge—*look out!*"

Down from the sky swooped a vulture of tremendous size with a thunder of wings that knocked men sprawling from their horses.

The scimitar-like beak was slashing for the Devi's soft neck, but Conan was quicker—a short run, a tigerish leap, the savage thrust of a dripping knife, and the vulture voiced a horribly human cry, pitched sideways and went tumbling down the cliffs to the rocks and river a thousand feet below. As it dropped, its black wings thrashing the air, it took on the semblance, not of a bird, but of a black-robed human body that fell, arms in wide black sleeves thrown abroad.

Conan turned to Yasmina, his red knife still in his hand, his blue eyes smoldering, blood oozing from wounds on his thickly-muscled arms and thighs.

"You are the Devi again," he said, grinning fiercely at the gold-clasped gossamer robe she had donned over her hill-girl attire, and awed not at all by the imposing array of chivalry about him. "I have you to thank for the lives of some three hundred and fifty of my rogues, who are at least convinced that I didn't betray them. You have put my hands on the reins of conquest again."

"I still owe you a ransom," she said, her dark eyes glowing as they swept over him. "Ten thousand pieces of gold I pay you——"

He made a savage, impatient gesture, shook the blood from his knife and thrust it back in its scabbard, wiping his hand on his mail.

"I will collect your ransom in my own way, at my own time," he said. "I will collect it in your palace at Ayodhya, and I will come with fifty thousand men to see that the scales are fair."

She laughed, gathering her reins into her hands. "And I will meet you on the shores of the Jhumda with a hundred thousand!"

His eyes shone with fierce appreciation and admiration as, stepping back, he lifted his hand with a gesture that was like the assumption of kingship, indicating that her road was clear before her.

Acknowledgments continued

Please Stand By by Ron Goulart. Copyright © 1961 by Mercury Press, Inc. From *The Magazine of Fantasy and Science Fiction*. Reprinted by permission of the author.

What Good Is a Glass Dagger? by Larry Niven. Copyright © 1972 by Mercury Press, Inc. From *The Magazine of Fantasy and Science Fiction*. Reprinted by permission of the author.

The Eye of Tandyla by L. Sprague de Camp. First published in *Fantastic Adventures*, Vol. 13, #5, for May, 1951, C#B. 294 742 by Ziff-Davis Publishing Co. Copyright renewed by L. Sprague de Camp 1979 RE 26 977. Reprinted by permission of the author.

The White House Child by Greg Bear. Copyright © 1979 by Terry Carr. Reprinted by permission of the author.

Semley's Necklace, by Ursula K. Le Guin. Copyright © 1964, 1975 by Ursula K. Le Guin. Reprinted by permission of the author and the author's agent, Virginia Kidd.

And the Monsters Walk, by John Jakes. Copyright © 1952 by Ziff-Davis Publishing Co.; originally published in *Fantastic Adventures,* July, 1952; © renewed 1980 by John Jakes. Reprinted by permission of the author.

The Seeker in the Fortress by Manley Wade Wellman. Copyright © 1979 by Gerald W. Page and Hank Reinhardt. Reprinted by permission of Kirby McCauley, Ltd.

The Wall Around the World by Theodore Cogswell. Copyright © 1953 by Galaxy Publishing Corporation; © renewed 1981 by Theodore R. Cogswell. Reprinted by permission of the author.

The People of The Black Circle, by Robert E. Howard. Copyright © 1934 by Popular Fiction Company. Reprinted by permission of CONAN Properties Inc.